Deadly Trilogy

DEADLY TRILOGY

Complete Series: Books 1-3

Ashley Stoyanoff

Ashley Stoyanoff Books
London, Ontario

Cover Art by Lily Dormishev
Edited by Kathryn Calvert

Published by Ashley Stoyanoff Books
http://AshleyStoyanoff.com
Produced in Canada

Also by Ashley Stoyanoff

CHEATING DEATH SERIES
Going Rogue
Secrets and Lies

DEADLY TRILOGY
Deadly Crush
Deadly Mates
Deadly Pack

PRG INVESTIGATIONS SERIES
Two Truths and a Lie
Play It Again

THE SOUL'S MARK SERIES
The Soul's Mark: FOUND
Waking Dreams, A Soul's Mark Novella
The Soul's Mark: HUNTED
The Soul's Mark: BROKEN
The Soul's Mark: CHANGED

OTHER TITLES
If I Could Do It Again
Jingle Bells and Witchy Spells
Halloween in Hell

Deadly Crush

Deadly Trilogy Book 1

Dedication

For my sister, Jonel, because you are awesome!

CHAPTER 1

JADE

I should have taken my own advice.

It was good advice. Simple advice. Advice that I had lived by for two full years. All I had to do was stay clear of the pack. They were just a bunch of dogs. That was it. Nothing special. Just dogs with a superiority complex. Nothing good ever happened by getting mixed up with them. I had seen the proof of their destruction over and over, and what had I done? I had let one of them help me. *Stupid. Stupid. Stupid.*

The thing was, it wasn't easy to avoid them. The pack had been a part of Dog Mountain since, well, forever. I was pretty sure that the town was even named after them. Why else would they have called it Dog Mountain? Anyway, they were everywhere; in school, on the streets, at the stores; you couldn't go anywhere without running into one of them. Everyone knew about them. That would have freaked people out in most towns, but not here. Here, everyone welcomed the werewolves, well, everyone but me.

Personally, I couldn't stand them. They walked around as if they owned everything. I guessed they kind of did, or their families did. But that wasn't the point. They were possessive, territorial, and a serious pain in the butt. Especially the *she-wolves.* The *she-wolves* were the worst.

And it was because of one of those nasty *she-wolves* that I was trapped in the girls' locker room in my underwear.

I should have figured something like this would have happened. Erika and her little gang of dogs had been on my back ever since Dominic — the alpha's beta — drove me home last week. It had been completely innocent. It had been pouring rain, my car had broken down, and he had stopped to help. That was it. But Erika, well, Erika wanted him all to herself, and she couldn't seem to get it through her thick head that it had only been a ride home.

I opened up another locker in the long line of metal doors and slammed it shut. Empty. They were all empty. *Why did gym have to be my last class of the day?*

Frustrated, I plopped down onto the cold bench and pulled my knees to my chest, hugging them closely. They didn't even leave my backpack, and, of course, that's where my phone was.

How could I have been so stupid? This year, I had Mr. Townsend for gym, and gym with Mr. Townsend meant running laps. Only laps. He thought running was the only kind of fitness anyone ever needed. Personally, I thought that that mentality had to be a werewolf thing because, well, running laps sucked. And yes, my gym teacher was a werewolf. Needless to say, by the time class ended, I was all sweaty and gross. I had planned to go shopping after school, just to kill some time before Marcy, my best friend, and practically sister, got home, so understandably, I had decided to grab a quick shower. Clearly, leaving my clothes unattended was a big mistake.

I glanced at my watch, 3:30. Another hour or so before the after-school clubs would finish. *Maybe I could make a dash for my locker then and grab my extra set of gym clothes?* The idea of running around school almost naked made my stomach roll.

For years, I had managed to avoid those ... those ... dogs. And now, I couldn't get away from them. I didn't even understand why Erika cared so much. Dominic hadn't spoken to me since that day. And honestly, I didn't even know why he had stopped to help me in the first place. Since he had become one of them, he had barely glanced my way.

I'm going to throttle that she-wolf!

The pack had always made their presence known in everyday Dog Mountain life. They prowled the streets, taking what they wanted when they wanted it. Well, maybe not really *taking*. Most of the residents of Dog Mountain willingly gave whatever it was that one of those stupid dogs wanted, but that wasn't the point. The point was that they never actually worked for anything; they just took. What happened to the days when werewolves had kept hidden?

The time ticked by slowly. I was starving, but then, I was always starving, and since I had just finished gym, I was extra-starving.

My stomach rumbled, and I was starting to get a headache. I could feel it at my temples, radiating in circles through my head. *What a fan-freakin-tastic way to end the first week back at school.*

"Jade, you in here?"

Dominic. His deep voice rumbled through the door as he pushed it open a crack. My heart jumped in my throat, and I was pretty sure my whole body flushed. I felt it like a flash fever. Hot and sticky.

"Go away, Dominic," I yelped, scrambling from my seat. I whipped open one of the lockers and hid behind the metal door. "Don't come in here."

"Why not?" he asked, and I could hear the laughter in his voice. "It's not like I haven't seen you in your underwear before."

"Just stay out!" I hissed at him.

He didn't open the door any more than a crack. "I'm sorry, Jade. Erika ..." He paused, sighing long and loud, and then his hand slid through the small opening. "Look, I have your clothes. I'll just leave them here at the door, okay?"

I didn't say anything, and he didn't either. He just stood there, only his hand visible for a long moment. My stomach twisted in tender knots, and my heart beat loudly in my ears. The door inched open a bit further, and I couldn't stop the squeal that rushed from my lips. *Jeez, he's going to come in!* My brain was certain of it.

I frantically searched around for something, anything to hide my body. But there was nothing. Not even a towel. Those darn wolves probably would have stolen my bra and underwear, too, if they hadn't been in the stall with me.

But then, Dominic sighed again, and thankfully, he dropped my clothes onto the floor and pulled the door shut.

CHAPTER 2

AIDAN

I slinked behind an oak tree, pressing myself tightly against the rough bark, and held still as Dominic stomped out of the school. He walked by, without even a glance in my direction, and he was muttering something about *'Jade being impossible.'* Who Jade was, I didn't have a clue, and what he was doing here when he was supposed to be meeting me seriously had me annoyed. I may not have been the alpha for that long, but I was still the alpha — his alpha.

I had been tailing him all day, and so far, it had been a disappointment. The pack (or I guess it was *my* pack now) liked Dominic. I had been banking on the fact that it was only because he was a better option than Ray, the last alpha, if only slightly. But so far, following him around had only shown me that they actually liked him and what was worse, they trusted him. The problem was that I had a gut feeling that I couldn't trust him. Dominic was power-hungry. I could see it, feel it, and I was sure that he would be my biggest threat at the ceremony tonight. He had been Ray's beta, and now he was mine by default. Sure, I could choose someone else, and I wanted to, but as I said, the pack liked him. Stripping him of his title could lead to something I didn't want to face — yet.

I was beginning to feel a bit foolish, though, hiding behind a tree and stalking my beta. It didn't feel very alpha-ish. But then, I had never meant for this to happen. It wasn't that I didn't want to be the alpha. I did, and I was sure I'd be good at it, but that didn't change the fact that I hadn't meant to take out the last alpha.

I peeked around the tree trunk and scanned the parking lot for

Dominic. He was leaning against his car, arms crossed, and, by the look of it, he was still muttering about something. This was the first time in the last twelve hours that I had seen his cool persona ruffled. And right then, as I watched him, I didn't know whether to be happy (or even more disappointed) that maybe I had been right about him.

He had been there when I had *disposed* of Ray last night, or I guess it was this morning, and he hadn't done much to stop it. Although it would have been against pack rules for him to step in, still, he didn't seem to care that much that Ray was gone. I figured that that was a good thing, seeing as the only reason I challenged the jerk in the first place was because I had found him beating his mate.

Just thinking about it made my stomach roll. Tammy had been covered in blood and barely breathing, huddled at Ray's feet when I had walked into the bar.

I had scented the pack at the border of this little hick town, and I had come close to just driving straight through. The last thing I wanted to deal with was a pack that I didn't know. And if I hadn't been so exhausted, I would have kept going. I'd been driving for thirteen hours straight, trying to put as much distance between my father and me as I could.

After checking into a motel, I searched for the pack and found them easily enough at a little hole-in-the-wall bar in the center of town. My plan had been to let the alpha know I was in town and just passing through. This was purely out of respect for the pack, but when I saw him kicking the girl over and over, and not a single one of the pack members were doing a thing to stop him, I kind of lost it.

He was a big guy, dressed like a biker with a leather jacket and a green bandana wrapped around his head, and by the way the others were watching him, I knew right away that he was the alpha. They were all cowering back, clearly afraid to interfere. I shot them all disbelieving looks. They were all pack members; even the bartender had a distinctive wolf scent. Fury raged through me. I started toward the alpha and was about to pull him off the girl when Dominic stepped in front of me. "Leave it alone. She's the alpha female."

"The alpha female deserves more respect than this," I growled, staring him down. The alpha was still kicking her, oblivious to us, and for the first time in my life, I actually channeled my father.

I shifted, recalling everything the man had taught me about

showing dominance. My legs were stiff and tall. My ears were erect and forward. My tail, vertical and curled. The hair on my back bristled, and I growled long and low. I stared at Dominic, advancing slowly. It didn't take long for him to drop his human gaze and shrink away from me, submitting. It was then that I knew he had to be the beta. The rest of the pack members followed him, moving back, hunching their shoulders, and making themselves look smaller. Not a single one of them shifted.

I let out a low warning growl, and the alpha stopped, motionless. The copper scent of blood was stronger in my wolf form, calling to me, reminding me of the thrill of the hunt. I took slow and sure steps toward her, baring my teeth, curling my lips, and claiming the prey as mine. If the alpha hadn't shifted, I don't know what I would have done. At that moment, all I saw was easy food.

He snarled at me, his fur bristled, and he crouched, ready to attack, guarding his food. The silver-white light of his alpha's imprint shone through his chocolate-brown fur as he gathered his scent, giving me a silent warning to back off. I growled again, and all at once, his scent blasted at me with a staggering force. The pungent, bitter scent overwhelmed me, reminding me of the days I'd spent locked away while my father tortured me — taught me — to ignore the call of an alpha with his own alpha scent. It was crippling, demanding me to give in. Submit.

He channeled his scent again, pushing it out at me in a steady stream. I tried to shake it off just as my father had shown me, and I pushed my own scent at him. He cocked his head to the side, confused for a moment, but without the imprint to enhance the power of my scent, his confusion was short-lived.

I kept my dominant posture, my lips curled even further, exposing my gums, and right then, he launched at me. For half a second, I almost submitted to him. I was exhausted and hungry, and I couldn't think straight, but then his teeth sank into my shoulder, and rage rushed through me again. Hotter and deadlier.

Swift clarity came back to me in a rush. An image of the girl curled on the floor, bleeding while Ray kicked her over and over surged through my brain.

I twisted, biting back. My teeth sank into his side, and then his legs, and in less than a second, he was pinned under me, his vulnerable neck exposed. The years of training under my father had paid off, making him an easy target, but he didn't submit. He snarled and kicked up, trying to throw me off him. He snapped out at my neck, his teeth grazing my fur.

I could feel the rest of the pack watching. Their tension and unease were palpable, and my inner-wolf responded to it. They had submitted, and he would, too. I pinned his neck down with my teeth, not biting, only holding him on the ground, but still, he fought, bucking and twitching under me. He snarled again, and a chorus of whimpers rang out behind me.

"End it," Dominic growled. "He will not submit."

And I did. My teeth found purchase in his neck, and I tasted his blood seeping into my mouth. And then, he stopped moving, stopped fighting, stopped breathing, and I let go.

I couldn't say how long I stood over the dead alpha, staring at him, waiting for him to take a breath before I had shifted back. I remember thinking that my father would have been proud if he knew that I had found my own pack and claimed the alpha rank. I had followed in his footsteps, just as he wanted. I could hear his words as if he were standing right beside me, *'You can run, but alpha is in your scent. You can't hide from it, Son.'* And I also remember thinking that I didn't know how I felt about it.

I didn't reach for my clothes piled behind me, marking where I had become a wolf. I was too stunned that I had won to realize that I stood in the middle of the bar, stark naked. I saw the beta pull the girl to her feet from the corner of my eye, and I noticed that she wouldn't lift her head. She kept her body curled, staying small and passive, and all I could think was, *How had that girl won the challenge?* How many females had she beaten to become the alpha's mate? And what had he done to her to break her so badly?

"The new alpha pair," Dominic said, once she was firmly on her feet and standing in front of me. He waved a hand at us as if he were introducing us to the world. The words shocked me. I hadn't considered everything before I challenged him, and the reality of my actions was slowly sinking in. Alphas do not lose their status if one of them passes on. What was his was now mine, and I was now hers. We were the new alpha pair.

"No," she whispered. "Please. I just want to go. Let me leave. I don't want the rank, and I don't want the pack." She looked up at me; her eyes were full of tears, pleading with me to let her walk away.

I slid my thumb across her cheek, wiping some of the blood away, and she cringed at my touch. "Are you sure?" I asked. I needed to know if she understood what she was doing. If she stepped down, there would no longer be a place for her in this pack. She would be ostracized, marked as weak, and, in time, killed or run out of town.

She didn't hesitate and said, "Yes, please take a new mate. Please. I'll leave town." Her voice was weak, and she dropped her gaze back to the ground. She quivered, shrinking closer to the floor with every passing second. I should have felt sorry for her. An alpha female should never show fear, not like this, and I couldn't even begin to imagine how broken she must have been. But right then, I had no sympathy for her. I only felt relief. I would not have to babysit a mate that I did not want, and clearly, she did not want me either.

"Go," I said. Just that. A simple command I had heard my father use countless times.

She let out a shaky pent-up breath and whispered, "Thank you," still refusing to meet my eyes, and she scurried from the bar without as much as a backward glance.

I had never seen a pack like this in all my nineteen years. Werewolves were supposed to be a protective bunch. It was ingrained in us. In our blood — our bones. But this pack ... whatever Ray (and I was certain it was because of Ray) had done had ruined them. Right now, though, my biggest worry was how close Dominic really had been to his old alpha. I needed to be sure he was with me. Tonight could change everything, and if he wasn't backing me ... I didn't even want to think of the chaos that could happen.

My phone began to vibrate against my hip, jerking me from my thoughts, and I fished it out of my pocket. Dominic. His name flashed on the screen. I tapped the flashing call button and brought the phone to my ear.

"I'm going to be late," Dominic barked into the speaker before I even had a chance to say hello.

"Anything wrong?" I asked, keeping my voice low and peeking at him again. He had folded one arm across his chest, and his body tensed as he leaned against the car.

He looked like he was considering what to tell me, and then, after a moment, he said, "No. I just need to deal with something." He relaxed slightly and sighed into the speaker, or at least I thought it was a sigh; it sounded like a crackly burst in my ear.

"With what?" I pressed, wishing I could get closer. I could barely pick up his scent from this far away, and I wasn't entirely sure if he was lusting after someone or completely frustrated. The scent was so diluted, mixing with the grass and leaves, and most of it was taken away on the breeze before it reached my senses.

"It's personal," he snapped with a rumbling growl.

I was about to tell him that nothing — absolutely nothing — was personal when his alpha was asking, but right then, the double doors banged open, and a girl stormed out of the school. She was of average height, maybe five-foot-six, slim with curvy hips and long brown hair, curled softly at the edges and around her shoulders. She was cute, and she looked furious, which in my opinion, made her look even cuter. She had a fiery spirit; anyone could have seen it just by looking at her. Her hands were clenched at her sides, and her cheeks were bright red. She squinted against the glare from the sun, and then her eyes landed on Dominic. If she had been furious before, she was murderous now.

For a second, she looked as if she were about to dart back into the school, but then Dominic turned to her, and she froze.

"I've got to go," Dominic growled into my ear, and the phone went dead.

CHAPTER 3

JADE

As soon as I walked out of the school, I spotted his silver VW. And then I saw him. Dominic was waiting for me. He was leaning against the driver's side door with one arm folded across his chest and his cell phone glued to his ear with the other. His short blond hair was sticking up as if he had been running his hands through it over and over. His jaw was set in a rigid line, and he really didn't look happy.

I probably should have guessed he'd be waiting for me, but in my defense, I was a tiny bit flustered. I figured I had an excuse, though, seeing as my clothes had been stolen, and my head was pounding as if it had its own heartbeat. I was about to turn around and run back into the school to find another exit when his hazel eyes met mine. He snapped his phone shut before I could make a move and strutted up to me. Yes, strutted. It wasn't a walk or a stroll; it was full of coolness, confidence, and more than a little conceit.

Dominic closed the distance between us faster than I would have liked, and when he was only inches away, he asked, "You okay?" although the tone of his voice insinuated that he really didn't care if I was or not, and he scanned me over, from head to toe — twice.

I wanted to yell at him because, really, I wasn't fine, far from fine. And it was his fault that Erika was picking on me. He could stop it. He could make them leave me alone. He was the beta, for Pete's sake. They had to listen to him. But he hadn't done anything about them, and clearly, he knew what they had been up to. He had just brought my clothes back.

I looked up at him with narrowed eyes, and I straightened my shoulders, masking myself with an air of confidence that I really didn't feel. "I'm fine," I said through clenched teeth, and with my chin held high, because I seriously didn't want him to know how much the *she-wolves* had upset me this time, I walked past him and into the parking lot. And the whole time, my werewolf survival mantra echoed through my brain, *Don't show fear. Stay strong. Be the dominant one.*

"Jade, just get in the car," he called after me.

I huffed and kept walking. "Leave me alone, Dominic."

"I don't think you should walk home alone." His footfalls echoed around me, and I almost started running — almost. It took a heck of a lot of restraint not to. Dealing with werewolves was kind of like being trapped in a horror movie; no matter how fast you ran, the evil villain would still catch you at a walk.

Suddenly, Dominic was in front of me, blocking my path. I gritted my teeth and glared at him. "I don't care what you think," I said, sidestepping him.

"Come on, Jade." He groaned and darted back in front of me. "Just get in the car. I said I was sorry. What more do you want?"

He towered a good six inches over my five-foot-six frame. I glared up at him; his broad shoulders blocked out the glare from the sun that was starting to make its slow descent, and he smiled sheepishly down at me as if his perfectly white smile could wipe out what had just happened. And dammit, but I missed that smile so much that I almost caved right there and then.

But I didn't. I rubbed my temples in small circles, wishing the headache away. I needed a clear head to deal with this. It helped a little. I forced my lips into a smile and said as sweetly as I could, "What I want is for you and your stupid pack to disappear." I batted my eyes at him in a way that I hoped was a little bit mocking, and then I stepped around him and started for the trail at the back of the parking lot.

I hadn't made it two steps when he grabbed my arm, not unkindly, but still with a firm grip, and started pulling me over to the car. "Just get in the car. The pack is stressed, and you're the last person that should be walking around alone right now."

"Let go of me, Dominic!" I squealed. My heart jumped into my throat, and my stomach twisted into a painful knot. I pulled back, trying to rip out of his vice-grip hold. I was pretty sure he was just trying to look out for me, but the thing was, he was creeping me out — just a little. I didn't like *this* Dominic. He was cold and intense, and he made my skin crawl.

Dominic stopped pulling me. He grabbed my other arm, spinning me in front of him and holding me tightly. He looked down at me and rolled his eyes. "I know you think I'm an ass, but I'm really just trying to help you here."

I laughed, but there was no humor in the sound. "It's your *so-called* help that got me into this mess." I yanked again, and he clamped his grip a bit tighter, pinching my skin. I could feel the bruises forming under his grasp, but he seemed oblivious to it. He looked ... distant ... hurt, gazing down at me but not seeing me. I almost felt bad for saying it. Almost.

After a long moment, Dominic blinked. "Jade ..." he growled. His eyes started to shimmer, golden yellow, around the edges, and I shuddered, completely involuntarily. Deep down, I knew he wouldn't hurt me. Out of all of them, Dominic was one of the best. Most of the time, he tried to keep the others under control. Well, he did when Ray wasn't watching. I knew it was Ray's fault that the pack was the way they were. They were being run by a drunken jerk that didn't care about anyone but himself.

Dominic opened his mouth, but he didn't get a chance to spit out whatever he was about to say. "The girl said, 'Let go.'"

Dominic didn't move, and he didn't let go. He glared down at me, still holding me tightly in front of him, as he growled, "Stay out of this, Aidan," sounding more animal than human.

Aidan? Who was Aidan? I looked over my shoulder, spotting the owner of the voice. He smiled and winked at me. "I don't think I will," the new guy — Aidan — said, folding his arms over his chest, making his broad shoulders look even larger. "Let her go."

I stared at him, and my jaw dropped. He was definitely new. He had to be because I knew I would have recognized that face if I had seen it before. He was smiling or smirking. It was hard to tell. It was one-sided, and his jaw twitched a little with tension. He was trying to look gentle, but there was a rough side to him that he couldn't quite mask. It shone through his chocolaty eyes, deadly and sweet all in one.

Dominic's grip tightened again, and a low growl rumbled from his chest. I winced, pulling my eyes away from Aidan's brown ones. "Dominic, you're hurting me," I said, just barely audible.

Dominic flinched as if my words were a physical slap, and the shimmer of golden yellow in his eyes vanished. For about half a second, he looked like he was actually sorry.

It didn't last.

"Whatever," Dominic snapped as he dropped his hands from my arms. He shot me an ice-cold look. "You want to walk home with Erika lurking about, then fine. Don't blame me when she finds you."

Dominic stepped around me then, glaring daggers at the new guy as he went to his car. The new guy didn't flinch. He stared back with the same intensity as if he were daring Dominic to come back. When Dominic opened the driver's side door, he growled something unintelligible and then jumped in, slamming the door shut, and his car rumbled to life.

What just happened? a voice in my head asked as I watched Dominic peel out of the parking lot. In all the years I'd known him, I'd never seen Dominic back away from anyone, even before he became a werewolf.

"You okay?" the new guy asked, pulling me back to the parking lot.

I glanced at him and offered what I was sure was a scary-looking smile. It felt forced and strained. "Um, yeah, thank you, um, Aidan, was it?" I asked. Confused didn't even begin to explain the turmoil swarming my brain.

"No problem," he said with a wink. His voice was deep but warm and held a bit of laughter in it, and I had to admit, the sound of his voice made tiny little butterflies flap in my belly. Or were the butterflies from relief? I wasn't entirely sure.

"You know Dominic?" I asked, squinting up at him and raising my hand to shield the glare from the sun. He was cute, in a rugged sort of way. His hair was shaggy, light brown, and uneven, and his strong jawline was rough looking with stubble. He looked about six-foot, and he was built, but not in a muscle builder kind of way — it was softer — but still showed his undeniable strength.

Aidan chuckled. It was deep and soft and the best sound ever, and he gave me a knowing kind of smile as he watched me take him in. I blushed. "Doesn't everyone in this town know him?" he asked.

"Yeah, they do, but you're clearly new." *Because if you weren't new, you would have pretended not to see Dominic dragging me to his car.* Aidan may have looked strong, but human muscles were more decoration than anything else against the werewolves.

"What's that supposed to mean?" he asked. A wide grin curled his lips. "I can't know people because I'm new?" Aidan chuckled again, and I couldn't help but smile at him. I just loved that sound. It vibrated through me and made my skin tingle.

"Okay, so that probably came out wrong." I dropped my gaze to the ground, trying to hide the burning blush that was rushing up my neck.

Then, a thought dawned on me; maybe he didn't know what Dominic was. Maybe the new guy wasn't stupid, just ignorant. And maybe that was why Dominic walked away. Dominic was giving him a chance to learn the pecking order, giving him a free pass this time. I looked up at him and blurted, "You should be careful. You don't know what you're getting into talking to Dominic like that."

He cocked his head to the side, searching my face. He frowned and sighed softly, and right then, I wished I could read his mind. The look he was giving me was so complex, full of sympathy and anger and something else that I couldn't place, except it did vaguely resemble guilt. He stared at me for a long time, long enough that I started to feel awkward, and it took everything I had not to start fidgeting. After what seemed like hours, he cracked a small smile. "Let's start again," he said, and he stuck his hand out to me. "I'm Aidan Collins."

"Jade Shaw," I said, accepting his hand and pumping it twice and effectively lifting the tension that had been brewing between us. "What are you doing here anyway?"

Aidan smirked. "Just finished registering for classes," he said in a way that made me feel like it should have been obvious.

"On a Friday when the school is closed." It was supposed to be a question, but it came out as a challenge. Maybe it was because new people never moved to Dog Mountain. It was a pack thing. There were never houses available for new residents unless they had the pack's endorsement, and with the way Dominic had acted, Aidan clearly didn't have it.

If Aidan caught my tone, he didn't let on. He just shrugged his shoulders as if to say *obviously*, and asked, "You need a ride somewhere?"

Yes. That's what I wanted to say. The way he was watching as if he wanted nothing more than to get to know me had my heart jumping like crazy. It was such a tentative look as if I were the only person around. But then I guess I was. We were standing in an empty parking lot, except the look in his brown eyes gave me the impression that it wouldn't have mattered if the lot was full. And it made me want to know him, too, even if it would be stupid to try. Aidan had just placed a huge target on his back, and he didn't even know it. Strangely enough, knowing that he was trouble, or more like knowing he had pissed off the beta, only made me want to know him more. But no matter how much I wanted to say yes, what came out was, "Actually, I don't live that far. I'll walk. But thanks."

"Sure," he said, sounding a little disappointed, or maybe that was just me hoping he was disappointed because, well, he was a cutie. He looked at me awkwardly for a second and raked his hand through his hair before sticking his thumbs in his back pockets. "I guess I'll see you around?" Was that a hint of hopefulness I heard in his voice?

"Yeah, um, sure," I said, stuttering slightly over my tongue. "See you." I turned from him, which was actually more of an effort than I had thought it would be, and started for the path. After a few steps, I glanced over my shoulder, and I was a bit shocked, and more than a little thrilled, that he was still standing there watching me. "Oh, and really, thanks," I called and gave a little wave, and then, before I lost my nerve and fully turned back to him, I headed for the trees.

CHAPTER 4

AIDAN

Jade disappeared into the trees. I wasn't sure if I wanted to follow her or pretend as if I had never met her. The one thing that I knew for sure about Dominic was that he didn't get angry or anything, really. He kept his emotions bottled up, hidden behind a mask. But that girl ... the way he had looked at me when I stepped in ... if I had to guess, I'd say he was jealous.

But then I really didn't have to guess. I could smell it on him, and I also caught a whiff of her hatred. It's funny how emotions could tamper with someone's scent. It made them an open book, really.

What was going on between them? Dominic hadn't taken her as his mate. Their scents were still distinctly separate. But there was something about the way that he had looked at her. It was as if she were his. It was full of safety — guarded protection. He may have been angry, but it had been clear that he would have never hurt her. Not really.

And I didn't know how I felt about that. When a wolf picked a mate, that was it. It was for life, and the thought of her being someone else's made my stomach clench. It was stupid. I didn't know anything about the girl other than that she was cute and she had pissed off more than one of my pack members, but when I spoke to her, I couldn't deny that I never wanted to stop hearing the sound of her voice. Even when she was clearly nervous, she had been confident about it. Her voice hadn't wavered. It was strong and sweet. Sure and stable. She knew exactly who she was, and she was so positive about it that I wanted nothing more than to know her, too. She was definitely ... intriguing.

Why had I told her I was registering for school? I should have come up with a better lie than that. I graduated last year. *Ugh!* I should have just left it alone. She was obviously on the verge of being spoken for, and besides that, I no longer had the luxury of choice. Alphas don't get to choose. A frustrated growl rumbled up my throat, and after another long look at the path that Jade had disappeared down, I turned and started for my car.

The cool breeze was refreshing as I made my way to the front of the school. Everything was still green, but soon it would change. The grass would die, the leaves would fall. Longer nights under the moon. For the first time in years, I was excited for the winter to come. I actually had a pack to run with. One that was not my father's.

Dog Mountain was small. Everything connected to the one street that ran through its center. There were a few shops, a handful of restaurants, a grocery store, and a hardware store. I was told that it was a busy place in the summer months, packed full of tourists coming to enjoy the hot springs that were tucked in the mountain, but it was hard to imagine it as I drove through the empty-looking town. A few people were walking on the street. Out of the ten people I saw, six of them were werewolves. At only 4:15, most shops were already closed for the day, with only the grocery store and restaurants still open.

I pulled into the driveway of the shabby-looking motel that I now called home and wasn't the least bit surprised to see Dominic's VW sitting in front of my room. He was leaning against his car, arms folded over his chest, and his legs crossed at the ankles.

I parked beside him, shut off the engine, and jumped out. "You were following me, weren't you?" he asked, not even bothering to look at me.

I walked past him, digging out the flimsy plastic key-card from my pocket, and unlocked the room door. I thought about ignoring the question, but seeing him leaning there, so calm and cool and with an obvious lack of respect, annoyed the hell out of me. "I was," I snapped. "Spread the word through the pack; Jade is off-limits." As soon as the words came out, I regretted them. I could almost feel the anger rolling off him instantly.

I pushed the door open and went straight for the curtains, pulling them closed. The room was an eyesore, and the sunlight dancing off the dust that coated the dark wooden surfaces of the desk and dresser only made it worse. I made a mental note to get cleaning supplies. I wasn't a clean freak by any means, but the dust was starting to drive me crazy.

"Dude, you can't claim her." Dominic was right on my heels, coming into my room and slamming the door with a jarring thud. "You lost that privilege when you became the alpha. You know how it works. You can't just pick a mate." There was a protective edge to his tone that cut through me like a jagged and dull knife.

Dominic pulled out the desk chair and spun it around before dropping down into it. I could feel the hostility rolling off him in waves, even if he did keep his tone even and the usual mask tightly in place.

"That's not what I meant," I said with a huff, except it kind of had been what I had meant, but I wasn't about to admit it. I knew the rules better than most of this pack. My dad had been drilling them into me since I was old enough to understand. "Make sure Erika knows to leave her alone. Same goes for everyone else, including you." I narrowed my eyes, and I could feel my eyebrows knit together as I glared at him. "This pack is going to learn to treat people with respect."

Dominic held my stare for a long moment, his hazel eyes shifting more yellow with every passing second. For a moment, I thought he was going to try to lecture me *again* on why an alpha wasn't free to pick a mate, but he didn't. Instead of arguing with me, he said in an acidic tone, "Yeah, sure, whatever you want."

The tension in the room was thick as we both glared at one another, neither of us willing to back down. Secretly, I kind of admired his gall. He had only known me for half a day, and in that time, he had watched me kill the alpha, and still, he stood up to me. This was the kind of beta I needed. One that wouldn't hesitate to tell me I was wrong. One that would stand up to me when I was making dumbass decisions. That's what my father's beta had done for him, and that's what I wanted, too. Except Dominic didn't stand up to me because he was trying to help, he did it because he had absolutely no respect for me.

"You will start showing me some respect," I said evenly, forging an authority into my voice that I didn't feel, but I was already getting sick of the way he challenged my every decision, and it had only been twelve hours now. It had to stop. "This is your last warning."

"You think you can run this pack without me?" He tensed in his chair, and his muscles shuddered under his skin as if he were on the verge of shifting.

I narrowed my eyes further and gritted my teeth. "Are you challenging me?" It came out as a growl.

Dominic considered it. He looked me up and down, insolently, and the first snap of a bone-breaking and grinding sounded loudly in my ears. Bristles of coarse hair littered his cheekbones, and his eyes glowed yellow as his shift to a wolf began.

Okay, so that wasn't what I had expected. My jaw hardened, and I widened my eyes, staring him down. My inner-wolf squirmed in my stomach, itching to come out, but I held it back, if only barely. Pins and needles rushed over my skin as my fur began to sprout. I stepped closer to him; a savage growl erupted from deep within my gut and rumbled through my lips.

Dominic's eyes widened, and for a split second, fear passed across them. It didn't last. "Nope," he said, shrugging his shoulders; any trace of the wolf vanished. "Just stating the obvious. Ray couldn't do it, and you won't be able to either." He spun the chair lazily in slow circles, and all the tension in him melted away, replaced by the cool conceit that I was getting used to seeing in him. "Once Bruce's pack finds out about you, they'll be here, ripping this town apart while you're weak, and I know them. I'm the one with the contact. I know how they work and where they'll hit." He chuckled and grinned. "You just focus on the games. Without a strong mate, you're as good as dead."

Again, I wanted to tell him to get out. How was I supposed to work with him? I didn't like him, didn't trust him. Everything about him screamed authority, and he wouldn't back down. He had made it clear more than once that he didn't want to be the alpha, but I wasn't buying it. No one would go to such extremes to show their dominance if they didn't want the position. There was just something about him that got my defenses up, and whatever it was, it only felt more intense with each passing minute.

He was still spinning the chair around in slow circles when I finally dropped my glare and padded over to the lumpy bed. I sprawled out, staring up at the off-white popcorn ceiling. I couldn't say how long we sat there, neither of us bothering to say anything, when I asked, "Why haven't you made a move for her?" I hadn't even really realized that I wanted to know his reason until the words were out of my mouth. I glanced over at him then, and he was smirking.

Dominic's smirk turned into a smile, and his shoulders began to shake as he tried to hold in a laugh. "Is that what you think?" He burst out into laughter and choked out, "Dude, I'm into men."

That hadn't been the answer I had expected, and I was sure that if I hadn't been able to smell the truth in his scent or hear the steady beat of his heart, I wouldn't have believed him. As I looked at him, though, even without those other things, I could see the truth written all over his face, and it confused the hell out of me. The kind of hatred I saw between him and Jade was the kind of hatred that stemmed from a lot of hurt feelings and a deep connection. *Maybe they were together before he realized?* I wondered.

"Why does she hate you so much?" I asked.

His smile vanished, and his laughter died abruptly. "She doesn't hate me." His tone was insolent, his jaw clenched. It was as if he dared me to say that Jade didn't like him.

"I'm not an idiot, Dominic," I growled and sat up, glaring at him.

He threw his hands up in surrender. "Seriously, she doesn't hate me exactly," he said with more than a bit of contempt. "Jade just hates the pack. She thinks we ruined her life. She'd be happy if there was no such thing as a werewolf." He was lying. I could hear it in his voice. It was defensive and wavered slightly. I was about to call him on it when he smirked and chuckled. "But don't worry about it too much. Soon enough, she'll hate you, too."

I lay back on the bed, forcing my tense muscles to relax. I didn't want to think about her, or anyone hating me just because I shifted into a wolf every once in a while. It was still hard to wrap my head around the town dynamics. Humans knowingly living with werewolves. It seemed wrong and utterly perfect all at the same time. I figured it would make life easier, not having to hide, and from what I'd heard about Bruce's pack, not hiding would make these people a whole lot safer. But still ... it was weird.

"We've got to get going," Dominic said. "You ready to defend your title and start the games?" There was laughter in his voice, and when I shifted on the bed to look at him, he was giving me an odd kind of look.

"I'm defending the title against you?" I asked, forging my voice to sound cool and uncaring as if he were a pesky flea and nothing to worry about, but in all honesty, out of all the males I had met so far, Dominic was the one I worried about.

He didn't answer. His eyes were dancing with amusement, and he chuckled as he rose from his chair and headed for the door. But then, I guess his laughter was enough to answer my question.

"I won't go easy on you," I said, sitting up. "I might not have meant to take over this pack, but I do intend on keeping it."

Part of me wanted to launch at him right then and there and end this ... whatever this was that was brewing between us, but I couldn't. No. I wouldn't. I was going to do this by the rules. Every male had a right to challenge me once I overthrew the alpha. That was the point of this ceremony, and I needed to defend the title with honor and witnesses, not in a brawl in a grungy motel room. Tonight, I would either be taken down, or I would remain standing. I intended to remain standing.

Dominic stopped at the door and glanced over his shoulder at me. "Hurry up, man," he said with a smirk. "Let's get this over with."

CHAPTER 5

JADE

The walk home was quiet. Too quiet. I took the trail that cut through the woods. It ran from the school right past my house. It was probably just Dominic's insinuated threat that Erika was lurking about, but the whole way home, I was on edge. At every bend in the path, my heart literally stopped until I could see that nothing was hidden around it, and the hair on the back of my neck stood on end, sending prickling shivers down my spine. After the first two minutes or so, I was seriously kicking myself for not taking Aidan (or Dominic, for that matter) up on the ride home.

Me and my stupid pride! That's pretty much what it all boiled down to. I was too proud to ask one of those stupid dogs for help. And Aidan, well, I couldn't think of a good excuse for that. Stupidity was pretty much all I had there.

I wondered if Aidan knew about the werewolves. I was pretty certain that he didn't. If he did, he wouldn't have faced off with Dominic as he had. I thought about telling him, warning him to stay clear of the pack, but each time the words ran through my mind, all I saw was his smirk and laughing eyes. He'd probably think I was a lunatic.

"Jade, where have you been?" Marcy yelled from my porch step as I stepped out of the tree line. "I've been waiting for hours." She raced over to me, throwing her arms around me in a too-tight hug. "Don't scare me like that again."

Laughing, I pried her too tight arms off my waist. "Really, Mac? Hours?" To say she was a little dramatic would have been a complete understatement. Marcy was one of those all-or-nothing kinds of people, and she applied it to every aspect of her life. There was never a middle ground with her. And that was one of the things I loved about her the most.

She wrinkled her nose at me and tucked her long blond hair behind her ears. "Okay, maybe it was only ten minutes. But it felt like hours." She grabbed my hand and dragged me over to the porch swing. "Did you hear the news?" she asked as she plopped down, taking me with her. The swing creaked and cracked under our weight. She didn't even take a breath for me to answer before she huffed and muttered, "No, of course, you didn't. I shouldn't even know yet."

"What news?" I asked distractedly, noticing that the oversized driveway was empty, and the house was quiet. I glanced at my watch, 4:15. Where were my parents?

"If I tell you, you have to swear not to breathe a word," she said, giving me a stern look.

"Of course," I grumbled and rolled my eyes. Marcy had been going through this gossip phase. It started about a month ago, and each day since, there was another big piece of 'news' that I couldn't breathe a word about. It usually consisted of who was dating who, or what one of the *she-wolves* had worn; a bunch of useless information, really. But like I said before, she was an all-or-nothing kind of person, and gossiping was no different from anything else. At least her information was harmless to those she talked about. Marcy didn't have a malicious bone in her body. I leaned back on the swing, getting comfortable, and waited to be bombarded with whatever had sparked her interest today.

Marcy leaned into me; her vanilla spice lotion tickled my nose, and she whispered, "Ray is dead."

If Marcy had wanted my attention, she got it. "Holy sugar sticks!" I shrieked, and I swiveled on the swing, making the chains creak. My eyes felt as if they were bulging out of their sockets. "He's dead? You sure he's not just on a bender again?" It wasn't uncommon for the pack's alpha to disappear for a few days (or weeks) when he started drinking again. Clearly, Dominic wasn't kidding when he said the pack was stressed.

I felt sick. Guilt washed over me in nauseating waves of hot and cold. Had Dominic been reaching out to me because he needed a friend? Did I want to be that friend? *Yes. No. Yes. Maybe.*

Marcy held a finger to her lips and *shushed* me, and then she began wrapping a chunk of her hair around her finger, a nervous release she did often. That's when I noticed her puffy, bloodshot eyes and her wrinkly T-shirt. Marcy was a girly girl. She always looked perfect, and come to think of it, unless she was sleeping, I was pretty sure that I'd never seen her in a baggy T-shirt before. She tried to smile, but I could see through the act. Her lips were tight, forced into an exaggerated curve. If she had been wearing red lipstick, she would have resembled a demented clown.

She leaned into me again, dropping her voice even lower, as if she were worried someone would overhear her. "I overheard Dad talking about it at the station this afternoon, so I snuck into his office, and ..." she let her words fall short and visibly shuddered before whispering, "I saw the pictures from the investigation. Ray had bite marks all over him. You know what that means, right?" Her eyes were as wide as quarters, and that creepy smile twisted at the edges of her lips again.

I just sat there, staring at her speechless, and a small shiver rushed over my skin. *A new alpha,* a voice in my head, whispered, but I couldn't believe it. "Impossible," I said, more firmly than I felt. "We would have known already if someone had challenged Ray. The pack doesn't keep that stuff a secret. Are you sure the pictures were of him?"

Marcy pursed her lips and glared at me. "Of course, I'm sure. I do work there."

I rolled my eyes. I didn't think a co-op class was classified as actually working anywhere. Well, maybe it kind of was work, but really, she had only been doing it for a week now. There were two detectives in Dog Mountain, Marcy's dad being one of them, and he wanted her to follow in his footsteps. Or at least that's what he said, but truthfully, I thought it had more to do with her mom walking out on them last year than career training. He wanted to keep a closer eye on her, and what better way than to have her spend half of the day on the job with him.

A gust of cool wind blew over us, rustling the leaves in the towering oak tree that sat in the front yard, and I shivered again. Fall was coming. I could feel it in the air, crisp and fresh. It wouldn't be long now before the leaves changed. They were already starting; a slight hint of red and yellow-tinged the oak and maple trees surrounding my yard.

"I'm just saying," Marcy said with a shrug. "He was a werewolf. I highly doubt it was a *random drunk man falling into a ditch and being mauled to death by a wild animal* kind of thing." She arched a puffy brow at me then and asked, "What took you so long anyway?"

"Erika stole my clothes and left me pretty much naked in the gym locker room," I said absently, my mind reeling with the threat of a new alpha. The recruiting would start again, and then the power struggle, all wolves fighting each other for a higher standing in the pack. I had seen it happen twice in the last seven years, and each time had been worse than the last.

Marcy gasped and grabbed my arm. "You're kidding."

I let out a strangled kind of laugh. She was wiggling about on the swing, dying to hear the gossip. "Nope, and out of all the people who could have come by, it was Dominic that brought me my stuff back."

"Dominic? Really?" she squealed. "Please tell me you two have worked it out, and the two-year silent treatment is over."

With a long and drawn-out groan, I said, "Mac, seriously, he's a jerk." I cut her a look that I hoped showed how much I disapproved of the way she still idolized him. "You need to forget about him already. It's been two years."

Marcy, unlike me, had nothing against Dominic or the pack for that matter. It made no sense to me. It was their fault that her mother left, even if it wasn't intentional. Marcy's mom had never been okay with the whole werewolf thing (not that I blamed her), and last year she finally cracked — literally. She started doing drugs, drinking, and then a few months later, she just up and left without even saying goodbye. But, instead of blaming the pack, Marcy blamed her mom. I guessed there was something rational behind her blame, but seriously, shouldn't she hate the wolves just as much?

She smacked my knee playfully. "I miss him, and he's really not that bad. He hasn't changed as much as you think. If you'd just give him a chance ..." She looked at me, giving me one of those *I feel sorry for you* looks, and said, "I think he misses you, too."

Misses me. The idea of Dominic missing me made the hair on the back of my neck, and my arms stand on end and a small, but very noticeable, chill prickle over my skin. I tried to pretend that the shiver was from the brisk wind, but it wasn't. My stomach twisted and jumped; my body was alive with a craving — a longing — for him, one that I was beginning to think time would not dampen.

"Have you heard anything about a new alpha?" I asked, steering her back to the important stuff. My palms were starting to sweat, clammy and cold. My heart was aching. It was as if, with every frantic beat, a hand gripped onto it, squeezing it tight in my chest.

The last thing I wanted to think about was the gaping hole that Dominic had left behind when he walked out on Marcy and me two years ago.

"Nope. Nothing," Marcy said. "The pack's not talking. Dad won't say a thing. I even tried to bribe him with that father-daughter day he's been begging me for after he caught me looking at the pictures, and still, nothing. He won't even tell me when it happened." She looked me square on and leaned in so close that our noses were almost touching. "They're trying to cover it up, Jade. Dominic came into the station, and Dad actually shoved me in a closet so I wouldn't be seen. He hid me from Dom. Our Dom," she paused for a second, and her skin turned a pasty white. "Dominic doesn't want a single breath spoken about Ray's death. Shit, I really shouldn't have told you."

No shit, I thought. Why the hell would they want to cover it up? It made no sense. Alphas die. It happens ... sometimes. And Ray was a class A douche bag. Why did Dominic care if people knew or not? He didn't even like Ray, and he never tried to hide it, not for a second.

Right then, I felt all kinds of guilty. It rushed over me like a flash flood, cold and wet. I started to sweat, my stomach turned, and for a second, I thought I was going to be sick. Since when did I become such an insensitive bitch?

"Jade," Marcy whispered and shook my hand as if she were trying to get my attention, and she ripped me from my thoughts. "Jade, please don't say anything. Not even to Dominic. Please."

"Please," I said, waving her off. I stomped down the turmoil that was swimming through my stomach and smirked. "Tell Dominic? Not a chance. You know I won't say a word."

The blare of a car horn made Marcy jump. We both looked up to see Mom's blue minivan pulling up in the driveway. She waved at us and turned off the engine. "Hi, girls," Mom said as she opened the door. She jumped out and then reached back into the car, pulling out two big brown paper bags. When she turned back to us, she smiled, but I thought it looked too big and too nervous. Or maybe that was because I felt so nervous that everything around me was suddenly looking ... wrong.

"Hi, Mom," we said in unison, both jumping up from the swing. Marcy gave me a pointed look as if to say *Not a word.* I grimaced at her and then rushed over to help Mom with the bags. Marcy was right on my heels.

"Dad's busy tonight, so it's just us girls." Mom grinned, letting us take the bags, which smelled deliciously like fried chicken, and then she reached back into the car and produced an armload of movies. "I brought home KFC and movies."

CHAPTER 6

AIDAN

Steam curled around me. I stood rigid on a platform of rock, looking down into a pool of black. The hot spring-fed the air with a misty fog, effectively reducing visibility for me as well as my challengers. Tonight was not just about strength. It was about the ability to fight with what you had around you. And I was ready, kind of, sort of, maybe.

The night air was cool but far from cold, and the canopy of trees blocked out any moonlight from above. I looked out over the crowd of twenty-nine werewolves standing just on the edge of the challenger's ring, defined by blazing torches which lit their faces. They all watched me with leery eyes. All but one. Dominic.

He stood in the center of the ring and nodded to me for the second time, a clear indication that it was time to start, and I gritted my teeth. Even when he was on the verge of trying to overthrow me, he still felt the need to act as my second and feed me cues. It was positively infuriating.

I moved to the side, stepped around the pool of water, and started down the carved rock staircase. "All of you who wish to challenge me, step forward," I said, my voice strong and firm and cold, not giving any indication to the fury that was brewing within me. For a moment, I'd thought that maybe, just maybe, Dominic and I would be a great team. Too bad the thought didn't last.

I continued downward, keeping my chin even and my shoulders back. Dominic held my eyes, and a smirk grew upon his face. I smirked back and raised an eyebrow. What was he playing at?

Surely, he had to be a little bit nervous, but if he was, he wasn't showing it.

I reached the bottom of the stairs and stepped onto the damp grass. I paused for a second, scanning the crowd, and as I did, most of them cringed back or dropped their curious gazes to the ground. The only ones that stayed firm were the pack enforcers, but they were the least of my concern. Enforcers rarely challenged for alpha. For the most part, they were more than content with the power they already held over the pack, and I was sure that I wouldn't be going up against anyone from that team of five tonight.

I laughed a deep and belting sound that echoed through the clearing. I couldn't help it. My nerves were jumping like grasshoppers in my belly. All these people watching me. It kind of sucked. I could fight. I could be a leader, but public speaking was really not my thing.

"Is no one going to step forward?" I asked as I made my way into the center of the circle, feeling more confident with every step, and I took my place in front of Dominic. Part of me was hoping someone else would step forward. If I had to fight tonight, I seriously didn't want Dominic to be the only person I fought against. I wanted ... no, I needed a warm-up.

Dominic's grin widened, and he took a step closer to me. And that's when I noticed it. There was something in his scent. Something ... not right. Everything was too calm about him. No trace of adrenaline and no anger. Nothing.

He took another step. He was close enough that I could feel his hot breath puffing against my face and his hazel eyes shimmered with flecks of gold. He held my stare for a long moment, his muscles taut and his stance ready, and just when I thought he was going to attack, he asked, "I didn't fool you for a second, did I?"

"Nope," I lied, keeping my face hard as stone. I felt a sigh of relief inching up my throat, and I quickly swallowed it down. Relief washed over me in hot waves. From what I knew of Dominic, if he had wanted to fight, it would have been a fight to the death, and at that moment, I was shocked at how much I didn't actually want to kill the jerk.

He clasped me in a hug, smacking my back. "Now the fun starts," he whispered, except the tone he used made me think of anything but fun, and I stiffened slightly.

Dominic stepped back from me and looked out over the crowd once more, checking for anyone to step forward. When no one moved, he pulled the short wrought iron branding stick from his back pocket and walked over to one of the torches, holding it in the flame to heat. My jaw twitched. I could already feel the pain, and it hadn't even been done yet.

I turned to the crowd, a touch surprised at the silence. They were all watching me expectantly, waiting for me to speak. I swallowed hard and said, "You all have spoken by staying silent. Today marks a new day for this pack. New leadership and some much-needed change. Together, we will bring balance back into this pack."

It all felt too easy. All of it. What had Ray done to these people? The silence was deafening, and for a split second, I thought that someone might step up. Surely at least one of the males wanted to take the pack. They didn't even know me. I just couldn't believe that they would allow some new blood to walk in without fighting. But then I heard it. A soft clap. Just one. And that one was followed by another and another, and soon the clapping was louder than the silence.

I smiled, and warmth rushed through me. Acceptance. I hadn't let myself think that it could happen this quickly, but it was. Whether it was because they actually wanted me or because they were too scared to cross me, I didn't know, and right then, I didn't really care. This was mine. All of it. My life was changing and morphing before my eyes. In just a matter of hours, I had gone from a lone wolf, running from my father to an alpha. It was a rush. Adrenaline pumped through my veins, and my smile grew wider.

I stripped off my shirt, turned my back on the crowd, and closed the distance to Dominic. He held up the branding iron; the 'A' on the end glowed, burning like embers. This was the last step to claiming my new rank. The branding irons had been created long ago, back when werewolves ran wild and killed innocent people recklessly. They were infused with magic from the first pack and were distributed as new packs formed. When an alpha was branded with it, the magic bonded with their skin and bones. It gave them the power to use their scent, channel it, enhance it, and call upon it to control their wolves.

He mouthed, '*You ready*,' which turned out to be a pointless question because he didn't wait for my answer before he stabbed my right pectoral with the magic-infused, burning metal.

I locked eyes with him. My skin sizzled, and my jaw clenched, but somehow I managed to stay still and not make a sound. It hurt like hell. The metal burning and melting my skin. Leaving the alpha's imprint on my chest, but I didn't flinch. I wanted this too much. Craved it. Needed it. I could already feel the magic seeping into my bones as my flesh melted around the smoldering metal.

When he finally pulled it away, my skin stung as it quickly stitched back together, leaving a raised scar that looked as if it had been there for years. Dominic dropped the branding stick to the ground and snagged up a bottle of rye. He handed it to me, straight-faced, with awe shining in his eyes, and gave me a firm whack on the back before moving back into the center of the circle.

I quickly twisted the top and took a deep swig from the bottle. The rye burned down my throat and warmed my belly. My skin still stung, but the pain was tolerable. The soft buzz of the crowd drifted around me, and it grew louder and louder. I turned back to them just as Dominic raised a hand, silencing them.

The crowd inched forward, moving in closer to the edge of the circle, and I cringed on the inside as I watched the females shuffling in, snapping and growling at each other, even in their human forms.

Dominic stood still, waiting for them to settle, and as I watched him, I was certain that this was not the first time he had made this announcement. He waited patiently, playing his role of my beta perfectly. And right then, I got the feeling that Tammy may not have been the first alpha female Ray had had. Dominic seemed ... practiced. Sure of himself and what needed to be said.

"Ray's death has not and will not be leaked," Dominic said, belting out the words so loudly it was as if he had a microphone. "As you know, Tammy has left us, and with her gone, a new alpha female must rise up. So tonight not only marks the night of a new alpha male for our pack, but it also marks the start of the games for a new alpha female."

Hoots and hollers rang out through the night, and Dominic smiled, patiently waiting for them to die down before continuing, "Once the alpha pair has been established, we will let the news travel. You all need to be vigilant with your patrols. If any of you pick up the scent of Bruce's pack, we need to know immediately. He can't know that the females don't have a leader."

"You sound pretty cocky there, Dominic," someone shouted. "Last I checked, you lose your status when a new alpha male takes over."

Dominic laughed, a cruel sound. "You want to fight me for it, Joe?" Everything about him was relaxed as he spoke, his shoulders loose, his smile easy. He waited for a moment before another laugh fell out, and he said, "Yeah, that's what I thought." Then he turned to me and said, "You want to settle this, Aidan? Are you going to appoint a new beta?"

The pack erupted in a mess of noise. "Enough!" I yelled over the chaos. "Dominic will remain as my beta." I paused, waiting for any objections, but when none came, I said, "Let the games begin."

CHAPTER 7

JADE

I woke up feeling gross and greasy. The KFC had been delicious going down, but I wasn't used to eating that much grease at once, and it really wasn't sitting well at all.

Last night had been ... weird. Dad hadn't come home. Mom said he had a *boy's weekend*, and there was nothing to worry about, but the whole fact that she said there was nothing to worry about had me kind of worried. And it had been clear that I wasn't the only one. Mom had been hyperaware of every bump and thump. At one point, I had shifted on the couch, making the leather squeak beneath me, and she had jumped, tossing a full bowl of popcorn all over the floor.

Mom was never jumpy. She took everything in stride, and even when she was nervous, she always hid it well. It was a survival technique that I frequently used while dealing with the oddities of our town. But last night, she had been a nervous wreck.

Rolling over in bed, I looked out the big bay window. The sky looked like a dirty ball of wool had been unraveled, covered in clouds. I couldn't say how long I had lain there watching the little rivers of rain slide down my window when my door squeaked open, and Mom peeked around it. "Honey, you need to get up."

"It's Saturday, Mom," I said with a groan and rolled over.

Mom pursed her lips, pushed the door wide open, and flicked the light switch on. The pot lights seemed overly bright against the dreary day outside. "You have company," she said evenly.

"Mac's not company," I groaned. "She's been a permanent fixture here for a year now." Since her mother took off last year, Marcy had pretty much moved into our house, and my mom had unofficially adopted her into our family. The only time she went home now was when her father forced her, or rather when he begged her. It wasn't that she didn't want to spend time with her dad, it was more that he was never home, always working, and Marcy wasn't really a solitary kind of person. She needed people, noise, and action.

I rolled up on my elbows and scrunched my forehead as my sleepy brain tried to process why I needed to get up. I guess I took too long because she marched into the room, shooting me one of that *stern mom* kind of looks.

"I'm not talking about Mac," she said with her hands on her hips, scowling down at me. "Get up. He's waiting for you."

"What?" I asked, squinting at her. "Who's 'he?'" I scrubbed my eyes, wiping the sleep from them, and yawned loudly.

Mom looked more put together today, not as jittery, that was for sure. She had her dark brown hair tied up in a loose bun, and she was dressed in a long, simple black knit dress. It hung on her slim figure loosely. She arched a brow, and a small, devious-looking smile curled her lips. "Dominic's downstairs."

"You let him in the house?" I hissed and sat up with a start. I fought against my comforter, which was wrapped around my legs like a cocoon. "What's wrong with you?"

As soon as I said it, I heard his rumbling chuckle. *Darn those dogs and their impeccable hearing!* I glared at the door and gritted my teeth.

"Of course, I let him in. He's been your best friend since you were a baby," she said hastily and a bit too loudly as if she were trying to make sure he heard her reprimand me. "He stopped by to drop off your backpack, and he wants to talk to you." She walked over to my bed, flung the covers back, and glared down at me with her hands on her hips. "Now get up. I'm going out."

I gritted my teeth. *My backpack,* I thought, completely annoyed at myself for forgetting about it yesterday. I thought of a million reasons why I didn't want to talk to him or why I wasn't going to get out of bed, but each one sounded like a child throwing a tantrum. "Where are you going?" I asked instead. Heat settled in my cheeks, and my jaw was starting to ache from clenching it so tightly.

"Shopping," she said, not unkindly but with a definite edge, and then she grabbed hold of my feet and started to pull, dragging me off my bed. "Now get in the shower and make yourself presentable," she said.

Mom didn't leave my room until she watched me walk into the bathroom, and knowing her, she probably stood there until she heard the shower turn on. I couldn't believe she was still pushing her little dream on me. It was the only reason I could think of why she would leave the house with me in the shower and Dominic sitting just downstairs. Well, okay, maybe it wasn't the only reason. My parents knew he was gay, but still, they wanted nothing more than for me to date a werewolf, and pushing me toward Dominic would push me toward the straight ones. Twisted, right? They wanted their only daughter to hook up with an animal — literally.

I took my time in the shower and even longer blow-drying my hair. I was kind of hoping that if I stalled long enough, he'd just go away. I spent ten minutes staring into my closet before I finally decided on a pair of jeans and a powder blue T-shirt, and then, since I couldn't think of any other way to prolong the process further, I went to see what he wanted.

Dominic was lounging in my dad's recliner, and when I spotted him, I almost forgot how much I didn't want to see him. He looked ... good. Really good. His short blond hair was gelled, with the front flipped up. He was in jeans and a light blue polo shirt with the collar popped up, and he was smiling, something that he rarely did anymore, and darn it, but I missed that smile. It was a lot easier to hate him when he was all jerky and serious. But right then, at that moment, if only for a second, he was my best friend again.

I stood at the top of the stairs for a moment, watching him run a finger along the stacked bookcase beside him as if he were trying to pick something to read. He looked comfortable — at home — sitting in our country-style living room, amongst the blue and green-checkered curtains and the cherry wood floors. But then, I figured he should look comfortable since he was the one that had made and hung the curtains, and come to think of it, I was certain he had recommended cherry wood for the floors, too. I knew he had helped install them, at least.

As I padded down the stairs, trying to prepare myself for what I was sure would be a replay of yesterday, I stumbled, tripping over my own feet. I hadn't thought he'd even noticed me coming down the stairs, but the moment I slipped, Dominic jumped out of his chair, leaped over the coffee table, and caught me just before I did a face plant on the floor.

"That was graceful," he said, his voice oozing with sarcasm, and he helped me regain my balance. His lips twitched, and a cocky grin spread across his face.

"Wow, thanks," I said, snatching my arm from his hand. He chuckled, and his smile grew wider. I gave him my best *shut-up* look and said, "And you wonder why I don't like you. You do something slightly nice, and then you always ruin it by speaking."

Dominic crossed his arms over his chest; they bounced softly with his shoulders as he tried to hold in a laugh. His eyes shimmered with humor. "A simple thank you would have worked, too," he said. "You know, you're still so adorable when you're all mad, scrunchy-nosed, and flushed cheeked."

"Whatever," I snapped, putting every bit of snark I had into my tone. "Where's Mac?"

"She went home," he said, and then he gave me a serious look. "Jade, I want you to stay away from Aidan."

I laughed dryly and rolled my eyes before making my way into the kitchen. So that was what this little visit was about. The new guy. And by the look I was getting from Dominic, I'd guess it was also about a bruised ego. "And I care what you want because?"

Dominic followed me, stopping at the fridge to grab milk before moving to the cupboard and snagging two mugs. He scooped three heaping spoonfuls of sugar in one, added only milk to the other, and then filled them with steaming coffee. I watched him, stunned. The way he moved around the kitchen was as if he were supposed to be there as if he had never left. Once he had finished stirring in the sugar, he slid the mug over to me and grinned. "You still like it that way, right?"

I took the mug and drank a long, deep mouthful before looking back up at him. "What are you really doing here, Dominic?"

He stepped over to me and tucked a few strands of loose hair behind my ear, a gesture that used to be common, but now, it just felt wrong. "I saw the way you were looking at him. He's no good for you." There was more emotion in his voice than I was used to. It was gentle and pleading, strong and caring. It was as if we had stepped back two years, and he was still my Dom. My rock. My stabling force. My best friend. And I don't know why, but it pissed me off.

I almost pointed out that I didn't know anything about Aidan. I came close to telling Dominic that there was nothing to worry about because honestly, since finding out about Ray, I hadn't even given Aidan another thought, but I couldn't bring myself to do it. As far as I was concerned, it was none of his business who I looked at. "You don't have the right to play the concerned best friend card. Not anymore."

Hot guilt pulsed over me, and I almost took the words back. I felt like an insensitive jerk. Again, I wondered if he was trying to reach out because he needed someone to talk to about Ray's death. I almost asked him if he was okay, but just before I opened my mouth, Marcy's pointed look from yesterday flashed through my head and I bit my tongue. There was a reason Ray's death was a secret. I didn't understand why, and I really wasn't sure if I should let on that I knew about it — yet.

He narrowed his eyes, not harshly, but as if he were trying to get a better look at me and see something that may have been hidden under my words. "You're not being fair," he said after a long moment.

I glared at him. There really was nothing to say. He had abandoned me when I had needed him. Blew me off to climb the pack ranks. He had no right to try to tell me what was and wasn't good for me. Not anymore. If he wanted to talk about Ray, then fine, I'd be there for him, but I wasn't about to stand there and listen to him tell me what I could and couldn't do.

He must have seen what I was thinking, or maybe he still just knew me that well because he groaned. Dominic had a variety of groans. There was the long and drawn-out, annoyed groan. The short but loud *you've got to be kidding me* groan. But this one was one that I knew well. It was the *you are being so stubborn* groan. "Jade, you've got to forgive me already. It's been two years."

I clenched my teeth, trying to keep my jaw from dropping. If it wasn't for the look he was giving me, I probably would have laughed, but I could see that he was dead serious, and that made my head spin. "Exactly, it's been two years since the last time you made an effort. Two years since the first time you pretended not to know me, and two years since you left me to find my own way home because the pack was more important. You've never even pretended to be sorry."

Dominic crumbled at my words as if I had hauled off and punched him, and I almost felt bad — almost. He jammed his thumbs into the front pockets of his jeans and leaned against the counter, his shoulders hunched, and his gaze dropped to my stomach as if he couldn't look me in the face any longer. "I had to prove myself. They would have eaten me alive if I showed weakness, and you know it."

"Don't give me that crap," I snapped and banged my mug down

on the counter. "Being a friend isn't being weak. You're just like the rest of them. You don't give a crap who you stomp on."

He groaned. It was the annoyed groan this time. "I'm trying to fix things. Stop being so stubborn."

"It's my natural defense, Dom," I said, giving him a dirty look, "the one I use against idiots, bullshit, and stupidity, and since you're here ..." I waved my arm around, in an exaggerated gesture in his direction.

He smiled a sad sort of smile, and it caught me off guard. My stomach dropped, and my eyes prickled. I quickly blinked the tears away. There was no way he was going to see me hurting. Mad was one thing, but seeing me in pain ... it wasn't happening.

"You haven't called me Dom in years." His voice was soft, just barely a whisper, and I may have been mistaken, but I was pretty sure his eyes looked a bit misty.

I couldn't even begin to count how many times I had wanted to have this conversation. How many times I had sat up all night waiting for him to call and *want to fix things*, but now that it was actually happening, it was the last thing I wanted to hear. "It's too late to fix things." I sighed, frustrated and angry and hurt, and I turned my back on him. "Just get out."

I didn't hear him move, and I jumped when the front door slammed. Seconds later, his engine rumbled, and then his tires squealed as he peeled out of the driveway. My body shook, my fingers trembled, and with him gone, it was even harder not to cry.

CHAPTER 8

AIDAN

I was a wolf, and she pretended not to see me.

Jade sat on the covered porch of a large log house, rocking back and forth on one of those dainty-looking, wire porch swings. She stared at what appeared to be a sketchbook in her lap. From where I sat, just past the tree line, in clear view of anyone who may have passed by, I watched as her blackened hand made sure and gentle strokes across the page. Every few seconds, her hand would pause, and her head would tilt in my direction as she stole a glance, but she never once made eye contact.

That was a mistake.

If I had been any other wolf, she would have looked submissive. And submission would not get her to where I was starting to think she should be. It would only put her at risk. But as I watched, it was clear that this was not actually submission. It was power. A cool and calm remoteness. She did not look as if she were giving in. Instead, it was as if she were too important, too high in the ranks, to pay me any attention. She was above me. And my inner-wolf craved her attention and acceptance.

It was an odd feeling, one that I was not used to. She should have been the one feeling this way, not me. It was maddening and confusing. She wasn't even one of us. And in all honesty, part of me didn't want her to be. The strength she emanated was intimidating. Crippling. What would it be like if she was part of the pack?

That morning, I had woken up, determined to avoid her. There was no point in knowing her. Not now. The games had started. The challenging females had made themselves known. Getting to know her now would only put her in danger. I had sparked her interest when we first met. Her scent had given her away, and she wouldn't give in easily; I was sure of it. And letting her know she had caught my attention would only make it harder. Jade didn't strike me as the backing down type, and that would be deadly, definitely, maybe. This was my life now, and for the most part, it was a life that I wanted. And she was just a girl.

But Jade ... she seemed to weasel her way back into my thoughts at the least expected moments. I wouldn't say I liked her, but she was undeniably intriguing. But then, that could have had something to do with Dominic hounding me last night to stay away from her, or maybe it was the way she had fought back yesterday. Whatever it was, she had caught my attention and refused to let go. And no matter how hard I tried to pretend that I had never met her, my brain wouldn't let me forget.

For a few minutes, I had successfully pushed her out of the forefront of my mind, or I had until Dominic had shown up late for our meeting this morning. Not just a little late, but thirty minutes late. At first, I had thought that his hard eyes and pasty-looking skin were directed at me, but then he had placed a hand on my shoulder and said, *'Sorry I'm late.'* Except, it hadn't been his words that had given him away. It had been the scent on his hand.

It was a scent that I knew or that I thought I knew. Almonds with a splash of fruit punch. It tickled at my memory, like a niggling reminder of something that stayed just out of reach.

And it was because of that scent that I had found myself as a wolf, sitting under an oak tree, outside Jade's house.

I hadn't known where I was going until I had arrived here. The rain had temporarily stopped, but it was bound to start again by the look of the blackened sky. My fur was drenched from running through the sodden woods, and I was starting to get cold, but I couldn't make myself leave.

What was it about her that made Dominic so uptight? I had to know. Each time her name had been mentioned last night, whether it was by one of the girls bragging about their little stunt or me, he had stiffened, each muscle visibly coiling beneath his skin.

I stalked closer, inch by inch. I didn't want to scare her away, but I had to get closer. Every animal instinct I had was insistently urging me to get her attention.

"Dominic, if that's you, you can screw off." She didn't look up as she spoke, and her hand continued to move deftly across the page, stroke by sure stroke.

Her commanding tone stopped me, pinning me in place. *Who was this girl?* I felt myself shrink, crouching lower and bowing my head. My brain was screaming at me to show my dominance, but my inner-wolf shrank anyway.

I whimpered. I tried to swallow it, choke it down, but I couldn't, and Jade's head snapped up. Her stare was piercing, penetrating, and I bowed my head further. *Who was this girl?*

I didn't move. I couldn't move. When she finally dropped her eyes back to the page, my legs were trembling beneath me. I needed her approval. I didn't think as I bounded up the porch steps. I whimpered again and sat beside her, pressing my soaking wet body against her leg.

Jade stiffened, and a gasping sound hissed from her lips. I nosed her notebook, pushing it until it slid onto the swing beside her, and put my head on her lap. As I looked up into her big brown eyes for a moment, I thought she was going to push me away. She certainly looked as if she were considering it. But then, she smiled, a thin, tight-lipped smile, and placed a soft hand on my head. "I know, buddy," she said, stroking my fur. "I miss you, too."

JADE

It felt weird speaking to a wolf. I didn't know if he understood me, but I thought he probably did with the way he watched me. I buried my hand in his coarse fur, scratching his back, and he pressed into me further. He was soaking wet, and as he leaned against me, my jean-clad leg absorbed the moisture, and the fabric clung to my calf and knee.

I wanted to say more. I wanted to yell at him, laugh with him, and hug him. I wanted my Dominic back with every fiber in my body. This was the most attention he had given me in two years. I had tried so many times to talk to him, and he always pushed me away. This was my chance to get it all out, but instead of talking, I wrapped my arms around his neck and hugged him as he littered my face with sloppy kisses.

It seemed like only yesterday that he was bitten. The memory was still clear in my mind, cemented there, unwavering and unyielding. We were walking through the park, after watching a stupid horror movie. Dominic was a *Freddy Kruger* fanatic, me, not so much. There was just something about dying in a dream that made my skin crawl.

Late-night walks after scary movies were kind of a ritual of ours. It gave me time to unwind and reassure myself that it was only a movie. We were walking, arms linked, looking up at the star-speckled sky, when Dominic had stopped short and said, "You hear that?"

I smacked him playfully with my free hand and said dryly, "Not funny, Dom." He gave me an odd look, one that I really didn't understand, and then started walking again.

One of the things I had always loved about our friendship was that we had never needed to fill the silence with pointless conversation. We could spend hours just being together, doing our own thing without talking. And that night had been one of those nights. It was peaceful and perfect.

"Jade, there's something I need to tell you," Dominic said after we had walked for at least twenty minutes. That was when I had noticed how stiff his arm was in mine as if I were holding onto a steel pipe.

"Mmmhmm," I mumbled, hugging myself closer to his side, trying to keep myself out of the chilly fall wind. But instead of holding me closer, he only stiffened further.

I stopped short, looking up at him. A muscle in his neck twitched under his skin, throbbing like a heartbeat. His face was lined with crevasses, branching out from the corners of his eyes and lips like wild vines. "Ray wants me to join the pack," he blurted, all the words running together.

It took me a long minute to understand what he was saying, but sweat began to trickle down my back when I did. My stomach sank, and a chill rushed over my skin. For a moment, I thought I was going to be sick. I could taste the sour bile rising, burning up my esophagus. "You can't. They're a bunch of jerks, Dom. You can't." My voice screeched on the last word, loud and piercing.

"I know," he said. He hadn't needed to say more; I understood everything he wanted to convey in those two words. They would eat him alive. They were hard on him now, and we both knew they would be even worse if he was one of them. The pack had changed drastically since Ray became the alpha. They were vicious, even toward their own, and Dom ... well, Dom had a soft heart.

But Dominic never had a choice, not really.

The chilly night turned bitter. I remembered thinking that Erika must have been following us the whole time, waiting for the perfect moment to step out from the trees. I heard the crunch of gravel before I saw her. She stood in the center of the winding path with a purely evil smirk. The moonlight cast an unnerving silvery glow around her, making her black jeans shimmer in the light.

"Dominic, you have been summoned," Erika said. Her voice rang out, splitting through the silent night.

I moved in front of him without thinking, trying to block him from her sight. Thinking about it now, I realized that it would have never worked; he was half a foot taller than I was, but at the time, all I wanted to do was to hide my Dom. "No, you can't have him." My voice was strong, giving no indication of the twisted knots in my stomach.

Erika threw her head back and laughed. She locked her eyes with mine, and her skin rippled. Snaps and pops echoed through the cool night, and hair sprouted along her exposed flesh. Her face hazed over, distorting and shifting. Her legs snapped back, her arms extended and thinned. My stomach rolled as another deafeningly loud snap reverberated around me, and she dropped to all fours.

"Dom, run!" I yelled, glancing behind me, but he didn't move. I shoved him, trying to push him into action. It was as if he didn't even notice me; all he did was stare blankly at Erika.

A snarl ripped through the air, and I snapped my gaze back to where Erika had stood, just as a white wolf lunged at us.

Dominic hadn't screamed. He hadn't made a sound. It had been as if he had known all along what was about to happen. As if he had already given up. Before I could move, her teeth were embedded in his thigh.

That had been the night that I had lost one of my best friends. The night he had left me stranded. Erika held onto him until her muzzle was stained with red. She let go and chomped down three more times before sitting down on her haunches and staring up at him, his blood dripping from her muzzle. After an agonizingly long moment, she barked once and swung her head toward the trees.

Dominic hadn't looked at me. And he didn't look back while he trailed after Erika, head held high and shoulders stiff and straight. He left me there, tears streaming down my face, in the dark, alone.

I looked down at the big black wolf, his head still in my lap, and ran my hand along his fur, scratching lightly behind his ears. He huffed, a content kind of sound, and his sad-looking, golden eyes met mine. I smiled a little and muttered, “I’m sorry I kicked you out earlier.”

CHAPTER 9

JADE

Monday came too soon. I wasn't ready to face Dominic. Not after confessing that I missed him, even if it was true. He always had a way of making me forget my anger, and as it turned out, even after two years, he could still worm his way into my heart. When he had whimpered, looking up at me with those sad dog eyes, I don't know, I had just ... caved. Part of me wanted to run to him and catch up on everything we had missed, but a bigger part of me wanted nothing to do with him. The pack had ruined him, and if I let him in, I was sure they would ruin me, too.

Dominic had followed me around as a wolf for the rest of the weekend. He had kept his distance, but I could feel him watching my every move. He had sat at the edge of the woods while Mac and I had lunch at Lucy's Diner on Sunday, and he was there, waiting when we had left the boutique. His presence had been comforting and nerve-racking and annoying all rolled into one. Why he felt the need to stalk me as a wolf, I had no clue, but that was exactly what he had done.

My alarm clock's insistent beeping started again, and I smacked the snooze button for the third time. For a split second, I thought about faking sick, but deep down, I knew that wasn't really an option. Sooner or later, I'd have to face him, and I figured it wasn't going to get any easier with time.

Marcy was waiting in the kitchen when I dragged myself downstairs. She was back to her old girly girl self, decked out in a cute, and way too short, pink dress that ruffled around her thighs. She was perched at the island with a jumbo-sized jar of strawberry jam and a plate of toast in front of her. She was giving me an odd look, as if she had something to tell me, but couldn't decide if she actually wanted to say it.

"You stayed here last night?" I asked, too groggy to try to figure out what the look was about. I padded over to the coffee pot and dropped my backpack to the floor. After our shopping trip yesterday, I had hidden in my room, tackling a stack of homework, and frankly, I couldn't remember hearing her leave.

Marcy, I assumed, had set out my travel mug and prefilled the mandatory three heaping spoonfuls of sugar. I snagged the coffee pot and filled it to the brim with steaming goodness before switching off the coffee maker and dumping the last little bit down the drain.

"Nope, came in about twenty minutes ago," she said. She opened the jam, slathered a thick layer onto her toast, and then took a bite. "Mom left while you were in the shower," she continued after she swallowed her mouthful. "She's back on mornings this week. Oh, and Dad's coming home today."

"Huh," I said as I made my way over to the fridge and rummaged through the crisper. Mom being gone already wasn't really a shock. Being an emergency nurse at the hospital meant that she often left the house before me. But Dad, on the other hand, well, I was dying to know where he had been all weekend.

I glanced over my shoulder at Marcy and didn't miss the fidgety way she was sitting. She crossed and uncrossed her legs and slid the butter knife around; she just couldn't sit still. Her lips kept parting as if she were about to say something, but then instead of speaking, she shoved the last of her toast in her mouth.

"You ready to go?" she asked, around another mouthful of toast. She gave me an overly bright smile, popped up from her chair, and made her way over to the fridge, putting away the jam.

I snagged an apple from the crisper. "Yeah, I guess," I said and shut the fridge. I dragged myself over to my coffee and snapped the lid onto my travel mug. I shouldered my bag, and with a quick glance around, finding nothing that could delay leaving, I followed her out the door and locked it.

Not having a car sucked. It wasn't a bad day outside, but this whole walking to school thing was not for me. I really wasn't an exercise kind of girl, especially not in the morning.

The air was relatively warm for September, although by no means was it hot. I could already see the tiny goosebumps popping up on Marcy's bare arms as we walked against the breeze. The forest was a bit redder than it had been on Friday, and a few leaves had already fallen, scattering the gravel path with rich fall colors.

"I talked to Dominic," Marcy said casually, breaking the silence.

Hearing his name made a vein at my temple throb like a pulse, and I really didn't know if it was because I was nervous about seeing him or because he talked to Marcy about me. I cut her a look and said, "Don't want to hear about it, Mac."

She grabbed my wrist, pulling me to a stop. "He told me about this Aidan guy."

I groaned and shook her hand off. "He's overreacting. I met the guy for like thirty seconds, and I haven't seen him since." I shrugged my shoulders and took a deep gulp of coffee as I started walking again. The gravel crunching under my shoes suddenly sounded too loud. "And besides that, Aidan was only trying to foil Dominic's kidnapping attempt."

Marcy laughed. Hard. So hard that she actually snorted. "Wow, seriously? And you say I'm dramatic," she said and shot me a rueful look. I opened my mouth to snap out a defense, but she threw her hands up and silenced me with a hard glare. Her laughter died instantly. "Don't even try it. Dom told me the whole story."

Two years had gone by without so much as a glance from my former best friend, and now this. I huffed noisily. And men said women were confusing. "Why does he even care? If I *was* into this guy, what does it matter to him?"

"Jade, he loves you," she said solemnly, giving me one of those looks that said that I should have already known it.

Ha! Loves me. What a joke. I didn't even bother to acknowledge that comment, and thankfully, Marcy didn't push it. If Dominic loved me so much, then where the hell had he been all this time? Ignoring me. That's where. Or playing cruel pranks on me and pretending he couldn't remember my name. Sure, the cruelness wasn't only directed at me, it was directed at all the *outsiders*, but still ... one weekend of playing nice didn't make up for all the nastiness.

We broke through the trees, stepping off the gravel path and into the parking lot, just as the warning bell rang out. The lot was full of empty cars, with only a few stragglers rushing into the school.

"We need your car back," Marcy said as we both began to sprint across the parking lot.

The hallways were packed with students rushing to their

lockers or darting into homerooms. Marcy and I quickly parted, both mumbling, '*See you,*' before taking off to our lockers.

Dominic's locker was only a few down from mine, and I heard his laughter even before I rounded the corner and he came into view. He was leaning against the metal wall with Aidan, and they were laughing. Laughing!

I was stunned, gawking at them. Aidan was the first to notice me, and he smiled and winked at me. The way he looked at me was as if we shared a secret. And darn it, but those pesky butterflies started to wake up in my stomach. What was it about this guy that made my nerves all jumpy? He was cute, he had helped me out, but really, this was a bit ridiculous. I wasn't, and would not become, one of those boy crazy girls just because a boy winked at me, even if he did have a knee-melting smile.

Aidan hadn't shaved. That was the very first thing I noticed after getting over the shock of seeing him acting all buddy-buddy with Dominic. He was in dark blue jeans and a deep green hoodie that almost looked black. His hair was messy, not in a messy style, but just messy, flipping up at the sides. Everything about him, the way he held himself and dressed, said that he didn't care what people thought. And that alone made him, well, it made him seriously attractive. I loved confidence, and he emitted it like a tidal wave.

I snapped my mouth shut, realizing that my jaw had started to drop, and steeled myself, letting the thick doors within me slam shut, sealing off my emotions. It was something my father had taught me. '*Just imagine big doors, honey,*' he had said. '*And when you want to hide, just pull them closed.*'

It worked for about two seconds.

All the doors were sealed tight. I took a deep breath, gripped my travel mug a bit tighter, and I started down the hallway again toward my locker, focusing on my footfalls instead of staring at them. I could figure out why they were suddenly friends later.

I focused on walking, counting the tiles as I went. Anything for a distraction. I didn't get far. A pair of bright red heels came into my line of vision, and I looked up. Erika. The black leggings and a black, frilly empire cut shirt made her look extra-thin. Her pouty lips were painted to match her shoes, which, personally, I thought seemed like way too much effort for school, and her jet-black hair fell straight over her shoulders.

"I'm only going to tell you this once," Erika said, drumming her fingernails on her hips. "Stay away from them."

My eyebrows lifted so high it felt as if they were in the middle of my forehead. I didn't have to ask who she was talking about. It was clear by the way she stood in front of Dominic and Aidan as if she were trying to block them from my view. "And if I don't?" I asked with a strangled laugh. I don't know what made me say it, but it came out before I could stop it.

She made a *tsk* sound and wagged her finger from side to side. "It's really not up for debate, Jade. I know you've been sneaking around, trying to get Dom's attention. And I saw you checking out Aidan. They're mine. Both of them."

Erika held my stare, and she looked ... threatened as if I were standing in her way, and all she had to do was knock me over, and the prize would be hers. And that was confusing as all hell. Out of the corner of my eye, I noticed that Aidan was watching me intently with a half-smirk and curious eyes, and Dominic, well, Dominic looked as if he were about to burst out laughing. I couldn't say if it was at Erika or at me. His eyes were darting too quickly between us to really tell.

I smirked. "We'll see about that."

Her jaw dropped, and I stepped around her, feeling almost giddy from the dirty look she shot me, and I went straight for my locker. I know it was a horrible thing to think, but honestly, I was absolutely thrilled (and royally pissed off) that one of the *she-wolves* was considering me a threat, even if I really had no clue why.

AIDAN

Jade was livid when she stormed past me, and it was the cutest thing I had ever seen. It was also the most confusing thing I had ever seen. She shot me (or maybe — hopefully — it was to Dominic) an ice-cold glare. It was penetrating and commanding, and my inner-wolf clawed at my stomach, wanting to run after her and make her happy.

"I know what you're thinking," Dominic said.

My blood ran cold. He couldn't know that she was making me crazy. None of them could. If they knew ... "What's that?" I asked, glad that my voice sounded uncaring, and I glanced his way.

He laughed. "That she's adorable when she's mad."

"That she is," I agreed, watching as Jade disappeared around the corner and Erika scowled after her. My heart started to beat again, and the knot in my stomach loosened. He didn't have a clue. *Who was that girl?* The question echoed through my mind again, relentlessly. I just didn't get it. I could take down an alpha, command an entire pack of twenty-nine werewolves to submit, and grovel at my feet, but this ... this ... human girl could make me cringe with just one glance.

Erika turned to us with a big grin on her face and started over. I snapped my gaze to meet hers and said, "Don't you have somewhere to be?" It came out harsher than I had intended, but it worked, and without a word, she backed up a step and then took off down the hall.

"Stay away from her," Dominic said casually as if he were talking about the weather and not really trying to tell me what to do. I had heard the line more than I could count in the last forty-eight hours, and each time I heard it, it only made her all the more interesting.

"That's her call to make, not yours," I retorted, keeping my tone just as light. He still refused to enlighten me about his obsession with Jade, and spending the weekend following her around hadn't helped me figure it out either. The most I had gotten from that was confirmation that she missed him.

Dominic pushed off the locker and stretched his arms lazily over his head. He smiled a little. "She wouldn't even look at you if she knew who you were."

The second bell rang, signaling that we were late for homeroom, and we started down the hallway, neither of us in any rush to get to class. "Why are you so concerned about her?" I asked.

"I'm not," he said, cutting me a murderous sideways look.

I chuckled. "Not sure if I believe that this is your *I could care less* face."

Dominic stopped just outside our homeroom. The morning announcements began, and our principal's voice's distorted buzz droned through the old speakers. "She's lost enough to this pack," he said in a low whisper, just barely audible over the announcements. "She doesn't need to lose more than she already has." His voice, body language, scent, and everything about him said he was guilty. I just wished I knew why.

I pulled the classroom door open and gestured for him to go in. "You're really going to go through with this class stuff, aren't you?" he asked with a huff. "You know I don't need a babysitter."

I grinned. "Think of it as bonding time."

CHAPTER 10

JADE

Erika watched me. I felt her eyes burning a trail along my back in homeroom, then in English, and still in Math. Every move I made, she was there, watching. And it was starting to drive me batty. But she wasn't the only one that watched me. So did Dominic.

And I watched Aidan, if only to piss them off. Well, that and I couldn't bring myself to directly look at Dominic.

What was it about this guy that had them on edge? I really wanted to know. When Dominic wasn't staring at me, he was watching Aidan and Erika ... Well, Erika looked as if at any moment she was going to cock her leg and pee on him to mark her territory. Did female dogs do that? Well, if they did, I was sure she would do it soon. The whole thing was starting to make me feel a little sick.

Erika wasn't the only *she-wolf* acting like that, though. Linda, Becca, and Tiffany were all following Aidan around, giving dirty looks to any girl that looked his way. And they were snapping at each other just as much. They stared each other down and shoved each other around. It was the strangest thing I had ever seen. Weren't girls usually more tactful than this? What happened to the snide comments and mean girl manipulation?

Aidan took it all in stride. It was as if he didn't even notice. He talked to everyone. He was friendly. He smiled. Everyone seemed to like him, especially the pack, and darn it, but I did, too. And it made my stomach sink. No matter how hard I tried, I couldn't come up with anything that would get the pack away from him. It was clear that they were recruiting him, and the more I thought about it, the more the sinking feeling in my stomach grew.

But the weirdest thing was that no one was talking about Ray. The police still hadn't said anything. His death hadn't been in the paper, and as far as I knew, the pack hadn't had any kind of service. The only thing I managed to find out was that Ray's wife had vanished. Their house was empty. It was almost as if neither of them had ever existed.

I still hadn't talked to Dominic, but then, he hadn't made an effort to talk to me either, and I was beginning to think it was better that way. All I was getting from him was a bunch of what I thought were supposed to be meaningful glances, except I didn't know what the meanings were. I figured he was trying to make a point, but the joke was on him because whatever the point was, I wasn't getting it. I was pretty much ready to chalk up the weekend to a weak moment. It was probably better to just forget it. And if he had stopped watching me, I would have done just that.

I sat in class, watching the clock slowly tick the minutes away. Lunch couldn't come soon enough. I needed a break, not that I had been doing much in class. I couldn't focus on anything other than the burn of Dominic's eyes and the sneer on Erika's face.

When the bell finally rang, I forced myself to stay in my seat until they left. For about half a second, Dominic looked as if he was going to approach me, but before he could, Aidan slung a loose arm over his shoulder and led him out the door.

The cafeteria was already packed by the time I got there. I glanced at the overly long line of students waiting to be served and spotted Marcy at the front. She waved what I thought was a boxed salad at me, and then she pointed to a table and mouthed, '*I got it.*'

Ben and Ann were chowing down on French fries and gravy when I plopped down at my usual table. The fraternal twins were dressed the same, as always, in blue jeans and black hoodies. I've always thought that they secretly wished they were identical. They sure tried hard enough to look the same. Ben had even dyed his blond hair brown to match Ann's, and Ann always wore blue contacts, the same shade as Ben's natural eye color.

"Hey, Jade," Ann said and smiled. "I'm surprised you're sitting with us." She didn't mean it to be unkind; I could see that from the soft smile she was giving me, but the statement got my back up anyway.

"What? Why?" I asked. My voice sounded harsher than I had intended.

Ben cut Ann a narrowed eye glare and said, "We heard that you and Dom made up." He smirked at me and then dropped another fry in his mouth.

I snorted. "Hardly." I leaned forward, resting my elbows on the table and my chin in my hands. *Rumors*. How did kicking Dom out of my house translate into us making up? It took everything in me not to turn around and look at him. I could hear his laughter, and it made my heart twitch. It wasn't quite a squeeze or a twist, but it was enough of a twitch that I noticed it.

Thankfully, Marcy slid into the chair beside me and pushed a salad (or what was considered a salad by high school cafeteria standards: a bowl of lettuce and a single cherry tomato) in front of me. I was about to ask her when she was leaving for the police station, desperately wanting to change the subject, when she said, "And another one gets taken."

"Another what?" Ben asked, looking at Marcy with an utterly blank face, and Ann let out a loud groan.

Marcy rolled her eyes and then nodded in Aidan's direction. "The new guy seems pretty close with Dominic."

There goes trying to change the subject. "He doesn't look like he was taken," I said dryly. "He looks willing." And that made my head spin. I could have sworn they hated each other, or at least that Dominic really didn't like Aidan. Why else would he tell me to stay away?

Ben sighed, and he dropped the fry he had been about to shove in his mouth back into the container. "I didn't think it was possible, but Dominic is getting hotter."

"I know, right?" Ann said with a grin and elbowed her brother playfully. She didn't even try to hide the long and very appraising look she gave Dominic, and as she stared, the grin melted away. "Jade," she said, still watching him closely, critically, "have you noticed the way the pack is hovering around Dom?" Frown lines began to litter her forehead, and she scrunched her nose. "It's like he's ... more important somehow."

My breath caught in my throat, and my heart stopped. I swiveled in my chair, not bothering to try to hide it. Dominic sat at the head of the lunchroom table, which was ridiculous because really, it was just a plastic fold-up table, but he made it look ... regal. Aidan sat on his right, Erika on his left, and along the edges, six other pack members watched him, engrossed in whatever he was saying.

Dominic was smiling. His eyes were bright. He looked ... happy ... content ... proud. My heart started to pound again, and my stomach rolled. Dominic never looked happy. Not anymore. He always had the same mask. Hard and cold and cruel. Not happy. Never. And the way the others were watching him, listening to him ...

I locked eyes with Marcy and whispered, "No." I didn't mean it as a whisper, but the rock-hard lump that had suddenly formed in my throat wouldn't let my voice rise any louder.

Her eyes were wide, and the color rushed from her face. "He ..." she started, but she must not have believed what she was about to say because she promptly snapped her mouth shut.

I pushed my chair out, the legs scraping across the linoleum floor with a screech, and I stared at Dominic for a long minute. Clippings of the last few days flitted through my mind as if I were looking at newspaper articles. *The pack is stressed. He's no good for you. I'm trying to help you.* All his subtle little hints and warnings rang out through my head, and heat burned in my cheeks. Suddenly, I felt sick and utterly stupid. I wasn't part of the pack. He wouldn't have been able to warn me of anything without seeking permission unless ... The thoughts were swarming so loudly in my brain that I couldn't understand any of them.

And then I was standing over him, and I heard my voice, cold as ice, say, "Dominic, we need to talk."

Dominic didn't even look up. "Kind of busy," he said dismissively.

I gritted my teeth, and I really don't know what came over me, but I grabbed hold of his ear and pulled. "We need to talk now."

That got his attention, as well as the attention of all the werewolves at the table. They all glared at me. Even Aidan was giving me a death stare. Dominic jumped up from his chair and smacked my hand away from his ear. He took hold of my bicep firmly and said, "I'll be right back, guys," before he dragged me from the cafeteria.

As soon as we were through the doors, he dropped his hold and asked, "What do you want?" His tone was sharp, and his shoulders, rigid.

"It's you, isn't it?" I asked. I guessed the look on my face wasn't sweet because he backed up a step and the pink flush in his cheeks turned white. I poked him in the chest, and he flinched back another step. "You took out Ray."

Dominic trembled slightly under my stare, and he sucked in a noisy breath. His shoulders sagged a little as if he were trying to shrink further away from me. He dropped his eyes to the floor, and then he gave his head a forceful shake, pulled in another loud, sucking breath, and hesitantly met my gaze. "You threw me out of your house. Blew me off, and now you think you can just ... just ..." He grunted and threw his hands up in the air, completely frustrated.

"Stop it," I snapped, and he flinched again. "Just cut the crap, Dom. You followed me around all weekend; you can damn well answer my question!"

Dominic cocked his head slightly and searched my face. His brow furrowed in confusion, and any hostility that had marred his body softened. "What are you talking about?" he asked.

"Come on, Dom, I know that the black wolf that trailed me all weekend was you," I shouted. I didn't mean to shout. It just sort of happened, and a burning blush rushed up to my neck. I took a deep breath and smiled awkwardly. "Look, it doesn't matter. You've made your point, okay. I'll stay away from Aidan, but don't be like Ray. Don't start the recruiting. You're better than that."

"Jade, I'm a brown wolf, and I'm *not*," he punched out the word, letting it hang in the air for a moment as if he wanted to make sure I grasped it before he continued, "the new alpha. And it would be really smart for you to forget that you know anything about Ray."

AIDAN

Crap! It seemed like that was the only word my brain could formulate as I listened to Jade and Dominic. It was also the first time in my life that I hated having enhanced hearing. It would have been nice to pretend that they were just having a friendly conversation.

Erika leaned into me. "You were following her?" she snarled in my ear and then leaned back. Her lips curled into a sneer, and she laughed darkly. "Did you hear that, ladies? It looks like we have another contestant."

Crap! Crap! Crap! The banter stopped instantly, and four sets of glowing yellow eyes landed on me, expectantly. Waiting. I slouched a little, trying to look relaxed, and shrugged my shoulders, brushing it off as no big deal. I held their eyes for a long minute before I said, "She's nothing."

"I don't know about that," Erika said and laughed again, but there was no humor in it. "She seems smitten, and by the sound of your wild heartbeat, I'd say you are, too."

CHAPTER 11

JADE

"Dom, what do you mean it wasn't you?" I asked. My voice was barely a whisper, and the metal-lined hallway suddenly seemed ... small ... tight ... airless. I had hugged that wolf, and I had let it smother my face with wet kisses. I felt ... violated. At least I knew why Dominic hadn't tried to talk to me yet, although knowing it didn't really make me feel any better.

"I'm not a black wolf," he said again, a little helplessly this time. He took a step toward me, and when I took a step back, he put up his hands in surrender. "Jade, you're not looking so hot. Are you okay?"

I focused on breathing. In and out. In and out. I wasn't entirely sure why I was so upset, but my throat was burning, and I fought hard to swallow the tears that were threatening to break loose. My heart was breaking — again — just like it had two years ago. And I realized, unexpectedly, that part of me, even though I had been fighting it, had really hoped that I was going to get my Dominic back. That he'd heard my confessions. That he wanted to start over and *fix things* like he'd said. And I was pretty sure that the fact that he hadn't heard me say all those things was distressing me more than knowing some other wolf was stalking me.

I shook my head. "Nope," I said calmly, and before he had a chance to make me even more *not okay,* I turned from him and started down the hallway.

"Jade, wait!" Dominic called. His footsteps were extremely loud in the vacant hallway as he jogged to catch up to me.

I spun back around and put up a hand to stop him. "I can't do this right now, Dom. Just tell Mac I'm not feeling well. Please." My voice sounded as hollow as I felt, and it really didn't sound like my own. I tried to close the doors. I wanted to hide my feelings, but I couldn't. I couldn't focus. I could barely breathe. Each small breath I managed to suck in hurt, burning down my throat like a lit fuse and into my lungs.

But Dominic didn't seem to have the same problem. His face hardened as he closed himself off from me, and it made my stomach drop. I could see the doors slamming shut as he proceeded to lock me out and cut me off, and I hated him for it. He nodded. "Take the sidewalks."

I offered a weak smile and a little wave, but he didn't respond. He just looked at me with those cold, uncaring eyes and waited for me to leave. And that's exactly what I did. I left. Just like he had left me two years ago. Without a backward glance, I weaved through the empty hallways and out the school's front door.

♥

My key was stuck in the lock. It wouldn't turn, and I couldn't get it out. It was frustrating as all hell, and without thinking, I kicked the door. Hard. It hurt. I yelped, and my big toe throbbed.

But it was worth it. I yanked on the key again, and it came out just as the door flew open.

Dad smiled at me. It was the kind of smile that only a dad could give. A bit excited, a touch worried, and a lot happy. It was one of those smiles that encompassed every emotion he had, and it was exactly what I needed.

"Hey, Dad," I said, and without warning, I launched myself at him for one of his epic bear hugs. "Welcome back."

He caught me just as I knew he would, squeezing me tightly and spinning me over the threshold. But the hug didn't last nearly long enough. He put me down and held me at arm's length, giving me one of those concerned fatherly looks. "Hi, honey. What are you doing home?"

I wiggled out of his soft grip and slid by him, kicking the door shut with my heel. "Wasn't feeling good," I lied and padded into the living room. I dropped down on the couch, focusing all my effort on looking sick.

He didn't buy it for a second. "You never get sick," he said bluntly, following me into the room. He sat down beside me and asked, "What's going on?"

Dad looked tired but relaxed. His silver-dusted black hair was flat on one side as if he had been sleeping on it, and he had pillow creases indented on his cheek. He had on his favorite navy blue jogging pants and a gray T-shirt, and by the tightness of his lips, I guessed he was fighting against a yawn.

"Sorry I woke you up," I said. "How was your trip?"

"Jade," he said with a no-nonsense tone, "what are you doing home?"

I bit my bottom lip and wiggled on the couch as I considered lying again. But then I looked into his bright blue eyes, and I saw the concern painted on his face, and the floodgates burst open. Everything rushed out in a mess of words. I told him about Erika and the locker room. I blurted about the black wolf. About Dominic. About Ray. About how no one was supposed to know he was dead. I told him about Mom being all jumpy. I talked about losing Dominic and about how much I missed him. It was as if I were stuck in a tornado, gushing everything out in a spinning gust of wind, unable to stop.

But just like a tornado, I touched down and ran my course, and when there was nothing left, I flopped back on the couch, feeling drained and a little deflated.

Dad considered my story for a long and way too silent moment before he asked, "Does Dominic know about the black wolf?"

"What does that matter?" I asked a little breathlessly. He had to focus on the black wolf out of everything that I had blurted out. I wanted to be upset, or angry, or anything, really, but I couldn't. It all seemed like too much energy. And all I felt was empty. Not in a bad way. It was more of a contented kind of empty as if I had expelled all the badness, and all that was left was ... exhaustion.

"He has always watched out for you, honey," he said softly, and he reached out, brushing some hair from my forehead. "Even if it didn't feel like he was there, he was. He always will be. You know that."

Did I? Not really. But I nodded and smiled anyway. "I'm going to lie down," I said, hauling myself up from the couch.

"Wait," he said, taking hold of my wrist and pulling me back down. He wrapped me in a hug, leaning his chin on the top of my head. "I know you think we are pushing you, your Mom and I, to join them, and I don't want you to think I'm trying to give Dominic an excuse. He hurt you. He knows that. You know that." Dad sighed, and his shoulders slumped a little against me. "But you can't judge them all from his stupidity. I just want you to be safe, honey. I know you can't see it, but the pack is safe. They always have been, and having the wolves as friends isn't as bad of a thing as you think it is."

I knew he was trying to be comforting, or give me some kind of life lesson full of wisdom, but it really wasn't helping. There was nothing safe about the pack. It didn't matter which way he tried to spin it; werewolves were not safe.

I pushed out of his arms, giving him what I hoped was an agreeing look. "I'm going to take a nap," I said, and I left him sitting there with concern marring his face, and I headed to my room.

It wasn't until I got to my room that I realized he hadn't told me about his weekend, but at that point, I was just too drained to care.

♥

I screamed. There was something on me, smothering me. I couldn't breathe. I tried to push it off, flailing my arms around, pulling at the comforter. I couldn't move. It was dark. Too dark. I was drowning. Suffocating. Another scream ripped from my lips, but it was muffled and distorted with barely any sound to it.

"Chill out, Jade." Marcy's voice belted out, wrapping around me like a soothing blanket. She grabbed hold of the comforter and pulled it down. I sucked in a ragged breath, and it burned through my empty lungs. She was laughing and grinning, and she was sitting on top of my stomach.

I pushed her off me, giving her a dirty look. "What the hell?"

Marcy giggled. She flopped onto her stomach and made herself comfortable on my bed, resting her chin in her hands. "What happened to you today?"

I grabbed my powder blue comforter, pulled it back up to my chin, and wiggled under the covers, trying to find the sweet spot again and hoping that she'd just go away. I closed my eyes and kept wiggling, but I just couldn't get comfortable.

Marcy cleared her throat dramatically loud. I opened my eyes and gave her another dirty look, but she just grinned.

"Nothing happened," I said. "I just wasn't feeling well."

"Liar," she said, pursing her lips. "You never get sick."

I groaned and rolled onto my side. "Whatever."

My curtains were open, revealing the star-speckled night sky.

The silver moon was almost full, and there didn't appear to be a single cloud. I must have slept for hours, but yet, I was still exhausted, and I was sure if Marcy would just leave, I would have no problem falling back to sleep.

Marcy had another plan. She smacked at my legs. "Get up. We're going out."

"Just let me sleep, Mac," I said, snuggling a bit deeper under the blankets.

"Not happening." She laughed evilly and crawled over me, so we were nose to nose. She was grinning mischievously, and her eyes danced with laughter and what looked a lot like secrets. "We're going to get ice cream, and you are going to spill everything. Especially the part about why Erika was asking about you. Whatever you said to Dom, she's fuming about it." Her smile widened, and she giggled a little. "And I have awesomesauce news of the boy variety."

CHAPTER 12

AIDAN

That night, Dominic was the moody one. Not that I was overly moody per se, it was just that Dominic was never really anything, except when Jade was involved. Again, I found myself wondering what that girl had done to make my pack so uneasy around her. It wasn't just Dominic and Erika; it was most of them. They all watched her with leery eyes, and she seemed oblivious to it. The girl was too busy being overly sure of herself, and I couldn't help but think it was a complete act. No one could be that tough, not when they knew what they were up against.

Dominic hadn't spoken a word to me since lunch. After Jade left, he had talked to her friend and then stormed off. I still couldn't believe that Jade tried to drag him out of the cafeteria by his ear, and if I hadn't been the reason for her anger, I'd probably be laughing about it now.

We were sitting in my motel room watching the night descend upon us; well, I was sitting. Dominic was pacing. I had figured he would have come around by now, but he hadn't. Every once in a while, he would stop his relentless pacing to slam something around, but still not a word.

The first challenge was scheduled for tonight. I was sure Dominic wouldn't be here otherwise. Erika wasn't wasting any time. She was determined and strong and competent, and I absolutely hated it. She was a bitch and not really someone I wanted to spend the rest of my life with. But then, none of the challenging females really sparked my interest. They were all just so ... bitchy and conceited and fake.

But Erika, she had to be the worst of them. Actually scheduling a challenge ... it just wasn't normal. Females were usually more creative, not relying solely on strength to beat their opponents. They picked their times carefully and rarely broadcasted when the attack would happen. It gave them the edge of surprise. As long as there was one witness to testify to the outcome, the winner would move forward.

Erika, though, wanted an audience. Most likely, she was trying to intimidate the others, letting them see what she could do. And I didn't like it. She was too full of herself, and conceit wasn't really a great leadership quality.

A frustrated growl penetrated my eardrums, and Dominic slammed a coffee mug onto the dresser, shattering it.

"Stop slamming things around and just spit it out already," I said, sprawled out on my lumpy bed, staring up at the popcorn ceiling. I couldn't take much more of his brooding. The stress of tonight was eating at me, and he was only making it worse. And at the rate he was going, I wouldn't have a single mug left in this crap hole of a room.

"I asked you to stay away from her," he said through clenched teeth.

"And I told you that wasn't your call to make." I tried to hide the amusement from my voice, but it leaked out completely unintentionally. Seriously, he sure acted like a crazy jealous person for a guy who didn't even like women.

He stiffened, every muscle in his body tensed, and he glared at me. "She's not going to join the pack."

I offered up a smile. "I never said I wanted her to."

The smile worked ... a little. Dominic sat down in the desk chair and leaned forward, resting his elbows on his knees. "Then what are you doing with her?"

Now that was the question, wasn't it? What was I doing with her? I didn't even know. I hadn't meant to go to her. I hadn't even realized it was her scent that I was following, but once I was there ... I just didn't want to leave. No, that wasn't entirely true. I wanted to go, but my inner-wolf had wanted something different. She was born to be an alpha. She had the strength. She had compassion. She could make me tremble with a single look. Jade had it all, or she would if she was one of us. *And I'd have her.*

The sudden and completely unexpected realization made my stomach squirm in a nervous, happy kind of way. I could almost picture her standing beside me, not a step behind. From the way the other females treated me, I knew they would always be hiding in my shadows. But Jade ...

I shook off the thought, or rather my inner wolf's elated dream. Instead of telling Dominic all of that, I said, "You know, I hate to point it out because this whole thing is actually quite entertaining to watch, but haven't you considered what could happen if you keep telling me to stay away from her? It's like she was just a girl, and now she's forbidden fruit. You are making her so much more intriguing." He shot me a foul look, and I chuckled. "Oh, and not to state the obvious, but I didn't even speak to her."

"We only have one black wolf in the pack," Dominic snapped, but then he chuckled, and a mischievous grin began to pull at his lips. "You think I'm worried about her safety, but really, I'm not. Jade can take care of herself. It's you I'm looking out for here. She'd tear you apart if she knew who you were."

I laughed and rolled my eyes. "A bit dramatic, don't you think? She's just a girl," I said, except I kind of believed that it wasn't all that dramatic.

Right then, my phone rang, a loud shrill, and the sound felt like doom. Okay, maybe not doom exactly, but definitely one step closer to it. And by the way Dominic was watching it vibrate across the nightstand, I figured he was thinking close to the same thing.

"You going to answer it?" he asked, without lifting his gaze from the phone.

I reached over and snagged it up, tapping the flashing call button, and then held it to my ear. "What's the verdict?"

"You've got to come down here," Joe said in a rush, panting as if he had been running and was completely out of breath. "Erika's lost it."

My jaw clenched, and I gripped the phone a bit tighter. "Against the rules, man. I can't interfere." This was the part I hated the most about the games. Alpha males were not allowed to attend the challenges. It was supposed to stop distractions and provide each female with a fair playing ground.

"Aidan, she's going to kill Becca," Joe said. "Get down here."

My gut twisted. *Dammit!* I had hoped it wouldn't come to this. I took a deep breath and said, "I can't. They knew the risks. If Becca won't submit ..."

"Becca already submitted," Joe snapped, cutting me off. "She submitted five minutes ago."

"Where?" I asked, jumping off the bed and snagging my keys.

I mouthed, '*Let's go,*' to Dominic, and threw the door open. According to pack law, fighting to the death was fine if neither of them would give up. But killing after submission was punishable by death.

"The park, and hurry up," Joe said, clearly flustered. I could hear shouting in the background, tinted with panic. "She's already bit a few of us that have tried to step in."

"I'll be there soon," I said and hung up.

When I jumped in and started it up, Dominic was already in the car. I threw it in reverse, and the tires squealed. My muscles were so tight they burned.

"What going on?" Dominic asked as I shifted gears and spun onto the road.

"Erika's trying to kill Becca. Where the hell is the park?"

It was a tense and silent drive to the park. I was actually a bit stunned that Dominic didn't have anything to say. He always seemed to have something on the tip of his tongue. He listened as I told him the little bits Joe had said, which took less than a minute, and then he sat there staring out the window with a locked jaw.

It took four and a half minutes to drive across town and reach the park. I figured that was one of the pluses to living in a small nowhere town, but it still felt like a long drive. As soon as I parked, Dominic was out of the car and running toward the crowd gathered in the center of what looked like a soccer field. The sky was clear, and the extra-bright moon cast the ground in dull silvery light. I took a deep breath and emerged from my car, letting the door slam, and I started over.

The field was set back in an alcove. On three sides, tall pines hid most of the view from the rest of the park. If the parking lot hadn't been directly in front of it, I wouldn't have even noticed it. Raised bleachers outlined the playing area, and a walkway skirted the open end.

As I approached, Dominic was already pushing everyone back, opening up the circle of onlookers. With a quick scan, I was relieved to see that they were all part of the pack, and for half a second, my focus settled on the head of the enforcers. Jared stood just outside the crowd, watching. He smirked at me, and my blood boiled. "You couldn't have dealt with this?" I snarled.

"Not my job to keep the peace, alpha," he said with laughter in his voice. "I only deal with those who have broken pack law, and that hasn't happened here yet."

I gritted my teeth, focusing back on the crowd. I had never liked the enforcers in my father's pack, and the ones here were no different. Always waiting on the sidelines to deliver punishment, but never stepping in.

And then my eyes landed on Erika.

She was in wolf form, her white coat speckled with blood. She was snarling, circling around a gray wolf that lay motionless on the ground. The wolf was still breathing; I could just see the slight rise and fall of its stomach. Erika stalked toward her, growling, low, and menacing.

"Enough!" I shouted, closing the last few steps to tower over her.

Erika swung her head, fixing her eyes on me. She let out another growl, baring her teeth. A rush of raw adrenaline coursed through my veins, and my skin prickled. I pulled off my shirt and pants and tossed them aside as my bones started to break, reshaping and changing. It was a rush, hot and cold. Spine-tingling and thrilling. A hot chill slithered over me, and my body shifted, forming into a black wolf.

I growled and snapped out at her. My fur bristled along my spine, and I curled my lips, exposing the full length of my canines. Erika backed up a step, her eyes darting between Becca and me. Blood dripped from her muzzle, and she snarled again, savagely.

I held her eyes and stalked toward her, a low growl rumbling from my throat. I gathered my scent, letting it trickle through my imprint and into the air. It was as if she just realized who I was because a flash of panic suddenly flitted across her eyes. For a second, she looked as if she were going to bolt, but then she dropped to her stomach, shimmied across the ground until she was at my feet, and began to lick my chin.

I snapped at her to stop, and she whimpered, rolling onto her back, exposing her vulnerable neck and belly to me. I looked down at her for a moment, disgusted, and then I turned from her and let my body reform to human.

As soon as I stood up, Dominic handed me my jeans, and I tugged them on. The crowd was silent, still as marble, watching to see what I would do. I dug my keys out of my pocket and tossed them to Dominic. He snatched them out of the air. "Get Becca out of here."

"What about her?" he asked, nodding toward Erika, who was still on her back, whimpering softly.

I looked back at Erika and gritted my teeth. I could have her locked up, but it wouldn't hold. Technically, she hadn't done anything wrong yet. Becca was hurt, but she was breathing. The enforcers would let her walk no matter what I said. If I hadn't stepped in ... I gave my head a shake, banishing the thought. If I hadn't stepped in, I would have lost both of them.

"Let her go," I said, more than a little reluctantly. I heard Jared chuckle, and I didn't doubt for a second that he'd been hoping I'd slip up and make a stupid call. The enforcers were the only ones who had the authority to deal with reckless or unfair alphas, and they were the only ones who wouldn't be punished for standing up to me. "She hasn't broken any laws."

I glared at Jared for a moment, and his dark, laughing eyes held mine. He smirked at me and gave me a nod that looked like approval. I knew what he was doing. Testing me. He was trying to decide if I would abuse my rank and whether I needed to be under constant watch. I figured I passed the test, though, because he turned his back on me and walked away.

I scooped up my shirt, and as I tugged it over my head, I heard someone say, "Shit, Jade. We need to go."

CHAPTER 13

JADE

Marcy was worked up. So worked up that I had absolutely no clue what she was saying as she spoke. She was speaking in half sentences, starting the thought in her head, only giving me bits and pieces, and then jumping from one topic to the next so quickly that I was completely lost. The gist was that I had pissed off the pack ... again, which really wasn't a new thing. I tended to piss them off a lot. Not that I meant to. It just kind of happened. I've always liked to believe that it was because Erika couldn't deal with the fact that Dominic and I had a past, although I couldn't swear on that, because really, it wasn't just Erika that I seemed to piss off.

Marcy was dragging me through the park, hell-bent on getting freakin' ice cream. The wind was cold. The sky was black. And all I wanted to do was lie in bed and pretend as if nothing was wrong. I wanted to forget about the black wolf that wasn't Dominic. I wanted to pretend I had never met Aidan, and I seriously didn't want to think about Ray's death and why no one was talking about it. But no, of course, I couldn't do that. Marcy needed ice cream.

Baskin Robbins was just on the other side of the soccer field. We stuck to the path, rounding the field, and from this distance, it looked as if the shop lights were dancing through the night as the silhouettes of customers moved past the window.

"Shit," Marcy said. Her arm weaved through mine, and she jerked me to a stop. "Jade, we need to go." She started tugging on my arm, pulling me back the way we had come.

"I thought you wanted ice cream," I said, cutting her a sideways glance. Even in the dark, she looked guilty.

"Marcy!" someone shouted, and I swiveled, looking into the secluded field. Someone was walking toward us, but I couldn't tell who it was. Behind him, a small group of people, maybe ten, were gathered.

"Shit. Shit. Shit." Marcy looked up at me with wide eyes and chewed on her bottom lip for a second, thinking. "If he asks, you begged me to go out, okay?" she whispered, her eyes pleading.

"What?" I asked, completely lost, and I glanced back at the group. Had they been there the whole time? I didn't know, and not knowing made me crazy nervous. I should have noticed them. I should have been alert, not worrying about some boy that I had hardly talked to. If Aidan wanted to be part of the pack, that was his problem, not mine.

"Trevor," she said urgently. "He told me to stay home tonight. Please, Jade. Just please say this was your idea."

I wanted to shake her by her shoulders — literally. "What does Trevor have to do with anything?" I asked, not bothering to try to hide how pissed off I was.

"He's my awesomesauce news," she mumbled, averting her eyes from mine. She started kicking at the ground, digging a little hole in the grass with the toe of her shoe.

Clearly, she needed more than just a shake. Awesomesauce news and Trevor seriously didn't mix. Trevor was not awesome anything, werewolf or not. He was a complete douche bag. And I was about to tell her as much until I caught movement out of the corner of my eye. Trevor was moving in on us, closing the distance quickly, so I bit my tongue and started pulling her down the path. I didn't move fast enough.

"Mac, what the hell are you doing here?" Trevor shouted, snagging her arm and tearing her away from me. He spun her around to face him. "I told you to stay home."

Trevor stood stiff, looking down at her. He wasn't much taller than I was, but his bulky frame seriously increased his intimidation factor. His hoodie was snug, hugging his thick arms and chest, and his white baseball cap shielded most of his face. His jaw was locked, and his grip on her arm looked painfully tight.

Marcy shot me a desperate look before focusing on him. "Um, Jade wanted ice cream. It's a girl thing. We eat ice cream when we're upset." As she rushed out the explanation, her voice squeaked unnaturally high, and Trevor shifted his glare to me.

His scrutiny made the hairs on my neck prickle, and like a wave, they slowly rose as a shiver traveled up my back and neck. I took a step toward him, trying to hide how nervous I was, and clenched my fists. "Take your hand off of her, Trevor, before you lose it," I said, glad my voice was strong and didn't jump the way my stomach was.

"You're not helping, Jade," Marcy hissed at me and moved closer to him, wrapping her arms around his neck. "I'm sorry. She was upset about the whole Dom thing. I couldn't say no."

Trevor stood stiff, not moving closer but not moving away from her either, and he kept his gaze focused on me. "You should have called me," he said through gritted teeth. "I told you I didn't want you walking around alone. Is it really going to be like this again, Mac? Not even a day, and you're already trying to push the limits."

"I didn't want to bother you," Marcy said sweetly. She brought her hands up to his cheeks, pulling his gaze back to her, and she batted her long lashes at him. "You said you had pack stuff to deal with tonight, and it's not like *Baskin Robbins* is far." She glanced over her shoulder at me and laid the sweetness on thick. "Look at her, honey. She's a mess. Ice cream is totally mandatory right now."

Trevor cupped her face with both hands, thankfully not looking back at me. I was sure that he would have known she was lying if he had. "You make me crazy, you know that, right?" He bent a little, planting an incredibly hot kiss on her, so hot, in fact, that I blushed and had to turn away.

I glanced back at the field as I waited for them to stop, and relief washed over me. The group had pretty much dispersed, with only two of them left watching us.

The relief died fast.

The two left were heading over, and as they neared us, I realized who they were. Dominic and Aidan. Dominic gave me a completely fake smile and cleared his throat. "Sorry to interrupt, guys, but did she just tell you that Jade wanted ice cream?"

Marcy made a throaty whimpering kind of sound, and Trevor chuckled. "Yeah," Trevor said, his voice muffled by Marcy's lips.

My body temperature dropped and a painfully tight knot twisted in my stomach. *He wouldn't,* I thought. Dominic grinned at me and winked, and sweat beaded up on my upper lip. "Shut up, Dom," I hissed, and his grin widened.

"Jade's allergic to dairy," he said. "Trev, your girl is lying to you."

I felt my jaw drop. Aidan moved a bit closer, and Dominic

laughed. I was stunned. Absolutely stunned. Did he really hate me that much? Really?

"You lied to me?" Trevor asked, pushing Marcy back and holding her at arm's length. His eyes raked over her as if he wasn't really sure if he should believe Dominic or not.

"Wwwhat?" she stammered, her eyes growing wide and panicked. She cut Dominic a disbelieving and completely betrayed look and said, "No, of course not. Why would I lie about ice cream?" It probably would have been believable if her voice hadn't trembled so much.

Knots twisted in my stomach. I couldn't think. We had been so close. So close to just walking away.

Trevor growled. It came from the back of his throat, and his eyes flashed yellow. Marcy started to squirm, trying to shake him off. I shot Dominic the coldest look I could muster, and he chuckled and mouthed, '*Do your thing.*'

It took me a second to process it, but once I did, I almost laughed. If I hadn't wanted to kill Dominic at that very moment, I probably would have roared with laughter. He was setting us up. Except, we had been seconds away from walking away, and Marcy had been handling it just fine without Dominic's seriously unneeded help. I wanted to march over to him and smack that grin off his face, but instead, I groaned and stomped up to Marcy. "Have you lost your mind?" I snapped, grabbing her arm and tugging her out of Trevor's hold. "Mac, he's already broke your heart once. What the hell is wrong with you?"

Marcy didn't miss a beat. Confusing Trevor had always been the easiest way to get his temper down to a bearable level. And Trevor, well, he wasn't exactly the smartest werewolf of the bunch. She jutted out her bottom lip in a pout. "You're supposed to be happy for me."

Dominic chuckled, swiftly moving between Trevor and Marcy, cutting off Trevor's attempt to grab her again. I tugged her a bit further away before throwing my hands up in the air. "He cheated on you."

Dominic's chuckle turned into a full-bellied laugh, and I shot him a murderous glare. Why he felt the need to set up a distraction was lost on me. He could have just ended it, pulled rank on Trevor, and made him walk away, or even better, let us handle it.

"It was a misunderstanding," Marcy said, pacing around me

until both Dominic and I were effectively blocking Trevor from her.

I followed her movement, crossing my arms over my chest and rolling my eyes. "Oh, I've got to hear this," I said dryly. "A misunderstanding? How exactly did you misunderstand seeing his tongue down Erika's throat?"

"Okay, so maybe it wasn't entirely a misunderstanding. But he promised he won't do it again." She went up on tiptoes and glanced over my shoulder, smiling sweetly. "Right, honey?"

"And you believed him?" I said before Trevor had a chance to answer.

"I'm happy, Jade," she said and stomped her foot. "Can't you just let me be happy?"

Dominic was roaring with laughter, and it took everything I had not to burst out, too. Trevor looked so lost, his gaze shifting back and forth between us as if he were watching a game of tennis. Another minute or so of this, and we'd be able to walk away; I was sure of it.

"Babe," Aidan said, stepping in front of me, "give her a break." He slung an arm around my waist, pulling me against him, and nuzzled my neck. "Trust me," he whispered in my ear, his lips brushing against my earlobe. My breath caught in my throat, and I tried to push him away. He looked down at me with that knee-melting smile of his and whispered again, "Trust me."

AIDAN

Jade gave me a dirty look. Not just a little dirty, but mud puddle dirty. I tried to pretend that it was directed at someone, anyone else, but it wasn't.

I should let go, I thought. *I should let go and just walk away.* But watching her manipulate one of my wolves without a shred of violence ... It was amazing. She was amazing. And all I could think about as I watched her was touching her. Being closer to her. I needed her.

I held her tightly against my body, and she tried to push me away, but it was a halfhearted attempt. I could feel her frantic heartbeat pounding against my chest, and her breath was coming fast and short. I pulled her a bit closer, and she melted against me. Too bad she still glared up at me with hatred. It was frustrating as all hell, and all I could think of was wiping that look off her face.

I smirked at her and bent forward, brushing my lips against hers lightly, teasingly, and she responded instantly, wrapping her arms around my neck.

A primal need surged through me, crippling me. And before I could stop it, the teasing kiss changed ... morphed ... into something close to savage. Jade bit my bottom lip, sucking it between hers. She moaned and dug her hands into my hair, pulling me closer, crushing me against her.

This crush is going to be the death of me.

That's all it was. A crush. Simple attraction. Something to forget. I knew that. I just wished my gut (and my heated lips) would accept it, too. She had been doing just fine without my interference, but if I was being honest with myself, I had only interfered for a chance to get closer to her.

"Aidan!" Dominic growled.

I didn't want to stop. I really didn't want to let her go, but at the sound of his voice, Jade jerked away from me. I held on tight, keeping my arms firmly around her waist, and after a second, she relaxed against me again. She looked up at me through hooded eyes. They were the sexiest eyes I had ever seen. They had this bedroom quality, deep brown, with full, thick lashes. I brushed my lips against hers, just a featherlike sweep, and let my hand travel slowly down her silky smooth arm, entwining my fingers with hers.

"You have my keys, Dom," I said, keeping my eyes locked with hers. "I'll see you back at the motel." Then, I stepped back from her, giving her hand a little tug, and started walking. I knew this was stupid, but I couldn't let go, not yet, so I said, "Trevor, the girls want ice cream. You coming?"

Trevor looked as if he had no clue what was going on, and I bit back a laugh. Dominic had said he knew what he was doing, but this was not what I had expected. He shook his head as if trying to clear it and then grinned. "Yeah, sure, come on, Mac." He held his hand out to her, and she rushed over, grinning.

We had only made it a few steps when Jade stopped abruptly and spun back around. "Dom, wait," she called. There was desperation in her voice, which lit my nerves on fire. She tried to pull her hand away, but I didn't — wouldn't — let go. Not only did I not want to, but Becca was already in the backseat healing, and the last thing I needed was to try to explain to Jade why there was a naked and very bloody girl in my car.

Dominic didn't turn back. He reached for the car door and

swung it open. "Not now, Jade," he said and climbed in, shutting the door quickly.

She stood still, watching him pull out of the parking lot as if she thought he'd stop. He didn't. The car disappeared down the road, yet she still watched, even after any shred of taillights was gone.

"You okay?" I asked as I took a quick glance over my shoulder. Trevor and Marcy had already disappeared into the shop.

"What the hell are you doing?" Jade asked, keeping her voice low. She tugged on my hand and started walking. Her hand was stiff in mine, and she made a point not to look at me, but she didn't let go.

"Hanging out with friends." That wasn't really a lie, was it? The pack was sort of my friends. I wanted to tell her who I was so bad it hurt, but I just couldn't do it. What if Dominic was right? What if she hated me just because I was one of them? I didn't think I could live with that.

"They're not your friends, Aidan," she snapped. "Are you blind or just stupid?"

"Stupid," I said, looking down at our hands laced together. "Definitely stupid." But everyone needed to be stupid once in a while, right? What fun would life be if I always played by the rules?

CHAPTER 14

JADE

My mocha was cold. Not just cool, but freezing, and I sipped it slowly, trying to make it last. The coffee shop was busy. The chatter of students buzzed in the air. Each one of the cracked up red, faux-leather booths was occupied, and for once, not a single pack member was invading the space. I fiddled with the saltshaker, twirling it around, watching the tiny grains shift through the glass. Marcy was talking about, well, I really didn't know, because I honestly wasn't listening.

Once she started gushing about Trevor, I zoned out, and well, I was too busy forcing myself not to look at Aidan again to really hear what she was saying. I was really beginning to feel like a crazy stalker. Aidan had been sitting in the booth a few down from us, reading for close to an hour now, and he still hadn't glanced my way. It was maddening. Never in my life had I been ignored as much as he ignored me. It had been almost two weeks since we kissed in the park. And since then, he had been more than a little distant. He was always polite when I forced him into a conversation, but that was it. A distracted politeness, as if he always had somewhere else to be that was more important.

And that attitude made me want him more. He'd only been living in Dog Mountain for a short time, but Aidan had quickly climbed to the top of the social ladder at school. The pack loved him, and with the pack's endorsement, so did the rest of the students. I figured being popular in a small town wasn't all that hard. It wasn't as if there were a ton of competition. Except, I knew that being popular in my small town was a challenge. But Aidan hadn't needed to even work at it. Even after standing up to

Dominic, he had managed to penetrate the popularity ranks. And he had done it with a cool detachment as if he didn't care one way or another.

This was the first time I had seen Aidan without Dominic or one of the other werewolves flanking him in the last two weeks. It was also the first time I had seen something other than aloofness on his chiseled face. His hair was spiky with gel, and his brown eyes were wide as he flipped the pages of his textbook as if it were the most absorbing thing he had ever read. He was gentle with the pages, letting his fingertips caress them delicately. I got the impression that he was one of those people who could read a book ten times without making it look like it had been opened. I didn't know whether I liked that about him or if it was another thing that drove me crazy about him.

"I like him, Mac," I said, still twirling the saltshaker in my hands. "Like really like him." It seemed like such a stupid thing to admit. I hardly knew him. How could I possibly know if I liked him or not? But my stomach didn't seem to agree. Every time I saw Aidan, birds took flight in my belly.

Marcy cocked her head to the side, looking at me as if I were nuts. She arched a brow. "Who?"

I tilted my head and jutted my chin in Aidan's direction.

She glanced over her shoulder and then turned back to me, wrinkling her nose. "Really? But he's ..."

"Perfect," I said, cutting her off and shooting her a dirty look.

"Dominic is perfect. Trevor is perfect. He's...," she paused, and her eyebrows moved together as she tried to find the right words. She snatched the saltshaker out of my hand, smacking it down on the table. "Cold."

I laughed. I didn't mean to. It just came out. "He is not, and Dominic doesn't count in this."

"Yeah, he kind of is," she said, and her frown grew. "He's barely spoken to you since the park."

"It's an act," I said defensively and with a lot more conviction than I felt.

Marcy considered this, and as she did, a sly smirk spread on her lips. "Then go get him."

"I can't." I sighed, looking down at the table. What was it about him that made me lose my nerve? Anyone else, and I wouldn't hesitate, but Aidan, he seemed so out of reach. Above me. As if he were above us all.

"Why the hell not? Who says you have to wait for him to make a move. We're not in the Middle Ages, Jade."

I sighed. "He hasn't even noticed I'm here."

"Wow, really? When did that ever stop you before? You want him, then get your skinny butt over there and make your presence known." I gave her a look, and she grinned her epic idea grin. She leaned in across the table and dropped her voice to a whisper. "Remember back in eighth grade, before Dominic came out, and you wanted his attention?" she asked.

"Um, not sure ..."

She cut me off. "Yes, it's perfect."

AIDAN

Keeping a straight face was a challenge. Jade and Marcy sat a few booths over from me, but I could hear them as if they were right next to me. Jade looked, well, hot. But then, she always did. It wasn't just her perfect figure with all of those peaks and curves, or her glossy hair, or her full lips that made her hot. It was her confidence. Even when she doubted herself, she was still confident about it. It was far from conceit, though, nothing like Erika and the others. Jade was a girl who knew exactly who she was, and she let the world know it, too. It made her even more appealing, really.

Staying away from her these past few weeks had been brutal. But I didn't really have a choice. Erika had taken down another one of the challenging females, and with only four of them left, it wouldn't be long before I was tied down to one of them. There was absolutely no future for Jade and me, and the sooner I accepted that, the easier it would be for her. So far, Erika hadn't caught wind of our little moment in the park, and she had forgotten the absurd idea that Jade was a threat. And I wanted to keep it that way.

From the corner of my eye, I watched a storm of emotions pass across Jade's face before she settled on the confidence that always burned in her eyes. She slid from the booth, stood up, and ran her hands down her thighs, smoothing out her jeans.

"Okay, I'm going to do it," she said, looking at Marcy as if she wanted Marcy to stop her.

Marcy grinned and leaned back in the booth. "Good luck."

Jade's shoulders rose and fell three times before she spun on her heels and walked up to me, or marched was more like it. Everything about her said determined. I had expected her to say *hi* or slide into the booth across from me, but she didn't. She dropped down beside me, and before I could even get a word out, she grabbed the collar of my shirt, balling it in her fist, and yanked me toward her.

Her lips were on mine before I could even think. They were soft, warm, and tasted like mocha. They felt even better pressed against my mouth than I remembered. She worked her lips over mine with the same passion that she had for everything else she did. Urgent and hot. My lips parted as did hers, and as soon as they did, she flicked her tongue against mine, and suddenly, my hands were wrapped in her silky hair and ...

"Sorry, I'm late." Dominic. At the sound of his voice, we broke apart, both of us breathing more than a little heavily. She looked at me; her eyes were full of heated excitement. She licked her lips as a smile pulled at the corners of her mouth. "Jade?" Dominic asked in disbelief. "Out of all the pack members in this town, you go after him again!"

Jade made a sound. It came from the back of her throat, a mix between a gasp and a growl. The heat that had been in her eyes iced over, and she leaped out of the booth.

"You're one of them," she spat.

I narrowed my eyes at her, searching her over. My brain was foggy, and my eyes kept landing back on her swollen lips. It took a few long seconds for me to figure out what she was talking about.

"I'm not just one of them," I said just as nastily, and every muscle in my body tensed as I slid out of the booth and glared down at her. I had never had someone look at me with so much hatred, so much disrespect. "I'm the alpha."

All the color drained from her face, and I instantly regretted telling her. For half a second, she looked as if she were going to pass out. She wobbled a little, and Dominic placed a hand on the small of her back, keeping her steady. He was smirking at me, a cocky smirk, and all I wanted to do was punch him.

Jade rocked on her feet for another second, and then, scarlet streaked up her neck, settling in her cheeks. She spat on the floor and wiped her mouth so hard with her sleeve that her lips were burning red when she stopped. "I feel sick," she whispered.

JADE

I needed air. Aidan was the alpha. I kissed the alpha. And I wanted to kiss him again. So much so that it hurt. He was staring down at me with cold eyes, and his jaw was twitching as he clenched and unclenched his teeth. Dominic was saying something to him, but I couldn't hear it. My ears were ringing too loudly, and my heart was pounding even louder.

I swallowed hard, but it didn't help to move the bristly lump lodged in my throat. *I kissed the alpha.* The birds flapped in my stomach, begging me to move closer to him and do it again.

Suddenly, a montage of images invaded my brain. I saw Dominic. His smile. The way he held me in the picture that sat beside my bed as if I were the only thing that mattered. The proud big brother. The best friend. Then I saw him as the beta. The cold eyes. The hatred. The aggression. His back faced me as he walked out of my life. And my irrational mind blamed Aidan for it all.

I felt my face twist into a sneer, and for a moment, I saw the pain in Aidan's eyes. It didn't last long, and in a blink, he had his cold mask back in place.

Aidan didn't see it coming, but then I hadn't either. I took a step toward him and slapped him with everything I had. A burning sting rushed through my hand. Dominic chuckled, and I spun on him. Whatever it was that he saw in me made him take a quick step back, and without even a small glance over my shoulder, I left the coffee shop.

CHAPTER 15

AIDAN

Jade was like a flash thunderstorm, calm one second, and the next, a burst of ferociousness. It was amazing and troubling and more than a little confusing. And she could really hit. My cheek burned, and I was pretty sure there was a nice red handprint there. I really hadn't seen that one coming, not after the seriously hot kiss she had just planted on me. I could still taste her mocha on my tongue, and dammit, but I wanted more.

The door slammed behind her, and the glass shuddered from the impact. "You okay?" Dominic asked, although his tone clearly said that he really didn't care one way or the other. He was smirking and looking as if it were an effort not to burst out in laughter.

"Fine," I said, scanning the coffee shop. Everyone was silent, waiting, watching, and the reality of what I had just done sank in fast. I dropped down into the booth, noticing the weary eyes and the stiff postures of everyone around me. Ray's death, and my position, had been kept quiet for a reason, and because of that ... that ... girl, it was all going to go up in flames. "Shit," I blurted, resting my head in my hands. "Did I really just announce that?"

The silence was ruthlessly loud. The pounding hearts and breathing of all the people around me were like bad music blaring in my ears. Too loud to think. I wanted to run after Jade. Force her to listen. Make her see me again for me. But I had a pretty good feeling that that would be a useless effort, and Jade hating me seriously wasn't the important thing. Not now. But Bruce's pack getting wind of a new alpha, one without a mate, was.

"I'll make the call," Dominic said abruptly and pulled his phone from his pocket. Any humor that had been on his face vanished. His back stiffened, his jaw hardened, and he paced to the back of the shop, his phone already to his ear as he began barking out orders.

Shit! The pack wasn't ready for this. I didn't know enough about the cougars yet. How they worked. How many there were. The last count Dominic had been able to get hold of was eighteen, but that was only a count of the males. From what I understood, the female numbers were and always had been an unknown factor.

I knew Bruce was vicious, and he was always looking for more females to lure into his clutches. I still couldn't figure that one out. From what Dominic had told me, Bruce only recruited females, and so far, his contact wouldn't reveal the why. I also knew that they had been coming closer to town these last few days. Their scents were scattered along the edges of our woods.

How could I have been so stupid! This little game with Jade ... this stupid crush, was putting us all in jeopardy. Not just the pack but also the town. But still, even knowing that all I wanted to do was run after her.

For about half a second, hot regret washed over me. If I had just kept driving. If I hadn't stopped in this stupid hick town, I wouldn't have to deal with any of this. I wouldn't have to worry about a pack of werecougars. I wouldn't have to deal with twenty-nine werewolves that acted as if they were the only things that mattered. I wouldn't be an alpha with a beta that fought me at every turn. And I wouldn't have met Jade.

I sighed. Not meeting Jade ... My fists balled in my hair, and my jaw tensed. That girl was ruining everything. But then, I figured it was my fault. I had been letting her and the pack walk all over me. Maybe I had been too nice, too forgiving. Maybe Ray had had the right idea all along. Evoke fear in the pack and the town. I wanted to call my dad. I needed advice, but I couldn't bring myself to dial the number. He would only tell me what I already knew. I was being too soft with them all.

I didn't hear the door open or her footsteps, but I felt her slide into the booth, pressing up against me. Erika. I glanced at her. Nervous whispers and the synchronized clattering of mugs against tables suddenly invaded my brain. I glanced up to find the booths around me were now empty as people filed out the front door or moved to the opposite side of the coffee shop, giving me a wide birth.

I inched away from her, pressing closer to the wall. She wore her typical skintight black tank. It was cut so low that her breasts were barely covered, and she also sported black jeans and a leather jacket that fit like a glove. Her bright blue eyes and even brighter red lipstick were the only color on her.

Her nostrils flared, and her eyes sparkled. She studied me long and hard, taking in deep breaths, and when her lips started to curve, my stomach sank.

"Leave it alone, Erika," I warned, putting every bit of authority that I had into my tone. "She's not part of this."

She smiled, not a nice smile, and it sent a chill over my skin. "Too bad what you say doesn't really matter, not when it comes to this. She's left her stench all over you."

CHAPTER 16

JADE

I could still feel Aidan pressed against me. The warmth of his body. The softness of his lips. The sweet taste of his tongue against mine. The butterflies in my stomach turned into a flapping nest of birds just from the thought of him. But then they stopped. How could someone so ... so ... perfect be such a monster?

It was strange how my perception of Aidan could change drastically with a single word. I thought I had known who he was. Not that I really knew him, but I had this idea of who he was supposed to be, except that idea crumbled as soon as I heard *alpha*. In a split second, everything had clicked into place with surprising clarity. The pack loved him not because he was a nice guy but because they had to. And it made me wonder how much of what I thought I knew about him was a lie.

The last few rays of the sun had long since flickered out on the horizon, and the sun-warmed ground that I sat on had grown cold. The wind was fierce, cutting through my jeans and sending goosebumps rushing over my skin. Leaves flew around me, falling from the trees, and were yanked from the ground as another gust of bitter wind rushed through the park. I should have gone home. Marcy would be worried, and so would Mom and Dad. But I didn't want to leave. Not yet.

To be honest, I was a bit surprised that no one had come looking for me yet, but I figured Dominic had a hand in that. He was really the only person that Marcy or my parents would have listened to if they thought I was missing. I guessed I should thank him for that. For giving me time to breathe.

I traced the engraved stone, running my fingers along the

grooves. The moon cast light in silver strips on the stone, cutting through the trees. I had always loved this place. The wall of faces. The monument stood in the center of the park. It was supposed to be a tribute to the alphas, their faces engraved there as they took over the pack. For me, though, it wasn't a tribute. It was a reminder that they were not invincible.

Leaves crunched under shoes in the distance. I listened as they approached, not bothering to look behind me. I probably should have, but I couldn't make myself care. The crunching stopped at what sounded like only a few feet from my back, and her voice cut through the air, making the already bitter night turn arctic. "You should have stayed away from Aidan."

"Go away, Erika," I said, letting my finger trail along the grooves of another face.

She laughed darkly. "I don't think so."

I straightened a little as tension flowed freely, thick and suffocating, between us, but I still didn't bother to turn around. Erika was one of those girls that thrived on others' fear, and I wasn't going to let her think that her presence bothered me, not even for a second.

A string of snaps and pops echoed through the park. I leaped up from the ground, but not out of fear. I was furious. Why couldn't she just leave me alone? I spun toward her and gasped. She was a white wolf, larger than I remembered her to be. Her eyes were wide, staring at me, and she bared her teeth, snarling.

I snarled back. I felt it in my belly, vibrating up my throat. All of my anger bubbled up, and it burst out into a growl. I stalked toward her. It was probably stupid. A voice in my head was screaming at me to run, but I couldn't. I wasn't going to let her think I was scared, and in all honesty, at that moment, I was too angry, too hurt, to feel the fear that should have been jolting through me.

Erika snapped out at me and let out a rumbling growl. But I kept moving in on her, my eyes locked with hers. "You're not going to win," I taunted. My voice sounded wrong — savage — and my lips twisted into a sneer as I snarled at her again. I sounded feral like an animal. It was wrong. So wrong. But at the same time, it felt ... right. Strong and fervent. Eager to end her reign of terror once and for all.

I towered over her wolf form. She pulled her lips back further, the pink of her gums exposed. For a second, I froze, and white-hot anger surged through me as I stared into those yellow eyes. I blinked, only a quick flutter of my lashes, and when I opened my eyes, she lunged forward.

Raw adrenaline pumped fiercely through my veins. I jumped out of the way, hitting the ground hard. Grass and dirt bit into my side as I skidded along the ground. I rolled out of the skid, jumping back up to my feet.

Erika stalked toward me again, snarling savagely, and right then, my stomach rolled. *What the hell am I doing?* She circled to my right, and I swiveled, matching her movements. I swallowed the dread that had begun to trickle over my skin and scanned around me, looking for something, anything, I could use.

My eyes fell on a branch, and another frustrated growl ripped through me. The branch looked thick, sturdy, and perfect, and it lay on the ground just behind the snarling white wolf.

The fur along Erika's back bristled, standing on end along her spine, and her ears straightened as she pushed them forward. With stiff, straight legs, she sidestepped, continuing to circle, and I kept moving, matching her pace. The branch was getting closer with each cautious step. Her eerie, glowing eyes never strayed from me. They were intense and cold and calculating.

Suddenly, Erika stopped and leaped into the air, moving faster than my eyes could follow. And then she was on me. I barely felt her teeth sink into my ankle. My blood was pumping fast, and my breath coming short as a new burst of energy coursed through me. I did the only thing I could think of. I kicked out at her, throwing her off balance enough that she let go, and before she could sink her teeth into me again, I lunged at her, grabbing her muzzle with both hands, and held it closed.

Erika bucked and swung her head from side to side, but I held tight. Now that I was actually touching her, all the fear I should have felt in the first place was pressing at me from all sides. She growled and yanked, and I held on certain that if I let go, I'd be dead. My arms were throbbing and shaking, and my hands were slick with drool. I didn't know how much longer I would be able to hold on. With every shake of her head, my hands slipped, and I had to scramble to keep hold.

A low, rumbling, and more than a little frustrated growl ripped from me. "Stop it!" I yelled in a voice that did not sound like my own. It sounded too cold and too forceful, full of command that I had never known I had in me. And then, Erika just ... stopped. She looked up at me, her eyes widened, and her entire body trembled. She bowed her head, breaking eye contact. Her ears flopped down, and she whimpered, lowering herself to the ground at my feet as I let her muzzle slip from my hands.

AIDAN

"Did she ...?" Dominic started, his voice trailing off.

We tracked Erika since she rushed out of the diner, watching and waiting. She had been right. I had no say in the alpha female games. I couldn't stop Erika from challenging Jade, but Jade was just a human, and I figured that that fact alone could overrule the *no alpha males allowed at a challenge* rule. If Erika had tried to pull the crap she had with Becca, Jade wouldn't have stood a chance. Or at least that's what I had been trying to tell myself to justify my proximity to the challenge. Clearly, I had been wrong.

"She did," I said as Erika bowed her head and sank to the ground. The copper scent of blood filled the air. I felt sick, and a cold sweat broke out over my back. I should have stopped this. I could have stepped in. And if I had, Jade wouldn't be ... *She'll hate you even more when it sinks in,* a voice echoed through my head, triumphantly, as if my conscious was actually happy that my life was crumbling all around me.

Dominic looked at me, stunned. "Aidan, you're not going to ..." he started, but his voice trailed off again as he looked back at the girls. Erika lay silent, her tongue darting out as she licked at Jade's ankle.

I nodded. "I am." I wanted to smile; I could feel it in my belly, but I didn't. The scent of blood was growing, wrapping around me, and I watched as Erika's tongue darted out again, coating Jade's bleeding ankle with her saliva. My conscious was yelling at me, telling me this was nothing to be happy about, but I couldn't stop it. I was happy and sick and stunned.

"She doesn't know what she did."

"Doesn't matter. You know the rules. She probably won't win anyway. She'll give up." Even to my own ears, my voice sounded cold, uncaring, and it was ... odd. My heart was thumping; my nerves were alive, rushing and sparking over my skin. But my voice ... my voice was like my conscious. Cold and disappointed.

"But she's not one of us," Dominic said, a pleading note to his voice. "And she doesn't know how to give up."

"Dominic, go help Jade," I said, cutting him a look. "She's bleeding."

CHAPTER 17

JADE

She bit me. She bit me. She bit me.

My ankle was bleeding. Erika's tongue tickled my skin as she lapped up the scarlet trail that leaked from my flesh, catching it before it reached the ground.

She bit me. She bit me. She bit me.

I couldn't move away. I wanted her to stop. My stomach rolled, and bile rushed up to my throat.

She bit me. She bit me. She bit me.

Erika whimpered, and her tongue flicked out again, sending a hot rolling chill up my leg and over my skin. She was salivating. Her drool was warm and cool all at once. She nosed my leg, trying to get my attention.

She bit me. She bit me. She bit me.

"Erika!" The voice was loud. Commanding. Furious.

Erika whined and pressed her head against me, cowering at my feet. She looked up at me. Fear shone in her eyes, and she whined again.

"Erika, get away from her," the voice demanded, but she didn't move. I didn't know how she could resist the urge to obey. That voice. It made my insides shiver, not in a good way.

She held my eyes and tilted her head to the side. She barked once, just a little yip, and then bowed her head again.

"Shit," the voice said. A hand touched my shoulder. It was gentle and warm and familiar. "She's waiting for your command," it said softly in my ear.

"She bit me," I said. I felt empty. Hollow. Vacant. "She bit me."

A growl rumbled through the air. I shuddered. So did Erika. I felt her trembling against my leg. I bent beside her. I don't know why. I didn't want to, but I couldn't stop it. "It's okay," I whispered and patted her lightly, letting my fingers trail down her back.

The growl came again. Louder. Stronger. And the white wolf cringed into me. She licked my chin and flattened her ears.

"Jade, stand up. Don't let her hide behind you. You can't protect her from her alpha. It's not your place."

"She bit me," I said again, hating myself for saying it. I looked up, and Dominic smiled a sad, sad smile.

"I know, honey," he said. "But you need to step away from her. Tell her to go with Aidan."

I furrowed my brow and looked around. What was he talking about? There was no one else here. I opened my mouth, ready to demand an answer when suddenly, I was face to face with *the* black wolf.

I jumped a little and rocked on my feet. Erika whimpered, and Dominic snapped, "Don't show fear. It'll ruin what you've already done." I started to look up. The realization of what had really happened hit me hard and fast. "No, don't look away from him, Jade. Stand up slowly, keep your eyes open and fixed on him."

The black wolf snarled and bared his teeth, and I fought the urge to close my eyes. This was Aidan. Aidan was the black wolf. I thought I would be sick, and I swallowed hard, pushing the rising bile back down my throat. I stood up on shaky legs and held still. I wanted to run. I fought against the scream, trying to push up from my stomach.

We locked eyes for an agonizing and terrifyingly long moment, the black wolf and me, and then he shifted his focus, growling at Dominic. And Dominic ... Dominic dropped his eyes and shrunk, rolling his shoulders over and making himself as small as he could without dropping to the ground.

Erika crawled toward Aidan, her belly dragging along the ground, and licked his chin until he snapped at her to stop. With one last piercing glare at me, he left, with Erika trailing behind him, her tail between her legs.

"Why did you make me do that?" I asked, my voice cracking over the words. The last bit of Erika's white form disappeared into the trees.

"Because Erika is treating you like an alpha, and if you bowed to him, you would lose that respect," Dominic said as if it was matter-of-fact.

"But you bowed to him," I countered. I wish I hadn't said it. I didn't want to talk. I didn't want Dominic's help. Cold sweat was dripping down my forehead, and the bitter, sour bile was fighting its way back up my throat.

"Yes, but I'm his beta," Dominic said. He sounded so distant. So far away. "I'm lower than him."

The world around me was spinning and shifting. The night seemed darker, blacker, and bitterer. My stomach rolled, and my head spun. I looked at Dominic and whispered, "She bit me."

♥

I woke up to a wonderfully familiar smell. It was musky with a hint of apple, and I pulled in a long, deep breath, savoring it. His hand brushed lightly across my forehead, pushing away my hair, and I cuddled up closer to him, burying my head in his chest.

"How are you feeling?" he asked. His voice was whisper soft, and he pulled me closer still, wrapping his strong arms around me.

"Tired and thirsty. Really, really thirsty." His sweater muffled my voice, but he still heard me and laughed.

"Thirsty?" he asked and chuckled again. "I think that's the first time I've heard that one."

I kept my eyes closed. I didn't want to look at him. I didn't want to see the pity or the understanding that I was sure would be on his face. The sun was beating through the window. Its warmth touched my exposed skin, and it felt so ... real. All of it felt real. I wondered how long I had slept. Was it a few hours? A few days? Was I already in transition? I wanted to be angry, but I couldn't bring myself to drudge up the feeling. What point was there? It was done. I was, or soon would be, one of them. Anger seemed like such a waste of effort.

We lay there silently for a long while. Dominic rubbed soft and soothing circles onto my back, and although I couldn't say it, I was glad he was there. Who would have thought that this would be what brought us back together? I surely hadn't, but in a way, I was glad for it. His arms around me made everything a bit brighter. Fuller. Easier to handle. I could still feel Erika's wet tongue on my ankle, tainting my blood.

"What's going to happen, Dom?" I asked. I squeezed my eyes tighter, wishing I could just go back to sleep and pretend none of this had happened.

"Well, um ..." he started and squeezed me a bit tighter before continuing, "the first thing that's going to happen is that you are going to have a shower, and then you'll get dressed, and then you need to talk to Aidan."

I bolted up, pushing him off me, and a surge of white-hot rage rushed over me. "What!" I shouted and then took a long breath, trying to rein in my voice. I narrowed my eyes at Dominic. He was still lying back on my bed, cool and calm, smirking at me. "I'm not going to talk to him. I never want to see that jerk again." Okay, so maybe anger wasn't all that hard to feel after all.

That wiped the smirk from his lips. "Jade," he said, with a commanding force that made me sit a bit straighter. "There's no place in this town for a lone wolf, and with what you did to Erika ..." he trailed off and took a long, deep breath. "If you don't join the pack, you'll run the risk of creating your own, and trust me, you don't want that. Not here."

AIDAN

Dominic's voice was loud. It drifted down the stairs as if it were seeking me out, making sure I didn't miss a beat of his conversation with Jade. I wished I had missed it all. The venom in her voice when she said she never wanted to see me again had my inner-wolf doing backflips in my stomach, just itching to run to her and beg her to accept me.

She was meant to be an alpha. Not just an alpha, but *my* alpha mate. I could feel it with every fiber, every vessel, every nerve ending in my body. I wasn't sure how Dominic managed to speak to her the way he was. His voice held so much command. It didn't waver in the slightest. I assumed it was because of their past, whatever that was, but still, the rest of the pack had been treating her with hostile caution, and he acted as if she were just a girl. And right then, I wished I had done exactly that right from the start.

As it was, it took everything I had in me not to run up those steps and punish him for speaking to her that way. It was as if my inner-wolf had already claimed her and accepted her as my equal.

Mr. Shaw didn't seem to notice my turmoil. He just stared at me, long and hard. It was distracting and annoying, and I could feel my blood pressure rising with every passing second.

He seemed like an okay guy. And I figured he had a right to be a little pissed about his daughter, but the longer he stared at me, the more I felt as if he wasn't really that angry. It was as if he were sizing me up, taking in every little detail and trying to decide my worth. He reminded me of my first girlfriend's father, which made me overly nervous.

Mrs. Shaw had been a lot easier to deal with. I'd met her briefly this morning, and it had only taken a few short minutes to convince her that Jade would be fine. She didn't even bother checking in on her daughter before running out the door to work, entrusting her fully to my care. And she had actually seemed happy about the fact that Jade had been bitten.

We had been sitting in the living room for about an hour waiting for Jade to wake up when he finally cracked an odd kind of smile and said, "So my daughter is part of the competition."

"Yes, sir," I said, a bit stunned. I looked him over again and furrowed my brow. The inner workings of a pack's rank were not something that a human should know. He was staring at me, waiting for more, and he was giving me a no-bullshit kind of look, one that had me certain he knew exactly what was going on. Most likely more *Ray* damage, I figured, and I continued with caution, "She broke Erika last night. And she didn't back down from me after the challenge."

That shocked him. I saw a quick flash of it in his eyes, but he covered it up quickly. "I don't doubt that. Jade has spent a long time hating your pack. She wouldn't back down." He stretched his long legs in front of him and crossed them at the ankles. "Has she accepted the rank?"

I held his eyes, unblinking and unflinching. "There are still three other females fighting for it. Nothing to accept yet. And as far as I know, Jade doesn't have a clue what she's signed up for. She might step down when she does."

He laughed, a full-bellied laugh. "Jade doesn't give up," he said and laughed again. He sounded so much like Dominic, it was a bit ... weird, and it added a whole shitload of questions to the rising pile in the back of my mind that centered on Jade. Again, I found myself wondering, *Who was this girl? And how deep of a connection did she have with my beta?*

Mr. Shaw's laughter died down, and he gave me a somber look. "Be honest with me, kid," he said, sounding a little deflated, "does she have a chance, or should I be packing her up and taking her away?"

It was a fair question, and I had to really think about it before answering. "If she left now, she'd have Erika following her. It was a struggle to get her to leave Jade's side last night." I paused, collecting my scattered thoughts, and scrubbed at my face before looking back at him. "I think she has what it takes, sir."

Mr. Shaw considered my answer. He folded his arms over his chest, and one eyebrow rose. "And how do you feel about my baby girl?" There was no-nonsense in his tone as he asked the question, and I got the feeling that there was only one right answer. Too bad I didn't really know what the right answer was.

"Doesn't matter," I said with a shrug. "Alpha pairs are about strength and dominance and leadership. How I feel, or who I want, doesn't make a difference in who will win."

"You don't know who I am, do you, son?" he snapped, and I got the sinking feeling that sticking with the truth of the situation wasn't the right answer.

I shook my head from side to side. "No, sir. Should I?"

"He works for you, dumbass," Dominic said as he padded down the stairs. "Who do you think I called yesterday when you were stupid enough to tell the whole town who you are?"

Every muscle in my body coiled like a spring. "You," I said, snapping my gaze back to Mr. Shaw. My nostrils flared as I sucked in breath after breath, but all I got were wolves and humans. No trace of cougar. Nothing but human was coming from this man. "You can't be."

Mr. Shaw chuckled. "Nice little trick, isn't it?"

CHAPTER 18

JADE

The doorbell rang again in three short and shrill bursts. I could hear Dominic laughing and the deep rumbles of Dad's voice, but yet, the doorbell was still ringing. I secured my towel around me, tucking it tightly, and whipped the bathroom door open. "Answer the door," I yelled, and with a glance down the hall, just to make sure no one was there, I slipped out of the bathroom and headed for my room.

I didn't get far.

Someone cleared their throat and started shuffling up the steps behind me. I spun around, figuring it was just Dominic. I was about to give him an earful about the door, but the words clogged in my throat. "Aidan," I said, and I hated how my voice squeaked on his name. I sounded like an awkward teenager, and I was sure I looked it, too.

He wasn't smirking. His jaw was locked tight, but he didn't look unhappy, annoyed, maybe. He reached the top of the stairs and just stood there, staring down at me. And right then, I didn't find him intriguing. It was a weird feeling as if something that should be there was just ... gone. I figured that it was because I knew who he was now. The mystery was gone, and at that moment, all I saw was barely concealed power and authority, and it made me shiver. My stomach constricted, twisting tight as a corkscrew, and I chewed on my bottom lip nervously.

Aidan took a step forward, and I almost did the same. Almost. His fitted gray T-shirt hugged his muscled chest and sculpted arms, and as I looked at him, I suddenly felt alive, as if someone had flicked my power switch on. All I could think about was touching him. An urging need ran through me. It was primal, deep-seated, and more than a little bestial. It was nothing like the butterflies or birds that I usually felt when he was near. This was so much more that it consumed me like fire consuming a fluttering piece of paper. My skin burned, and my heart pounded. I wanted to know what that power felt like under my fingertips. His eyes raked over me, and he licked his lips, and Jesus, but my knees started to tremble. He had that look in his eyes, the one he had had when we first met as if he saw nothing but me. It was so intense as if I were the only thing in the world that was worth looking at.

And that's when my senses came back to me. I flushed. It burned over my skin like a fever, and I reached up, pulling my towel around me tighter. I blinked, and I took a step back. He took another step toward me. Everything about his tense posture urged me to move away, but I couldn't. Dominic slid his hand to the small of my back, pressed his lips to my ear, and whispered, "He's testing you, Jade. Don't back down."

I jumped then. I hadn't even seen him approach us. I had heard him downstairs, and I knew he must have walked right by both Aidan and me. "You didn't tell me he was here," I hissed back. My heart was racing, and my knees still shaking.

"Well, I am," Aidan said, "and we need to have a chat." He shifted his hard gaze to Dominic and said, "You've got to stop helping her. She needs to win this one on her own."

"I don't think I want her to win," Dominic said, his voice full of defiance. His hand pressed a bit harder on the small of my back, and I slapped it away before he forced me to move closer to Aidan.

Aidan laughed, a shocked and strangled kind of sound. "Not your call, Dominic."

"What the hell are you two talking about?" I snapped, but they ignored me. I looked between the two of them. Aidan stood a bit straighter, and so did Dominic, rolling his shoulders back and puffing out his chest. Aidan's chocolaty eyes brightened, and a golden ring shimmered around the edges. He growled. Yes, growled. It was deep and low and rumbling, and it made me shiver again. The power behind that sound was intoxicating. Alluring. And something deep within me responded to it. I wanted it. I wanted that power more than I wanted to breathe.

The face-off didn't last long. Dominic slunk back a step and dropped his gaze, but the tension lingered. Silence fell over us, thick and awkward, and with every passing second, I became hotly aware that I was standing in the hallway wearing only a towel.

Aidan was staring at me as if I were some hot fudge sundae that he really wanted to lick.

"Aidan, let my daughter get dressed," Dad hollered up the stairs, breaking the seriously uncomfortable tension.

Aidan smirked then and winked at me. "Sure thing, Jeff," he yelled back in a way that was far too friendly. He turned from me then and started down the stairs. Dominic followed him, his eyes on the ground and shoulders still hunched.

"Stop right there," I said. Aidan glanced over his shoulder and smirked. "How do you know my dad?"

He chuckled. "Again, I ask you, can I not know people just because I'm new?"

AIDAN

I think walking away from Jade was the single hardest thing I had ever done. I had expected her to be dressed, not almost naked. That little white towel had left little to the imagination, hanging just below her bottom, and cinched tightly over her chest. Each silky curve of her body begged me to get closer and see if her skin was as soft as it looked. All I could think about was seeing what was underneath that thin cloth. I had never wanted something so badly. Never.

And that scared the hell out of me.

Wanting wasn't in the cards for me. Not until she won. Not until she was mine. And my gut was telling me that once she knew the score, she'd happily step down. I had seen it in her eyes. The loathing. The hatred. I was certain that's what the look had been. The girl who had been haunting my every move had been unattainable before, and she had just moved even further out of my reach.

Dominic followed me down the stairs, not saying a word, and her father stood at the bottom, eyeing me suspiciously. I waited for the soft click of her door and looked the man straight in the eyes, and said, "We're not going to tell her. She won't stand a chance if she knows." And then I spun on Dominic. "If you go against me again, I will strip you of your title and kick you out of this pack. I'm not playing your games anymore."

Anger flared in his eyes for about half a second, but it quickly vanished when he noticed I was serious. Clearly, playing nice hadn't worked yet, and I was done. Done with all of it. If this pack was going to continue to push me, I would push back. Especially now. With Jade's transformation, I couldn't risk her inner-wolf losing respect for me. I wouldn't risk it. If that happened, if I couldn't maintain a position as her equal, even as a hated equal, I'd risk losing the entire pack. And I wasn't ready to lose yet. Not when it meant another male would take her.

"I'm sorry," he whispered, dropping his eyes to the ground.

Jeff turned gray, all the blood rushing from his face, and he sucked in a loud gasping breath. "You can't keep this from her."

"She won't fight for me," I said calmly, even though saying it out loud sent rage coursing through me. "I'm pretty sure your daughter hates me, Jeff, and you know what will happen if she doesn't fight. It's not just my pack I'm worried about. Now that the news of a new alpha is out, your pack will be hovering, and she needs to be focused."

"Are you kidding me?" Erika's voice screeched through me, like rusty brakes on a car. "She'll fight for you. She wants you."

"What are you doing here?" I asked, well, okay, I demanded, and Erika flinched.

"Jade didn't show up at school," she said. Her voice was whiny, and she sounded as if she were going to cry. She lifted a stack of books and stepped closer to me as if she thought I hadn't noticed them. "I brought her homework."

I just stared at her and gritted my teeth. My own scent wafted around me — pungent and commanding. I pulled on my alpha wolf, pushing it forward, channeling it into my human form. The vibe was unmistakable. I might as well have ripped off my shirt, beat my chest, and yelled, *'I am alpha.'*

"Aidan, we get it," Dominic said with a slight tremor to his voice. "You're the alpha. Could you tone it down a little?"

I didn't have a chance to respond. "Erika?" Jade snapped. I swiveled and looked up the stairs, and for a second, I started to smile, but it died fast. Her scent was just as strong as mine was, and it came close to overpowering me. "Seriously, you have a lot of nerve," she spat. "Get the hell out of my house!"

"Um ... I'm just ... homework," she said, jutting a stack of books out. Her arms were shaking, the books sliding around in her hands. "Please don't hate me," she whispered. "I won't be a problem. I promise. Just ... I can't live with my alpha hating me. Don't make me go." She started inching toward the stairs, keeping her eyes averted from Jade, and it made my blood boil.

"Erika, she is *not* an alpha," I said more harshly than I had intended, but with Jade so close ... projecting so much authority, I just couldn't pull it back. "She's not even part of *my* pack."

Erika stopped at the base of the stairs but didn't turn back to me. She curled her shoulders over and dropped her head as if she hoped that I wouldn't notice her. "Jade and I have some business to deal with. She'll see you tomorrow," I said as gently as I could, which still turned out to be sharper than I wanted, and Erika shuddered, but she still didn't move. I turned to Dominic. "Take her home. Don't come back here tonight."

"No," Jade growled from deep within her belly. She fixed an icy stare on me and held it for a long minute. When I didn't flinch, she said, "We have no business. Erika, come up here. You can help me with my homework."

Erika started up the steps, and Jade smiled at her encouragingly before she glanced at her father. "Dad, if Mac comes home, send her up, okay?" And then she shifted her gaze to Dominic and said, "Oh and Dom, I'm starving." Her tone was sharp, commanding, and impossible. I loved it and loathed it. She smirked at me, clearly pleased with herself, and started to turn her back on me. She hadn't even made her first shift, and she was already falling into the ranks with ease as if she had been there all along.

Dominic's laugh pulled me out of my stupor. "Sure thing, boss," he said. "One Lucy's Griller coming up."

Everyone was moving, jumping at her orders. My whole body went rigid. "Stop!" I shouted. I couldn't make my muscles relax. My jaw flexed, and it took everything in me to just stand still. Dominic froze, and Erika blanched. "Get out."

"Aidan," Jeff said. His voice was calm, but I heard the warning in it, and he squeezed my shoulder with a firm, pinching grip.

I didn't let him finish. I didn't want to hear it. This wasn't going to help, I knew that, but I couldn't stop it. She was being impossible, even if she didn't know it. I turned to Jeff and looked him straight on. "I said get out."

CHAPTER 19

JADE

Okay, maybe I took it a bit too far. But in all fairness, Aidan was pissing me off. Who the hell did he think he was coming into my house and commanding my guests as if they were nothing more than slaves? It was wrong on so many levels. But what was worse was that something inside me growled when I caught his scent. It was intoxicating, and in seconds, my own scent ramped up and matched his. I didn't know what was happening to me, but I loved it almost as much as I loved the idea of being alone with him. It was all completely animal, and it excited and scared me all at once.

My dad gave him a crazy disappointed look but didn't argue. But then, of course, he wouldn't. He was the pack's number one fan. "Mom and I will be at Joe's tonight if you need us, pumpkin," he called, and then to my horror (and absolute pleasure), he left, pushing Erika and Dominic out the door.

"You need to leave," I said, but my voice betrayed me. It shook, and all of the command I had had just moments ago was gone.

"Has Dominic told you what to expect?" Aidan asked, completely ignoring me. His tone was as sharp as his body language. Commanding and demanding answers. Every part of me screamed to give him anything and everything he wanted. I wished he hadn't ignored me. Really, I wished he would just go because all I could think about was jumping down the stairs and ripping off that shirt of his. I wanted to kiss every inch of his body, taste it, lick it, and oddly, I really wanted to rub against it. It was driving me crazy. He was driving me crazy. I had never wanted something so much before. It hurt in a wonderful kind of way.

"I already know," I said and let my eyes trail down his lean body again. "Grew up here, remember? I'll shift in three days unless my blood rejects it, and in that case, I'll die." His muscles looked deliciously strong, and as I descended the stairs, moving closer to him, I could feel the heat radiating from his sun-kissed skin.

"You won't die," he said. He started to smile. I saw a hint of it touching his full lips, but it vanished quickly. "I can already smell the wolf coming from your skin. You'll shift."

"Huh," I said. He was watching me closely as my foot fell on the last step. I wanted to run at him, but I fought against it. What had Dominic said? Don't back down? I tried to imitate Dominic, keeping my head high and shoulders back. I pictured his strut and his confidence, and I channeled it. Honed it in and projected it.

Aidan noticed. His face lost a little color, and he sucked in a loud breath. "I'm not going to tolerate you stepping over me. If you want to be part of my pack, you better learn your place."

"Who says I want to be part of your pack?" I purred. *Purred!* I almost laughed at myself. I really wasn't the purring type. Blunt and direct was more my style. But this guy ... I licked my lips. Completely involuntary, I swear, and my eyes raked over him again.

He arched a brow and smirked ... a little. "Your hatred towards me is a bit much, don't you think?"

Hatred? Clearly, he was misreading me. He squirmed a little, and his face went a bit whiter. And I grinned. I couldn't help it. I had never had a guy squirm from my stare before, and I had to admit, it was a bit exhilarating. "Actually, no, I don't," I said, playing along. "You lied to me."

He sighed, a frustrated kind of sound. "You never asked, Jade. You just assumed I was human. I never lied."

We were only a few feet apart now, just a couple more steps, and I'd be able to run my hand over his chest. I shrugged lazily and took another step. "Lying by omission. It's the same thing, genius."

He chuckled. The sound was like velvet. Soft and strong, and it made my knees go weak. He noticed that, too, and chuckled again. "I can't omit anything that I wasn't asked about."

I was about to tell him that he was an ass-hat. What a stupid cop-out. And by the look he was giving me, he knew exactly how stupid he sounded, but I didn't get a chance because Marcy came barging through the front door.

"Jade, I'm so sorry. Dom made me leave this morning." She slammed the door behind her, turned around, and ran smack into

Aidan's chest. "Oh," she squealed, surprised. She took a step back, realized who it was, and then she gave him the dirtiest look I had ever seen. She put her hands on her hips and narrowed her eyes further. "What are you doing here?"

Aidan gave her a quick once over and said, not cruelly, but with a definitely uncaring tone, "Trying to decide if I want her in my pack or not."

Marcy gasped and hopped another step back. "You can't ban her."

He smiled and then laughed uneasily. "Yeah, I can. It's not an automatic entry. She wasn't recruited. She picked a fight and got bitten."

"I didn't pick a fight," I said, folding my arms over my chest. My bottom lip jutted out, and I hated myself for it. Really? Was I really going to pout about this? Technically, I had picked a fight. I could have walked away. But still, hearing him say it, seeing that look on his face, it was as if he thought I was nothing more than trouble.

"Aidan, dude, you're being a douche bag," Marcy blurted. Aidan's eyes flared, and her hands flew up in surrender. "Settle down, boy. I'm all about team werewolf, but she hasn't even shifted yet. Can't this, you know, wait? Maybe you could come back tomorrow or something?"

Aidan didn't even think about it before he shook his head and said, "Nope, someone's got to stay with her."

"I'm not going anywhere," Marcy said, standing a little straighter, and she fixed her glare back in place. She was aiming for fierce, I was sure of it, but right then, she looked more like a little kitten testing out her claws.

"I mean a pack member, Mac," he said with a groan. "Someone needs to monitor her just in case ..."

"You said ..." I started, but Aidan promptly cut me off.

"Things can always go wrong, Jade."

"Trevor," Marcy blurted. "Can he stay with us?"

Aidan gritted his teeth, and it almost looked as if he were trying to find a reason to say no, but after a moment of consideration, he fished his phone out of his pocket. He scrolled through his address book, tapped on the screen, and then brought the phone to his ear. "Trevor, come to Jade's. I need you to stay here with the girls." There was a long silence, and Aidan stiffened. One by one, deep lines began appearing on his forehead. "When?" he asked. Another pause. "How many?" He must not have liked the answer because a growl slipped out, and he turned his back on us. "Just get here," he snapped, and then he shoved his phone back into his pocket.

"What's wrong?" I asked, although my voice didn't sound like I cared even to my own ears. His back was stiff, the muscles under his skin coiled and bulged, and the urge to touch him again was unbearable. I took a step, moving toward him, and he spun around.

Aidan's eyes were golden. Not a speck of the delicious brown left. Strands of coarse hair littered his cheeks, and his skin looked as if it were crawling. Seeing him on the verge of shifting awoke something in me. Something ... deliriously physical. My muscles began to ache in an amazing kind of way, and prickles ran over my skin. It was as if my body wanted to shift with him. Anything to be closer to him.

"Jade, you will not let anyone other than Trevor and Marcy through those doors. Am I clear?" His voice was a deep growl, and his eyes held me with such intensity that I couldn't move.

"Crystal," I whispered.

I couldn't say how long we stood there watching each other. It could have been seconds, minutes, or hours, but it didn't matter. Right then, I could have stayed there forever, lost in his shimmering eyes.

"Trevor's here," he grumbled, shattering the perfect moment into millions of sharp-edged shards.

There was a loud bang on the door, and Aidan turned away from me, grabbed the handle, and pulled it open.

Trevor looked ... rattled, and there was a jagged rip across the front of his blue sweater. There was also a gash along his right cheekbone that looked like it was starting to heal. It was still bright pink, and there was dried, crusty blood along the edges.

"What happened?" Marcy shrieked and rushed over to him. She started fussing over his sweater and his cheek, making a bunch of anxious gasping sounds.

Trevor grabbed her hands, holding her still, and exchanged a long look with Aidan that I couldn't even begin to understand. And then Aidan glanced at me and said, "By the way. You'll need to learn how to control that."

"Control what?" I asked and hated the pout I heard in my voice. He stepped out the door, keeping his back to me, and I hated that, too. He was leaving, which was a good thing, maybe, kind of. Well, it should have been, but darn it, I didn't want him to go.

He glanced over his shoulder and winked. "Your lust. Your

scent is screaming sex." And then he walked out the door, shutting it quickly behind him.

CHAPTER 20

AIDAN

It was easier leaving than I had thought it would be. My inner-wolf wanted Jade so badly that it took everything in me not to shift. With Jade's enthralling scent and Trevor's news, I really hadn't thought I would have been able to walk out that door and leave her alone, but I did it. As soon as I shut the door behind me, I let out a pent-up breath that I hadn't even realized I'd been holding, and I dug my phone out of my pocket. I fired off a text to Dominic telling him to meet me at my motel room and bring Jeff. I had some questions for both of them, and it was time that they started talking.

I got into my car, started it up, and pulled out of the driveway before I could change my mind. She was handling it all better than I had expected. She didn't need me. And knowing that she didn't need me made it so much harder to deal with. I wanted her to need me.

But what I really needed was a shower. Preferably a cold one.

Jade's scent had held a distinctly alpha quality to it, and she was responding to me exactly how I had hoped she would. I was an unclaimed alpha, and her inner-wolf had picked up on it immediately, even if she didn't know that it had happened. Female wolves' hormones tended to go a touch haywire when there was an unclaimed alpha nearby, and since she had liked me beforehand, well, it was all a little more ... intense.

Thankfully, when I arrived back at the motel, the parking lot was empty. I darted into my room, and knowing I probably only had a few minutes before Dominic would get there, I stripped off my clothes and jumped into the shower, turning the taps as cold as I could stand.

The shower helped ... a little. I had just turned off the ice water when I heard a thudding knock at my door. I got dressed in a rush and yanked the door open, and just as I did, Jeff's fist slammed into my jaw.

I stumbled back a step, and a sharp pain shot through my face. What was it about the Shaws that made them want to hit me? Yesterday, Jade. Today, her father.

Dominic was on him in a flash, grabbing his arms and holding them behind his back. Jeff didn't struggle. He stood just outside my door, glaring at me.

"Okay, yeah, I probably deserved that," I said, rubbing my aching jaw. The skin was already hot under my hand. "But I warn you, Jeff, don't do it again. I'm not Ray, and I will not humor you." I turned from them, padded over to the lone desk chair in my room, and took a seat before I said, "Let him go, Dom."

"Yeah, you did deserve it," Jeff said, shaking his hand out. "Don't you ever try to kick me out of my own house again."

Dominic slid by Jeff and sat on the desk beside me. He wouldn't look at me, but I wasn't really surprised about that. I was surprised that he was taking his place beside me. I really hadn't expected it. After ripping him away from Jade and threatening to boot him out of the pack, I had figured he would have stayed clear of me, at least for a while.

Jeff looked stunned, too. His jaw dropped slightly, and his eyes widened. Clearly, Dominic had said something to him when they had left. Jeff looked as if he were about to say something, but he held it back. After a second, he crossed the room, letting the door slam behind him, and he took a seat on the edge of the bed.

"Where's Jade?" Dominic asked. He tried to sound casual, but it was a useless effort. His voice was like gravel, and his scent was a mix of hot fury and concern, and it held a tangy edge of jealousy.

"At home," I said with a chuckle, as the dirty look she gave me flashed across my mind. "She kind of kicked me out. But I have some good news. She doesn't entirely hate me, although I think she wishes she did."

"I never thought she did," Dominic said through clenched teeth. "You sparked her interest the first second she laid eyes on you."

"How could you leave her alone?" Jeff asked. His complexion paled quickly, and it looked as if it were a struggle for him not to jump up and run out the door. "What if one of them attacks before she's ready? What if ..."

I raised my hand, and he sucked in a breath, holding in whatever he was about to say. "She's not alone. Mac and Trevor are there. And she did beat Erika as a human. I'm sure the other three won't be a problem for her."

Dominic shifted on the desk and finally looked at me. "What if she rejects the change?" He held my eyes, and I saw his fear. It was shining through his mask, although by his tense posture, I was pretty sure he was trying to hide it.

"She won't," I said, keeping my tone light. "Actually, I wouldn't be surprised if she has her first shift today. She smells more wolf than human."

"Aidan, please let me go stay with her," Dominic said. He reached out, placing a hand on my shoulder. "She hates Trevor, and she needs someone to help her through this."

I shrugged his hand off and stretched my legs out in front of me, crossing them at the ankles. "Bad news, too, though," I said, ignoring his plea. "It's time for you to come clean. Because honestly, if I catch another whiff of jealousy on you, I'll rip you apart." I said it all with a smile, but there was no mistaking how serious I was.

Jeff sat still. So still, in fact, that I was pretty sure he was even holding his breath. His hands were clasped in his lap, and his graying hair looked like it could use a good brushing. When I had first seen him, he was kind of intimidating, big, and burly. The father of the girl I liked. Right now, he looked small and scared. It was ... weird and a little perfect. All I had needed was to show my authority, and I could make this man tremble before me.

Dominic sighed and hopped off the desk. He padded over to the big window and pulled open the curtain, letting the sunshine glitter through the glass. He was nervous. I could smell it, and his heartbeat picked up, thrumming a little quicker against his ribs.

"There's nothing to come clean about," he said and glanced around the room. He snagged the garbage can and made his way back over to the desk, picking up the scattered protein bar wrappers and empty coffee cups.

I watched him pick up all the garbage and then begin to straighten the textbooks on the coffee table. The tension was growing; his nerves were making his hands tremble slightly. "I know something's up with you two, Dom, and I want to know what it is."

He turned to me and gave me a blank look. "Shouldn't we be dealing with your exposure? The pack needs to prepare. If we aren't ready, she's the easiest target."

"She's not an easy target," I said, not backing down. "She doesn't even need to move to pin someone in place. I know you felt it. You jumped pretty quickly when she said she was hungry."

I let my scent roll off me, filling the room, and folded my arms over my chest. He was giving me an insolent look, one that clearly told me that he did not, and would not, agree with me, and I was done putting up with it. I hadn't wanted to use my alpha scent like this. I hadn't wanted to turn into my father, but I couldn't fight him and deal with everything else.

Dominic held my stare for a moment before his body visibly started to shake. He laughed a strangled sound and put his hands up, backing up a step. "I swear nothing is going on between us," he said with a desperate note in his voice. "We grew up together. We were best friends. She kissed me once. I told her I was gay. Without the whole sex issue between us, we got closer. I got bit. I ditched her. She hated the pack and me for it. That's it."

I felt the change in my eyes, the soft sting as they began to glow, and he shuddered back another step. "If that were all true, you wouldn't be so jealous," I said, watching him drop to his knees before me.

Guilt washed over me hard and fast. Dominic's face twisted with agony, and a quick flash of how this felt slammed into me. I remembered the pain burning over my skin when my father had let his alpha wolf out. I remembered the scent clawing through my body, making my inner-wolf convulse. I remembered the power behind it, and that memory was what made me pull it back.

Dominic gasped in a breath. "I love her like a sister," he said, panting and crumbling to the floor as I pulled back the last of the invasive scent. He took a few breaths and pulled himself up, propping his back against the wall. "I don't want her hurt. She hates hard, she loves even harder, and if she doesn't win, she'll be crushed when she realizes that means she won't get you." He laughed, but there was no humor in the sound. He gave me a look, and if I didn't know better, I would have thought he actually cared about me. "And you'll have to walk away from her. How many times do I have to tell you I'm looking out for you! Not her. If she lost right now, could you walk away? I'm not blind, Aidan. You're attracted to her, and that's dangerous. If you help her, give her any kind of advantage, she'll be killed, and you won't be able to stop it.

The pack won't stand for it, the enforcers will step in, and I don't trust you enough not to help her. You've already interfered with her once."

The cocky strength was back in his voice, and the color was quickly returning to his cheeks. As I listened to him, I felt as if he had swung a baseball bat into my gut. "That's different," I scoffed, but I knew it wasn't. "You were dragging her to a car."

Dominic got to his feet, still a little shaky, and paced toward me. "Yeah, I was. But if she had have been my mate, she'd have been put on trial for crossing me. And you would have had to hand down the sentence."

I scrubbed at my face. "You're going to tell her, aren't you?"

"Nope. You were right. She won't fight for you. Not because she doesn't want you but because she's stubborn. She's pissed at you, and with Jade, that can last a while." He sighed long and loud and ran his hands roughly through his hair. "She'll lose everything while she chews on her hatred."

I didn't say anything because I was pretty sure he was right. Sooner or later, Jade would gain control of her inner wolf, and when she did, I was pretty sure she'd turn her back on me. Dominic let out a gusty huff and took his place beside me, sitting on the desk.

"I want to be free to help her with the change," he said with determination. "I want to be able to help her win, and I can't do that without your consent. Before you shoot me down, just think for a second about how close you are to having two packs in this town. Erika will follow her anywhere, and I'm sure others will, too."

"Dominic, she needs to know what's happening," Jeff pleaded. It was the first time he'd spoken in a while, and honestly, I had kind of forgotten he was even there.

"Shut up, Jeff," Dominic snapped. "This has nothing to do with you. She's our problem now, and if you still want us to protect your wife, you'll stay the hell out of our way."

Where the hell did that come from? Dominic could be cold. I knew that. I'd seen it, but this ... this was more than a little cold. Jeff inched back a little before he could catch himself. Just hours ago, I would have sworn they were close. Really close. They were so much alike, the way they spoke, the way they held themselves. It was as if they were related. But just like everything else that confused the hell out of me, it pointed back to Jade. *Jade.* That girl was going to be the death of me. I was sure of it.

I glanced over to Dominic and said, "I'll think about it. That's all I can give you right now. But I promise I'll consider your request." He offered a small smile, and then I shifted my gaze to Jeff. "You know, I've been thinking," I said. "You're the only person in this town that would have the ability to leak the information of a new alpha. Even with my slip up yesterday. You're the only one that could have gotten it to them."

Jeff sat up a bit taller and glared fiercely at me. "My alliance has always been with this pack."

I narrowed my eyes. "Three of the cougars attacked one of my wolves on the outside of town today."

"Shit. Who?" Dominic asked.

"Trevor. He's fine. The cougars aren't, though." I hunched over in my chair, leaning my elbows on my knees and leveling my glare on Jeff. "There's something that just doesn't add up here. Why didn't you change your daughter, and why are you so intent on her being part of my pack?"

For a moment, I didn't think Jeff was going to answer me, and white-hot rage simmered in my veins. He must have noticed the change in me because, in one breath, he blurted, "Our pack would have used her. She's young. They don't take mates the way you guys do. Women are a community possession. I couldn't let that happen to my baby. As far as they know, Jade and my wife died three years ago when their bodies rejected the change. Dominic, please talk some sense into him. Jade needs to know what she's gotten herself into." A small tear snaked down his cheek and dripped off his chin, soaking into his sweater.

"Nothing has changed," Dominic said icily. "We aren't friends. I have always tolerated you for Jade's sake only. I can see through you, Jeff. You only want her to know because you want her to hate Aidan more than she is going to hate you when she finds out what you are and what you've done."

Jeff bolted up from the bed. Red rushed to his cheeks, and he balled his fists. "I haven't done anything!"

Dominic slid off the desk and stretched lazily before closing the distance between them. "I watched you do it," he snarled and then hauled off and punched Jeff. Jeff grunted, and he dropped back onto the bed, out cold.

CHAPTER 21

JADE

I'm a werewolf.

I laughed. I'd been laughing since I heard Aidan drive away. Marcy was sitting on the couch looking at me as if I were a nut case, and well, I probably was. This wasn't really something to laugh about, but the irony of me becoming a werewolf, well, it was just funny in a sick kind of way.

Once Aidan left, Marcy had promptly showed Trevor to the bathroom so he could get cleaned up, and then she had made her way back to me. The cut was supposedly from screwing around with some of the guys, but I wasn't sure if I believed him. When he'd said it, his heart rate had picked up, and the scent that pulsed from him smelled like a lie. It was tangy and salty, and it just didn't feel ... true. But whether he was lying or not didn't really matter.

I sat in Dad's recliner, feet up, arms sprawled over the armrests, staring at a lot of nothing. My stomach was starting to ache, but the laughter just kept coming. I figured it was a form of shock, although it really didn't feel anything like shock.

"Jade, what the hell did he mean about you smelling like sex?" Marcy blurted out. She was clasping and unclasping her hands nervously as she watched me.

My laughter died fast, and my cheeks burned. "Um ... well ... dammit, Mac, if you hadn't shown up ..." I let my words fall short, and heat flushed over my skin. I didn't want to admit what he'd done to me, just by being in the room, or how much I wanted to run after him right then.

"You want him?" she asked, and her eyebrows shot up. "After the coffee shop, you still want him?"

I sighed and something pressed against my stomach as if it was trying to chew its way out. "More than ever, and I hate it. He makes my body burn and tingle."

"Maybe it's part of the change," she offered. I thought she was trying to be helpful, but she wasn't. There was so much disgust in her voice that I felt sick for even considering him.

"It's not part of the change, but it is normal," Trevor said, walking into the living room. He glanced at me, just a quick look before he dropped his gaze to the ground and made his way over to sit with Marcy. He had scrubbed the dried blood off his face and had replaced his torn sweater with one of my dad's zip-up hoodies.

"What the hell is that supposed to mean?" Marcy shouted.

"Mac, I've had a bad day," Trevor snapped. "Don't push me." He went to put his arm around her, and she smacked it away.

"You've had a bad day?" she said, jumping up from the couch and glaring down at him. "My best friend is turning into a werewolf. She's lusting after some jackass alpha. My boyfriend thinks he has a right to treat me like dirt. You think you had a bad day? Stop being so goddamn selfish, Trevor, and answer my damn question."

I bit back another laugh. I wanted to jump up and clap. It wasn't often that Marcy got mad, but it was an awesome sight when she did. And for her to finally tell off Trevor, well, I had never thought it would happen. Her petite frame was all puffed out, and she balled her fists. She looked as if she was ready to haul off and punch him.

"When there is an unclaimed male alpha, female wolves get a bit crazy," Trevor said, looking up at her with barely concealed rage. He held her stare for a moment before he shifted it to me. "Jade, your inner-wolf is reacting to him. It's natural."

"Clearly, I'm missing something," Marcy said with a noisy huff. She dropped down beside Trevor again, and this time when he tried to pull her into his arms, she let him, but then that was Marcy. She didn't know how to stay mad, and Trevor knew it. I was a bit disappointed.

"Why did Erika come after me, and why did she call me her alpha?" I asked once they were settled. Marcy cuddled into his side and rested her cheek on his chest as if she hadn't just blown up at him.

"She did?" Trevor asked as if his brain couldn't understand what I was saying.

"Yeah, and Aidan kind of freaked out about it. He said I wasn't an alpha, and I needed to learn my place."

Trevor chuckled. "He's threatened."

"You've got to be kidding me," I said with a groan. Aidan, threatened? I didn't believe it. Not for a second.

Trevor shook his head and chuckled again. "You don't get it. You make him nervous. You make all of us nervous. Even before you were bitten, you've always projected power. You've always been dominant. It's why you've never been recruited. Ray didn't want someone who would stand up to him. And everyone knew if you were changed, you'd make your way into the alpha pair."

"The alpha pair?" Marcy questioned before I could and shifted her head to look up at him.

"Packs have alpha pairs, or they're supposed to," Trevor said as he brushed some hair out of her eyes. "Two alphas. One male and one female. We've never really had that." He shrugged a little as he looked back at me. "There's always been an alpha pair, but the females have constantly cowered behind the males."

"Hold up," Marcy said and sat up a little. "Are you trying to say that Jade's the alpha?"

"Not yet, but I think she could be."

Marcy looked at me with wide eyes, and she made a gurgling sound from the back of her throat as she choked on whatever she was about to say. She started to cough, a wet and painful sound and Trevor rubbed circles into her back.

I sat up slowly, pushing on the footrest of the recliner until it clicked, locking into place. I was pretty sure that this was where I was supposed to crack. I sure felt like I was going to crack. *Me ... an alpha.* The idea was almost laughable ... almost, and if it weren't for the rush of energy that shot through me at the thought, I probably would have actually laughed. And what the hell was an alpha pair? I had an idea of what that might entail, and I was suddenly a bit ashamed, enough that my skin began to tingle at the thought of being paired with Aidan.

I stood up abruptly. I needed air. It was too hot. I was starting to sweat. It beaded up on my forehead and ran down my back. I spun on my heels without a word and darted for the door.

Trevor got there before I did. "Where are you going?" he asked. He folded his arms over his chest and leaned against the door.

"Out," I snapped and tried to shove him out of the way. It was like trying to move a thousand-pound boulder; he didn't move an inch.

"I can't let you do that, Jade," he said with more than a little caution. He eyed me hesitantly.

"You're going to stop me?" I growled, and I was stunned at the viciousness that coated my voice.

Trevor unfolded his arms and grabbed my shoulders firmly, pushing me back a step. "Jade, don't make me call Aidan back here. He has more important things to deal with than your change."

That hurt. Really hurt. Even if I didn't want to admit it, part of me wanted to be the most important thing on Aidan's mind. I deflated like a popped balloon.

♥

I didn't go out. Not because I thought Trevor would actually stop me if I pushed the issue (or at least that's what I had been telling myself) but because I knew if I had left the house, I would have run to *him*, and I really didn't want to do that. I sent Dominic a slew of text messages, begging him to come over, but he still hadn't replied.

Marcy had given up trying to talk to me hours ago. She was curled up on my bed, snoring softly, and Trevor lay beside her. He pretended to sleep, but I knew he wasn't. I could feel him watching me through slitted eyelids.

I sat on the window seat in my room, watching the stars slowly fade into the gray-blue sky of predawn. My bones ached but in a good way. I could feel the change coming, and it scared me. It had only been about forty hours since I had been bitten. The change shouldn't have been happening this quickly. But it was.

I had expected it all to be unbearably painful. It had always sounded painful. Bones snapping and reshaping. But each time a bone began to crack, a rush of steamy adrenaline pumped through me. It was like a high, and I was actually starting to crave it. So far, only a few bones here and there had tried to reshape, but as soon as they snapped, they quickly mended back in place.

My stomach was a tender ball of knots, and every few minutes, a burst of heat rushed over my skin as coarse hair sprung out and receded again. My nails were the only thing that stayed constant. They had morphed into claws about an hour ago and had yet to change back.

"We should go outside," Trevor whispered, sitting up and

sliding off the bed, careful not to wake Marcy. "I've been timing it. It's only about seventy seconds between each break now."

"I'm not ready," I said, looking back out the window. During the last twenty minutes, an increasing number of wolves had been gathering along the edge of the woods in my backyard. At first, it was just one, a rusty brown one that sat at the edge of the tree line watching my window. But as the minutes ticked by, more gathered.

"You are ready, Jade," he said, although I didn't believe him. I rolled my eyes dramatically, and he laughed a little awkwardly. I knew Trevor didn't like me, and I couldn't stand him most of the time, but it was kind of *nice* having him here. He shuffled in place for a second and then grinned at me. "You're going to make an awesome werewolf. You just need to let it out," he said as he fished his cell phone out of his pocket.

"What are you doing?" I jumped up from the ledge and rushed over to him as he tapped the screen. Panic gripped my throat, and my heart jumped in my chest.

"Calling Aidan. He ..."

"No, please don't call him," I said, a little desperately, cutting him off. "Trevor, please."

He cut me an apologetic look and raised his hands helplessly. "He told me to call him when you started to shift, Jade. I don't have a choice. I can't ignore a direct order from him. He'll throw me out of the pack."

Right then, I caught a scent. It was a scent that I knew, one that I would have recognized anywhere, and one that made sparks race over my skin and birds take flight in my stomach. I looked back out the window, and my breath caught in my throat. "He's already here," I whispered, locking eyes with the black wolf.

CHAPTER 22

JADE

He howled to me. The sound wrapped around me, and warmth pooled in my stomach. My heart fluttered for a second and then drummed fast in my chest. I was transfixed, unable to look away from his midnight black coat. Behind him stood at least fifteen other wolves, all a mix of browns, grays, and whites, and they joined in his song.

The black wolf looked up through my window. His golden eyes searched my face, and then he tilted his head back and let out another skin-tingling howl.

"It's time, Jade," Dominic said, and he placed a hand on my shoulder. I jumped. I hadn't heard him come in, but darn it, I was glad he was here. "You need to pick."

"Pick what?" I asked, and my voice shook. I looked up at him, and my eyes burned with the threat of impending tears. Everything was falling into place and falling apart at the same time. I was becoming what I hated most, but by becoming that, I was also getting back what I wanted most: Dominic.

He smiled a crooked smile and took my hand, pulling me up from my seat. "He's giving you a choice to pick the pack. Aidan brought them for you."

"I ... I don't understand," I stammered and snuck another quick look at the black wolf.

Dominic reached out and tucked some loose hair behind my ears. "Every wolf has a choice. Pack or solo. It's simple. You can walk away from us, or you can join us."

I glanced back out the window. My skin was crawling, and my face was starting to feel ... wrong. Different. I could feel the coarse hair poking out along my arms and the pressure on my bones. The wolves continued to sing below me, and the sound of them called to me. It was as if they were calling to me and only me. Asking me to join them. Waiting for me to sing with them. And every fiber in my body wanted exactly that. To be a part of them. I wanted to throw up and laugh, scream, and cry.

"Um, Jade ..." Marcy's voice was shrill, and as I looked over at her, she scurried back on the bed. "You have a muzzle."

AIDAN

Maybe I was wrong about Jade. Maybe she wasn't ready. But the truth was, whether she was ready or not, I couldn't wait any longer. She was vulnerable until she shifted, and I couldn't worry about her not being able to defend herself.

I had rounded up as many pack members as I could, hoping that with this many wolves present, her inner-wolf would respond to them. But having them here meant leaving very few watching the perimeter of Dog Mountain.

I tilted my head back and let another long howl out. I waited, listening to my pack calling her for what felt like forever. I was about ready to give up, but then I heard it. The click of a door. The soft drop of clothes onto the ground. A gasp. A moan. A grunt. The pat of paws on cement.

And then I was flying through the air and crashing onto the ground.

She stood over me. Her fur was black as pitch, and her eyes, a brilliant gold. She grinned, a toothy grin, and hopped a little, ready to play.

The pack was silent, and the tension was thick. Her scent was powerful, sharp. I rolled back up to my paws and shook the grass from my coat. My scent ramped up a notch, and a chorus of whimpers filled the air. But Jade ... she didn't back down. I straightened, and I let a warning growl rumble from my chest. My lips curled up, and my eyes widened.

She cocked her head to the side as if she didn't understand, and I growled again. I needed her to fall in line. She had to choose to follow me. She had to choose the pack. I wished I could speak to her. I wished she would grasp it. But she nudged me again, nipping playfully at my side.

JADE

I thought Aidan was trying to tell me something, but I couldn't focus on it. His scent was wonderful. Powerful. Perfect. And all I wanted to do was run and play and rub against him. I had so much energy. Too much energy. It was soaring through me, and I couldn't stand still.

He seemed ... annoyed, and I wished he would stop growling at me. The tension that rolled off the other wolves was suffocating, and he was only making it worse. Each time he growled, they would whimper and shrink further away from us.

And I didn't want them to go.

I nosed his side, and he snapped at me. He growled again, louder, longer, and my insides shivered at the sound.

I stood a bit straighter and pushed my ears forward. I growled and snapped back at him. *I want to play.* Why wasn't he getting it? It was so frustrating.

Aidan shivered. I could see it move along his fur. It was amazing. Tantalizing heat surged through me. He growled again, and I growled back.

Aidan took a step closer to me, his canines bared, and he snarled. His scent changed then. It became stronger, and something in me trembled. He barked and followed it with another growl that made my knees shake. A voice in my head screamed at me to stay standing, but my knees started to buckle, and with each second, it was harder to hold his stare. I felt my head dropping inch by slow inch.

Something tore into my skin. I yelped and tried to jump away. My flesh ripped. It felt as if a bunch of little and very sharp knives was stabbing into my hip over and over. The silence was painfully loud. All the growling and howling stopped. The knives bit into my flesh again, and a snarl exploded from me.

The copper scent of blood drifted up to my snout. I pivoted on my hind legs, my right side burned, and I came face to face with a dirty-gray wolf. Her lips were curled back, and blood — my blood — covered her teeth and dripped from her muzzle.

Sounds of a scuffle rang out from behind me, but I didn't take my eyes off the wolf in front of me. She crouched down, snarling and snapping at me. I tried to mimic her movements, but my back end hurt so badly. I could feel the warm trickle of blood running down my leg and matting my fur.

She lunged at me, tackling me to the ground. I landed on my

back with a breathtaking thud, and her teeth came at me, aiming for my neck. I kicked out, my back paws planted in her stomach, and I kicked her off me before her teeth could sink into my neck, and I pushed back up on all fours.

I could barely put weight on my injured leg. I didn't understand what was happening. Dominic had said they had come to welcome me. Why wasn't he helping me? And where was Aidan? The gray wolf was circling around me, and she looked as if she was ready to jump on me again.

What's happening? a voice in my head shrieked. *Why were they letting her do this to me?*

I snarled at her, and for a split second, she froze, and her eyes widened. But then she growled and came at me again.

I stood my ground for two reasons. One: Dominic told me not to back down from them. And two: I couldn't run even if I wanted to. I stretched my body, standing as straight and as firmly on the ground as I could, preparing for the impact. I growled a menacing and slightly freaked-out sound.

The gray wolf was barreling toward me with her canines exposed, and my heart was jumping around like a rabbit in my chest. Her teeth sank into my right shoulder, and she wrestled me to the ground.

Dirt and grass burned against my side as we slid and rolled over each other. I bit out blindly, desperately, and I instantly tasted the salty sweat in her fur and the iron taste of her blood. The blood seeped into my mouth, and I latched on tighter. I growled and yanked and flung her onto her back.

She made a whimpering sound, and I sprung up and towered over her. Rage and fear and something that I really didn't want to understand fed through my veins. I felt my lips curl, the cool air brushed against my gums, and the world seemed to stand still, vanishing away and leaving only the gray wolf cowering at my feet.

It scared the hell out of me, but at that moment, I wanted to kill her. I wanted to rip her apart and roll in her blood. It was as if the animal that I had turned into was taking over, and all I could think about was the taste of her blood. I felt a growl rumble around me. Her shoulder was gushing blood, a large chunk of skin was gone from where I had bitten her, and her meaty muscles were exposed. It would have been so easy to kill her. I could see it all. My teeth in her neck, tearing out her throat. The taste of her blood. The rush of victory.

The growl came again, followed by a soft whimper, and then a cold nose pressed against me. I swiveled, baring my teeth and snapping out. A rusty brown wolf dropped to its belly and then rolled onto its back and licked my chin. Standing right behind that wolf was the midnight black alpha.

I snarled at him furiously, and he snarled back. For half a second, I thought about lunging at him. I was so mad, so hurt ... but instead, I shook off the thought, turned, and limped away from him and the pack.

CHAPTER 23

AIDAN

"What the hell did you do to her?" Marcy screamed. She ran at me, her fist balled, and she punched me over and over in the chest. And I let her. She was crying. Her shoulders convulsed as gasping sobs fell from her, and she continued to punch me.

Trevor rushed over, ready to pull her off, but I shook my head. I hardly felt her weak hits, and I figured she probably had a right to be mad. So I just stood there until she was done. Playing the tough alpha seriously wasn't easy. It's not as if Marcy knew I had no choice but to let Jade fight it out. I hadn't expected the attack to happen, not on her first shift, but the females had a right to fight her, and I couldn't do much to stop it.

It took a full sixty-four seconds for her tears to win out, and Marcy crumpled against my chest, crying uncontrollably. "Mac, I didn't do anything to her," I said softly.

"You should have stopped the wolf!" she shrieked and pulled away, glaring up at me. "I told Jade you were cold. I told her to stay away from you. I was right. You're just like all the alphas before you." She pulled her arm back and swung at me, open-handed. I caught her wrist tightly in my grip.

"Marcy," I snapped, my patience wearing thin. "Don't think you can talk to me like this just because you are dating a member of my pack." She struggled, trying to jerk her hand away, but I held onto her wrist firmly and looked at Trevor. "Take her. I don't want to see her again."

"Aidan, Jade wants her here," Trevor said, refusing to look at me. He stepped up to us and wrapped his arm around Marcy's stomach, pulling her away.

Fury spiked through me, and I hated it. I hated giving orders and using my alpha status to get what I wanted. I loathed demanding things from the pack and forcing them to submit. I hated my father for doing it, and I hated myself just as much. But this pack was just too screwed up. They didn't listen when I asked nicely. And now Jade, the wolf I intended to make sure won the challenges and became my mate, aided their disobedience. *That damn girl is going to be the death of me.*

"I don't really care what Jade wants," I said, seething. I let my scent roll off me, and Trevor started to tremble under the weight of it.

"I'll take her to her room," he said with a desperate note in his voice. "You won't even know she's here." He still wouldn't look at me as he started to drag Marcy away and up the stairs. She shouted at me through a garbled mess of tears that I couldn't even begin to decipher.

When he reached the top, he looked back in my direction, his eyes fixed on the floor at my feet. "Aidan, please stop." His voice was like gravel grating under tires. "She's just as much my alpha as you are. Don't make me pick one of you." He turned on shaky legs, with Marcy still crying in his arms, and disappeared down the hallway.

I gritted my teeth for a long moment. I'd never seen anything like this. Never. How in the hell was Jade able to dig into Trevor so quickly? She wasn't branded. She didn't have the extra power that came with the alpha's imprint. Her scent was strong, but without accepting the position, it was still bearable. I cursed myself for letting Trevor stay with her, waiting for her to shift. His loyalty was shifting, just as Erika's had, and I didn't have a clue what to do about it.

I stood at the bottom of the stairs, counting them, up and down, attempting to relax my nerves. It wasn't working. My fists clenched and unclenched, seemingly on their own, and each second that passed, my skin grew hotter, and my blood boiled further. "Dominic!" I shouted.

Dominic was out of Jade's bedroom and standing in front of me in a flash. Surprising relief washed over me at his quick response; at least it did until he said, "Just go, Aidan."

I laughed. It sounded cruel even to my own ears. "I'm going to see her, Dom." I took the first step, and he grabbed my bicep, yanking me back from the stairs and pulling me into the kitchen. He stopped in front of the stove and turned on the fan before glancing at me. When he did, I figured I looked just as pissed off as I felt because he skittered back a few steps.

"She doesn't understand what's happening," he whispered. "She thinks we allowed the attack."

I shot him a cold glare and, through gritted teeth, said, "You should have told her to submit once she walked out of the house. You were supposed to guide her. You're the one who asked to help her." I was already regretting letting him. I thought he got it. I thought he'd tell her what to do; clearly, I was wrong.

"I did tell her. Dammit, Aidan! You're such a jackass! You can smell it. She's an alpha. It's in her scent. Her inner-wolf will only submit to you if yours submits to her." Dominic's voice rose with each word until he was flat out yelling in my face.

I wanted to punch him. Just haul off and punch him. Somehow, I really don't know how I held the urge back. "She has to prove herself for that, and so far, she hasn't."

"She took down another challenger," Dominic said as if that was proof enough.

I shrugged. "There's still two more."

He looked at me then, as if I was an idiot and an even bigger fool, and said a little helplessly, "She just wanted to play."

JADE

I could hear him. Aidan was whispering. I couldn't make out the conversation, but the sound of his deep voice made me shiver. I shouldn't have been able to hear the notes of his voice. He was downstairs, and my bedroom door was sealed tightly. But his voice wasn't the only thing that found me. His scent, musky and powerful, wrapped around me.

I sat on my bed, watching the last of the scars on my hip fade away to nothing. By the time I finished showering and scrubbing my body clean of blood, my wounds had closed. It had only been thirty minutes. Thirty freakin' minutes since that wolf attacked me, and the marks were already gone. I didn't know whether I wanted to pass out, hyperventilate, or jump around. My senses were hyperaware of everything around me, and it was terrifying and exciting and a little sickening. I had never had so much energy before, and I didn't know what to do with it all.

Aidan's voice rose and fell as he argued with Dominic. He was beyond mad. I could hear it in his growled murmurs and smell its heat in the air. It was almost like the scent of hot pavement as the first drops of rain fell, except stronger. Each time it got louder, my body shuddered with a mix of pleasure and spine-tingling fear. My inner-wolf was doing backflips in my stomach. One second my skin was burning with desire for him, and the next, my inner-wolf was cringing and begging me to lie down at his feet.

I wanted my dad. I wanted to talk to him. I needed to hear the reassurance in his voice. He always knew the right thing to say, and since Dominic wasn't explaining anything that made sense, I thought maybe, just maybe, Dad would know what was happening to me. He'd been involved with the pack for as long as I could remember and knew a lot about how they worked. I dialed his number for the last five minutes, and each time I called, it went straight to voicemail.

The front door slammed, and footsteps pounded up the stairs. I pulled my blankets up around me, listening to the scuffling as Aidan and his amazing scent made his way down the hallway. It was weird knowing instinctively who was walking on the other side of the walls, but I did. I could feel his presence in my bones. With each step closer to my room, my heartbeat quickened. My bedroom door squeaked open, and he stepped into my room, closing it behind him.

He was wearing black jeans that sat low on his hips and a snug black T-shirt that showed off the ripples of his abs. He had toned up since I first met him; his muscles were more defined, not as soft-looking. He leaned against the bedroom door and folded his arms over his chest, flexing his biceps as he did. His eyes were yellow as they looked me over, and my breath caught in my throat. The man was perfect and completely flawed, and I loved it all. I wasn't sure if that made me stupid or crazy, but either way, right then, I knew I needed serious help. *Was this how all werewolves felt when they were in the presence of an alpha?* I wondered as my eyes drifted over him. I tried reminding myself that he had let this happen to me, but it was useless. Each time the thought passed through my mind, my inner-wolf growled as if it were trying to banish it.

"Jade, let's go." His voice was sharp, and I jumped to my feet without an ounce of hesitation, my tangled mess of blankets falling to the floor.

I couldn't pull my eyes away from him, and right then, I was glad for it. I watched as he took a step toward me. His eyes traveled down my neck, along the strap of my tank top, and then they paused on my cleavage for far too long before he glanced down at my skimpy pajama bottoms and took in my bare legs. If I hadn't been watching him so closely, I probably wouldn't have even noticed it. His nearness, his scent, it all screamed power and authority, and it was fogging my brain.

I snapped out of it in a rush, grabbed a pillow, and whipped it at him. "Get out!" I shouted as he batted the pillow away, and it dropped to the floor.

He frowned. "I'm not asking, Jade."

"I don't give a shit," I snapped. I grabbed the pile of blankets and dropped back into bed, pulling them around me.

Aidan took up his post again, leaning against the door. "It's Tuesday. You have school."

His scent thickened, and a soft glow, an outline of what looked to be the letter 'A,' lit up on his chest, shining white through his shirt. My skin buzzed, my inner-wolf pressed against my chest, and my throat tightened.

I got up. I couldn't stop myself. I needed to get closer to him. That power. It was unbelievable. It rolled off him in waves of delirious heat. It was as if I floated across my room. I barely felt my feet touch the floor. I stood in front of him for a second before I couldn't hold back any longer. I lifted my hand and traced the glowing 'A' on his chest.

The sensation was like nothing I had ever felt before. My finger lit up as soon as it connected with what felt like a raised scar beneath his shirt, glowing with the same white light. It sparked and heated my entire body. I shuddered with pleasure. The unbelievable power ... authority ... command ... I wanted it. It called to me. It was like a little whisper in my ear telling me to take it. Claim it — *him* — as my own.

Aidan's hand snaked around my wrist and pulled my hand away from his chest. "Jade, focus. You need to get dressed. We're going to be late."

"Seriously?" I asked a little breathlessly, still staring at his chest. I lifted my other hand, wanting to touch it again, and he quickly snagged it. "You're worried about my education, but you'll let one of your wolves attack me. What's wrong with you?"

"You missed yesterday," he said dryly, pushing me back a step and holding me at arm's length. "I promised your parents you wouldn't miss anymore. Get dressed. You're going."

"My parents ..." I licked my dry lips. "You know where my parents are?"

"Yep, your dad went out of town for a few days, and your mom's at work. Get dressed." He dropped my wrist then, and his scent all but vanished into a thin and ultra-light film in the air.

I sucked in a deep, fresh breath and my insides shuddered with a deep-seated longing. I glanced up at him, meeting his golden eyes, and asked, "You going to let me change?"

He chuckled and crossed his arms over his chest, making his broad shoulders look even bigger. "I'm not stopping you. Go ahead."

I blushed from head to toe. He couldn't actually think I would give him a strip show, could he? He leaned back on the door casually as if that was exactly what he intended. "God, Aidan, get out."

He smirked. "How cute. A modest werewolf. You worried I won't like what I see, sweetheart?"

"I couldn't give two shits what you like," I lied, spun on my heels, and stalked toward my closet.

He chuckled, and it was positively infuriating.

CHAPTER 24

JADE

Aidan really made me go to school.

After a few minutes of shuffling through my clothes stalling, I heard the soft click of the door as he left. I let out a pent-up breath, thankful he wasn't actually going to make me change in front of him. He hadn't gone far. He was standing right outside my bedroom door when I emerged after tugging on blue jeans and my favorite plum hoodie.

When we got into his black Mustang, I tried to ask him about the mark on his chest, but all he'd say was that it was none of my business. He pulled up to the coffee shop and left me in the car, with a firm warning not to move an inch, while he bought coffee and donuts. He shoved them at me without a word.

Aidan escorted me to my locker, and he hovered over me in my classes, making people move so we could sit beside each other. Things had ... changed. Something had shifted in him. For the past few weeks, he had been approachable. Now, not so much. He was testy. His eyes flashed a lot. And he was seriously turning into a jackass. He was snapping at everyone, including the pack.

He wouldn't let me sit with Ben and Ann at lunch, and he wouldn't let Marcy sit with the pack or Trevor. He dragged me — literally dragged me — around, his hand always gripping on my wrist, or his arm looped around my waist, everywhere he went.

I had never been so happy to hear the bell ring at the end of the day. News had already traveled about my new *status,* and between the cautious looks from the student body, and Aidan's retardedly possessive behavior, I couldn't wait to get out of there. I left the computer lab, very aware that Aidan was right behind me, and I turned left, heading for my locker.

"Jade, come," Aidan snapped. I stiffened and spun around. I didn't want to, but that tone ... I just couldn't ignore it. I whimpered, and my inner-wolf stirred in my stomach. He gave me a stern glare and pointed to the floor in front of him.

My jaw dropped, and I put my hands on my hips, attempting to glare, and fighting the urge to run at his command, although I was sure I failed miserably because he didn't even flinch. Thankfully, though, my feet stayed firmly in place. "Did you just beckon me like a dog?"

His eyes flared, and he pointed again to the floor in front of him. "Jade," he growled.

At the sound of his growl, all of the *end of the day* chatter died, and tension rose all around us. Students rushed by so quickly it was as if they were running for cover from a bomb that was about to explode.

We stared off for a few long minutes. *He's serious,* my inner-wolf reminded me over and over, and it was a struggle not to run to him. But dammit, I'd had enough. Since I had been bitten, he had been acting like a complete jackass. But the worst part about it was that this new attitude made my body sing. The way he looked at me with those wide eyes, the tone of authority in his voice ... it spoke to me in a whole new way.

I wanted to walk away and turn my back on him, but I couldn't. His glare pinned me to the floor. My knees were shaking, my hands started to tremble, and damn him, but he grinned as if he had just won a battle. He paced toward me, never once looking away from my eyes, and he leaned in so close that I felt his warm breath push against my lips as he whispered, "Do you know what the penalty is for defying your alpha?" I shook my head, just a small side-to-side bob. My mouth and throat were too dry to answer. He chuckled softly. "Death, Jade."

He locked his hand around my wrist. The touch of his hand on my skin sent a rush of sparks and chills through me, and he pulled me to his car. And I hated myself for following along like an obedient little dog.

AIDAN

Jade locked me out of the house.

She didn't say a word to me as I drove her home, and she even smiled that sweet smile she used to give me before she knew who I was when we got out of the car. I figured she was coming around. I thought that my little threat had done the trick. For half a second, I was sure she was going to fall in line and accept me as her alpha. But clearly, I was wrong.

I didn't have time for this crap. Not with the werecougars and the constant issues with the pack. Not to mention the fact that if she didn't submit soon, I was sure we'd have more than one pack running around town. Jade was putting out more signals of her dominance than I was able to mask, and I was pretty sure that she didn't even know she was doing it.

All through our classes, I had rolled Dominic's words around in my mind, but the problem with his solution was that I just couldn't submit to her until she was officially my mate. She needed to first claim her place in the alpha pair and be recognized as my equal. I might not have been able to submit to her like he had suggested, but I had figured out a loophole. A small gap in the laws allowed me to take her under my guidance even as a challenging female, and what did she do? She locked me out of the damn house!

"Open the door, Jade," I growled for what had to be the twentieth time. I was starting to think I'd have to break a window. The top of her head was just visible through the small window in the door as she leaned against it.

"Looks like I'm smarter than you," she said through hysterical giggles. She must have rolled up on tiptoes then. Instead of seeing just the top of her forehead, her big brown eyes and wide grin peeked through the window.

"Jade, open the damn door!" I shouted again and banged my fist against the wood.

She jumped back quickly and called, "Don't think so," still giggling like a crazy person.

I had always liked to think of myself as a calm man. Patient, caring, rational, but all I saw was red at that moment. Her scent was stirring something in me that I had never felt before, and her *screw you* attitude was driving me mad. My inner-wolf clawed in my chest. That part of me, my animal side, had already accepted her. It didn't care about the rules or the laws or the challenges. It saw her as my equal — my mate.

The image of her wrapped in the thin towel the other day and the one from this morning in those skimpy little shorts and tank top flooded my mind. My skin heated, burning hot. I wanted her more than I wanted to breathe.

"Jade, you are going to be mine," I growled without thought. I slammed my palm against the door so hard it shook. "Fighting me will only delay it, but it won't stop the inevitable. I know you feel it."

That stopped her laughter abruptly, and I chuckled under my breath. "I'm not a piece of property, you jackass," she retorted.

"Yeah, you are," I said and sighed loudly. *You are as much my property as I am yours.*

I felt as if I were standing in quicksand, sinking deeper and deeper. What the hell was wrong with me? I hated this feeling of helplessness. I'd been a werewolf all my life. I knew how to control my inner cravings and the erratic behavior. But Jade ... her inner-wolf ... the wanting ... I shook my head, pushing the thoughts away.

She let out a strangled laugh. "Yeah, and that's the way to get me to open the door. Have a good night under the stars or go home."

I listened to the soft pat of her footsteps as she made her way through the house, and then I heard the whoosh of air as she sat, most likely on the couch.

I had to stop going easy on her. I'd been trying to tame my scent for her. The last thing I wanted was to cripple her under the full force of the alpha power. I wanted her to want me willingly. I wanted to see that lust in her eyes again without forcing it out of her. But I was running out of time. I could see it, her, slipping away. She wasn't mine yet, I didn't have to hold back, and maybe I shouldn't be, at least until she won.

I don't know how long I stood there staring at the door before I took a seat on the porch steps. I was starting to wonder if alphas were banned from the games not because of the interference issue but for their own sanity. I felt as if mine were teetering on a cliff, ready to tumble and shatter in the rocky cove below. Watching Jade beat the last two challengers had been amazing. She was amazing. And each time she pinned someone in place, a challenger or not, by just her glare ... it sent my inner-wolf crazy with want.

I scrubbed at my face roughly and then raked my hand through my hair. I didn't need this kind of distraction. Not now. Jeff claimed that he could distract the cougars and give me more time, but I wasn't so sure. Even now, I could smell them. The cougars were coming closer and closer to town, marking my woods as their own.

And there was just something about Jeff that wasn't sitting well with me. It turned out that the incident Dominic had been referring to when he had punched him was the moment he had caught Jeff cheating on his wife. That kind of thing happened, I knew that, but after finding out what the women were used for in his pack, and with the way, he could hide his scent ...

"You're breaking the laws," a voice said, yanking me from my tortured thoughts. "You cannot hide her."

"I'm not breaking any laws, Trisha," I said, not bothering to look up. I scrubbed at my face. "She's a new wolf, and with that status, I'm allowed to train her." Couldn't I just get five minutes alone? Five minutes with my thoughts. I really didn't think that was too much to ask for, but it was as if my pack could sense when I wasn't doing anything.

"You're interfering in the games," she said coolly. "We have a right to fight her."

I would have been lying if I tried to say I wasn't stunned at the aggression I smelled pulsing from Trisha. I was floored that the woman even wanted a shot at Jade after this morning. A part of me had hoped that the last two standing would drop out now when they saw what she could do and save us all the hassle. But I figured that just would have been too easy. I looked up at her then and said with a chuckle, "I'm not stopping you from challenging her."

Trisha crouched in front of me, leveling herself to my gaze. She was the oldest challenger, in her mid-forties, I guessed. She was lean and long like a dancer, wearing yoga pants and a long-sleeved, bright pink T-shirt. Her blond hair was pulled back in a severe ponytail.

"You're playing favorites, Aidan," she said. "You want her. I can smell your desire." She laughed cruelly and reached out, running a long fingernail along my chin. "When you're mine, the first thing I'm going to do is mate her to another. Trevor maybe. She despises him, and it will break her little friend's heart. Or Jared. He'll keep her in line."

Jealousy rushed through me at the idea of anyone else touching Jade. My eyes flashed. "You're walking on dangerous ground, Trisha," I snarled. I had never felt jealousy like this before, and it scared the crap out of me. Right then, I knew I'd rather be dead than see Jade mated with someone else.

The deadbolt on the door clicked open, and I swiveled to see Jade standing in the doorway. She looked furious. Her nose was scrunched, her cheeks were red, and her body was trembling as she stepped over the threshold and onto the porch.

"Jade, get inside," I said. Her inner-wolf was on the verge of breaking out. Her skin looked as if it were slithering over her bones and the hair on her arms was coarser, darker. She didn't have the restraint yet. I didn't want her to fight again. Not so soon. Not until I worked with her a bit. This morning I had been certain that she would have killed her opponent. If it hadn't been for Dominic drawing her attention ...

"Shut up, Aidan," she growled, not even glancing my way, and she pointed at Trisha. "You touch him again, and I'll rip you apart."

"Oh, is the little puppy coming out to play?" Trisha said with a snicker as she rose from her crouching position in front of me. She backed up a step and then flicked her hands as if to say, *Bring it on.*

I stood up and stifled a groan. Seriously ... all I wanted was five minutes of peace. I turned to Jade and folded my arms over my chest, giving her a look that I hoped would make her turn around and run back into the house. I could feel the warm burn of my alpha imprint, and I let my scent grow and grow.

She didn't even notice.

"How old are you?" Jade snapped and moved to the railing, leaning on it. "Like forty? Don't you think he's a bit young for you?"

"He's going to be mine, Jade." Trisha's voice was strained, and her face turned paperwhite. She gave me a leery look, and it looked as if she were struggling to stay on her feet. "Aidan, you can't interfere like this!"

At least my scent was working on one of them, I thought before I pulled it back. She was right, even if I didn't want her to be. My interference could render anything that happened between them void. I moved to the side, leaning up against the railing, and folded my arms.

"I'll give you a chance," Jade said, a smirk spreading across her lips. "Submit now, and I'll let you walk away without a scratch."

Holy shit! Did she really just say that? I almost laughed. She was falling into her new life faster than I would have thought possible. Jade's eyes flashed and then settled into a golden glow. Her scent ramped up and more dark hair sprouted along her neck. My skin felt like it was on fire. It was a fight not to move from my spot. The sweet smell of power was intoxicating, and all I wanted to do was pull her into my arms.

Trisha looked ... nervous. She was jittery, hopping from one foot to the other. She sucked in a deep breath. Her knees were starting to shake, and her shoulders were beginning to sag. "Submit to a pup?" she asked, her voice quivering. "A big demand for someone so young." Trisha looked at me, just a quick glance before focusing on Jade. "Time for you to leave, alpha."

"Nope," I said, holding in my laugh. Trisha looked as if she could barely keep Jade's gaze, yet she still seemed determined to go through with the challenge. Jade's scent rocketed up another notch, and my heart quickened. "Not going anywhere. I've put her under my training." I shrugged my shoulders, making it clear that there was nothing she could do about my presence. "Besides, you need a witness."

Jade didn't wait for me to finish my sentence before she leaped over the rails on the porch and landed on the balls of her feet in front of Trisha. She growled, a lethal sound, and her skin started to shudder. "Last chance, old hag," she said, snarling the last word. "He's mine."

Trisha sucked in a noisy breath. She held Jade's gaze for half a second before she turned and ran down the driveway as quickly as she could.

"What the hell was that about, Aidan?" Jade asked. She tried to sound tough, but I heard the laughter in her voice as she watched Trisha run down the street.

"I'm yours, am I?" I said, feeling a little cocky. I raised an eyebrow and chuckled.

Jade gave me an adorable dirty look. "Don't let it go to your head, jackass."

"Of course not," I said with mock sincerity. She rolled her eyes dramatically, spun away from me, and marched into the house, leaving the door wide open. *Three down, one to go, and then ... you'll be mine*, I thought and smiled as I followed her inside.

CHAPTER 25

JADE

My veins pulsed from his scent. Its power pressed against my bones and toyed with my muscles as I fought the urge to turn back to him and pull him to me. I had never really believed the stories about alphas or about the imprint that helped channel their scent. Obviously, I should have, but how was I to know that an alpha's scent would have such a powerful effect on me. Why would I care when joining the pack was the most ridiculous and inane suggestion anyone could ever make to me.

I had heard these stories all my life, but really, I honestly never thought a scent could do this to me. I should have figured it out this morning when I saw that soft glow under his shirt. He was trying to manipulate me then, and by the pressure, I felt on my skin now, he was doing it again. And the thing that freaked me out about it was the feeling that he was still holding back, and part of me wanted to feel the full extent of his control.

But according to the stories, this was not the sensation I should have felt. It should have been piercing and shuddering, forcing me to bow to him. Painful even if I tried to fight it. But Aidan's scent didn't make me feel like that at all. It was a wild feeling. Full of desire and overwhelming confusion. It centered me and tore me apart. It spoke to the beast inside me like a song. Slow and sensual, and then fast and out of control.

I wasn't sure what was happening to me or what had come over me when I stepped outside. When I'd heard that woman talk to him as if they were lovers, something inside me just snapped. And when I opened the door to see her looking at Aidan as if she wanted to jump him right then and there, I lost it. I had never felt jealous of anyone before. Not like this. I might have felt a bit jealous when Dominic left me for the pack, but that had been like a mosquito bite compared to the blinding anger that had spiked within me when I saw her touching his face.

I was shaking from the inside out, and my skin was moving, sliding over my bones in a fast rhythm. My inner-wolf was begging me to let go of my restraint and shift. It felt as if that was the only thing that could give me an ounce of relief from the torture of seeing that woman so close to *my* alpha and from his invasive, mouthwatering scent, which was demanding that I make him mine. I was changing. I could feel it in my bones. I was no longer the prey but the predator, and he was what my inner-wolf wanted to hunt.

It's natural. Trevor's reassurance played through my thoughts. *He's an unclaimed alpha.* But this ... this wasn't natural. I was losing control. A control that I had fought so hard to keep. It was the only thing that kept me safe from the wolves. I had let it slip once with Erika, and look at where that got me. But right at that moment, I wanted to let it all go. It was as if something else was taking over. Something deep within me knew, without a doubt, that Aidan was mine. My mate. And I'd kill anyone who stood in my way of getting him.

They are your wolves now, a small voice in my head whispered. My skin heated, burning like wildfire.

My wolves. My pack. My alpha. It scared the hell out of me how possessive I felt of the things that I had spent so long hating. Of the pack that I would have been happy to see vanish from this earth only a few days ago.

I focused on my slow steps, making my way down the airy hallway. The hardwood floors felt cold and unforgiving with each step I took. I could feel him behind me, following me into the house, and I cursed myself silently for not locking the door. I passed by the arched doorway leading to the kitchen and kept my gaze firmly on the staircase in front of me that would take me to the sanctuary of my bedroom. His scent wrapped around me. It was sexy as hell. It fogged my brain and made my skin buzz.

"You need to shift?" Aidan asked, shutting the door behind him. "We could go for a run. That will take the edge off."

I took a deep breath, trying to clear my head. It didn't work. Aidan and his stupid scent worked its way over and through me. I turned slowly, backed up a few steps until my heels hit the staircase, and then I dropped down, taking a hard seat.

I looked at him. His expression was full of humor, and he looked way too cocky as if he knew exactly what he was doing to me. A morsel of my sense came back to me, and I gave him the dirtiest look I could muster up. "That's the third wolf that wanted to fight me in three days, and she was also the second one that made it clear you were the reason for it."

He chuckled, still wearing that cocky grin. "Your point?" He stood in the hallway, looking pleased with himself, his grin stretching further, and the corners of his eyes crinkled softly.

"I'm not buying this jackass thing you're trying to pull," I said with a groan. I tried to look away from him, but I couldn't. His laugh and his chocolaty eyes captured me, making my skin grow warmer. "I know you, Aidan. This isn't you."

A strong wave of his scent hit me, and his grin faltered for a second. "You've known me for two weeks. You have no clue who I am." There was bitterness and challenge in his voice, coated with authority, that made me want to crawl across the floor to him and beg at his feet not to be mad at me. My body trembled with a need that I didn't understand, or maybe it was one that I didn't want to understand.

"I swear if you don't tell me what's going on, I'll walk away. I'll leave town without another thought of you or your stupid pack." I tried to stand up then to prove a point that I knew I wouldn't be able to follow through on. I failed miserably, my knees shook too much to hold my weight, and I plopped right back down. I was lost to him. Completely and irrevocably lost.

That shook him. His jaw dropped a little as he looked me over. His nostrils flared as he sucked in deep breaths, searching for what I didn't know, but on the fourth one, his smile returned. "Mmmm, I love a challenge," he said. His voice turned deep and husky. "You're making this so much more fun, sweetheart. You and I both know you'll submit to me. You'll be mine."

"Excuse me?" I snapped, trying to hide the surge of pleasure that unraveled in my stomach. *Submit to him! Be his!* My body came alive, and my inner-wolf stirred. But just as quickly as the pleasure came, fiery rage burned it away. "You're just digging a bigger hole, jackass."

He chuckled and took a slow, teasing step toward me. "I can smell it, Jade. Your inner-wolf is practically salivating for me. And you've had your eye on me since the first day we met."

"A little full of yourself?" I scoffed, hating how right he was. I managed to stand up and step closer to him. He was only a few feet away, but the distance felt like miles.

"I could put you on trial for your disobedience," he said. "But I'm feeling a little generous. Submit now, and I'll consider letting you off the hook, and maybe I'll even pretend I didn't notice that Dominic and Marcy helped you defy me."

"You're threatening me with my friends?" I asked as the spark of anger from before reignited within me. My muscles stiffened, and my face burned with heat.

"Submit to me or let them fry." Fire flared in his eyes. It was dangerous and intense, and it suddenly hit me that I knew nothing of the man that stood before me. I was also certain that he meant exactly what he said. I had been right. He had been holding back. He'd been keeping the alpha authority at bay with me, but what I saw in him now scared me to death. My anger froze. He moved closer, backing me into the wall, and released a trickle of his scent, enough to make me want to throw myself at him and run from him at the same time. "I have them in custody as we speak."

I said nothing, not wanting to provoke him and knowing that it would only make things worse if I opened my mouth. His scent was fogging my brain and blurring my vision. I wanted to melt against him and run away as fast as I could. He smiled faintly. It was clear that he knew the effect he had on me. He started to move away, receding toward the door, and as he did, I felt stripped to the core.

"Aidan, wait," I said a little desperately. I didn't want him to leave, and I hated myself for it. The further he got from me, the more I shook. That man was mine. Every part of me knew it, wanted it. "Let them go. I'll do what you want. Just leave them out of this." After the words were out of my mouth, I felt sick. I didn't know whether I was saying it to get him to stay or for my friends.

He stopped and gave me a sexy half-smile. "Will you submit, Jade?"

Yes! I wanted to scream it, but the word wouldn't come out. I didn't know what to do. It was as if he were speaking in another language. My body shook as my inner-wolf, and my human side battled against each other. One wanted me to stay strong and claim him as mine, and the other wanted me to drop at his feet. And I couldn't figure out which one wanted what or which one to listen to.

He must have taken my silence as a rejection because he started to turn from me again. "Aidan, please don't go," I whispered.

"Submit to me." His husky voice wrapped around me, demanding and gentle, a confusing mix, and for a second, I couldn't breathe. My lungs just ... stopped working. His eyes were full of desire and longing. If I had to guess, he and his inner-wolf wanted me just as much as I wanted him.

"But Dominic told me not to back down to you." I didn't know what else to say. I'd had boyfriends before, but not one of them did this to me. Not that he was my boyfriend ... yet, but every part of me wanted him to be. It felt as if I were being torn down the middle. His intense gaze was as if he could see through me, into my head, my soul.

He laughed. It was a cool sound, one that held little humor but no malice. "It's your choice, Jade. You will give in sooner or later." He held my stare for another long minute as if he were waiting for me to say something, and when I didn't, he shook his head with clear disappointment. "I'm going out. Do not leave this house without permission. My number is on the fridge. And by the way, you're not smarter than me."

CHAPTER 26

AIDAN

Damn, but that girl could really push my buttons. I seriously wasn't looking forward to going back and seeing her. She was weak to me for a moment. I hadn't held back this time, letting every ounce of my scent wrap around her and merge with her. It was the most incredible thing I had ever felt. For a split second, we had been one. Her scent mingled with mine, teasing me in a way that made me want to forget the rules and claim her. And I was pretty sure that if she actually knew that there were rules, she would have felt the same. I had never thought I'd find a mate that would fill me the way she did. Not in this town.

But without my scent taming her, I was sure that when I went back, there would be hell to pay. She'd shake it off, and when she realized I had the house surrounded, keeping her locked up tight ... I shuddered at the thought. My only saving grace so far had been the fact that she was new ... unstable. She didn't know how to manipulate her scent yet. Every time she let it out, it was random, not really directed at anything or anyone in particular. But when she figured it out, and when she claimed her imprint, I knew I'd be just as lost to her as she was to me. But then again, I was pretty sure I was already lost. Jade was the only thing I was sure of — my clarity — when everything else around me was a jumbled mess.

There had already been moments where she had made me want to submit to her. She was the strongest female I had ever met. She would be mine. Maybe, possibly, that is if she didn't kill me first. And after the crap I just pulled, I thought she just might try when she figured it all out.

I was so close to telling her about the games. So close to ruining my chance at having her. She lusted for me now, but lust was far from love, and the hatred that burned behind it was just as fierce. She wouldn't fight if she knew it was for me. I was sure of it. And I needed her to fight. She was my perfect match in every way. She was my home.

When did I start thinking that I could have love? The thought shook me. Love didn't, and shouldn't, matter to me. Not as an alpha. But the idea of being with Jade had my heart pounding. I could ... no, I did love her. I loved her fire and her lippy responses. The way she challenged me and kept me on my toes. I loved everything about her.

I sat in my new living room, not really listening to Dominic and Trevor as they went over the plan to deal with the werecougars. The house had been vacant for a while now. It had belonged to the alpha before Ray, and as pack property, it was now mine. It wasn't much. Two bedrooms, two bathrooms, a tiny kitchen, and a living room were better than the motel. The paint was peeling on the walls, and the carpet needed to be ripped out. But the furniture was still good. A black leather sectional couch and a matching armchair pretty much filled the room.

Dominic had gathered my few things earlier while I was with Jade, and he had been here when the bed was finally delivered. And right then, I would have killed to be able to go lay down on it. Marcy had even picked up and washed a new set of sheets for me, and she had also cleaned and stocked the fridge. Trevor had been right when he said Marcy didn't know how to stay mad. I didn't think she'd ever forgive me after her little flip-out this morning, but as Trevor promised, it was as if it never happened.

Their kindness was ... weird. I got the feeling that they hadn't done all this because I was the alpha, but because they actually wanted to. I hadn't expected it, not after the way I had been treating them since Jade had been bitten, but I figured it was Marcy's doing. After watching her for the last few weeks with Trevor, I knew she thrived on making the people around her happy. And for a human, it was pretty impressive that she had Dominic and Trevor wrapped around her finger.

After Jeff had woken up from the Dominic-induced nap, he had divulged Bruce's sick obsession with recruiting females. The women were never changed. As Jeff had said, they were community property, used only to breed males to be changed. When a female was born, they raised her until she was old enough to be used. Ray had had an agreement with Bruce. He'd ignore the twisted use of the women as long as the werecougars stayed away from his town. I couldn't ignore it, though. Dominic swore he hadn't known, so did the pack enforcers, and each one of them was behind me, eager to put an end to the sick use of the women.

Right now, we were waiting for a full count from Jeff. We had sent him back to his pack to investigate how much Bruce knew about me and report back with exactly what we were up against. At the last check-in, he had reported that Bruce had him tied up, and he would let us know once he had something we could use.

Dominic's phone buzzed on the coffee table, and the voice caller display chirped, *Jade Shaw,* in a mechanical female tone.

"Don't answer that," I said and grabbed his reaching hand before he could get the phone. "She kind of thinks I locked you up."

"What?" Dominic asked, and he gave me a look that clearly said he thought I'd lost it. He glanced at the phone again and then leaned back, settling into the couch, with a raised eyebrow, waiting for me to explain.

The oven door slammed, and the scent of hot pizza filled the room. "Jesus, Aidan, what the hell did you do this time?" Marcy yelled from the kitchen. She clattered around, slamming cupboards and banging plates against the counter.

I groaned and watched the phone until it stopped skittering across the table. "She wouldn't submit. She also thinks I have you locked up, Mac. Oh, and I kind of left the enforcers with her to make sure she doesn't leave the house." Saying it out loud made it worse, and dread pooled in my stomach. *Yep, she's going to kill me.* And I knew I'd let her if she really wanted to. I'd welcome it. I deserved it. *I really am a jackass.*

"Really, Aidan? Really?" Marcy said, aghast. She came through the small doorway juggling two pizzas and a stack of plates and stomped over to us.

"I want her to win," I said lamely. Trevor and Dominic were both chuckling, and Marcy rolled her eyes.

"Dumbass," Dominic said and shook his head. "I didn't think you were this stupid."

Marcy giggled. "She's going to kill you when she finds out you've lied to her again." She placed the pizzas on the coffee table and started filling the plates, handing them out before taking a seat next to Trevor.

I gave them all a dirty look, biting back the urge to tell them off.

The only thing that stopped me was the fact that they were right. I certainly felt like a dumbass. So I leaned back on the couch, propping my feet up on the edge of the coffee table, and let them laugh.

"Aidan, do you really want her to submit?" Trevor asked curiously. "I thought alpha pairs aren't supposed to submit to each other. You know, to keep them both in control."

I hadn't expected the question, and I took a large bite of pizza as I thought it over. The spicy sausage and pepperoni made my stomach growl with hunger, and I devoured the slice before I finally said, "She's being impossible. She needs to learn some respect." *And she is not an alpha ... yet*, I said silently. There was no point in reminding them. The two werewolves in the room had made it clear on more than one occasion that they had already considered her their alpha female. I just wished that I could ignore the rules, too.

Marcy shot me a stern glare. "Lying to her and manipulating her isn't going to get her to respect you."

I scrubbed at my face roughly, attempting to rub away all the confusion that that girl had brought into my life. "I thought she wanted me. I thought ... I thought ... dammit. After she beat Trisha today ..." I let my words fall short, and I glanced at Dominic, waiting for the lecture that I knew was on the tip of his tongue. I almost wanted to hear it. Dominic watched me, chewing on his pizza. I'd never seen him so quiet. He was pissed off, that much I could tell, but the rest was hidden under his carefully placed mask. "Look, I didn't have much of a choice," I said to Dominic. "Her scent was overpowering me. My inner-wolf has already accepted her as my mate. Whenever I get near her, all I can think about is claiming her. I had to let my alpha out."

"You haven't been using it with her?" Trevor asked and laughed again.

"Not fully, well, at least not until today," I admitted guiltily. I knew I should have been. Dominic had even advised me to do it. We had all hoped that it would encourage the alpha in her out, but every time I thought about doing it before today, I felt like an ass. "Call me crazy, but I was kind of hoping she'd feel the same thing for me as I do for her. I didn't want to force her inner-wolf to realize she's meant to be my mate. And I didn't really lie to her completely. You both have violated laws."

"Dude, not part of the pack," Marcy said around a mouthful of pizza.

"Dude," I said, mimicking her snark. "Trevor claimed you. He did two nights ago. Even if you haven't been changed, a mate is considered part of the pack. You're bound by my laws."

I instantly knew I'd said something stupid. Marcy turned ten different shades of red before she shrieked at Trevor, "You told him!"

I held back a laugh, but Dominic didn't. He let out a deep belting roar, and he started to cough, choking on his pizza. Trevor turned white as a sheet, and his eyes widened. It was more than a little obvious he didn't tell Marcy what would happen after they hooked up.

"It's a scent thing, Mac," Trevor said in a rush. "I can't hide it. Our scents have synced together since we ..."

"Don't you dare say it!" she said, jumping up from the couch. "God, isn't anything private with you guys?" She spun on me then and snapped, "Jade does want you, but she'll never bow down to you. She's not going to fight for someone who is trying to force her either."

"Okay, I get it," I said, throwing my hands up in the air, and all my pent-up laughter fizzled away. "I'm a moron. How the hell do I fix it?"

"You let the people that know her best out of jail," Dominic said with a chuckle. "She'll win the games tomorrow." He laughed again and focused on Marcy, "Mac, you up for it?"

Marcy considered it for a second before a grin inched its way on her lips. "She's going to kill us. But I'm in."

CHAPTER 27

JADE

My heart dropped when I heard the engine of a car pull into my driveway. It was a rumbling, clunking sound instead of the purr of Aidan's Mustang.

I stood at the fridge, cell phone in hand, staring at the sharp scrawl of his handwritten number. Last night after he left me, I had realized four things. One: He might have been smarter than me. Two: He was hiding something from me. Three: I needed to play nice and get Dominic and Marcy out of jail. Four: I was falling for him — hard.

His alpha wolf spoke to my inner-wolf in a personal way. It took the control that my inner-wolf craved. But it wasn't just his alpha that spoke to me. It was him. This jackass thing was an act. I knew it without a doubt, and I was determined to break through it.

As soon as Aidan left, I had snuck out the back door. He had been right; I needed to shift. I had too much energy coursing through me, burning me up from the inside out. I hadn't noticed the wolves until I walked out the door, and they surrounded me. But Aidan hadn't just left some wolves at my house. No. He had stationed the pack enforcers to make sure I didn't go. The enforcers were a team of five. And they were ruthless. Their sole purpose was to enforce the alpha's commands. I had seen them in action before, and when Jared shifted and stood nose to nose with me, stark naked, demanding to know where I thought I was going, I almost threw up from the sudden fear of facing them.

The enforcers were the only wolves that I never had, and would never, pick a fight with. No one walked out of that alive. They had no compassion. They didn't ask questions. They didn't have to follow the normal rules of the pack. In a sense, when they were called upon, they held just as much power over the pack as the alpha did, except they always executed that power with death and violence.

But Jared had given me a choice, which had shocked the hell out of me. Jared wasn't known for his patience or for giving options. Kill first, ask questions later. That was pretty much his motto. But instead of attacking me, he let me decide: call Aidan or go back inside. In the end, my stupid pride had won ... again. Jared made it clear that I wasn't allowed out unless I spoke to the alpha, and since I refused to call him, I was escorted back into the house. But before Jared closed the door on me, he had looked me up and down and said, *'We're going to have a lot of fun once you lose the alpha games, little girl.'* There had been no mistaking his meaning. The gleam in his eyes when they settled on my breasts told me everything I needed to know. He planned to take me as his mate. I wanted to ask Jared what he was talking about. What were the alpha games? But instead, I slammed the door and locked it.

That was when I decided that Aidan just might have been smarter than me and when I realized that he was hiding something from me. It was also that moment that I knew I was falling for him. The idea of anyone else touching me other than him was something I didn't want to think about, and it made me feel a little queasy for more than one reason. I was supposed to hate him. I was supposed to hate the pack.

I'd been trying to call him for the last hour, but my inner-wolf had been fighting me. For reasons that I couldn't begin to understand, it didn't want me to submit. *Not yet*, a voice chanted over and over in the back of my mind. *You need to win him first*. It just sucked that I really didn't understand what that meant.

"Jade?" Mom called from the hallway. "Honey, are you home?"

"In here, Mom," I said, bracing myself for what I was sure was going to be a lot of tears. I hadn't seen her since I was bitten, and knowing my mom, I knew that wasn't by her choice.

"Oh, honey," she said as she came into the kitchen. She looked exhausted, but she tried to hide it with an overly bright smile. Her pink scrubs were all wrinkly, and her hair was a mess, falling out of her ponytail. She set her bag on the counter and rushed over to me, wrapping me in a hug. "I've been so worried about you. How are you feeling?"

"I'm fine, Mom," I said, squeezing her back. She sniffled in my ear and swallowed loudly as if she were trying to choke down her tears. "I'm good, really," I said softly, trying to sound reassuring. "I shifted. Everything's fine."

"If everything's fine, then why are there wolves surrounding our house, Jade?" she asked as she released me and folded her arms over her chest, waiting for my response.

"Because the alpha is trying to show me how smart he is," I said with more than a little bite to my tone. I was on edge, fighting with everything I had not to shift. My skin was crawling, and quick bursts of adrenaline shot through me every few minutes.

Mom laughed and sniffled as she wiped at her misty eyes. "You should be happy that the alpha is showing interest in you." She looked me over from head to toe, taking her time as she searched my body as if she needed to see every part of me to make sure that I really was okay.

"The alpha is being a jackass, and those wolves outside are the enforcers," I said. I grabbed my steaming mug off the counter, took a seat at the table, and drank a deep gulp of my coffee.

A spike of tangy fear flitted through the air, reaching my nostrils, and Mom lost a little color to her cheeks. "Let me guess, you haven't submitted to him and recognized him as your alpha yet." She made her way through the kitchen and sat down at the table, giving me a stern look. "You really should do it before he loses patience with you. The pack has always been about the rules."

She was serious. I could see it on her face. But there was something else there. A small knowing smile. A slight twinkle in her eyes. Pride that her only daughter had joined the pack and caught the alpha's attention. And right then, I was sure she knew exactly what Aidan was hiding from me.

"Don't you have an issue with the fact that your daughter is a werewolf?" I snapped. This was the first time I had seen her since I was bitten, and she looked ... happy about it. Freakin' happy! I started to shake with hot anger, and I glared at her. "You want me to give myself to some guy to use me as he chooses? Seriously, Mom, I think you and Dad need therapy or parenting classes or something. This is not something to be happy about."

I might as well have slapped her across the face. She certainly looked like my words had hurt her just as much, and a rush of guilt washed over me. Her eyes misted up, and she took a few breaths before she was able to look at me again.

"Jade, Aidan is not Ray," she said in a shaky voice. "I won't have you speaking about him that way in my house. Use you as he chooses." She shook her head and made a *tsk* sound, clearly disappointed. "He's not a monster. It's just the way of the pack. He's the leader. You need to show your respect. And besides, once the games ..."

The front door opened and slammed shut. Mom looked up, and I watched as the blood drained from her face and her complexion turned to a sickly gray. I didn't need to look to see who it was; his scent hit me hard and fast.

"What games?" I asked, fighting to ignore his presence. "What were you going to say?" I may have been too freaked out to ask Jared, but Mom was a totally different story.

"Nothing, honey," she said in a rush, still looking over me at Aidan. "Better hurry. You'll be late for school."

I jumped up, and my chair rocked back, crashing to the floor. "School! Really? I'm not going. It's not like I need an education now. I'm never getting out of this stupid hick town."

"Jade!" Aidan barked from the doorway. I spun around; anger sparked over my skin, and I met him straight on. *There goes playing nice,* I thought. What was it about him that made my blood boil and my heart melt at the same time?

His eyes flared with that dangerous warning that shook me to my core. The sweet Aidan was gone, replaced by the alpha that scared me to death. I tried to hold his stare. I fought for the control and the authority I had had only days before. The command that had made this man trembled under my stare.

His scent hit me again, strong and sweet and powerful. It pulled at me, making my body convulse with the effort to stay standing. His gaze hardened, and he nodded in my mother's direction. "Apologize."

It wasn't a request. There was no mistaking the tone. I wanted to tell him off and kick him out of the house just as much as I wanted to tell him that I was his if he still wanted me. But I couldn't do either. The words lodged in my throat. "Now, Jade," he said tightly, and he closed the distance between us. He took my chin in his hand with surprising gentleness and forced me to meet his eyes.

"Aidan, please ..." My bottom lip trembled as I spoke. His eyes were wide, glowing yellow, and his scent thickened in the air until I could hardly catch my breath.

"You need to learn," he said, and I was sure I heard a hint of regret in his voice.

"I'm sorry," I whispered. I didn't want to whisper, but my voice just wouldn't work. I was lost in his eyes, in his scent, and my world was crashing down around me.

Aidan held me in place for another long moment before he dropped his hand from my face. I sagged against him almost instantly. Without his hand supporting me, my knees began to shake, and they refused to hold me upright. His arm snaked around my waist, holding me close, and my heart hammered in my chest, thrilled and terrified of the man that I was falling for. He spoke to my mom, but I felt as if I were drunk with his scent so strong. His voice was garbled and slurred in my ears.

Aidan took my hand in his and led me out of the house. I vaguely registered the smirk on Jared's face and his team of enforcers standing behind him, watching me as I got into the car. A moment later, Aidan jumped in and backed out of the driveway. He didn't say anything to me, and his brain-numbing scent was hardly noticeable now. His jaw was tight, twitching as he clenched and unclenched it.

"I don't mean to be so, um, difficult ..." I started. He snorted and gave me a quick sideways look that made me want to giggle. "Okay, maybe I do mean to be. But really, you've been a bit of a jerk."

His hand clenched the steering wheel, and his knuckles turned white. "Jade, when you walked out that door and shifted with us, you chose the pack. With that choice comes rules. You may not care about the rules, but I don't have that luxury."

I was certain I heard the regret return to his voice. Silence stretched awkwardly between us. This was a side of Aidan that I had never imagined. He'd always seemed so carefree. So confident. I had never pegged him for a *rules* kind of guy.

"I need a freakin' handbook," I muttered under my breath, breaking the silence.

He chuckled softly, and the velvety sound made my heart flutter. "Did you have a nice time sneaking out last night?"

"I ... I ... needed to shift," I said softly. "You were right."

He grinned. "I told you I was smarter, Jade," he said with a confident-sounding chuckle. "I told you not to leave the house without asking me. Did you really think the enforcers weren't going to tell me?"

CHAPTER 28

JADE

Aidan didn't take me to school.

He left me sitting in the pack's headquarters' sterile-looking, white waiting room. The smell of bleach and various lemon-scented cleaners was overwhelming, and they were seriously making my head hurt. I would have preferred school.

I'd never been inside their headquarters before. But then, I hadn't even known they had one until today. Really, what could a bunch of werewolves need with a headquarters? It seemed ... stupid, and it also reminded me again that I had so much to learn about the pack. Number one on my list was to figure out the rules that Aidan had been talking about. Again, I found myself seriously wishing for a handbook.

For the last three and a half hours, I'd been sitting there watching the door to Aidan's office. After he had deposited me in an uncomfortable, bright orange plastic chair, he gave me a stern warning not to move, and then he went into his office and closed the door. About ten minutes after that, Beck, one of the enforcers, escorted a sobbing Marcy and a furious Dominic into the room.

They didn't even look at me as they went by, and I wasn't sure if they didn't notice me or they didn't want to see me. I wouldn't have blamed them if that were the case. It was my fault that they were in this mess, but the idea of them hating me burned anyway. I had started to get up to talk to them when Beck focused his golden gaze on me and mouthed, '*Not a word*,' and I froze.

Beck was about Aidan's height with the same kind of thick and muscular build, but unlike Aidan, he was kind of scary. He was a lot like Jared in the no patience department, and since I had pissed him off more than a few times before, I didn't want to risk pushing it. Not with the vicious warning that burned in his eyes. Damn, I hated the enforcers.

About thirty minutes after the three of them went in, and Beck never came out, I thought I was going to lose my mind from nerves. If Aidan kept one of the enforcers with him, it probably wasn't a good thing. I snuck over to the door, and I pressed my ear against it, trying to hear the conversation. The door must have been reinforced with something because I couldn't make out anything even with my enhanced hearing. Not even a second later, the door flew open, and I tumbled into the room.

Before Beck scooped me up, I didn't even get a peek at Marcy or Dominic. He carried me back over to the waiting room and set me down. "If I catch you moving again, I won't be this gentle," he growled, and then he vanished back into Aidan's office, slamming the door behind him.

I hadn't moved an inch since. My butt was tingly, my feet were pins and needles, and my back was throbbing, but I refused to move. I could deal with Aidan — kind of. I was pretty sure he wouldn't actually follow through on his threats, but Beck ... there wasn't a doubt in my mind that Beck would.

The sound of shoe-clad feet slapping against the white ceramic tiles down the hall drew my attention. As soon as my eyes found the source, I shuddered. Jared was coming toward me.

Jared was shirtless, and his gray track pants hung low on his hips. He had a small white towel wrapped around his neck, and his sculpted abs and chest glistened with sweat. Even though they were resting at his sides, the roped muscles in his forearms and thick biceps seemed as if they were flexed. His short black hair was messy and damp, and when his eyes, which were such a dark brown that they looked black, met mine, a one-sided grin twitched at his lips.

"Hey, little girl," Jared said, closing the distance between us and taking a seat beside me. "You in shit again?"

I shrugged my shoulders because I really didn't know if I was or not. "How many times do I have to ask you to stop calling me *little girl*," I said and rolled my eyes in an attempt to make him think that his closeness wasn't at all nerve-racking. He had started calling me *little girl* back when I was in seventh grade. He had been in grade nine then, and I had a horribly stupid crush on him. Right then, I wished I was back in seventh grade when he didn't scare the crap out of me.

He chuckled. "Will you relax," he said. "I'm not here for you. I was at the gym." He nudged me in the ribs playfully and winked.

I tried to relax, but it wasn't an easy task with him beside me. I hadn't really spoken to him since seventh grade, and I had avoided him at all costs when he became the head of the enforcers. Just like when Dominic had joined the pack, Jared had turned cold. Heartless. Ruthless. But then, Jared had always been a little cold.

"Who's he with?" Jared asked, nodding toward the closed door. He stretched his long legs out in front of him and draped an arm around the back of my chair.

"Dom and Mac," I said, leaning forward a little, so it didn't feel like his arm was actually around me. After last night, I didn't want to give him a single reason to think I was interested. "They're in shit for helping me."

My palms were starting to sweat, and I roughly wiped them on my jeans. A pulse of sugary sweet power hit me, not like Aidan's scent, which made me think of nothing else but ripping off his clothes, but it was strong enough to make my heart hammer against my ribs. My breath caught. I heard it, and so did he. His chuckle gave it away. The pulse turned into a trickle and then to a stream. "He's not the only one who can speak to your inner-wolf, little girl," Jared said. "You're strong. What you crave is the power, not him. I can give you what you need."

I sucked in breath after sweet, sweet breath. My inner-wolf clawed at my stomach like a crazed lunatic. It was a weird feeling, nothing like the passion that Aidan brought out in me. This was vicious. It filled me with something that resembled anger and made me feel like a savage beast. I fought against it. Hated it. Needed it. Wanted it. And really, really feared it.

My own scent changed, ramping up and swirling around us. The stronger it got, the more stable I felt, and after a moment, my inner-beast settled — a little. "Jared, can I ask you something?" My voice was a throaty whisper. I looked over at him, meeting his glowing yellow eyes.

He arched an eyebrow, looking at me as if he were waiting for me to do something. When I didn't do whatever he had expected, his scent slowly dissipated, and his expression turned stony. "Shoot," he said, coating the word with a growl.

I shivered. I didn't know if it was his growl or the lack of the mouthwatering smell that made my insides freeze, but whichever it was, I didn't like it. I opened my mouth, then closed it, and cleared the prickly lump in my throat before I asked, "Why did you give me a choice last night? I didn't think you guys did that. Like ever."

His hand clasped my arm, and he pulled me back into the chair, draping his arm securely and a little possessively around my shoulder. I fought the urge to jump away from him, terrified of what he might do if I did. "You'll be more fun to me alive," he said, his voice husky. "You ready to give up yet?"

"Give up what?" I asked, and a chill ran up my back, forcing my spine to jolt and straighten. *He knows,* a voice in my head hissed. He knew what Aidan was hiding. Everyone knew. My mom, Jared ... Right then, I bet the whole freakin' pack knew. I didn't know whether to freak out or feel hurt. Both seemed like a viable option right then.

He chuckled and pulled me closer. "Step down from the games, little girl. I'll be more entertaining than the alpha. Promise."

"What games?" I asked. He ignored my question, leaned into me, and nuzzled at my neck. "Keep your hands off me," I snarled. It burst out of my mouth before I could stop it. His touch felt wrong and cold and forceful. It made my skin crawl and heat up at the same time. My inner-wolf stirred again, and a low growl rumbled from my throat, and I tried to wiggle free of his arms.

He didn't let go. His arm wrapped tighter around me, pulling me closer. "Mmmm, love that fire, but I'll have you purring like a kitten in no time," he whispered in my ear, and his hot breath played with the fine hairs on my neck. "Give up. Let Tiff be his mate."

All the hints and warnings that I had received over the last few days played through my mind in a blast, fighting over each other to be heard. *Stay away from him. She's treating you like an alpha. Don't back down from him. I can't live with my alpha hating me. Packs have alpha pairs. Two alphas. One male and one female. He'll be mine. When you lose the alpha games ...*

"Tiff's the last one fighting for him?" I asked. The frost I heard in my voice was bittersweet. *He really is a jackass,* I thought, as all the pieces slid together. My body began to shake, and I hardly felt Jared's arm around me anymore. Red-hot fury blazed through me. The bastard had me fighting for him! He'd been playing me all along. Was I a werewolf because of him? Was it his idea to ruin my life and then sic his wolves on me? Would he have even cared if they killed me? I'd seen the murder in that dirty-gray wolf's eyes. And because of a stupid crush, I had walked right into his games.

At that moment, I thought I hated myself even more than I did him for letting myself care about a stupid dog.

Jared's arm slipped to my waist, and he yanked, pulling me onto his lap. I gasped, and my hands flew to his chest, pushing him away. "Hands off, Jared," I snapped, but he didn't let go. He pulled me against his chest, placing a trail of hot kisses down my neck.

"Mmmhmm, it's just you and Tiff," he said against my neck. "You don't want to be an alpha. With your fire, you'd make a great enforcer. We don't have to play by the rules." I pushed at him harder, and he pulled me closer, pinning my arms between our chests. "Jade," he murmured into my ear, "I know you want me. I can smell it." He flicked his tongue against my earlobe.

I gasped, and every muscle in my body went rigid. Tight knots twisted in my stomach and a nervous laugh slipped out. I tilted my head back, trying to move away from his kisses. "This is not happening," I snarled, pushing away as hard as I could.

CHAPTER 29

AIDAN

"Answer my question," I said with a lethal note in my tone. I was on edge. Even with the door closed, I could smell her. That sweet scent slid through the crack under the door and wafted around me. Her inner-wolf was calling me, seeking me out, and begging me to claim her. I needed this to end. Now. Before I completely lost my mind.

And Beck wasn't making it any easier. It had been just over three hours now since I had him drag Marcy and Dominic in, more than enough time to make Jade believe that they were actually in deep shit. But for the last three hours, Beck had lounged in one of my leather chairs with his feet up, and eyes closed, making comments about what pack member we should stick Jade with when she lost.

"Yeah, he called," Beck said, keeping his eyes closed. "Talked to him last night while Jared was playing with your newbie." He cracked one eye open and smirked at me.

"Beck," I growled a clear warning. I leaned forward, placing my palms on the oak desk. Dominic gripped my shoulder before I could stand up, holding me in my chair. The enforcers had their own set of rules they played by. It was supposed to keep some balance in the pack and gave them the authority to deal with alphas that didn't follow the rules or punish those who needed it. And Beck seemed to be intent on reminding me at every turn.

He chuckled softly. "Easy alpha, I'm not your enemy." He clasped his hands, lacing his fingers together, and stretched his arms over his head. "If she doesn't win, Jared would be a good match for her. He'll tame her. Or we could always do what we do best. Jade's broken more than a few rules."

I growled. It ripped out of me before I could stop it, and Beck laughed. He was toying with me. He had been since he came into the room, seeing how far he could push me before I snapped. I knew they had no plans to take Jade down for the rules she'd broken. While she was in the games, she had a free pass for most of them.

Beck was about my height and build, maybe slightly bulkier, but not by much. And he carried himself just like the enforcers from my father's pack. They all had the same air about them. Confident. Cocky. They knew they could get away with pretty much anything. Without them to carry out and enforce the rules, most packs would crumble. They didn't just keep the wolves in check, but they kept alphas from abusing their power.

"Beck cut the shit," Dominic snapped. He gave my shoulder another squeeze before letting go. "What did Jeff say?"

Beck chuckled, and I let my alpha scent trickle into the air. Enforcer or not, he still had to obey me to some extent, and right then, I was out of patience. As soon as I did, his eyes hardened, and he fixed a burning glare on me. "Bruce is sending him out on a recruiting mission," he said through gritted teeth. "There was an *accident*, and they lost the last of their females. He says Bruce doesn't know about you, and the cougars Trevor ran across were a fluke."

"What kind of accident?" Marcy asked. She'd been sleeping, curled up on the leather couch for the past hour. I wished she had stayed asleep. She yawned loudly and then propped her head up with her elbow, looking at Beck groggily.

"You know what they're used for," Beck said coolly before I had a chance to come up with a lie. "Do you really need to ask how they died?"

Marcy jolted upright, and her hands flew to her mouth. She gasped. "Oh my God." Her eyes widened, and she started to shake.

Dominic squeezed my shoulder again, most likely trying to warn me not to flip out, and then he went to Marcy, pulling her into a tight hug. Heat rushed up to my neck, and my muscles tensed as she started to sob into Dominic's sweater.

"Were you planning on telling me?" I growled, settling my glare back on the enforcer.

He raised an eyebrow and shrugged. "Just did."

"How many?" I demanded. My imprint started to heat up, and my scent rolled off me like a tidal wave. I gripped the armrests of the chair, feeling the plastic snap within my hands. If Beck wanted to push me, I'd push back.

He winced, and he let out a mix between a growl and whimper before he said with a slight tremble in his voice, "Two. Jeff is trying to stall things so you can claim your mate. He says that's why he took the mission to bring in the women they want. With them dead, we've got time."

"Beck, you're a heartless bastard," Marcy shrieked. Her face was tear-stained, and her shoulders were shaking. She pushed out of Dominic's arms and stomped over to him, balled her tiny fist, and swung at him.

Beck caught her fist easily, closing his hand around it, and his eyes flared. "Maybe, but it is my job to kill people." He squeezed her hand, and Marcy yelped and tried to tug out of his grip. "You've been claimed," he said to Marcy, letting his voice drop to a growl. "You're part of this pack now. Learn the rules. I'm not going to warn you again."

"Let her go, Beck," I said and scrubbed at my face in an attempt to cover up my simmering rage. Things just weren't adding up. No one seemed to know why Ray would have made a deal with the cougars. Something was missing; I was sure of it, and I just couldn't figure out what it was. What could Bruce offer that Ray wanted?

Beck cut me a look and let Marcy go. She jumped back from him a few steps as he dropped his feet from the table. A yellow ring glowed around his blue eyes, and his jaw twitched with tension. He growled, letting his inner-wolf come out in his voice. He flexed his hands, balling and un-balling them, as he glared at me with a silent challenge. "Tone the scent down, alpha," he said. "The enforcers are behind you now, but that can change."

I laughed, a cruel kind of laugh that didn't sound right coming from me. I pushed my chair back, and as I did, Dominic skirted around my desk and leaned on it, blocking my view of Beck. "Has your team picked up anything?" he asked with an edge. He shot me a quick pleading look, and I reluctantly pulled the scent back ... a little.

"Not yet, but we will," Beck said tightly, and I smiled, more than a little glad that I was affecting him so much. "And now that we don't have to worry about the humans, we can clean them out when we find them."

A sick feeling rushed over me as I listened to the enforcer. I didn't want to admit it, but he had a point, and I actually agreed with him. Without any humans left to worry about, we had time to track them down. We could watch them. Figure out their weaknesses. It would give us more of an edge against them. And with Jeff stalling and feeding us information, we could hit them and clear them out in one shot. I hated to admit it, but overall, the deaths would make everything ... easier.

The tension slowly started to break and fizzled away as I pulled back the last of my scent. Dominic's rigid shoulders sagged, and he let out a loud puff of a breath. "I think we've freaked her out enough," he said, turning back to me.

"Yeah, probably," I agreed. "You sure you guys want to do this?"

Marcy was all splotchy, but her tears had dried up, and she gave me what I thought was supposed to be a reassuring smile. "Jade will forgive us later. She always does. Besides, Jade is an act first ask second kind of person. If she thinks she's losing you, she'll finish this off."

"You're really going to tell her you're taking Tiff as your mate?" Beck asked, leaning back in his chair, the smug and cocky smile back on his face.

"Yep, that's the plan," I said, pulling myself up to my feet. My legs felt like they were tied down as I made my way over to the door. I still wasn't sure that Dominic and Marcy were right about this little idea, but everything I tried had failed epically, and I was out of options. I just hoped Jade didn't try to kill me after telling her.

"You've got guts," Beck said and chuckled. "That girl has bite to her."

I glared at Beck hard. His commentary was not helping, and he damn well knew it. He grinned and got up, joining me at the door. I took a deep, steadying breath and then stoned my expression, forging cold remoteness into my body, and I pulled the door open.

As soon as I opened it, I froze. Jared had Jade on his lap, his face buried in her neck. And Jade ... Jade was giggling. Her hands were on his bare chest, and her head was tilting to the side as if she were trying to give him better access.

My inner-wolf went wild, clawing at my stomach and tearing at my heart. Raw heat pulsed through me, and my chest started to hurt. A cold sweat broke out on my back, and the plan to tell her that I was picking someone else vanished from my mind. "Jared," I growled. "She's off-limits. This is one rule you can't break."

Jared chuckled and looked up. His golden eyes met mine, burning with a silent challenge. "I think she's ready to give up, alpha," he said. He took his time untangling himself from Jade, stood up slowly, and pulled her to him. "She's free game."

Jade looked at me a little desperately as she tried to wiggle out of Jared's arms. Jared leaned into her, whispering something so softly in her ear that I couldn't make it out, and she stopped moving. She held my eyes, and as Jared spoke, something passed across her face. It was cold and hateful and vile, and her scent pulsed into the air. Jared smirked and let his arms drop from her waist, but Jade didn't move. She kept her back pressed firmly against his chest, and his smirk turned into a wide grin.

I started toward her, slowly, carefully, wishing I knew what was going through her mind. She'd looked at me with hatred before, but it was nothing like this. I was halfway across the waiting room, only about fifteen steps from her, when she snarled, "You had me competing for you. When did you plan on telling me?"

"Jade ..." I said, and dammit, but my voice cracked on her name. The hatred in her eyes ... it was just too much. My heart crumbled like a piece of dried bread.

"Did you think I wouldn't find out? That I'd just ... just ... become an alpha, be your mate ..." She was visibly shaking, and her skin flushed cherry red. Her scent burst from her wildly, hitting me with a deadly force, and I stopped instantly, unable to move. My throat closed up as if someone cinched a rope around it and started to choke me.

"Jade," Marcy snapped, stepping toward her.

Jade's eyes flared, and a shudder rushed over her skin. "Shut up, Mac," she growled, and her canines sharpened. "Let me guess. You weren't really in jail with Dom. You two have known all along."

"Jade," Dominic said, with the stern tone he always used with her, and he groaned long and loud. "You're overreacting."

"I think I hate you guys," she said. There was so much heartbreak in her voice. Her invasive scent receded, and I sucked in a breath. She looked at me then; her golden eyes shimmered with what I was sure were tears. "How many more things are there, Aidan? What else have you lied to me about?"

I took a step toward her. I wanted to pull her into my arms and comfort her as she cried. She was breaking; I could see it in her shivers as her inner-wolf tried to take over and in the small tears that slid down her cheeks. I wanted to tell her it was all going to be okay. I wanted to hold her and tell her how sorry I was, but as I moved toward her, she put her hands up and leaned further into Jared.

He grinned over her head and snaked an arm around her waist possessively, and she let him. She didn't wiggle or try to move out of his arm. She sagged against him a little as if she were taking comfort in his presence. My inner-wolf stirred restlessly, and my scent ramped up.

Now was my chance to tell her everything. I knew that. I could tell her about her father. About the cougars. About the humans that died. But the only thing that came out of my mouth was, "I graduated high school last year."

Jade stiffened, and another shudder rushed over her skin. She clenched her fists and sucked in a few noisy breaths. She met me straight on, her expression an emotionless mask, and said, "I won't fight for you, alpha." She grabbed Jared's wrist, pulling his arm from her waist, and she started for the door.

Jared chuckled and went after her, slinging an arm over her shoulder. She shrugged it off and turned into him, "Jared, I need space," she said, putting a hand on his chest.

"Sure thing, little girl," he said and leaned into her, brushing a light kiss on her lips, and dammit, but she let him. She even smiled at him a little before she dropped her hand and walked out the door.

I lost her. I really lost her. I deserved it. I knew that, but it didn't make it hurt any less.

"Looks like the games are over," Jared said, snapping me back to the room as the door slammed behind Jade. He folded his arms over his chest and leaned against the wall. I crossed the room, feeling oddly calm, and when I was directly in front of him, I pulled my arm back and punched him. His nose crunched and snapped under my fist. Too bad it didn't make my shredded heart feel any less broken.

CHAPTER 30

JADE

I ran through the woods. I couldn't stop. I didn't want to stop. My heart was pounding in my ears, and my breath was coming fast and ragged. Branches whipped at my face, and the underbrush ripped at my ankles, but I didn't care.

The trees around me were covered in fall. Oranges and reds, deep and rich. Leaves scattered the ground and crunched under my feet. The fall leaves used to be soothing, but right then, the fiery colors only added to my rage. Betrayal hurt more than I had thought it would. It was like an icy pick jabbing and twisting into my heart. I'd watched Dominic turn his back on me before, and Marcy, well, Marcy pulled crap like this all the time, but this ... this was too much. They were playing with my life. I could have been killed. Erika could have ...

All of this for a stupid crush, I thought bitterly. I should have listened to Dominic from the start. I should have stayed away. Found someone else. But I walked willingly right into Aidan's game. I had never felt as utterly stupid as I did right then.

I felt stripped to the core. And vulnerable. And stupid. Really, really stupid. Each step I took, my inner-wolf fought me. It wanted Aidan. It wanted the power. It wanted its mate. Aidan felt like ... home. But that home was gone. Ruined with lies and deceit. It just sucked that my inner-wolf didn't care about that. She wanted out. The bursts of raw adrenaline were only seconds apart now, but I fought against it. I knew with every part of me that if I shifted, I'd end up right back at his feet.

My stomach rolled, and I swallowed the bile. I felt dirty. I shouldn't have let Jared touch me. I shouldn't have let him kiss me, but when he had, all I could think about was hurting Aidan as much as he'd hurt me. How could he endorse women fighting over him? It was sick ... twisted ... *What did you expect from an alpha?* My heart twisted and split down the center. He was no different from the rest of the pack, using and manipulating people to get what he wanted.

My legs burned, and my skin was numb from the beating of the tree branches as I ran. I didn't want to stop, terrified that if I did, I'd run back to him. What was wrong with me? Even with the cold truth, a part of me still wanted him. *He's your perfect mate,* a voice in my head whispered.

Suddenly someone grabbed my arm and yanked me to a stop. I spun and snarled viciously. My skin felt like it was on fire, and my blood was boiling. "Back off, Erika," I snapped in a voice that did not sound like my own. It was like gravel, rough and jagged and sharp.

She jumped back, dropping her hand from my arm, and averted her eyes from mine. "I tried to see you last night," she said softly. "The enforcers wouldn't let me in. I've been worried about you." She looked at me then and smiled a little. "I heard what happened with Aidan."

"Leave me alone," I growled and turned my back on her. I needed to keep moving, keep fighting my inner-wolf from breaking free.

"Tiff's been searching for you," she said as I started walking away. "She wants to end this. You need to get ready."

Another shudder rushed over my skin, and my ankle buckled and snapped. I sucked in a breath and waited, willing my body to relax and stay human. "Let her have that lying piece of crap," I said, gritting my teeth against the rush of power and adrenaline as my ankle began to piece back together. She grabbed me again, spinning me around to face her. "Erika, back the hell off!"

Her fear was thick in the air, tangy mixed with salty sweat. It was so thick that I could taste it. "She's made a deal with your dad, Jade. I'm the first female she's going to send to the cougars." She was shaking, her hand trembled against my wrist, but she squeezed harder.

I forced myself to relax. She was terrified, and the urge to hug her and tell her everything would be fine was overwhelming. My inner-wolf calmed slightly, and I asked, "What cougars? What are you talking about?"

"Jade, please," she begged. She dropped to her knees before

me, grabbing at my jeans. "They'll kill me. Your dad ... he's ..." A gasping sob fell from her, and she jammed her hand into her pocket. "Here, just watch this." Erika pulled her iPhone out of her pocket and tapped the screen, bringing up a video.

"So we have a deal then?" my dad's voice crackled through the speaker, and my heart stopped. The image was fuzzy and dark, but I knew the voice well, even if I couldn't make out the face.

"Yeah, I'll send you some females, but why wolves?" a female asked, that I assumed was Tiffany. The image zoomed in a little, and her carrot hair came into focus, confirming my assumption. She was the only person I knew with hair like that.

"They'll heal faster," Dad said, his voice cold and impossibly cruel. "These humans break too easily, and my boys like some fight in their women."

"And your daughter?"

There was silence for a second, and then my dad laughed. "She's Aidan's weakness. The boy is lovesick. Give her to one of the enforcers. We'll use her when we're ready, but someone might as well have a little fun with her in the meantime."

The video stopped, and the play icon appeared in the center of the screen. My body temperature dropped to ice cold. I snatched the phone from Erika and played it again. I couldn't believe it. I didn't want to understand what was being said. I'd never seen anything like this in my father before. He sounded twisted, cruel, wrong. *They heal faster. My boys like some fight. Give her to one of the enforcers.*

My inner-wolf stirred again, restlessly. My chest felt tight, and the adrenaline rush hit me again. "Did you show this to Aidan?" I asked harshly, trying to hide how much I was hurting. My father, Aidan, Marcy, Dominic ... I couldn't handle much more. How many more people were going to betray me? "Shouldn't you bring this up to the enforcers or to him?" I glared down at her, trying to stay strong. I never thought for a second Erika, of all people, would come to me before her pack. She hated me, attacked me, and changed me into a monster only days ago. She'd done everything she could since she had become a werewolf to make my life hell. *She's treating you like an alpha,* Dominic's voice clouded my brain.

"Challenging females don't have to follow pack rules," Erika said. "As long as they don't kill an opponent after they've submitted ..." she let her voice trail off for a second, and a flash of guilt passed across her face, but she shook it off fast. "Once the alpha female steps up, Aidan has no control of what happens to the rest of us. Alpha female rules the females, alpha male handles the males. The enforcers could do something, but they scare the hell out of me. I tried to show Jared, but he was all 'get out of my face, and he wouldn't listen. And Aidan hates me because I'm following you." Her voice was getting higher and higher as she spoke. She was desperate. I could see it in her eyes, and it scared me to death. "Jade, you can't let her win. This pack is screwed up enough. I need you. We all need you. We need a strong alpha pair. You'll stand up to him. I know you can stop this."

My brain was spinning, and my stomach rolled. I paced a few steps away from Erika. What the hell was I supposed to do? Mate with Aidan and try to fix this screwed-up pack? Walk away and keep the little bit of self-decency I had left? I didn't want to do either. *I should have just stayed away from the pack!* Did I want the responsibility of the females? Could I handle it? Could I actually walk away knowing what would happen to them and leave them in the clutches of Tiffany? If I walked away now, I could leave town and never see that lying jackass again, and that idea wreaked havoc on me. I couldn't imagine not having Aidan around, even if I did want to kill him at that very moment. But if I took alpha female, it's as if I've condoned what he's done.

An idea began to form, slow and a little sketchy, but it was something. Something that I thought I could live with ... maybe. I turned back to Erika. "I've got an idea. Do you have Jared's number?"

CHAPTER 31

AIDAN

My office felt empty. It wasn't, but it felt it. The average-sized, beige room felt huge and dull and vacant. Jared sat on the edge of my oak desk with a smug grin, and Beck stood nearby fighting back a laugh. They were playing with her, I was sure of it, just as they were toying with me, and they were enjoying every second of it. What I didn't get was why? Why did the enforcers give a shit about Jade? And what were they getting out of ripping us apart? I couldn't bring myself to believe that Jared actually wanted her or that she was attracted to him. I knew it was possible; I'd seen them all over each other, but the thought of her with him, or anyone else, made me feel sick.

Jade had been gone for twenty-eight minutes and forty-two seconds. Each minute that passed by and she didn't walk back through the door, my heart died a little more. I thought about all the lies, about the way I manipulated her and used her, and I figured I deserved the gut-wrenching pain that spread through me with every beat of my heart.

"Aidan, it's going to be okay," Marcy said. Except she didn't sound too sure about it. "She'll be back once she calms down." She offered up a shaky-looking smile as she pulled her knees to her chest and rocked slowly, back and forth, on the couch.

"Mac's right. Jade always comes back," Dominic said. It sounded like he was trying to convince himself just as much as he was trying to convince me. He paced the room restlessly, glancing at the door every few seconds. I didn't need to ask what he was thinking; I was sure it was the same thoughts going through my head. There was no way to cover up that she stepped down. Too many people had heard her say it. The games were ... over.

"I can track her if you want," Beck offered. I glared at him and gritted my teeth. He was enjoying this. Enjoying every second of watching me crumble as I lost the only thing that mattered, the only person that brought an ounce of good into this screwed-up pack.

"No," Dominic and Marcy shouted in unison before I answered, which was probably a good thing because I wanted to say yes.

"Dude, don't drag her back before she's ready," Marcy said frantically. "If you force her to fight now, she'll never forgive you." She flushed and cut Jared a dirty look. "Dammit, Jared! What were you thinking?"

Jared shrugged his shoulders in a bad attempt to look innocent. "Figured she knew what was going on. She did take down three of them."

"You damn well know she didn't," Marcy snapped.

"Enough!" I yelled, glaring at Marcy. I knew she was only trying to help, but I couldn't take the constant bickering anymore. She started to cry and hugged her legs tighter to her chest. "Mac, you should go," I said and scrubbed at my face roughly. "Trevor's probably waiting for you, and Jade already stepped down. Doesn't matter anymore. Tiffany won."

"Aidan, she's going to come back," she said, her voice hitched on her tears. "I promise."

I tried to smile at her, but I was sure it fell flat. The reality was it didn't matter if she came back or not. I couldn't restart the games. I didn't have a choice. Tiffany had won by default when Jade walked away. My fate had been sealed the second she said she wouldn't fight.

A phone rang, breaking the silence, and Jared groped in his pocket, digging out his phone. He looked at the screen and chuckled before tapping it and bringing the phone to his ear. "Miss me already, little girl?" Jared said and smirked at me. "Your house or mine?" he asked and then paused. "Be right there, kitten." He chuckled softly, "Get used to it, Jade." He hung up and slid his phone back into his pocket. Looking at Beck, he said, "See you in a bit," and then he pushed off my desk.

"You're not going anywhere," I growled, pushing my chair back and standing up. My hands were shaking with rage, and I pushed them down on the desk to keep them steady. I couldn't believe she had called him. She wasn't wasting any time replacing me. Not that I was really hers to start with, but right then, whether I had been hers or not didn't matter. Jared chuckled, obviously enjoying my reaction, and white-hot fury flooded over me.

"Enforcer business," he replied coolly and padded over to the door, pulling it open.

"Screwing my mate isn't enforcer business," I snarled. I shouldn't have said it, and I really didn't mean to, but it just came out. As far as my inner-wolf was concerned, Jade was mine. She always would be, and the lust-filled scent that Jared gave off right then sent the beast inside me over the edge.

"Jade's not your mate, alpha. Tiff is. Beck, track down Tiffany and bring her in," he said, keeping his eyes on me. There was a warning in his voice, and his muscles visibly coiled, as if he were just waiting for me to step over the line and break a rule.

Beck chuckled. "Sure thing, boss," he said, and right then, I felt as if I were dead.

CHAPTER 32

JADE

I waited impatiently as Jared made the call. He had been waiting for us on my porch when Erika and I had emerged from the forest. For the last hour, I'd sat in my bedroom and listened as they filled me in on everything they knew about the cougars and the alpha female games. The gist was that the cougars were sick bastards and had been tormenting the town for more than a hundred years. Jared said that the wolves started to fight back about forty years ago, which was when the pack decided not to hide their presence in Dog Mountain.

As for the alpha female games, well, it all sounded stupid. I found it hard to believe that all these girls would fight for a guy just to become the alpha female. Erika said it had nothing to do with the guy. She claimed that love didn't matter. Alphas were paired together because of dominance, leadership, and strength. She said that she didn't even really like Aidan, and she had been fighting for the pack, not for him. I hated to admit it, but I thought she was crazy. How could she not like Aidan? And why did I still want him?

When Jared walked out of my bedroom to make the call, I told Erika about the scent. I told her what Jared had done to me and what Aidan did. I was hoping for some kind of explanation from her, anything to make my cravings for the two men make an ounce of sense, but all she said was that my inner-wolf had an alpha in its scent. When dominant wolves of the opposite sex meet, it causes a different reaction. She figured my inner-wolf was recognizing them as potential mates. She explained that for most of them, the scent was crippling, basically telling me things I'd already (somewhat) figured out and not really helping with the things I hadn't.

Needless to say, the last hour had been ... tense. I had a few meltdowns, learned more about the pack than my brain could really absorb, and overall, came up with a plan that would probably get me killed. The whole time I tried to tell myself that this near-suicidal idea had nothing to do with Aidan. It was for the pack. That was it. But my heart (and my inner-wolf) wouldn't believe me.

Jared rubbed his sandpaper-looking jaw as he strode back into my bedroom, his cell phone still in hand. "It's done. Tiffany has just accepted the position."

"And even without the games, I can still challenge her, right?" I asked. I was more than a little glad that my voice was strong and not showing the nerves that were jumping around as if I had a circus of juggling acrobats in my belly.

He considered it for a moment and then nodded. "Yep, at any point, an alpha can be challenged. It's just harder to beat them once they're branded, which, by the way, is happening to Tiff right now."

I threw my hands up in the air, frustrated, annoyed, and more than a little confused. "What the hell is the point of the games if she can be challenged at any time?"

"It's entertaining," Jared offered dryly. I could have smacked him. Entertaining? Really? I'd been put through hell for the last few days to entertain them? He started to chuckle as he padded across the room and sat beside me on my bed. "I'm just kidding. The games happen when more than one female wants to be alpha." He ran his hand up my leg and winked at me.

"Cut the crap, Jared," I said, slapping his hand away from my knee. "Will the plan work?"

"Don't know. Never heard of a female winning and then not taking the alpha male as her mate." He leaned back on my bed, propping himself up with his elbows. He hadn't bothered to put on a shirt before he came over, and his abs flexed and rippled as he got comfortable.

"But is there a rule against it?" I asked, forcing myself to look away from him. He may be a complete dick, but he was hot, and the last thing I needed was more temptation. His scent was more than enough to drive my inner-wolf crazy, and the visual seriously wasn't helping.

"Number three?" Erika asked meekly from the other side of the room.

"She can't screw him over if she doesn't claim her rights to him," Jared snapped, glaring at her, and she pressed herself further into the corner, hiding behind my dresser.

"Stop freaking her out," I hissed, giving him a dirty look. "If I win today, she's going to be my beta, so be nice."

He rolled his eyes and rubbed his jaw as he looked me over. "I really don't know about you joining my team, little girl. No offense, but you don't have what it takes."

I stood up, spun around, and put my hands on my hips, glaring down at him. "No offense? Really, that was an offense. I'm seriously offended. Did you miss me taking down three challengers, one of which when I was still human?" *And hadn't he just told me that I'd be good at it?*

It felt weird admitting it out loud and even weirder knowing what I had done. But I'd be lying if I said it wasn't all a little amazing, though. I'd beaten three werewolves that I hadn't even known why I was fighting in the first place. And right then, as I glared down at the enforcer, who only a few hours ago had me sweating with fear, I was pretty sure it was going to my head — a little.

Jared didn't move. He stayed on my bed and grinned at me. "The enforcers go up against alphas, too, not just pack members."

"Tiff is the alpha right now," I scoffed, "and I'm going up against her."

"You're too soft, Jade," he said with a chuckle. "You care too much." He glanced over at Erika then, and I had a pretty good idea what he was talking about. Maybe I was too soft. Erika had put me through hell and back, but even with that, I hadn't been able to walk away when she needed help. Did that make me soft or just a good person? I wasn't entirely sure. I didn't really feel like a good person right then. Not while I planned to attack someone and fight until only one of us was left alive.

I narrowed my eyes. I wasn't going to back down on this. As far as I was concerned, the enforcers needed just as much work as the rest of the pack. They were all screwed up, and I figured the best way to try to fix them was by becoming one of them. Well, that, and if I actually won, working with them would give me a distraction, and I was pretty sure it was a distraction I'd need if I wanted any chance at staying away from the alpha male. "If I win, you take me on your team and train me."

"If you lose and survive it, I'm taking you as my mate," he countered. "You will not compete in the next round of games after we take her out."

I didn't think about it because I knew if I did, I'd back out of the deal. I nodded, a stiff bob of my head, and said, "Fine," as quickly as I could.

"Jade, don't make a deal with him," Erika said, still cowering in her little corner by my dresser. "Rule number four: You can't screw over an enforcer. You won't be able to back out of this."

"Rule number one: Always obey your alpha. When I win, he won't be able to back out either." I shrugged and cut her a straight-faced look. "It's a fair deal."

"But he can just deal with this himself," she said, her voice rising and pitching. "We have proof. The enforcers can handle it. You don't have to challenge Tiff."

"Erika, stop," I said, forging calm into my tone. "If I don't, then it leaves the door open for the games to start again." I sighed and shook out my trembling hands. "I want this to end."

CHAPTER 33

AIDAN

Tiffany screamed when she received her imprint, and I had to hold her in place while the metal seared her skin. If she moved too soon, it would just heal, and we'd have to do it again. It was painful to watch and even more painful to listen to. I thought what made it hurt the most was that the girl screaming in my arms wasn't Jade. But then, I couldn't really see Jade screaming. She'd have put on a brave face and hid the pain, just as I had when it was done to me.

I reminded myself that it had nothing to do with love as Tiffany sobbed against my chest. I held her loosely, like I was supposed to, and rubbed her back gently. It was better this way. Love was an unneeded distraction. Jade would be better off, and so would I, definitely, maybe.

It had been ten minutes since the branding was done, and she still sobbed against me. I didn't feel the need, nor did I want to comfort the girl. I knew she had already healed, and there was no pain, and knowing that made it all so much harder to stand still and hold her. I did it solely out of duty. To keep up the appearance of us united. *Detachment is better,* I thought and rubbed another circle on her back. This was what I needed to take back the pack. A partner, not a lover, not someone I would worry about every second. At least, that's what I tried to convince myself.

Marcy pulled Tiffany's dress back up over her shoulders. "Come on, sweetie, let's get you cleaned up," she said, taking Tiffany's hand and pulling her off my chest. It should have sounded sweet and comforting. Marcy always did, but right then, she sounded hollow. She sounded how I felt.

"Don't think I've ever seen an alpha cry before," Jared said, strolling into my office. "What did you do to her?" He took up a post beside Beck, leaning against the wall, and folded his arms over his chest.

"She took her imprint," I said and dropped down onto the couch. I hadn't expected Jared back, not this soon, and I was more than a little stunned that I didn't really care that he was. It was done. I lost her. I had a mate now. And even though I wanted to tear him apart, I figured there wasn't much point, and it would take a lot of energy that I just didn't have.

"You should have heard her scream," Beck said with a snicker. "Where've you been?"

"Jade's," he said, watching me closely as if he were expecting some kind of reaction. When I didn't give it, he said, "Sorry I missed it all."

I looked him over, taking in breath after breath, looking for any difference in his scent. I didn't find any, and I didn't know whether to be happy about that or not. He hadn't claimed Jade ... yet. I sighed. "I'm not giving her to you, Jared," I said, after a moment, keeping my voice even. "I'm not going to force her to mate."

"My little kitten doesn't need to be forced," he said and winked suggestively. "She'll come to me willingly soon enough." He looked toward the door and called, "Jade, anytime now."

My stomach dropped at the sound of her name. I should have figured he'd drag her back here just to rub it in my face, but honestly, I had never thought he could be that cruel. Clearly, I was wrong.

Jade stormed into the room and growled, "Shut it, Jared." She swiveled around, looking everyone over, and then snarled, "Where is she?"

She looked wired. Her brown eyes were rimmed with gold, and her fists were clenching and unclenching rapidly. She was fighting her inner-wolf; its scent was thick in the air, and by the looks of her, if she relaxed at all, she'd shift instantly. I'd never seen a newbie with so much restraint before. But then, I'd never seen one as strong as she was either.

"Jade, tread carefully," I warned, looking her straight on. What the hell was she doing? I could have strangled Jared right then. How could he have let her walk in here like this? Didn't any of them give a shit about what happened to her?

"Tiffany broke pack rule number five," she said, marching up to me. Her skin was twitching, and dark hair had already started to litter her cheekbones. She put her hands on her hips and stared down at me, scrunching her nose.

I sighed. Why did she have to be so damn cute when she was mad? "Jade, stop. She's your Alpha now."

"Are you even listening to me!" she yelled and stomped her foot. "She's not my Alpha. She's turned her back on this pack."

"Jade!" I stood up and stepped closer to her. I was vibrating with anger. Wasn't it enough that she walked away? Even if it was completely my fault, she ripped out my heart without a second thought, and now she was on a one-way path to getting herself killed. "Dominic," I barked. "Take her and teach her the rules before she gets herself killed."

Right then, I hated myself even more. I should have forced her to submit. I should have taken control. Jared and Beck were watching her closely as if they were just waiting for her to do something stupid now that her free pass was over, and I couldn't do anything to help her. It was hard enough standing here, seeing her in so much pain, and not being able to pull her into my arms. *Dammit! What was she thinking, throwing out random accusations about an alpha?*

"Let her speak, Aidan," Beck said. He pushed off the wall and strode over to her, a glimmer of curiosity shining in his eyes. "Do you have proof?" he asked when he was standing in front of her.

"Erika, show them the video," she said, with more gentleness than I expected her to have with the girl that changed her life.

CHAPTER 34

JADE

Aidan watched the video. Twice. And as he did, I started to lose control. Jared tried to help. He rubbed my back each time a bone snapped and whispered random nonsense into my ear as if he were trying to talk over my father's betrayal, but it didn't help. My inner-wolf had been trying to break out for hours now, and I didn't know how much longer I could hold her in.

"I want to challenge her," I said, pacing back and forth before they could watch the clip again. "Where the hell is she?" My voice didn't sound like my own anymore. Each word that I said was slurred and growled. But if Aidan noticed, he didn't care, or if he did, he hid it well.

"Jade, you don't need to," Aidan said coolly. "She'll be killed for this." He looked at me with cold detachment, and I hated how much it hurt. I wasn't supposed to care about him. He was a lying jackass. I was the one who walked away. But I just couldn't help it. Everything about him made my body sing.

"Not good enough," I snarled, using the pain he'd caused me to fuel my determination. "The games aren't starting again. I want to end this."

Aidan cocked his head and looked me over, and as he did, I knew I had picked the wrong words. He started to smile, a soft smile, and for a split second, his desire burned brightly in his eyes. I was about to take it back and try to rephrase it when Tiffany's nasally voice pierced my ears. "I won't submit to you."

I pivoted, following the earsplitting sound. She stood in the doorway, grinning at me. Her carrot-colored hair was pulled back in a ponytail, and her light blue dress was dotted with what looked like dried blood on the right side of her chest. She was shorter than me by a few inches and thinner, too. Instead of my soft muscles, she was skin and bone.

I grinned as I took in my opponent. "Yeah, you will, or I'll kill you. You pick," I said. I stripped out of my clothes quickly as the first snaps of my bones rang out around me. I let my body remold in a rush of steamy heat, and my fur sprouted from my skin. Shifting felt like a high, a fast-acting drug, one that I would never get enough of. Energy pulsed through me, hot and cold and blissful.

I growled, and my lips curled back over my gums as I stalked toward her. She had her eyes closed, and her nose was scrunched. The outline of her mark flickered to life with that soft white glow that I had seen on Aidan's chest. Her bones started to break, and her dress fell to the floor.

Tiffany's wolf was a deep brown with scattered flecks of white. She backed out of the office, growling, and I followed her into the gleaming white waiting room. My claws clicked against the tiles, echoing around me.

I didn't wait. I didn't want to give her a chance to make the first move. As soon as I was through the doorway, I lunged at her, and my teeth found purchase in her hip before she could fully jump out of my way. I held on tightly, throwing my head back and forth until a chunk of her flesh gave way.

Maybe I should have waited. She spun on me as soon as she was free, and I felt her teeth tear into my side and then into my shoulder. She danced back, snarling, and then came at me again, biting into my hip. Her movements were fast, and her bites were clean and effective. In seconds, a sharp pain shot from all over my body.

I twisted, biting out at her. She was fast, dodging out of the way before I could get my teeth into her. I snarled. The coppery scent of blood wafted around me, mixing with an overwhelming scent that was spicy and bitter and strong and near-crippling. I backed up a step, confused. I didn't know what it was or where it was coming from. It made my throat constrict and my knees shake.

She circled around me, growling and snarling, and I shook my head, trying to clear the pain that coursed through me. Between her bites and that scent, my body was screaming with agonizing, burning pain.

I focused on her, swiveling with her slow circles. Her chest was glowing, the white light pulsing through her fur, and I was certain the scent was coming from her alpha's imprint. Right then, I knew I needed to end this before it consumed me.

I crouched down and pushed off with my hind legs. Sharp, hot pain slid through my joints and muscles, and I collided with her side. We smashed breathtakingly hard into the tiles, snarling and rolling together in a jumbled ball. I bit her, tearing through her flesh over and over, as we tumbled across the waiting room, a trail of crimson laying the path behind us.

We hit the wall, and suddenly she was on top of me. Her razor-sharp canines flew at my neck, and I bucked under her, trying to throw her off. Blood sprayed across the floor as her teeth sank into the hollow side of my neck just above my shoulder, and she tore out a chunk of skin and fur. I kicked and clawed at her, tossing her off before her teeth could find me again and finish me off.

I scrambled to my feet. Blood dripped off me, pooling at my paws. I tried to growl, but it didn't sound right. My breath shortened, wheezing and gasping, and I trembled as I tried to keep my feet under me.

Tiffany stood in front of me, her scent thickening in the air and blood dripping down her muzzle and hindquarters. I felt my scent pulse from me in a warm, hazy burst, trying to mask hers. She staggered slightly to the side before letting out a menacing growl, and my body convulsed with a shiver.

"Jade!" Aidan yelled, and out of the corner of my eye, I saw him struggle to get to me. Jared and Beck held him by the arms, pulling him back.

I'm going to die, I realized, as my legs gave out from under me. I could barely breathe, and dizziness was consuming me, turning the world gray around the edges of my vision. I'd known it was a possibility, but I'd never really believed it would happen. I fell to the floor. I heard the thud, but I didn't feel it.

"Jade, don't give up!" Aidan shouted again. There was pain in his voice and desperation that I had never thought I'd hear in him, and it made my heart quicken in painfully fast beats.

Tiffany landed on top of me, snarling down at me. I tried to roll out from under her, but she pinned me, holding me on my back. Her lips curled back, and some of my own blood fell from her mouth, splattering on my face.

"Jade!" Aidan yelled desperately as Tiffany's muzzle came down at me with bared teeth. It was all happening so slowly. I could feel her breath ruffling my fur, see her teeth closing in on my neck, feel the cold of her wet nose as it got closer and closer.

Someone let out a guttural cry, and heat rushed through me. My scent ramped up, and my body burned, fever hot. I bucked again, rising up to meet her attack, and then my teeth were in her neck, and I ripped out her throat.

The limp body of the brown wolf fell against me, and a whimper burst out of me.

The silence was loud as I kicked the wolf off me and shifted back to my human form. I looked down at the wolf, hardly believing that the mangled body at my feet was dead because of me. My mouth tasted of blood, and it chilled me when I realized that I didn't mind the taste. Someone put a sweater over my shoulders, and I was vaguely aware of my arms being pulled into the sleeves and the zipper tugging up to my chin.

I looked around, following the sprays and splatter of blood that covered the walls and floor. My body hurt, and warm blood trickled down my neck, soaking into the sweater. My skin began to tingle as it slowly pieced back together, and I found myself wondering if I would have scars. I knew it was a stupid and irrational thought, and I almost laughed. Almost.

"I am yours now," Aidan whispered. He placed a hand under my chin, tilting my head and giving me a look that said, *Accept it and deal with it*. "And whether you meant to or not, you made yourself mine."

"I'm not a possession, you big jerk," I growled, still sounding more wolf than human.

He chuckled a deep velvety sound that made my knees go weak. "Actually, yeah, you are. You're my possession. Mine. To protect and love and have. Mine." He grabbed me then, coiling his arm around my waist, and pulled me tightly against the length of his body.

"Get your hands off me, Aidan!" I shrieked, but I couldn't make myself move out of his arms. I breathed in his scent, and I felt the smile spread upon my lips.

He smirked down at me, and my heart pounded loudly in my ears. "Is that what you want? For me to let you go?" His voice was just a whisper, his warm breath brushing against my lips as he spoke.

I stared up at him, feeling some multicolored emotion of guilt and desire and self-loathing all rolled into one and tied with a neat little bow, keeping the confused emotions clustered together. "Yes," I murmured.

He didn't let go, and dammit, I was furious at myself for being glad about that. But then his lips crushed against mine, roughly, greedily, and it was intoxicating. And for that moment, I simply forgot that I wasn't supposed to want him anymore.

CHAPTER 35

JADE

They branded me. Freakin' branded me! After I had cleaned myself up, Dominic heated what looked like a cattle prod until the metal 'A' on the end glowed red, and he stuck me with it in the chest. It hurt like hell, and it took everything I had in me not to scream out. Half the pack was right outside the door dealing with the mess in the waiting room, and the last thing I wanted was for any of them to think I was weak. I was having a hard enough time hiding how wrecked I was over killing someone. I knew she had to die. I knew she would have died whether it was by my hand or one of the enforcers, but knowing it, and dealing with the fact that I had actually done it, was an entirely different story.

Jared stood in front of me, glaring at me for the entire five minutes it took for the imprint to stick without my skin completely healing the scar. Disappointed didn't even come close to describing the look he gave me, which made me feel sick. Was I really that weak? Maybe he was right when he had called me soft. It was clear that he sure thought I was. The first chance I got, I flew back into Aidan's arms like a lovesick fool.

When Dominic pulled the burning metal away, Aidan leaned in to kiss me, and I forced myself to move my head, letting his lips brush my cheek instead of his intended target. Aidan didn't seem to notice, and I was glad for it. I backed up a step, putting some distance between us, and said, "Tell me what you know about the cougars."

It was a long conversation. Aidan relayed every bit of information he had, which turned out to be not much more than what I had already known. The part I found most interesting was that no one had ever met Bruce. Dominic said that Ray had handled everything when it came to them, and Jared and the enforcers had never had a need to seek them out. For the most part, the cougars stayed away. And it was that piece of information that made me wonder if Bruce was even real. The way my dad had spoken in the video, it was as if the cougars were his.

I did a lot of pacing, mainly to keep myself away from Aidan. I was pretty sure that what I was planning to do would hurt me more than him. Even so, I knew I'd spend every minute I had regretting it if I let him think I was okay with everything that had happened between us.

I wondered how I didn't know that my father was a werecougar. The thought of living with the enemy my whole life made me feel sick. And then I spent some time thinking about how the enemy had changed. Only a week ago, I would have sworn that it was the pack, and now, everything in me wanted to protect them. They were mine. My wolves. My life.

When an idea hit me, I almost laughed. It was more from nerves than anything else, but I managed to hold it in as I divulged my thoughts to our little group. The idea was simple: let Dad think Tiffany won. We had all come to the same consensus. We needed to buy some time to track the cougars. We knew Dad wanted to use me, but we didn't have a clue for what. And I didn't really think he was actually out *recruiting*. Not when he thought Tiffany would send some wolves to him if she won.

Aidan and I took turns calling him. Although it wasn't that hard, I put on a big show of being heartbroken. My heart was, after all, completely shattered. And when Aidan called him, he even agreed to mate me with one of the enforcers. When it was all said and done, Dad promised to try and stall, giving Aidan a few days to settle in with his new mate, and Aidan swore he'd call as soon as he had a plan to deal with the pack of cougars.

Aidan leaned back in his chair, folding his arms across his chest. His forehead scrunched a little as he thought, and he scrubbed at his face. "Okay, we've bought ourselves a few days. You guys can go," he said, waving a dismissive hand. "Jade and I need to discuss this, and we'll call a meeting when we have a plan together."

Crap! That was the last thing I needed. One on one time with Aidan. I wasn't strong enough, not yet, not when every part of me wanted to pretend as if nothing had happened. "Wait," I said before anyone had a chance to leave. Everyone froze, and I glanced back at Aidan. "Aidan?" I said cautiously, stepping back from him, and I met him straight on, squaring my shoulders and stoning my face. I took a deep breath, and then another and another, trying to calm my nerves. It wasn't working. My inner-wolf fought me, and my heart started to crack again. My palms were sweating, and my stomach twisted into painfully tight knots. "We need to find them before we can do anything else," I said in a rush.

Aidan watched me with confusion marring his gorgeous face. He arched a questioning brow, folded his arms over his chest, and leaned further back in his chair.

I shook out my trembling arms, and before I lost every bit of my nerve, I blurted, "Aidan, I'll be the alpha female of this pack, but I can't be your mate."

The silence was thick in the air. No one moved. No one breathed. I glanced back at Jared. I didn't mean to, and I was sure it would give everyone the wrong impression, especially him, but as I met his eyes, I was glad I had. He gave me an encouraging smile and nodded his silent approval, and I hated how much that approval steadied me. "And I'm going to join the enforcers," I said, looking back at Aidan, focusing on his chest, so I didn't have to see if I was hurting him or not. Either way, I knew I couldn't handle it. "I want to help find the bastards."

"Jade," Aidan said, uncertainty in his voice. He pushed back his chair and stood up, taking a few steps toward me. I stupidly looked up then and wished I hadn't. A swarm of emotions flew across his eyes, devastation being the most prominent. But he also looked ... scared ... no, more than scared ... terrified. "Jade, what are you doing?"

"You were right," I said, putting my hands up in a desperate plea for him not to come any closer. "I know nothing about you, and what I do know, I don't really like."

"Jade, have you lost your mind?" Dominic barked. He was furious. His fists clenched, and his neck tensed. He started toward me, red streaking his face and settling in his cheeks.

"Careful, beta," Jared said with a laugh. He grabbed Dominic's shoulders, pulling him to a stop. "My little kitten has claws. You don't want to get too close."

I shot Jared a murderous look. *Kitten* was seriously worse than *little girl*. And really, this wasn't the time for his stupid pet names.

"Jade, please ..." Aidan whispered, ignoring them and bringing my attention back to him. I almost cracked. Walking away from him was by far the hardest thing I'd ever done. Everything in me wanted him ... needed him. My inner-wolf stirred in my stomach and tears bit at my eyelids. I quickly blinked them away, but by the broken look on Aidan's face, I didn't do it fast enough. The problem was I knew I couldn't live with letting him think that I was okay with all the bullshit he had put me through. I wasn't okay with it, and I really didn't know if I ever would be.

I turned away from him then. I had to. If I didn't, I knew I would have caved, but caving wasn't an option right then. "Beck, can you organize the team and start tracking them?" I asked. "I know Jared should be doing it, and I'm sorry to dump this on you, but I want him to take me home for appearances, just in case my mom's in on this. Maybe we can get someone watching her?"

Beck grinned and cut me a knowing kind of look, and the blood rushed from my cheeks. I hadn't meant to give any of them the impression that I wanted it to be Jared because I really didn't care which one of the enforcers it was. He just seemed like the most logical option, or at least that's what I tried to tell myself. In a rush, trying to cover it up, I said to Beck, "Or Jared could do it, and you could take me home."

Beck didn't get a chance to answer. "I'm taking you," Jared growled with a possessive edge.

I glanced back at Aidan then, hoping to see anything other than the pain I was causing. I did, but what was on his face now was far worse. His eyes were lined with gold, and his glare was fixed on Jared. Hot jealousy spiked through the air, suffocating and thick. His fingertips were clawed, and he ground his teeth so hard that I could hear the enamel grating together. God, I hated being able to smell their emotions. It was as if nothing was secret anymore. Could he smell my heartbreak just as I could his?

"I'll get the team together," Beck said, stepping in front of me. He gave me a warm smile that looked completely out of place on him and then wrapped me in a hug. "Welcome to the team." And then, for my ears only, he whispered, "You're doing great. I can barely smell your nerves or anything else coming off you."

I froze, stunned at what he'd said. He let me go and winked at me. I smiled a little, wondering if he had any idea how much his reassurance meant to me. Maybe the enforcers weren't as completely heartless as I thought. He chuckled then, and I groaned. "Beck, don't you dare get all mushy on me."

He elbowed me playfully and then turned to Aidan. "You have any issues with the order?"

"Go ahead," Aidan snapped through clenched teeth. Marcy jumped, and Erika grimaced. But Dominic ... Dominic just stared at me with fierce disappointment and clear disapproval. I knew he was just itching for everyone to leave so he could give me one of his lectures. And I realized something. I didn't want to hear it. I didn't care if I ever talked to him or Marcy again. This was the last time I was going to let the two of them play me to get what they thought was best for me. This time, they'd gone too far.

"As for you two," I said, pointing at Marcy and Dominic, "stay away. I don't want to see you guys for a while."

Marcy started to cry and garbled something that sounded like an apology, but Dominic didn't show an ounce of emotion. He was a mask of cold indifference as he went to Marcy and looped his arm around her, dragging her out the door.

I started to follow. I needed to get out of there, away from Aidan, and I desperately wanted a nice hot shower. I didn't even get halfway across the office when Aidan asked, "Jade, can we talk? Alone?"

I gave him what I was sure was a sad smile and shook my head. "I can't do this right now, Aidan. With my dad and the cougars and everything ... I just can't. I've appointed Erika as my beta. She'll spread the word about what happened, or you can get Dom to do it. But please, work through her for now. I need some space."

He let his scent trickle out, just a soft brush, and I stood stiff, wishing he would stop. He must have noticed my effort not to throw myself at him because he smiled ... a little, and he pulled it back instantly. Jared took my hand, and Beck took the other, and I let them, thankful for the support, and as I left, I couldn't stop the tears from finally breaking through and trailing down my cheeks.

CHAPTER 36

AIDAN

I followed the scent of almonds and fruit punch and mouthwatering power around the large log house and into the backyard. The air was brisk, but I didn't mind it. It was refreshing and helped alleviate some of the nervous sweat that beaded along my forehead. I jammed my hands in my front pockets and kept my head down as I made my way across the grass to where she lay, staring up at the sky.

I hadn't seen Jade in two days. She needed space, and I'd been determined to give her that, but two days ... it felt more like a year. She wouldn't even accept my phone calls. Text messages were all I got, and they were only status updates on the progress of tracking the cougars.

I pulled in another deep breath, and my heart thudded wildly in my chest. I hadn't been sure what to expect, but I had figured her scent would have changed by now. From what Beck had relayed back to me, Jared had moved in, or maybe not officially moved in, but he hadn't gone home since she claimed alpha status. But her scent was the same, unclaimed and perfect.

I stopped a few feet away, watching her for a moment. Her dark hair covered the grass like a fan around her head, and her chest rose and fell rapidly as she pulled in deep breaths. She knew I was there, she was breathing me in, and it killed me that she forced herself to pretend I wasn't.

You did this, and you deserve it. I knew it was true. I'd driven her away. I'd caused this, but it didn't change how much I still wanted her. She was my mate or should be. My perfect match in every way, and I'd ruined it.

Her muscles had toned up. The black yoga pants that clung to her hips and thighs revealed the firm skin underneath. She had the sleeves of her plum hoodie pushed up to her elbows, showing the tight and lean muscles of her forearms. She was breathtaking. The most beautiful creature I had ever laid eyes on.

The wind picked up, bringing her scent right to me, and my skin heated and tingled. I drank it in, savoring every breath. My inner-wolf scrambled in my stomach, begging me to move closer. It wanted her just as much as I did, and it was torture staying away. I pulled in another deep, calming breath and closed the last few feet between us, lying down beside her in the cool grass.

"That one looks like an ice-cream cone." I pointed up to the sky, letting my finger trail along the sharpened point of the cloudy cone and the rounded top.

"Go away," she said, tensing but not moving from her place beside me. I probably should have just gotten up and left her alone, but I decided to take her not moving as an invitation to stay.

"I used to spend hours watching the clouds," I said. "Always found it calming." I pointed up to a thick gray cloud that looked like a ball of dirty fluff more than anything and said, "Cheeseburger."

She sighed a deep-bellied sigh. "What do you want, Aidan?" She sounded ... tired. But I figured she probably was. From her short text messages, I knew she'd been training with Jared a lot, learning how to fight and use her scent as an advantage.

"That one's spaghetti and meatballs. And that one there, it looks like a loaf of bread," I said, ignoring her question, not because I didn't want to answer, but because I didn't know how to.

"They all look like food?" she asked with a laugh. It was a musical sound, and it made my heart leap and my inner-wolf stir in my chest. My breath caught, and I swallowed hard.

"It's subliminal messaging," I said. My voice hitched, and I cleared my throat. "I figure if they all look like food, you'll get hungry and won't be able to say no when I ask you to come with me for dinner."

She was quiet for a long moment, and I tilted my head to look at her. Her typically soft features were tense, her jaw tight and clenched. "Not happening," she finally said.

I'd expected the rejection, but even knowing it would happen, it didn't hurt any less. "Is Jared really living here?" I asked.

"Yeah," she said, her voice was a bit airy as she let her pent-up breath out with the word.

I rolled onto my side, resting upon my elbow, and I traced the twitching line of her jaw. She glanced at me, her eyes shimmering with tears, and she leaned into my hand. "You deserve better than him, Jade."

"Aidan, don't do this," she whispered as she rubbed her cheek against my palm.

Her inner-wolf was craving me, I thought, surprised that she was rubbing against me. It gave me a small ounce of hope, but there was also a pleading note to her voice that crushed my heart all at once.

"Hey, little girl, you ready?" Jared said, and she jumped away from my touch.

Jade flushed bright red. "Just give me a sec," she said, looking up at Jared with what could only be guilt. She sat up, glancing back at the house, and then quickly locked her eyes on him. She smiled the kind of bright sunshine smile she used to give me.

"Sure, kitten," Jared said in a husky voice. He crouched down in front of her. His hand snaked out, wrapping around the back of her neck, and he pulled her into him. And she let him. She even looked ... happy about it ... eager. I wanted to look away, but I couldn't, and I watched as he crushed his lips against hers. It was a possessive kind of kiss, one that made my blood boil and adrenaline rush through my veins. There was nothing sensual about it. But then, I was sure it wasn't meant to be. Jared was marking his territory, attempting to give me a clear sign that she was no longer on the market, and it took every ounce of willpower I had to not pull him off her and snap his neck.

He broke the kiss as abruptly as he started it and stood back up. His eyes flared as they settled on her, and then he smirked at me. I fought the urge to growl and let my scent loose on him. I wanted to see him crumble at my feet and inflict as much pain on him as I could. Jared chuckled and gave me a knowing kind of look as if he knew exactly what I wanted to do before he glanced back at Jade. "Don't be long," he said, and then he turned and walked away.

Jade watched him walk with a soft smile on her face, and that smile hurt more than watching the kiss. It was ... contentment. She looked happy. I should have been okay with that. She deserved happy after what I put her through, but I figured I wasn't that good of a person because the last thing I felt was okay with it.

"Jade?" I said, pulling her attention away from Jared's backside.

She looked at me, and her smile disappeared almost instantly. "Yeah?"

"Would you have fought?" I asked. I dreaded the answer. I wasn't really sure if I could handle it, but I had to know. "Did I ever have a chance?" *Do I still have a chance to make this right?* I wondered, unable to voice the last question.

She smiled a little. "Yeah, I think I would have." She rolled up to her feet then and glanced at Jared leaning against a tree at the edge of the forest. "I've got to go."

"Jade," I called, a little desperately, as she started to walk away. This wasn't going as I had hoped, although I had to admit, it was better than I expected. She turned back; her face was blank — emotionless — as she waited to hear what I had to say. "I know it doesn't mean much, but I'm really sorry."

"I know, Aidan," she said with a smile that didn't even come close to reaching her eyes, and then she turned away from me. She took a few steps and then glanced over her shoulder. "My dad called this morning. He'll be home in two days."

JADE

Jared watched me cross the backyard, and it took everything I had not to lash out at him. What the hell did he think he was doing kissing me like that? Or better yet, kissing me at all? It was degrading and overly wrong. What was it with these stupid dogs that made them feel the need to treat everything like a possession? I'd be damned if I was going to be part of a pissing contest between the two of them.

Sure, my mom had been watching from the window, but a smile or a peck on the cheek would have been more than enough to keep her thinking we were together. The fact that he'd been sleeping in my room (on the floor) for the last two days was more than enough as it was.

I could feel Aidan watching me and his eyes trailing along my back was the only thing that kept me from attacking Jared. I desperately wanted to turn back and tell Aidan that none of this was what it looked like. I wanted to beg him to believe that it was all an act for my mother's benefit and tell him it was all part of the plan to deal with my father. But I couldn't. No matter how much I wanted to fall into his arms and tell him everything, I couldn't. Not yet. He had to believe the act as much as everyone else did. It was the only way we'd be able to beat my dad at his own game. The less people that knew, the less likely my dad would be to pick up on it. As he said in the video, I was Aidan's weakness, and I was beginning to believe it. Right now, Aidan needed to be strong, and when he was near me, he wasn't. He was lost and confused and hopeful when he was with me, focusing on fixing us instead of dealing with my dad and the cougars. And right now, I needed him to be strong. But not just me. The pack needed him to be strong.

Seeing him again was harder than I thought it would be. I had trained with Jared every waking minute for the last two days, just to avoid him. My body ached everywhere, and I was exhausted, but having Aidan lying beside me for those few minutes, gave me more energy than I knew what to do with. My body was alive, my skin sparking, and my inner-wolf did summersaults in my stomach, begging me to go back to him.

I stopped in front of Jared and glared at him fiercely with my hands on my hips. He chuckled and reached out a hand, caressing my face. "You okay?" he asked and then dropped his voice to a whisper, "We still have an audience."

"Nope, not really," I said through gritted teeth, but I forced myself to lean into his touch. The hardest part about letting Jared touch me was the simple fact that my inner-wolf responded to him just as much as it responded to Aidan.

It was a different feeling with Jared, though. Wilder. Reckless. It made my heart thump and my body come alive in an entirely different way, and I hated it. I despised how he made me feel. I loathed the way he spoke to me. And it made me sick that, at times, I wondered what it would be like to just let myself go and become his mate. However, the thing that stopped me was the lack of birds in my belly. Jared only spoke to my inner-wolf, but Aidan ... Aidan spoke to my human heart as well. He made me feel ... alive. Alive in a complete and utterly perfect kind of way.

He chuckled. It was infuriating, and I bit back a slew of nasty words I wanted to spit at him. "Wow, I never thought I'd see the day that a werewolf would make your heart go thumpaty-thump."

"Me neither," I snapped with a frustrated huff, banishing the thoughts from my mind. I glanced over my shoulder then, seeking out the person that had put me in this position. Aidan still sat on the grass, watching, with an utterly blank look on his face.

"Come on, kitten," Jared said and pushed off from the tree. He slung an arm over my shoulder, and he led me into the forest.

I let him. I didn't have much choice until we figured out how deep my mom was in all of this. So, I snuggled into him, wrapping my arm around his waist as we walked the trail.

As soon as we rounded the bend in the trail and were out of sight, I said, "Seriously, you have to stop calling me kitten, and news flash — you and I are never going to happen." I shrugged off his arm and cut him a sideways glare. "And if you pull that kissing crap again, I'll kill you myself. It's bad enough that I have to lie to him and make him think we're together. You don't need to rub it in his face."

"I don't know about that," he said with a wink. "I think you're warming up to me. Oh, and it's not just us today. Beck and I thought it'd be fun to see if you could stand up to both of us."

"Bring it on," I said, stifling the groan. My whole body ached from yesterday, but I'd be damned if I was going to admit it. And in all honesty, I knew it would be a good distraction. It would give me something to think about other than Aidan and Jared and how crazy they were making me and my inner-wolf. I smirked. "I can't wait to kick your asses."

Acknowledgments

Deadly Crush owes a lot to my editor, Kathryn Calvert, so thank you, Kathryn, for having such a great eye, and for being so invaluable to me and my work.

To my mom, Jo-Anne, and sister, Jonel, thank you for all your support and for keeping me sane through the writing process.

A quick shout out to all my awesome coworkers. Thank you so much for acting as my trusted sounding boards, and for vetoing the twists and turns that made no sense. You all are the best!

And to my husband, Jordan, thank you. You are my inspiration.

But most of all, I would like to thank the readers, reviewers, and bloggers for your support and for sharing your love of books. You all are the reason I keep writing.

Deadly Mates

Deadly Trilogy Book 2

Dedication

For my husband, Jordan, because you have always believed in me.

CHAPTER 1

JADE

I shuddered as flares of hot adrenaline shot through my limbs. My legs crunched and snapped, a hollow, echoing sound as they twisted and reformed. It was weird shifting; I could feel each bone in my body bend and break, but it was also a rush — electric. My face was numb and tingly as my snout became a nose. I still expected it to hurt. It sure sounded painful. But it wasn't. The adrenaline that came with the shift was invigorating, coursing through my blood and sending each nerve ending into a breathtaking current of delirious heat. *God, how I love this feeling.*

The cool fall breeze prickled along my bare skin, littering it with goosebumps, but I hardly noticed. My heart was thrumming against my ribs, and my breath, short and fast. I lay on my back, the cold grass tickling my sensitive skin, as I gazed up at the canopy of trees overhead, catching my breath. The leaves danced in the wind, a mixture of pumpkin and cherry and lemon. A few fell from the branches, floating to the ground around me.

The sound of a wolf's whimper and grunt flitted through the air, and with a groan, I pushed myself up to my feet, feeling each achy muscle in my body as I rose. I pivoted in place, scanning the small clearing for the wolves I knew were close by, keeping my muscles tight and ready.

A rumbling growl filled the air, and I swiveled to the right. There wasn't much light in the small clearing. The sun was just starting to rise; peeking through the trees, the sky was a deep denim blue with soft veins of gold. I strained my eyes and senses, keeping my stance ready. It took me a moment to find the wolves, but when my eyes landed on them, I couldn't stop the burst of laughter that erupted from me.

Jared and Beck were heaped together in a tangled mess of paws and legs, nestled at the base of a thick oak tree in a pile of leaves. I may not have been physically stronger than they were, but I was by far faster. I laughed again. I just couldn't help it. I'd only been a werewolf for a week, and already, I'd managed to outsmart and outmaneuver the big, bad enforcers.

Beck poked his gray snout out from underneath one of Jared's paws. His eyes shimmered with flecks of gold, and he gave me a big doggy smile and let out a playful yip before squirming out from underneath Jared. They both managed to get back on their feet, and as soon as they did, Jared's deep brown coat started to ripple as he began to shift.

I shook my head and smirked, swallowing the giggle that bubbled up in my throat and darted into the trees to fetch my clothes before Jared could finish his shift. It was one thing to stand stark naked in front of them as wolves, but I still wasn't all that comfortable doing it while they were human. Well, okay, to be honest, it was more that I wasn't comfortable standing in front of Jared naked. I didn't trust my inner-wolf to behave. She was pulled to Jared, enthralled by his dominant scent more than I liked or cared to admit.

I had just made it behind the broad pine where my clothes were stashed when Jared called, "Where are you running off to, kitten?" The huskiness of his voice made my inner-wolf squirm and my spine straighten. I sucked in a breath, trying to calm the beast within me. *Darn it!* I loathed the effect he had on her. Even the sound of his voice made her perk up, sending excited shivers along my skin.

"To get clothes on," I called, snagging my underwear and bra from the pile and yanking them on hastily.

"We've seen you naked before," Jared said, chuckling.

I bristled, seriously not needing the reminder of Jared seeing me naked. It had happened yesterday after seeing Aidan for the first time in two days. My inner-wolf had been crazy worked up. She'd been furious at me for walking away from him — her mate — and when training started, Beck and Jared had gotten the brunt of her fury. I'd had them both cowering at my feet within five minutes. When I'd shifted, my stomach was growling. I couldn't get the food-like clouds that Aidan had pointed out, out of my mind. And my inner-wolf couldn't let go of the way rubbing against his hand made her feel. The contentment, the tingling skin, the frantic need to get closer to him, to have him.

After we'd shifted, Jared had tried to use his scent to soothe her. It didn't work. She'd gone wild, taking me over. If it weren't for Beck, I would probably be mated right now, and it wouldn't be with the wolf that I knew, without a doubt, was mine. No matter how pissed I was at Aidan, my inner-wolf and I both knew that he was my mate. It was a feeling, something deep within my bones. My inner-wolf recognized him as hers — as mine — even if I wasn't ready (didn't want) to claim him.

Jared's chuckles echoed in my ears, and I felt my heart beat a bit faster. I huffed and shouted, "Doesn't mean I have to stand there and let you gawk." I didn't mean to shout it, he probably would have heard me at even a whisper, but right then, I couldn't control my tone. A blush flared along my skin; it started at my toes and spread all the way to my cheeks.

"I don't gawk, little girl," Jared growled. He was trying to sound fierce, but I caught the humor and something that sounded a whole lot like longing in his tone.

I rolled my eyes. Jared didn't exactly gawk, but he also didn't hide the fact that he looked. And that appraising gaze he gave me after I shifted yesterday, well, it made my inner-wolf shudder. But the thing was, Jared was a dick, plain and simple. Other than his enthralling scent and the undeniable strength he had within the pack, there was nothing about him that I really liked, well, at least nothing that would make me want to take the mating jump with him. He was friend material, loyal beyond sanity, but nothing more, and each moment that passed, I regretted it a little bit more that I hadn't asked Beck to pretend to be my mate. Beck was hot, but nothing about him made me, or my inner-wolf, sing. It would have been a safer choice.

"Uh, yeah, you kind of do," Beck said, laughing. "Why'd you shift, Jade? It was just getting fun."

I grabbed my jeans, tugged them on, and grinned. *Fun.* I had to admit, learning to use my scent and manipulate them with it was kind of fun, but no matter how much fun it was, I was exhausted and achy, and I'd had enough for the day. "Because I'm freakin' tired, is why," I said, as I buttoned up my jeans. "We've been at it for hours already, and besides, I have school." *And you guys haven't let me get a full night of sleep since I became alpha female,* I thought, not bothering to remind them. They only insisted that it was all part of my training each time I did.

"Your dad's coming home tomorrow, and you're going to school?" Beck asked, amusement clear in his timbre.

I cringed a little at the mention of my dad. I wasn't ready to see him or talk to him. I sucked at lying to him, and I had no clue how I would act as if nothing was wrong. I still didn't want to believe the video Erika showed me. I had watched it at least fifty times since the first time I saw it, and each time I watched it, I wanted to throw up. How didn't I know he was a shifter? How didn't I notice that he was like an evil spawn of Satan? I sighed and said, "Yep, Aidan said ..."

"When were you talking to Aidan?" Jared's breath was hot against my neck, and his voice was a low growl. I stiffened, and my breath caught in my throat. He pressed against me, his skin warm against my bare back, and I cursed myself. I needed to pay more attention. I couldn't let them sneak up on me like this. I couldn't let down my guard.

"He sent me a text message last night when you were in the shower," I said, hating how raw my voice sounded and how crazy guilty I felt all of a sudden. I cleared my throat. "We are the alpha pair. It's not like I can ignore him forever." Except, I had kind of planned on doing just that. Well, at least until the whole werecougar mess was dealt with. He didn't need the complication, and honestly, I already had enough to deal with. The last thing I wanted to think about was whether or not I could get over all of his lies. He may feel like home to my inner-wolf and me, but I just wasn't ready to forgive and forget.

Jared placed a hand on my bare shoulder, letting his fingers trail down my arm. My inner-wolf stirred restlessly as his heady scent engulfed me. "Stay home with me. I promise it'll be a hell of a lot more fun."

"Why in the world would I want to do that?" I asked sweetly, stepping away from him and yanking my T-shirt over my head. I didn't give him time to snap out a response before I started to walk away. The hot, salty scent of sweat and anger spiked in the air, and my inner-wolf fought me with each step I took away from him, trying to force me to stay. I didn't think I would ever understand that part of me. Why my inner-wolf reacted to him so strongly, I still didn't know. Sure, Erika had said it was because she recognized a dominant male — a potential mate — but as far as I was concerned, Jared had no potential, not as my mate at least. And my inner-wolf had already picked her mate; we just hadn't claimed him yet. Shouldn't knowing that her mate was close by change her reaction to other males?

I'd only made it a few steps before Beck's rumbling warning reached my ears. "She's his, Jared. She has been from the day they met. You've got to back off. Let all this shit go before you have both of them out for you, man."

For about half a second, I thought about spinning around and telling them that I wasn't *his*, that I didn't belong to anyone, but I didn't. The truth was I belonged to Aidan just as much as he belonged to me.

Jared and Beck followed me, keeping their distance, but I still caught their murmurs as they discussed the plan for tomorrow when Dad got home. I was dreading it. Dreading all of it, I hated how glad I was that Jared would be with me, staying in the house, helping me deal with it all.

When I stepped out of the forest into my backyard, the scent of Belgian waffles and bacon frying drifted around me, and my stomach growled. Mom hadn't been working since Jared moved in, and to my dismay, I really didn't think his presence bothered her much. She doted on him like crazy, always cooking for him and cleaning up after him. They chilled out, watched movies together, and joked around — a lot. I knew the mouthwatering scent wasn't for me. It was for him. Not that it really bothered me. It was just something I noticed. If I knew anything about my mom, she loved to take care of people.

But Jared, on the other hand ... He'd only been living with me for three days now, but he was already getting on my last nerve. He was taking our little act way too seriously, and he was enjoying it far too much. Especially when Aidan was watching. I didn't know how Aidan could stand to watch Jared and me together. I was certain that I wouldn't be able to do it. And God help the wolf or human that tried to move in on him. Yes, it had been my idea to make the act look real. Yes, I knew that we needed to successfully fool the pack and the town to actually fool my dad. The more people who knew it was an act, the more chance my dad would catch wind of it. It had been Dad's idea to mate me to an enforcer when he thought I'd lost the games, and if we had any chance of figuring out exactly what he was doing, playing along with his suggestion seemed like the best way to do it. But honestly, I was beginning to think that Jared believed I was, or soon would be, his mate.

"Mmmm, she made me waffles again," Jared said, coming up beside me and draping a loose arm over my shoulder.

"And bacon," Beck added.

"That's what it smells like," I said dryly, shrugging off Jared's arm. "Way to point out the obvious, guys."

I rounded the house, and I wasn't surprised to see the driveway full. The team hadn't missed a mealtime since Jared had moved in. I climbed the porch steps and reached for the doorknob, my arm stiff and heavy, my muscles screaming at me to rest. I clenched my hand around it and yanked the door open. And then I heard it, a light, bubbly laugh that really shouldn't have been coming from within my house.

Marcy was here.

For about half a second, I stood in the doorway, frozen, before forcing myself to follow the sound. I didn't know whether to be thrilled because, well, I'd been missing my best friend like crazy or pissed off because she'd actually come by. She might be like a sister to me, but she had gone too far. I couldn't help but wonder if things might have played out differently between Aidan and me if she'd just stayed out of it all.

"Jade, look who finally came home," Mom said, waving a hand toward Marcy as I padded into the kitchen. By the look of her, it was a cleaning day. Her thick, dark hair was tied up in a messy knot at the top of her head, and she was wearing faded jeans and a bleach-stained T-shirt.

The team, plus Erika and Marcy, gathered around the table. Landon looked well, hungry, but then he usually did. His tall and lean frame was hunched over the table, his chin resting in his hands. His bleach blond hair was gelled and spiked, and his baby blue eyes met mine for a brief second, and he winked. Beside him was Mark, the youngest member of our team, only seventeen. He was leaning back, slouching in his chair, a thick arm draped over the back. He had on a light grey hoodie, the hood pulled up, covering his mop of curls. A few of them were poking out, framing the hard lines of his face. And then there was Craig with his soft features. Out of all of them, he looked the most unthreatening, sweet even, but his smaller size and warm smile were deceiving. When he was on, he was deadly, but right then, he was too involved with trying to get Erika's attention to even notice we had come in.

Over the last few days, mealtimes had become a bit of a circus with them all here. Our house wasn't really small, but it wasn't big enough for this many people. We bought another table, a bigger one that barely fit within the kitchen, but at least it was big enough for us all to sit down at.

I finally let my gaze drift to Marcy. "Hey," I said, giving her a little nod. She looked awkward sitting with the team. Her cheeks were flushed, and deep crevasses marred her forehead.

"What are you doing here?" Jared questioned, stepping past me. He hadn't bothered putting on his shirt, instead draping it over his shoulders. He gave Marcy a bored once over before sliding into his chair.

"Jared! Marcy lives here, too." Mom scolded, cutting him a disappointed look. It didn't even faze him.

"I thought maybe we could walk to school together," Marcy said, or I guess croaked would be more like it. "Aidan said you were going back today." She made sure to keep her eyes on me as if she were trying to imagine that it was only us and that she wasn't really sitting at a table with the pack enforcers.

I didn't get a chance to answer before Jared said *No*, as if he actually had the right to answer for me.

I pursed my lips and rolled my eyes at him. "Oh, shut up, Jared." I didn't care what *game* we were playing. I was still one of his alphas, even if he didn't want to acknowledge it.

"Now, kitten." Jared's voice was a low growl. He didn't bother looking at me, but his shoulders tensed, and I was sure his eyes were a nice shade of gold right then. "Is that any way to talk to your mate?"

"Will you shut up, please?" I said through gritted teeth, biting back the reminder that I wanted to spit out. I wasn't his mate — never would be — no matter how much my inner-wolf craved him. This was an act. Something to fool my dad. Nothing more.

My response earned me a few chuckles from around the table, a long, drawn-out groan from Erika, and an annoyed huff from Mom. She pursed her lips and cut me a dirty look.

I rolled my eyes. Mom had always wanted me to hook up with one of the pack members, and to say she disapproved of the way I spoke to Jared was definitely an understatement.

Jared looked up, meeting my eyes. His flared brighter, and he said, "No, I don't think I will. You're not walking to school." And then, as if it were settled, he grinned at my mom and said, "Breakfast smells delicious, Pam."

I watched him in stunned silence for a moment, my jaw dropping a little. My blood was boiling. It was a serious effort to calm down and not blurt out all the nasty things I wanted to say, but after a few deep breaths, I managed to simmer down.

I glanced at the table; Jared and the team were already digging in, and although my stomach was rumbling, I turned, heading out of the room. Right then, the last thing I wanted to do was sit down with my *so-called* mate and play the sweet girlfriend part. "Come on, Mac," I said, waving a hand.

I hadn't even made it to the doorway when Jared's growled command reached my ears. "Jade, sit down and eat."

"I want to talk to her," I said, turning toward him like an obedient mate would do, loathing myself for doing it, and if Mom hadn't been there watching us, I wouldn't have, or at least that's what I tried to tell myself.

Jared dropped his fork, letting it clatter to his plate, and pushed his chair back. His expression was lethal. "I don't like the idea of you walking alone." There was an underlying threat to his tone.

"I won't be alone," I said. "And besides, we're just going up to my room for now."

He opened his mouth to say something else, but I didn't want to hear it. I channeled my scent, feeling the burn of my imprint as it heated beneath my top, sending out a clear warning for him to back the hell off. He stiffened, and his jaw started to tick. He tried to hold my glare, but he couldn't, and I watched as his eyes began to drop.

Marcy didn't miss what was happening. She scrambled from her chair and darted over to me. "Come on, Jade," she said, nudging me with her elbow, "let's go."

CHAPTER 2

AIDAN

It took five minutes for my head to clear enough to realize that the insistent knocking sound was actually someone at the door, and by that time, the knocking had turned into a head-splitting thud, thud, thud. And even then, I stayed in bed, staring up at the ceiling.

Slivers of light streamed through the cracks along the edges of my blackout blinds as the sun began to rise. I shifted my pounding head; the glowing red numbers on my alarm clock read 6:05. I knew I should probably get up, see who the hell thought banging on my door at sunrise was a good idea, but honestly, right then, I didn't really care.

I felt like hell. My head was throbbing as if it had its own pulse, and my eyelids were sore, heavy. I'd only been asleep for about fifteen minutes, and that fifteen minutes had been the longest I'd managed to sleep at once in the last three days. Between the pack, the threat of the werecougars, and the constant, relentless urge to run out, find Jade, and drag her — kicking and screaming, if needed — away from that damn enforcer, sleep had become a luxury; a luxury that I was seriously craving.

I groaned and snagged a pillow, putting it over my head, hoping to drown out the banging. Maybe if I ignored it, whoever it was would just go away.

It didn't work.

The thudding came again, loud enough that it felt as if it were shaking the entire house. Where the hell was Dominic? He was supposed to be dealing with the pack and their petty issues. He was supposed to be giving me time to sleep.

I heaved myself out of bed, stumbled over a pile of clothes, and banged into my dresser. "Dammit!" I growled, kicking the pile of laundry out of my way. The room I now called my bedroom was small cluttered, with a king-size bed and a worn mahogany dresser taking up most of the space.

I sucked in a deep breath, trying to calm my sour mood. It helped — a little. Gritting my teeth, I headed downstairs, not bothering to get dressed. Whoever it was wasn't staying.

The banging came again, hard enough to make the windows rattle. I took the last few steps two at a time and crossed to the door in a few long strides, throwing it open. "What the hell do you want?" I growled before it was even fully opened.

"Missed you, too, pup." The deep, rumbling voice made my entire body stiffen, and the temperature around me rocketed up at least twenty degrees. My inner-wolf woke up, clawing at my chest, itching to break free, and I swallowed hard, fighting him back.

I looked up slowly. I didn't want to. I wanted to slam the door shut, but I couldn't make myself do it. The two men standing on the deck were people I had wished to never have to see again. Chris and Tommy, my dad's most trusted enforcers, the ones that had helped Dad teach — torture — me as a kid, looked almost bored standing in front of me. My eyes swept over them. They looked the same as I remembered: Chris, tall and thick, chiseled face and goatee, and Tommy, short, stocky, and bald. They were twice my age and had been with my dad since I was born.

"Get the hell off my deck." My tone was calm and controlled, masking the blazing anger that filled my core. I moved forward, filling the doorframe, rolling my shoulders back, lifting my head, keeping my hard glare fixed on them. My nerves were already fried, my patience at a breaking point and this unwelcome visit only managed to send my stress level sky-rocketing.

Tommy smirked. "Your parents sent us." He held out a hand, a folded piece of paper clasped between his fingers.

I narrowed my eyes, glancing down at the paper, and my skin shuddered as my inner-wolf tried to push free. It took a moment for my groggy, pounding head to catch up, but when it did, I groaned. *Mom.* I knew I shouldn't have called her yesterday. And I sure as hell shouldn't have told her where I was or about the pack I had taken over, but after seeing Jade, the way Jared touched her, the way she smiled, that damn kiss ... I'd caved. I needed advice. I needed ...

Tommy waved the paper in front of me, waiting for me to take it. "You going to just stand there, or let us in, kid?"

"Haven't decided yet," I said, snagging the paper and unfolding it. I scanned the simple note, my jaw tightening with each word I read. *Your mother filled me in. Use Tommy and Chris however you see fit. They are there to help, and they will stay as long as you need them. I know I haven't said this enough, but I'm proud of you, son.*

It wasn't signed, but I would have known my father's sloppy scrawl anywhere. I read the note twice before crumpling it, balling it in my hands. Proud of me. What a joke. My father didn't even know the meaning of that word. I was sure of it. I lifted my glare back up to theirs. "Turns out I don't need you guys. Go home." It was a command. They heard it. They felt it. For a quick second, I saw surprise pass across their faces, but then their wolf nature took over. Their shoulders started to sag, and their gazes began to drop. I channeled my scent, giving the command a bit more punch, and as I did, their eyes fell to the deck.

"Your mom filled us in," Chris said, his voice hoarse, strained. "We're here to help, kid."

I didn't budge from the doorway. It wasn't that I didn't need the help because I did; it was the principle. My father had absolutely no right to send anyone from his team. Not without speaking to me first. I hadn't asked for his help, and the last thing I wanted was to owe him anything. My jaw clenched, and my face heated. *This is my pack — my territory.*

Chris snuck a quick look at me and jammed his hands in his pockets. "Come on, Aidan. We've been driving all night, and I'm starved. At least let us eat and grab some sleep before you throw us out."

I wanted to stand firm, slam the door, and kick them out of town. But even if I wanted to, I couldn't bring myself to do it. Guilt wormed its way through my stomach. I knew it was stupid. I shouldn't have felt guilty about sending them away. It wasn't as if I'd ever been close with either of them; my feelings for them had always been a tossup between sparks of admiration and all-out hatred. And the last thing the pack needed right now was two more hard-headed enforcers hanging around. As it was, I was already struggling to keep control of the fragile balance I had attempted to create here. But even if I knew that having them stay, even for a quick bite, wasn't a good thing, I still felt my resolve slipping. The idea of having someone that I knew, really knew, close by, even for a short time, started to eat at me. I was pretty sure I would regret it, but I stepped back from the door, letting them in. Really, what harm could a little food and sleep do?

They stepped into my house, keeping their gazes tight to the floor. "I'm going to take a shower," I grunted, shutting the door and nodding towards the kitchen. "Food's in there. Don't leave the house."

I didn't wait for a response before heading upstairs, taking the steps two at a time. I went straight for my bedroom, grabbed my cell phone from the dresser, and fired off a quick message to Dominic telling him to get here, now, and then I scrolled through my contacts. When I found the number I was looking for, I started to pace the narrow length of my room, glaring at the phone in my hand. I attempted to rack my thoughts, organize them, sort them, and line them up, but it was a useless effort. The only thing that kept surfacing in my exhausted brain was that my father had no right to send anyone to me. This was my pack, not his. My territory, not his. My life. I let out a frustrated growl. I knew part of the anger that was building in my chest was from a lack of sleep, but I couldn't seem to stop it. I glared at his name again, and the anger burned red-hot. I sucked in another breath, let out another growl, and scrolled down a few more names. I found the one I wanted, tapped on it, and brought the phone to my ear.

She answered on the first ring, most likely waiting for my call. "Hi, sugar." Her voice was soothing and warm, so warm that I could actually hear her smile.

"Is there something you forgot to tell me, Mom?" I asked. I tried to sound firm, but I couldn't, and before the full question was out of my mouth, I felt a grin tugging at my lips. Being annoyed at her was impossible, even if she was out of line. I dropped down, taking a hard seat on the edge of my bed.

"I'm going to assume my gifts showed up this morning," she said with a wicked giggle.

"Gifts?" I chuckled, but there was no humor in the sound; it was more stunned than anything. "On what planet are Chris and Tommy considered gifts?"

She laughed at that, the throaty sound rupturing through the speaker. "Be nice, Aidan. They volunteered. Believe it or not, I think they missed you."

For a second, I was taken aback. I couldn't imagine Chris and Tommy volunteering for anything that involved me. "Yeah, sure they did," I said, disbelief thick in my voice. I paused for a second, pulling in a deep breath, trying to pick my words carefully. Letting the breath out with a long sigh, I said, "Look, I know you mean well, but you can't just send me your enforcers. I'm an alpha now, Mom. I have my own pack, my own team. You and Dad need to respect that. You can't just butt in, trying to fix everything."

She made a *tsk* sound. "Oh, Aidan, I think you're forgetting that you're also my son."

"They can't stay," I said adamantly. "I'm feeding them, letting them sleep, and then they're leaving."

"You can't send them back," she countered, her voice losing all motherly compassion, taking on the firm tone of an alpha. "Trust me. Chris and Tommy are exactly what you need to fix that pack of yours." She paused for a second, inhaling a deep breath that sounded like static in my ear. "And they're what you need to get that mate of yours back."

My grip on the phone tightened, the casing digging into my palm. "She's not my mate." I felt myself say it, except I couldn't hear my voice. The words sounded like a wave crashing in my ears — reality trying to drown me in my own stupidity.

Mom sighed a gusty sound. "She'll come around. I don't know a single female that can run from her mate. Believe me, I tried to run from your dad. I couldn't run from him any more than I could run from the alpha in me."

I swallowed hard, trying to fight the uneasiness that squirmed within me. I wasn't so much worried that Jade would run from anything. It was more that she would do something stupid just to spite me — to get even. If I knew anything about her, it was that she was the kind of person that held a grudge.

The thing was, most alphas never found their true mate, or if they did, they couldn't act on it. My parents were one of the few. I had always believed that my mom won the games simply because she couldn't walk away from Dad. Her inner-wolf wouldn't let her.

And I knew — my inner-wolf knew — Jade was my mate. The feeling was profound, unexplainable, and undeniable. I felt it with every fiber of my body. I hadn't truly understood the feeling until she walked away. I'd known I liked her; hell, I'd even known that I could love her, but I didn't understand how much, how deep the feelings ran until I'd stupidly pushed her to the point that she turned her back on me. I knew she felt it, too, even if she was hell-bent on fighting it. And just like that, another piece of my resolve snapped and broke.

"You couldn't have sent Lance with them, could you?" I asked, hating how bitter I sounded. *Damn, was I really even considering this?*

That earned me another laugh. "If you needed a father figure, I would have. It sounds to me like you need brute strength and discipline with that pack of yours."

"Yeah, you're probably right," I said, running a hand through my hair. I hated to admit it, but maybe, just maybe, having some help wouldn't be the worst thing ever. Surely it would give me a bit more time to try and fix things with my mate, if nothing else.

"So you'll be letting them stay." It wasn't a question. The certainty of the statement was as if she knew she had already won.

Shit! If Jade was pissed at me now, what would she be like with Chris and Tommy here? But even though I knew she would probably kill me for bringing new members into the team without asking her first, I found myself relenting, and I said, "For now."

CHAPTER 3

JADE

Marcy sat on my unmade bed cross-legged, hugging one of my pillows to her chest. The crisp white comforter was balled up beside her, twisted around the emerald sheets, and she nudged at them absently, as if she were trying to push the mess of blankets out of her way. She looked a bit tired and a lot flustered, but then, that wasn't really anything new for her. Her long blond hair was down, hanging around her shoulders, and she was in black leggings and an off-white sweater dress. She wasn't looking at me; instead, her stare was fixed on a strand of photo booth pictures that was wedged in the dresser mirror. They were of us, four silly photos from a shopping trip last summer.

On the floor beside my bed was another pile of blankets — Jared's makeshift bed — a telltale sign that we weren't actually sleeping together. It was a serious effort not to rush over and pick up the pillows and blankets. But if Marcy had noticed them, she wasn't letting on, and the last thing I wanted to do was draw attention to them. My dresser was scattered with his things — deodorant, cologne, cell phone, wallet, keys. His clothes were strewn all over the place, and I found myself hoping she'd chalk up what looked like a bed on the floor to Jared being a slob and not see it for what it really was.

I leaned against the closed door to my bedroom, gazing out the window at the forest, listening to the sounds of the team joking around and eating downstairs. I didn't really know what to say, and by Marcy's silence, I figured she felt the same. I opened my mouth and then closed it. Each time I tried to say something, it just felt ... wrong. It wasn't that I didn't have anything to say, because I did. Loads. I just didn't know how to say everything or even if I should.

I sighed, a heavy sigh, and asked, "Why are you here, Mac?"

Marcy shifted her gaze, focusing somewhere around my belly. "I ... Jade ..." She huffed and started twirling a long strand of hair around her finger. "Wow, I didn't think this would be so awkward." She huffed again, letting it draw out until she'd expelled every drop of air from her lungs.

"Did Aidan send you?" I asked cautiously, folding my arms over my chest, more to stop the chill that slid through me than anything else, as I braced myself for the answer.

My question caught her full attention. She screwed up her face, still staring at my belly, and blurted, "Really? You think I'm here because of Aidan? God, Jade, I can't believe you'd even ask me that."

She was lying. I heard it in her outburst, the way her voice rose and fell and trembled. I could smell it in the air, the salt, the thickness, the staleness. And it stung. Bad. Worse than I really thought it should. "Mac, please don't be like him." My voice was soft, filled with the sting piercing my heart. "Don't lie to me."

"Dom sent me, okay?" She met my eyes then, hers were rimmed with glossy tears, and she squeezed the pillow tighter. "Maybe it was Aidan's idea, maybe it wasn't. I really don't know whose idea it was. But I swear that's not the only reason I'm here. I miss you. So much crap is happening. Trev hasn't been home in two days now, and I think Dom is going out today, too, and Aidan has been a moody prick since you left with Jared and ... and ... I need someone to talk to. I need my sister back."

For a moment, I forgot to breathe as I watched her bottom lip tremble. I didn't need an awesome sense of smell to know everything she'd said was true; it was written clearly in that quivering lip. I pushed off the door and stepped over to her, perching on the edge of my bed. "Where's Trevor been?"

She looked at me as if I should already know the answer, and I figured she was probably right. "Aidan has him and some of the others searching for the cougars. They keep finding tracks around town, coming closer and closer. Trevor said that they lead to the mountain, but once they get to the base of it, the tracks just vanish."

"What?" I asked. "How don't I know they're trying to track them?" I didn't expect an answer, and I was sure Marcy knew that, but it didn't stop her from snapping one out even if she did.

"Because you've been ignoring the pack. You've been ignoring Aidan." She tossed the pillow at me, smacking me in the chest with it, and yelled, "Jeez, Jade, you've been blowing off everyone except that team of yours, and as far as I can see, they aren't in any rush to find your dad or those nasty beasts."

"What's that supposed to mean?" I asked, keeping my voice just above a whisper, "and keep your voice down." I was sure the whole team could hear her, and I knew they had to be listening. The house was quiet, so quiet it was as if the house itself were holding its breath.

She didn't keep her voice down; instead, she let it rise higher. "You know exactly what it means. You and those enforcers haven't even tried to help find them. Do any of you even care that they're actually coming into town? I woke up this morning to find tracks all over my yard. The pack is supposed to keep our town safe. You and those enforcers are supposed to keep us safe."

"Shut up, Mac," I hissed, squeezing my eyes shut, listening. It felt like an eternally long moment before I heard chairs scraping along the floor, shuffling footsteps, and the round of *thank-yous* for breakfast. And then, just as I was about to let out my pent-up breath, my bedroom door swung open, and Jared walked in.

He didn't say anything as he padded across the room, snagging his phone and stuffing his wallet into his back pocket. Taut, strained muscles lined his neck and shoulders. He opened the closet, reached in, tugged a black long-sleeved T-shirt off a hanger, and then pulled it on.

Marcy kept her head ducked, but I could see her watching him from the corner of her eye, and when he turned to face us, her complexion paled just a little.

He didn't seem to notice. He was giving me an expectant kind of look, although I really didn't know what it was he was expecting, so I said, "I take it you're going out?"

"Yep." A cocky smirk twitched at his lips. He crossed the room in two long strides and reached out, running a finger along my cheek, before wrapping his hand around the back of my neck, pulling me to him. His lips were on mine, hot and rough before I had a chance to even register what he was doing. Thankfully the kiss ended just as quickly as it started. He feathered a light peck on the tip of my nose and then let his hand drop from my neck. "You better hurry up, kitten. You're going to be late," he said before turning away and leaving the room.

I sat in stunned silence, staring at the empty doorway. I had expected him to growl something at Marcy, to defend his team, even defend himself, or at the very least tell her to keep her nose out of enforcer business. I had figured he would give me a lecture about walking to school or snap at me for the way I had spoken to him downstairs, but he hadn't done any of that. Actually, he had acted normal, and that normalcy kind of freaked me out.

"Well, that was um ... interesting," Marcy squawked at the sound of the front door slamming. She cleared her throat. "What's going on with you and Jared? He hasn't given you the time of day since we were in seventh grade, and you had that crush. And even then, he wasn't interested, and you know it."

I hesitated, wanting to tell her the truth, but not sure if I could trust her to keep it to herself. I had never been away from Marcy for this long, and right then, seeing her sitting there, I wanted to blurt out everything. I knew it was a bit hypocritical of me. I had told her I didn't want to see her for a while. It was my fault she hadn't been here, but really, she was practically my sister. And it had been three days already. Three long days of having no one to talk to about the mess I had gotten myself into with Jared.

Sure, there was Erika, and theoretically, I should have been able to talk to her, but I just couldn't. She didn't get it. Anytime I tried, she was all like, *It's not about your feelings, Jade, it's about the pack,* or, *You're the alpha, suck it up.* In all fairness, Erika didn't know the truth. She really thought Jared and I were together mainly because I didn't trust her enough to tell her any different, and thanks to the way my inner-wolf reacted to him, she believed the lie. Yeah, I had named her as my beta, but that had been a heat of the moment kind of decision, and as the days slipped by, I realized how little I knew about her and how much I just didn't like her. It wasn't that she was completely awful. We just didn't click. She wasn't Marcy.

The thing was, even if I was sure that what I was doing with Jared was right, it felt sickeningly wrong. It felt wrong to have him sleep at my house, let alone in my room. And honestly, I hated having to lie to the pack, letting them, and everyone else, think we were together. But I didn't know what else to do. We had all agreed that my dad couldn't know that I'd become the pack's alpha female, and pretending to be with an enforcer seemed like the best cover-up. Really, until we had a clear picture of exactly what my dad's plans were, it didn't seem like I had much of a choice.

Maybe that wasn't entirely true. There was a choice, but I knew one thing for sure: choosing Aidan right now had to be the worst of two bad choices.

Marcy nudged me. "Talk to me, Jade. What's going on?"

"It's complicated," I said, glancing at the clock. It was already 7:30, and I still needed a shower. I got up and trudged over to the closet, riffling through the hangers. My mind was reeling. I couldn't understand why Aidan would send anyone out searching without talking to me about it. Didn't I have a say in what the pack did now? And he knew the team was working on it, kind of, well, okay, maybe not really. Most of their time was taken up on working with me. But they had been spending at least an hour a day looking. That was something, wasn't it?

"Well, un-complicate it," she snapped, following me to the closet. She reached in and snagged my plum hoodie, tossing it on the bed. "Because you're going to end up regretting this. He's playing with you. I know it, and I know you know it, too. There's something else behind this." A thought dawned on her then; I saw it pass across her eyes a moment before she visibly shuddered, and when she continued, her voice was whisper quiet. "You haven't slept with him yet, right? Please tell me you haven't because I did with Trevor and well ..."

I yanked a pair of jeans off a hanger and grabbed a white tank from the shelf before turning to look her straight on. "I know, Mac. You're mated. I can smell it. You have two distinct scents, yours and Trevor's. It's weird, though. I thought you had to be a werewolf for that."

"Um, yeah, well, you and me both." She blushed, a light pink, dropped her eyes and smiled — a little. "I just ... you can't, not with Jared. You don't even like him and Aidan ..."

"My inner-wolf likes him," I said, cutting her short, not wanting to hear anymore. "And really, who I end up mating with isn't important." I grabbed the hoodie she had tossed on the bed and started for the door. "I need to take a shower. You can wait or go, whatever."

"This wasn't Aidan's fault," Marcy blurted. "It's all on Dom and me. If you have to hate someone, then hate us. Don't take our bad advice out on him."

I didn't turn around. I couldn't. I was sure my face was crumbling just like my heart, and I didn't want her to see it. I kept my hand on the doorknob, but I couldn't bring myself to twist. "You didn't make him lie, Mac." I swallowed hard, hating how raw my voice sounded. "You didn't make him manipulate me. You didn't force him to put me in danger. He was the one stupid enough to follow through with it all."

"We just wanted you to be happy," she pleaded, coming up behind me. She squeezed my shoulder. "You can fool everyone else, but not me. I see through you. I always have. Aidan's the cheese to your macaroni, and you know it."

"The cheese to my macaroni?" I asked as I dropped my grip on the doorknob and turned around. I arched a brow and pursed my lips.

She grinned, wrapping me in a too-tight hug. "I've missed you, Jade. Three days is way too long."

CHAPTER 4

AIDAN

Dominic looked uncomfortable. He leaned against the kitchen counter, watching Tommy fry up some bacon and scrambled eggs. His blond hair was gelled, but that was pretty much the only thing he'd bothered to do before coming over. His jeans were stained with dirt, and his olive hoodie looked as if he'd been wearing it for weeks. His eyes were bruised veined red. It was clear that he'd been sleeping just as well as me.

My unwelcome guests had made themselves at home while I'd taken a shower and gotten dressed. They had raided my fridge and cooked up the last breakfast food I had. A heavy layer of greasy smoke filled the room, and the small, dusty-gray countertop was covered with pots and dishes.

Chris drummed his fingertips on the table, watching the coffee pot as it gurgled and dripped. "Your dad was telling me your beta is in high school and the head enforcer is about your age."

A strained tension shifted through the cramped space. For the last five minutes, Chris and Tommy had been chatting with me as if Dominic weren't there, and Dominic looked as if he were about ready to snap.

I scrubbed at my face and leaned back in my chair, stretching my legs out in front of me. "Yep, Dominic's graduating this year, and Jared's a year older than me."

Tommy grunted. "He looks like a pup." He cut a quick look at Dominic. "How long have you been in the pack, kid?"

"Two years," Dominic said, his tone more hostile than I would have liked, but I guessed I couldn't really blame him. They were being dicks. He pushed off of the counter and headed to the cupboard, pulled it open, and grabbed four mugs, setting them on the table before pulling out a chair and taking a seat.

"And Jade, the alpha female, she's only eighteen?" Tommy asked, his tone calm, friendly even as if we were old friends just catching up. He switched off the burners and began dishing out scrambled eggs onto the plates lining the counter.

"She is," I said, keeping my tone just as friendly. I knew what they were doing. Trying to loosen me up. Looking for the foothold. They were under orders to stay and help me out, and they were looking for a reason to do just that. I probably should have told them that they would be sticking around for a bit, but honestly, I was kind of enjoying watching them sweat a little.

"So every pack member in a position of real power is under twenty-one." The coffee pot rumbled and spat out the last of the brew. Chris reached for it, pouring himself a cup. He took a deep drink before glancing over his shoulder. "You ever heard of anything like this before, Tommy? Because I sure as hell haven't."

"Nope," Tommy said as he made his way over to the table, juggling the heaping plates of eggs and bacon, and passed them out.

"Ray replaced all the enforcers with newly turned werewolves," Dominic offered. "He ran his last beta out of town, too, when I was turned. He wanted people he could mold, ones that didn't know any different, didn't know pack law."

"Huh." Tommy sat down, grabbed his fork, and shoveled in a large mouthful of eggs. His forehead creased, a sharp V forming in between his eyes, as he tried to make sense out of what Dominic said. We ate in silence for a long moment before he said, "And you've let your head enforcer move in with your mate."

"She's not my mate." The words felt like gravel on my tongue. I hated how screwed up this whole situation was. I figured I deserved it all, but really, Jade was taking this too far. Yeah, I'd hid things from her and lied to her, but right now, she was screwing with the delicate balance that I'd created within the pack, and whether she knew it or not, she was on the verge of shattering it completely. We were supposed to be a team, and her ignoring me wasn't showing a united front. It made the pack nervous, and a nervous pack of werewolves was really not something either of us needed.

Tommy waved a fork at me. "She's the alpha female, which makes her your mate."

I rolled my eyes and let out a long, windy sigh. "According to her, it doesn't."

"You know what I'd do?" Chris said casually as if he were just making small talk and not giving me advice. "If I was the alpha, I'd force that enforcer out of her house. You said they aren't mated. There's really no reason why they should be living together."

"I don't know about that," Tommy said. "If she's as hard-headed as I hear, she'd probably just follow him. I'd send him out of town; get him away from her altogether."

I groaned. I was way too tired to play this friendly chat game. "Guys, I know what you're doing. I've watched you work with Dad long enough to know what this is, so cut the small talk crap." I snagged the coffee pot and poured myself a cup, thinking. They knew damn well they were gaining ground with me, but then I was sure that they'd both known they weren't going anywhere the moment I let them in the door. After a long moment, I said, "I can't send Jared anywhere. Jade's dad is coming home tomorrow, and I need every pack member I have to deal with the cougars."

Dominic's eyes flared, and a spasm worked its way along his jaw. "You should send him out hunting them." His voice was growled, and an angry red flush settled over his face. "The team has barely spent any time looking for them. He's been too busy with Beck, teaching Jade how to fight."

Chris chuckled and leaned forward, resting his elbows on the table. He looked Dominic over, a flash of curiosity passing across his face, before he asked, "What's the deal with these cougars, anyway?"

I almost told him it was none of his business. The words were right there, on the tip of my tongue, but the truth was, I wanted to hear someone else's thoughts. Dominic was too close to the issue, too close to Jade, and well, the pack didn't have much of a clue about what was really going on. Before I knew it, I was telling them everything. I told them about the video of Jade's dad and about how the cougars used women. I explained the town's dynamics, and I even talked about Jade, telling them about the games, about the lies, about tricking her into competing.

And just like they did with my father, Chris and Tommy listened, throwing in their thoughts and pulling apart the problems, separating them and categorizing them. Breakfast turned into lunch, and lunch turned into early afternoon, but we actually had a plan by the time we were done. A real, solid plan. It was too bad it was a plan involving Jade and Jared staying together.

JADE

School was well ... it was school. Nothing spectacular. I knew I was supposed to be learning something, but I couldn't focus. All I could think about was that Aidan had been sending *our* wolves out to track the cougars — to track my dad. I should have been okay with it all. Clearly, my dad was evil. He'd even said that he would be using me at some point. But even if I knew all that, there was this little nagging voice in the back of my head that kept reminding me he was still my dad, and no matter what I tried, I couldn't shake it.

The walk to school with Marcy had been insightful, if nothing else. She'd warned me that most of the pack members that should be in school wouldn't be. Aidan had them all running on fumes. From what she'd said, he'd turned into a bit of a slave driver over the last few days, but the pack had really warmed up to him. They respected him trusted his judgment. Although, she also let me know that even if they respected him, they were also getting fed up with his short fuse, especially the females. Personally, I couldn't picture Aidan with a short fuse. He'd always been so laid back and carefree. Well, at least most of the time, he was.

Marcy spent most of the walk and all of lunch trying to convince me that I needed to talk to Aidan. Really talk to him. I hated to admit it, but she was right. The thing was, yesterday hadn't gone so well when I saw him. Just thinking about the broken look on his face when I walked away with Jared made my chest squeeze and my breath shorten.

And that feeling led me to another issue. The one I'd been trying to pretend didn't exist. Was I lying to Aidan about Jared because it was needed? Or was my subconscious trying to inflict some kind of petty revenge for all the lies he'd told me?

Yep, the whole situation really sucked.

Word had spread about me joining the enforcers, and as the day went on, I heard a few whispers about Jared and me. Really, I should have been happy that people were buying it, but I wasn't.

Instead, it only made me feel sick. God, I hated lying. Nothing, *nothing*, good ever came from a lie.

Dominic hadn't shown up yet. But then, I guess I'd never really believed he would. I knew he would be with Aidan, but still, I'd hoped to see him nevertheless. I'd fought with Dominic before.

Hell, I'd even shunned him for two years. But still, after patching things up with Marcy, I wanted to see him, too. I wanted to make sure he was okay.

I shifted in my chair and glanced at the clock: 1:49. Six more minutes until gym, until laps. Oddly enough, I was looking forward to running for the first time in my life. I felt restless, confined, and running would help — hopefully.

And after gym, I would go see Aidan.

I hadn't quite figured out what I would say when I got there, but I knew, just knew, that I needed to tell him how I was feeling about the whole dad situation, if nothing else.

The six minutes dragged. When the bell finally sounded, I hastily shoved my books into my backpack. I was just about to stand when the classroom door opened. My senses came alive as an aroma assaulted my nose. It was musky and woodsy and sharp, and on top of that, I could smell the wolf. A wolf that I was sure I didn't know. My inner-wolf perked up, and my heartbeat doubled.

I slid out of my chair, a soft flare of adrenaline pushed through my veins. Unease started to claw in my chest like an animal trying to break free, and a slow growl started at the base of my throat, working its way up. The room fell silent, completely silent. I breathed in the scent again, and I caught something else. Dominic.

But there was something ... off. I could feel it, knotted and tangled in my gut. My classmates rushed into the hallway, most likely to get out of my way. My skin was crawling with shivers. I didn't wait for everyone to clear out. I couldn't. My inner-wolf pushed me, begged me to move. I quickly shouldered my bag and headed out the door.

Dominic stood beside a man who was casually leaning against the lockers. I would have said he was in his early forties if I had to guess. He was short, an inch or two shorter than my five-foot-six, but he was thickset — sturdy looking. His head was clean-shaven, and as he looked at me, I caught a fleck of gold in his eyes.

"Dom, who's your friend?" I asked, eyeing him closely. He didn't answer, didn't even bother to acknowledge that he'd heard my question. Instead, he just kept that infuriating expressionless mask of his in place.

I took a step toward him, and as I did, the man's nostrils flared, and then he smiled a surprisingly friendly smile. "You." His voice was raspy, and he was pointing a stubby finger at me. "You're coming with me." He didn't take the chance that I might not agree. Within a second, he was across the hall, grabbing my wrist and yanking me forward.

"Let go of me," I growled. A fast shiver cut across my skin, and my inner-wolf brushed against my chest as if she were asking if she could come out and play. I pushed the sensation back and pulled on my alpha scent, focusing on everything Jared had taught me. I imagined it thick and heavy and suffocating, and as I did, my imprint began to heat up like a flare of a match tip.

He shuddered, only slightly, and the friendly smile melted away. "That's really not a nice way to greet a guest."

"Wasn't meant to be," I said and yanked hard, pulling my wrist from his grasp.

The man chuckled, not a nice sound. "Apparently." He snatched my hand again, yanking me forward as he started down the hallway. Students jumped out of the way, pressing against the lockers and trying darn hard to pretend they didn't notice us. "The alpha asked me to retrieve you, but he didn't tell me how to do it. Rein in that scent of yours, kid, or I'll drag you out of here and tie you up in the back of my truck."

I tried to yank free again and snapped, "I'd like to see you try it."

"Jade, Aidan sent us to get you," Dominic growled. "Give it a rest." He wouldn't look at me as he fell into step beside us. He was nervous — I could smell it — but I couldn't tell if it was because of me or the dumbass holding onto me.

I gritted my teeth. I was pretty sure it was true. Dominic wouldn't have been there if it weren't. Obviously, he wasn't being forced into helping, but really, wasn't the dragging thing a little extreme?

"Who the hell are you?" I demanded, letting my scent fade a little, as he pulled me through the doors into the harsh sunlight. A cool breeze cut through my hoodie as he tugged me toward the parking lot.

"That doesn't really matter," he said. It wasn't unkind, just cool and brisk as if he'd written me off as a low-ranking pack member (although clearly from the way he'd shuddered under my alpha scent, he knew I wasn't).

"You do know who I am, though, right?" I asked, a little baffled.

He chuckled, stopping beside a steel gray pick-up truck. "Sure do," he said and winked. "You're the alpha's mate."

I laughed. Hard. I didn't mean to, but it bubbled up and out before I could stop it. "Clearly, you have no clue who I am." I poked him in the chest with my free hand. "I'm the mate of an enforcer. The head enforcer, actually. And I'm also the alpha female of the pack in town."

The man was totally unfazed. He pulled the door open, and Dominic jumped into the back of the extended cab before he finally let go of my wrist, gesturing for me to get in. "Exactly what I said. You're the alpha's mate."

A growl rattled around in my chest. I opened my mouth, ready to tell him again, when Dominic said, "Jade, get in the damn truck. Don't make me call him. Trust me, right now, this is the better option."

I snapped my gaze to him, taking in the hard lines on his brow and the bruises under his eyes. He looked like crap. He held my glare, unrelenting. I was tempted to tell him to make the call for about half a second, but I didn't. Right then, I didn't think I could handle talking to Aidan in a civil way, so I bit my tongue and hopped into the truck.

The man slammed the door as soon as I was in and then made his way around to the driver's side. When he was in the truck, and his door was shut, I swiveled, looking him straight on, and asked, "Where are you taking me?"

"Home," he grunted, starting up the truck and shifting it into gear.

Home, I thought. Relief swelled in my chest. At that moment, home was exactly where I wanted to be. I would take a hot shower, calm down, and then go and see the jackass who had me pulled from school. Yep, home was perfect.

The drive took less than five minutes, and for those five minutes, I sat rigid in my seat, my gaze fixed to the floorboards. Dominic didn't try to talk to me, and neither did the man driving, and I was seriously glad for it. The last thing I wanted was to have to talk. Frankly, I was just too busy stewing over being dragged out of school.

I didn't look up until the truck came to a stop in the driveway, and when I did, my jaw clenched tight. As it turned out, the bald man did take me home; it just really wasn't the home I wanted to go to.

CHAPTER 5

AIDAN

Jade was, to put it mildly, pissed off.

I was sitting on the couch, my legs stretched out and arms folded behind my head, trying to stay awake as I waited for the inevitable when she burst through the door. She looked like she was ready to punch someone, most likely me. She stalked toward me, Tommy and Dominic trailing along behind her, neither of them looking impressed.

I had kind of hoped she would have calmed down a little by the time she got here, but by the look of her, she hadn't. I'd known she would be fuming. I'd expected it. But the thing I hadn't expected was that even though she was furious, her skin didn't shudder, her eyes didn't flare. She was in control of her inner wolf. Completely in control. I hated to think it, but whatever Jared had been doing with her was helping. And that thought made my blood boil. I knew a lack of sleep and stress made me so edgy, but knowing it didn't make the thought of Jared helping her any easier to swallow. *It should have been me.*

She stopped a few paces away from me, and as her eyes swept over me, a layer of ice settled in her glare. "You ever hear of a phone, jackass?"

I kept my expression blank, which was harder than I thought it would be. *Home.* The word filled my mind, my body, as I took her in. Her long, brown hair was loose, hanging around her shoulders. As my eyes raked over her, my skin warmed, my heart raced. She was in jeans and that plum hoodie she always wore, nothing out of the ordinary, but on her, well, everything looked good on her. Her scent, fruits mixed with almonds, made my inner-wolf stir, and a deep-seated craving spread through me. She was mine. My inner-wolf agreed, echoing my thoughts, *Mine.*

I pulled in a deep breath, letting her scent reach every nerve within my body, and then I met her cold gaze. "Jade, sit down. We need to talk."

Jade's jaw dropped a little, and the layer of frost that had settled over her eyes thawed slightly. Her nostrils flared. She was breathing me in. Her inner-wolf heard the command in my tone — in my scent — even if she didn't want her to.

Dominic made a sound. It wasn't quite a laugh, but I was pretty sure that's what it was supposed to be. It was choked, gurgled as if he had tried to swallow it.

Jade ignored him, but his laugh seemed to clear her head a little. She swallowed hard and fixed a lukewarm glare back in place. "Talk," she said, putting her hands on her hips, drumming her fingertips impatiently. "Come on, I'm dying to hear what reason you could possibly have for sending Dom with a complete stranger to drag me out of class — literally drag me — when it was your idea for me to go in the first place."

I smirked. I couldn't help it. Jade was just so damn cute when she was pissed off. Her peach complexion was slowly turning to an adorable shade of pink. "Actually, that was Dom's idea, not mine."

I held her glare in total silence until Chris shattered it by clearing his throat. Jade shifted her fuming gaze to him. She started to vibrate a little. Adrenaline, most likely. Her fingers stopped drumming; instead, they trembled slightly as she pressed them against her hip bones.

"So this is the girl," Chris said, bemused. "This is your mate? Really?" He folded his arms over his chest and chuckled, leaning against the doorframe to the kitchen.

"I'm not his mate!" Jade pivoted, and I caught another shudder of her skin as she faced Chris head-on. "Who the hell are you?"

I chuckled softly. I knew it was completely horrible, but part of me was seriously glad that she wasn't as in control as I initially thought she'd been.

The glad feeling was short-lived. Her scent flared, and I almost flinched — almost. I glanced around the room, taking in the smirks from Tommy and Chris and Dominic's scowl. Suddenly, my stomach twisted and sank. Maybe having them all here wasn't such a great idea. She looked as if she were ready to launch herself at Chris. But I knew that Chris and Tommy needed to see what I was dealing with if they were going to help at all, and as for

Dominic, well, if I was being honest, I had kind of hoped having him here might chill her out a little. I knew she was mad at him, but they had a history. One that I had really hoped would bring her down a notch or two. And, yeah, I probably should have called her instead of sending Tommy, but I knew she wouldn't have answered. I'd barely gotten a response when I told her to go to school, and she hadn't answered a single one of my calls since she became alpha female.

"Jade." I said her name carefully, keeping my voice firm, forceful, hoping it would speak to her inner-wolf, if nothing else. "These are the newest members of Jared's team. The guy you're thinking about attacking is Chris," I said and then nodded toward Tommy, "and you've already met Tommy."

"We aren't looking for new members." Her voice was growled, harsh, and when she looked back at me, her eyes flared with a challenge. "You have no right to ..."

"Stop," I said, raising a hand in warning. "I have every right. This is my pack. I've made my decision."

"It's our pack," she said, throwing up her hands. "You just can't ..."

"No," I said, cutting her off. I stood up and stepped toward her, closing the distance until we were so close that if one of us pulled in a deep breath, our chests would touch. I glanced down at her, and she met my gaze with something that looked a hell of a lot like hatred, but underneath that hatred, I swore I saw a lick of fire just waiting to ignite. I swallowed down the urge to take her into my arms and said, "It's not ours. It's mine. Until you decide to step up and get involved with the pack, you don't get to make decisions involving them."

"Screw you, Aidan," she said, exhaling the words on a breath. She closed her eyes, squeezing them tight, and then blinked a few times before meeting my gaze again. She opened her mouth as if she would say more, closed it, and then turned her back on me — again.

It wasn't the first time she had turned away from me, and knowing her, it wouldn't be the last. But still, it burned. I reached out without thinking, wrapping my arms around her waist, and pulled her back flush against me. Leaning forward, brushing my lips against her ear, I said, "Don't walk away from me, Jade."

JADE

Aidan's breath brushing against the back of my neck — warm and sweet — sent a hot chill careening through me. My breath hitched. I could feel every ripple of his abs and chest against my back as he held me close. His strong arms tightened around my waist, pulling me closer still, and darn it, but I leaned into him.

His command and this show of dominance should have bothered me, but it didn't. I felt delicate, like a flower, with his arms around me, surrounding me with his power. My inner-wolf lapped it up as if hearing him, feeling him, having him so close was the best treat she could have asked for, and even though I hated it, I completely agreed with her. The last thing I actually wanted to do was walk away from him. Doing it once was pretty much all I had in me. Right then, I was sure of it.

I could feel the others watching us. Their breathing, their heartbeats, whispered around me like a breeze rustling through the forest, but at that moment, I didn't care.

Aidan's steady heartbeat thrummed against my back, and his heady scent ... I licked my lips and took a deep breath. *Home. I was home.* His betrayal had hurt. I was sure that I would never be able to trust him again, and yet, as I stood there incased in his arms, I knew that I would never be able to stay away from him either.

And then, my phone rang a sharp pitch, sharp enough to clear my head.

I wrapped my hand around Aidan's wrist, pulling his arm from my waist. He didn't stop me. Instead, he let his arm fall, then the other, and then the warmth of his body pressed against mine was gone. I felt the separation like losing a limb, and I almost turned into him. God, I wanted those arms back around me, but then my phone rang again, and I hastily fished it out of my pocket, glancing at the screen.

Jared.

Guilt pooled in my stomach, which was completely asinine. I had no reason to feel guilty. It wasn't like Jared, and I were really an item, but I felt it, like searing hot water pouring over my skin. I forced a smile, took a breath, and tapped the screen as I brought the phone to my ear.

"Hey, baby," I said. My voice was raw as if I'd swallowed a handful of tacks, and I swallowed hard, trying to clear the lump from my throat.

"Where the hell are you, Jade?" he yelled.

I cringed from the blast of his voice piercing my ear, and I almost glanced around to see if anyone noticed, but thankfully I caught myself. I forced my smile wider, hoping it would ease the rockiness of my voice. "I'm at Aidan's. You should probably get over here."

"You're supposed to be in school," he barked.

I could feel Aidan's eyes on my back, and I found myself hoping that he couldn't hear Jared. I didn't want Aidan to hear the possessive edge in my *so-called* mate's voice. I didn't even want to hear it myself.

"I didn't have much of a choice," I said. Was my tone sweet enough? I didn't know. I wanted to walk outside. I wanted to tell Jared off, but I couldn't. Not with everyone watching. Darn it! I hated having to play the sweet girlfriend. I wasn't even sweet on a good day. I sighed and felt my forced smile stretching further. "Can you find Erika and bring her with you? Oh, and maybe call the team. I want them all here."

"I'm not your damn secretary, Jade," he growled. "Call them yourself if you want them. Better yet, get your ass home."

I sucked in a deep breath. I was vibrating all over, and I felt the twitch in my jaw as I bit down, swallowing the urge to rip into him. "Jared, I'm not asking."

Aidan stepped into my line of vision and tapped my chin, forcing me to look up. He smirked, a knowing kind of smirk, and reached out, taking the phone from me before I could stop him and bringing it to his ear. He chuckled, and an amused grin curved his lips. "Jared. Come. Now." He barked out the order, grinning the entire time, and then thumbed the screen, disconnecting the call. His grin spread wider, and he winked at me, tossing the phone back.

I caught it easily and jammed it in my pocket. "You look a little too proud of yourself there," I snapped, glowering at him.

"Yeah?" he asked, chuckling. "Well, I kind of am."

CHAPTER 6

JADE

Aidan's house was comfy. I was pretty sure it had belonged to one of the previous alphas of the Dog Mountain pack, but I had never been inside before. It wasn't much, a living room done in browns and greens, soothing just like the woods, with a smallish kitchen off to the side and a set of stairs leading up to the second floor. The carpet was kind of gross, and the paint was chipped and peeling in spots, but other than that, it was cozy. And it smelled like him. Strong, a little sweet, and green. It was a peaceful scent, one that I was pretty sure I would never get enough of. Every few minutes, it would get stronger and then fade, as if he were using it, trying to stir a reaction from me, and it was a crazy hard effort to keep the stoic expression on my face and not let him see how much he was affecting me. I had already slipped up once since I walked through the door, and there was no way I was going to do it again.

I sat on the couch, my feet pulled up underneath me, waiting for Jared and the team to show up. Aidan sat across from me in a big, beat-up leather chair, with Chris and Tommy standing behind him. His light brown hair was askew, and his jawline was rough with a couple days' growth. His brown eyes were tired but alert, and he wore an easy smile as if the five of us together weren't awkward at all.

Dominic paced the small space, five steps one way, five steps back. His calm mask was starting to splinter. Every few minutes, he would steal a glimpse at me, and when he did, I caught the slivers of pain and regret spreading through his eyes like ice cracking under pressure.

While I waited for Jared, Aidan filled me in on why he had me pulled from class. He had a plan. As far as I could see, though, it wasn't much of a plan, and I was eighty-nine percent sure there was more to it than he wasn't telling me. The gist: he was calling the team together, and tomorrow, once Dad got back and I played up my relationship with Jared a little, they were going into the mountain to hunt the werecougars.

But my doubts about his plan could have also had something to do with the new additions to our pack. Aidan said they were temporary, help sent from his parents, and I really didn't know what to make of that. I hadn't thought about Aidan belonging to another pack before now. I guessed it made sense; he had been a werewolf before he'd shown up in Dog Mountain, but the information only managed to fill me with questions and reaffirm the fact that I really knew nothing about him. Another item to add to the growing list of things he hadn't told me.

Chris and Tommy were like statues behind him as he spoke. Seriously, it was as if they weren't even breathing. The only thing that moved on them was their eyes, constantly sweeping the room and windows, alert and ready. Was this how enforcers were supposed to act? If it was, then our pack was more screwed up than I had thought.

"Don't think you've actually thought this one out," I cut in when Aidan paused to yawn for at least the twentieth time. "Have you considered that Dad's going to notice Tiff isn't around? If you're not here, who's going to stop him from trying to seek her out to get the wolves she promised him?"

Tiffany had won by default when I refused to fight for alpha female, accepting the role and technically becoming Aidan's mate. Her reign hadn't lasted long. She had been the star of the video Erika had gotten, her leading man, my dad. She had conspired with him for reasons none of us knew, agreeing to send some female wolves to the cougars because, as my dad put it, his boys liked some fight in their women, and the werewolves would heal faster. Once I saw that video, everything changed. I hadn't been able to not fight. I couldn't stand back and do nothing. Not when *my* wolves were in danger. So I fought. And I won. I killed her.

I shuddered at the memory. There were times when I swore I could still taste her blood on my tongue. I knew I should have felt sick over the whole thing, but I didn't. Really, the only thing that got to me was that for a short time, Aidan had belonged to someone else. I couldn't feel bad for taking the life of someone that would willingly risk the lives of my pack members. My inner-wolf wouldn't let me hold onto the feeling even if I had wanted to.

"Yeah, I thought about it," Aidan said and yawned again. "That's why I'm going with the team. It would make sense that Tiff would be with me since she's supposed to be the alpha female, my partner."

A pang of jealousy worked its way through my chest. *Partner.* I guessed I should have been thankful he didn't call her his mate, but nope, I wasn't. *Partner* was just as bad. I swallowed down a growl. "And me?" I asked and winced inwardly at the bitter tone in my voice. I swallowed hard. "What am I supposed to do?"

He arched a brow, and a crooked smirk appeared. "You're part of the team now, aren't you?"

"Hold up," I said. A shocked laugh worked its way out of my throat, and my eyes widened. He couldn't be serious. He just couldn't. I fixed him with what I was sure was a stunned glare. "You really think going with Jared and me to hunt them down is a good idea? 'Cause, it's not."

God, it really wasn't.

How was I supposed to spend that much time with him and not let my struggle show? How was I supposed to pretend that Jared was the one I really wanted? Even sitting here in the same room as Aidan was a challenge. My inner-wolf was restless; I was restless. I could still feel his arms around me, the heat of his body pressed against me. And I couldn't believe the way my body was responding to his scent as if it belonged to me and no one else as if I had to have it or die trying to get it. It was crazy but as crazy as it was, I found myself drawing in another deep breath, letting the sweetness and the greens and the power of his aroma fill my lungs.

I trembled, and my inner-wolf stirred, swirling my own scent around me. *I need to tell him the truth,* I thought, as I watched him close his eyes. His nostrils flared, and then he winced as if I had just hurt him. Really not the reaction I had wanted, that was for sure, and just like that, my confessions died on the tip of my tongue.

Aidan shook himself, readjusting in his chair, and his smirk turned into a full smile. He chuckled. "Jade, whatever it is that you think is happening here, it isn't." The smile died, and his lips thinned. "My pack is being threatened. Like you just said, Tiff would give some of *my* wolves to them, and your dad is still expecting that to happen. You can hate me all you want later. Right now, the pack is more important."

That hurt and I groaned, trying to hide the pain his words were causing. It wasn't that I hated him. I just didn't trust him. "Get over yourself, Aidan," I said with as much snark as I could muster. *This was your choice,* I reminded myself sternly. *You're the one that walked away.* But even if I knew that it didn't lessen the pain, it didn't change how I really felt. I tried to spit out the truth, but the confession was stuck in my throat. I swallowed a few quick swallows, then I sighed. "We don't even know why she was going to do it. What was she getting out of it? We need to be here. We need to try and get the information out of him."

"No, we don't," Aidan said. He held my eyes for a long moment and let out a windy breath. "This really isn't up for discussion."

The rumble of a diesel engine pulling into the driveway caught my attention, stopping me from snapping out something that most likely wouldn't have helped. I glanced over my shoulder to the window. Jared. His truck was a monster, diesel with dual back tires. He killed the engine, and the team slowly piled out.

Jared didn't bother to knock, instead just barging in as if it were his house. The team hung back as he walked in the door, kicking off his shoes. His gaze swept the room before settling on me. He looked calm enough, although I could see he was pissed. It was in his eyes, the flecks of gold, the hard edges. I grinned at him, hopping off the couch. "Hey, baby, what took you so long?"

Jared watched me closely as I made my way across the room. He was in black jeans and a black, form-fitting tee. His fists clenched at his sides, the muscles in his forearms roped and straining. I stopped in front of him, overly aware of everyone watching us, specifically Aidan. My inner-wolf bucked and fought me, begging me to back up walk away. But I didn't.

Jared stared down at me, unblinking and unmoving, for a moment longer, and at that moment, he was impossible to read. His face was a mask, his scent calm-ish. His arm snaked out, wrapping around my waist, pulling me against him, and I squealed in surprise. "Couldn't find Erika," he said, finally. He leaned down, pressing his lips to mine. His lips were warm and moist, his kiss was rough and demanding.

Something dark and wild, and frantic surged through me. I stood rigid in his arms. I knew what he was doing, marking his territory. Showing Aidan I was taken. My inner-wolf bucked some more, furious with me. The only thought I had as I fought against her protests was that Jared was so not the cheese to my macaroni. *Darn you, Mac, for putting that thought in there!*

I sighed when he broke away, and he grinned, clearly taking the sigh as something more than just relief that the kiss was over. He winked and then let go. As he stepped past me, he asked, "What's my girl doing here?"

"She's my partner," Aidan replied coolly. "We had some business to deal with."

I cringed. I couldn't stop it. And I couldn't turn around. I felt dirty, filthy, letting him kiss me like that, mark me as his, but I didn't know what else to do. As far as everyone else was concerned, I was with Jared. Beck was the only one who knew the full truth, and he was keeping it quiet, just as Jared and I had planned.

The guys stood just outside the door, grinning at me as if they actually thought this was funny. Landon leaned into Beck and whispered something that I was glad I couldn't hear because I was sure I would want to deck him if I had. He was grinning at me, a grin that was both knowing and condemning. Whatever he had said, it made Beck laugh hard.

I was about to tell them to shut up and get inside when Jared said, "Jade, come here."

I cut a dirty look at the team before turning around. I mustered up the sweetest smile I could and started toward him. "What do you mean you can't find Erika?"

Jared was already sitting on the couch, his arms draping over the back, and his glare was fixed on Aidan. "Exactly what it sounds like," he said without looking in my direction. "I don't know where she is."

I sat down beside him, pressing close, and nudged him with my shoulder, trying to pull his death stare off of Aidan. He didn't respond, so I nudged him again and wiggled against his side.

I risked a look at Aidan. His glare was fixed on me. His jaw ticked. His nostrils flared. His hands gripped the armrests, his fingers turning white. The butterflies in my stomach made themselves known, flapping and fluttering. The jealousy that flashed in his eyes stole my breath, and a hot blush streaked to my cheeks.

"Who are the statues?" Jared asked, tensing further. I knew he could smell the spike in my scent and hear my frantic heartbeat, but I couldn't make myself calm down.

I shifted my focus to Jared, snuggling a bit closer. "They're friends of Aidan's." My voice squeaked a little, and I cleared it. "Um, they're kind of joining your team."

"Your idea?" he asked, glancing down at me. The warning in his eyes was clear, and again I tried to tone my scent down.

I shook my head. "No. But we could use the help, don't you think?"

For an incredibly tense moment, Jared didn't say a word. The team crowded around us, along the back of the couch, and Beck, Landon, Mark, and Craig touched me one by one. Whether the hands were there for support or to show Aidan they'd staked a claim to me, I didn't know.

"Anything you want, kitten," Jared finally said. His arm draped around me then, pushing off all the hands that had found their way to my shoulders, and his body relaxed as he pulled me into his side. He kissed the top of my head, breathing me in, and then asked, "So what's this business about that was so important that you forgot to call me before ditching school and rushing over here?"

CHAPTER 7

AIDAN

I was sweating. My boxers, yeah, were soaked. I felt as if I were sitting in a puddle. No, it was more like a lake. Had the team agreed? Had Jared agreed? I scrubbed at my face. I felt as if I were losing my mind. Her scent worked through my system, screwing with my brain. I didn't know if the constant flares of her scent were for him or for me. Damn, it almost seemed as if the fragrance was spiking for both of us. My biceps flexed. My inner-wolf shifted. I started to get up, but my legs wouldn't move. This was a nightmare. It had to be. The kind where I knew I needed to run, but my legs wouldn't obey. Did any of that just happen?

Jade smiled. She waved. Jared wrapped an arm over her shoulder and kissed her lightly. He winked at me; clearly, he knew this was torture for me, and I was sure he loved every second of it. I was living in a damn nightmare. The door shut. The truck started. And I sat there watching as my mate left me again with Jared.

"Well, that was ... interesting," Tommy said, running a rough hand over his clean, hairless head. He paced a few steps, tugged at the collar of his polo shirt, and then dropped onto the couch.

"He sure has some hold on her," Chris added with a long whistle. He was sitting on the arm of the couch, his arms crossed over his chest and legs stretched out, folded at the ankles. "I've never seen an alpha female or any female fight so hard to ignore the call of her mate." His chiseled face looked harder under all the creases lining his narrowed eyes.

I swallowed hard. Her scent lingered. Fruits and almonds. My muscles flexed again. *Shit!* "She's not ..."

"Yeah, she is," Tommy said, cutting me off. "It's pretty obvious, kid. She feels it. Jared sees it, too. Her inner-wolf may want him, but she sure as hell doesn't."

What the hell just happened? I took another breath. I shifted in my chair. No one had argued. No one had challenged my decision. Jade agreed to everything. She even told Jared she wanted Chris and Tommy on the team, that she wanted me with them on the hunt. Where was the fight she had before Jared showed up? How the hell had he calmed her into a docile, obedient ... *Shit!*

For a second, I'd thought I still had a chance. A real chance. She'd melted against me like putty. I had smelled it. Her desire. Her need. But then he showed up. He calmed her. Her inner-wolf wanted him. The scent was there. She had been throwing it off like crazy when he had walked through that door. He possessed her in a way that I'd dreamed of having her since the moment I had met her.

I shifted again, sweating even more. "Dom?"

He looked just as confused as me. He sat on the couch beside Tommy, one arm over the back, staring at the door with a big question mark on his forehead. His brow furrowed, and he shook his head from side to side a few times before his hazel eyes finally focused on me. He shrugged. "I told you before she's stubborn, but if I had to guess, this whole Jared thing really has nothing to do with you. Jade might hold a grudge, but she wouldn't do this just to hurt you. She's not that much of a bitch. My best guess is she actually likes him. It's obvious her inner-wolf does." His tone was dry as if his throat had closed up, and the look he shot me said he didn't really believe what he was saying, but that didn't matter. All I heard was *likes him.*

"Likes him," I echoed. My jaw ticked. My eyes flared. *Get it together!* "Likes him," I said again. Every muscle in my body screamed as I forced myself to stay put and not go after her.

Dominic didn't miss my sparking rage. He stood up, moving behind the couch, putting a safe distance between us. "I can call Mac," he blurted. "See if she found out anything this morning."

"This morning?" My voice was a growl. My scent flared. His mask splintered and cracked. He paled. His head bowed. I was falling apart. I could feel it deep within my gut. My nostrils flared as I sucked in more and more of her lingering scent. *Mine,* my inner-wolf, growled into my mind. Dammit! She was mine. Every instinct I had was urging me to go after her. *Pull it together!*

"Yeah." Dominic tugged a hand through his blond hair, his head bowing further. "I sent her over there this morning."

"Dammit, Dom!" I jumped up and started to pace. My skin was crawling, my inner-wolf howling, begging to be let out. "Can't you follow anything I say? I told you both to keep away from her. She wanted space."

"Aidan," Tommy choked out in a hoarse voice. He stood up and stepped in front of me, placing a hand on my shoulder, and squeezed. "Keep it together, kid."

I closed my eyes, taking in a deep, centering breath. It didn't help. God, was her scent getting stronger?

"Jade doesn't know what she wants," Dominic whispered. "And Trevor found tracks outside Mac's house this morning. She can't stay at home. Her dad won't let her move in with her mate, and he won't let Trevor stay there, so being at Jade's with the team always hanging around is the safest place for her."

I glanced at him then, my scent still flaring, and he shuddered. His eyes were full of concern, full of misery.

"Aidan," Chris growled through his teeth. "Tone the scent down. It went well. She'll see her dad in the morning. Play up the Jared bit and then meet us. He won't see it coming. And it will give you exactly what you need. The more time you spend with her, the better chance you'll have at getting her away from Jared. We went over this."

"You don't get it!" I snarled. "That team has never agreed with anything I've said. And, Jade, she's not that easy to convince of anything. Something's not right here. Something else is going on." The rational part of my mind knew he was right. Everything was going as planned, and tomorrow I would have the entire day to try and talk to her, begging her to forgive me, but the other part was crazed, furious that she had left with him — again. Right then, I was certain she had given up on me.

An uneasy silence crowded the room. Tommy dropped his hand from my shoulder and took a step back. He huffed out a breath. "Look, kid, we have to get going," he said. "You heard Jared. He wants us to stay with Landon. Don't want to give that team any reason not to trust us. We'll email you with anything we find out. Get some sleep. It'll look better tomorrow."

JADE

I had to force myself out of the house, one foot in front of the other. I felt wrecked. Shattered. Jared wouldn't talk to me. I got in the truck. We dropped off the team. And still, he hadn't said a word.

Aidan's scent clung to me. On my skin. In my hair. Could Jared smell it? Was that the reason for his maddening silent treatment? He had to know I let Aidan take me into his arms. He had to know that my heart was still racing, that my inner-wolf was doing backflips, begging me to go back. That had to be it. The problem was I didn't really care if he knew. Did that make me a bitch? *Probably.*

He pulled into my driveway. Turned off the truck. He didn't move. I shifted in my seat, opened my mouth, and then shut it. His knuckles were white. His jaw clenched. The muscles in his forearms, straining. He had never been this mad at me before, not even when I wasn't one of them and despised the pack. I swallowed hard, popped the door open, and got out. He would talk when he was ready. Hopefully.

Mom was sitting on the couch when I walked in. She glanced at me as I went by and frowned but didn't say anything. I figured I looked as bad as I felt.

I went straight to my room, sat on the bed, and waited. And waited. And waited.

The glowing red numbers on my alarm clock flipped by, minute by agonizing minute. An hour passed, and still, Jared hadn't come in. I wondered for a moment if he had left, but I knew I would have heard his monster of a truck startup if he had.

I sighed and spent a few minutes debating on whether I should go back out there and try to talk to him. But instead of facing him (yeah, I was being a coward), I dug my phone out of my pocket and fired off a message to Erika asking her where she'd been all afternoon. She should have been accessible. She should have been by my side through that meeting. Erika answered immediately. *At home studying.*

I stared at the message for a long moment. Had Jared even tried to find her, or was she lying to me? I wasn't sure. Jared didn't like Erika, like at all, and she loathed him. I wouldn't have been surprised if she'd simply ignored his calls, and at the same time, it wouldn't have shocked me if he hadn't even tried to reach her.

God, I hated feeling like this. Lost and confused and sad.

Really, really sad. The pack had always seemed so close from the outside looking in. A tight-knit group. But the reality was so different. It was like living in a constant power struggle, never knowing who you could trust and who wanted to watch you crash and burn. I was certain Aidan was up to something with his little plan of spending time with Jared and me, and I knew Jared was up to something. He always was. And I was stuck in the middle, wanting someone I shouldn't want, and with someone I didn't want. On top of all that, if Aidan's plan worked the way he wanted, I would be forced to pass judgment on my dad. As a friend of the pack, his betrayal meant I would be issuing a death sentence. The thought of sentencing my father to death was just too much, way too much. No matter how evil he was, he was still my dad. I was still his little girl. Was it completely wrong that I didn't want to be part of the hunt? *Most likely.*

Another twenty minutes passed, and the front door finally opened and closed. I heard Jared's whispered conversation with my mom, too low to really make out what was said. Then his footsteps, clunking up the steps. A knock on a door. "Trevor knows you're staying here?" Jared asked.

"Um, yeah, you want me to call him?" Marcy asked. She sounded nervous.

"Yes." Jared didn't sound happy. I squeezed my eyes shut, pulled in a deep breath, and pushed myself up. Jared didn't turn around when I opened the door. He stiffened, his neck tensed. "Jade, go wash that smell off of you," he said, the words clipped, brisk.

I felt sick. Hot and cold and sick. "Is everything okay?" I asked, looking at Marcy. I took a step and placed a hand on Jared's back. He flinched, and I let my hand fall away. *I'm such an ass-hat.* "She can stay here if she wants, Jared."

"Not if her mate hasn't okayed it, she can't. I'm not housing her without speaking to him. Jade, go." His tone was cold, challenging even.

Marcy smiled. It was forced, a little shaky. She mouthed *It's okay*, and made a shooing gesture at me.

I hesitated for a second, staring at his back, willing him to turn around, but he didn't. Marcy scrolled through her contacts and gave me a pointed look before thumbing the screen and bringing the phone to her ear.

I turned away, took the few steps to the bathroom, and let the door click shut behind me, sinking to the floor. At that moment, I hated, *hated*, being at home. It didn't feel like home, not anymore. It just felt like one big lie.

I hugged my knees to my chest. I hated feeling like this. Since taking over as alpha female, I'd spent the last few days doing what I thought was right. I had stayed away from everyone, the pack, Aidan ... I'd been convincing myself that working with the team was the right thing to do. Pretending to be with Jared was the right thing to do. Stay away. Keep them safe. But as I sat in Aidan's house, listening to his plan, realizing that he needed help, something had dawned on me. I was no better than him. I had condemned him for lying to me, for manipulating me, but really, I was just as guilty. And watching him glare at Jared made me realize that I was hurting him just as badly as he had hurt me.

God, I suck!

Marcy was already sleeping by the time I finished scrubbing Aidan's scent from my body. I stood outside her door for a few minutes listening to her soft snores, debating on sneaking in there and hiding until the morning. But I didn't.

The lights were off in my room when I eased the door open. Jared's steady breathing came from beside my bed. I listened for a moment, trying to judge if he was really sleeping. I couldn't tell. I tiptoed across the room and eased myself into bed, trying not to disturb him. His breath hitched. He shuffled around, and I let my head hang over the bed, glancing down at him. "Jared, I know you're awake. Will you just yell at me already and get it over with?"

He was lying on his back, the comforter pulled to his waist. Moonlight streamed in from the window, basking him in a silvery glow. He didn't have a shirt on, and his hands were folded behind his head. He sighed. "I don't know what you're talking about."

"Come on," I said, hating how raw my voice sounded and how guilty I felt. "This cold shoulder crap is getting old. I know you're pissed."

"Pissed is so not what I'm feeling right now, little girl. Not even close."

I shimmied off the bed, sinking down beside him on the floor. "Then enlighten me."

He groaned, long and loud. "Go to sleep, Jade. It's going to be a long day tomorrow."

"I can't sleep knowing you're pissed off at me." I inched a bit closer. "What was I supposed to do? Refuse to go? He sent that Tommy guy. He literally had me dragged from school."

Jared opened his eyes then and rolled over, propping his head up on an elbow. "You think this is because you were at his house?"

I threw my hands up in the air. "Well, what else could your mood be about?"

"This was your idea." He waved a hand between us. "You wanted this to be believable. You wanted us to be believable." His eyes flared bright gold. "His scent was all over you. In your hair. On your neck. What did you do? Trip and fall into him? This may just be a game to you, Jade, but to me, it's not. So stop jerking me around."

I felt his words like a slap in the face. Something splintered inside me. It was as if I were being held underwater. The pressure built and built until my insides felt as if they were filled with hairline fractures. Tears — damn tears — filled my eyes. I would have preferred him yelling or telling me off. But this ... this hurt. I couldn't breathe. I gasped for air, and it burned through my lungs. There was just so much pressure. Be an alpha. Claim a mate. Stop the cougars. Deal with my dad. Maybe even have him killed. Forget or forgive Aidan. Learn pack laws. Fix the pack. Run the pack with a man that made my body sing and my blood boil and one that I couldn't trust. Pretend to be in love with Jared without hurting him. I gasped again. The tears stung, brimming in my eyes and spilling over.

"Don't do that," he said, brushing a thumb hastily across my cheek. "Don't make me feel like the asshole here. You were practically panting over him. Do you really think no one noticed?"

"I'm sorry," I said and hiccupped. "I ... I ..." I huffed and hiccupped again. I shrugged my shoulders. "I don't want to feel this way about Aidan, but I'm his. He's mine. I can feel it in my bones." I pressed my hand to my chest, gripping my shirt in my fist. "I feel it here."

Jared rolled onto his back, and he closed his eyes. Clearly, he was done with the conversation. I watched his chest rise and fall for a few breaths, noting the tension, the unevenness of each lungful.

"I'm going to tell him the truth about us, Jared," I whispered, turning from him and climbing back in bed. I pulled the comforter up to my neck and waited for a response, but when all that followed was another unsteady breath, I continued, "I'm sorry that this situation sucks so much for you. And I'm really sorry that I'm such a crappy fake girlfriend. I won't blame you if you want to call it quits, but I have to tell him the truth."

"I'm not going to give up on you, Jade," he said, his voice thick with emotion that sounded more like anger than anything else. The man didn't have a warm cell in his body. At that moment, I was sure of it. Anger and hatred always won out with him.

"You should," I said, meaning every word. "You really should." *Because you don't have a chance,* I thought, not able to say it out loud.

AIDAN

I was a wolf, and I stood below her window.

I knew I shouldn't have come here, but after seeing Jade today, I needed more. Maybe I was just a sucker for punishment. Yeah, that was probably it. The window was open, just a sliver, and her sweet, sweet scent washed out. She sounded ... sad, angry, frustrated. Her voice was just barely a whisper by the time it reached my ears, just loud enough that I could pick up bits and pieces of the conversation. I shouldn't have been listening. I shouldn't have come. And I knew I needed to leave, but I couldn't.

Maybe it was my guilt that held me in place.

There were many things a wolf could do that wouldn't actually complete mating, and in the last hour, I had done pretty much all of them.

After everyone had left my house and I'd been alone with Jade's tormenting scent, I'd needed a distraction. And I found it in the all too willing arms of Erika. I wasn't proud of it. Truthfully, I felt more than a little sick about what I'd just done, but even if I felt bad about it, I had still done it.

I had left my house five minutes after Dominic went home, and I'd ended up on Erika's doorstep. I told myself it was because I wanted to know why she hadn't been available for Jade. Erika was her beta, and as far as I was concerned, there should never, *never*, be a reason for her not to be reachable when Jade needed her. Dealing with Erika was the one thing I knew I could do. But one thing had led to another, and before I knew it, I was in her room with her tearing off my clothes. She had been more than happy to provide her alpha with the relief that I'd needed, and dammit, I'd been more than willing to let her. Her lips, her hands, caressing my entire body was ... a short-lived relief, effectively shattered by a text message from Jade.

I couldn't believe how easy it had been for Erika to lie to Jade

— her alpha. She had glanced at the phone and quickly fired off a message: *At home studying.*

That small interruption had been more than enough to stop everything. I had grabbed my clothes, yanking them on as she tried to convince me to stay.

And now here I was planted on the lawn outside Jade's house, listening as she begged Jared to forgive her.

I'd been telling myself that Jade was probably doing the same things with Jared as I had been doing with Erika. She might not be mated with him yet, but I knew they were sharing a room, and I was sure her bed.

Jade's voice rose. I could hear the tears. Damn, I could feel the heartbreak as her voice reached my ears. "I don't want to feel this way about Aidan, but I'm his. He's mine. I can feel it in my bones." She paused and then whispered, "I feel it here."

Clearly, I'd been wrong. So very, very wrong.

I'm his. He's mine. The words beat at my mind, repeating over and over. My throat started to close up. My heartbeat started to race. The beginning of a growl built in my chest, and I fought against my inner-wolf to keep quiet. I began to back away. Self-disgust filled me like a nest of snakes writhing in my gut. My inner-wolf tried to hold me in place, demanding me to go and retrieve her, get her away from Jared, but I fought it. I'd been sure she'd been hiding something from me, but I hadn't imagined it would be something like this. Not with the way her inner-wolf reacted to Jared. I backed up a little more. I needed to get out of there. I needed to think. I needed to process this. And after a few steps, I pivoted and ran.

I'm such a jackass.

CHAPTER 8

JADE

I woke up alone. Jared's bed was gone, the blankets, the pillows, all put away. It was weird. He never picked up anything. Never. His wallet wasn't on the dresser, neither were his keys. I rolled over, glancing at the clock: 6:08. My heartbeat doubled, and a nervous knot yanked tight in my belly.

Panic fluttered through me. I yanked the blankets off. He wouldn't just leave. He wouldn't. Not with Dad coming home today, even if I was a crappy fake girlfriend, even if I'd said I was going to tell Aidan the truth. Jared wouldn't …

I was out of bed in a flash, and just as my feet hit the floor, the door swung open. I skidded to a stop. Jared stood in the doorway, a towel cinched low on his hips. His black hair was wet. Beads of water slid down his sculpted chest. My breath hitched. A hot flush rushed to my cheeks, and I dropped my head, peeking at him through my lashes. My heartbeat skittered within my chest, and my panic eased slightly.

His nostrils flared, and he shuddered — a little — as he scanned me over. "What's wrong, kitten?" he asked, his voice husky. He crossed the few steps to me and cupped my cheeks, forcing me to look at him. He searched my face. Whatever he saw there made him smile.

"I thought you left," I said, hating the tremor in my voice. "I thought you just up and left."

He frowned. "I told you I'm not going to give up on you."

"But your stuff?" I flailed a frantic hand toward the dresser and then to his missing bed. Right at that moment, I realized something. Jared wasn't just the leader of my team. He wasn't just my pretend mate. At some point in the last few days, he had become a friend. A person that I could count on.

He smirked and chuckled, clearly enjoying my panic and knowing him, reading something into it that wasn't there. "Put it away. You're always bitching at me to pick up after myself."

He was looking down at me in a way that was far too personal. His hands fell from my face, dipping to my shoulders. A whole new panic bloomed within my belly. I took a step back, wanting to put some much-needed space in between us. Jared's presence in my life might have started to feel comfortable, but he wasn't home — he never would be. "Nothing's changed, Jared," I said evenly. "I'm going to tell him today."

He opened his mouth, and he looked as if he were about to protest when I heard someone clear their throat and a familiar gruff voice said, "What the hell do you think you're doing?"

I'm not ready for this, a voice in my head shrieked. The temperature in the room dropped to freezing. My stomach twisted, my throat closed up. Jared turned and backed up a few steps, and I swiveled and blinked.

"Daddy?" I said. He looked furious. I took a step back, right into Jared. His face was streaked red, his hands balled. His large frame filled the doorway, and his jaw started twitching. I'd never seen him like this before. Never.

His clothes were rumpled, his jeans filled with dirt stains. Tired lines littered his eyes. Dad's lips thinned. "Get some damn clothes on, boy!" he shouted, his fists clenching tighter.

A rock-hard lump formed in my throat, and the door across the hallway swung open. "Mr. Shaw, what's going on?" Marcy asked. I couldn't see her past the wall that was my dad. Dad didn't turn around, didn't give any indication that he had heard her. His face reddened further, and his gaze was fixed on Jared.

"Jeff," Jared said coolly. He slipped a possessive hand on my hip. "Nice of you to finally come home."

Dad took a step into the room. He was a big man, burly and thick, but he had never looked so much like a bear before, snarly, angry. "Don't test my patience, Jared."

I brushed Jared's hand off me and took a step away, my cheeks burning with a flush. "Daddy, we were just ..."

"In the middle of something," Jared said, cutting me off. He snaked an arm around my waist and pulled me back against him.

"Let go," I said, tugging at his hand. His arm was like a vice grip. Maybe it was the decision I'd made last night, but Jared's hands on me felt more wrong than they ever had before. Even my inner-wolf squirmed and shrunk, wanting away from him.

Act the part! a voice screamed through my head. I stiffened, fighting back the growl that worked its way through my chest, and I softened my smile and batted my eyes. "Daddy, you knew he was living here. I told you. I thought you were happy about it."

His eyes landed on me then, burning like fire. "And you also told me you were mated, but you're not."

Crap! Crap! Crap! This was so not the plan. I sucked in a breath. He wasn't supposed to know. We needed him to believe I was mated. *Crap!* I didn't know what to say. I sucked in another breath and blurted, "What? He is my mate."

He stepped closer. "Don't lie to me, Jade. By now, I'm sure you've been told what I am. I can smell it. You haven't mated. And you're not going to. Not with him." His blazing gaze rose, looking over my head. "Now, you listen to me closely. Take your hands off my daughter and call the alpha. I want him here, now." His tone was nothing short of a challenge.

Jared bristled, and he growled, long and low, tightening his grip on me. His muscles started to shudder, rippling beneath his skin.

"Mac," I shouted. "Mac, get back in your room and call Aidan!"

AIDAN

The wind cut through my fur as I broke into a full run. Her scent was thick in the air, teasing my senses, making my heart race. She yipped, a playful sound, and I set chase. I needed to find her.

From the corner of my eye, I saw her dash out of the trees. She skidded to a stop in front of me. I slowed. Stopped. Sunlight streamed through the branches overhead, winking off her midnight black coat. She licked my nose and rubbed along my side before sitting on her haunches in front of me. Her body trembled. Her fur receded. My heart stopped. Anticipation clawed through me. If I were human, my palms would have been sweating. Her face started to shift. Her smile was shy but bright, like the sun and the moon basking me in light.

And then my phone rang.

I groaned, sitting straight up. The phone rang again. I groped at the nightstand, snagging it up. I thumbed the screen, brought the phone to my ear, and said, "Aidan."

"You need to get to Jade's, like now." Marcy's voice screeched through my groggy brain, and I jerked the phone away, waiting for the ringing in my ears to stop before pressing it back in place.

I groaned again. "Breathe, Mac," I said, scrubbing at my face. "What's going on?" My voice was thick and heavy with sleep. I blinked a few times, clearing my fuzzy eyes.

"I can't breathe. Mr. Shaw is about to take off Jared's head." She sucked in a loud, shaky breath. "The team's not here yet. Jade's starting to freak out. Jared looks like he's about to shift. He's holding onto her, Aidan. He won't let her go."

Shit! I was out of bed and yanking on my jeans before she'd finished her tirade. *This isn't the plan!* I launched out of my room, taking the stairs at a run. "Mac, go to your room, okay? Lock your door." I grabbed my keys off the table and bolted out the door. "Don't come out until I get there, no matter what. Call Dom. Call the team. Get them there. And call your mate."

"Aidan, she needs ..."

"No," I snapped, cutting her off. My chest squeezed tight. *Shit! Shit! Shit!* I got in my car and started it up as I sucked in a steadying breath. "Jade can take care of herself. Stay in your room." I thumbed my phone and tossed it on the front seat, praying I was right.

JADE

Dad's nostrils flared. He stood deathly still, his blazing gaze fixed on Jared. Where the heck was Aidan? It had to have been five minutes since Marcy had retreated, locking her door. I really didn't know how much longer I could keep this up.

Dad's lips thinned. He waved a hand, beckoning me to him, and I shook my head. He didn't try to come closer. I figured he could see how close Jared was to losing control. As it was, he was just barely holding onto his human form. The tension in the room was suffocating, pressing against me from all sides. Right then, I knew I couldn't wait any longer. I needed to calm Jared down. I needed to act like an alpha.

I turned in Jared's arms, reaching up, resting a hand on his cheek. I smirked and said, "No dogs allowed in the house."

He growled. His eyes were completely gold, not a speck of the typical black-brown left. They were fixed on the doorway, on my dad. His claws dug into my back, sharp enough that I gasped as they shredded through my shirt. Any harder, and he'd break the skin, too.

My imprint heated. I needed to get his attention, to calm him. My scent gathered, and I sent out a small short burst. Jared snapped his gaze to mine. He growled again. His muscles rippled. I grinned, rolled up on my toes, and pressed my lips to his. His claws dug deeper, and I bit back a screech as a sharp pain shot through my back. I looked up, my lips still against his, and whispered, "I said no dogs allowed in the house."

Another growl sounded from behind me. Lower. Deeper. I stiffened. So did Jared. A familiar scent filled the air. My nostrils flared. Raw power trembled around me. Jared's knees buckled. Another spasm raked through him, rippling against me. He stiffened and then gave his head a good, thorough shake, and he let his arm fall from me. His breathing evened out, and darn it, mine quickened.

A short burst of adrenaline rushed through me. "Aidan, stop!" The challenge was there, the command clear in my voice. He was going to ruin everything. My inner-wolf clawed through me, trying to rip free. His scent worked through me, stronger, pushing on my nerves, speaking to my inner-wolf in a way only he could. I spun around as another growl ripped through my room, and my gaze met his.

The alpha. I couldn't breathe. *The alpha.* I'd never seen him like this before. *My alpha.* His presence filled the room. His broad shoulders rolled back, his chest puffed out. Corded muscles lined his neck, shoulders, arms. I licked my lips and pulled in a breath. *Home.*

Aidan studied me for a few seconds, and the power, hunger, and strength in that stare left me feeling dizzy. "Jade," he whispered on a breath. He held out a hand, and I reached for it. I saw my hand moving, my inner-wolf forcing me forward, and I couldn't stop it.

Dad barked out a laugh. It slid through me like ice in my veins, and I stopped mid-step. He stepped toward me grabbed my shirt, tugging the neckline down just enough to reveal the burning imprint on my chest. "So my daughter won the games."

AIDAN

Rage pounded through me like a series of waves crashing against my skull. I couldn't think. A growl worked its way out from my chest. There was another man, basically naked, pressed against my mate. Her lips were on his. His claws raked along her back. The rational part of my brain told me this was okay. She was playing a part. She'd confirmed that last night, even if she didn't know, I knew it yet. The guy holding onto her wasn't a real threat, but my inner-wolf growled anyway, *I'll kill him.*

Jeff's voice barely registered in my ears. I heard nothing but the rage. Saw nothing but her. I reached for her whispered her name. She froze. A hand tugged at her shirt. A light shine of sweat covered her forehead as she stared down at her imprint, flickering with a soft white glow.

And then a fist swung at me. It connected. My nose snapped and crunched, and blood rushed down my face.

"Dad!" Jade shouted. Her voice was panicked, scared.

The rage pounded again. Harder. Faster. Her fear fed it. I could taste my own blood seeping into my mouth. My scent thickened. I had to protect my mate. Nothing else mattered. My chest heaved with each breath. Right then, I was more animal than human. I grabbed Jeff, tossing him against the wall, the meaty palm of my hand pressed against his throat.

"Aidan, stop it!" Jade commanded. I felt her voice in my bones, vibrating through me. She growled. Her hand wrapped around my wrist, tugging, as she tried to dislodge my palm from her father's neck. "Think!" she screamed. "You need to think!"

"Take her and get out," I growled, shifting my gaze to the useless enforcer, standing off to the side of the room with his gaze cast to the floor. "You touch her, though, and I'll kill you." It was more than a threat; it was a promise.

"Screw off, Aidan," Jared snarled. He lifted his head slightly, and his face contorted with fury.

I got in his face, tight and fast, dropping my hand from Jeff's neck. "You'll do what I say."

CHAPTER 9

AIDAN

My nose throbbed. Blood still flowed freely down my face. Jared squared his shoulders, dipped his chin, and let out a low growl. The look he gave me was pure challenge.

Every muscle in my body stiffened. I rolled my shoulders back and puffed out my chest only an inch from his. A growl built in my throat, and at that moment, all I saw was red.

"Jared, you need to go," Jade said, her tone a sweet melody of power and authority. She turned to me, jutting her arm between us, and placed a hand firmly on my heaving chest. She shoved, trying to push me back a step, and I let her. "Aidan, you need to calm down."

My nostrils flared, and my throat tightened. I wanted to rip him apart from limb to limb. *No one touches my mate. No one.* Not now. Not after hearing the truth of how she felt last night.

Jade shoved at me again. My nerves were on fire, searing within me. I fixed my gaze on her. Shivers chased down her shoulders and back. She was breathing hard and fast in ragged bursts. The sight of her shivers broke through the murderous haze that was clouding my brain a little, and instead of launching at Jared and ending him, which, yeah, was exactly what I wanted to do, I growled, "Get him out of here." My scent ramped up, and I hated to admit it, but I thoroughly enjoyed watching Jared shudder under its weight.

"Aidan, I'm serious," she growled. Golden veins streaked through her eyes, and she gritted her teeth. "I can't deal with all this testosterone. Everyone needs to calm down."

I watched as another shiver rushed over her skin, and then I forced my eyes closed, and I took a long, long moment to breathe. It was the only thing I could think of doing, to try to calm myself down. Her hand stayed on my chest, shaking. I was exhausted and torn up from the inside out. My self-control was cracking under the pressure of the rage that crashed through my veins, but for her, I would do just about anything. So I breathed and breathed, forcing my inner-wolf to stand down. When he finally receded to a far corner of my mind, I looked down at her, and my heart pulled and squeezed as if a hand had wrapped itself around it and was determined to rip it from my chest.

Her hand dropped from my chest. I almost reached out to grab it. I hated the disconnected feeling. Hated it. But I didn't stop her. Her shivers increased, and she shouted out a slew of obscenities that I'd never heard from her before. And as I listened, resolve tightened in my chest. Whatever game she was playing with Jared was going to stop. Now.

I watched her closely. Couldn't pull my eyes away from her, actually. She looked up at me, really looked at me, and she whimpered a deep, throaty whimper. Her swearing stopped, and her eyes softened as she brought her fingers to her full lips. That small gesture almost did me in — almost — and again, I found myself fighting not to take her in my arms.

And then Jeff laughed, a deep rumbling sound. "You son of a bitch," he said. I glanced at him over my shoulder before I turned to meet him straight on, ready to throw myself in front of Jade if I had to. Sharp clarity washed over me. Jeff — the monster who had been ready to take some of my wolves for his sick, twisted pleasure — stood in front of me laughing.

The blood still trickled down my face, but it was starting to slow. The pain was dull, just a small throb as my nose began to heal. The rage was beginning to fade, and in its place, something cold settled in my bones. *There goes the plan.*

But as I watched him, if I hadn't known any better, right then, I would have thought he actually cared. Although he was still chuckling, his eyes were glassy as they shifted between Jade and me. His expression was a mix of shattered amusement. He pulled in a breath, shook his head, and said, "You made her fight. Tricked her into competing in the games, and then you just let her go. You've been lying to me for days while I've been out there risking everything I have for you and your damn pack." He laughed again, a shocking kind of sound, and his lips curved into a bemused smile.

"You broke my nose," I said and grabbed the hem of my shirt, pulling it up to mop up some of the warm blood that was still dribbling down my chin. I kept my glare focused on him as I tried to make sense of his reaction. But, oh hell, I couldn't. He had to understand that Jade being alpha female, put a gaping hole in his plans to secure female wolves from Tiffany, but if it bothered him at all, he wasn't showing it. But then, he wouldn't know that we knew his plans.

I let my now bloody shirt drop, and Jade whimpered again, her eyes fixed on my face. I smiled at her, just a small twitch of my lips. I couldn't help it. Honestly, it was kind of nice to see that she cared for once. It was just too bad. It took a broken nose for her to show it.

"You deserve more than a broken nose," Jeff said with a chuckle. "You're the sorriest excuse for an alpha this pack has ever had. She's supposed to be your mate, and you let Jared move in here." His grin widened, and he smacked me on the back as if we were old friends. "Why the hell haven't you claimed her yet?"

Okay, so that wasn't what I had expected. Jeff was grinning at me, all the tension he'd had moments ago was gone, and he looked ... happy? I looked him over. His eyes were bright with curiosity, not even a stitch of fear. His scent seemed ... calm and way too human. I didn't know if he could mask his emotions the same way he could hide the cougar smell. My gut told me that he didn't have a clue how much we knew. He wouldn't seem so relaxed if he did, so I went with it. I shrugged, a lazy lift of my shoulders. "Jared was your idea," I said, lifting a brow in question.

Jeff rolled his eyes and grunted. "Because you told me she lost. Mating her with one of the enforcers was the next best option."

JADE

"Enough," I hissed. "I'm not some darn prize. I'm not a piece of property you guys can just give away to any random guy you choose." I spun on my dad, the back of my neck and face burning with a flush. "God, Dad, how can you even talk about this in front of me? I'm supposed to be your little girl, remember?"

Dad looked a little ashamed. He cleared his throat and shifted awkwardly from one foot to the other. I threw my hands up in the air. This was so not cool. My dad chatting about me having sex was just not cool. I figured it shouldn't surprise me. I knew what kind of animal he really was, but still, he was my dad. Blood rushed to my face. Talk about embarrassment. At some point, the entire team had crowded in the doorway. Dominic was there, smirking, so were Marcy and Trevor. Leave it to my best friends to enjoy this epically embarrassing situation.

Aidan turned to me, staring down at me. The hem and collar of his shirt were soaked with blood. I scanned him over, watching the muscles tick in his arms and neck. His gaze went to Jared, hard and cold, before shifting back to me. The blood on his face was starting to dry, crusting up under his nose, down his chin.

And just like that, my humiliation shattered. I made a sound, a mix of a growl and whimper. I swallowed hard. He'd never looked so powerful before, so much like an alpha even with the blood and broken nose. His muscles were bunched, straining beneath his shirt. His chin dipped. His broad shoulders, squared. Confidence. Authority. It emanated from him.

My lips parted, my jaw dropped. *My alpha. My mate.* The words echoed through my mind. Right then, I couldn't remember why I had been so determined to stay away from him. My inner-wolf stirred as I deeply breathed in his scent.*Mine,* she agreed.

Something had changed with him. Something big. It was as if he were just now, in that very moment, finally stepping into his full authority as alpha male. I'd seen him do this before with the pack, but never with me. Never. He was soft with me. I made him weak. Even when he tried to stand strong, he always relented way before his point was made. But now he didn't look weak, not at all.

The butterflies in my stomach awoke, flapping and fluttering with excitement. *My alpha.* At that moment, all I saw was him. Everyone else faded, melted until it was as if they were just gone. It was just us.

Jared's hand settled on the small of my back, pulling me back to reality, and I quickly stepped away. If the plan hadn't already been blown apart, that small step had done it. None of them of my dad, Aidan, Jared, or the team missed that step. The step away from the man I claimed to want. I felt cold. Cold and drained and tired, as if every ounce of fight I had in me was just gone. Everything was ruined. Aidan's plan. My plan. All of it ruined.

I needed to get out of the room.

My thoughts began to leap and jump, nothing making sense. I needed a new plan, that was for sure, but my brain wasn't working. My dad looked so calm, caring even. It was wrong. Everything that was happening was just completely wrong. I glanced around a little frantically. There were enough pack members here to make sure he didn't go anywhere. I stepped toward the door. "Move," I said, pushing at the wall of enforcers blocking my way out, but they didn't budge. Clearly, I wasn't the only one feeling the power shift in our alpha male.

I shoved at Beck's chest, none too gently, but he stood firm, blocking my exit. He wouldn't look at me, his gaze fixed over my head, most likely on Aidan. He lifted a questioning brow, and after a long second, he stepped out of my way.

I glanced back at Aidan, waved a hand, beckoning him to follow me, and I headed into the bathroom.

CHAPTER 10

JADE

The bathroom door clicked shut behind me as I grabbed the washcloth from the towel rack. I didn't have to look to know that it was, in fact, Aidan that had followed; his presence filled the room with waves of power. I took the cloth to the sink, turned on the hot water, and shoved it under the flow. My muscles bunched and rolled beneath my skin, my inner-wolf begging to come out.

I kept my eyes fixed on the porcelain top of the vanity, and the bottom edge of the ornate, copper framed mirror, studying the swirls and twists of its floral design. The bathroom was large. My parents had renovated it a couple of years ago, pushing walls back and turning it into a spa-like retreat, with double sinks, a walk-in shower, and a separate soaker tub, but with the door closed and Aidan's heady scent filling the space, it felt tight and small and airless.

Once the cloth was soaked, I turned off the tap and slowly rung it out before finding enough nerve to turn to him. His expression was void of emotion, a blank slate. He leaned against the door, arms folded over his chest, his brown eyes watching my every move.

My hands were shaking, my heart pounding. I closed the short distance between us. I looked back up at him, and darn it, but I whimpered again. *So much blood.*

The sound softened him a little. He reached out and caressed my cheek, but when I pressed into the touch, he let his hand drop, hanging loosely by his side. His eyes searched my face, looking for something, but what I didn't have a clue. I felt the sting of tears welling up. I don't know why. The last thing I wanted to do was cry. Not for the alpha that had destroyed my life and ripped out my heart. His nose had already healed. He was fine. *But there's just so much blood.*

I blinked fast, banishing the tears. "Does it hurt?" I asked and then swallowed hard. I lifted my trembling hand and dabbed at the blood, wiping it away as best I could. "I hope it does. You've ruined everything." Even though I said the words, they held no real meaning. My voice was weak, straining against an onslaught of emotions blooming within my chest.

"No," he grunted. "It's already healed." He grabbed my wrist, holding my shaking hand still. "I did what was needed. You're not staying here any longer, Jade. This little game you're playing ends now. I'm taking you home, where you belong."

I clucked my tongue and dropped my gaze. More butterflies surfaced in my belly, and I breathed, "This is where I belong."

"Look me in the eyes and tell me that," he said. When I didn't lift my head, he chuckled a deep rumble that turned my knees to mush. "You can't, can you?"

"I can't trust you," I whispered, my voice wobbly. My heart started pounding painfully fast. "I don't even know who you are."

He tipped my chin up with his free hand, forcing me to meet his eyes; his eyes were pleading. "Your wolf knows me, Jade. She trusts me. You feel it. I know you do. We can work on the rest. I can make this right."

I shook my head, pulling in a deep breath. He was right. He was so bang on, and it scared me to death. At that moment, I wanted nothing more than him. I wanted to feel delicate, wrapped in his arms. And I never ever wanted to feel the dark, frantic need that Jared brought out in me again. But the tendrils of longing and desire that weaved throughout my chest scared the heck out of me. How could I feel this way about a guy who had done nothing but lie and manipulate me?

I heard the shuffling steps outside the door and then the thump of feet on the staircase. I listened until the last step had been taken and strained to hear if anyone else had hung around upstairs. The silence that greeted me seemed too loud, and uneasiness wormed its way through my belly. My nerve started to falter, and I squeezed my eyes closed, and then I murmured the words that I was sure could only lead to my heart being ripped out again. "I don't know if you can make it right." I sucked in a full breath and let it hiss out slowly. "But I guess that doesn't really matter. I need to ..."

He growled low in his chest. My eyes snapped open as his grip tightened on my wrist. I searched his face, trying to read what was there, but all I saw was rage. "Don't say it, Jade," he spat. "Don't even think of saying you need to stay with him."

AIDAN

Jade was still trying to play the game, and it confused the hell out of me. Maybe she had changed her mind from last night. Maybe she wasn't going to tell me the truth anymore. I didn't really deserve it, especially after what I'd done with Erika, but damn, I wanted to hear her say it.

She knew I'd seen her shudder away from Jared's touch. She felt the connection, the chemistry, between us. I could see it in her eyes. I knew she didn't believe she should stay here, stay with him, but she still tried to convince me that she wasn't mine. It was wrecking her — wrecking me. Her expression was shattered, her body trembled.

"Will you just shut up," she hissed, keeping her voice low so no one would overhear, and her defeated gaze dropped to my chest. She shook off my hand, which was still clamped around her wrist, and when I let go, she hugged her arms around her waist, pressing the damp washcloth into her side. The water seeped into her light blue nightshirt, the thin cotton soaking it up and darkening where it touched, but she didn't seem to notice. "I'm trying to confess here," she huffed, "and you are so not making it easy."

"Confess?" I asked. I shook my head. Damn, clearly, I had read her wrong. The way she had closed her eyes, squeezing them shut, as if she couldn't handle looking at me, and that sad, sad smile that curved her beautiful lips. I sucked in a breath, steadying my racing heart, and I tapped her chin again, tilting her face back up to meet mine. "You want to confess?"

"Never pictured this happening in a bathroom," she muttered. She puffed out a breath and tugged her bottom lip between her teeth. She held my gaze for a moment before pushing my hand away and letting her eyes drop again. "Jared and I aren't really together," she whispered.

I held my breath, waiting for more. I craved to hear her say that she was mine, that I was hers. I needed to hear it, needed to watch her say it, but she didn't say it. Her shoulders slumped, her breath hitched, as if talking to me was physically painful for her.

My inner-wolf howled within me, and the alpha in me shot to the forefront of my mind. Pieces I hadn't even considered last night started to fall into place. I'd been so busy feeling like an ass that I hadn't seen the whole picture. But at that moment, I saw it all in crisp, clear threads playing out just behind my eyes. Not only had my mate been lying to me, but the head enforcer, probably the whole damn team, had also been. My inner-wolf took over, and through my teeth, I said exactly what my inner-wolf wanted to do, "I'm going to kill him."

"Oh no, you're not." Jade shuddered back a step and jammed a pointed finger into my chest, the cloth still clutched in her hand, leaving a wet print on my shirt. "You're going to stay away from Jared."

A growl rumbled in my chest, and I closed the small space she'd placed between us, pressing against her and glaring down at her. My biceps flexed, and my eyes washed over with a golden haze.

"I'm serious, Aidan," she whispered. She took another step back and then turned away from me. The back of her shirt was shredded and angry. Red welts littered her skin, the remnants of Jared's claws raking over her. Her shoulders rose and fell quickly, and she said in a soft, airless tone, "You will leave him alone. None of this was his idea. I care about him, and I'm asking you to leave him alone."

I growled again. I couldn't seem to do anything else. Right then, I was more animal than human. Coarse hair layered my forearms and then receded. Shots of adrenaline pounded through my veins. Another growl erupted, and another shot of adrenaline followed.

Jade spun on me, narrowed her eyes, and planted her hands on her hips. "Will you stop this! God, when did you turn into such a freakin' caveman?" She sighed long and loud and shook her head a few times. "Jared was following my orders. I put him up to it all. I didn't want you to know. He lied to you for me. Maybe I wanted to hurt you as much as you hurt me, I don't know. I tried to tell myself I was doing it for the pack, for you, even. But I guess that doesn't matter anymore. I asked him to keep it real and keep it quiet. And he did exactly what I wanted."

"You're just digging his grave, Jade," I said in a low growl. "Word of advice, keep your confessions to yourself. Don't give me another reason to get rid of him."

Her eyes narrowed further until they were only little slits. She swallowed a few quick swallows and then asked, "Who are you?"

"I'm still the same person you fell for. The same person you fought for a few days ago. The same person you killed for. I haven't changed. I'm your mate." She made a shocking noise from the back of her throat and brought her fingers to her lips. Her eyes widened. "What? Did you really think I didn't know how you felt?" I'm not sure what made me say it. The truth? Until yesterday, I'd actually believed she hated me.

"Of course, I didn't think you knew," she muttered, turning the cutest shade of rosy pink. She took a step back toward me and reached out, running a finger along my cheek. She cocked her head to the side, and her nostrils flared, then she smirked. "You need to chill out before you end up shifting in my bathroom."

I chuckled, but it sounded strangled and forced. I needed to know something, and I was pretty sure the answer would completely suck. "I can't believe I'm going to ask this, but why him? Why would you pick someone that you knew wanted to mate with you?"

She lifted her shoulders in a small, delicate shrug. "Because at the time, he was a better choice than you. At least with him, I knew where I stood."

Yep, completely sucked.

Her answer burned, and the small ounce of peace I'd started to feel under her touch splintered. I growled again. I couldn't stop it. My inner-wolf was going crazy. I was going crazy. I reached out, cupping her cheeks in the palms of my hands. "I'm taking you home. Your Dad knows who you are, Jade. The best thing we can do right now is walk out of this house together." I paused for a second, searching her face, waiting for her protest, but she said nothing, so I pushed on. "You're going to tell him you freaked out after taking Tiff's life. You'll tell him you were scared about mating, that you weren't ready for that kind of commitment, and that the pressure of it all was too much. And then you're going to pack your bags, and you're going to finally come home."

For about half a second, she smiled, a soft, sweet smile, but it didn't last, and before I knew it, she was frowning. I ran a hand over her forehead, desperately wanting to smooth out the lines and bring the smile back. As I tried to brush them away, she said, "This is my home."

"Not anymore." I dropped my hands from her face and took a step back toward the door, ready to walk away. I couldn't listen to her try to tell me any different. I didn't trust myself to keep in control. Not right now. "I'm not arguing about this. Right now, I need to fix what just happened. I need to cover this up, and the best way to do that is to take you home with me."

I waited for a second, hoping to see something — anything — to tell me that she agreed, that she felt the same as I did, but she gave me nothing. I sighed and started to turn away from her, but as I did, she placed a hand on my chest, stopping me. "Lean back," she said. "You still have blood all over your face."

CHAPTER 11

JADE

I finished cleaning the blood from Aidan's face. My pulse was pounding, my ribs aching, as if my heart was trying to break through with each frantic beat. I had to admit that telling him the truth had a freeing effect, even if I hadn't been able to say everything I had wanted to. It was as if there had been a barbed wire cage around my heart, squeezing and cutting, but as I told him that I wasn't actually with Jared, the barbs had loosened, although they hadn't completely vanished.

I wanted to say something. He had to know how ridiculous he was being. He had to know that there was absolutely no way I would just pack my bags and follow him home just because he said so, even if that was exactly what I wanted to do. He'd had his chance, and what had he done with it? He had set it on fire and watched it burn. And I really didn't think I was ready to give him a chance to do it again.

The problem was I couldn't make my voice work. Maybe it was because deep down, I didn't really want to fight it, or it could have been that my inner-wolf was clamping down on my protests, reminding me that I had essentially done the exact same things that I'd been blaming him for. Whatever it was, it was definitely annoying.

His shoulders were set, a determined glint in his eyes. There was no reasoning with him, at least not now. His scent raked through me, calming my nerves and, at the same time, doubling my heartbeat. All I could do was focus on breathing, slow, steady breaths.

I rinsed out the cloth and draped it over the edge of the sink. I sighed. I could feel his eyes on me, scanning down my backside, most likely inspecting my tattered shirt. I'd felt the gashes close up some time ago, and the dry crustiness of blood was starting to itch. I grabbed another cloth from under the sink, wet it down, and tossed it to him.

Aidan caught it easily and moved in behind me as if he knew exactly what I needed. His fingertips, warm and smooth, teased my skin as he lifted the hem of my shirt, and I really had to focus on not leaning into him as he gently stroked the cloth along my tender skin. But darn it, I wanted to.

I knew he was waiting for me to tell him no. During the last few minutes, while I couldn't find my voice, he had been coaching me. Telling me exactly what I had to do. He was sure my dad didn't know everything. He claimed that the *Jared cover* being blown was just a hiccup. And he had made it very clear that I would be in a crap-load of trouble if I didn't make the story I needed to tell Dad believable.

On the other hand, I had been trying to think of a way out of this. I knew I could make the story believable. It was all the truth. I had freaked out. But really, who wouldn't have? I had killed someone. I had fought to the death for a pack that, for the last two years, I had loathed with every fiber of my body. And, yeah, Aidan was right. When I really thought about it, in the end, I'd been fighting for him. It had been his voice, his encouragement that had helped me win. His cries to me had been full of heartbreak, desperation, fear, and it was all of that that had given me the strength in the very last second to finish Tiffany off; I was sure of it.

But I knew in my gut that moving in with Aidan wasn't such a smart idea, even if it was only until we dealt with my dad. I didn't trust him, I didn't trust myself to be alone with him, and I was sure that staying here, near my dad, would be more useful. Really, that had been the reason behind everyone agreeing that I should pretend to be with an enforcer, so we could keep an eye on things.

When Aidan finished up on my back, he tossed the cloth into the sink, and I slowly, almost reluctantly, turned around. And again, I found myself wanting to tell him how stupid he was being. He was acting like a freakin' caveman, puffing out his chest, giving me a look that clearly said, *You're mine, accept it and deal with it.* The same look he'd given me when I had won the games and had melted into his arms. But again, I couldn't because, darn it, no matter how I looked at it, I was his.

Like the earth needed rain, I needed my mate.

He leaned back against the wall and gave me a thorough once over before he asked, "Is there anything else you want to tell me?"

"I'm not sure I can do this," I said, feeling a slight tremor in my bottom lip. "He's still my dad. I feel like ... like I'm betraying him."

He frowned. "Your dad betrayed your pack."

"You're not helping, jackass," I snapped, cutting him a dirty look. "It's not that simple, and you know it." But then, maybe it was that simple. I knew I was desperately trying to hold on to an image of my dad that couldn't have ever really existed. It was just that a part of me, the scared little girl within me, really, really wanted her father not to be the devil.

"Come here, sweetheart." Aidan's voice was soft, soothing. He held a hand out to me. I took a tentative step and then another, and as soon as I moved close enough, his arm coiled around my waist, pulling me flush against him. The gesture felt so incredibly right, so perfectly natural that I found myself liquefying, melting into him, and leaning my head against his chest. As he brushed some stray hair from my forehead, the barbed wire around my heart loosened a bit more.

He pressed a kiss onto my brow line, and all it took was just a light brush of his lips, and my heartbeat tripled. "You're the strongest person I know. You can do this." He squeezed me tighter and rubbed a small circle on my back. "Nothing needs to be decided today. We can go on the defensive. We'll watch and learn what we can about his pack and his involvement. Figure out what they want with our town. That's it."

"Okay." I nodded against his chest. "Okay, I'm ready." He didn't say anything else as I wriggled out of his arms, straightened my shoulders, and raised my chin. And he didn't try to stop me as I nudged him out of the way and went out the door, but then he'd already said everything he'd needed to, giving me the strength I needed.

I found everyone in the living room. Dad sat in his recliner, completely at ease. Dominic was grinning at me. Trevor, too, with Marcy pressed against his side. Jared was scowling, but thankfully he had ditched the towel and gotten dressed. The team, all five of them, were squashed together on the couch. Tommy and Chris stood behind them like statues. They looked incredibly out of place amongst our young pack members, but for a split second, I was really glad they were there, their strong, controlled presence balancing out the youthful recklessness of my team.

The glad feeling didn't last nearly long enough. There was so much tension I could barely breathe. Aidan was behind me. I could feel the heat of his glare hitting my back in waves. I could only imagine the furious, determined glint that had to be in his eyes because, honestly, I was a bit too freaked out to turn around and actually see it. *You can do this*, I coached myself. Too bad my little pep talk wasn't working for me.

As we approached, heads bowed and shoulders drooped. I gritted my teeth. Again, I felt like something big had changed. And I really didn't know if I liked it. Since when did my team show any kind of respect to the alpha? They hadn't been with Ray, and they had challenged Aidan's every move since he took over. I knew the show of respect wasn't for me. For me, they would have grinned and said something ridiculously annoying. Whether they meant to or not, their silent show of reverence only managed to make my nerves waver.

I stopped beside the couch, wishing I could squeeze in with the guys and hide. I was about to try it, too; I even took a step closer.

Aidan must have figured out what I wanted to do. His hand clamped down on my shoulder, stopping me. The profound silence that followed the gesture and the dark look from Jared twisted my stomach into pinching knots.

My dad spoke up first, and I couldn't stop myself from cringing at his question. "Is what Dominic told me true, Jade? Did you turn your back on your mate?" The disappointment I heard in his tone pulled the knots in my belly tighter and made me want to throw up. My cheeks cramped, and my mouth flooded with water. I didn't know how he could sit there looking all heartbroken like he actually cared. Not with everything he'd done, was doing, and was going to do again and again until we stopped him. I swallowed a few times, trying to bury the sick feeling.

At least his question explained Dominic's grin, and I cut my former best friend a dirty look. He winked, clearly enjoying my discomfort.

"I did," I whispered, dropping my head. Aidan squeezed my shoulder, probably trying to reassure me, but it didn't help. I pulled in a breath. "I was scared. I'm still scared."

"Do you understand that he could have you killed for this?" Again, the disappointment. Again, the heartbreak. Bile rose in my throat again, and I swallowed it down.

"At the time, no, I didn't," I said, shaking my head from side to side. "I thought I actually had to go through the mating process to break that law."

Dad sighed and said, "As soon as you won the games, your mate was chosen, pumpkin. The alpha male and female always mate. It's what makes the alpha pair such a strong force. The combination of your scents mixed with your imprints, it would give you both complete authority over your wolves, being able to draw on each other's scents or use them both together ..." He sighed again, long and loud. "A mated alpha pair is the strength behind any pack."

I blinked. I hadn't really thought much about the whole scent merging thing. Really, I had kind of figured that the purpose was solely to ward off other wolves, like a *mate nearby* warning function. But hearing it all put so bluntly, well, it made me feel a little sick. I knew love wasn't supposed to have anything to do with it. Erika had told me as much when I'd stepped down from the games. The alpha pair was never supposed to be about love. Call me crazy, but I still thought love should be a factor. It was the reason why I won in the end. I figured there was something to be said for that. Love had given me strength when I needed it. I had killed for Aidan, and I would do it again. But in the pack's eyes, it was about strength and dominance and leadership. And with our scents merged, working together ... *Oh God, I think I really am in love with Aidan.*

I blinked again and shook myself a little. I sucked in a breath and another. I needed to stay focused. I quickly shrugged off Aidan's hand from my shoulder, stepping over to my dad. I crumbled to my knees in front of him.

"I'm scared, Daddy. I'm not ready for this. Any of it. I'm only eighteen." My voice held a high squeal of terror, and I held onto that feeling as I launched into the story. I told him how I had stepped down and walked away before the games ended. I explained that when Tiffany had won by default, she'd told Erika that she'd made a deal with Bruce and that Tiffany had promised Erika would be the first to go to the cougars, all the while dodging around the video that condemned him. It was Aidan's idea. He had wanted to see Dad's reaction, see if we would get anything out of him, but to my dad's credit, he looked shocked, disgusted even, and I went with it. I cried about killing someone, and he tried to soothe me, telling me that as a wolf and as an alpha, it was expected and probably wouldn't be the last time I would have to kill to defend my pack.

When I finally finished, tears were streaking down my cheeks. Dad brushed them away with his thumb before his gaze shifted to Aidan. He was in full diplomat mode now. A side of him I'd seen from time to time when Ray had come pounding on our door, usually in the middle of the night, waking the entire house. "Are you going to officially bring her in front of the enforcers for this?"

Aidan didn't answer for a long moment. He took his time, looking the team over. To my surprise, Beck actually looked a bit misty. His eyes were fixed on me, and Tommy and Chris had their hands planted on his shoulders as if they were holding him in place. When Aidan finally looked back at my father, his expression was like stone. "There won't be any need. My mate will be coming home with me today." A crooked smirk curved his lips, and he looked over his shoulder at Jared. "She'll also be stepping down from her role as an enforcer."

What? Okay, I hadn't agreed to that. There was no way I would step down abandon my team. I jumped up from the floor and closed the space between us. My emotions ran wild, and a new wave of tears brimmed in my eyes. I grabbed Aidan's bloodstained shirt, bunching it in my hands, and cried, "Aidan, stop this. Please. I'm not ready for this. I don't want this. Please."

"That's enough, Jade." He took my hand, prying my fingers off his shirt. "I've let you have your fun for the last few days. It's ending now. Your Dad's right, you know. If you fight me on this, you'll force my hand. I'll put you on trial if I have to, and the enforcer you've been screwing around with will stand right there beside you."

"I think I hate you," I whispered. I pulled my hands from his, letting them drop to my sides. He held my stare for a long moment, and I knew exactly what he was waiting for, what he'd told me I had to do. And darn it, but I did it. I bowed my head, showing my submission to the only person I was actually allowed to submit to — my mate.

I heard a few quick intakes of breath from behind me. The significance of that bow spoke volumes to the team. And when I shifted, presenting my vulnerable neck to Aidan, the intakes turned into loud gasps that resonated around me.

Aidan took a moment to press his nose against my throat, taking in a deep breath, showing everyone that he was accepting my submission. As he did, his lips fluttered little kisses, sending hot shivers cascading down my back. I figured he was trying to reassure me; with the angle, we were standing at, no one would notice the kisses, but when he pulled back, his eyes still held that hard glint. "I'm fine with the hatred," he said coolly. "Alpha pairs aren't about love, sweetheart. They never have been."

I straightened, looking up at him. I knew he didn't mean it, but it hurt. Bad. Really, really, bad. A hissed cry slipped out of my lips.

Suddenly Dominic was in between us. "Dammit, Aidan," he growled. "You have no right to speak to her like this!" His fists were balled, knuckles turning bluish-white.

I placed a hand on his bunched forearm. "Dom, don't do something you'll regret," I whispered. I met his eyes for a brief moment, pleading with him to shut up. He cocked his head to the side, understanding burned in his eyes. His jaw clenched, his eyes blazed brighter, but he stepped back, clamping his lips shut.

I turned to my father, pulled in a deep breath, and held my head high. "I want to stay here. I've shown the alpha the respect he wanted, now please, talk some sense into him."

But Dad only shook his head, and a disgusted sneer spread across his lips. His gaze morphed into an ice-cold glare. "You don't want to go, then step down and let the games start again. It's the only way out of this, Jade. Step down. Let someone else run the pack with him and leave town. Either way, you won't be staying here."

I gasped. I didn't mean to, but really, that wasn't the reaction either Aidan, or I had expected. His words were like a physical punch in the gut, knocking the wind out of me, crippling me. Where was the man I had called Daddy, the big teddy bear that was always there for me? Where was the man that, a few moments ago, while locked in Aidan's arms, I had wanted to protect? Tears streaked down my cheeks in earnest now as I searched his face for any resemblance to the man I had loved all my life, but all I saw was the monster I didn't want to believe he was. I backed up a step. Something dawned on me then, my last thread holding me here, to this house, to this man. "Where's Mom?" I asked, looking around. I knew there was no way she would have been able to sleep through all the commotion. "I want to talk to Mom."

My dad frowned and looked at me as if I were crazy. "She's at work, Jade, but even if she were here, you wouldn't get a different answer. Your mother knows pack law. She knows how this works."

But she hasn't worked in days. Why would she go back the morning her husband came home?

I glanced over my shoulder, looking at Jared. I must have looked pretty freaked out because he offered up a smile and said, "She left around 5:30 this morning."

A hand slipped into mine, and then another, squeezing silent support. I glanced from one side to the other, not missing the grim expressions marring my best friends' faces. "Come on, honey," Dominic said. "We'll help you pack."

CHAPTER 12

AIDAN

Jade's tears had looked real.

I dismissed the team, Tommy and Chris included, as Jade disappeared upstairs with Dominic and Marcy. Trevor followed them. I was sure he didn't want to leave Marcy alone, not with the enemy so close. Jeff rambled on, trying to make sure I wouldn't hurt his *baby girl*, and I tried not to think about how real her tears had felt.

A strong swell of sensations stirred within me. It started with fury and ended somewhere near disgust. This man, the one that claimed to love his daughter, was using her as a puppet in his sick, little game; I was sure of it.

At first, I had expected him to fight, beg for her to stay under his roof. I had never expected him to kick her out, basically disown her, and then in his next breath, beg for her life. None of it really made sense. He would have more control over her if she stayed, but I started to understand as he spoke. He had known Jade would follow me. He could see that we were *attached*, hell, I was sure everyone could see that, and he was simply playing into our weaknesses. And that was when I learned something very valuable about this man. He didn't care who got hurt, but instead, he took pleasure in watching the pain. He was certain that he would win the end game, and he planned on enjoying every second of the battle in between.

By the time Jade finally came downstairs with her bags, I was sure of two things. One: I needed to know what the hell the end game was. Two: his certainty that he would be victorious was by far his greatest weakness.

Jade didn't say goodbye to her dad, didn't even look at him. She took her bags out to my car, piling them in the trunk, and then climbed in the front seat, waiting.

Jeff made me promise to take care of his baby girl. He even went as far as to tell me not to wait any longer to make our mate status official. It was one hell of a struggle to accept the hug he offered, and really, all I could do was nod my agreement on the not waiting thing because I knew if I opened my mouth, I would regret whatever came out.

Outside, Trevor asked me to call Marcy's school and her father, pulling her out for the day on pack business. He made it clear that he didn't want her out of his sight, and honestly, I couldn't blame him, so I did it. Marcy's dad hadn't been happy about it, but in the end, he hadn't argued, which was probably a good thing because I wasn't in the mood to deal with it.

Once that was settled, I sent them back to the pack headquarters with Dominic, asking them to call all available pack members together. I figured it was probably better to let them see Jade and me together before the word spread about her show of submission. Dominic hadn't said much, only that he hoped to hell I knew what I was doing, but the truth was so did I.

Jade didn't look at me when I finally got in the car. Her gaze was fixed on the forest, but her eyes looked blank as if she wasn't really seeing anything. I started the car. I didn't know what to say. I'd never seen so much turmoil in one person before. As I sat beside her, I didn't know whether to pull her into my arms and let her cry or leave her alone and let her pretend that she was okay. She needed time to process, that was for sure, but I could see that she was holding this all on her shoulders, even if it was my fault everything had gone to shit in the first place. She was struggling to keep her tear-filled eyes dry and not let her shoulders sink in defeat.

The urge to pull her to me, to give her some comfort, was physical, winding through my body, my soul, like a living organism, but I couldn't do it. Jeff was watching out the window, and after our little show, well, hugging her wasn't really an option. So I put the car in gear and backed out of the driveway.

"If you're ever that cold to me again, you'll be sorry." Her voice was hoarse and raw.

My entire body stiffened, and a sharp ache settled in my chest. I sighed, shifted the car into gear, and eased my foot off the clutch.

"It wasn't real, sweetheart." I gave her a quick sideways glance, but she was still gazing out the window.

"It felt pretty real to me," she whispered.

I didn't say anything as I gave the car more gas, let up, pressed on the clutch, and shifted again. The truth? The coldness felt pretty damn real to me, too.

JADE

My brows were drawn in severe slashes over my eyes. I tried wiggling them. Anything to ease the tension from my face, neck, and shoulders, but each time I began to relax, I would take another breath and catch a scent that shouldn't have been coming from Aidan.

I had missed it earlier. I wasn't really sure how. Maybe it was the stress, or maybe it had been his scent overpowering the light spring fragrance that now seemed to cling to him. But right now, enclosed in this car, I couldn't smell anything else, and it was really starting to make me feel sick.

I figured I couldn't blame him for carrying her scent on his clothes. As far as he had been concerned, I had moved on. I'd been with Jared. And the fact was, we were never actually together — really together. Sure, we'd had a strong attraction to each other, but the second that we'd been able to act on it, be more than just two people who liked each other, I had walked away. So yeah, I couldn't blame him, but that didn't change the fact that it hurt. Bad.

The five-minute drive back to Aidan's house felt like five hours. For the last few days, I had craved time alone with him. But now that we were actually alone, my nerves replaced the cravings, jumping around like a field of grasshoppers in my belly. I wondered if my nerves were because of the scent that stuck to him or if it was because I knew exactly what I wanted for the first time since I'd joined the pack, and with that darn smell, I didn't know if I could still have it. I figured I could thank my dad for that. His bluntness made something click inside me, gave me clarity, and forced my irrational brain to accept what I had known all along. Aidan was mine. The pack was mine. And there was no way I would let someone else have either. Not without a fight.

Most likely, though, the nerves were just something else for my stubborn brain to think about. I guessed they were better than dwelling on my father kicking me out, which pretty much sucked.

When Aidan pulled into the driveway, I still hadn't looked at him. I would have killed to know what was going through that gorgeous head of his, but yeah, I was a chicken, way too scared to ask. So I got out grabbed my two bags, a backpack, and a duffle bag out of the trunk. They weren't heavy, only about half full. I hadn't really wanted to stick around long enough to really pack. I made a mental note to ask Marcy and Dominic if they would go back and pack up the rest of my things because there was no way I was going back there with my father home.

Aidan waited by the car door. He looked exhausted, maybe a little defeated, and the ache in my chest grew and pulsed. He met my eyes, smiled a little, and held out his hand to me. I was at his side in a breath, lacing my fingers through his. The scent may have been there, clinging to him like glue, but he was making it clear what he really wanted. So he slipped up a little. No big deal, right? My inner-wolf was so calm, elated, content, just being near him. Clearly, she wasn't freaking out about it, so I probably shouldn't be either, definitely, maybe. He squeezed a little, his silent reassurance, and together, we headed in.

I let my bags drop to the floor just inside the door. I sighed and then sighed again. The scent was still only on him. I hadn't realized how freaked out I'd been to walk in and smell it in his house, too, but it wasn't any stronger than it had been in the car. At least he hadn't brought her back to his house. Another sigh hissed from me in a long stream of air.

Aidan chuckled a bit nervously. "Don't know whether to take all your sighs as a good thing or not." He squeezed my hand again. "Want to talk about it?"

Yes! That's exactly what I wanted to do. Talk. I'd known him for just under a month, and we had never really talked. I wanted to know him — really know him. And I wanted him to know me, especially since it looked like I would be staying with him at least for a bit. But instead of answering, I only shook my head. Sometimes opening up and letting someone in was the hardest thing to do.

I tugged on his hand, pulling him from the doorway and over to the couch. I plopped down none too gracefully, dragging him with me. I sat there for a moment, sinking into the leather, staring at nothing. I could feel him watching me, waiting, but for the first time ever, I had absolutely nothing to say to him. No snippy remarks, nothing.

Another long-winded sigh pushed out of my lips.

I shook off his hand. I needed to get comfortable. I needed to get closer to him, and I wanted to feel his arms around me. I scanned the length of the couch and smiled a little before shifting toward him. Then I placed a palm on his right hip and another on his right knee, and I pushed.

Aidan chuckled, and he was looking at me as if I had lost my mind, but really, I was pretty sure I actually might have. Maybe I was just tired of being pissed off at him. Who knows, but right then, I felt beyond relaxed. I grinned up at him, what I hoped was verging on a flirty grin, and pushed again. "Move. I need more room."

"Yeah, sure," he said, chuckling again and shaking his head. He went to get up, most likely to move over to his chair and give me space, but as he started to stand, my hands slid to the top of his thigh, pushing him back down.

"No," I said, glaring up at him. "Just shove over."

He chuckled again, still shaking his head, but he shoved over. I nudged him again, and he kept sliding until I had him pressed tightly against the arm of the couch. Satisfied, I flipped around, my back to him, and swung my legs up. I'd thought about sitting like this with him more times than I could remember. I flopped back, my head landing square on his lap, and then I grabbed hold of his arm and brought it around me, pulling it tight, just below my breasts.

He stiffened suddenly, his thigh turning into a rock under my head. His scent changed, thickened, leaving a sour taste in my mouth. *Guilt,* a voice within my mind chimed in, and my inner-wolf growled within me.

I closed my eyes, trying not to let it get to me. I tilted my head into him, my nose pressing against a clean patch of his shirt over his stomach, and I inhaled a long breath, letting it out in a strangled growl. I almost told him to go change. I wanted to get rid of that smell so bad it made my teeth itch. And the dried blood along the hem wasn't helping either. For a split second, my entire body went rigid against him — or was that his body going ridged against me? I didn't know for sure. Whichever it was, it didn't last, and he, or maybe it was me, relaxed again.

He ran a finger along my cheek, letting it drift down my neck. The sour scent thickened, masking everything else for a moment.

"Sweetheart, I can't stay here." His voice sounded strained. "I have work to do. The pack is unsettled, and I really need to meet with the team about your dad." I snuggled deeper into his lap. I had no intentions of letting him up, not anytime soon, at least. Not until we settled a few things. I was about to tell him as much when he huffed and said, "And there's something I really need to tell you before whatever is happening between us goes any further."

Crap! Was he actually going to tell me? My breath hitched. I didn't think I wanted to hear it. "I'm pretty sure I already know what you have to tell me," I said, my voice tight and my body stiffening again. I took a breath, let it out, and took another. "Work can wait, so can the pack. This, right here, is more important."

He laughed, but there was no humor in the sound. "You wouldn't say that if you actually knew what I need to say."

I pulled his arm a bit tighter around me and swallowed a few times. I was pretty sure I knew exactly what he was going to say. My nerves jumped again. I opened my mouth, closed it, swallowed, pried my eyes open, and decided to just get it over with. "I can smell Erika on your shirt and jeans, Aidan. Guess you didn't think that one out when you threw on the same clothes from yesterday, did you?"

"Guess not." He frowned, searching my face. "And you're okay with that?"

"No, not really," I said, deflating like a popped balloon. I'd really hoped there had been another reason for the scent. "But I'll get over it, just like you're going to get over Jared sleeping in my room for the last few days."

For a long moment, Aidan just stared down at me before he finally said, "Huh." He ran his free hand through his hair, blinked, fixed his blank stare back on me, but said nothing more.

"Really?" I asked sharply, elbowing him lightly in the ribs. He winced. "All you're going to say is 'huh.'"

His jaw twitched, so did his forearm that was lying across my chest. "Um, yeah, right now, huh is pretty much all I've got." The blankness began to recede from his brown eyes, and in its place, something that looked a heck of a lot like panic settled in. "Wait, why aren't you pissed at me? You're always pissed at me. This can't be a good thing."

I laughed, a cold, empty sound. "I can assure you, alpha, that on the inside, I'm a blazing ball of fire. Of course, I'm pissed, but

..." I paused, and my inner-wolf brushed against my chest, urging me on. She knew what I wanted — what I needed — and she wasn't about to let me chicken out. I sighed. "Well, I figure you lied to me, I lied to you. I was with Jared, and you moved on. It'd be pretty horrible of me to hate you for the same things I was doing." Something dawned on me then, something I probably should have clued into yesterday. Erika never studied. "It's really too bad, though," I continued. "Guess I need to find a new beta."

A swarm of emotion passed across his face so quickly that I really couldn't pinpoint exactly what I saw there. His scent told me he was guilty, angry, hurt. He growled, a deep rumbling sound, and his eyes filled with specks of gold. "Screwing around with the alpha isn't grounds for stripping her of her title, sweetheart." The roughness from the growl tinged his voice, dropping it lower, but I wasn't going to let it stop me.

"No, but blatantly lying to me when I needed her is," I said with a matter-of-fact air. He looked a bit confused, and I furrowed my brow. "Tell me you weren't with her when she sent the text message last night." His lips parted, and his scent spiked with more of that throat closing, tongue-tingling sourness, and I huffed. "Yeah, that's what I thought." I closed my eyes again, pressing my cheek against the hard contours of his stomach, and muttered, "I guess I should be glad you weren't stupid enough to go all the way."

Aidan petted my hair, just a light touch. "It went pretty far last night, Jade." His voice was low, just barely a whisper. "You should know that before you make any decisions here."

Okay, I really didn't need to hear that, but I had to admit it, I was impressed. I was so used to Aidan holding everything back, hiding things that would hurt me or piss me off. It was kind of nice hearing the truth directly from him. It gave me hope that maybe, just maybe, things could change. Warmth spread through my chest, swelling and pulsing. "I can't condemn you for doing the same thing you thought I was doing."

"Are you really saying you want to just start over?" He looked so serious and incredibly confused as if he were just waiting for me to lose my cool and storm out, but I was done with that. If my dad had shown me anything today, it was that I needed to suck it up, get over everything, and, in one way or another, move on. The thing was, I didn't think I could handle moving on to a life that didn't have Aidan in it. It was a truth I'd been trying to ignore, one that I hadn't wanted to accept. And it was a truth I wasn't going to brush off any longer.

Right then, though, I needed to fix all the seriousness that was marring his expression, so I smiled wickedly. "Yep, that's what I'm saying, but I do want to know something. How far exactly can you go without the whole scent merging thing happening?"

His jaw dropped a little, and he coughed a choked sound, and yep, he actually blushed a bright fire truck red. His eyes widened, and he gave me a look that begged me not to force him to give me all the details.

I smirked. It was totally evil, but I loved his awkwardness. "Seriously, I need to know in case I get the urge. Landon was looking pretty yummy today, oh, and Beck. Yep, Beck has potential." I laughed and winked.

His eyes flared with a dangerous warning, and his arm tightened around me. "That's not funny, Jade," he growled.

"I think it's only fair," I said, pushing at his chest half-heartedly and giggling. "If we're really going to start over, then we should even everything out. I only ever kissed Jared when people watched to make our fake relationship believable, and I can assure you, there was no pleasure in it. You had some fun. I should, too."

He folded over me in a blink, and his lips came crushing down on mine. It was a possessive kiss, rough and demanding and oh-so-amazing. I squealed in shock, my lips parting a little under his. His tongue was suddenly in my mouth, claiming every deep crevasse and fold, marking my mouth as his. He dug a hand into my hair, settling it at the nape of my neck, pulling me closer, holding me still, and before I knew it, my body was liquid against his.

Aidan broke away way too soon, only moving an inch from my swollen, tingly lips. I was panting. My heart was racing. "Let me make one thing clear," he growled. "As of this moment, you're mine. I'm not letting you out of my sight again, and I'm not stupid enough to let you go twice." I jutted my bottom lip out in a fake pout, and he nipped at it before he said, "By the way, I was also outside your window last night. I heard everything."

My eyes widened, and it was my turn to blush. I felt the heat blaze up my neck and settle in my cheeks. *Oh, God.*Last night I'd told Jared that I belonged to Aidan. Was he really saying he heard that? "Everything?" I asked. My voice was choked, and he chuckled and nodded.

I squeezed my eyes shut for a quick second, wishing I could just vanish. I didn't know if I would regret this, but I didn't care right then. The truth? I'd spent the last few days lying my face off, and it felt so amazingly good to have it all out in the open. And I was kind of regretting never talking to him before now. So much pain could have been avoided if I had. I was sure of it.

I felt him shift, and my eyes popped open. He lowered his head, coming in for another kiss, but I lifted my hand, placing a finger on his lips. I took a deep breath and said, "I'm Jade Valerie Shaw. My favorite color is plum, not purple. I'm eighteen, and before I joined the pack, I spent my free time drawing. I love using charcoal and my favorite time of the year is fall. There's just something so perfect about being able to wear jeans and a hoodie. It's not too cold, not too hot."

Aidan's eyes lit up with amusement, and he laughed, a full belly roll of a laugh. "What are you doing?"

"I think it's time we got to know each other," I said, grinning.

He laughed again, giving me a wide smile. He lifted a brow and asked, "You ever going to stop surprising me?"

"Probably not." My smile stretched almost painfully wide, and more warmth pooled in my chest. Right then, I was pretty sure I could love this man, really love him.

"Good," he said with a bob of his head. He took my hand, the grip was awkward with my head still in his lap, but he made due, shaking it once before lacing his fingers through mine and letting his arm fall back to my chest. "Nice to meet you, Jade Valerie Shaw. I'm Aidan David Collins."

CHAPTER 13

AIDAN

When we pulled up to the pack headquarters, the parking lot was already full. Jade was quiet beside me. She was a bit nervous, but she was still smiling.

It was her smile that made my stomach sink and my nerves light on fire. The pack, especially my males, were a little ... upset with Jade. I'd been trying to explain it to her, but I didn't think she was taking me seriously. Maybe she was at her maximum stress limit for the day. Maybe she just didn't want to believe that they were all that pissed off. I didn't know for sure, but I was starting to think I should have just left her at home because that smile wasn't going to help matters. It was a sweet smile, a happy one. It reached her eyes and lit up her face, and I loved it. I really did. It was just that I was sure it would give the wrong impression as if she were trying to lighten the seriousness of what they believed she had done.

The thing was, most of the males felt as if she had abandoned them while she'd been hiding away with the team for the last few days. And then there was the issue that she had turned away from me. That alone had gotten a lot of backs up. I didn't really know what the response would be when she walked in. I hoped that seeing us together would ease some of the tension, and if she would just stop grinning, it might actually work, but I just didn't have the heart to tell her to stop.

I pulled into a spot at the back of the lot and turned off my car. This was the last place I wanted to be. I wanted to be alone with Jade, but my phone had been buzzing nonstop against my left hip for the last twenty minutes; Dominic had been trying to let me know everyone was waiting.

Pack members milled about outside the glass double doors, the team of enforcers among them. I watched their cagey pacing for a moment, the way their muscles shuddered as they moved along the concrete exterior of the building as if they were wired, ready to shift without a second's notice. They were alert, working as a team to scan the tree line for any sign of a threat. Even from this distance, their tension was evident. Tommy and Chris were with them, but Jared wasn't. I didn't know whether to be happy he wasn't among them or pissed off that he hadn't bothered to show up.

I puffed out a breath and pulled the keys from the ignition. "Erika's going to be in there," I said.

Jade stiffened in her seat, but her smile didn't fade, not even a little. "I know. I'll be discreet, Aidan. I don't want your night broadcasted any more than you do."

"Okay, good." I nodded a few times quickly, more to reassure myself that this was actually good, but really, who was I trying to kid? Her calmness about the whole thing was kind of eating at me. I understood her theory, that she couldn't blame me for doing things that I had believed she was doing, but still, it was just ... odd and not what I had expected from her. And it made me uneasy. I wanted to kill Jared for even looking at her, let alone touching her. My inner-wolf wanted blood, but Jade, Jade was the picture of calmness.

I puffed out another breath. "You ready for this?" I asked as I popped my door open.

Jade nodded, a stiff bob of her head, as she got out. She met me in front of the car, holding her hand out to me, and I took it. Her smile widened further as she weaved her fingers through mine. Damn, I loved that smile and the content glint in her eyes. I really didn't know how I had gotten so lucky or why she had decided to forgive me, but I wasn't about to question it. I didn't want to give her a reason to rethink her decision to start over. I was pretty sure if she thought about it, she would realize that I had done so much more wrong than she had, even if she claimed we were even, and then she would walk away again. There was no way I would let that happen, so, yeah, I wasn't going to ask. I was going to just suck it up and not worry that she didn't seem to be all that bothered about the whole Erika thing. I didn't need to know the full why of her decision. All that mattered was that she was with me. Yes, that was all that mattered, definitely, maybe. I breathed in a deep, calming breath of the crisp air, and together, we started for the doors.

As we crossed the parking lot, our pack began filing inside. I tugged on Jade's hand, slowing our pace. I wanted everyone inside before we walked in. I wanted them to see our clasped hands, our nearness, but most of all, I wanted them to see that I'd accepted her submission and that I wasn't going to hold her actions over the last few days against her.

When we reached the door, she squeezed my hand. "Will you relax," she whispered. "It's going to be fine. I can handle this."

I looked down at her and forced a smile. "I know you can," I said. Jade didn't buy it, not for a second. She rolled her eyes, reached for the door, yanked it open, and pulled me inside.

"Look at this. The alpha female is finally deciding to grace us with her presence," Phil, one of the older pack members, spat as the doors shut behind us. His eyes sparked with speckles of gold. He wasn't a big man, slim and lanky, but the hatred that burned in his eyes as he scanned Jade over made him look threatening, and my inner-wolf stirred restlessly. I tugged on Jade's hand, pulling her behind me, and a growl built within my chest.

The silence that followed was deafening. I could barely hear the whispered breaths of all the people around me as the buzz of anger built in my ears. The pack, minus Jared, were all gathered in the sterile waiting room. The stark white floors and walls and the scent of bleach and various cleaners assaulted my senses as I made my way into the center of the room, tugging Jade along with me. Some sat on the hard orange plastic chairs, some paced, and others just stood there, glaring at Jade. Whispered criticisms invaded my ears, too many for me to even try to comprehend. The stress coming from my pack was palpable, rippling through the air like an electric current.

Phil sneered at Jade, and I let out a low warning growl. "That's enough," I said. The words were snarled, and by the way his eyes dropped to the floor, and he slid back a step, I figured he knew I wasn't asking.

"Aidan, I don't need you to defend me," Jade said calmly. She pushed out from behind me, tugged her hand free of mine, and moved to stand a few paces away from me. She took her time to look at every one. The urge to grab her and pull her closer, to keep her safe, was unbearable, but as she moved, the division within the pack had never been clearer, and that was what held me still. She needed to see it. She needed to understand what had happened within the pack over the last few days.

Our werewolves began shifting to positions that clearly reflected who they considered their alpha to be. The females crowded in behind Jade, the males moving closer to me. She didn't need me to keep her safe; she had her pack at her back.

"You've been alpha female for three days, and you're already destroying this pack," one of the men said under his breath. It came from behind me, a mumbled whisper, so low that I really wasn't sure who had said it.

I let out another growl, pivoting in place to glare at my wolves. "She's one of your alphas, and you'd better start addressing her as you would me."

"No, she's not," Phil countered. He waved a hand toward the females. "She's the females' alpha. She's nothing to me. Not without you as her mate."

I blinked, stunned at the defiance, I saw stoning his face. Yes, he was right. Without us mated, without our scents combined, the pack was divided, but damn, she still deserved their respect. I opened my mouth, ready to tell them all exactly what I thought, but Dominic jumped in before I could.

"We called you all here to tell you that our alpha female made a public display of her submission to Aidan this morning." He stepped up, standing in between Jade and me. "I was there, so was the team, and Aidan accepted it." He paused, letting everyone process the information for a moment before he continued, "The alpha pair will now be living under the same roof and are to be considered mated from this moment on."

Jade made a strangled sound from somewhere at the back of her throat. I glanced over my shoulder just in time to see the vibrant red flush rushing to her cheeks. "Dom!" she called, her voice strangled. "We are so not discussing that."

For a split second, everyone was silent, but it didn't last. It started with a chuckle and then a giggle, and in no time, the entire pack was roaring with laughter. I met Jade's eyes, smirking, and she blushed brighter.

CHAPTER 14

JADE

My face was on fire, and darn it, Aidan was smirking. The tension that had filled the room moments ago was almost completely gone, although the visible split between the pack was still very evident. The laughter continued, I even heard a few snorts, and my face burned hotter. I planted my hands on my hips, scowling.

Aidan closed the space between us. He was chuckling, too, and his eyes danced with amusement. I figured the laughing was better than the tension, but this was just not funny, well, at least not to me. He leaned into me and planted a sloppy kiss on my cheek. "Have I ever told you how cute you look when you're all embarrassed?" he asked.

I shoved at his chest, rolled my eyes, and pursed my lips. I was about to tell him that I didn't find any of this funny. Really, how many more times would my sex life (or lack thereof) be brought up and discussed today? I guessed it shouldn't bother me. Mating was a huge part of pack life. I thought it had something to do with a werewolf's protective and oh-so-possessive nature. Claiming and possessing that one person you couldn't live without. At least that's how I felt when I thought about mating with Aidan. The idea of possessing him in a way that no one else ever could sent hot chills careening through my body.

My embarrassment clearly dissolved a lot of tension, so I figured that was a good thing — kind of. But really, there were so many more important things to talk about. Like my dad being home or how the search was going for the cougars' location. We needed to find them before they moved again, but no, discussing the status of my mating was so much more important. *Ugh!*

And then I spotted Erika. She was in red leather pants and a jacket with a black tank underneath that was cut so low the black lace of her bra was showing. Her midnight-black hair hung straight over her shoulders, and her lips, coated in a devil red, were parted. Her lust-filled eyes were fixed on Aidan. Any embarrassment I had felt vanished, replaced by an ugly surge of jealousy.

I placed myself in front of Aidan and growled. Yep, I growled. Somewhere in the back of my mind, I knew, just knew, I would regret the reaction. I was so not this person. I wasn't psycho jealous, and I was secure enough with myself that I didn't need to worry, but right then, none of that mattered. Aidan was mine, and that tramp was basically drooling over *my* man. I didn't care that technically she was still my beta or that Aidan and I weren't even officially together. God, we'd just barely passed the forgiveness point. But as far as my inner-wolf was concerned, no one — absolutely no one — could look at him like that.

My growl didn't faze her. She actually sidestepped and tilted as if she were trying to look around me. Her eyes dropped to his chest and then back to his lips.

"Erika, you did hear Dom, right?" Even I felt the chill rolling off my tongue. My tone was so cold. "The alpha male has a mate. I suggest you fix that gaze of yours elsewhere."

Erika shook herself like a wet dog shaking water out of her fur. She slowly pulled her gaze from Aidan, fixing it on me. She opened her mouth as if she were about to say something but snapped it shut just as quickly.

My reaction earned me another round of laughter from the werewolves who didn't know me all that well. But the ones that did, my team and Dominic, they moved in, flanking me. "Is there something we need to know about?" Beck asked, letting his booming voice carry throughout the room.

The laughter died abruptly. No one missed the pointed question or the lethal glint in Beck's eyes. The lobby was so quiet that the only sound I heard was my racing heartbeat pounding in my ears.

My blood was pumping, hot and fast. My skin, shuddering. All I could see was her with her hands all over my mate. *There goes being discreet,* I thought. I opened my mouth, ready to tell the team about her little rendezvous with Aidan and the text message she had sent me, but I snapped it shut when Aidan said, "Meeting's over." He weaved his arm around my waist, holding me still. He glanced down at me and grinned, a sexy as hell half-grin, and winked. If I had to guess, he actually looked happy about my reaction.

Aidan held my eyes for a long moment. His were dancing with humor and what looked a heck of a lot like relief before he finally looked back up at the stunned crowd. "Thank you for coming on such short notice," he said, his tone light and, yep, happy. "We didn't want to wait to share the news with you all that Jade has finally come to her senses and moved in with me." There were a few chuckles, and Aidan paused, grinning like a fool as he waited for them to die down before continuing. "As you know, Jade's father came home this morning. Jade and I will be working closely with the team, and we'll call you all together again when we're ready to act. Remember, our phones are always on, and our door, always open. If you need us for anything, come find us."

No one questioned Aidan's dismissal, which shocked me a little. Marcy had told me that the pack had warmed up to him, that they listened to him, but even so, it seemed weird to me how quick they moved toward the door, no questions asked.

I barely noticed the curious glances in Erika's direction as people started shifting toward the door. I was too busy trying to tone down the swarm of jealousy-induced emotions that kept thrashing around within me, and on top of that, I couldn't figure out why Aidan was happy about it. I received a few hugs, some whispered congratulations on my move, and it sucked that pretty much all I could manage was grunted responses.

I don't really know how long I stood pressed into Aidan's side before he stepped away from me. I vaguely noticed him talking to Beck and then whispering something to Dominic. My focus was fixed on Erika. Her complexion was paling fast, going a little whiter with each person that left the building.

When the last person left, and all that was left were the team and Dominic, Erika whispered, "I thought you were with Jared." She put her feet in motion, coming closer, and when she was only a foot away from me, she dropped to her knees. "I swear. I would have never let him in the door if I knew you were going to take him back."

She dropped her eyes to the ground, tilted her head, and presented her neck to me. I wanted to take a step away from her. I wanted to ignore her offer and tell her to get the hell away from me, but the team stopped me before I could. Beck and Landon were suddenly beside me again, their hands pressing into the small of my back, holding me in place.

I heard the growl the second they touched me. It was a predatory and extremely possessive sound, and I shuddered. I shouldn't love it, but coming from Aidan, I did, so very, very much, and just as quickly as their hands had settled on my back, they were gone. Aidan growled again, and his scent swamped my brain, bogging me down, although I wasn't complaining. Man, I loved that smell, the power mixed with the greens of the forest — best smell ever. My heart skittered in my chest, and my inner-wolf decided to wake up, moving around within me as if she thought that my belly was the perfect stage to do the salsa.

The team moved, so did Dominic, clearing a safe distance from me, and my stupid mate secured me around the waist with a stiff arm. Erika didn't move from her position, her neck still craned out before me, but she did whimper.

"Will someone explain what's going on?" Craig asked. He crouched down beside Erika, his freaked out light blue eyes met mine, pleading, and his usually soft features were sharp and hard.

Erika squeezed her eyes closed and pulled in a noisy breath. Her shoulders drooped a little more, and she blurted, "Jade's upset because the alpha came to see me last night."

Craig looked at her and blinked. His jaw started to drop, and he gave his head a shake, and as he did, he growled, a deadly sound. He stood up slowly, his jaw ticked. "Is that why you were late?" His cheeks flamed, his eyes flared. "Why you showed up at my place freshly showered, hair still dripping, with all that awful perfume?"

Erika straightened, rising up to face him, and she shrugged. "I wanted to keep my options open."

Right then, I wanted to slap her, if not for me, for Craig. I hadn't known that they were actually seeing each other. Erika hadn't said a word, and Craig was more of the quiet type. If I had known, I wouldn't have said anything, not with him here.

Craig's fists flexed, released, flexed. He was vibrating, his skin starting to ripple. He glared at her, grinding his teeth so hard that I swore I could hear the enamel chipping.

I pried off Aidan's stiff arm from around my waist and went to him, placing a hand on his forearm. "Why don't you go take a walk," I said.

"No, I need to hear this," he growled, shaking off my hand, never taking his fuming gaze from Erika. "She promised herself to me last night." His voice cracked, and another shudder rushed along his skin. "She's supposed to be mine."

Aidan cleared his throat, drawing everyone's attention. "Craig, it was my fault," he said, looking everywhere but at me. "I'm the one who sought her out. I'm the one who let it get out of hand."

I spun on Aidan, my eyebrows shot up. "You've got to be freakin' kidding me! You're defending her?"

Aidan's mouth twisted into a wary frown and his hands rose in what I thought was supposed to be surrender. "No, not defending," he said. "You have every right to ignore her, strip her of her title, and throw her out of the pack. I'm just thinking we should consider showing her the same kindness you showed me."

Erika huffed and planted her hands on her hips. "You can't throw me out of the pack just because I gave the alpha the relief you wouldn't give him."

Craig's eyes fell back on her, slicing like blades, and his stance stiffened. He lifted one side of his mouth in a sneer, and as he did, I got a glimpse of the tips of his lengthening canines.

"You're right," I said. "But that's really not the problem. When I was looking for you last night, you told me you were at home studying."

Erika smirked. "Well, yeah," she said, waving a hand in Aidan's direction. "I was studying, and I was thoroughly enjoying it, too."

My jaw dropped. Honestly, I didn't know where Erika was getting the balls from. It wasn't that long ago that she had cowered in my bedroom, trying to hide from Jared. Maybe she was just getting used to the enforcers, or maybe she knew there was really no way out of the shit pile she had found herself in. More likely, she was just reverting back to the epic bitch she had been for the last two years. My mom had always told me that people could only hide who they really were for a week or two before the truth came out. Whatever it was, though, it was making me see red.

I took a step toward her, my fist clenching. I saw it all play out in my head, the satisfaction of smacking that smirk off her face. And I was going to do it, too, for Craig, if nothing else. I took another step, my jaw clenched.

And then Tommy stepped in front of me. "Jade," he said. He ran a hand along his shiny head and then met my eyes. "This is the girl that brought you the video, right?"

"Yes," I said through my teeth. "This is the girl. But right now, I don't really care about the damn video."

He grimaced, and he dropped his eyes from mine. "I've been

wondering how she got it without the enemy picking up her scent. Before you sentence her, maybe we should consider that."

I gritted my teeth and almost snapped at him. I was just too mad to think. Aidan must have noticed because suddenly, his scent wrapped around me, and I pulled in a long breath of fresh greens. I shifted, glancing at him over my shoulder, and he gave me a look that clearly told me I had to hear her out before I made any decisions. I hated that he was right.

CHAPTER 15

AIDAN

"Hold up a second, Aidan," Tommy whispered, placing a firm hand on my forearm as Dominic began leading the group down to the meeting room.

Jade must have heard his whisper. She stopped abruptly and gave us a funny look. Her eyes drifted to Tommy's hand clamped on my arm, and then she looked back up at me, arching a brow.

I sighed and then forced a smile. "I'll be right there," I said. "Don't start without me, okay?"

She frowned a little, but then Chris moved in beside her and placed a hand at the small of her back, nudging her forward. She quickly stepped away from his hand and cut me another questioning look. I smiled what I hoped was an *everything's okay* smile. It must have been convincing because she nodded and then followed the others down the hallway, with Chris right behind her.

I turned to Tommy, squinting against the bright sunlight that streamed through the glass doors. He wasn't frowning, but he also wasn't smiling; his expression was stuck somewhere in the middle. "Can this wait?" I asked.

"No." He rubbed a hand over his hairless head as he waited for the others to clear out. Once they were far enough down the hallway that they wouldn't overhear, he said, "Jared took off."

I huffed a loud gusty sound. "What do you mean Jared took off?" I asked. I didn't need anything else to deal with. Not today. Out of every possible scenario I'd considered after what happened this morning, Jared leaving hadn't been one of them. I had figured he would give me the cold shoulder, or he might even try to challenge me, but leaving, well, he didn't strike me as the giving up type, and leaving was definitely giving up. He'd be giving up his home, his pack, his friends ...

"Just what it sounds like," Tommy said. "He took off. But I got to say, I don't think it was because he wanted to go. Pretty sure the guys told him to get lost for a bit and cool down. I came in at the tail end of it."

It's temporary, I thought, surprised that I actually felt glad about that. I knew it would kill Jade if he left because of her — because of us. I folded my arms over my chest and frowned. "You think the guys pushed him out?"

Tommy nodded. "Yep. They're pissed at him, and I'm sure that if he showed up right now, they would go at it. Specifically Landon. With the way he talked last night, it sounded like he was ready to kill Jared. Don't have a clue why, though."

Charming. Just what I needed. The team at each other's throats.

Through my teeth, I said, "So you haven't really found out anything." I knew it wasn't a fair statement. Tommy and Chris had only just gotten to town yesterday, and in all fairness, I hadn't really expected them to find out anything from the team anyway.

Tommy glowered at me, and when he spoke, his voice was a gravel pit, rough and jagged. "Not fair, Aidan. We've only had one night with them, but I do know that Jared hasn't been sticking around at your mate's house just because he wants her. There's more to it than that, but thanks to Beck, Landon clamped up when I pressed."

I laughed, a cold, frustrated sound, and scrubbed at my face. "Well, I can't very well act on your speculations now, can I?"

Tommy was uncharacteristically quiet for a minute. He studied me closely; his eyes were alight with a curious seriousness. "You are nothing like your father, you know that?"

I didn't respond immediately. My father most likely would have taken the information as grounds to throw the whole team in lockdown and tortured them with his alpha scent until he got what he wanted to know out of them. And although the idea was an appealing one, since the last thing I needed was the team fighting right now, I wasn't going to do it. Jade would never forgive me for it, and well, I didn't want to run a pack by inflicting fear and pain on my wolves. It just wasn't me.

I finally looked back at him and asked, "Did you really volunteer to come here?"

Tommy hadn't expected the question. He furrowed his brow. "Sure, why wouldn't I?"

"Oh, I don't know," I said with a lazy lift of my shoulders. "Maybe because you've hated me since I was born."

He gave me an odd look, one that I couldn't even begin to understand, and in a low, calm voice, he said, "Never hated you, kid. If we were all soft on you like Lance was, you'd never be where you are now. Probably would have died in your fight for alpha."

I really didn't know what to say to that. He might have had a point, but I wasn't ready to admit it, so I just shrugged and started down the hallway. "Come on," I said. "Jade's waiting."

JADE

Time, even the last twenty minutes, had given me some perspective as well as a much-needed reality check. To put it simply, the pack was a freakin' mess, clearly divided. There had been no mingling between the males and females, no friendly gestures. If anything, there was a hostile tension wrapping around the room, well, until they started laughing at me.

I hadn't believed Aidan when he had tried to explain how upset everyone was with me. Really, I figured he was exaggerating, but after seeing them all together, one thing was clear: I couldn't hide behind the team any longer.

I had never gone further than Aidan's office in the headquarters before, and I was a bit shocked at how large the building actually was. Tommy had suggested we move our little meeting from the lobby to a more appropriate setting, so Dominic had led our group down the main hallway to a meeting room at the back of the building. There was a network of hallways that branched off the main one, and every few feet, there was another closed door. I had no clue what all the rooms were for or why we needed such a big building, but after this was all over, I was definitely going to check them out.

I was in a meeting room with the team: Beck, Landon, Mark, and Craig. Tommy and Chris were there, as were Aidan and Dominic. Jared still hadn't shown up, but I was starting to think he probably wouldn't. The room smelled of wolves, angry, nervous wolves. And there was a hint of lingering staleness as if the space had been sealed up tight for some time. That was the first thing I had noticed when I had stepped in.

And it was quiet. So very quiet. Everyone was looking at me, waiting expectantly, but I didn't know what to say. I hadn't been in the pack for all that long, not to mention I had no clue what I was doing as an alpha. The sound of my footsteps was loud, echoing around the room as I paced back and forth. Heat pooled in my cheeks, so hot that I was certain my face was a bright scarlet.

Once Aidan and Tommy had come in, we had listened as Erika recounted the events leading up to her capturing everything on video, and I hated it. Still, her story had an undeniable ring of truth. She had driven Tiffany to the meeting with my dad. Her best guess was they didn't notice her scent so close because they had known she was there, although they had thought she was waiting in the car. She'd been certain that Tiffany would win the games, and she had done what she could to get in Tiffany's good graces before that happened.

But after waiting for a little over thirty minutes, Erika had wandered into the woods, following Tiffany's trail. She said they were just beyond the tree line, and the moment she had picked up what they were discussing, she had crouched down, hiding behind a bush, and started recording. When they had broken up their little meeting, Erika had bee-lined it for the car. She drove Tiffany home, listened to Tiffany brag about her little get-together, and as soon as Tiffany was out of her car, Erika had found me. According to Erika, Tiffany had been so certain she would win the alpha female games that she hadn't felt the need to hide her plans, especially since Erika had sworn her alliance.

Once she finished her story, I had dismissed her, sending her back to Aidan's office to wait. I needed time to think everything out, figure out what to do with her. I wasn't sure if she would stick around, but then I guessed she really had nowhere else to go, and she knew we would hunt her down if she left.

The light coming into the room was dim; the windows, covered by light filtering roller shades, the same sterile white as the shiny ceramic tiles, were pulled down and the lights off. A long, rustic wood table that looked like a slab was taken from the center of an enormous oak tree filled the room, with the enforcers surrounding it, sitting in matching wooden chairs.

Aidan smiled. It was a bit shy, a lot sweet, and it made the butterflies in my belly dance and shiver. The air around me warmed as if I stepped into a patch of sunlight. He sat at the head of the table in jeans and a light gray zip-up hoodie, the sleeves pushed up to the elbows. His light brown hair was sticking out a little, but then he'd been running his hands through it constantly as he listened to the recount. He hadn't shaved, his jawline looking rough with stubble, and as I scanned him over, if I had to guess, I'd say he hadn't been sleeping much lately.

"Sweetheart, she's telling the truth. You can smell it." The smile that Aidan gave me shifted to something that looked like a challenge as if he were daring me to disagree, and I resisted the urge to groan and roll my eyes. I knew she was telling the truth, but darn it, I wanted it all to be a lie. He noticed and got up, crossing the room to me. He leaned in close, his voice dropping to barely a whisper as he pressed his lips to my ear. "I love the whole jealousy thing. It's hot as hell, but you need to be sure your decision wasn't because of my bad choice last night. You need to be fair to her."

When he pulled back from me and retook his seat, my heart was pounding, and I seriously hoped I didn't look as guilty as I felt. I looked at Aidan, silently cursing him for pointing out what had already been eating at me. I swallowed down a frustrated sigh.

"Okay," I said. "Okay." I nodded a few times, more to reassure myself than anyone else. "I think we can all agree that Erika can't be my beta. And I can't very well throw her out of town. She may suck most of the time, but she's loyal to the pack, and right now, we need all the loyalty we can get."

Craig didn't look happy, but he grunted, "You're right," along with the rest of them, and I started my useless pacing again. I just didn't know what to do with her. I knew the way the pack worked to a certain extent. If I stripped her title, they would eat her alive. She would be marked as a weak link, which never went well. *God, I don't want to make this decision.*

"Where the heck is Jared?" I blurted, stalling. "He should be here for this."

The second the words left my mouth, I heard Aidan's growl. I stopped in my tracks and cut him a dirty look. "Will you stop that? Seriously, what's with all the growling?" His response was a sexy smirk and another soft growl.

"Jade, he can't help it," Tommy said, chuckling. "Give him a break. It's his inner-wolf voicing his claim on you. It'll ease up after you two are officially mated."

Tommy grinned when I shifted to face him. It was a playful grin, one that told me I was, in fact, as red as my cheeks felt. I laughed a little and smiled sweetly. "The next person who brings up my sex life is going to be sorry. I swear it."

Beck laughed, Landon rolled his eyes, and Mark snickered. I groaned. "Okay, if she stays here, she needs a mate. The threat of a pissed-off mate should keep the pack off her back, and I think we owe her that much for what she's done for us."

I glanced at Craig, and he quickly shook his head. "I won't mate with her, and I won't house her either." He let out a painful-sounding sigh. "I just can't do it. I won't be her fallback plan. I can't deal with the fact she was with him or anyone just before she crawled into my bed." He glanced at Aidan then, and I was a bit stunned that there was no hostility or blame in his gaze. "At least I understand why she said she wanted to wait." He stood up slowly, glancing at Beck. "Will you watch out for her? The pack owes her protection. The team owes it to her for bringing Jade to us. Once she's stripped of the title, she'll be looked at as weak, and with how unsettled the pack is, that won't end well. I just can't do it."

Beck nodded, and Craig shifted his focus to me. "You good with this?"

I nodded. I couldn't really do much more than that. My throat was burning and my eyes stinging. I wanted to hug him. I wanted to tell him I was sorry, but the words were jammed in my throat. But the nod seemed to be enough.

"Good," Craig said. He nodded, too. "Good." He looked at Aidan and said, "We need Jade on the team. I know you want her to step down, but it'll be a mistake. We need her. She's the only thing that's keeping Jared sane right now."

"Is he okay?" I asked before Aidan could say the blunt *no* that I could see written all over his face.

A ripple of tension passed through the team, and Landon said, "Nope, he's far from okay. But you need to stay away from him. And I don't agree with Craig. You need to step down, keep clear of him until everything is ..." he smirked and chuckled, "settled between you and Aidan."

I clucked my tongue and began fidgeting, playing with the strings on my hoodie. Aidan was frowning, but at least he wasn't growling. My stomach dropped, and I huffed. "He's still my friend, guys. I'm not going to just ditch him."

"He's not your friend, Jade," Landon said. "I hate to point it out, but he didn't give a shit about you until Aidan showed his interest. Might want to ask yourself why."

Ouch. That was pretty much the only thing that went through my mind as I stared at Landon, my jaw-dropping.

"Landon," Beck said. "Not your place, man. Let it go."

"What's not his place?" I asked. My voice was a little rocky, and I swallowed hard. I glanced at Beck, but he only shrugged. He gave me a look that clearly said *Let it go* and glanced in Aidan's direction.

Mark leaned forward, his elbows on the table, and he rested his chin in his hands. "Did anyone else pick up on Jeff's eye twitch when Jade told him about Tiffany's deal with Bruce?"

CHAPTER 16

AIDAN

Looking back on it, I thought I should have known that there was more trouble with the team than just their normal jerkiness. But with my pack, pretty much everything equaled some kind of trouble, and it was beginning to become extremely hard to see the real problems when they surfaced. They were all so testy and high-strung right now that even looking at someone the wrong way caused an issue. So when Jared failed to show at the pack's headquarters, I really hadn't thought much of it. I figured he was pissed off, and not showing was his version of throwing a tantrum.

Except this wasn't just a tantrum. Whatever the problem was, it went further than Jared being pissed off at me. I hadn't wanted to believe what Tommy uncovered, but after listening to Landon tell Jade to stay away from Jared, I was sure this really did have something to do with the entire team.

Awesome. Another problem to solve. Just what I need.

I pulled up to a stoplight and glanced at Dominic in the passenger seat. He looked as if he were somewhere else, completely lost in his own thoughts. His face was utterly blank, not guarded as usual, and it made him look a lot younger than eighteen.

It only took about five minutes for everyone to agree that I needed to chat with Jade's dad and get a briefing on the cougar situation. As far as Jeff was concerned, I'd sent him back to the cougars to gather information for me, and if I never bothered to ask him what he found out, sooner or later, he would clue in that something was up.

It didn't take long to set it up. Jeff had been more than happy to meet, and within fifteen minutes, I was back in my car. And although I tried to convince Jade to come with me, she'd ended up hanging back at the headquarters with the guys claiming she wanted to work on strategies.

The light changed, and I eased off the clutch, feathering the gas. After another moment of silence, I said, "So, Jared's gone. Tommy said that he thinks the guys forced him to leave for a bit."

Dominic blinked and pulled in a loud breath. "Yeah, figured as much," he said. He fiddled with the window button, letting the glass fall an inch and then rise again. "Maybe it's a good thing. Gives you both time to simmer down."

"I don't need time to simmer down," I said, making a right on Clearmont Drive. "I promised Jade I wouldn't touch him, and I won't. God, I can't believe I'm saying this, but we need him. We need all of them right now."

Dominic grunted and cut me a sideways look that clearly said he disagreed. Whether his disagreement was about me needing to cool down or us needing Jared, I really wasn't sure.

The park came into view, and I pulled into the lot, parking at the far end. It was vacant, not a single car other than mine, and I wondered if maybe, just maybe, Jeff wouldn't show. As I pulled the keys from the ignition, Dominic said, "Aidan, be good to her, okay? I know you were just following my advice the last time around, but don't hurt her again."

So that was what his quietness was about. I should have guessed. The only time Dominic got that remote look on his face was when he was thinking about Jade. I sighed as I opened my door. "She wants to start over. Clean slate and all that."

He smiled a little and nodded as we got out of the car. "Yeah, I figured she'd do something like that." He scanned the parking lot quickly and asked, "You think he'll show?"

"Hopefully not," I said. "It'll give me a reason to go after him."

Unfortunately, Jade's dad was exactly where he said he would be. Jeff was sitting on a worn wooden bench nestled under a large oak tree, sporting a lime green windbreaker and khakis. When he spotted us coming across the field at a leisurely pace, Jeff got to his feet, leaving the bench behind as he came toward us. He was smiling a casual *nice to see you*kind of smile as if he hadn't just broken my nose this morning.

He stopped a few feet away from us, jamming his hands in the pockets of his jacket. "Didn't expect to hear from you so soon," he said. "Did Jade settle in at your place, okay?"

I had to give him credit; he was great at the *concerned father* act, so good, in fact, that I could almost believe it. Almost.

I returned his caring smile and ignored his question. "Where are they, Jeff?"

Jeff raised his hands, obviously noticing my no-nonsense tone. "Okay, fine, right down to business then." He let his hands drop, and a frown curled his lips. "I'm not too sure. They were relocating when I left. Supposed to get a call in a day or two when they settle in."

"Did you know the cougars have been coming into town?" Dominic asked in his typically calm, cocky demeanor. He smoothed a few non-existent wrinkles from his sweater.

"Nope," Jeff said. He smiled, a cool and confident kind of smile, but his eye started to twitch. "Maybe they're looking for Tiffany. She made a deal, right? They're probably trying to find her to collect on it."

I studied him for a moment as a gust of wind blew through the park. His eye was still twitching, and I wondered if it was because he was lying or if it was nerves. Either way, it made me smile. I might not have been able to pick up the scent from him, but the eye twitch, that was something to go on. *Thank you, Mark.*

"I got to say, Jeff, I figured you'd have something to tell me by now," I said, folding my arms over my chest, my biceps curling up thick. I might have promised Jade I wouldn't hurt him, but I said nothing about trying to intimidate him. I narrowed my eyes. "What were you doing with them?"

Jeff's smile lost confidence. "Like I told you," he said. "I was stalling the recruitment for more women. And I was trying to get a full count for you."

"What's the count then?" Dominic questioned.

"I'll know in a couple days," Jeff blurted a little too quickly to be believable. His throat worked fast in a bunch of swallows, and his smile returned. "Some of the guys were out, and no one knows how many were gone. They're not an organized bunch. I blame it on having no females."

I took a step closer, and he took a step back. "You know, I'm starting to feel like you're jerking me around."

His eye started to twitch again as if it had a pulse. "I'm not your enemy, Aidan."

"Oh yeah?" I chuckled. "You're one of them. Kind of makes you the enemy."

Jeff froze like a snapshot, blinked, and then shook his head, and he laughed a humorless laugh. “Careful there, alpha. My daughter might be upset with me, but she’s still my daughter.”

I shrugged. “She’ll forgive me,” I said, except I really wasn’t sure if she would.

JADE

Landon was trying to draw.

Okay, so it wasn’t really a drawing. It was supposed to be an attack plan. There were stick figure wolves, what I thought were supposed to be trees, and I had no clue why there was a half-moon in the background.

Aidan had been gone for forty-two minutes, and I thought it was totally lame that I actually knew the minute count. But, yeah, I did. I didn’t like that he was meeting my dad. I knew he was more than capable of handling himself, and Dominic had gone with him, but still, it didn’t seem like enough. And it also seemed like a waste of time. It wasn’t like Dad would tell him anything, but Aidan said we had to play it cool and keep my dad thinking we didn’t suspect him of anything.

I hated that he was right.

I glanced back at the drawing, tilting my head. Maybe if I looked at it from a different angle, the thing would make sense. Nope. I tried the other way. It didn’t work. I seriously had no clue what I was looking at.

I got up from my chair and went to the jumbo pad that Landon hovered over. “What is that supposed to be?” I asked, pointing at the half-moon that couldn’t really be a half-moon.

Landon stopped drawing and made a tragic face as if I had insulted him by asking. “It’s the mountain. I was trying to give it a backdrop. To make it look realistic.”

“You drew the wolves as stick figures,” Beck pointed out, chuckling. “I think you lost the whole realistic feel with that.”

“What’s the point of this?” I asked as I turned from the drawing and returned to my chair, pulling my legs up and crossing them.

Landon shrugged. “Just trying to be prepared,” he said. “And we could use a playbook, don’t you think?”

Craig groaned and leaned forward, planting his elbows on the table and resting his chin in his hands. “If you are going to be drawing our playbook, we’re in serious trouble.”

"Come on, it's not that bad," Landon said, cutting everyone an exaggerated *I'm wounded* kind of look.

"Yeah, man, it is," Mark said as he looked over the drawing. He patted Landon on the back roughly in mock consolation. "But keep practicing. You might get better at this whole drawing thing."

I rolled my eyes at the guys as they continued badgering Landon about his lack of art skills and glanced at my phone, wishing again that it would beep or ring or do something. I'd sent Jared at least five messages since Aidan left, and each one had gone unanswered. I understood why. Really, I did. But still …

"Jade." Beck's tone was a harsh bark, letting me know he knew exactly what was on my mind as I started to reach for the phone. He moved silently to the table and leaned against it to face me. "If you even think about texting him again, I'll confiscate that damn phone."

I let my hand fall back into my lap. Not for the first time today, I grew angry with the guys, and when I spoke, it showed in my tone. "I just want to know where he is."

"Not your concern anymore," Mark said softly and firmly as if he were trying to be absolute on the subject, but at the same time, he wanted to be compassionate.

I felt a little hurt, but not so much for myself. I felt it for Jared. Beck looked troubled, but I didn't think he had the right to be. I rubbed my face, my gaze drifting again to the phone.

"What is that?" Aidan said, drawing my attention to the doorway. He was staring at Landon's drawing with a seriously confused expression painted on his face.

"It's supposed to be our playbook of attack strategies," I said, uncrossing my legs and twisting around. "Did Dad tell you anything?"

He shook his head and said, "Nothing useful, but I think the eye twitch happens when he's nervous."

CHAPTER 17

JADE

My head hurt, a throbbing pain right behind my eyes. With each throb, a needle prick pinched at the bridge of my nose. My butt was beyond numb, and I couldn't feel my toes anymore. Aidan's hands kneaded at my shoulders and rubbed up my neck. His touch felt like heaven — simply amazing.

It was closing in on three in the morning, and still, the team was in strategy mode. Each one of them had picked up on different things during our interaction with my dad at my house yesterday morning. Mark noticed the left eye twitch. Beck picked up on a light apple butter scent when my dad had passed him in the hallway. Craig heard a hint of excitement lining Dad's tone when he had kicked me out. Dominic noticed how Dad watched Aidan as if he were waiting for an opening to rip out his throat. And Tommy and Chris, well, they seemed to notice a lot about Jared. Like the way, he watched me as if he wanted me dead. I didn't really blame Jared for that. If I were him, I figured I would probably want me dead, too.

We had taken a quick break at noon, long enough for Beck to sneak out and stash Erika at his house until he could figure out what to do with her. Craig had gone with him, and when they had gotten back, he looked completely wrecked, and as the hours passed by, he didn't look any better.

The table was scattered with empty pizza boxes and burger wrappers. Someone had pinned up a town map on the wall, and beside it was a jumbo pad of white paper hanging from an easel. Since Aidan had gotten back from the useless meeting with my dad, they had been mapping out each area they had searched for the cougars. Aidan pinpointed each spot he'd sent Trevor to as well. They marked each location with a red X and then placed a blue X on every place they had found tracks.

I'd thought we had made progress, but as I scanned the map from my seat, all I could see was how much territory we still had to search. Dog Mountain was secluded, surrounded by thousands of acres of bush, and there was also the entire mountain to cover. There were three times as many blue marks as there were red.

Aidan's fingers moved up my neck again, working the muscles along my spine, and I released a long groan when they hit the tender knot. I wasn't really sure how we had gone from barely speaking to this in less than twenty-four hours, but I didn't really care. Since seeing him yesterday, a longing, deep and close to unbearable, had settled within me, and having him close eased it a little. He leaned forward, resting his chin on my shoulder. "How you holding up, sweetheart?"

Sweetheart. It sounded so perfect and, at the same time, so weird. His fingers kept working at the kink in my neck, and his breath tickled along my cheek.

"I think my brain died about five hours ago," I said with a groan.

Aidan chuckled. He pressed his lips to my ear and whispered, "I'm taking you home."

Home. Another way too perfect-sounding word. His hands dropped from my neck, and his chin lifted from my shoulder, and then he was in front of me, taking my hands in his and pulling me up from the chair. He fired off a bunch of quick commands, telling everyone to get some sleep and meet back here at eight tomorrow morning, and then he led me out of the building and to his car.

I must have dozed off in the car, and Aidan must have carried me inside. The last thing I remembered was buckling up my seatbelt. Now I was tucked in a big bed, surrounded by Aidan's scent. My jeans were gone, so were my hoodie and socks. All I had on was my underwear, bra, and tank.

A number of sensations struck me all at once: the emptiness of the bed, the coldness of the room, Aidan's scent clinging to the sheets. But above all that, I felt a bitter stab of loneliness. I shivered, and a sharp roll of needles chased down my spine.

The room was black as pitch. Not even a stitch of light came through the drawn curtains. It took a few blinks for my eyes to adjust, but once they did, I tugged on the comforter, wrapping it around my shoulders, and then wiggled off the bed. The last thing I wanted right now was to be alone.

The upstairs of Aidan's house was as empty as it felt. There was a bathroom just off to the left of the room I'd been sleeping in, the door open and lights off. I kept moving, tiptoeing down the hallway. A bit of moonlight streamed in through a small window, casting shadows that I swore were trying to jump up and trip me. I picked up my pace, passing another bedroom that was again empty, not even a stitch of furniture, and I kept going, sneaking down the stairs as quietly as I could.

I found Aidan snoring on the couch. The curtains were drawn. The only light coming into the living room was through the tiny frosted peek-a-boo window on the door. He was on his back, one leg on the floor and one arm draped over his eyes. There was a blanket pulled up to his waist.

I stood at the base of the couch and tugged the comforter more snuggly around me, cocooning myself in its warmth, as I watched his chest rise and fall with each steady breath. My chest expanded, my heart warmed. He looked ... happy in sleep, a soft smile on his lips, his muscles relaxed and loose.

I sighed. My chest expanded a little more. I didn't know exactly what I was feeling, but it felt a heck of a lot like love. I sighed again and smiled as I turned away from him. I figured I should probably go back to bed even if I could have stood there all night and watched him sleep. I took a small step, a floorboard creaked, and Aidan's soft snores stopped. He didn't move, but his abs and pecs flexed. He pulled in a loud breath, and his muscles relaxed again.

I waited for him to say something, but he didn't, as if he were waiting to see what I would do. I hesitated for a second, watching him pull in breath after breath, and then I sat down, squeezing myself into the small space on the couch between his bent knee and stretched-out leg, pulling my feet up underneath me.

I felt him tense again and then relax. He kept an arm draped over his eyes but lifted the other and wound it around my waist, pulling me closer. He kept tugging until I shimmied around, and then he tugged some more until I was settled on top of him, my comforter still snug around me. I buried my head at the hollow of his neck. I could feel him swallow, his Adam's apple bobbing against my forehead. He tightened his arm around me. "Thank you," he said.

I leaned up, tucked my comforter under my arms, and planted my forearms on his chest. "For what?" I asked.

He smiled but still kept his arm over his eyes. "For forgiving me."

I grabbed his arm, lifting it so I could look at him. My heart skittered within my chest as he settled his beautiful brown eyes on me. "I'm really glad you stuck around long enough for me to come to my senses," I said.

Aidan cupped my cheek. "I would have waited forever," he said.

I sighed, and once more, my heart expanded. I really didn't know how this would work out, but I was determined to try. He let his arm fall back over his eyes, and I put my head back down on his chest, listening to the steady thump of his heart. He lifted his leg from the floor, and I wiggled around, tugging at the comforter until it loosened enough that I had one of my legs on either side of his thigh. I thought about telling him that we should move, head to the bed where there was more room, but I was too comfortable wrapped up in his arms, lying on top of him, and frankly, I didn't want more room.

We lay there in a perfect kind of silence for a few moments when a thought surfaced that effectively rocketed my blood pressure up about ten notches and set my skin on fire. I planted my forearms back on his chest, lifting myself up again to look at him. "Did you undress me?" The question came out as a whisper.

"What?" he asked. He slid his draped arm from his eyes to his forehead and squinted down at me.

"Did you undress me?" I asked again, louder this time. The butterflies in my belly became soaring birds, and my skin heated just about everywhere.

Aidan shifted, scrubbed at his face, and groaned. "Don't get all modest on me, Jade. I'm too tired. It's not like I left you naked. You're still covered. And I'm pretty sure I saw more of you that day when you were in that little towel than I did tonight."

"Chill out, alpha," I said teasingly, settling my head back down on his chest. "I was just asking. I don't remember coming in."

He chuckled. "I tried to wake you up, but you were completely out," he said and finished it off with a long yawn. "We've got to be up in a few hours." He lifted his head from the armrest that he had been using as a pillow and pressed a light kiss on my forehead. "Are you staying down here?"

"Would it bother you if I did?" I asked, snuggling deeper into his arms.

He squeezed me tighter and whispered, "It would bother me if you said no. I love having you this close."

I smiled. I was sure we would both be seriously cramped in the morning, but I didn't care. I closed my eyes, breathing in a deep drag of his scent, and the world softened and then dissolved as sleep took me.

CHAPTER 18

AIDAN

Two days after Jade moved into my house, her dad asked for another meeting.

I probably shouldn't have been relieved that Jade refused to come with me to see her dad, but I was. I needed a break. I never thought living with Jade would be easy, but I never imagined it would be this hard.

The biggest problem: Jade wouldn't let Jared go. He had been MIA for the last two days. The team said he needed some distance, and frankly, I was glad for it, even if we could have used his help with the hunt. I didn't want to see him, and I didn't want Jade to see him, either. I had promised her that I would leave him alone, and I planned to keep my word, but it was seriously getting harder and harder to do.

All Jade could talk about was Jared. She claimed she was just worried about him, but I knew it was more than that. Even after telling her everything Tommy found out, she still held onto him. She cared about him — a lot. I knew we had agreed to move on, forget about the past, and start over, but I just couldn't do it. Maybe I didn't trust her; I knew she still didn't trust me. And I was sure that our trust issues were the reason we still hadn't moved forward, why we still hadn't made our mate status official, and it made the whole living together thing seriously tense.

I'd lost track of how many times over the last few days I'd found her outside trying to call him. It wasn't that I cared that she was checking in on him. It was more that she felt the need to sneak outside and hide it from me. How was I supposed to move on when she was sneaking around? I even asked her as much this morning. Her response: an intense kiss, a cute smile, and then she told me I worry too much.

So now Jade was at home getting ready to meet up with the team, and I sat in the coffee shop, sipping a steaming cup of java. I needed time to clear my head before seeing her dad again, and I needed some peace and quiet to review the latest email report from Tommy and Chris.

The faux red leather booths were lumpy and uncomfortable, and the coffee was burnt, but I sipped it anyway. The coffee shop was relatively quiet, with only a few tables occupied. The waitress rushed by with steaming cups of coffee and a tray of pastries.

I scrolled through my phone, brought up the email from Chris, and scanned through it again. The report wasn't much. Chris said the team had something they figured they should probably share with me. Chris was leaving it up to me on whether I wanted to hear whatever it was from the team or if I wanted to meet with them first. The email was clear that they thought I should let the team tell me. I didn't know what to think, and honestly, with all the crap going on at home, I didn't think I could take many more confessions.

I hit the reply and was about to start tapping in my response when a woman said, "Aidan, could you spare a minute?" I glanced up to find a short blond moving over to my booth, looking nervous and out of place. I'd seen her before, but I couldn't place her. She looked to be in her mid-thirties, and she wasn't part of my pack. She wore the typical fall Dog Mountain outfit: jeans and a heavy sweater. She smiled, showing a brilliant flash of white teeth, and stopped beside me.

I glanced back at my phone; I still had about ten minutes until I was supposed to be at Jeff's. I gestured to the empty seat across from me and said, "Sure, what's up?"

She slid into the booth and extended her hand to me. "Rachel," she said as I clasped her hand. "I don't think I actually introduced myself when I ran into you a few weeks ago." She had a firm, steady grip as she pumped twice before letting go. "How are you liking Dog Mountain?"

I chuckled. I couldn't help it. The look she was giving me was all business. "I know that look," I said. "You're not here to chat. What's on your mind?"

She laughed and tucked a lock of her shoulder-length hair behind her ear. "Oh, you're good."

"Well, I do live with Jade," I said and chuckled again. "She's the queen of that look. I get it at least five times a day."

Her expression sobered a little more, and she leaned forward, placing her hands on the table. "Those guys at the bar," she said, jutting her chin and keeping her voice low. "They've been in here a lot over the last few days. Asking a lot of questions about Jared and the enforcers."

I glanced over my shoulder, spotting Tommy and Chris, and groaned. I hadn't even noticed them come in. Tommy nodded to me, and Chris chuckled. "Morning, boss," they chimed in unison.

I rolled my eyes and groaned again. "Please tell me you guys just walked in," I said, hoping that was the case because I seriously should have noticed their scent as soon as the doors opened and they came in.

Tommy laughed, a loud rumbling sound. "Been here for about ten minutes," he said. He got up and made his way over; Chris followed along. "You had that *I want to strangle Jade* look again, so we figured you needed the space."

I shook my head, turning my attention back to Rachel. "Next time they pester you, tell them to screw off," I said.

"Oh." She brought a hand to her mouth, and her eyes widened. "I didn't know you had new members. Shit!" She blushed, a deep crimson, and glanced at Tommy, her cheeks reddening further, and then she looked back at me. "I'm sorry for giving them a hard time, then."

I smirked. "Don't be sorry, knowing them, they deserved it."

"Hey," Tommy said, punching my shoulder playfully. "Don't give the lady the wrong idea about us, kid."

"See what I mean?" I said to Rachel, rolling my eyes. "They deserved it."

Rachel laughed, a nervous kind of laugh. "You're nothing like Ray, are you?" she asked, arching a brow and tucking more of her thick hair behind her ear.

I wasn't really sure what she meant by that, but I really hated how nervous she was sitting across from me, so I smiled the crooked smile that always worked to mellow out Jade and shook my head. "Nope. Nothing like him."

♥

Jeff was sitting on the porch steps when I got out of the car. He didn't look up as I approached. He was in jeans and a light gray fleece sweater, and he wore a black baseball cap that shadowed his face.

The sun was obscenely bright without a cloud in the sky, but the wind was brisk and heavy. The chain links that held the porch swing creaked and cracked as it swayed in the breeze. The van was gone, the driveway empty, but then I guess I hadn't really expected Pam to be home. According to Jade, she had been working like a dog since Jeff got back, furious at him for kicking her daughter out.

"My daughter didn't bother to come?" he asked, a hint of hopefulness in his voice, as he glanced back at the car as if he might have missed her at first. He kept his chin dipped and his face hidden under the brim of his cap.

I took a deep breath, trying to keep calm. I figured he knew I didn't like him; I was sure he could smell my distaste, but I didn't really care. "She doesn't have anything to say to you right now," I said evenly. "You did kick her out of her house."

He shrugged as if kicking out his only child was no big deal. "You were going to make her leave anyway."

A gust of wind hit my back as I stopped in front of him and my nostrils flared. The copper scent of blood was thick on the wind, and it carried the now familiar smell of cougars. It was an odd scent, almost like a house cat, but not. It was stronger, harsher, and had a hint of dried birch bark mixed with lemon.

"I don't have time for this shit, Jeff. She'll talk to you when she's ready, or she won't," I said, forging calm remoteness. I took another breath, trying to determine which direction the smell was coming from, but the wind was making it seriously hard to pin down. "What was so important that you needed to see me in person for?"

He lifted a hand, tipping up his cap with a fingertip, giving me a clear view of his blackened and swollen eye along with a busted up lip.

"What the hell happened to you?" I asked, scanning him over. There was a tear in his sweater, right at the neckline, and what looked like the remnants of a bruise on his cheek. His lip was healing, although it seemed slow for a shifter, or maybe he just really got his ass kicked. Either way, I didn't really care. The man deserved what he got.

"Jared came to see me this morning," he said. "He's on the outs with his brothers again. It never goes well when those boys are fighting. People get hurt."

I narrowed my eyes, folded my arms over my chest, and glared down at him. "Jared doesn't have any brothers, and I doubt he could do this."

Jeff smirked, causing his lip to split open again. "You sure about that?"

Was he joking? Damn, I couldn't tell. His scent gave nothing away. I was pretty sure Jared wouldn't show up here just to beat the crap out of him. If he was going to try and beat someone down, it would most likely be me. And I was certain he didn't have any brothers. From what Dominic had told me, Jared was the product of a one-night stand. He was the only enforcer that grew up in Dog Mountain. He'd never met his dad, and his mom died three years ago from an overdose.

Another gust of wind brought the scent of blood swamping around me. I breathed it in and turned, looking toward the tree line. The wind shifted, blowing from the other direction, and again, it brought the coppery smell back with it.

"He got a phone call while he was here, and he took off pretty quick," Jeff said and chuckled, a cruel sound that put ice in my veins. I shifted my gaze back to him, and he smiled wide. "I'll give you one guess who called him."

I gritted my teeth. I didn't need a guess. I knew exactly who had called him. "Jade."

Jeff didn't confirm it, but I guessed I didn't really need him to. I'd known something was up with her when she practically shoved me out the door this morning. But I had really been hoping it had nothing to do with Jared.

Jeff stood up and walked to the door. He was still smiling, enjoying the pain he was inflicting on me; I was sure of it. "Before you go running off to track down that mate of yours, I called you here to tell you I finally got a full count of the cougars, and I also picked up a little something for you that will lead you right to them." He shoved the door wide open and stepped back.

For a long moment, I didn't have a clue what I was looking at. The stench of cougar and blood was suddenly so thick that I almost gagged. I moved up the steps, holding my breath as I did. Sitting on a chair, tied tightly enough to cut through the skin, was a man about my age. His eyes were closed, his head lolled to the left. Blood dripped to the floor around his feet.

"Richard," Jeff said. The man lifted his head and slowly opened his eyes. "Meet Aidan, the alpha of the Dog Mountain pack."

CHAPTER 19

JADE

"It's official. I'm going to flunk out of high school," I said, slapping my textbook shut. My whole plan of studying for an hour before meeting up with the team was not going to happen. I couldn't focus my mind on anything other than what my father could possibly want. He had been lying low, avoiding us completely, and Aidan had sat back and watched, just like he'd promised me. But this morning, Dad had called, waking Aidan and me up, demanding a meeting.

Marcy giggled a trill sound that burst through the speakerphone of my cell. "You're not going to flunk out, Jade," she said. "Half your teachers are part of the pack. They wouldn't dare fail you." Clunking footsteps and a rustle of fabric flitted through the phone suddenly, and she squealed a little breathlessly. "Trevor, stop it. Alpha on the line."

Trevor grunted something that I thought might have been an apology, and I rolled my eyes, flopping back on the couch. "Don't you guys have Erika duty today?" I asked, picking up the list of late assignments and scanning it over. It was ridiculous how much homework could pile up over a week. As far as I was concerned, there should be some kind of law about homework. How the school system expected people to sit in class all day and then spend hours each night cramming in more knowledge was beyond me. Not that I had been sitting in class much lately, but that was beside the point. It was a sunny Saturday morning, and I was stuck on the couch surrounded by a mountain of work. Where was the home/school balance?

"Don't remind me," Marcy said, her voice sounding further

away and a bit fuzzy as she switched me to speakerphone. "She's driving me insane. Tell me again why we're putting up with that … that …" she groaned. "See, she has me so pissed off I can't even think of a good name for her. I get the whole going after the single alpha thing, but I don't know how she could do this to Craig."

"I'm supposed to be diplomatic now," I said, dropping the list to the couch. "And protecting a wolf that helped the pack is diplomatic."

Marcy snorted. "You, diplomatic? Yeah, right."

"Hey, I totally resent that," I said, except she probably had a point. I really wasn't the diplomatic type, but still, I was trying to be somewhat reasonable. "I can be diplomatic. You've got to admit it, I've got skills. If I didn't, you wouldn't be lounging in Trevor's bed right now, would you?" And pulling that one off had taken mad skills. I'd sat with her dad for hours trying to explain the whole mate status thing and what that actually meant. In the pack world, she was literally married now. I'd done a crapload of bargaining and more negotiating than I'd ever done before, but in the end, we'd finally come to an agreement, and Marcy had moved in with her mate. Seriously, the whole thing had been a perfect example of exactly how diplomatic I could be when I needed to.

"How's everything going with Aidan?" Trevor asked casually.

I took a deep breath. "I don't know. He's been crazy bossy, and I swear he hasn't left me alone for even a second in the last two days. It's like he thinks if he turns his back, I'll just vanish." I'd known that trying to start over would be work — a lot of work — but he was being impossible. Whenever he was around, the problem was that birds flapped in my belly, and my heartbeat pretty much tripled. He made my body sing and my inner-wolf dance. And I loved him. I really did. There was no denying it, not anymore. I just didn't have the strength or energy to do it anymore. But sometimes, space was a good thing, and Aidan hadn't been giving me much space (or any space) over the last two days.

And yet here I was alone. Actually alone. Sure, I had basically shoved him out the door this morning, but still, after two days of his hovering, it felt weird not having him standing over my shoulder, and whether I liked it or not, his absence made my inner-wolf uneasy.

"He's your mate, Jade, and an alpha," Trevor said. "Of course, he's bossy. His inner-wolf wants to keep you safe. It's probably all he can think about. Give the guy a break."

"He's not my mate," I countered, the weight of my words close to unbearable, and I suddenly found it hard to catch my breath. "I don't know if this whole starting over idea was such a hot idea."

That wasn't entirely true. I didn't regret starting over. In truth, even with Aidan's constant closeness, and his increasing possessiveness, I was glad I was here — with him. But if I took that step, I wasn't sure who I would be anymore. I wasn't even really sure who I was now. I had adapted to my new life. I had survived. I thrived as a werewolf. And well, it had become comfortable. The truth? I was terrified that if I took that step with Aidan, I'd lose myself, that I'd become just another piece of him. There had to be a balance — somewhere.

Never fall so hard that you can't live without him. You need to stay your own person. Mom's advice to Marcy when she'd broken up with Trevor for the first time never strayed far from my mind these days. I thought they were supposed to be words of wisdom, except I didn't know how to stop myself from falling, and I was falling fast. It didn't help one freakin' bit that our inner-wolves knew there would be no one else. They were done with waiting, and darn it, but the thought made me glow from the inside out.

"Has the last few days really been horrible?" Marcy asked.

"No," I said a little grudgingly, staring at the phone on the coffee table. "They've been perfect. He cooks, cleans. He's considerate, and he even lets me have the television remote. It's sickening. He's not supposed to be this sweet. But I need to just be *Jade* for a while. I need to find my way through this make a place for myself in the pack. I might have won the games for alpha female, but it's almost as if the males can't see me as my own person, like I'm just another arm of him, not important but there anyway."

If I had been hoping they would disagree with me, I was left disappointed. The silence stretched on for a long moment before I asked, "Have you guys seen Jared? The guys won't tell me anything, and with Aidan hovering, I haven't really been able to check on him."

"It's for the best, Jade," Trevor said. "You need to forget about him. If you would move on and embrace your mate, you'd see a shift in everyone's attitude." His tone was firm but not cold. Trevor was one of the few male pack members who hadn't shunned me over the whole Jared thing, although I was pretty sure it was only because he was mated to my best friend. He had to play nice, and so did I.

"How is this fair?" I asked. "Aidan actually messed around with

Erika, and no one batted an eye at it. All I did was pretend to have a boyfriend, a few public kisses, that's it." A frustrated growl rumbled around my chest.

"Aidan hasn't hated the pack for two years," Trevor said, his tone measured and tense. I figured Marcy was probably giving him a look to stop him from telling me off. "We all know how you felt about us. It's not like you hid it. You didn't bother to try once you became one of us. You showed complete disregard for our ways, decided you didn't need to follow our laws, and you publicly humiliated our alpha — your mate — and walked away with an enforcer."

He was right. Yes, I had done all that, but in all fairness, I hadn't known that I was doing it. No one had bothered to tell me the rules.

The sound of a car pulling into the driveway drew my attention, and I glanced out the window. I watched for a moment as a white Honda pulled to a stop, and then a pack member got out. "Got to go, guys. Luken's here," I said as I watched him walk up the driveway. He knocked on the door, thumping three bangs that rattled the hinges. "Get to Beck's. He needs a break." They both mumbled a reluctant agreement before ending the call.

I crossed over to the door, pulling it open. I didn't even get a chance to say hi before Luken asked, "Where's the alpha?" His arms were folded over his massive chest, and he focused a dark glare on me. The werewolf was close to enforcer status, just one row down in the pack's pecking order. He was built like an enforcer, too, tall with more muscle than any one person needed. He was in jeans, a black baseball cap, and an off-white fall jacket.

"You're looking at her," I said, aware that I had hesitated way too long before answering him.

He stood perfectly still for a moment as his nostrils flared, and then he leaned forward, taking a deep sniff of my scent. His lips curved in disgust. "You're not my alpha. Where is he?"

I laughed, a startling sound, and brought a hand to my chest in mock hurt. "Ouch. You know if you guys keep this up, I might actually start to believe you don't want me here."

He lifted one shoulder in a small shrug. "We don't," he said. An easy smile curved his mouth. "Where's Jared been?" He sounded cautious as if he were testing how far he could push me without crossing the invisible line that would lead to me telling Aidan or unleashing my alpha scent on him. Even so, tension slid down my spine, awakening my inner-wolf and ratcheting up my anxiety.

I was sure that the pack males knew I was clutching onto my independence with a fiercely tight hold. Luken wasn't the first in the last two days to talk to me like this or ask me about Jared, and I was sure he wouldn't be the last.

"What do you need, Luken?" I asked, planting my hands on my hips and giving him my best *no-nonsense* look. The wind ruffled his jacket, filling the space between us with a light rustling of fabric. "I've got stuff to do."

I held onto my inner-wolf tightly, keeping her growing annoyance balled and contained. She was getting tired of the constant challenge of our authority, but really, so was I. In my mind, it shouldn't matter that I wasn't a mated alpha. I had taken out every challenger. I deserved their respect even if I had walked away from my mate.

"You wouldn't understand." He paused for a moment and then said, "Just tell him to call me." And with one last disgusted look my way, he turned from me and stalked down the driveway to his waiting car.

I stood there for a moment, feeling like a piece of crap, at least until the car door slammed. It was amazing how much damage I had done to the pack without even trying, and I was actually starting to feel guilty about it. I blinked, watching him pull out of the driveway before retreating back to the couch.

So that sucked, I thought. I didn't want to believe it, but maybe Trevor was right. Maybe I needed to move on. But I knew I wasn't wrong either. Wanting to be my own person, not be defined by who I was with, wasn't wrong.

I glanced at my phone, reached for it, and pulled back. I knew there really was only one thing to do. I had to fix things, and I knew exactly where I needed to start. I reached for my phone again, snagged it up, and made the call before I could change my mind.

CHAPTER 20

JADE

I sucked in the fresh air. My lungs couldn't get enough of it. Clean and crisp and cool. The jog over to the clearing had been refreshing and relaxing. I stood hunched over, my hands on my knees, pulling the air into my lungs and expelling it in slow, deep puffs.

The sun was out in full force this morning, coating the clearing where I had spent many hours in training with Jared and Beck in a warm glow. Leaves rattled across the dried-out grass as they were carried in a cool breeze.

I knew he was behind me, watching from the tree line, but I needed a moment to just breathe. His scent was thick in the air, a mix of caution and a hot spike of tempered anger. I figured he was waiting for someone else to show up. I didn't really blame him for that, but it hurt a little that he assumed I'd try to set him up.

Another couple of minutes passed before I heard the crunch of leaves underfoot behind me. I pulled in a few more deep breaths and slowly straightened, turning toward him.

"Hey, little girl," he said, looking me over with cool eyes as he walked toward me. I didn't really know what I had expected when I saw him, but what I saw definitely wasn't it. Jared looked ... good. Really good, actually. He had gotten a haircut, his black hair short, spiked, and gelled. His face was clean-shaven, smooth, and fresh-looking, and there wasn't a stitch of darkness under his eyes. The tension he had carried around with him while he had stayed with me was gone. I didn't recognize the leather jacket he was sporting, and underneath he had on a light green tee that I was sure I had never seen him wear before. He usually kept to blacks. It hugged his sculpted chest, outlining his thick pecs.

He stopped a few feet away from me, and his eyes swept over me in a thorough inspection. His nostrils flared a few times, and then he smirked. I knew what he was looking for, a change in my scent, and I seriously hated that smug look that was etching itself onto his face. "Does he know you're here?" he asked, amusement thick in his voice.

"Does it matter?" I countered blandly, lifting a brow. A gnawing sense that I was walking in a gray area surfaced, and it scared the crap out of me. My muscles tensed, my stomach started to twist, and I tried to breathe through it, hoping he wouldn't notice.

Jared chuckled, a husky sound. One that usually sent my inner-wolf into a round of manic backflips, but oddly enough, she was calm and steady. It was strange and, well, amazing. But then I guessed living with Aidan had calmed her. But still, I had kind of expected the franticness, the racing heart, but it didn't come, and my coiled muscles began to unwind.

"Nope," he said. His smirk widened. "Just didn't figure he'd loosen up on that short leash he's been keeping you on long enough for you to sneak away."

Ouch. Okay, the truth of his statement kind of sucked. I tried not to frown, but it happened anyway. Yeah, Aidan had been keeping me close, but frankly, I was just as bad as he had been. I hated having him out of my sight.

But was I really so transparent that Jared could see that I had snuck out, or did he just know me that well? I could feel the scrunch in my forehead and a knot deep in my belly twisted and yanked. The gray area flapped in front of me again. *I probably should have told Aidan,* I thought. I should have given him a choice to come with me, too. But honestly, I hadn't wanted to get that look again. The one who told me he didn't trust me enough to go alone; the same one I would have given him if he had told me he wanted to see Erika.

"I didn't sneak away, and he doesn't have me on a leash," I snapped, except it didn't sound believable. I took a step toward him, and he backed up a step, putting up a hand as if he were asking me not to come any closer.

My frown deepened, tugging at my lips. I huffed. He looked at me as if I were the dangerous one out of the two of us, which was pretty much a laughable notion. I never thought I would see the day that I would make the head of the enforcers nervous. And, man, had I tried to make him nervous in our training. But Jared didn't get nervous, not usually. He fought. Sometimes he lost, mostly he won. His job as an enforcer was black and white for him. *Fear and nerves are for the weak*, he'd told me. *Win or lose, don't show fear.*

I plopped down onto the grass, stretching my legs out in front of me, and leaned back, propping myself up on my elbows, trying to make myself look unthreatening. "Where have you been?"

"Around," he said with a lazy lift of his shoulders. He scanned the length of my body again, letting his scent thicken in the air. When I gave him no reaction, he lowered himself to the ground, sprawling out on his back still a few feet away from me.

"Really?" I asked. "That's all you're going to give me?"

Jared sighed long and loud as he stared up at the cloudless sky. "What did you expect, Jade?" he asked in a hushed tone. "You made your choice. I didn't want to stick around and watch."

I groaned and cut him an exasperated look. Too bad he still wasn't looking at me. "There was never a choice, Jared. I never hid that from you. You knew from the start I was his. Don't you dare try to make this about *us* because you know damn well that there never was an *us*."

He lay on his back as still as rocks except for the steady, even rise of his chest as he breathed. He was quiet for a crazy long moment before he finally said, "I needed a break. The team is a nightmare with Aidan's newbies hanging around."

I laughed. "Nightmare?" I said and laughed again. "You want to talk about nightmares? Hell, I'm living in a damn nightmare."

Jared chuckled. He shifted onto his side, propping his head upon his hand. His dark brown eyes searched my face with an intensity that made me shiver, not a pleasurable one. His eyes were cold and calculating and hard, and they traveled along my skin as if he were watching the shiver spread down my body. His lips quirked into a cocky, one-sided grin. "Awe, kitten, is that soon-to-be mate of yours not treating you as good as you thought he would?"

I bristled like a porcupine, and my inner-wolf became seriously agitated within me at his insinuation. "He treats me just fine," I said through my teeth. "It's keeping him from hunting you down that's the freakin' nightmare. On top of that, most of the males hate me. And you hiding away like I've ripped out your heart is only fueling their anger. It makes us look guilty."

That wiped the smirk off his face. His brown-black eyes hardened and cooled again. "Maybe we are guilty."

I rolled up to my feet and paced the few steps over to him. "I'm not buying this *poor me* act," I said, smirking. "And by the way, you suck at it."

That earned me a throaty chuckle. "Come on, I know you felt a little bad."

"The team needs you, Jared," I said, ignoring him. "Aidan needs you. He might not want to admit it, but he does." I extended a hand to him. For a minute, I didn't think he was going to take it. He schooled his expression into a blank mask of indifference, and as he did, I whispered, "Please."

As soon as the whisper left my lips, he took my hand and pulled himself up. He stood in front of me for a moment before he tugged on my hand and wrapped me in a tight hug, resting his chin on the top of my head.

I stood stiff in his arms, waiting for my inner-wolf to perk up at his nearness, but she didn't, not in the way she usually did, so I wrapped my arms around his waist and squeezed back.

CHAPTER 21

AIDAN

"What am I supposed to do with this?" I asked, waving a hand toward the man, tied and bleeding out onto the floor. I felt cold and tired. I probably should have been mad, but I just couldn't drudge up the emotion. Jade was with Jared. Cold and tired and disappointed was pretty much all I had right then. Ice slid over my skin. I wanted to dig out my phone and call her. How long had I been gone? An hour? She didn't have a car, but he could have picked her up. My brain raced and swirled with all the things she could have done with him in the last hour. My stomach rolled. I swallowed hard. "He can barely hold his head up."

Jeff chuckled and shook his head. "He'll heal," he said. "The count's eighteen." He chuckled again. "Seventeen now." He moved into the house, rounded Richard, and placed a hand on his shoulder, his grip hard. "I was supposed to kill this one, but I figured he could be of use to you. Like I told you, they were moving locations when I left, and he's been to their new hot spot." He dug his fingers into Richard's shoulder hard enough that the man groaned and winced, and then he let go, shrugged his shoulders, and said, "But if you don't want him, I can dispose of him."

I couldn't focus. I knew I needed to. I knew that Jeff was playing me, and I needed to pay attention, read between the lines, but all I could think about was Jade. Was it so wrong that I wanted to keep her close, protect her, hold her, to have her in every possible way? She seemed to think so. *"Stop being such an overbearing dog,"* she'd said to me this morning, laughing. She had kissed me, kissed my cheeks, my lips, my neck, a flutter of delicate presses along my skin. *"I'm yours, Aidan. You have nothing to worry about."*

But she wasn't mine. Not really. Not fully. Most of all, I wanted her to want me the way I wanted her. To be with me. I thought that was the part that was eating at me the most. When she was with me, she wasn't really with me. Her mind was with him. I was lost to her. Completely lost. At some point, those ideas of love had gripped me, turning into so much more than just ideas. And knowing that she was out somewhere with Jared, that she clearly didn't feel the same as I did, was wrecking me.

I guessed that was probably why Jeff had told me where she had run off to. I figured he wanted me distracted. "What's his death sentence for?" I asked, trying to push her out of my mind, even for a second.

"He fell in love, took off with one of the women just before the accident." Jeff's tone held a note of remorse, remorse that I knew he didn't feel. "He was stupid enough to go back, and when he was caught, they called me to get rid of the problem."

The rage I had been missing surfaced and thrashed against my skull. *Accident.* The way he said it was as if it were actually an accident such as a car crash or a house fire. But it was nothing like that. His pack had brutally used two women, used them until they died. It wasn't an accident. He didn't care that they were dead. I was even willing to bet he had known they would die.

"I can help you," Richard rasped. He struggled to lift his head enough to meet my eyes. His were a cool blue, hard and full of conviction. "I want to help you."

"We'll take him," I said, fished my phone out of my pocket, and thumbed the screen. 9:30. Jade had been alone, or with *him*, for an hour and a half. I should have killed him. I could have, too. In the eyes of pack law, Jared had done enough to be put down, but Jade ... she wouldn't even let me throw him out of the pack, claiming none of his crimes was his fault. They were hers.

Another rush of ice pushed through me. I stared at the clock. A minute ticked by. I knew I needed to call the team in the back of my mind. Get them here. Deal with the cougar. If nothing else, I wanted time to question him before he met his death, but I stood there frozen, staring at the clock. Another minute passed, and then another.

"I know what you're thinking," Jeff said blandly. I glanced up as he stepped away from Richard. There was a pitiless, callous glint in his eyes as he approached me. "You're wondering how long she's been gone, counting the seconds, minutes, maybe even hours since you left her this morning. She probably told you she would take a shower and meet up with the team. She's been trying so hard to help, and you wanted to believe her. You want to trust her, but you can't, not really. Not when you know he can speak to her inner-wolf and that she cares about him enough that she has to hide it from you." He paused, smiled, and chuckled. "I bet you're trying to figure out how long she's been with him this morning. Did she actually take that shower? How long could that have taken?" He stopped in front of me, his smile widening. "You should have taken my advice. You shouldn't have waited to claim her as your own. If you had done it, you'd see Richard as something of value to you and not just another problem for you to solve."

Listening to him speak about his daughter as if she were a piece of meat was like walking through the pits of a garbage dump. Stomach-turning and vile. But even if listening to him made bile rise in my throat, he'd summed up everything that was racing through my head. I forced out a laugh that I hoped sounded somewhat believable and lied, "Actually, I was thinking you have a lot of cleaning to do before your wife gets home from work."

He chuckled and said, "I'm sure that's exactly what you were thinking."

For half a second, I entertained the idea of shifting and ripping out the man's throat. Oddly enough, it was my inner-wolf who pushed the thought away. I'd promised our mate that I wouldn't hurt her father, and it seemed as if my inner-wolf was determined to make me keep that promise. He wasn't willing to make a move that could jeopardize my chance at claiming her.

I thumbed my phone again, bringing up Beck's number, and tapped it as I headed down the steps of the porch, putting some distance between myself and the bastard Jade called a father. It rang twice before he answered. "How'd the meeting go?" he asked.

"Gather the guys and come to Jeff's," I said, walking down the driveway, away from Jeff. I let my voice drop low and added, "And send someone to track down Jade."

"What do you mean 'track down Jade?'" he asked, his voice taking on a hard edge.

"She's with Jared," I said and swallowed the rotten taste that had filled my mouth that was full of my useless anger.

"You let her go see him." It wasn't a question. I didn't miss the blunt accusation in his voice. Beck had taken on a *big brother* kind role with Jade. The whole team had, actually. She had them wrapped around her finger, and they loved it, loved her, and right now, Jared wasn't in their good graces.

"She told me she was going to study and then meet you guys," I growled. The rotten, rusty taste filled my mouth again, and I tried to swallow it down.

"Shit," he said, summing the whole situation up perfectly. He growled out a few more obscenities before he said, "Let me go for her."

I clenched the phone tighter, feeling every muscle in my body flex right along with my fingers. His reaction wasn't helping my mood, even if it was exactly what I had expected. "I don't care who goes for her. Just send the guys to me and have someone bring her back to the headquarters. Jeff is giving us one of the cougars." I didn't wait for his response before ending the call. I shoved my phone back into my pocket and focused every bit of energy I had on reining in my emotions.

JADE

Jared's arms felt solid wrapped tightly around me. He was taller than me, not a lot, but enough that he had to bend a little to whisper in my ear. "You sure about this?"

I nodded. "Yes. I wouldn't be here if I weren't. Aidan's never going to get over it if you keep running, and like I said, he needs you now more than ever."

He moved back slightly to meet my eyes and brushed a strand of hair from my cheek with a big warm hand. "He might not agree," he pointed out.

I shuddered. No, Aidan probably wouldn't agree. I had no doubt that he would want to throttle me when I brought Jared back, but it was a risk I had to take. The longer he stayed away, the guiltier we looked. The pack needed to see the three of us working together. They needed to see my reaction. They needed to know that I wouldn't turn back to Jared when things got tough, that I was with them, and most of all, that I was with Aidan.

And I knew Jared wanted to be different. I saw that. Over the last few days, he'd worked so hard to show me that he did care about the pack. He may be a cocky pain in my ass, he may push all of my buttons, but he was loyal. He was pack. He was family.

I grinned. "You leave Aidan to me. He'll come around." Okay, I wasn't entirely sure that he would come around, but I was hoping he would.

Jared chuckled and shook his head, clearly thinking I was mental. Right then, I wasn't sure that I disagreed.

"You have a death wish, don't you?" Beck, his voice rough, pierced through me like a row of sharpened teeth.

"It was just a hug," I squeaked, jumping out of Jared's arms. "What are you doing here?"

Beck was tense but trying not to show it. I could see it in his set face and the way his shoulders bunched, emphasizing the muscles under his jacket. "Aidan sent me to find you." He didn't crack his usual *you're a pain in the ass* smile, but then, neither did I. "Haven't you put him through enough of this bullshit?"

Nice. It was going to be one of *those* days.

"You've got to be kidding me," I said in a stronger voice, although there was a bit of a whine to it. I couldn't help the small smirk, and Beck rolled his eyes. "I'm not doing anything wrong here. It's just a hug."

"Just a hug," he repeated as if I'd said the words in some foreign language, and he couldn't quite grasp the meaning. There wasn't a doubt in my mind that he was disappointed with me, and, man, did it make me feel like an ass. I probably should have stopped at, *"I'm not doing anything wrong here,"* because the look he shot me made me want to find a rock to crawl under, full of animosity and frustration. He paced toward me. He looked as if he wanted to grab and shake some sense into me. "If you really believed that, you would have told Aidan where you were going. You were warned to stay away from him."

I opened my mouth and then closed it when nothing came out. He stopped only inches from me, folding his arms over his chest, still giving me a god-awful expectant kind of look as if he were waiting for a detailed explanation. It was the kind of look Dominic or Marcy would give me, but really, I had nothing that would make this look better, so I kept my mouth clamped shut.

"Beck, lay off," Jared said, pressing in closer to me again. "She was trying to convince me to come back. That's all. Give her a break."

"If you speak again, I'm going to punch you," Beck said softly, but it was clear that he meant it. He glared at Jared. There was a warning in his eyes that I couldn't even begin to understand, but I figured Jared did. He moved in a blink, propping himself against a tree about ten feet away.

Beck's nostrils flared as he fixed his eyes back on me. "His scent is on you," he said, gritting his teeth and digging out his phone. He tapped on the screen, brought it to his ear, and after a second, he said, "I've got her." He paused, scanned me over, and moved a little closer. He grabbed my shoulder, spinning me around, and then he lifted my hair, inspecting my neck and shoulders. "I'm checking, Aidan, just hold on," he barked. He did a thorough once over of my clothes and then said, "There's not even a hair out of place on your mate." He paused, cut a furious look at Jared, and said, "Yeah, I'll bring them both in."

I could hear the heated tone of Aidan's voice as he gave his orders but couldn't quite make out the words. *Oh, God.*Nausea rolled in my belly. I held out my hand and said, "Give me the phone. I want to talk to him." Beck started to pass the phone but hesitated, listening for a moment to whatever Aidan was saying. He scowled at me, shaking his head, and then thumbed the screen and jammed the phone into his pocket. "Beck, what the hell?"

"He heard you and said 'no.'" There was a dry, cutting edge to his tone that I really didn't like.

"Is he mad?" I whispered, my throat closing up. My chin started to dip on its own, and my shoulders sagged. It wasn't that I hadn't secretly seen this coming, well, okay, not exactly this, but I'd had a hunch that Aidan wouldn't be all that pleased with me dragging Jared back into the mix. But I knew that what I was doing was right. If anything, we needed to keep the pack together — keep them safe — and even if Aidan didn't like Jared, as the head of our team of enforcers, he was a big part of the pack.

Beck frowned. "Disappointed, definitely hurt. You've got to stop this shit, Jade. You threw the guy away because he lied to you. Do you really think this is any different?"

"Jared and I are just friends," I said. "It was never anything else. You know that."

Jared's temper flared. The heat in his scent pulled my eyes to him. His face shifted slightly, his eyes flashing gold, and then it faded, but the heat in the air lingered. Beck flashed him another cold glare just as Jared opened his mouth, and he closed it, biting back whatever he was about to say.

"It doesn't matter what I know," Beck said, softening a little. "Finding you in the bush alone with him doesn't look good. What if it had been someone else? What if he'd called Craig or Landon instead of me? You need to start thinking, Jade. You can't just run off like this. You wouldn't do it with the team, and you can't do it with him. He's your partner; you need to treat him like one." He huffed, and then a wicked smirk curved his lips, and he chuckled. "You are going to be in so much shit when he smells Jared on you."

"Not funny, Beck," I said with a sigh and then ran my fingers through my tangled, windblown hair.

"Yeah, it kind of is." His gaze was still dark with disappointment, but at least he was smiling now. "I love seeing that look on your face when he growls at you. It's priceless."

I smirked and stretched out my arms. "Want a hug?"

He shook his head and took a large step back. "Oh, hell no, you screwed up, you pay the price. I'm not getting in the middle of this shit."

CHAPTER 22

JADE

Aidan didn't look happy. He was leaning against the concrete side of the building. His arms folded over his chest, glowering, when Jared, Beck, and I emerged from the woods.

My heart did a little flip-flop against my ribs, and I stopped abruptly. Even glowering, he was a sight; tall and broad, with so much muscle. He was in jeans and a long-sleeved white T-shirt. His shaggy, light brown hair was flipping at the sides and disheveled on top, and all I could think about was running my hands through it. His intense brown eyes met mine, and I watched, frozen in place, as they flashed gold. He pointed at me, wagging a finger, beckoning me. My inner-wolf perked up, pushing at my skin, desperate to break free and run to her mate.

But I didn't move. It was as if my feet were pinned in place, no longer connected to my body. A rush of wind kissed my cheeks, bringing with it an assault of scents: leafy greens, hot power, the tang of anger and anxiety, and mixed with it all was a coating of spice. It was the spice that freaked me out the most. I knew exactly what it meant. He was jealous, which was, well, annoying, but it was also a little hot, and I shuddered hard.

Aidan's lips parted, and he growled. His eyes flared brighter. He beckoned me again, his finger stiff as he flicked it. I took a shaky, unsure step. The emotions in his scent were seriously nerve-racking, and they were also overly exciting my inner-wolf, sending hot chills over my skin and warmth pooling in my belly. It wouldn't take much for his inner-wolf to push to the forefront, for him to go all *alpha* on me, and I fought back the feeling that maybe, just maybe, I had made a mistake. I shuddered again, and his nostrils flared.

I took another step, and Beck snagged my wrist, pulling me to a quick stop. "Jade, play nice," he warned.

I shook off his hand. Now was so not the time to touch me, like at all. Not when my inner-wolf was all squirmy, wanting her mate. I put my feet in motion and picked up my pace to a jog. "Hey," I said, meekly, as I approached. "How did your meeting go?"

Aidan didn't answer. His jaw was tense, the muscles along his neck, roped and straining. I picked up my pace further, closing the distance between us as quickly as I could, and as soon as I was close enough, I threw my arms around his neck, pressing myself flush against him. He shifted his gaze, glancing down at me, and I rolled onto tip-toes. I meant to kiss him, ease some of the jealous rage I saw flaring in his eyes, but he wasn't having it. Before I knew it, his nose was pressed to my neck, dipping to my chest, and then back up to my hair, pulling in long, deep hauls.

I felt the growl bouncing around in his chest just before I heard it. His hands wrapped around my wrists, pulling them from his neck, and he glared down at me. His jaw worked as he clenched his teeth, and he growled, "Gym shower. Now."

"Wow, really?" I asked, leaning back. I smiled the sweetest smile I could, hoping it would soften him. It didn't. He let go of my wrist, folding his arms back over his chest. I huffed and glanced over my shoulder, watching Jared and Beck make their way to us. Beck was already chuckling, a deep rumbling from his chest. "Two guys telling me I smell in the last few days. You know, if you all keep it up, I'm going to develop a serious complex."

"Jade," Aidan said in warning, clearly not seeing the humor in my statement.

"It was just a hug, Aidan," I muttered, feeling about fifty different kinds of guilty. My inner-wolf squirmed and sunk in my stomach as if she were feeling just as bad.

He studied me with a strange intensity, almost as if he were seeing something new in me, and if I had to guess, whatever he was seeing wasn't something that he liked much. "Go wash that smell off of you," he said roughly as if his throat had been shredded and was raw.

I laughed nervously, placing a hand on the swell of his rounded pec. "There's no way I'm leaving you with him, not with you all growly." I poked him in the chest. "And don't look at me like I've done something wrong because I haven't, and you know it. You need him."

If Aidan heard me, he clearly wasn't processing my words. "Jade, please go shower," he said and nudged me toward the door.

I took his hand. It felt warm, good, solid and strong, and perfect. "Come with me?"

I figured it was the right question to ask because his sudden grin was one hundred percent male. He bent, scooping me up in his arms in a motion so quick that I squealed. My arms flew around his neck, holding on, as he yanked open the door and stepped inside.

AIDAN

"How many times do I have to tell you that I'm yours before you believe me?" Jade asked. Her head was cradled in the hollow space between my neck and shoulder as I carried her through the network of hallways to the gym.

Jared's bitter scent clung to her, but it was the underline sharpness of his arousal that stirred the beast within me into a wild, rage-induced frenzy. Another male had been turned on while touching *my* mate. Another male touched *my* mate. Another male ... A growl ripped from my throat.

"If it were really true, we wouldn't be waiting." I knew I shouldn't have as soon as I said it, but I couldn't hold it back. My inner-wolf was pressing under my skin, itching to break free. He wanted his mate, craved to mark her with his scent, claim her as his. But, oh hell, so did I.

"That's such a guy thing to say," she said, cuddling closer. It was as if she were oblivious to the turmoil thrashing around within me. My muscle flexed; my grip on her tightened. "I don't need your scent in me to make us real, Aidan." Her lips, soft and moist and warm, brushed along my neck, but it did nothing to calm my inner-wolf. Her brush-off only agitated him — me — further. "You shouldn't need it either."

I shouldered the door to the gym and stalked to the back changing rooms. My nostrils were flaring, my heart was thundering with adrenaline. My inner-wolf urged me to lock her up, shift, and kill the bastard who had dared to touch her. He wanted to hunt. He wanted blood. And then he wanted to bathe his mate with his scent. It was as if I'd lost all rational thought. I needed to hunt. Kill. Claim. Protect. My mind was functioning on the most primal level, lost within the need of my inner-wolf.

Two pack members ran on treadmills in the far corner of the room. "Out. Now," I growled, my voice sounding far more animal than human. The whirl of the treadmills halted immediately, and they vacated the gym in a rush, keeping their eyes glued to the floor as they went.

I pushed through the doors to the changing room and flipped the deadbolt on the door, locking us in. I set her down, and she twirled around. Her head came to the bottom of my chin as she faced me. She glanced up, her big brown eyes full of concern, and when she met my furious gaze, she took a fast step back.

"You're right. I probably shouldn't," I said, following her as she continued to back up with every step I took. Her eyes were wide, and I watched closely, waiting for alarm or fear to show. If she showed fear, I would have stepped back in a second, but her scent was screaming excitement, so I continued my advance. "But when you throw yourself at another male, come back to me smelling of him, of his arousal, it makes it hard to believe you."

Her lips quirked into a sexy as hell smirk. She backed into the long row of showers, unzipping her hoodie and shrugging it off. My pulse quickened.

"How am I supposed to lead this pack when I can't even keep tabs on my mate?" I growled. "You blatantly lied to me, Jade. You were supposed to be here with the team, but you snuck out to meet *him* instead."

She kicked off her shoes, hopping around from one foot to the other as she yanked off her socks. Her eyes, flecked with gold, were trained on my lips as she licked hers. I continued my slow advance, and she stopped, letting her eyes rake over me.

I was pretty sure she wasn't listening, her scent thickening in the air, calling me to her, but I had to get it out. She had to hear it all. "Do you really think no one notices this crap? That the pack doesn't see it? You're single-handedly ripping apart our pack, and you're doing it with a damn smile." I took one more step and reached out, cupping her cheeks in my hands. "I love you, Jade. Probably more than I should, and I'm beginning to think that's the problem with us. We're the alpha pair. Caring complicates our job."

Jade flushed a rosy pink. "I didn't throw myself at him," she said, her voice husky. "And I don't think he was aroused. We're just friends, Aidan."

I let my hands fall from her face. My jaw locked with tension. "I can smell it, Jade. He wants you." My voice was stiff, low, furious, and my inner-wolf howled for blood.

My inner-wolf challenged me for dominance. I pressed against Jade, letting him take control, and I leaned in, taking her mouth with mine. She whimpered. Liquid fire ran through my blood. There was nothing careful about how I held her. I was done with being careful. She was mine. And by the sugar-sweet change in her scent, I could tell she didn't mind what I was doing.

I stepped into her, pushing her back until she was pressed against the tiled wall, caging her between my arms, and she melted against me. Heat crawled across my skin as her lips parted and her hot tongue pushed and tangled with mine.

The kiss helped to calm my inner-beast, but having our mate near, tasting her, wasn't enough. I broke the kiss and growled against her plump, swollen lips, "You're mine, do you understand me?"

"Yes," she whimpered, her inner-wolf flaring up in her golden eyes. Her fingertips ran along my back, her nails lengthening into claws as they descended along my spine.

"Say it," I growled against her mouth, my voice thick with need even to my own ears. "I want to hear you say it."

Jade took in a shuddering breath. I could scent the alpha within her, pushing for control, and it shocked the hell out of me when she tilted her head back and cocked it to the side, presenting her delicate throat to me. My inner-wolf howled with joy at her quick submission. "I'm yours," she murmured, her voice knotted and rough.

I growled, a soft rumble in my throat, and her alpha scent thickened in the air. Almonds and mixed fruits came at me in waves. My heart was pounding hard.

Her lips curved into a bemused smile. She cocked her head a little further, exposing more of her neck. "Looks like you're stuck with me, alpha," she said, lifting her shoulders in a delicate shrug. She sounded totally confident in that, but then she clucked her tongue, shifting her gaze to her feet. "Something happened that I should tell you about."

"What's that?" I asked, dreading the answer.

She looked up and touched my face with her fingertips, delicately running them along my cheekbone. "My inner-wolf ..." she started, stumbling over her words. Her face paled, and she pulled in a ragged breath. "Well ... she didn't respond to him."

She shook her head, her hair falling forward, covering her eyes, and she dipped her chin, fixing her gaze on my chest. "Like at all." Her voice was whisper quiet as if what she was telling me was wrong to say out loud, and I waited for the bad part because I was certain there had to be a bad part to this, but so far, I wasn't seeing it. "She was quiet, calm, even when he hugged me. It was as if she didn't even notice he was there."

"You say that like it's a bad thing."

"No, not a bad thing." She took my hand in hers. "I didn't really get it at first. Actually, I kind of thought something was wrong with me. But I understand now."

She didn't seem willing to say more, but I was still simmering over her meeting up with Jared, and I needed to know. "You're killing me here, sweetheart," I said, trying to keep my voice gentle. I brushed her hair from her eyes, tucking it behind her ears. "What do you understand?"

She sighed, a painful and more than a little frustrated sigh. "That I'd never give you up. Not ever again. As soon as I saw you, even all growly and pissed off, my inner-wolf wanted to come out. She wanted to run to you, rub against you, feel you. But it's not just her. I wanted to do it, too. Me. All of me." She ran her fingers over my lips, and I shivered. "I adore you, Aidan David Collins, and it scares the hell out of me."

She straightened then, leaned up, brushed her lips against mine, and smiled up at me. The featherlight brush was nowhere near enough, and I tried to capture her mouth again, but she giggled, pushing at my chest. She tucked a long strand of dark hair behind her ear as she tried, and failed, to force her smile away. "I wasn't really inviting you *into* the shower with me."

"Sure sounded like it to me," I said, giving her the crooked, half-grin that I knew made her knees weak.

Jade giggled and ducked away from me. I reached out to pull her back, but she sidestepped and headed toward the line of showers.

I stood there, looking after her for a stunned moment, and she glanced over her shoulder, grinning. That grin was all it took for me to follow. I closed the distance between us in a few long strides, letting a low growl rumble from my throat. She squealed, a delighted kind of sound, and I pulled her into my arms.

I dipped my head, pressing my lips to hers. She gasped as I pulled her bottom lip between my teeth. Her gasp quickly turned into a soft moan. She wound her hands around my neck, stepping back into one of the open stalls, pulling me with her.

Her silky hands gripped at my shirt, tugging and pulling, lifting it up. Her fingertips traced along my stomach and up my chest, and she pulled back from me, just enough to tug off my shirt, before leaning in and placing a trail of burning kisses along my shoulder.

I buried my lips against her neck, kissing and nipping my way up to her ear. Her skin was warm, smooth, sweet. I let my hands roam down her back and slip under the edge of her tank top, pulling her as close as I could get her.

"Aidan!" Dominic shouted as a round of thumping bangs against the locked door reverberated through the change room. "Open the damn door!"

"Not now, Dom," I shouted back before focusing back on Jade's sweet and smooth neck.

"You live with her, man," he bellowed. "You can do whatever you're doing later. Get out here!"

I opened my mouth to tell him to screw off when Jade said, "He's right. You should probably go." She squirmed in my arms, pulling back and breaking away, as she blushed, a deep red.

"He can wait," I said, smirking down at her and leaning in for another kiss.

"Aidan," she said against my mouth. "I don't think I'm ready for this. You should go."

I leaned back a little, searching her face. Her lips were red, plump, and swollen. Her skin, flushed, and her scent was full of need, but her eyes held a hint of uncertainty that twisted my gut. I nodded, stealing a quick kiss, and smiled down at her. "I'll go get you a change of clothes," I said, and before I could change my mind, I turned from her and went straight for my locker.

CHAPTER 23

JADE

Aidan grabbed me his spare gym clothes, jogging pants, and a T-shirt, told me not to even think about putting back on the clothes that smelled of Jared, and then left me alone to shower.

My entire body was thrumming. My inner-wolf was a bundle of tender nerves, pressing against my heated skin. I didn't know whether to be glad or furious that Dominic interrupted us. I was trying to be sensible about the whole thing. Yes, I wanted Aidan, but I was only eighteen and him, nineteen. Wolves mate for life. It wasn't like we could change our minds later. It just didn't happen. And really, once our scents mixed, it couldn't happen. I would be his, and he would be mine. So yes, I was trying to be sensible, but my inner-wolf didn't want to be sensible. And her instant need to claim him was driving me crazy.

Keeping Aidan's jogging pants up on my hips took three bunching knots along the waistband. His T-shirt was baggy on me, too, but I didn't care. After securing the clothes the best I could, I gave my wet hair another tight ring-out and twisted it into a messy knot, and then I went to find Aidan.

The headquarters was relatively busy for a Saturday morning, or I guess it was early afternoon now. As I walked through the brilliant white hallways of the hulking maze-like building, I passed quite a few pack members. A few cut me dirty looks, and a few offered causal greetings, but most of them just ignored me, which kind of sucked. But I was working on that, and it would change, definitely, hopefully.

"He hasn't woken up yet. There's a stench to him, but that

could just be him. The boys have clammed up, too, since Jared got back."

I heard the lazy, gravelly voice drifting past the slightly ajar door of Aidan's office as I walked through the lobby. I paused for a moment and took a deep breath. Aidan's scent flooded my nostrils, and I went to the door, nudging it open. "Who hasn't woken up yet?" I asked.

Aidan looked up, smiled, and then exchanged a look with Tommy, Chris, and Dominic, sitting on the couch. He gestured for me to come in, and I shook my head, cracking a smile, because, well, I wasn't really asking for an invitation. As I padded across the room and rounded his desk, he pushed back his chair, and I hopped up on the edge, facing him. "Well?" I said, folding my arms over my chest. "Who hasn't woken up yet?"

He scanned me up and down a couple times before his eyes settled on my chest. He let out a frustrated groan and tugged a hoodie off the back of his chair. "Put this on," he said hastily, tossing his sweater at me.

I glanced down at myself, not sure what his issue was. I noticed it fairly quickly, though, and I rolled my eyes at him. I pulled on the sweater and said, "You told me not to put my clothes back on, Aidan. I was wearing a tank with a built-in bra."

"I want you to go home, sweetheart," he said.

"Good for you, but I'm not going," I said, glancing over the scattered papers that littered his desk. Status reports on the team, bank statements, and income statements for the different establishments the pack owned in town were strewn everywhere. "I've got work to do. I was thinking about going out with the team, too, help them search the next section of land." I folded my arms over my chest, looking back at him. "Now tell me, who hasn't woken up?"

Dominic chuckled, and I was pretty sure the gravel-sounding snicker came from Tommy. I swiveled, cutting them each a dirty look, and the laughter died abruptly, although all three of them were grinning.

Aidan's warm hand clasped my hip as he moved in closer. His emotion shone brightly in his eyes, a deep stormy sea of anger and adoration and dread. He puffed out his chest, his lips drawn tight. His scent increased, and, well, I laughed. I shouldn't have, but I couldn't help it. I knew what he was doing, trying to distract me, and it wasn't going to work.

He leaned forward and kissed me on the lips, sweet and warm, with none of the intensity from before. It was gentle, tender. Full of all the emotion that I knew was growing inside him, the same emotion that was building within me. "You're not going anywhere with Jared," he said. "If you wanted to go out with the team, you should have thought about that before you brought him back." He said it as if it were simple and something I should have already thought of.

"Be serious, Aidan." I nudged him back a little and tried to laugh it off.

He let his scent trickle into the air and gave me a grin that was at least half-wolf. "Oh, I am, sweetheart. I'm very ..."

I put my hand over his mouth, stopping him from saying something stupid, and I stared him right in the face with a no-nonsense glare. "Tell me what's going on, Aidan."

I took my hand away slowly, keeping my glare fixed in place. He laughed a little as if he were in shock. "Go home, Jade." There was an unmistakable command in his tone, one that clearly told me he was the dominant one. He was to be listened to.

"Aidan, cut it out," Dominic said dryly. There was a little smile on his lips and amusement in his eyes. "Of course, she isn't going home. You wouldn't be able to watch her if she did." Clearly, whoever was sleeping was important to them if they felt the need to hide it from me. I wasn't sure if that was a good thing or not.

"Don't think he's interested in watching her anymore," Chris said. His face twisted into a frown, and he cut a sharp look in my direction.

Aidan's body went tense, but he didn't break eye contact with me. I cocked my head to the side, narrowing my eyes, trying to ignore the others as he was. I could feel the push of his alpha-wolf, trying to bend me to his will. It was strange. I had no idea what was happening or why there was a shift in him. But there was a shift, one that sent my inner-wolf into a panicked, angry frenzy in my belly. Was he trying to protect me from finding out the truth or manipulate me?

Silence fell. I wasn't really sure what Chris meant, but his words rattled me nonetheless. After what had just happened in the showers, I hadn't thought Aidan would let me out of his sight, at least not anytime soon. But as the silence stretched and I tried to make sense out of what was happening, Jared's first piece of training surfaced. *"The moment you show weakness, you'll lose my inner-wolf, Jade,"* he'd said. *"No matter what, you need to stay dominant. No matter how much you want to submit, don't. There is a place for submission, but only to your mate and only when it is necessary to appease his inner-wolf. You do it to show your respect. You do it to show you agree, to show others you are backing him. But submit when you shouldn't, and my inner-wolf will decide you are weak. He'll forget you. Never let him forget because if he does, so will I."*

Aidan held strong, his eyes wide, unforgiving, commanding. Was his inner-wolf forgetting me? Had I already lost that piece of him? I had shown my submission to him twice. Once to show I wouldn't argue with his decision to take me home, and once to show him I was his during a heated moment, but I wasn't really his mate — yet.

I gasped and almost lunged into his arms. Almost. For a hot second, all I wanted was his comfort. I wanted to hear him say that I hadn't made another epic mistake as alpha female or as his potential mate.

It was his growl that held me in place, a low and commanding sound that left me short of breath.

And I thought that this probably wasn't the best time to be passive or look for comfort, and I growled back, yep, I actually growled at him.

Quick vibrations littered my skin. "Aidan." My voice was a low snarl. My nails dug deep into my palms as I clenched my fists. My claws were itching to come out. Hair brushed under my skin, waiting to erupt. The need to dominate rushed at me. It was ... weird and a little freaky. It was one thing to show him my submission when we made out. My inner-wolf was happy to let him take the lead there. But here, in front of Tommy and Chris and Dominic, I was his equal, and he would either treat me like one or he would submit. It was black and white in my inner wolf's mind — simple.

His scent thickened, so did mine. My breath quickened, my body started to tremble. Blood rushed from my face in a cold flush of fever as I struggled to keep my chin level, my gaze on him. It was as if I were fighting an exhausting internal battle with my inner-wolf. She clawed for control while I wanted to bow, present my neck, and feel his warm lips flutter across me in acceptance. Or was that my inner-wolf, and it was me that wanted control? I wasn't one hundred percent sure right then.

His nostrils flared for a moment, and then he sat back in his chair and gave me an amused smile as if he'd simply decided to humor me. "Your father gave us a cougar. According to him, the guy had a death sentence for helping one of their prisoners escape, and your dad was supposed to dispose of him. The wounds your father inflicted on him have healed, but he hasn't woken up."

"He gave you a cougar," I said slowly, processing this news. "Don't you think that maybe, just maybe, you should have told me that already?"

Aidan smiled his sexy, crooked smile that never failed to make my heart flutter. "I had other things on my mind, sweetheart," he said and winked. "More important things."

"Going all growly on me because I hugged a friend was more important?" I pursed my lips, trying for annoyed, but I was pretty sure I failed. "Might want to rethink your priorities there, honey."

♥

It seemed strangely unreal that my father would give us one of his own. I leaned against the countertop in the makeshift kitchen of the pack building, sipping on hot chocolate loaded with frothy whipped cream, wondering why he would when I thought it did seem somehow appropriate. Dad had to have guessed that Aidan hadn't believed him about not knowing how many cougars there were or where they were hiding. What better way to show he was on our side than by giving us someone who knew the ins and outs of the werecougars, even if he wasn't able to tell us anything yet.

I squinted against the bright rays of the setting sun that streamed through the window. The parking lot was half full, and a knot of people gathered by the cars. They mostly looked unhappy and on edge, but then I couldn't really blame them. Aidan had decided to tell everyone about the cougar we had acquired, and no one really knew how to take it. For the most part, the pack wanted the sleeping man dead, and no one was all that pleased with me that I wanted to keep him alive.

The thing was, I figured that if my dad had, in fact, been about to kill him, then he might be willing to help us if he woke up. And even if he wasn't willing, there was a reason he'd been given to us. I wanted to know what that reason was.

And I was also almost positive that I needed to get my mom away from my dad, which was absurdly ridiculous. We had no solid reason to suspect she knew anything about what was going on, but we didn't have a solid reason to doubt it either. Pulling her out would tip off my dad, but then, maybe that was a good thing. This defensive strategy wasn't really getting us anywhere, and I was beginning to wonder if going on the offensive was what we should have done all along.

Aidan hadn't strayed far from me since our little dispute in his office. I still felt the weird shift in him, and it hurt, but only a little. At least he still felt the need to stay close by. It was definitely better than ignoring me.

I snuck a peek at him. He sat at a scratched-up round table, nursing his coffee as he studied the map of the forest surrounding Dog Mountain. We'd made a lot of progress over the last couple of days, but there was still a lot of land to search before we could move on to the surrounding towns.

Aidan glanced up at me, and his eyebrows rose. "What?"

"I think we need to stop watching and act," I said, shocked that I actually voiced my thoughts. So was Aidan, judging by the wide-eyed look he gave me. I sighed. "I've been justifying waiting to myself because we didn't have enough information. Dad wants to use me, but we don't know what for. He also said I was your weakness. I'm going to take a wild guess here, but I figure he's going to use me to get to you, although I don't have a freakin' clue why. The longer we wait because I don't want to hurt my dad, the more people who could suffer — will suffer. And my mom ..." I swallowed, dropping the thought.

"We don't need to rush," he said, but it wasn't believable. I knew he was just saying it to make me feel better, to give me a sense of security that really wasn't there.

"Did you call Luken?"

Aidan nodded. "He wants to join the team. He wants to help find them."

"And he thought I wouldn't understand." It wasn't a question. It seemed crazy that he thought I wouldn't understand that. "What did you tell him?"

"I told him that he needed to talk it over with Jared," he bit out, annoyed.

I huffed. "I know you don't want Jared here, but we need him. The pack needs to see I'm with you, and the three of us working together will help. I should have talked to you first, but let's face it, you've been a bit overbearing lately. You would have told me no. We would have argued. I'm just trying to fix the mess I made." I waved a hand in his direction. "Clearly, it's a bigger mess than I thought."

"About earlier," he said, raking a hand through his hair and shifting his gaze.

"I get it," I said when he didn't continue. "We aren't really mates. I shouldn't have rolled over to you. But you try and pull that crap again, and you'll be the one rolling over."

He let out a soft growl and met my eyes again. His were crinkled with humor. "Sure, you keep telling yourself that, sweetheart."

I rolled my eyes. "I've got to get going." I downed the last mouthfuls of my drink and rinsed out my mug in the sink. I walked over to him and gave him a peck on the cheek before heading for the door. "They're probably waiting."

"Hey, hold up," he said, snagging my wrist and pulling me to a stop.

"Aidan, don't start," I said, turning into him. My voice was growlier than I intended, and I quickly cleared my throat, attempting to hide my frustration. "I'm going. I need to do something. I can't just sit here. And besides that, my skin is crawling. I need to shift." And it was. My skin was rippling and prickly and itchy. My inner-wolf needed out.

He chuckled, and I couldn't help but smile. Man, I loved his laugh. "I'm not going to stop you," he said. "I just wish I could go with you." He stood up and pulled me into his arms. I wrapped mine around his waist, looking up at him.

"Yeah, well, we don't always get what we want," I told him dryly. "One of us needs to stick around and be available, and you're the better option for that. They like you, me not so much. And I really think it will help my image with you agreeing that I should work with them. You know, let the pack see you're okay with it, with him."

He dipped his head and pressed his lips to mine in a quick kiss that left me breathless and, to my dismay, panting for more. "I don't know what I'm going to do with you." He chuckled. "One minute you're growling at me, and the next you're melting into me."

"I believe you growled first," I said, batting my eyes in an attempt to look innocent. "It's about time I growled back."

CHAPTER 24

AIDAN

I walked Jade to the doors, hating every damn step, and although I'd said all the right things to make her happy, I felt … on edge and a little empty. I knew she was right, but it didn't mean I had to like it. It just seemed stupid to let her go out to hunt down the cougars. It went against every protective instinct I had.

Oh, hell. There were so many other things to worry about right now, but the only thing on my mind was the weird-ass way my inner-wolf was reacting to her.

For a moment, I indulged myself and imagined what it would have been like to claim her in the showers. What her peachy skin would have felt like against mine. What her hands and lips, grazing all over my body, would have felt like. Seeing that fiery passion in her eyes. I could almost smell the change in her scent and in mine.

The fantasizing was a good diversion, but it didn't help.

It's going to be fine, I thought. I just had to breathe. She wasn't going to be alone. She'd have the team. She'd have Jared. Okay, so that didn't help either. But they wouldn't let anything happen to her, right?

And the cougars were smart. They changed locations frequently. They hid their tracks. Based on the last week of hunting them, the odds of her actually running into one of them were low.

Knowing that should have helped, too. It really should have. But it didn't.

There was still a good crowd in the parking lot when we got outside. At first glance, I didn't think any of them noticed Jade. It hadn't been obvious that they were watching her join the team, and for a moment, I thought that maybe her shifting in private was a bad move. Too discreet to draw attention. But as I followed her out the doors, I realized they were watching. I caught the sidelong glances checking out the matte-black wolf trotting away from me and the arched eyebrows in my direction, and I forced a smile to show I was supporting her.

When she reached the edge of the forest where the wolves were gathered, Jade twisted to look behind her, and her bright golden eyes settled on me. She let out a sound that was somewhere between a growl and an excited yip.

"Be careful, sweetheart," I called, lifting my hand in a little wave. *Just breathe. She's going to be fine. We are going to be fine.* Damn, it would be better not to feel anything right now.

As the team and Jade took off into the forest, I spotted Tommy and Chris leaning against the building with Dominic. And oh, they weren't happy. Even if Tommy's shiny head wasn't redder than a blistering sunburn, the hot spike in the air would have given it away. Clearly, they didn't appreciate Jared telling them to hang back from the hunt.

"Hey," Dominic said as I approached. He was frowning and giving me one of those looks that told me he knew I was on the verge of cracking. I had to give it to him; he knew how to read me. "She can handle herself. She'll be fine."

I nodded but didn't say anything. He was right. I knew it. He knew it, too. But knowing it didn't mean that I liked her going any better. But I made a conscious effort to dial back my anxiety.

My relaxed persona must have been somewhat convincing because as I settled in with them, Dominic chuckled and then said, "You know. She once told me that there's nothing sexier than a man who's in love with his woman and not afraid to show it."

Tommy and Chris chuckled, and both of them rolled their eyes.

Dominic flashed them a bright, pearly white grin, full of exaggerated smugness. "Laugh all you want," he said. "I may not date women, but I know what I'm talking about when it comes to impressing them." And then he grimaced. "Mac and Jade like to talk — a lot."

I had to laugh. If Dominic knew anything about Jade or Marcy, it was only how to piss them off. Except it really did sound like something Jade would say. The question was: how was I supposed to show how much I loved her without coming across as being possessive or overbearing? That's what I wanted to ask, but what I said was, "She's not really *my*woman."

"Keep thinking like that, and she never really will be," he said and clapped me on the shoulder.

Something inside me flinched hard. "Yeah, well, we're still trying to work out our issues."

"Whatever, I'm not judging, man. Just sharing my wealth of knowledge on the mystery of what women want." He smirked, cutting me an angled side glance, and then said, "Come on, these two want a meeting."

"Sure," I said with a nod and pushed off the wall. "I'm going to check in on the cougar. I'll meet you guys in my office in a few."

The headquarters had once been home to the pack. They had slept here, ate here. There was security in staying together. And the building had everything they had needed: beds, private rooms, kitchen, gym, media, and game rooms. It had been built to keep the pack together, and now it was just a place to conduct business.

The slap of my shoes echoed in the bright, empty hallways as I made my way through the building. I followed along and veered to the left where the old sleeping quarters were. Keeping the captive there was Jade's idea, insisting he be kept comfortable until we could determine if he truly was our enemy.

If I hadn't known where he was, I could have followed the smell of cougar, that odd mix of lemon and birch bark, all the way to where Richard slept. It gave the sterile pack headquarters a weirdly cold feel, smelling the enemy within its walls.

As I stepped out of the hallway and pushed through the doors that led to the rooms, Luken looked up and gave me a bright smile. He leaned against the wall, a phone in his hands, just outside the door to the captive's room.

"I didn't expect to see you here," I said. I knew he'd been planning to talk to Jared, but I figured he would have been shot down.

"Me neither," he admitted, hastily pocketing his phone and straightening as I approached. "Jared said he'd think about it and stuck me on guard duty while they're on the hunt." He shifted from one foot to the other and averted his gaze. "About Jade, sorry I gave her a hard time."

"I'm not the one you need to apologize to, man." The words sounded normal, but my tone was hard and direct. His smile dimmed, no longer looked bright but breakable, and I heaved a sigh. "If you would have talked to her, you wouldn't have to be stuck on guard duty. You'd be on that hunt with them right now. She would have gone to bat for you, and if that didn't work, she would have pestered him until he agreed."

He didn't look like he believed me, or it could have been that he just didn't want to believe me, but it was the truth. Jade would have welcomed the help, and she would have forced the issue until she won.

We stood there in silence; the only sounds were our breathing until he cleared his throat. "I'm guessing you came to see him," he said. He didn't wait for my answer before he turned and stiff-armed the door, letting it swing open.

"Any movement?" I asked as I stepped in and flicked on the light switch.

The room was simple, holding only a bed and dresser. The walls were painted in a pastel blue, and the window coverings were fringed with a pale green lace, the remnants of whichever pack member had once made it their own.

"Nothing yet," he said. "I've been checking every fifteen minutes."

My gaze locked on Richard lying flat on his back in the bed. He had passed out before the team had shown up at Jeff's. I hadn't thought much of it at first. He'd been so torn up and beaten at the time it had made sense that his body would shut down, try to heal. But the wounds were closed now, looking more like old scars than fresh cuts. And he didn't really look asleep. He was too still. His eyes didn't flutter. His muscles didn't twitch. It was almost as if he'd been drugged into a comatose state.

About ten minutes later, I made it back to my office, feeling about fifty different kinds of pissed-off. Not that I hadn't seen it coming, but I was now certain that the little gift from Jade's father was more of a distraction than anything else. The question was: what was he trying to distract me from?

Man, the urge to race out and beat the shit out of Jeff until I had the answers I needed was nearly irresistible. But then, so was the desire to keep Jade happy, and beating her dad wouldn't keep her happy. I seriously never thought loving someone could be this damn confining.

I heaved a sigh and settled in behind my desk. "I'm guessing this meeting is about your report on the team," I said. "What did you find out?"

I expected Tommy to tell me I was wrong and urge me to wait.

They'd made it clear in the email that I should hear whatever it was from the team, but from the look he exchanged with Chris, I assumed my guess was right and that waiting was no longer an option.

"None of them are going to talk to you now that Jared's back and breathing down their necks." He collapsed onto the couch across from my desk and stretched his legs out in front of him. A slow, grim smile twisted his mouth, and he said, "The team, all five of them are half brothers. Same father, different mothers. Jared was born here, but the others came along a couple years ago."

I frowned and began tapping the pen in my hand against my desk restlessly. I looked at Dominic and cocked a brow. He was frowning, too, and shrugged as if this was the first he heard about this.

"Who's their father?" I asked as a fast ripple of irritation passed through me.

"That's the interesting part. You killed their father," Chris said, his voice carrying a dark undertone. He leaned forward in his chair, resting his forearms on his knees. "According to Landon, Ray tracked them down and changed them just before he fought and won alpha. He was building a pack that wouldn't think about trying to overthrow him, even before it was his."

I felt Dominic's eyes on me, and I dropped the pen, splaying my hands out on my desk, as I settled a glare on him. "Why doesn't anyone in this damn pack know about this?"

Dominic stared at me for a moment, his expression unreadable, and then said, "Knowing Ray, he probably didn't want anyone to know they were his sons. It explains a lot, though. The team always looked the other way when Ray stepped out of line. It was smart not to let anyone know. Too many gray lines when you have that many blood relatives in power positions. If I'd known, I would have fought it, and I'm sure others would have, too."

His weak explanation didn't improve my mood, even if it did shed some light on why all those pack members had cowered back, clearly afraid to interfere, while Ray had been beating his mate. If the team had always looked the other way, then there was no one to have their back if the alpha abused his power.

I was starting to feel a bit ill. "Should I be worried about Jade out there with them?"

"No." Tommy said it with certainty. "Landon and Mark are loyal to you. Beck is stuck in the middle somewhere, loyal to the pack and to his brothers, but he wouldn't let any of them, not even Jared, touch her. He loves her, even if he isn't sure about you."

"None of them will talk about Jared," Chris added. "They're trying to cover for him. It's pretty obvious he would love to see you dead. And Craig hates you for touching Erika."

I leaned back in my chair. I didn't know what surprised me more ... that two of them were loyal to me or that two of them would be happy to see me dead. I guessed it could have been worse.

"Don't blame yourself," Dominic said after a stretch of silence. "When your mate's ex-whatever-he-was wants you dead, he wants you dead. There's nothing you can really do about it. And besides," he shrugged, "Jared always wants someone dead. He'll get over it."

CHAPTER 25

JADE

I had expected to be taken to the last trail that was uncovered, or at least to the base of the mountain where the cougar tracks were thicker, but instead, the team had turned off and headed straight for a new patch of land that hadn't been searched. And I really didn't like where they were planning on searching. We were heading straight into the hunting camps.

I knew that hunting season wasn't open yet and that even if it was, hunting wolves was illegal, but even knowing that, it still didn't seem like such a hot idea to go running into a place that potentially had men with guns.

But I figured the hunting camps were a good place to look. They had shelter. They had beds. And they were only used a couple weeks of the year.

Jared's deep brown wolf led the way, keeping a muscle-burning pace. The team stayed with him, running in watchful silence. We ran for a solid twenty minutes before he finally slowed to a light jog and cut right, heading down a dirt roadway.

The roadway hadn't been traveled recently. Not a single tire track was pressed into the dirt. Trees hung overhead, and sprigs of weeds and grass had popped up sporadically down the center of the path. The forest was darkening quickly, the sun almost gone for the day, and skeletal shadows crisscrossed along the path in front of us.

Jared slowed again, veering left as he followed a bend in the trail.

And then the first camp came into view.

The building ahead had a rotting sign hanging over the door

that read, *Brinkwell.* It was a large rustic-looking cabin made of logs. There wasn't much of a clearing, as if the owners had only cut down enough trees to make way for the structure, a few picnic tables, and a fire pit.

Beck moved in closer to me, hugging my side. He growled when I pulled back and away from him. It was a flat warning to stay close, and he reinforced it by nipping at my shoulder.

I stopped dead, cocking my head to look at him. His eyes stayed on mine as he dipped his head, pressing his muzzle to the ground. His nostrils were flaring with each long breath he took. He nosed at a small pile of leaves, pushing them toward me, and I breathed in the scent.

There was, I realized, a faint trace of cougar on those leaves.

Jared growled, and Craig, Mark, and Landon moved in around him. He pawed at the wooden door of the building, but it didn't budge. His coat began to shudder and ripple. The dry crack of bones sounded loudly in my ears. His fur receded in a quick, clean motion. And then he was human, standing on the rickety-looking deck. "Beck, don't leave her side," he said in a ragged pant, and then he shoved the door open.

AIDAN

"She's not going to like this," Dominic said, but he pushed the door open and hopped out of the car anyway.

I got out of the car and pressed the lock button on my key fob. "Yeah, well, Jade's worried about her, and I need to talk to her."

The Dog Mountain General Hospital didn't look different from a hospital in any other small town. The building was a nondescript brown brick structure. If it weren't for the big *Hospital* sign and even bigger *Emergency Entrance* sign, you wouldn't have even really known it was a hospital. There were two parked ambulances in the lot and a few cars, most likely belonging to the medical staff.

As I walked through the emergency doors, people noticed me. Everyone knew who I was, what I was. I didn't really like it, but I could do nothing about it. No one looked at me directly, but I could feel them watching from the corners of their eyes.

Mrs. Shaw sat behind the desk at the nurses' station, and she looked up as the doors slid shut behind us. She didn't smile as she said, "Hi, Dominic," and then she gave me a curt nod, "Aidan."

In her late forties, she was an attractive woman dressed in bright floral scrubs. Her dark brown hair was tied in a tight bun. She looked a lot like her daughter, same big brown eyes, same nose and cheekbones.

"Hey, Mrs. Shaw," Dominic said with a little wave. His tone was light, and he smiled. "Could you maybe spare a minute?"

"Depends," she said. She didn't meet his gaze. Instead, she kept her cool brown eyes locked on me. "Is he here about my daughter or my husband?" Her tone was casual, sweet even, but her face was tight.

I approached the desk and leaned against it. Keeping my voice just as light, I asked, "Would it make any difference which one I'm here to talk to you about?"

"Yes," she said tightly and nodded. "Yes, it would."

"He's here about the team, Mrs. Shaw," Dominic said and smiled again. She didn't smile back, didn't even pretend to. "And about Jared stopping by to see Jeff this morning."

Mrs. Shaw swallowed hard. Her entire body tensed, and then like a rolling wave, she relaxed. "As you can see," she said, nodding toward the waiting room, "I've got work to do."

I glanced over my shoulder at the empty waiting room and frowned. I hadn't expected to get a *no*, at least not right away, and my heart sank a little. "Look, Pam," I said. "We can do it now when your husband isn't here, or I can come by the house later."

"Where's my daughter?" she asked, her voice cracking over the words. There was a subtle change in her scent, the tanginess of fear or paranoia, so light that I almost missed it, but it was there.

"She's out with Jared," I said, watching her closely. I leaned a bit closer, and dropping my voice low, I added, "And his brothers." She stared at me for a long, hard moment. Her fingers were trembling now, and the tanginess increased in the air. "I'm not trying to scare you, Pam," I added, feeling more than a little heartsick. "Really, I just have a couple of questions, and I promise you, your answers will remain confidential."

I was pretty sure she didn't believe me, but she let out a pent-up breath, and her shoulders sagged as she gestured to the closed door of the triage station.

JADE

There were more hunting camps hidden in the woods than I had thought. Big log structures full of bunk beds. We'd found three more in the last two hours, all of them empty, but all of them had the same scent of birch bark and lemon and cat.

But this one was different. This one had been vacated in a rush.

And it hadn't been empty long. The scent was thicker here, and it still clung to the grass and trees in the area.

We were getting closer.

The problem with getting closer, though, was that we learned some truths that I seriously could have done without knowing. One of those truths: they kept the women in cages made of thick barbed wire. We'd found traces of old human blood around the crude structures. And there were thick chains and long leather whips on the ground, the kind of whips you saw in the hands of large animal trainers.

It was best not to look at it. Better to keep going. Stay focused.

Beck stuck close to my side, so did Landon. Tension was running high within the team, and I had a feeling that Aidan and Tommy were right; the tension wasn't just from the hunt. The only one that paid any real attention to Jared was Craig. The others stayed focused on me, and through me, on the hunt.

I put my nose to the ground, searching for the trail. But there wasn't just one trail. There were many. Each one I followed wrapped around, branched off, met back up, and then backtracked. Each loop took me back to the same place. To the cages.

I scanned the grounds again, looking for anything I could have missed the first time. There had to be something. Had. To. Be. It just wasn't possible for a full pack to vanish without a trace.

I trotted toward the base of a towering oak that was roughed with deep gouging marks. Someone barked, Beck nudged at my side, and I growled, snapping out at him to leave me alone.

The gouges looked like claw marks, and they shot up into the low-hanging branches. Could they have climbed the trees? They were big cats. They could climb, right? Leap from tree to tree, hiding their real trail.

Beck nudged me again and growled another warning. I dodged to the left, circling the tree, and backed up to look at the trunk better. I heard the loud snap at the exact moment I was ripped from my feet and tossed into the air like a ragdoll.

And then I was hanging upside down, dangling by a leg about five feet from the ground.

Adrenaline took over. My bones began to remold, breaking and shifting, as I swung, bobbing, back and forth. As I finished the change back to human, sharp pain lanced through my leg as if a fireball had been shot within my body. The rope seemed as if it were tightening with each small movement, cutting deeper into my flesh. I screeched, and my eyes stung with tears, and for a moment, I lost my breath to the skin ripping, muscle tearing pain.

I couldn't hear anything over the loud buzzing in my ears as my blood rushed to my head. Thick warm liquid trickled down my leg, and I fought the panic that began to claw its way through my chest. I started to pull myself up, using my arms and abs. I needed to get the rope off. I needed to get down.

After a few grunts and a lot of muscle burn, I managed to loop my arms around my knees. And then I saw my mangled ankle. The rope had cut deep, hidden in my skin and under the blood, and I lost my balance, falling back to dangle again.

"I tried to warn you," Beck said with a rumbling chuckle. "Next time, don't shift. Your skin and muscles rip more easily while your body is reshaping."

"Glad you find this amusing," I snapped, fighting against the pain. I'd be damned if I was going to let him, one of the tough enforcers, see me cry over a little rope burn and cut.

Beck chuckled again, pacing around and staring up. I tried not to watch him, focusing on anything but his lean naked body or his wide, muscular shoulders. And it was in that second that I realized that I was hanging upside down, stark naked. I felt a blush reach my cheeks, and a whole new panic settled into my belly. My anxiety ratcheted up when the others gathered around him and started to shift. Laughter echoed through the air, hard and loud.

I should have stayed a wolf, I thought bitterly.

"This is so not funny, guys," I hissed, folding my arms over my chest in an attempt to cover my breasts. "And it hurts like hell, so get me down and don't look."

CHAPTER 26

AIDAN

"Well, shit," Dominic said. "I really didn't see that coming."

I glanced over at my beta. He was grinning like a fool as we left the hospital. He walked beside me with restless, twitchy steps as if he were itching to shift and burn off some energy.

"Really?" I asked. "'Cause I thought it was pretty obvious." I dug in my pocket for my keys and unlocked the car. The headlights flashed, lighting up the parking lot.

Dominic laughed. "Yep, that's right. You knew all along that Jared went over there to beg her father to help him get her back. And then when he said no, Jared tried to beat a *yes* out of him because Jared's always been the desperate type, and it's not like I can smell the stench of lies coming off you or anything."

Okay, so yeah, it was a lie. Whatever. At least I was now certain that Jade's mom knew nothing of what her husband was really into. The woman truly believed he worked for my pack. And she also believed he was a good man. Knowing that lifted a little stress, although not enough.

I got into the car, slamming the door, and when Dominic jumped in, he was still laughing. I narrowed my eyes at him and wondered if I just kept my mouth shut, if maybe, just maybe, the conversation would end.

When the silence stretched, he laughed. "Come on, Aidan, lighten up."

"How I am supposed to lighten up about this?" I pushed back my hair. "Jade is just a trophy to him. A prize. Something to wave in my face. And she doesn't see it. You heard what Pam said. Jared's using her to get to me. The pain it would cause me was his damn bargaining chip this morning." *Oh, hell.* I was really starting to feel like a failure. As a male. As an alpha. And it was burning away my sense of self-worth.

"Start by picturing Jared begging," he said, chuckling. "Then picture the look on Jade's face when you tell her about this."

I winced and looked away. "I'm picturing the look, Dom, and it burns."

JADE

Beck cut me down — literally — and I fell five feet, butt naked, into Landon's arms. As I landed, all I could think was, thank God Aidan wasn't around for this one. He would have lost his freakin' mind.

Within seconds of landing, Mark had tossed a dirty old wool blanket over me, covering me up, and then Landon carried me inside the hunting camp. He'd put me down on a ratty old couch that had some odd patchwork pattern on it. The thing was faded and worn, but it was ridiculously comfortable, and after thirty minutes of sitting on it, I was ready to take the ugly thing home with me. It was that comfortable.

Having the rope pulled out of my skin was not fun, and yep, I screamed and cussed up a storm. The raw gash it had left behind ran all the way around my ankle and cut through the muscle, almost to the bone. But it was out now, the wound was healing, and the bleeding had stopped.

The guys had found some clothes: bright orange hunting jackets and coveralls. I felt as if I were drowning in them. The jacket was rough against my skin, and so were the stiff jean coveralls. But at least we were all clothed as we waited for my leg to heal enough to make the trek home.

A cold sweat broke out over my skin as I shifted on the couch, placing my foot down flat and putting some pressure on it. Pain shot through my body like fire, and I quickly swallowed the gasp. I'd been testing it almost every five minutes now, but still, it hurt — bad.

"That's going to hurt like hell for a few hours," Landon said. He was hovering, so was Mark. It was getting close to suffocating. And each time Jared moved, they slid closer to me, pinning him with heated glares.

The only reason I pretended to ignore their crazy aggression was because they looked as if they were ready to smack Jared around, and my instinct was telling me that if I called attention to it, it would only make things worse.

"I'm good," I hissed. "We've got to get back. Let Aidan know what we found."

"Jade, you need to heal," Beck said and gave me one of those firm *big brother* kind of looks. He stood under one of the light fixtures, and the way the light hit his face made his cheekbones look hollow and the creases above his brow, harsh.

"No," I said, shaking my head. "I need to get out of here. Seriously, this place creeps me out." I glanced over at Jared and wasn't really surprised to see him still brooding, leaning against the doorframe. "You done searching the area?" I asked him.

He looked me over with cold, harsh eyes, and as he did, I tried to remember a time when he'd ever looked at me with even a sliver of warmth. I couldn't. Jared didn't do warm. His voice might heat a little, but that gaze was pretty much always cold. Right then, all I wanted was to get home and see Aidan. See his warmth. Feel some heat. I forced a smile, trying to show I was good to go, even if I wasn't sure if I actually was.

He didn't answer me, and nobody else spoke up, so I finally said, "Jared, I want to go home now."

Then, without breaking the cold eye contact, he pushed off the doorframe. He stalked toward me with a slow, predator-like grace, his lips lifting into a sly grin. "Your scent draws him to you, but does he love you?" His tone was flat.

I stayed silent for a moment, wondering where the hell his question had come from. A flicker of unease tightened in my chest as he watched me expectantly, waiting. My forced smile faded, and I frowned. "Yes, yes he does."

"Then you don't love him." More coldness. God, I could almost feel it in the air, pulsing out from him.

"I do love him." I said it fiercely, so fiercely that I was pretty sure I shocked the entire team. For a breathless moment, they all turned to stare at me, stunned. The moment didn't last.

Jared took another slow, stalking step and stopped smiling. "Then why haven't you claimed him?" His question cut through me like a knife's blade.

Mark and Landon moved closer to me, their faces as hard as a stone. They growled, low and deadly, their gaze locked on Jared, watching his approach with trained eyes. Craig turned, moving in, flanking Jared. His eyes flared, and his muscles began to tick all along his neck.

"Jared, that's close enough." Beck's voice barely carried over the increasing sound of the growling coming out of Mark and Landon, and it didn't stop Jared from taking another step.

The five of them, Jared and Craig on one side, Mark, Landon, and Beck on the other, stared off. The growls increased as the tension rose. The air crackled with it, and I started to crack.

"What the hell has gotten into you all?" I shouted. My imprint heated, my skin shuddered. I let my scent thicken, hanging like a heavy mist over us, and I focused on calling their attention to my alpha wolf. The echo of growls slowly softened, and then there was only the heavy pumping sound of their breathing.

Jared recovered first as my scent began to recede, and he looked at me with a haze of violence clouding his face. His lips pulled up at the corners again, but his eyes stayed cold and black. "Come on, kitten," he snarled. "We all know why you asked me to come back. And don't think no one has noticed that it's you who's standing in Aidan's way from trying to kill me. It would take a moron not to see it." He took another step toward me.

Beck shoved him back so hard that Jared stumbled. "I said that's close enough." His voice was a low, menacing growl as he faced off with Jared. "Take one more step, and I will kill you."

Dammit! What the hell is going on with my team? I harnessed my scent again and forced their attention. It took a bit longer than the last time, but one by one, they each started to relax, thankfully not fighting the call of my alpha wolf. Jared even bowed a little. The show of respect was a shocker. And then he gripped Craig's arm and dragged him out the door.

AIDAN

Running on the treadmill turned out to be a good relief. It kept me focused and let me think as I waited for Jade to return. My thighs were screaming as I hit the tenth mile, but I wasn't ready to stop. I increased the incline, found my stride, and kept going.

Dominic had finally given up on trying to talk to me and left. I figured that was probably for the best. The more I thought about the information that Tommy and Chris had uncovered, the more I wanted to punch something. And listening to Mrs. Shaw confirm it all plus some, seriously hadn't helped.

I knew the team was a necessary evil to defend my pack, not just from outside threats but from me. But I kept coming to the same conclusion: I needed to disband them and build a new team. Blood was thicker than pack to some, and those boys were a perfect example of that. *Dammit!* Jade had had enough heartbreak. She didn't need this.

At that moment, the gym doors swung open. Jade. Her scent filled the air like a warm breeze through a farmer's fruit field. I glanced up. Landon had a loose arm around her waist, and she leaned into him as she limped into the room. Mark and Beck crowded in behind them. And none of them looked happy.

I hit the emergency stop button and was off the treadmill before the belt stopped rolling. Jade looked pale, and the scent of her pain mingled with her natural fragrance, causing anxiety to spike through my head. My instincts fired up because Jared and Craig weren't with them, and that had to mean something had gone wrong. More wrong than her being hurt. Even if he hated me, Jared wouldn't leave her like this. He wouldn't. My mouth went dry as if my tongue had shriveled up, and a low rumbling sound went through my chest.

Just as I was going to go to her, she said, "Before you get all growly ..." Pain laced her voice, and it showed in the deep lines on her forehead. She sucked in a breath. "I can't walk without his support yet." She wasn't looking at me. Knowing her, she didn't want me to see the pain in her eyes. She probably figured it was a weakness.

I went to her in a rush and gathered her into my arms. As soon as she was settled against me, I felt her soothing hands stroke down my shoulders as if she thought I needed calming. "What happened to you?" I demanded. My voice was too harsh, raw. Maybe I did need calming.

"Hunter's trap," she said. She leaned into me, kissing my cheek at the corner of my mouth. "I was looking at some claw marks on a tree when I got snagged in a trap." Her hand brushed over my chest and drifted up to my cheek. "I'm fine. Really, I'm fine."

I lifted my gaze, fixing it on the boys. "Where are Jared and Craig?"

"Taking a breather," Beck said. He fell into an attack posture, bending his knees, bringing his arms up. "And it's best they take it."

I glared at Beck and let out a bitter laugh. My chest burned so badly with white-hot rage that I thought if Jade wasn't pressed against me, I'd probably let him attack and then kill him for trying it. "Which one of them are you willing to fight me to protect?"

He didn't get a chance to respond. Jade stiffened and dragged in a lungful of air. "Aidan, let this one go," she said, brushing another kiss over my cheek. She glanced over her shoulder. "Beck, you'd better relax that glare you have fixed on my mate."

I was so pissed off that it took me a moment to see what was happening right in front of me. Without a word, Beck relaxed and whipped his head down, fixing his gaze to the floor, obeying her command.

My jaw dropped on its own, no matter how hard I tried to keep it up. I couldn't believe she had spoken to him with that kind of command. And I really couldn't believe that he had listened. Wait, had she just called me her mate?

I put a hand over my eyes and scrubbed at my face. Okay, this was good, right?

Her scent shifted then, and it confused the hell out of me. I could smell her pain, but there was also a thick flare of sweetness, the same sweetness she'd had in the showers. Her delicate touches were ruining my focus, and when I glanced down at her, it was clear that that was exactly what she was trying to do. Distract me.

Sitting down seemed like a damn good idea right then.

I shook off my fury and sucked in a breath, and then I scooped her up and carried her over a weight bench. I sat her down gently and kneeled in front of her. Once she was settled, I took the foot she'd been favoring into my hands, rolling up her jeans. Her ankle was swollen and raw-looking, with an angry red line encircling it. I looked over my shoulder, glaring. "How the hell did she get so hurt?"

Landon grinned, shaking his head. "She shifted while she was dangling upside down by the rope." He chuckled. "You've been too easy on her. Our girl stays with you for a few days, and she forgets everything we taught her."

"It's not funny," Jade hissed as a rosy flush crept up her neck. She managed to put the entire definition of embarrassment into it.

And that's when I fully understood her scent and the touches. The entire team had seen my mate naked, dangling by a rope, and she probably assumed I'd lose it. I knew I shouldn't have, but I smirked and chuckled. Seriously, I had never met a werewolf who was as paranoid about being seen naked as she was. It was adorable and incredibly impractical.

She must have seen me realize it because she said, "Not a word, Aidan." Her eyes blazed with fire. Her throat worked hard, and another brilliant flush crept up her neck.

I quickly swallowed my chuckle and put on my best serious expression. I figured it wasn't very good because Jade rolled her eyes and pursed her lips. "Tell him what we found, guys," she snapped.

"Uh-huh, sure," Beck said with a stiff nod and came over to us. He wouldn't look at me, but then that was probably a smart choice on his part because, yep, I was still simmering. "We searched four hunting camps. They'd been in all of them. I'm pretty sure the last one was where the *accident* happened." He looked a little green suddenly, and he swallowed a few times before continuing. "There were barbed wire cages with traces of human blood, whips, chains ..." Another hard swallow. "Jade found claw marks on the trees."

"They're climbing the trees," Landon added. "It's why we keep losing their damn trail." He was still in the doorway, stiff and straight. His tall, long legs were like thick boards, and his arms hung like metal rods, rigid and unbendable. He stared at me with wide, red-rimmed, baby-blue eyes. I could almost taste his anxiety in the air. He looked back at me with an intense focus, and I got the gut-twisting sinking feeling that he knew Tommy and Chris would have told me everything while they were gone.

"The marks were deep, not just one of them scratching, but really cut in," Mark continued. "I think Jade's right about them climbing, but I can't see how they could jump from tree to tree. It's not like they're small cats. You'd think the branches would snap on the landing."

"About Jade ..." Beck started, shoving his hands in his pockets. He glanced down as if he were trying to put some words together in his head but couldn't quite find any he liked.

"Don't worry about it, guys," she said in a low, calm voice. "I'm almost as good as new. Honest." But she wasn't. She started to tremble as she gave me a bright, brittle smile.

"Sorry we didn't take Tommy and Chris with us," Landon said. He looked overly calm, and his glare was still pointed.

Oh, hell. He must know they told me. With a shrinking feeling, I wondered if I should apologize for killing their dad.

Landon smiled then, a sad smile, and before I could think of anything to say, he said, "You should probably take her home. She's exhausted."

CHAPTER 27

JADE

I grabbed a steamy breath of air. My nerves were too tight, too bunched up under my skin, and the blistering shower wasn't helping much.

Aidan had been so quiet on the drive home as if he'd been waiting for me to open up. He hadn't asked anything, and I hadn't either. The words had been on the tip of my tongue, but they hadn't fallen from the safety of my mouth. Why was it so hard to admit that I may have been wrong?

Beck had threatened to kill Jared, hadn't he? And then he'd threatened to attack Aidan, too. Jesus, I'd been so surprised by the menace I saw in those guys tonight. I'd always known they could be scary. I even remembered when I went to all costs to avoid them. But they had always been close with each other. Always.

But they weren't close. Not now. Not anymore. And it was my fault. I didn't have a clue why, but I knew, just knew that it was.

If I hadn't stepped in, harnessing my inner-alpha, well, I wasn't really sure if we all would have made it back. No, I wasn't sure of that at all.

Commanding them the way I had really hadn't left a good taste in my mouth. It was the vicious look that Jared had given me that made me feel sick as if I'd stepped over a line by using my inner-alpha on him and his team. I'd stripped him of his authority without thinking, and I was pretty sure he would never forgive me for that.

Damn, I still felt sick.

My eyes watered, and I leaned my forehead against the tiled wall as the scalding water beat against my skin. I'd been such a fool to bring Jared back into the mix. I should have just let him go.

By the time I'd finally turned off the water, it had started to run cold, but at least I was beginning to feel a little more like myself. I dressed in a rush, pulling on jeans and a sweater, and went straight for the kitchen. My stomach was grumbling, and the house smelled deliciously like *Shake 'N Bake* chicken.

Aidan stood over the sink, elbows deep in suds as he scrubbed at a baking sheet. When he saw me, he grinned. "How's the ankle?" he asked, drying off his hands on his jeans.

"Hurts, but it's getting better," I said. I hobbled over to the table and sat down. It was set, which seemed out of place. Aidan just didn't set the table. He didn't usually eat at it either. Mealtime was more of a *grab-and-go* thing with him, leaving everything on the stove. Normally, we would dish out what we wanted before heading to the couch. But at the table were three lit candles, placed in the center, the flames tall and flickering. "What's all this?" I asked, eyeing the candles suspiciously.

Aidan went to the oven, pulled it open, and with a towel draped over his hands, he pulled out two heaping plates of chicken and vegetables. He placed a steaming plate in front of me. "I'm trying to make up for my crappy growling earlier."

I laughed a full-belly laugh, and darn, it felt good. "By lighting smelly candles?"

He rounded the table, set down his own plate, and took a seat. He gave me one of his lopsided grins and gestured to the plates filled with chicken and vegetables. "And I cooked dinner."

I smirked, trying not to laugh again. "You could also just say sorry, you know."

Aidan looked down at the table, furrowing his brow. "Isn't this better?" he asked. He was absolutely serious.

I blinked, shaking my head. "Nope, saying sorry is always better." I closed my fingers around my fork and scooped up a piece of broccoli. "That way, I get to feel like I was right."

He snorted and rolled his eyes. He looked as if he were about to say something, but he must have thought better of it, and dug into the food instead, which was probably the smart thing to do given the wicked smirk that was playing on his lips.

We ate in silence for a few minutes. The food, like always, was fan-freakin-tastic. One of the things I loved about Aidan, the man knew how to cook. The chicken was juicy; the vegetables warm but still had that nice crunch. Delicious.

I swallowed a mouthful of chicken and looked up. "Something is really wrong with the team," I said. As soon as the words were out of my mouth, I kind of wished I hadn't said them because it was pretty much the last thing I wanted to talk about right then.

Slurping his drink, Aidan leaned back in his chair. His smirk was gone. "Yeah," he said.

Considering what had happened with Beck, I really expected more than just *Yeah*, but it didn't look like I was going to get it. In fact, he was looking at me with a perfectly guarded expression, which was weird. Aidan wasn't much for guarding his feelings, at least not with me. With me, he kind of sucked at it.

I pushed some food around my plate, glanced back up at him, and heard myself ask a question that I wasn't sure I really wanted the answer to. "How did you know I was with Jared earlier?"

"Your Dad," he said, forking a piece of chicken and popping it into his mouth. He chewed it slowly, considering, and then swallowed it down. "Jared beat the shit out of him and then took off when you called."

I was thrown for a minute, and I was sure my eyes went saucer wide. "What was Jared doing with my dad?" I dropped my fork. "Wait. He hit my dad?"

Aidan nodded. His eyes were darkening, a rich brown velvet and some of the guardedness faded as if he had just then decided to tell me what was going through his head. "Jeff said something about people getting hurt when he fights with his brothers."

I stared at him blankly for a few long seconds, trying to understand what Jared's fighting had to do with anything. I puffed out a breath. Pulled one in and said, "He doesn't have any brothers." I was sure of that.

"About that." Aidan set his fork down. He watched me with an intense stare, the kind that he usually reserved for when I was pissing him off or when he was about to tell me something I really didn't want to hear. "He does have brothers, four of them."

And just like that, our nice dinner turned into a long, long evening.

Eventually, Aidan finished telling me about the newest piece of information that Tommy and Chris had found out. He told me about his concerns with everyone in the team being brothers and stressed that he thought we should take apart the team and rebuild it.

He went on to fill me in on how the pack had handled me taking off with the guys, which, as it turned out, was better than I had hoped, and he thought that some of the males were warming up to me. I thought that it was about time we had some good news.

But then he told me about his visit with my mother, and when he was done, I was pretty much numb.

He kept his tone detached and direct through the whole thing, only giving the facts and closing off all emotion. Except, he watched me as if he were assessing just how upset I was about the news, which, on a scale of one to ten, I was sitting somewhere near an eleven.

Given everything he told me, it was a surprisingly short conversation, and when he finished, I tried to tell him about what had happened at the camp, but he cut me off, gave me a kiss, and told me nothing had to be decided tonight, and then, he went to take a shower.

I puttered around the kitchen, washing the last few dishes. I thought about everything. About what I could fix and what was completely out of my control. But mostly, I thought about how this was the first time Aidan had talked to me, really talked to me, about pack stuff without trying to protect me.

I stretched and changed into a pair of boxers and a tank in the bedroom. I pulled my hair back, tying it into a loose knot, and waited for Aidan to finish his shower.

I had every intention of staying awake. I really did. I wanted to talk to him about what had gone down at the hunting camp and about what we found, but as I laid down and my head hit the pillow, sleep took me in a rush.

AIDAN

Jade was a bed hog.

I had an elbow digging into my ribs and a knee in my back. The covers were kicked off the bed, not even a sheet left. I went to roll over a little, but I couldn't. Somehow she'd managed to shove me to the edge of our king-size bed.

The space on the other side of her was loaded with the pillows she'd flung. She had even snagged mine, I noticed, which she was now using as her own.

I held in my laugh and worked to dislodge her knee and elbow without waking her up. She made a contented sound from the back of her throat and wrapped an arm around me, nuzzling her head into my side. She didn't fully wake up, stuck somewhere between sleep and awareness, and when I kissed her forehead, she sighed, and then her breathing deepened and evened out, and she was lost in sleep again.

I probably should have been asleep, too, but sleep was definitely not my friend tonight. My brain was too full of useless little bits of information. The team was all brothers. I killed their father. Jared wanted revenge in the form of taking Jade. The cougars kept their women in cages. They used whips. They used chains. We didn't know where to find them. Jade's mom was innocent and trapped in a house with the devil. The devil was Jade's dad. I loved Jade. Craig wanted me dead. Jade loved the pack. She wanted to protect the team. The information was starting to sound like a record, with a pounding base, playing on instant repeat through my head over and over. There was lots of information, but not enough on any one thing to really do anything with. Utterly useless.

I grabbed my phone from the nightstand, checking to see if there was any news about our sleeping captive. Nothing. It was just after three in the morning. Beck would have just started his shift with Erika in tow. Erika. I really needed to talk to Craig and Jade about that. She couldn't be babysat forever. Except, I really didn't have a clue how to broach the subject since it kind of was my bad judgment that led to her being stripped of her beta status. Just another thing to add to the *I don't know what to do with it* pile.

I set my phone back down and was about to close my eyes and listen to the god-awful stream of useless information in my head again when a tinkle of keys caught my attention. A lock clicked. A door opened and closed. And then I heard Dominic. "If you're awake, it's just me."

You've got to be kidding me, I thought, and held in the groan, not wanting to wake up Jade. I started to get up, slowly lifting her arm from my chest. She murmured something that sounded a lot like *Move over* and started shoving at me again as I slid off the bed. With a soft chuckle, I grabbed a T-shirt on my way out of the room and tugged it on as I headed downstairs.

I found Dominic sitting on my couch. He was in blue — a dark blue T-shirt, blue jeans, and a light blue jacket zipped halfway up, and he was looking happier than he should for three in the morning.

"What are you doing here, and why do you have a key to my house?" I asked, in a hushed voice, eyeing him from the bottom of the staircase.

"Of course, I have a key," he said cheerfully, flashing me a bright smile. "I'm your second in command. Why wouldn't I have a key?"

I didn't answer that. Over the last month of knowing Dominic, I found it better not to give him a reason to go off on one of his mind-numbing lectures. I sighed, sitting down in my chair. "It's three in the morning, Dom."

He was still smiling a way too sunny smile, and come to think of it, I didn't think I'd ever seen a real smile on him before. He might smirk or grin, but he never really smiled. "If you want it to work, you need to stop holding onto things that will keep you from moving forward."

So it wasn't the boundaries lecture he had in mind. Fantastic. I didn't particularly want to listen to whatever he had to say. Honestly, I wanted to crawl back in bed and wrap my arms around Jade. But it didn't look like that was going to happen. "If you're trying to give me more Jade advice, I don't want to hear it. I almost lost her once because of your advice."

Dominic stretched out on the couch, his arms behind his head, staring up at the ceiling. He was silent for a long moment before he said, "Did you tell her everything?"

"Of course I did," I said, furrowing my brow. "What kind of a stupid question is that?"

Dominic shifted. He steadied his icy blue eyes on me, and his smile turned cold. "She didn't call Mac, figured you were reverting back into that *I'm not going to tell her something that will piss her off* mode."

I hoped I didn't look as annoyed as I felt, but I figured I did, judging by his cool chuckle. "You woke up at three in the morning to come here and ask me if I talked to her," I said dryly.

His eyes narrowed. "Nope," he said. "I was over at the headquarters checking in. The hostage woke up. Oh, and I had to break up a fight between Jared and Beck."

CHAPTER 28

AIDAN

Jade had adorable bed head. Even though her hair was tied up, the indentations by her temples were visible, and stray strands flipped all over the place. Waking her up had been a bit of a challenge. It wasn't until Dominic had come in with a pitcher of ice-cold water threatening to dump it on her that she finally sprung from the bed. By the time I had finally hustled her out the door and into the car, it was closing in on four in the morning.

She walked a few steps ahead of me, her hands continuously running over her hair and then down her wrinkled hoodie and yoga pants, trying to smooth everything out, but she only succeeded in making herself look more rumpled. The hoodie she was wearing was mine, and every few seconds, I noticed her discreetly pressing her nose to her shoulder, pulling in a deep breath of my lingering scent, and each time she did, something in my chest expanded and warmed.

It felt complete. Perfectly whole.

The parking lot was pretty close to deserted, with only a sparse few vehicles, all of them belonging to the team. The air had a bite to it, stuck in that place where any precipitation could easily change from rain to snow in a heartbeat.

Dominic walked along beside me. He still hadn't patched things up with Jade, both of them too stubborn to apologize first, I assumed. Needless to say, the drive over had been on the tense side and painfully quiet.

Jade held the door open long enough for me to catch up and grab it before she took off down the hallway at a determined pace. She was focused, in some kind of zone, so she wasn't really paying attention, and when she reached the doors to the meeting room, and they flung open, she was startled, stumbling back a step.

Jared grinned as he let the door close and stalked toward her. He was in matte-black tonight — black jacket, black T-shirt, black jeans — there wasn't a speck of color except for the sparks of gold in his dark eyes. And he was sporting one hell of a shiner. He locked eyes with me as he closed the distance to Jade. He leaned into her, pulled her into a firm hug, and said, "Hey, little girl."

Clearly, he wasn't done trying to push my buttons.

Jade flinched away from him as if his touch burned and cut me a nervous glance. Her face went tight and still, and for the first time ever, she looked at me with something that resembled real fear. She stayed close to Jared and readjusted her stance, spreading her legs hip-length apart, squaring her shoulders. There was no doubt in my mind that if I made a move, she would place herself between him and me. The look she gave me had a strange intensity about it, as if she knew exactly who she was or who she wanted to be, and she wasn't going to let me change that.

The truth? I loved it. I loved her fire and never wanted it to change.

I swallowed my growl, and I folded my arms over my chest, hiding my clenched fists under my elbows. I grinned. It took a hell of a lot of effort to do it, too, but I managed a grin that I hoped looked somewhat real.

She arched a perfectly shaped brow and looked at me suspiciously for a second, and then she was suddenly crashing into me, and her hands were in my hair, and her lips were pressed to mine with a quick, warm kiss.

"What was that for?" I asked, wrapping my arms around her waist.

She giggled and grinned up at me. "I love that grin."

And right then, I thought that maybe, just maybe, showing her that I trusted her was a big step in the right direction for us. Hell, if it got me more of her kisses, I would keep the damn grin even if it killed me. I smoothed her hair and stole another kiss. "Let's go see what he can tell us."

Jared crossed his arms and frowned at Jade (she didn't even notice), and then he cut me a vile look. He held it for a long moment before he pivoted and followed Dominic into the room.

Richard had a few new bruises, and so did Beck.

That was the first thing I noticed when we walked into the meeting room. The entire team was there: Jared, Craig, Beck,

Landon, Mark. Tommy and Chris stood on either side of Richard, and Erika sat in the far corner, clutching a brown paper bag. The man was maybe nineteen or twenty, with a sharp face and intense smoky gray eyes that didn't stay still, roaming the room in a constant, jittery motion. He was sitting, unrestrained, in a wooden chair, his hands on his thighs and fingers splayed. He wasn't big, not like my wolves, but he wasn't small either, a medium build.

"Shouldn't he be tied up or something?" Jade sounded anxious, but she walked toward him with a sure purpose, even if she was.

"Come on, kitten," Jared said. "You know we don't need to tie him up." He was watching her in a far too personal way, and she didn't even glance at him when he spoke. From the way he was gritting his teeth, I could tell that he really hated that she ignored him. I, on the other hand, kind of loved it. She kept walking as if he weren't even there, as if she hadn't just protected him in the hallway.

"Jared," Landon snapped and shoved him back a step when he tried to follow her. "Show her and her mate some respect. She's the only reason you're here and still breathing."

"Which one of them hit you?" she asked. I wasn't even sure if she knew what was going on around her. She was focused in a way that I'd never seen in her before. She sounded concerned. She looked it, too, as she crouched down in front of him, inspecting his split lip.

Richard looked confused, leaning back in his chair, away from her. His eyes darted around, and he started to shake when Dominic moved closer. I gripped Dominic's shoulder, pulling him to a quick stop. I wanted to see what she did, how she handled him. And Tommy and Chris were close. They wouldn't let the cougar touch her. I locked stares with Tommy. He smirked and nodded, stepping in closer to Jade and Richard.

"It's okay," Jade said in a sweet, soothing tone. "I won't let them touch you again."

It seemed to take forever. Richard took a few hard breaths, searched her face, and then sighed. "Look, I already told them what I know." His voice was hoarse. "I already showed your boys where they are on this map. I was never involved in the decisions. I don't know why my pack is all male. I'm not important enough in the ranks. Women came in, they were used, and then they were gone, replaced by new ones. My mate was in the last batch, so I took her and ran. All I know is Dog Mountain used to be our town, our territory until you wolves came along."

"You're lying," she said. There was no malice in her voice, still soothing and calm. She stayed crouched in front of him, her eyes never straying from his. "Why are you really here?"

He let out a strangled sigh, and if I had to guess, I thought he looked relieved to be caught in the lie. "Because you'll kill me fast, Jeff would have made me suffer." His voice held so much anger, so much pain, and he was speaking the truth. He really believed we wouldn't torture him. He attempted a smile, but it wasn't quite right. It was shaky, and the look in his eyes made it clear he had regrets.

"What did you do to earn your death sentence?" she asked, clenching her fists, gritting her teeth. Richard paled, and he started to tremble as her skin darkened with hair.

"Jade," I said, calling her attention. She rocked back and lifted to her feet in a fast motion. She shook out her hands as if she were trying to shake away the adrenaline that I was certain was burning through her veins.

Jade took in a few sharp breaths and paced a few steps as she got herself under control. It would have scared me how close she was to shifting. She looked as if she were ready to kill him for his lies and we needed him, except the team wasn't concerned at all. They watched her, but it wasn't because they were worried she'd lose it. It was because of the man that sat in front of her.

"You're Jeff's daughter," Richard said and made a startling kind of sound which could have been a laugh but sounded more like a gasp.

Jade's eyes flared as she turned back to him and nodded. "I am."

Richard made that startling laughing gasp sound again. "How did you wind up a wolf?"

"Long story, involving that hardheaded, pain in my ass alpha over there," she said. "If you lie to me again, you'll wish you had stayed with my father." She crouched down again and met his eyes squarely. "Why do you have a death sentence?"

He shifted his gaze away from Jade and frowned. "Same reason you all are going to kill me." He looked back up then, fixing his eyes on me. "I'm the one that killed the girls."

CHAPTER 29

JADE

Some days lasted a lifetime. This was one of those days, and as the sun set, there was still no end in sight.

My stomach was a little queasy, flipping over and over. The team stood around, looking as if they were more than capable of brutal violence and completely willing to inflict pain. Except the violence and pain were directed at each other.

The team, a strong group of werewolves with a single-minded purpose of upholding the alpha's laws and protecting the pack, slowly drifted apart. It was almost tragic witnessing it. Even when I hated them, I always had kind of respected the bond they'd had. I wasn't really certain what had changed, but I knew it had something to do with Jared. Whatever ridiculous ideas he was holding onto was driving a wedge between them all.

We spent the entire day questioning Richard. After he finished explaining the real reason as to why my father was intent on killing him, Aidan had taken over with the questions because, well, I'd come close to attacking the bastard. He had executed the women. It hadn't been an accident. They were murdered after three months of being held captive simply because he thought they were no longer *fun* to play with.

Tommy and Chris finally took him to the cells about half an hour ago and had agreed to stand guard. It was either lock him up out of our sight, or one of us would have killed him.

But he had given us a piece of useful information. Ray had killed Bruce when he first took over the pack in a drunken bar fight, and it was because of that fight that there had been a deal struck with my dad. It was Ray's way of apologizing for taking out their leader. He would look the other way as long as they stayed off of his land. With Ray gone, so was the deal he'd had with my father.

"So, what do we do now?" I asked. I was still trembling with white-hot fury, and Aidan reached out to pat my shoulder, stroking my cheek as he pulled back. He smiled, his eyes growing warm as he released a little trickle of his scent to soothe me. He took a seat and stretched out a hand to me. There was no trace of the possessive, jealous edge usually there when Jared was around. It was simply a hand, an invitation. And I took it, settling myself on his lap.

"He'll confess his crimes to the team and us with the pack standing as witnesses," Beck answered.

I craned my neck, looking back at Aidan. "And then?"

His dark gaze turned serious, and his smile faded, and then it was just too much. "He'll be put down, Jade," he said.

I stirred in his lap, trying to hold back a shiver. He must have felt my unease because he started rubbing my back. I pulled in a deep breath and shut my eyes for a second. I wasn't sure why hearing it out loud was getting to me. I'd wanted to kill Richard myself not too long ago. I still did, but handing down his death sentence as if I were the judge seemed a bit too real.

But it had to be done. The longer we had questioned him, the more certain I was of it. He would kill again, whether it was with his pack or alone. The truth had been in his scent, in his eyes. Hell, he had even stated it bluntly.

And it wasn't as if we could hand him over to the police. Most people didn't even know about werewolves. Our town was special in that way. We lived in the open here, but it wasn't the norm.

When it all came down to it, shifters dealt with shifters.

"Why is what they're doing our problem?" Jared asked.

My eyes popped open at his cool tone, and I looked at him. He was straight-faced, as if he really didn't get why we had to do something. "Are you kidding me?" I said. "Of course, it's our problem."

Jared didn't respond immediately. He was staring at me. I didn't need to wonder what he was thinking. The detachment was clear on his face. He really believed we should look the other way. "It's really not," he said finally. "We've done just fine in protecting this town from them. They haven't threatened us outright."

My fury got a thorough kick start, and I growled, "Tiffany ..."

"Is dead," Jared said, cutting me off. "You killed her, Jade, and her deal died when you ripped out her throat." There was no emotion in his remark. He was stating a fact.

"We're dealing with it because it's wrong," Beck said with a frustrated growl, and I got a clear impression that this was not the first time the guys had had this conversation.

"People do wrong shit all the time," Jared said blandly. "I don't see us running out to stop it, so why now?"

"Because we know who's responsible," I shouted. "We can stop them. We can stop my father." I sounded desperate, and I hated it. "Don't make me regret saving your ass, Jared. I won't do it again."

Jared chuckled, a cold, raw sound. "You didn't save me, little girl, and I've got to say, I'm a bit hurt that you think he would actually win against me."

I bristled and sat a little straighter in Aidan's lap. A growl tore from my throat, and my inner-wolf flipped in my stomach. No one spoke about my mate like that. No one. "Watch yourself, Jared," I snarled. "I'll rip you apart if you come near him."

Aidan chuckled and pressed his lips to my ear. "Easy now," he whispered for my ears only. He brushed a kiss across my neck, and then he rose, bringing me up with him. He started toward Jared, approaching slowly. "You know, I think it's time we clear the air between us," he said to Jared.

Aidan's scent started to thicken in the air, a forceful punch of power and greens. That was never a good sign when Jared was around. My inner-wolf pressed against my skin, ready to break free and defend what was ours. I reached out for him, acutely aware that Landon, Mark, and Beck were moving in closer, their golden eyes fixed on him, but he stepped away from my hand.

"Nothing to clear, alpha," Jared said. He sounded calm, but his jaw ticked, and he stood a bit straighter, rolling his shoulders back.

"You sure about that?" Aidan asked, stopping a few feet away from him. "Because I heard something that's pretty damn interesting yesterday."

Crap! My body temperature dropped to freezing. This was not the time. Everyone was too strung out. "Aidan, not now," I said.

"No, Jade," Beck said. He looked at me gravely. "It needs to be out in the open. My brother needs to learn his place."

Jared blinked and looked at Beck in question. They held each other's eyes for a long moment as if they were having a silent conversation. Slowly, Jared's face went red with fury. He shifted his gaze to each one of his brothers. Disgust passed across his face in a quick flash before he forced a blank stare on Aidan. "Don't look at me like you regret killing my father."

"I don't regret it," Aidan said. It sounded harsh, but it was the truth. "I regret not knowing he had kids. I regret not giving him a service so you could have closure. If I'd known, I wouldn't have covered up his death. I would have given you guys time to mourn."

That was a little too much truth for Jared, I thought. He looked shaken and then angry. When he glanced at me, I immediately felt bad, bad enough to look away.

The silence stretched thin as Aidan waited for some kind of response from Jared, and as the seconds turned into minutes, I thought I was going to burst from the tension. But then Landon stepped forward. He looked weirdly calm. He took a knee in front of Aidan and bowed his head. Beck joined him, so did Mark, and then, after another long second, Craig took a knee, too.

"Our father failed this pack," Landon said. "Thank you for saving the pack from him."

"Don't bow to him," Jared shouted. I winced and brought my hands to my ears because when he yelled, it was so loud that it felt as if my eardrums were going to pop from the sound. "He doesn't deserve your respect. He doesn't deserve to be the alpha."

"You want to settle this now?" Aidan growled. "If you don't think I'm fit to be alpha of this pack, then I'll welcome your challenge."

They stared off for a long moment, Jared's scent was thick in the air, but Aidan held his at bay. I didn't really get it until he glanced at me, studying my expression, which was probably a little freaked out. His nostrils flared, looking for any trace of a reaction from my inner-wolf, and then he laughed, a shock and thrilled sound. When he shifted his focus back on Jared, a strong wave of leafy greens and power and sweetness filled the air. My heart started banging in my chest, and Jared, although he fought it so hard that the blood vessels along his cheeks looked as if they were about to burst, bowed his head.

"That's what I thought," Aidan said dryly. "Pretty sure if you actually believed you could take me, it would have happened already."

Jared met my eyes for a brief second before heading for the door. "I'm out," he said. I went after him, reaching out for his hand, but Aidan stopped me, snaking an arm around my waist.

Jared gave us a one-fingered salute, and without looking back, he went out the door.

CHAPTER 30

JADE

The team didn't want to talk. I figured it was a guy thing. They grunted a few *S'okays*, and *We don't blame yous* to Aidan.There were some awkward back slaps and a few rough-sounding chuckles. And no one said a word about Jared's freak out. I felt like an outsider watching them, not part of the alpha pair and not part of the team, just a bystander peeking in on a scene that made absolutely no sense to me.

Within five minutes, it was over, and so was our meeting. They set up a new watch rotation to guard the cougar, and then the guys trailed out with their heads hanging a bit lower than usual.

I shot Aidan a hard questioning stare once they were gone, but all he did was shake his head, and then he slipped a hand into mine. He squeezed, a reassuring press of his fingertips, and without a word, he led me out of the building.

The car ride home was a silent one. Aidan's scent was calm and relaxed, and his expression was similar. He held my hand the entire way, rubbing small circles on my palm.

When we got home, he gave me a distracted kiss and mumbled something about taking a shower. I wanted to say something, but I couldn't. My throat felt tight, as if hands were choking me.

Day from hell, I thought, as he disappeared up the stairs. I considered calling Marcy and Dominic but decided that even though I wanted to talk about everything that had happened with the team and the cougar, I didn't want to talk to them about it.

I went into the kitchen to grab something to eat, but I realized I wasn't really hungry once I opened the fridge. I paced around the house some. I wanted to call the guys, make sure they were okay, and then I wanted to find Jared and knock some sense into him. I knew he was hurting, but if he kept this crap up, he would find himself thrown out of the pack or worse. Alphas die. It sucked, but it happened. He couldn't blame Aidan, not for this. *It was the way of the pack.* The thought made me laugh, a harsh sound. How could I rationalize a death like that when I fought everything else?

Aidan was just turning off the shower as I padded up the stairs, and I headed for the bedroom, figuring I should get changed before he came in. I quickly kicked off my jeans and hoodie and tugged on a pair of boxers and a yellow tank, and then I crawled into bed, ready for the day to be over with.

Aidan pushed the door open a few moments later. He glanced at me and his sexy lips lifted in a crooked smile. His hair was a carefree mess and damp from his shower. He smelled so good. Fresh and clean. He was wearing nothing more than a pair of boxers. My eyes drifted over him, completely on their own, and settled on the raised scar of his alpha imprint on his right pec, a jagged letter "A," which matched my own. His carved face had a contented look to it as he moved toward me.

He crawled onto the bed, and as soon as he was settled, I snuggled in against his warm body. "Are you okay?" My hands were shaking, my lips tight, as I looked up at him, hoping for some kind of insight on what had happened between him and the guys.

"I'm fine, sweetheart," he said. The answer made me want to scream. How was he fine? I just didn't get it. I figured he noticed my confusion because he leaned down, pressed a kiss to my forehead, and said, "Did you just expect us to shed some tears and hug it out?"

"Yeah, kind of," I said, nuzzling my head against his bare chest. "Or at least show some kind of darn emotion."

He laughed as his hand drifted along my back and teased the hem of my tank top, and I shivered in delight as his warm fingertips brushed along the base of my spine. "What about you?" he asked. "Are you okay?"

I held my breath for a long moment. Was I fine? No, not really. My life had been one hell of a ride since I met Aidan, and it didn't seem to be stopping anytime soon. My father, the pack, the team, Aidan, they all seemed like problems, and I had no idea how to solve them. I let out my breath in a slow hiss and said, "Yeah, fine."

"Jade, look at me," his voice was full of command, and before I knew it, my body had complied. I twisted my head, resting my chin on his chest. His handsome face was hard. "Don't lie to me. We're past that shit."

"It's nothing." Another lie, but the thing was I really didn't know how to tell him I felt like I was being pulled in a million different directions. I didn't know how to say that I wanted the team to stay together, especially since he'd made it clear last night that we should take it apart and rebuild. I didn't want to talk about the fact that I wasn't okay with sentencing the cougar to death even if I knew he needed to die, and I really didn't want to talk about my dad.

"Still trying to protect him." It wasn't a question. His eyes hardened further, and his jaw started to tick.

I lowered my lips to his chest, littering it with teasing kisses and little nips. It was a distraction; I knew it, he did, too, but even so, a whole new tension tightened his muscles, and he let out a soft groan. "I don't want to fight," I whispered between kisses.

"I'm not picking a fight, are you?" His voice was husky, and his hand slipped under my tank, rubbing a tingling trail up my spine.

I sighed and shivered. "It has nothing to do with me protecting Jared." I lifted my head, meeting him square in the eyes. "Sometimes, the best move a leader can make is to step back from a battle when the potential loss is too high. Losing the head of the enforcers is a pretty big loss, don't you think?"

He didn't answer, and I continued the soft trail of nips and licks up to his neck. Another soft groan left his lips. "If you keep that up, I might not be able to behave myself."

"Who said I wanted you to behave?" I asked, nipping at his earlobe.

Aidan put a hand under my chin in a blink, lifting my head up. He kissed me, a dominant, thorough kiss, invading my mouth with smooth, powerful moves of his tongue. I really wasn't one-hundred percent sure how I came to my conclusion, but as his tongue tangled with mine and his hands ran along my skin, I knew one thing: I was sick of being sensible.

Funny, when it came right down to it, the decision was an easy one. Or maybe I was just completely and utterly overwhelmed with everything else that was going on, and that one thing was the only thing that made an ounce of sense. Either way, it didn't matter.

My body swayed closer to him, and I pushed on his chest to break the contact. He eased back, but only slightly. His warm brown eyes met mine, and I knew what he was thinking as he laid his head back on the pillow. He thought I was stopping him before anything unchangeable happened, and before he completely closed off the ideas that were burning in his eyes, I whispered, "I'm ready."

"Uh ..." He looked down at me, utterly confused for a moment. His nostrils flared then, searching my scent. His gaze darkened with desire, but there was something else, too, uncertainty, hesitation. I was a bit — a lot — terrified of that small spark in his eye. The one that pushed past everything else, showing me what I'd seen before. I was slowly losing his inner wolf. I could see it, God, I could even smell it.

I pulled in a shuddering breath. My nerves skittered and jumped. I pushed away from him, sitting back on my heels. "I mean, if you haven't changed your mind, that is." My voice (thankfully) was cool, not giving way to my jittery nerves, although I was pretty sure he could smell them anyway.

He shook his head in a violent shake against the pillow. "No, no, I haven't. You just kind of caught me off guard there. I figured ... well, I thought ..."

"You don't sound too sure," I said, knotting my hands in the hem of my tank.

Aidan scrubbed at his face and groaned. "I just don't want you rushing into this if you're still not sure, and I don't want this to happen if it's just to fix things with the pack or with me."

My inner-wolf was a traitor. I was trying, man, was I trying, to play it cool, but thanks to her, my body was burning wickedly hot. She wanted to fix that fading look in his eyes. I did, too, but that wasn't the only reason I wanted this. My mind, my body, my inner-wolf just knew it was time to stop being afraid of losing myself to him because the truth was, I'd been lost since the first time I met him. "This is for me," I said. "If it helps to fix the pack, that's an added bonus, but this is for me."

Aidan was ... nervous, like really nervous. It was kind of sweet and seriously unexpected. That deadly, predatory guard of his was gone. "This is forever, Jade. It can't be undone."

"Good," I said and smiled. "I want forever with you. I love you."

Aidan didn't seem sure, not even a little. He eyed me with doubt that pierced like a hot needle through my heart. And suddenly I couldn't breathe. His eyes narrowed, but not unkindly. It was as if he were trying to decide if he should take me seriously or brush me off.

After a painfully long moment, he said, "Come here."

And my body (or it could have been my inner-wolf) obeyed the command. Before I realized I was moving, I leaned into him again.

He sat up and caressed my cheek, a steaming brush of fingertips trailing along my jaw and dipping down my neck. "You sure?" he asked.

I nodded. I lifted my hands, pressing them against the hard lines of his chest. He continued caressing my skin, a slow trail back up my neck and my lips parted when his fingertips touched them, and he paused, slowly tracing their edges.

He kissed me, but it wasn't demanding. It was soft, testing, and he tasted sweet and minty. Warmth spread through my entire body right down to my toes, and suddenly I didn't want the sweet, soft kiss. I wanted more. I needed more.

Everything poured out of me. All the desire I'd been holding back since I first met him made me feel as if I were on fire. I leaned back from him, breaking the kiss, and stripped off my tank. I wanted to feel his skin against mine so badly it physically hurt.

Aidan watched me for an excruciatingly long minute. His eyes flared golden, his inner-wolf coming out. He let out a low growl of approval and licked his lips. And then his hands were on me, and mine on him. Our lips met. Gone were the sweet testing kisses. He didn't hold back, and neither did I. The world around us began to tilt and fade until all that was left was him and me, lost in scorching touches and feverish kisses.

CHAPTER 31

AIDAN

"Can this wait?" I asked. Okay, it was more like a demand into the phone. I tried not to look at Jade as she crawled back into bed, but not looking wasn't really an option. My gaze drifted back to hers, and I met her hooded eyes. With her long brown hair, still damp from her shower, hanging over her shoulders, and her perfect creamy skin, my blood was already running hot just looking at her. But then she gave me a seductive, hot as hell smile and wagged her finger at me, calling me back to bed, and my entire body went up in flames.

"No, kid, it can't." Tommy's voice, perpetually rough, held a lot more gravel than usual. "I'm bringing the boys to you now. We're ten minutes out."

I rubbed at my face and let out a frustrated growl. The sun was just barely up, and Jade was lying in my bed with nothing more than a towel on. Damn, all I wanted to do was get back in there with her, but of course, I couldn't. There was something else that needed my attention. "I need thirty," I said, watching her wind a strand of hair around her finger. I breathed in a deep lungful of air, catching her new scent, and a growl started to build in my throat. "No, make that sixty."

"Ah, hell, it happened, didn't it?" Tommy muttered. He paused for a second, letting out a long breath that crackled over the phone line. "Shit, kid, this really can't wait. It's about Jared. I'm so ..."

"Don't say you're sorry," I snapped before he could get the word out, and I forced myself to turn away from Jade. "I'm liable to kick your ass when you get here if you do."

"But I am." He paused for another long breath and then said, "Ten minutes."

I hung up the phone with a curse and walked over to the bed. I leaned over Jade, gave her a long and more than a little possessive kiss, and then as much as I hated to do it, I pulled away from her and said, "Time to get dressed, sweetheart. The guys will be here in ten."

Her reply was a purr that came close to undoing me. "We still have ten minutes."

JADE

Aidan laughed. I didn't think I had ever heard him laugh like that before. It was real and full of cheery energy. He was happy, and I loved it. He caressed my cheek and kissed my forehead, and then he pulled away again. "Ten minutes isn't long enough," he said, his voice low and husky. He backed up a step and smirked. "I'm going to jump in the shower, and you better have your cute butt dressed when I'm done." Aidan didn't wait for my protests before he turned around and headed out of the room. A second later, I heard the rush of the shower as he turned it on.

With a long sigh, I pulled myself out of bed grudgingly. I went to the dresser, tugging open a drawer, and began to riffle through the minimal clothing I had here at the house.

I had only just gotten out of the shower when Aidan's phone had gone off. I knew it was freakin' horrible to be annoyed at the interruption, but I couldn't help it. Really, was it too much to ask for just a few more uninterrupted hours with my new mate?

Then again, it wasn't as if they knew we had taken that step yet, so I figured I really couldn't blame them.

Letting my towel drop to the floor, I pulled on a pair of panties and then fastened my bra. Even annoyed, I was still grinning. Last night had been more than I had expected. So much more. It had been a slow, blissful hour, full of sensual exploration, discovering each other in an entirely different way. I had expected to be nervous, but after the first few minutes, my nerves had vanished. Being with Aidan was comfortable and exciting, and breathtaking. I had let myself go, and so had he.

I pulled in an idyllic breath, catching the change in my scent. I pressed my palm to my nose, grinning. I could actually smell the difference on my skin, a layer of leafy greens coating my natural aroma.

I'm really his, I thought, as I stepped into a pair of jeans. *And oh, God, he's actually officially mine.* My grin widened into a painfully big smile. My chest felt so full; I felt so complete. It was utterly amazing.

Banging, like someone was hitting the front door with a baseball bat, wiped the grin from my face. With a quick glance at the clock, I snagged a T-shirt and tugged it on, thinking ten minutes couldn't have possibly passed yet, but yep, it had.

I rushed out of the bedroom, and as I passed the bathroom, I heard the shower still going. "Hurry up, they're here," I called out, and then I hit the stairs at a jog.

The thudding at the door didn't stop until I yanked it open. I blinked against the bright sun, once, twice, and then my eyes went wide, and my lips parted with horror.

Craig stood in front of me, his left eye black and swollen shut. There was a blood-crusted gash running down his right cheek, stopping at the base of his chin. His neck was covered in bruises, and Jesus, I could actually see individual fingermarks there. Beck and Landon were behind him. They didn't look as bad, but each of them was sporting a nice shiner, and Mark, who stood off to the side, had a purplish bruise on his cheek.

"Where's Aidan?" Tommy asked, his voice all rough edges. He didn't wait for me to move out of the way before he started to shove the guys into the house, not too gently.

I blinked and cleared my throat. "He's upstairs," I said, backing up as everyone crowded into the living room. "In the shower." I chewed on my bottom lip, scanning the guys over. "I don't think I want to know what happened." I swallowed down the dread that was climbing up my throat. "Do you want some ice? Or something for the pain? Or ... Or ... What the hell did Jared do this time?" God, it had to have been Jared. I just knew it. He'd been so pissed yesterday. He'd been ...

"They're fine," Chris said in a lazy drawl, closing the front door. He flexed his arms, his biceps curling up thick, as he fixed a steady glare on the team. He was giving off a clear-cut vibe of a guy who didn't tolerate any crap. With the way he carried his tall, bulky frame, I didn't doubt for a second he wasn't opposed to using his fists to make sure everyone understood it. "Start talking, boys. You've got a better chance of making it out of this alive if you talk to her before Aidan." He smiled at me then, or at least I thought the rough curve of his lips was supposed to be a smile, and said, "She seems to have a soft spot for you boys."

The four of them exchanged tight-lipped looks. Landon started to shake — literally — and it was all wrong when he tried to smile at me. My inner-wolf shifted and stirred, and I growled. It came out before I could swallow it, fierce and all animal. "What have you done?" I demanded. My imprint heated, my scent flared, and all four of them dipped their chins, casting their eyes to the ground.

Tommy's shiny head took on a pinkish-red hue. "Please," he started and then cleared his throat. "Jade, control yourself, please. You're mated now, Aidan's scent mixed with yours is ..." He cleared his throat again and rubbed at it hard as if he were trying to massage away a lump that was blocking his voice.

I pulled in a deep breath, forcing my inner-wolf to stand down, which was, as it turned out, a crazy amount of work. Sweat beaded along my spine, and my hands trembled. But I managed to rein it in if only a little.

Tommy sucked in a noisy breath, and he shoved at Craig, growling, "Tell her."

Craig stumbled and fell to his knees. He wouldn't look at me, and I didn't know if it was because he physically couldn't look up or if it was that he didn't want to. "Jared," he croaked and winced. His voice sounded raw as if he'd swallowed a handful of broken glass. "He knew where the bastards were, Jade. He's known for a week."

Heavy footsteps coming down the staircase and a deadly growl told me that Aidan had heard what had just been said. I wanted to turn away. I wanted to go to him, but I couldn't move.

Craig might as well have punched me. It probably would have felt better. His accusations gutted me and left me raw and exposed and empty. "No." I shook my head. "No, he would have told me. You're lying. Jared's a dick, but he loves this pack. He wouldn't hide something like that. He wouldn't."

"You would scent that, Jade," Beck said, giving me one of those crappy reasoning looks. "You know he's telling you the truth."

Oh, God, I thought. Was this really how the rest of my life was going to be? Lies and betrayal? Aidan was behind me, close enough that I could feel his breath teasing the hair on the top of my head. I could hear his steady breathing and the rhythmic thumping of his heart. His scent was calm, and he was deathly quiet. It scared me a bit. As dread choked me, the only thing I could get out was, "Why?"

"Aidan took our father from us," Mark said. His eyes were dull when he looked up as if he had checked out and his mind was somewhere else entirely. "We wanted him to feel the same pain we felt when he died. Jared thought if he spent enough time with you, you'd mate with him. Aidan took something from us, he was going to take something back. He stalled on the hunt. We all did. We knew if you found them, you'd walk away from Jared. He just wanted more time to win you over."

Craig cleared his throat. "We didn't know he'd found them until this morning," he said. The smell of his desperation left a bitter taste in the air. "I swear it. We didn't know. He went ape-shit crazy when we told him we were done."

"You helped him." I was shaking all over. "You all stood by and helped him try to ruin my mate. You ... you ..." I growled. They all plotted against my mate. My mate. The people I trusted, my friends, my team. "How didn't I smell the lies?"

"You never asked," Beck said, again with that reasoning tone. "We never had to lie to you."

Landon lifted his chin a little and looked over my head. "Aidan, I thought she wanted him," he said, and damn him, he actually looked ashamed. "All of us did. Her inner-wolf reacted like Jared was to be her mate. She was throwing off her scent for him. If we'd known she wasn't into him, that it was just her wolf sensing his dominance, we wouldn't have helped stall things. We wouldn't have helped keep you from her." He swallowed a few hard swallows, and his face drained of color. "We stopped helping him when she submitted to you when you took her from Jeff's."

There was dead silence for a long breath. It was violent and cold, and when Aidan finally spoke, I found it hard to breathe. "You know I'm going to hunt him down, right?" Aidan's voice was a lethal toned whisper behind me. I turned to him and looked up. His expression was both striking and brutal. He looked me in the eyes and said, "And when I find him, I'm going to kill him. You are not saving his ass this time."

I knew I was probably supposed to reason with him, do the devil's advocate thing, but I couldn't. I wanted blood, too, so bad that my body lurched as my inner-wolf tried to break free. I'd always known Jared was loyal to a fault. I just never thought that loyalty could have been for Ray.

CHAPTER 32

AIDAN

It would have been better if Jade had defended him.

Jade didn't say a word. Instead, she gave me a terrible blank look and stood perfectly still. Her heart was slamming fast against her ribs. I could hear it so clearly. I could smell her bloodlust, too, a thick bitter-sweet aroma that had my inner-wolf pressing against my skin.

It struck me then, I was finally going to get my chance to kill Jared, and she was going to let me. Damn, by the look of her, she wasn't just going to let me. She wanted to do it herself. I really didn't know how I felt about that.

"You won't need to hunt him, kid," Tommy said. "He's challenging you for alpha. The pack has already gathered to witness."

The laugh that came out of my mouth was cold. "He thinks he can challenge me," I said and shook my head. "He lost his right to do that when he put his needs before the pack." I looked at the team. Their desperation, their fear, it all hung in the air like a pungent cloud of smoke. "But what should I do with you four," I said, stepping around Jade. "I find myself stuck here. I get revenge, and I can smell that you didn't know what Jared was hiding, but you helped him. You knew the cougars wanted our females and you helped delay the hunt."

Across the room, Beck shuffled his feet. "We meant what we said to you yesterday. You saved us from our father; I'm just sorry we didn't see that sooner." He raised his chin and stoned his face as he looked at me. "We will stand behind you if you allow it, and if you won't, we will accept your punishment without a fight."

"You knew she didn't want him, didn't you?" I laughed coolly. "Yeah, you did. You were always with them training, weren't you? You stuck close."

Beck nodded. "Because Jared wanted to force her, and I wasn't going to let him do that. No matter what, it was always her choice."

I rocked back on my heels a little bit as a punch of adrenaline shot through me. *Force her.* Another blast of steamy adrenaline rushed to my head.

"Easy," Chris said in a calm, low voice. "Easy there, kid, you need to think this one out. They came forward. They're giving up their own flesh and blood for you, for your mate."

I didn't want to hear that. I didn't care who they were giving up. *Force her.* He'd known. Beck had known that Jared was willing to force her. And he'd let the bastard sleep in her house, in her room. My inner wolf's savage nature took over. There was no logic to it. I was taken over by a possessive instinct.

At the sound of the first pop of bone, I heard a soft rasp, and I glanced over my shoulder. "Aidan, stop," Jade said. She reached out a hand to me, and I ignored it.

A series of pops and snaps broke out. My clothes tore and fell, my body remolded. And then I was a wolf. My lips peeled back, and I growled as I pivoted and stalked toward Beck.

Jade cut in front of me and said, "Aidan, remember what I told you last night. Sometimes the best move a leader can make is to step back from a battle when the potential loss is too high."

I heard a rustling and then a series of soft thumps. I glanced away from Jade, curled my lips further, and growled at the team. All four of them were on their knees, their necks craned out, their eyes closed. The silent offer reaffirmed what Beck had said. They would not fight me no matter what action I took.

"You are not this person," Jade said softly. "Your fight isn't with them."

JADE

Jared had called me soft once, and yeah, maybe I was soft. By pack law, I shouldn't have stopped Aidan, shouldn't have stopped his inner-wolf from killing the guys. By pack law, death was what they deserved. But I just couldn't let him do it. Not when they had willingly come forward. It may have been delayed, but they had done the right thing in the end. And I knew he would regret it afterward. I knew he was already bleeding inside from taking their father from them, even if he refused to show it.

It took thirty long minutes for everyone to get their heads back together and another ten after the guys told Aidan exactly where the cougars were for him to calm down enough to leave the house. I thought it was probably cold outside, there was a heavy wind, but I didn't notice the temperature. I couldn't feel it. I couldn't feel anything but the ice that shifted through my veins.

My werewolves were all gathered at the edge of the clearing, standing back — cowering — from Jared. He looked worse than the team had when they'd shown up on our doorstep. He was cut and bruised, and his right elbow was bending the entirely wrong way. His eyes were on me, though. They were so black, like bottomless pits. His pain and outrage rose up around him, hanging like acid in the air.

In front of him, discarded like a piece of trash, was Richard. He was dead. His blood no longer pumped through his veins, his heart no longer beat in his chest, and no breath would ever be pulled into his lungs again. A primal and territorial rage filled me. What struck me as odd, though, was that I was not angry that the man was dead, but because his sentence had been taken from me, even if I had dreaded having to issue his death sentence, it was my right to do it. This was my pack.

Luken was there, too, Richard's last guard. He was on his knees, although not because he wanted to be. He didn't look as if he could have gotten up even if he wanted to.

As I scanned the scene in front of me, there were, I realized, different shades of hatred, and until now, I had only ever felt a ghostly shadow of that emotion before. I hadn't really hated Dominic when he left me for the pack, although at the time, I thought I had. I hadn't truly hated Aidan for all his lies and manipulation or Marcy and Dominic for helping him. And I hadn't hated my father when I found out he was the devil. I'd been disappointed and hurt and angry and lost.

But, no, I hadn't hated them at all.

That had been a tingling sensation with a pinch, like getting a needle at the doctor or a blister. It was annoying, and it burned a little when poked at, but it hadn't been anything like what I felt at that moment.

Funny, but I never thought hatred would hurt so badly. It was like scorching heat, burning me up from the inside out, but at the same time, from the outside pushing in; I was cold as ice. My heart pounded so hard that it felt as if at any moment it would just stop beating as if it were about to give out on me. And God, did it hurt.

My mouth went dry, and I pressed closer to Aidan. His body was hot, solid, and strong against me. The silence in the clearing was voluminous. Aidan hadn't said anything yet. He was too calm. And right then, calm was, well, calm was scary. I thought I would have preferred to see the outrage he'd shown at home. At least that I could understand. But he just stared at Jared, an intense kind of stare that would have made pretty much anyone queasy.

"Who do you think you are?" Aidan finally asked. His tone was freakishly composed. "You are not the judge and executioner for this pack."

When Jared didn't answer, Aidan paced forward, leaving my side. He clasped his hand behind him. He wasn't looking at the dead body strewn out on the brittle grass. His eyes were fixed on Jared, a controlled stare that gave nothing away.

Aidan was only a few feet away when Jared gave a reaction. He shrugged and then winced from the movement. "Head enforcer is the executioner," he said dryly as if he were bored by the question. "And soon enough, I'll be alpha."

Aidan barked out a laugh. "You really think you can challenge for alpha with what you've done."

Jared's face grew red and furious. "Thanks to my brothers," he said with a venomous glare at them, "you will kill me if I don't."

Aidan seemed to consider Jared's words as he visibly measured the distance between them with a darting, calculating shift of his eyes. "You'll die either way, Jared."

Jared shifted his weight to the balls of his feet as if he were readying himself for a collision, but Aidan didn't move.

This was cruel, I thought. Really cruel.

Aidan flicked a small glance in my direction, and as if reading my thoughts, his eyes narrowed in warning. I knew then that I had to say something, even if I didn't want to.

Planting my hands on my hips, I stepped forward, and I said, "Last night, I told my mate that losing you would be a big loss to this pack. I defended you to him, again. I'm always defending you, Jared. You hid the cougars' location from me. You wanted to force me to mate with you. Have you told everyone how you plotted against us? That you betrayed us to get even for Ray's death? You tried to kill your own brother when he wanted to come forward. How am I supposed to defend you now? How? Give me a reason!" It all spilled out in a desperate tumbled mess, and I realized I actually wanted a reason to keep him alive. Maybe that was why the hatred hurt so badly; I honestly didn't want to hate him because he could be a good person somewhere under that cocky, jerk facade. I had seen it. I knew it was there.

Jared groaned and rolled his eyes. Not the response I had expected and definitely not the one I wanted. "They don't have to like me, Jade. They only have to fear me. And he's not your mate." He said it with a smile and a cocky wave of his hand.

I stepped closer, trying to not let my boiling hatred consume me. "Are you sure about that?"

CHAPTER 33

AIDAN

Jared's first mistake was striking Jade. His second was shifting.

The second she moved in closer, Jared's nostrils flared, catching the change in her scent, which was growing stronger with every passing second. He sagged, and his demeanor went from cocky to seething in a split second.

Jade was trying to give him a way out. She wanted him to live. I could hear it in her voice, that hint of desperation. Jared knew it, too. His eyes flared, and for a quick second, he even smiled a sad tilt of his lips.

But then, he moved and got in her face. He lifted his hand and backhanded Jade, hard enough that she stumbled. And then he shifted.

If he had stayed human, he might have had a chance.

Jade may have given him a way out of this, but she wasn't stupid. *Thank God she wasn't stupid.* She was out of her clothes a second later. She didn't hesitate in her shift, letting her inner-wolf out in a breath. And I was right there with her, my bones breaking and snapping. Hair sprouted over my skin, my canines lengthened.

It only took seconds, and then we were both wolves, big and snarling, black beasts. We moved like killers, stalking around him, waiting and ready for the strike. We moved together perfectly, Jade and me, completely in sync.

Jared shifted back and forth, pivoting to keep us both in his sights. He looked for his opening. He waited. He even backed up a step. And we stayed on him, stalking him like the predators we were.

Jade's breath was a constant growl, each inhale and exhale carrying the sound. At least until Jared looked her straight on, and she froze stiffly.

And that was the opening he had been waiting for. Jared launched at Jade, his lips curled, teeth sharp, and jaw open for the bite. That was his third mistake. It was also the mistake that solidified his death.

Males did not attack females. Especially not the alpha female.

My thirst for blood rose up, but I wasn't the only one who felt it. Growls erupted all around us, and wolves sprung forward from the sidelines.

Jade tensed, and a quick burst of her fear tingled at my nose. But her fear didn't last. She dodged his lunge just as I launched forward, tackling him to the ground. There wasn't time for anything fancy. I pinned his neck into the grass with a hard press of my teeth. With a graceful leap, Jade was on him, too, planting her front paws on his chest, snarling down at him.

Jared thrashed beneath us, growling and snapping. I saw the pack circling from the corner of my eyes, watching with hunger. Growls pierced through the air. The team had shifted, too, and closed in on us, but they did not attack, did not try to save their brother.

The pack moved in closer, snarling viciously. And I knew right then that if I didn't kill him, they would. The scent of savagery and bloodthirstiness clung all around them. Jared was not walking out of this clearing. The pack wasn't going to let him walk after attacking Jade. But then, neither was I.

Jared bucked hard, fighting with everything he had. Just like his father. But this time, I did not wait for his submission. I knew it would never come. No, this time, I ended it fast, burying my teeth in his neck, and biting down until he laid still. Until he was gone.

JADE

When Jared took his last breath, I backed up in a rush. Aidan let go of his neck as soon as I moved and looked up at me. It was a slow, searching look, and he didn't break it, not once, as he shifted back to human.

Wolves were howling all around me. The pack who had hated me had shifted to protect me. I'd seen them do it and rush in when

Jared launched at me. And now they howled, a sad, pain-filled song. My insides shriveled and twisted listening to it.

Aidan rose up, and his eyes were still on me. He moved slowly as if he was scared I would run. He found his pants, tugged them on, and then he was standing over me. He dropped down to his knees. His hand trembled ever so slightly as he reached out and ran it along my fur. He pulled me to him, wrapping his arms around my neck, and he hugged me close. His murmurs were soothing sounds, not really words, and I almost missed it when the words actually came out. "I'm sorry." His voice was raw.

I ached for him. I knew he really was sorry.

But it wasn't his fault. Jared could have made a graceful retreat. I would have let him bow out of town. I would have made Aidan let him, too, no matter what his crimes were against the pack or against us — the alpha pair. For that one desperate moment, I would have let him go. But he hadn't wanted that. He had wanted revenge.

I shifted in Aidan's arms, and he didn't let go, not even as my bones snapped and moved under my skin. I didn't respond right away when I returned to my human form. I simply gazed at him, hoping he would see that I understood.

"Thank you for making it quick for him," I whispered after a long moment. "I'm not sure the rest of them would have."

His gaze fell, and he nodded. His throat bobbed with a few quick swallows, and he released me from his arms. As he rose from my side, the pack began to shift back to human, and as they did, cheers rose up loud and quick. I took to my feet and swallowed down the bile that rocketed up my throat. My insides were twisting and clenching with pain.

They were cheering over his dead body.

"How can they be happy about this?" My voice was a whisper. I didn't expect an answer. I didn't really want one.

"They're not cheering because he's dead, Jade," Beck whispered from behind me as a windbreaker wrapped over my shoulders. "They cheer because the alpha pair is together. They cheer for your union. They cheer that you fought for them. That you didn't let them fall into the hands of Jared. They cheer for you, not for him. Never confuse that. It'll kill you if you do." The heartbreak in his voice made me ache for him. He slid in front of me and pulled the jacket closed.

Landon drew close, and he touched my arm. "Jared was already dead, Jade," he said. "My brother died the same night my father did."

I nodded because, really, I couldn't do anything else. Craig came forward, and so did Mark. The four of them surrounded me, and then I was in their arms. I don't know how long we stood there, finding support in each other's embrace, but by the time we let go, the cheering had dried up.

The pack had circled us, dressed once more. There was no malice in their movement, and I had the distinct impression that the circle they formed was one of protection.

I slid away from the guys and looked for Aidan. He hadn't gone far, just a few steps away. When my eyes landed on him, he smiled, although it didn't look real at all. I couldn't guess what he was feeling. Most likely because I was choking on my own emotions, and he had that calm fearless expression back in place.

He came to me, his warm weight settling in behind me, and his arms went around my waist. He squeezed me and pressed a kiss to my cheek, and then, he addressed our pack.

"Thank you, my friends," he said, his voice loud and strong. "Today, you've shown me that despite our differences, we can truly be a pack. You all didn't hesitate to rush forward when my mate was threatened, even though not all of you felt she was worthy of alpha, and I thank you for that. I will not forget it."

I looked out over the pack standing around us. I searched inside myself for a connection to them, that little thread of feeling that I had come to depend on. I found it in Dominic's hazel eyes and Marcy's sorrow-filled gaze. I felt it in Trevor's protective arms that encircled his human mate. I saw it in Erika as she looked at me with regret and admiration. I found it in all of them, that little piece of me. That sense of belonging, of possession, and of unyielding protectiveness. It swelled in my chest expanded my heart. We may have been splintered, but we were a pack. We were together, and we would support the cracks while they healed.

As a unit, the pack lowered to the ground, kneeling and bowing — a sign of their loyalty to Aidan. I found myself wondering if it might have been for both of us. Whether it was for him or for us, I felt the resolve tighten in my chest. This time, no matter what, I would not fail them.

As I looked out over the sea of bowed heads, I said, "Thank you." My voice was weak, very weak. I cleared my throat and blinked away the sting of tears. "Go now and rest. Grieve the loss of our brother, and comfort the ones he left behind." My voice still trembled, and Aidan's arm tightened around me, supporting me. My heart was pounding hard against my chest, and I strengthened my grip on my emotions. "But be ready. We know where the cougars are. The time is coming to take out our enemy."

As soon as they started moving, heading for the woods, I turned to those who had stayed behind. My friends: Marcy and Trevor, Tommy and Chris, the team, Dominic, even Erika, waited before Aidan and I. Waited for the words I figured neither of us wanted to say.

Marcy managed to whisper the question on all of our minds. "What happens now?"

"We bury our brother," Aidan said with compassion, choosing to ignore the real question behind her words.

A string of faint but heart-filled, *thank-yous* spilled from the guys, and a tension that I hadn't noticed was there until it lifted, dispersed into the air. And then the waiting started once more.

I swallowed hard, pulled in a breath, and said, "And then we tell my father I'm mated and watch for the next play of his game to drop."

Acknowledgments

An enormous thank you goes to my family and friends. When I think of your unwavering support, words fail to capture how truly grateful I am. I love you all.

To my husband, Jordan, thank you for talking to me about the characters as if they were real people. You make me laugh, you keep me challenged, and I love you for it.

And to my editor, Kathryn, your enthusiasm and insight makes me glad you are on my team.

Last, but not least, a big, huge thank you to all of my fabulous readers. You guys are the best and I couldn't have done it without you all!

Deadly Pack

Deadly Trilogy Book 3

Dedication

For Hazel, because you kept me sane.

CHAPTER 1

AIDAN

A ghost of a smile touched Jade's lips as I reached over and squeezed her hand. Wispy strands of hair framed her face, pieces that had worked their way loose from the twisted knot that was piled high on her head. Her scent was cluttered with emotions, the dense, sour-sweet aroma of sorrow being the most prominent.

Her gaze was calm, though, as it slid around our clustered circle, stopping for a beat on each face before moving on to the next. She held onto my hand with a loose, dry grip and nodded her agreement as plans were made and strategies were formed. She hadn't really said much of anything since the pack had left, and I didn't know what to think of that. Jade wasn't really the quiet type, and, dammit, her silent agreement to everything was unnerving. It made me think she had her own plans brewing inside that beautiful head of hers.

We were standing in the clearing, hashing out the last few details of what needed to be done. Dominic paced a few feet away, his phone glued to his ear, arranging Jared's cremation. Jade had been adamant about that. *"Jared's claustrophobic,"* she'd said. *"He wouldn't want to be buried, trapped underground, inside a small box. We'll spread his ashes here. He loved this place."* It had been the only words she'd uttered in the last twenty minutes that had held any trace of emotion; every other mumble that came from her lips had been blank and toneless.

Across from where we were gathered, Jared's body was being loaded into the back of Tommy's pickup truck. I didn't miss the fact that Jade was trying hard not to look, and I also didn't miss the way her throat worked hard when she caught sight of Tommy from the corner of her eye as he lifted the lifeless wolf form and carefully placed it onto a blanket in the back of the truck. Her nose was screwed up, wrinkling along the bridge, and her eyelashes fluttered quickly as she tried to fight against the fresh spring of tears that glossed her eyes.

Her inner turmoil was unbearable to watch. And it completely sucked that I didn't know what to do to make this easier for her.

Her gaze followed Tommy as he began folding the edges of the blanket over, cocooning Jared within it. A painful, gasping sound fell from the back of her throat as the blanket was draped over Jared's face, and in a beat, she swiveled, turning into me, and buried her face into my chest. Her hands fisted my shirt, and she held on to me as if I were her lifeline.

And my heart cracked, splintered, broke, as my strong, independent mate started to fall apart.

The guys fell silent as I wrapped my arms around her waist, giving her a moment to pull it together. I felt her body quake against me. She was breathing deeply but raggedly, her shoulders lifting and falling, and she pressed her face further into my chest.

I rested my chin on her shoulder, brushing my lips against her ear. "It's okay, sweetheart," I murmured. "It's okay." The words felt impersonal, and they sounded like a lie. I really didn't know if it would be okay. I didn't know if she'd be able to get past this, but I did know that I would do everything I could to make this easier for her. "Tell me what you need from me, and I'll do it. Anything. Tell me how to help you deal with this."

Jade didn't answer for a long moment, so long that I really didn't think she was going to, but then she whispered, "I'm okay, Aidan." Her voice was thick and raw, and her breath hitched on a hiccup. I felt her throat constrict and bob against my chest as she swallowed, and then she said, "I'm good. Promise. I'm just overwhelmed and a little ... um ... scared?"

"Are you asking me or telling me?" I asked, stroking my hand up and down her spine as I held her close, trying to soothe her. She sounded so lost, nothing like the fierce, feisty, bullheaded girl that I knew.

She craned her neck back and looked up at me. For a second, I saw her pain and anger blazing in her eyes, but it didn't last. She blinked a few times, smoothed out her expression, and pasted on a cool, fake smile. "I'm scared," she said with certainty.

My heart squeezed tight as if someone had wrapped it in an elastic band. Scared wasn't good. Fear could turn the best-laid plans into a disaster. A disaster that the pack (and the town) seriously didn't need right now. I squeezed her tightly and muttered, "Fear is only excitement in need of an attitude adjustment."

Chris chuckled, and my gaze snapped up to his. His eyes were dancing with humor, most likely remembering the first time my dad had said those words to me. He'd been there, so had Tommy, standing beside my father. I'd been just a kid, and I'd been terrified when they'd decided it was time for me to learn what an alpha's scent could do. Those words had been my dad's version of a pep talk, and I seriously couldn't believe that I was actually using them now.

Jade huffed and wiggled out of my arms. Her lips thinned, and she attempted (and failed) to give me a fierce scowl. She placed a hand on her hip, her bottom lip still trembling. "Are you saying I need an attitude adjustment?" she asked, quirking an eyebrow in question.

I nodded, grinning down at her. "Yep."

The guys stood motionless, watching Jade warily as if they were all waiting for her to flip out on me. The truth? I kind of was, too. Actually, I wasn't just waiting for it. I was hoping she would. I needed to see something other than the gut-twisting pain that marred her pretty face, and anger would have been better. It would give her something else to focus on, something other than fear.

But Jade didn't flip out. Instead, her lips stopped trembling. The corners of her mouth quirked up a little, and the elastic band that had been squeezing my chest snapped at the sight of her small smile.

The silence lingered for a long moment, but as Jade's smile grew, Marcy broke it and asked, "Is that a smile?" She inched closer to us and tried (unsuccessfully) to stifle a nervous giggle.

"No," Jade said, shaking her head and turning around to scan the group. "Definitely not a smile."

"It looked like a smile," Mark said. He was smiling, too, but it didn't come close to reaching his eyes. He had the hood of his sweater down; his crazy mop of curls was flipping all over the place in an unruly mess. He held Jade's eyes for a moment. His softened a little, and his pained smile tugged up a bit further.

Jade groaned and looked away quickly to hide the new flood of tears that pooled in her eyes, I assumed, and she said, "This is not the time for smiles, guys. We need to focus here."

"There's always time for smiles," Mark countered. "Life would be pretty damn depressing without them."

And I thought Mark was right. No matter how bad it got, making time for laughter and smiles definitely helped.

I knew the smiles I saw curving the team's lips were for Jade's benefit. They were trying hard to make her okay, to show her they were okay. And even if they weren't directed at me, those smiles, although small and pained, made it pretty damn clear that they weren't holding Jared's death against me. Well, at least that was how my brain decided to read them, and I found myself seriously hoping that my brain was right.

"It's all set," Dominic said, and he thumbed his phone as he made his way back to the cluster surrounding Jade and me. "They'll do the cremation today, and we can pick up his remains tomorrow."

There it was. The last piece we'd been waiting for before moving out.

The smiles faded, blurred, died, replaced by solemn expressions, and a determined vibe spread through the air. The hardness returned to the enforcers' gazes. We knew where the bastards were now. There was no more waiting. No more excuses.

"Time to move," I said, taking Jade's hand and giving it a little squeeze. "Landon, Beck, Craig, and Mark, you guys are with Tommy and Chris. Get as close as you can, but not close enough that they'll pick up your scent. You're just confirming what Jeff told us, nothing else. Seventeen cougars and no women. That's it. Then come straight back and report. Got it?"

I waited for the nods, watching them closely to make sure that they got it, but they didn't nod. Nope. Lips thinned, anger spiked in the air. And I found myself thinking — again — that sending them out was probably not the best plan. Not only did they just watch their brother die, but each one of them had been helping Jared screw me over in one way or another while he tried to get revenge for their father — another family member of theirs that was dead because of me.

I was about to voice my thoughts, tell them I'd find another group to go, when Jade said, "Guys, I know you're ready to take them out, but seriously, you're just confirming the location. Tell me you've got this because I cannot focus on what I have to do if I'm worried about you guys."

Their silence held for a second longer before Beck nodded.

"We've got it." His steely eyes focused on me, and he said, "I can see your doubt, Aidan. It's over. Let it go."

I held his gaze for a beat, searching for any hint of malice behind his guarded expression. He held firm, so did the others, and even though I wasn't sure I believed him, I couldn't pick up any trace of a lie. I nodded stiffly and pushed on. "Erika, you're with Dom. Take Jared and keep your phones on. Mac and Trevor, head back to the headquarters and work on something for when his remains are picked up. Plan for tomorrow night. Jade and I will take Richard's body to her dad." I looked down at Jade, squeezing her hand again, and asked, "Everyone clear on what you need to do?"

A round of *yeses* spilled from the group, and then everyone started moving.

Dominic hopped into Tommy's truck with Erika, starting it up, and with a quick nod in my direction, he eased out of the clearing. Trevor grunted a goodbye as he snagged Marcy's hand, towing her to his car. The guys started to shift, Tommy and Chris with them. It didn't take long before they were trotting off into the trees.

And as they disappeared, Jade started to shake again, and small sob-like whimpers escaped her lips.

"Hey," I said, dropping her hand and then tapping her chin up to meet my eyes. I brushed a thumb along her cheek to catch the stray tear that had managed to leak out. "Don't worry, sweetheart." I framed her face within my palms and kissed her chastely. "They'll be back soon," I said against her lips.

And they would. They were simply going to confirm that the cougars were at the newest location. Try to confirm Jeff's count of seventeen. Make sure we weren't going to walk the pack into a death trap when we attacked.

She blew out a noisy breath from her nose and whispered, "This morning, the happiness ... it feels like a lifetime ago." Her bottom lip started quivering, and she quickly tugged it between her teeth.

Damn, she really was breaking. I frowned. I felt it, the shift of my lips, the bunching skin along my brow, and I was sure my eyes didn't conceal the knot of panic that clogged my throat. The most perfect thing in my life was breaking, and I didn't have a clue how to fix it.

When I left my parents and my old pack, I never thought I'd have my own pack, let alone have someone like her in my life. Someone precious. Someone to protect. Someone to love.

But Jade Shaw had quickly become the center of my world. And

I was supposed to protect her, keep her from being hurt, but since we'd met, all I'd managed to give her was pain.

And I knew this was just the beginning. How would I put her back together when this was over, when her father was dead? Just thinking about it made my chest feel all knotted up.

I cupped her cheeks in my palms, caressing them as I stared into her big brown eyes, wishing for her smile, even a small trace of it, to come back.

Jade scrunched her nose up and pulled out of my loose grip. Her lips thinned, and she craned her neck back, cutting me a dirty look. "Don't look at me like that," she snapped.

"Like what?" I reached out, tucking a stray chunk of hair behind her ear.

She moved back a couple steps, out of my reach, popping her right hip out and planting a firm hand on it. Her face smoothed, her gaze turned serious, and she said, "Like you're worried I'm going to break."

I folded my arms across my chest and scanned her from tip to toe. "Are you?" My tone was casual as if I were just curious, but really, I was kind of freaked out that she just might break before this was over.

She shook her head slowly, deliberately. "No." Her voice was strong, certain. It was just too bad her tone didn't match the unstable and unsure spike in her scent.

CHAPTER 2

JADE

"You don't have to come with me," Aidan said.

I swiveled in my seat, looking over at him. I knew I was gaping, and I figured I looked completely stunned, but I couldn't help it. That was pretty much the last thing I'd expected him to say. His words should have sounded like a thoughtful gesture as if he were just looking out for me, but they didn't. His tone ... his scent ... well, if I had to guess, Aidan didn't want me to go with him.

But the thing was I had to go. There really wasn't a choice here. The man was my father, my flesh and blood. I had to be there. I had to do this.

"I'm not going home," I said. "I've got to do this."

Aidan dropped one of his hands from the steering wheel and squeezed my knee gently, reassuringly. He stole a small glimpse at me and smiled, just a tiny upward twitch at the corners of his mouth, before returning his gaze to the road.

And it confused me. Like really, really confused me. The gesture was supportive, just like his words were meant to be, but that scent ...

I figured he probably thought I'd interfere, try to delay things, and give my dad a fighting chance, and I didn't know how I felt about that. Hadn't I just proven that I'd stand behind his decisions? I didn't interfere with Jared, at least not a lot, and I wouldn't with my dad. My dad didn't deserve my interference.

And even if I wanted to delay things, it wouldn't — couldn't — happen. Except, I knew with everything in me that if I asked for more time, Aidan would grant it in a heartbeat. And knowing that freaked me out. A part of me, a small, scared part, wanted more time almost desperately, and it made no sense. Dad didn't deserve time. His pack didn't deserve time. Still, something inside me wanted that time. But I knew, *I knew,* I couldn't ask for it. I wouldn't let my pack down. Not this time. Never again.

Aidan's hand was still on my knee, his thumb rubbing a gentle back and forth sweep on the inside of my leg. I glanced back at him, noticing his tight jaw and the white-knuckled grip of his other hand on the steering wheel.

"I'm serious, Jade," he said. "I can take you home." He looked sideways at me, another little smile, then back to the road. "You could start getting things ready for tomorrow. Help Mac with the planning."

Tomorrow. I wasn't really sure how Dominic had pulled that off so quickly. I knew Marcy's dad, one of the detectives in Dog Mountain, had a hand in it, but still, Jared's cremation seemed ... rushed. But then, I guessed rushed was probably a good thing right now. It wasn't as if we had days to plan, and really, Jared would have wanted something simple and quick.

I wiggled in my seat, fidgeting with the seatbelt strap that ran across my chest. "I'm going with you, Aidan." My throat felt dry and prickly and sore, and I swallowed hard, trying to clear the sensation. "I need to see him. I need to do this."

Aidan's response was a frustrated growl. I glanced over at him hesitantly, watching his jaw tick and his fist clench tighter on the steering wheel. He didn't look at me this time, not even a little glance. His thumb stopped moving on my thigh, and his scent ... changed. I breathed in deep, trying to place the new aroma. It was thick, tangy. It was ... worry? Apprehension, maybe? I wasn't entirely sure.

"Talk to me," I said, reaching over and squeezing his thigh. Right then, I seriously wished I could read his mind because not knowing what he was thinking was knotting me up like crazy. "What's got you so freaked out?"

Aidan relaxed slightly under my touch. He sighed. "It's pretty clear you've hit your limit for today," he said. "I just think it might be best if I handle this one alone."

My inner-wolf squirmed uneasily in my belly, and I shifted in my seat, turning to face him fully. "Are you mad at me? Is that why you're trying to send me home?"

"No, sweetheart." He shook his head. "No, not at you. I'm mad at this whole screwed-up mess we're in," he said, with a ripple of irritation gliding through his tone. He let out another long sigh.

"But not at you. Never at you." His eyes met mine, serious but somehow warm. "I just don't want you to break on me. If you need time to get it together, then I'm going to make sure you have that time."

"I'm good," I said. A warm flood of relief washed over me, and I laughed a little. He was worried about me, not about what he thought I'd do when we got to my dad's. "I really am. And I have to do this, even if it kills me. I have to. I'm not going to let them down. Not again. I won't." I paused for a second, watching his jaw clench, and that warm feeling of relief started to fade. "There's something else, isn't there?"

"Later," he said, gently but firmly. "Let's talk about it later, okay?"

I opened my mouth, and just as quickly, I closed it because I really had no idea what to say to that. He was right. I'd hit my limit hours ago around the time that Tommy and Chris had shown up at our house with the guys and shared what Jared had been up to. I'd surpassed my limit when Aidan shifted in the house, ready to kill them. And by the time we'd confronted Jared, well, I'd been way past the point of keeping it together. But somehow, I'd managed. The truth? I really didn't know how much more I could take before I lost it completely.

So instead of pushing it, I leaned into him, kissed his cheek, and murmured, "Okay, later."

Moments later, Aidan turned onto my old street, pulled past my parents' driveway, and then backed in. He yanked up the parking brake and put the car in neutral, but he didn't turn it off. He looked at me, his face blank, and said, "Let me handle this."

I nodded once to appease him, but the burning glint that flared in his eyes told me he knew I didn't plan on sitting back and keeping my mouth shut. He let out a frustrated growl and dragged a hand through his hair.

"Aidan," I said a little hastily as he cut the engine and pulled the keys from the ignition. "He's my dad. I know how to talk to him." I let out a long stalling breath, and then I lied, "And I'm okay. Honestly. I'm good."

Aidan didn't believe me, not for a second. But really, I knew he wouldn't. He turned into me, cupping my cheeks in his hands. "I've got this." His voice was rough and full of some emotion that I couldn't place, or more accurately, it was one that I didn't really want to place. He brushed his thumb along my cheekbone, his eyes searching mine. "You trust me, right? As your mate, I need you to trust me enough to know that I've got this."

And with that, he dipped forward, touching his lips to my forehead, and then before I could reply, he popped the door open and got out. He didn't waste any time as he made his way up the steps of my parents' front porch and pounded on the door.

I'd like to say that I followed him immediately. That my head was in the game and I was totally prepared for everything. I wished I could say that I knew he had this. But I couldn't do any of that. Nope. Instead, what I did was sit in the car, watching out the back window, blinking at his back, stunned and more than a little confused.

The front door opened. My dad filled the doorway. He smiled at Aidan, and it looked so warm and sincere. Dad even clapped him on the shoulder in greeting. And still, I held my breath, and I didn't move.

I watched the arm gestures as they spoke, and I watched Dad's smile fade a little. And then his eyes roamed over the car, and they locked onto me. He furrowed his brow and cocked his head, and I heard him call, "Jade?"

His voice snapped me out of my stunned moment. I pushed the door open and hopped out of the car in a flustered rush. I was so flustered and rushed that my foot caught on the door well, and I tripped. My heart jumped into my throat as I lurched forward, coming close to doing a face plant on the driveway, but luckily, the door was there to catch my fall. I steadied myself and called, "Yeah, coming," as I let the car door slam.

I took in a few deep breaths, attempted to school my expression, and then, although my brain tried to fight me, urging me to run away, I turned and started toward the house.

"Pumpkin, what's wrong?" Dad asked, stepping out of the doorway, past Aidan. "You're looking a little pale." He looked good in jeans and a beige knit sweater, like an average working citizen. The clothes. The smile. The warm, concerned tone he used with me as if he actually cared. Lies. They were all lies.

I met his eyes, and I thought about making something up for a moment, but really what was the point anymore? So instead, I said, "I helped kill Jared."

Aidan cut me a warning look, which I completely ignored as I padded up the steps. I brushed my hand along his back as I went past him and took a seat on the porch swing. The old chains creaked as I pulled my feet up underneath me.

"Jared," Dad said, and his eyes widened just a little. He glanced at Aidan, then back to me. "Jared's dead?" And all his warmth was suddenly gone. He looked suspicious and a touch excited, and seeing it made my stomach roll.

"Yeah," I said, glad I'd sat down because I really wasn't feeling all that steady anymore. "He wanted to challenge Aidan for alpha. He ended up attacking me and I kind of held him down while Aidan ..." I broke off as my stomach rolled again.

"Jared wanted to challenge for alpha," Dad stated as if he didn't believe it. He narrowed his eyes, glancing between the two of us. His nostrils flared as he took in a few noisy breaths, and he chuckled, grinning at Aidan. "You claimed her."

I clamped my mouth shut, mainly to keep my jaw from dropping. A look passed between my dad and Aidan. I wasn't exactly sure what it meant, but it meant something. *Something* for sure. Whatever it was, it effectively ended any further discussion of Jared's death or the fact that I'd helped make him dead.

"No, she claimed me," Aidan corrected, cementing my theory that the *something* explained Jared's motives for challenging for alpha. He moved over to me, planting a hand on my shoulder, and squeezed, a firm reminder to me that he had this. He waited for a beat, most likely making sure I got the hint, and then said, "Richard's body is in the trunk. He's one of yours. You can deal with him."

Dad's eyes shifted toward the car, then back to Aidan. "The point of giving him to you was so he could help you." His tone was impassive as if Richard's death meant nothing to him one way or the other, and I assumed that was probably true. "He's not much use to you dead."

Aidan shrugged. "Wasn't much use to me alive, either." It came out on a growl, and his hand clamped, pinching tight on my shoulder.

Oh, yeah, my mate totally had this. I gritted my teeth and pressed my lips together, keeping my mouth shut, but I was pretty sure that the look I cut him told him exactly what I thought because he loosened up on my shoulder a little.

"You came here to get me to clean up your mess?" Dad asked, his voice carrying a bitter, dark undertone, and his distaste showed clearly on his face.

Aidan raised a brow and gave Dad a look that said, *oh yeah,* but he didn't say anything. I figured that probably wasn't what Dad wanted because his eye started twitching, and he clenched and unclenched his jaw as he glared at us. He was losing control over his calm persona. I could see it. The lines on his forehead deepened, his eyes hardened.

Dad looked back at the car and then glared back at Aidan, and it was at that moment that I decided I'd had enough. This conversation needed to end. Now.

"Dad," I said, drawing his attention. "Just deal with him." I looked up at Aidan. "And will you stop being a dick? He's been helping us. He doesn't have to, but he has."

A small, forced smile played at Aidan's lips. "I don't like it when someone hurts what's mine," he said. He reached out, brushing a thumb across my bottom lip, an intimate gesture, one that made me blush. "And he hurt you."

"Are we still on that?" Dad groaned. "You were going to make her leave. I helped you achieve that a hell of a lot more peacefully than you would have by dragging her out."

"Stop it," I said, hoping for annoyance, but it came out sounding a little too sweet. I totally blamed Aidan's lip touch for that. I stood up, shrugging off Aidan's hand, squared my shoulder, and met my dad straight on. I sucked in a few breaths, hoping to bury my unease, and spat, "We're close to finding them, no thanks to your little gift. You could save us some time and tell me where they are."

"I don't know their exact location, pumpkin." His voice was soft, careful, and so was his gaze. "They don't tell me until I'm called out. They think I'll slip up."

"I think that's bullshit," I said, and I was surprised that my voice came out calm and controlled because I felt far, far from calm. "I think you know. What I don't know is why you're trying to protect those monsters."

Dad jerked back a step as if my words were a physical slap, and at the same time, Aidan said, "Jade, that's enough." His tone was soft but packed full of command.

I chose to ignore him. So did my dad.

"I'm not protecting them," said Dad cautiously, raising a hand in surrender. "I'm trying to protect my family, and keeping them away from town keeps you and your mother safe."

"Safe!" My blood pressure rose, my heart pounding within my chest. "You call this safe? You pushed me into the middle of a war. You've made it my responsibility to act."

He laughed once, a startling sound. "You're the alpha female. You won't be fighting."

His assumption didn't improve my mood. My eyes flared, my fists clenched, and my entire body started to vibrate with anger.

"Hell, yes I will," I said with a fevered pitch. "Do you really think I'd send my pack out and not be there with them? What kind of a leader does that? We can't ask them to fight and then hide away until it's over."

I barely had time to suck in a breath before my feet were torn from the ground. Warm hands circled my waist, twisting my body around, and then I was dangling over Aidan's shoulder. I let out a gasping shriek and started to squirm as one of his hands gripped onto my butt, holding me firmly in place, and the other went to my thigh.

"Put me down, Aidan," I growled, smacking his back and kicking out because, really, kicking and hitting was the only rational thing to do while hanging over someone's shoulder.

Aidan chuckled and squeezed my right butt cheek. "Not a chance, sweetheart." And then he started moving, with me hanging over his shoulder.

"Wait a minute," Dad called. I heard the smile in his voice. "Jesus, Aidan, put my daughter down."

But Aidan didn't wait, and he didn't put me down.

He went straight for the car. He yanked the passenger side door open, dropped me in, and shut the door without a word. He turned his back to me and growled, "Get the body out of my car." And a second later, the trunk opened. The car bobbed a little as Richard was removed.

I blinked, stunned, staring at the window. Aidan stepped away from the door, moving toward the back of the car, and I reached for the handle, ready to follow him because, well, throwing me over his shoulder and tossing me in the car was seriously not cool, and I wasn't finished with my dad. Not even close. I grasped the handle and was about to pop the door open when I heard my dad's voice, and I froze.

"Aidan, we need to talk," he said. He sounded as though he were trying to hide his laughter, but there was a seriousness to his tone, too, and I swore there was an edge of desperation. "All of us. Your mating changes everything. There's more going on here than you think."

Aidan laughed. "Oh, yeah?" he said. "I thought you didn't know anything. Isn't that what you just told your daughter?"

"I said that I don't know where they are, not that I don't know what they want."

"I don't care what they want," Aidan said, and I was astonished by just how cold his voice was. "I won't negotiate with anyone that keeps women in cages and uses them like toys."

"It doesn't have to be like that," Dad said, and yes, he did sound desperate. So desperate that I swore I could almost smell it. Almost. And Jesus, had he just admitted that the cougars kept their women in cages? I felt shaken to the core. My chest seized up, and it hurt to pull in a breath. I swiveled around, trying to get a look at them, but the trunk was still open, blocking them from my view.

"No, it doesn't," Aidan said, and his voice had gotten impossibly colder. "You better figure out what team you're playing for, Jeff, and quick. We'll kill them when we find them, and if you're with them, we'll kill you, too." And then the trunk slammed, and the door opened, and Aidan was in the driver's seat.

He gave me a quick once over before he stuck the keys into the ignition, but he didn't say a word. He was pissed. I knew it, I felt it, but I was pretty sure it wasn't directed at me.

"What was that about?" I asked almost cautiously, *almost* being the keyword, because the truth was, I was kind of pissed off myself and more than a little shaken.

Aidan started up the car. "It's probably nothing," he said. "Just more of his games."

"You threw me over your shoulder." My voice was a hissed whisper, and I cut him a dirty look as my face flamed with heat.

"I told you to let me handle it," Aidan said. He sounded amused. He looked it, too. He dropped the emergency brake, shifted into first, feathered the gas, and pulled out of the driveway.

I huffed and buckled up. "You knew I wasn't going to let you."

"Yeah," he said cheerfully, giving me that crooked grin of his. "I knew."

I didn't respond to that. I figured it was best not to engage in this conversation while my blood was still boiling over.

CHAPTER 3

JADE

Aidan was still grinning when he dropped me off at the pack headquarters, and I had to admit, his grin was contagious. By the time he'd pulled up in front of the building, the majority of my anger had dissolved into pesky annoyance, although I wasn't about to tell him that. No, I wouldn't tell him because if I did, I might then have to tell him that he'd been right. I should have let him handle things with my dad. And telling him, that would have led to an even cockier grin that would have made me feel like even more of a failure than I already did.

The whole idea of bringing Richard to my dad was to make him uneasy, and hopefully, that would cause him to slip up somewhere. It was not to let him know, or give him even the slightest hint, that we were on to him.

But, of course, I let my emotions get the better of me. Damn, I might as well have told my dad that we knew everything. I'd clearly let him know that I didn't believe a word he said.

Yeah, I really should have listened to my mate and kept my mouth shut.

Since Aidan left, I'd been telling time by phone calls. They were becoming predictable. Every five minutes, my father would call. I hadn't answered one of his calls, and I had no plans to do it anytime soon.

I sat outside on a picnic table, shivering, with my phone clutched in my hands. The wind was brutal, cold, and blowing hard enough to rock me as it came barreling through the trees. Branches creaked, and the tops of the pines bowed under its furious attack. The sky was filling up with dirty, dark gray clouds and the air smelled of crisp, fall rain, damp and cold and fresh.

Each time my phone rang, I silenced it. After the fifth call, I'd given up on looking at the caller display. I didn't want to know what Dad had to say. Okay, that wasn't really true. I wanted to know. The issue was I was a little freaked out that he was calling to tell me that the team had been caught.

Okay, so that was probably a ridiculous worry. Dad had been trying to convince Aidan to stick around. He'd wanted to talk to us. He'd even hinted that the cougars actually wanted something from us. He was probably reaching out to me because Aidan had shot him down, but still, I was worried nonetheless.

I pulled my arms around me, hugging myself tightly in an attempt to stay semi-warm. How had my day turned sour so quickly? Just this morning, I'd woken up as the official mate of the alpha male of my pack. We'd been smiling — happy — planning to spend a lazy day in bed.

And then life happened.

It was really the only way I could think about what took place this morning. *Life happened.* Because within the pack, Jared dying for his crimes was life happening, and if I let myself think about it any other way, I was pretty sure I'd fall apart.

"Where's Aidan?" a hard voice asked from behind me, cutting through my thoughts.

I glanced over my shoulder. Luken. He'd healed up nicely from his run-in with Jared this morning, not even a scratch left. He looked annoyed and slightly hesitant as he closed the distance between us. "Dom needed him for something," I said with a sigh.

"You're shivering," he said, stopping in front of me. His arms folded over his chest, his biceps curling up thick with the movement. "Come inside. Mac's been looking for you."

"I'm not shivering," I said, my teeth clattering as I said it. I decided not to acknowledge that anyone was looking for me because, honestly, I wasn't ready to deal with anyone (especially Marcy). She'd want to talk about my feelings. She'd want me to let it out. And that was exactly why I was sitting outside freezing my butt off.

My phone rang again, chirping and vibrating in my palm, and I quickly silenced it.

Luken narrowed his eyes, looking down at my phone and then back up at me. After a couple of beats of silence, he said, "That better not be your mate you hung up on."

"Really?" I hissed, and he narrowed his eyes further. I gritted my teeth, giving him a pointed glare. "It's my dad."

Luken looked at me awkwardly for a moment as if he realized just how much of a jerk he was being. He let out a muffled sigh and unfolded his arms, taking a seat beside me. His eyes warmed, although not by much. "You should've answered it."

"He should be calling Aidan," I countered, which was a ridiculous thing to say, and by the look I got, Luken thought so, too. I was just as much an alpha as Aidan was, and the man (unfortunately) was my father. Of course, he'd call me.

I glared at him a bit harder, seriously wishing he would vanish. My glare didn't faze him. He made himself comfortable, propping his feet up on the bench. He had a pair of boots on, the edge of his jeans stuck at the top of his boot on one side. He unzipped his hoodie and shrugged it off, wrapping it around my shoulders, before leaning forward, resting his bare forearms on his knees.

"You should've answered it," he said again, but softer this time, almost caring.

I glanced back down at my phone and muttered, "Dad hasn't called me since he kicked me out." I met his eyes and whispered, "What if the guys got caught?"

"They weren't caught," he said. He sounded completely confident in that. "They're smarter than that. They'll be back soon, Jade."

I hoped he was right, but that ounce of hope didn't come close to chasing away all my doubts. My shoulders slumped, and I puffed out a slow breath.

"And then what?" I muttered as another shiver chased down my back. "We rush out on a mindless killing spree? I have my father killed? What if they're not all bad? What if they're just doing the only thing they were taught to do? It's not like they've ever lived among the human population like our pack."

Another gust of wind pushed at me, blowing loose strands of hair in my face. I shoved it back, tucking it behind my ears, and huffed. "I just can't figure out the *why*. Why were they raised like this? Why are only the men changed? Why was there a deal with our pack in the first place? I just don't understand. I don't get it."

My face felt hot — burning hot. I looked at Luken and cringed when I caught the hardness in his eyes. *Way to go, Jade,* I thought bitterly. *God, did I really just blurt all that out to him?* I should have swallowed it. It wasn't as if Luken and I were friends. Our one real conversation had been seriously tense, and he'd made it damn clear he didn't respect me or even acknowledge me as an alpha of this pack.

Luken must have noticed my unease. His expression softened and warmed further, and he said, "There isn't always an answer to the *whys*, Jade. Sometimes people do shitty things just because they can."

My phone started ringing again, and I went to silence it, but he snagged it from me before I could. He thumbed the screen and brought it to his ear. "Jade's phone, you've got Luken," he said and paused. "She's behind closed doors with her mate." He paused, listening. "Don't know." Another pause. "Tonight." His brow furrowed. "You'll have to take that up with her mate. Yep, I'll let him know. Later."

He lowered my phone and thumbed the screen. His brow pulled in, and he looked at me. There was a question burning in his eyes, one that I didn't think he wanted to voice and one that I was sure I didn't want to be asked.

The silence held between us as we searched each other's faces, and after a moment, I broke it, whispering, "Do I want to know?" I tugged my bottom lip between my teeth, trying to stop it from trembling.

He hesitated for a second and then said, "How about I give Aidan a call, fill him in, and let him decide." He said it cautiously as if he weren't sure what to do. When I didn't answer, he said, "Go on inside, Jade," making the decision for me.

And for probably the first time since I joined the pack (and maybe the first time ever), I did exactly what I was told without uttering a single syllable.

CHAPTER 4

AIDAN

Dominic was distracted, but then I guessed I was, too.

He was leaning against my car, watching Erika from the corner of his eye while he attempted to lecture me about the team. He talked in broken sentences, or maybe I was only listening to bits and pieces. Really, it could have been either at this point. But the parts I heard, I agreed on. I needed to pick a new head enforcer.

Erika was propped against the wall outside the funeral home, giving us space. Her eyes were glued to her cell phone as her fingers flew across the keypad. Dominic had been watching her since I pulled up as if he thought she'd run if he took his eyes off of her. I was pretty sure I should have asked what was up with that, but honestly, right then, I didn't really care.

I didn't have a good feeling. Not about the cougars, or about Jade, or the team. It all felt ... not right, leaving my gut pitted and twisted up in knots.

The sky was darkening quickly. Off in the distance, I could pick out the soft claps of thunder as a storm approached. The wind had picked up, carrying a damp chill with it, and I pulled my jacket closed, zipping it up.

Dominic paused in his half-hearted lecture, glancing up at the sky, and said, "It looks like rain."

"Yeah, it does," I agreed and let out a slow breath. I glanced at him; his features were blank, hidden behind his normally cool and collected mask. I knew he was trying damn hard to hide it, but I could still smell his worry in the air. I thought he was probably worried about the same shit I was. His thoughts never seemed to stray far from his best friend — my girl.

I let out a long breath and muttered, "She's breaking, Dom, and if she breaks, we won't stand a chance. The pack will feel it. They'll get nervous. They'll feed off her pain, her fear." I scrubbed at my face and raked a hand through my hair. "Damn, I already feel like I've been cut open like I'm bleeding from her pain."

"Dude, cut the drama. Jade's fine," he said distractedly. "She just needs some time in her head to work out how to feel about everything. I don't get it, but she loved Jared in her own way, and the same goes for her dad. What you're seeing is the normal Jade grieving process."

I felt even less good once he said that. In fact, I felt kind of sick. If anyone knew what she was feeling, it would have been Dominic. He knew her. Knew everything about her. I'd been hoping he would deny my worries, not confirm that she was hurting. And if he was right, and Jade was really grieving, it was because I'd taken someone from her, and it seriously sucked that I was going to take even more.

"That's what I'm worried about," I said. "Jade alone with her thoughts." My chest started to knot up again. I probably should have told her I loved her before leaving her at the headquarters. I probably should have said sorry, too. I should have said a lot of things. But I didn't tell Dominic that. Instead, I said, "I probably should have brought her here. It would have kept her busy."

That drew Dominic's full attention, and he gave me a long, measured look. He jerked his chin up. "You screwed up again?"

I figured that was a fair statement. I'd pretty much screwed up everything when it came to Jade, but even so, I felt my jaw tick and clench. "She flipped out at her dad, and I might have thrown her over my shoulder and put her in the car to shut her up."

Dominic chuckled, his ice-blue eyes steady on mine, and he smirked. "Dude, really? Are you ever going to learn?"

I smirked back at him, watching his eyes dance with humor, as I folded my arms over my chest and shook my head. "She accused him of trying to protect his pack and then started shouting about how she'd be fighting alongside us when we attack them." My smile widened as I spoke, and I chuckled a little. Yeah, I would have preferred it if she hadn't freaked out, but I couldn't deny that I loved the passion I'd seen in her. Standing up for herself, for our pack. She'd been amazing.

"Oh," he said and blinked. "And I have no idea what to say about that." He stared at me as if he couldn't quite figure out how Jade could have done that, and then once he'd gotten over his shock, he frowned, looking disappointed, as if he were sad he'd missed it.

Dominic's eyes went back to Erika and held there for a second before coming back to me. "You need to pick a new head enforcer, and she needs a beta," he pointed out, not for the first time since I'd arrived. "And you need to figure out what you're going to do with the team."

I didn't particularly want to talk about the team, but I knew he was entirely right. I should have dealt with it before sending the guys out. Even if it was temporary, I should have appointed someone to lead them. But I hadn't. I'd followed my gut instead. Appointing someone would have taken time, discussion, and time wasn't something I'd wanted to waste.

As for the team themselves, I knew Jade would fight me on it if I even mentioned building a new one, and that was definitely not a fight I was looking forward to having with her.

I shook my head, frustrated, and rested my weight against the car. "Yeah, I know, Dom, but it really isn't my top priority right now."

The severe line of Dominic's mouth made it clear that he disagreed with me. "Well, it should be," he said, missing (or choosing) to ignore my frustration. "You can't send those guys out, leading the pack into this without a head. And you shouldn't have sent them anywhere today if you're not sure that you can trust them." He sighed, long and loud, rubbing a hand across his forehead. "You also need to stop worrying about Jade. She's going to be fine. She loves you. She's got your back in this. Trust me."

"You got someone in mind to head up the team?" I asked, ignoring his Jade advice and pasting on what was meant to be an open expression, encouraging him to go on.

He groaned, and damn, I almost laughed at the sound. Almost. Dominic's groans were a sure way to know what he was thinking, and this one was one that I got a lot. It was the *you're being a pain in the ass* groan, and he cut me a look that clearly said the same thing. Through his teeth, he said, "Tommy, if he'll stick around. The team could use someone experienced, and they seem to respect him."

"Tommy?" I asked blankly. I took in his expression. He was serious. Damn, he couldn't be serious. My phone rang, and I jammed my hand in my pocket, kind of glad for the interruption. I shook off the dread that had started to seep in at the thought of Tommy sticking around and said, "That's not his call, or mine," as I yanked my phone out. "My father would have to release him before I could even consider it."

Glancing down at my phone, I saw *Jade Shaw* flash across the screen and thumbed it quickly as I brought it to my ear. "Hi, sweetheart."

"Your girl's been sitting outside freezing her ass off since you left." The voice on the other end of the line was deep and rough and not Jade.

A hot rush of adrenaline hit me, and my hand flexed tight around the phone. "Who the hell is this?" I growled.

"Luken," the voice replied, rushed as if he were cluing into the fact that he probably should have led with that piece of information.

Cold swept through me, and more of that awful dread filled the pit of my stomach. Luken and Jade weren't close. They weren't even civil to each other. She wouldn't just give him her phone. I glanced at Dominic and mouthed *Luken.*His eyes darkened, and he jerked his chin toward the phone stuck to my ear, urging me to find out what was happening.

I pulled in a breath and asked as casually as I could, "Where's Jade?" Which, as it turned out, didn't come out casual at all.

"Just sent her inside," he blurted and then continued more slowly. "Her lips were turning blue. Also just had a little chat with her dad. Wants his daughter back home. Says he doesn't like the way you were treating her at his house, so he's willing to make a deal to get her back."

I laughed, a cold kind of laugh. Well, that hadn't taken long. "He can have her back when I'm in the ground."

"That might happen sooner than you think," Luken said coolly. "Once the team gets wind of you raising your hands to her, they'll come for you."

"You accusing me of something, Luken?" I asked, my voice, deathly calm.

"Did you hit her?" he fired at me, not missing a beat.

I ground my teeth. Furious didn't even come close to describing the heat that surged through me from his question. "Did it look like I hit her?"

"I figure you wouldn't drop her off here until she healed," he said. "And it would explain the thick fear in her scent and the nervous look she gave me when I told her I was going to give you a call."

"I didn't hurt her," I said through my teeth. "I wouldn't, and I'm pretty sure you already know that."

Luken hesitated for a second before continuing with what sounded like a whole lot of caution as if he weren't sure that he was free to speak his mind. "Then he's making a play. This could be our in. And by the way, your girl's having some issues when it comes to taking him out."

That was true. Jade was having some serious issues when it came to her father. But confirming that to a pack member that was not her number one fan most likely wouldn't go over well. So instead, I asked, "You know what the deal is?"

"Nope, he wants you to call him," he said. "All he said was that there's something big in play, something that you and Jade would want in on and that if you work with him, he won't tell anyone else about what he saw you do to her."

Okay, that was good. It was probably better that no one knew whatever it was that Jeff had to offer until I figured out what the hell he was up to. "Did Jade say anything?" I asked.

Luken didn't answer right away. He sighed, and let out a frustrated growl, then sighed again. When he spoke, his voice was strained. "She said a hell of a lot, but she doesn't know what he wants or what he's accusing you of. She didn't talk to him. I told her I'd run it by you and let you decide if she needed to know. She agreed to it, Aidan. Without hesitation. No argument. Nothing."

That wasn't so good. Jade being fully agreeable with Luken should have been good, but because it was Jade we talked about and he was, well, Luken, it really wasn't good. My jaw clenched, and through my teeth, I asked, "What's she doing now?"

"I sent her inside to see Marcy," he said with a huff. "She's freaked out, and she's pissed off. Not a good combination." He didn't quite manage to hide the bitterness from his tone.

Dominic's gaze was hard and unwavering, stuck on my face, and I inhaled slowly, attempting to work through the sudden irritation Luken's call had brought on and keep it out of my tone. The breath didn't help.

"Don't remember asking for your opinion," I bit out on a growl. I paused and took another breath. "Set up her phone to have her calls forwarded to me before you give it back to her." And with that, I dropped the call, not waiting for a confirmation.

"That was harsh," Dominic said evenly, and his lips twitched up at the corners.

I shoved my phone back in my pocket. "Your point?" I snapped, not seeing the humor in the situation. My eyes sparked. I felt the tingle, followed by a quick pulse of adrenaline.

"No point, just an observation," Dominic said in a low, calm voice, raising his hands. He waited for a beat, and when I didn't offer up anything, he asked, "You going to fill me in?"

I heaved a sigh, thought about telling him to screw off, but instead said, "Yeah." I pushed off the car, rolled my shoulders, and then quickly filled him in.

When I finished, Dominic didn't speak immediately. He was staring across the parking lot. I didn't need to wonder what he was thinking about. The torn, stricken expression gave him away. I was sure he was thinking the same things I was. How far would Jade go to end this? How much could we ask of her before she broke? And he was probably trying to decide if we should even tell her about the call.

He pulled in a shaky breath, blinked, and focused on me, his gaze resolved. "Call him. Set up a meeting."

"No," I said firmly. There was no way I would hand Jade back over to him. She was finally mine. All mine. There wasn't a chance in hell I'd give her up now, and honestly, we didn't need to. Jeff was scrambling. Trying to find some hold on us. I was sure of it.

He groaned long and loud, rubbing a hand roughly across his forehead. "Aidan, think about it. When the team hears about this, they'll freak."

I shook my head. "I'll handle the team," I said. "And I'm not negotiating with him. Not yet. We don't have any need to. We know where they are. My guess is he clued in that something was off when Jade lost it on him, and he's scrambling to get his foot back in with us."

"I don't think I agree with you," he said, but he was smiling. That smile faded as he said, "You going to tell her?"

"Yeah, I'll talk to her tonight." I dug my keys out of my pocket and rounded the car. I pulled the door open and paused. "Wrap things up here and meet me back at the headquarters. I want you and Mac to take her home. She needs some friend time."

"Will do," he said with a nod as I slid into the car. He watched me for a moment as I started it up, giving me a look that I didn't even try to understand, before dropping his gaze and stalking off toward Erika.

CHAPTER 5

JADE

The rain sounded more like hail beating against the window. The downpour had started about twenty minutes ago, and it didn't look like it would be letting up anytime soon. It was a soothing sound, so soothing it almost washed away all the nervous turmoil that was shifting through my belly. Almost.

I was sitting on the couch with a cozy light blue fleece tucked around me, wondering if the guys had made it back before the storm hit and waiting (a little impatiently) for Aidan to come home. It had been a couple of hours since he'd shown back up at the headquarters to find me passed out on the couch in his office. He'd woken me with a sweet press of his lips on my neck, which had led to an even sweeter press of his lips on mine, which then led to a kiss that was not sweet, but it was delicious.

Once he'd finished kissing me awake, he'd sent me home with Marcy and Dominic, claiming I needed some *friend time*. He didn't say a word about Luken's phone conversation with my father, and I hadn't asked. I also hadn't protested, not even a little, about needing *friend time*.

Now, though, I was kind of wishing I had.

"I'm telling you, you need to get a new beta," Dominic growled, not for the first time since we'd walk through the doors. He was getting annoyed at me, but then that wasn't really anything new. Dominic was usually annoyed at me for one thing or another.

I pulled in a deep breath through my nose and let it out slowly. "And I'm telling you I'm not ready to pick one." And it was true. I wasn't. It wasn't as if the first one I'd pick had turned out all that well, and with everything going on, well, I didn't think it was smart to rush into a decision like that.

Dominic groaned. It was his frustrated groan, short and abrupt, and he cut me a look that matched his groan. He was sitting in the big leather chair in the corner, knees spread and leaning forward, his elbows resting on his jean-clad thighs. His bleach-blond hair was, as always, spiked and gelled, and his blue eyes bore into me as he clenched and unclenched his jaw.

"Don't start with the groan fest, Dom," Marcy snapped. She was testy, too. She'd been testy since he'd picked us up at the headquarters and brought us back to Aidan's. "If she doesn't want a beta, then she doesn't have to pick one." She was curled up beside me, her feet pulled up underneath her, hugging her arms around her waist. Her hair was pulled back in a ponytail out of her face, and she had a soft gray fleece tucked around her.

"Stay out of this, Mac," Dominic growled and shot her a dirty look. "There's a lot at stake here."

"You think we don't know that?" she shrieked. She tossed her hands toward me in a dramatic gesture, and the fleece fell, pooling on her lap. "You think she doesn't get what's at stake?"

"I thought this was supposed to be *friend time*," I muttered, pulling my blanket up and tucking it under my chin. When Aidan had first suggested *friend time*, I'd pictured the three of us vegging out on the couch, watching a movie, eating junk food, and avoiding talking about anything that could lead to tears or arguments. What I did not picture was us fighting about whether or not I needed to pick a new beta.

Dominic looked at me, and whatever he saw made his eyes warm and soften, and when he spoke, his tone matched his eyes. "Honey, you've got to understand that when we move on them, everyone's going to be watching you. They can't be worried about having your back. They need to be focused. You having a beta will relieve some of that worry."

"Dom, please drop it," I said softly, dropping my burning eyes to my lap. "I know you're worried, and I'm sure you're right, but I just can't deal with this today." And I really couldn't. My brain, my body, every part of me was exhausted. "I'm not going to risk the pack, and I won't do anything to jeopardize my mate. I get what's at stake here probably better than anyone. My pack, my mate, my family. I'm going to lose something no matter what happens." I paused, swallowed down the burn that was creeping up my throat, and then huffed. "We can assign someone to stick close to me and let everyone know."

"Are you having second thoughts?" Marcy asked delicately, inching closer to me on the couch and pressing her shoulder to mine.

"No," I said with a certainty that I didn't even come close to feeling. "My father needs to be stopped. I'm just worried about Mom."

"The pack will look after her," Dominic said. "We'll take care of her."

I offered him a smile that really didn't feel anything like a smile. The burn in my throat started again, along with my eyes. I knew they would look after her. But knowing that didn't change anything. She would be devastated, and I found myself wondering if I should call her. I thought that if I were in her shoes, I'd want to know what was happening. I'd want some kind of warning. I'd want to know everything. If it were Aidan, I'd want to know that he was a monster.

Silence fell. It wasn't a comfortable silence, but I had to admit, it was a needed one. It was a breath of air, even if that air was thick and heavy and stale.

It was Marcy who broke it with a small laugh. She nudged my shoulder and asked, "You remember when we were eight, and your dad caught the three of us hiding in the crawlspace under your house?" She shook her head and smiled. "You swore you saw a cat crawl in there."

Dominic chuckled. "And I wanted to rescue it."

"You were going to grow up to be a superhero," I said, smiling a little. "God, your superhero phase lasted two years. You were trying to rescue everything, whether it needed rescuing or not."

Marcy giggled. "We used to stage trouble just so you could save us."

"I remember that day," Dominic said. He shook his head and grinned. "Your dad lost his mind when we crawled out with that damn skunk. I'll never forget the look on his face when it sprayed him." I laughed, and Dominic flashed me a big wide smile. "Still don't have a clue how we managed to pull it out without getting skunked ourselves."

AIDAN

Looking at them sitting on the couch in my office, I wondered how I never realized that the four of them were brothers. They might not look alike, but they had the same mannerisms. The way they sat, the way they held themselves, their facial expressions; it was all a lot of the same.

Tommy and Chris were propped against the wall by the door. They looked exhausted. Hell, we all were. It had been a long day, already closing in on 8:00.

After sending Jade home, my office had been a revolving door. I was pretty sure I'd had face time with every pack member, although after the fifth one had stormed in, everything had sort of blurred together. They'd all said something similar, confirming (heatedly) in one way or another that they were behind Jade and me, ready to fight for the pack and our territory.

I drummed my fingers on my desk, waiting for one of the guys to speak up, but they kept watching the door, waiting. Waiting for Jade to show up. The storm had blown in just before they got back, and the rain was coming down in sheets now. There was no way I was going to drag her out in it just to see the pain return to her eyes when she saw them again.

"She's at home with Mac and Dom," I muttered after another long beat of silence. "I'm not calling her to come in either. What did you guys find?"

Six sets of concerned eyes landed on me, all of them asking the same question, a question that I wasn't ready to hear the answer to. I rolled my hand impatiently, prompting them to start talking, and then resumed drumming my fingers. I was restless, so was my inner-wolf, and all I could think about was going home. I needed — we all needed — this day to end.

"I counted twenty," Beck spoke up. For a split second, he looked disgusted before his face hardened. "Plus three kids. One girl, two boys. But we couldn't get close enough. There could be more."

Shit. I stilled my fidgety hand, only to drag it across my face and through my hair. Kids. *Shit!* Of course, there'd be kids. The women were there to be used, to breed males for them.

"The girl ..." I started and then paused, swallowing down a rush of bile that gathered in my throat. My inner-wolf pressed against my chest, and I bit the inside of my lip, tamping down the urge to let him out. "Was she ...?"

"She looked young," Mark said, but he didn't sound sure. "Too young. Maybe fourteen."

"They were smiling and laughing with her," Landon added. He sounded stunned as if he weren't sure he could believe what he'd seen. "They were playing with her. I don't think ..." He shook his head, letting his words fall short, and his frown deepened.

"Good." I nodded, although it sure as hell didn't sound good, but I found myself repeating, "Good. What about the boys? Any idea on their ages?"

"Toddlers," Tommy said. "Still in diapers."

I nodded. "Okay," I said and swallowed hard. "Anything else? Security? Lookouts?"

"There was no security, at least none that I could see," Craig said. "They seemed pretty relaxed, barbequing, drinking. I'm going to guess that Jeff isn't on to us. I figure they'd be on alert if he was."

"Or he is on to us and doesn't want us to know," I said, meeting each one of them in the eyes, searching for anything that showed they were holding something back — something that Tommy or Chris might not have noticed — but I didn't see or scent anything off. "He called after we dropped off the body. He wants Jade to move back home."

"Good for him. She won't be doing it," Beck bit out. His gaze darkened with anger. "What did she have to say about it?"

I sighed and raked a hand through my hair. "She doesn't know yet. Luken took the call, and I guess she was pretty upset, so he told her he'd talk to me, let me decide if she needed to know or not." Beck let out a laugh, and I held up my hand to keep him from saying what we were all thinking. "She agreed with him, guys. She didn't fight it. No argument. She even walked away so he could call me."

I quickly filled them in on the conversation, telling them about Luken's accusations and about Jeff's admittance that there was more going on than we thought. The entire time I spoke, I waited for one of them to snap because Luken was right. I was sure that if one of them thought that I'd actually hit her, they'd be all over me for it. Jade was, after all, one of theirs. She wasn't just their alpha female. As far as they were concerned, she was part of their team, and they loved her like a little sister.

But they didn't snap. Actually, I thought they even looked a little sorry for me, which was kind of weird.

"She okay?" Landon asked, concerned when I finished.

"Honestly," I said, shaking my head. "I don't know." I pushed my chair back, standing up. "Go home, guys. Get some sleep. I've got to go fill her in." I stepped around my desk and headed for the door. "Let's meet for breakfast tomorrow, all of you. Be at the diner for eight."

CHAPTER 6

JADE

My belly hurt, and I felt like I was about to pee myself, but I couldn't stop laughing. Each time I thought I was almost done, and I tried to catch my breath, Dominic or Marcy would start, and their laughter would set me off again. It was like a chain reaction; one of us started, and it caught on to all of us.

I wrapped my arms around my stomach, trying to hold myself together as my body shuddered through the side-splitting laughter. It hurt so much, but I had to admit, it also felt really darn good.

The skunk had definitely been the highlight of our summer that year.

Aidan crashed through the front door, which flung back and hit the wall with a startling boom, and then he slammed it shut. I jumped — literally jumped — flying off the couch, my heart in my throat.

"I hate rain," he muttered, wiping his face on his soaking wet sleeve. He was soaked through, his hair plastered to his head, and water running down his face and neck. He pulled off his jacket, and it fell to the floor with a watery smack.

"You scared the crap out of me," I muttered. He looked a little pissed off and really tired, and he continued to curse the storm under his breath, not even looking up at us.

My lips started to twitch as I watched him shuck off his water-filled sweater, and I swear I tried seriously hard to hold it back, but then he mumbled something that sounded like, *Stupid damn rain* and a burst of laughter tumbled out of me. And with that, Marcy and Dominic started howling right along with me.

Aidan snapped his gaze up, focused on mine. He looked a little shocked to see us all watching him, but the shock didn't last. He lifted a brow. "Something funny?" His voice was growled, but his lips were curving up at the corners.

I tried really hard to straighten my face and gave him my best serious look, which probably wasn't all that serious since I was still giggling. I shook my head. "Nope. Nothing funny." I darted over to him, went up on my toes, and planted a sloppy wet kiss on his cheek. He chuckled, and I swore he looked relieved. He reached out for me, and I managed to duck away before he could pull me into a soggy hug and called, "I'll grab you a towel," as I shot for the stairs.

By the time I got back downstairs with a towel, Aidan was down to his boxers, which only looked a little damp, leaning against the wall in the entryway. Dominic and Marcy were at the door, pulling on their jackets.

"You guys don't have to go yet," I said. "You can wait out the rain if you want or crash here." I padded across the room, and the minute I reached Aidan, his hand came out, wrapping around my wrist and pulling me in tight to his side. He plucked the towel out of my hand and rubbed it along his hair without letting me go.

Marcy smiled. "I promised Trevor I'd be home," she said and giggled. "And I think your man wants some attention." She pulled open the door, and she visibly shuddered as she looked out at the rain. "Is it unlocked?" she asked, looking back at Dominic. He nodded, and she said, "See you tomorrow, guys," and with a little wave, she ran out to the car.

Dominic held back for a moment, giving Aidan one of those expectant *start talking* kind of looks. I glanced up at Aidan, saw his frown and the slight shake of his head, and he said, "Give Tommy a call and get him to fill you in."

Dominic frowned. He held Aidan's gaze for a minute and then nodded. "Sure," he said, but he didn't sound happy about it. "See you guys tomorrow." And then he stepped outside, shut the door, and it was just Aidan and me.

Aidan was quiet, stroking a hand absently up and down my back, seemingly content to stand in the entryway holding me. His gaze was on the door, but I didn't really think he was seeing anything. He looked lost, buried under the weight of his thoughts.

"Everything okay?" I asked, shifting in his arms and eyeing him carefully, the same way he watched me.

Aidan smiled a little and caressed my cheek. "Not sure how to answer that, sweetheart. A lot of shit happened today." He leaned into me, pressing a soft kiss on my lips, and said, "I need a shower. Why don't you go get ready for bed? We'll talk when I'm done, okay?"

"Yeah, sure," I said, but I wrapped my arms around his waist, holding him to me, and inhaled a deep lungful of his scent.

He chuckled. "I won't be long. Promise." He gave me another quick kiss, a tight squeeze, and reluctantly, I let him go.

I stood there for a long moment after he vanished upstairs, just listening to the rain pelt against the window. I don't know how long I stood there waiting to feel the nerves that I was sure had to be just itching to fill my belly. I thought I should probably be nervous. Aidan was most likely going to tell me what my dad wanted and what the guys found out. But oddly enough, I wasn't. Maybe it was the *friend time,* maybe it relaxed me, or maybe I was just exhausted, but I felt stable for the first time today. Solid.

I made my way upstairs and paused, hovering outside the bathroom for a second, thinking again that at any moment, I would feel the nerves, but again, nothing. So I moved on and did what Aidan asked. I got ready for bed.

After changing into a tank top and pajama shorts, I curled up in bed. I must have dozed off because the next thing I knew, I was jumping at the creak of the door hinges.

Aidan chuckled softly. "Tired?" he asked as he walked over to the dresser. He rummaged around in the top drawer and pulled out a pair of plaid pajama pants.

"Yeah, I guess I am," I said. His back was to me, and I thought I should probably look away as he dropped his towel, but um ... well, I didn't. Instead, my gaze wandered along the muscular plains of his back, watching them ripple as he stepped into the pants and tugged them on.

He turned, catching me watching him, and smirked that sexy half-smirk. I wasn't really sure how I managed it, but I rolled my eyes at him, and somehow I didn't blush, not even a little at being caught.

Aidan's eyes never swayed from mine as he crossed over to the bed. He climbed in beside me, his arm went around my waist, pulling my front snug against his side, and I rested my cheek on his chest.

Once he had me situated where he wanted me, he let out a slow breath and said, "Your dad's making a play. That call Luken took, well, he wants you to move back home. He even went as far as saying that I hit you."

"Okay," I said, not sure what else to say. There was nothing, absolutely nothing that he could do to make me move back there, and his accusation was a joke. Aidan wouldn't hit me. He just wouldn't. "Um ... did you talk to him?"

"No. I'm not negotiating with him." Aidan's muscles were tense, jumping and twitching, and I rubbed my cheek against his chest, waiting for him to say more. His response made no sense to me. I wasn't arguing with him. I wasn't even acknowledging Dad's ludicrous accusation, yet, he was tense. Stressed. Wound up tight.

He made a noise from the back of his throat that sounded like a mix between a growl and a sigh. "The guys reported in, too." He paused, stiffened further, and then sighed, relaxing a little. "Your dad's pack has kids with them. A girl and two boys."

"What?" I went to sit up, but his arm tightened around me, holding me against his chest, not loosening until I stopped moving.

I held still, waiting for him to elaborate, but he didn't. He ran a hand through my hair and said, "We're meeting the guys for breakfast tomorrow, and if it goes well, we'll be going in for those kids immediately."

I blinked and tried to sit up again, but it was a useless effort. He held me tight against him. His breathing was strained, his heart thumping quickly against my cheek. It was then that I clued into what this was. He was reporting to me. He didn't want to talk it all out right then. He didn't want me to get upset. He was probably still worried I couldn't take anymore today, but he knew he had to keep me looped in.

So instead of telling him exactly what I thought about the little breakfast meeting tomorrow and demanding answers, I asked, "And if it doesn't go well?" My tone, unfortunately, came out sharper than I would have liked.

He noticed it, and his arms tightened again. Taking a deep breath and slowly letting it out, he loosened his hold but didn't let go. His fingers continued to shift through my hair, and when he spoke, his voice was firm. "I'll be picking a new team and then going in for the kids."

I listened to his words, heard his tone, and realized that I was completely wrong. It wasn't that he didn't want to talk it out. He'd already made his decisions, and he was simply telling me what the plan was. I pressed my face harder against his chest, trying to get closer, show him that I wasn't going to pull away, no matter what, and said, "Aidan, you can't ..."

"Jade, sweetheart, they betrayed me," he said, cutting me short. "They betrayed you. I can't risk that happening again. Not with this."

I opened my mouth and then snapped it shut because I couldn't exactly argue with that. He was right. No matter how much I didn't want it to be true, the team had betrayed us. "I'm with you, Aidan, and I swear I'm not as breakable as you think."

He leaned forward, pressing his lips to my hair. "I know, sweetheart."

I lay there, my cheek pressed against his chest, running a lazy trail with my fingertips along the ridges of his abs as I tried to process everything, which really wasn't working out too well. My brain was fried. I was exhausted. Processing tonight wasn't looking like a viable option.

Aidan shifted beside me, placing his hands on my hips, and pulled me up onto his body. His lips moved from my hair to my cheek, down my face, along my jaw, and settled at my neck. His tongue flicked out, teasing the sensitive skin below my ear.

Heat rushed over my skin and pooled in my belly as a whisper-soft moan pushed past my lips.

He rolled, trapping me beneath his hard body, staring straight into my eyes. "I forgot to tell you something earlier," he murmured. He planted his forearms on the bed, holding most of his weight off of me, and his hands came up, framing my face.

"What's that?" I asked and squirmed against his chest, my heart plummeting. I didn't think I wanted to hear anymore, at least not tonight. What I wanted was more of his kisses. More of the heat, the contact. Something good to cover up the bad.

He caressed my cheek with his thumb and lowered his head, pressing his lips to mine. "I love you, Jade."

My heart danced in my chest. I opened my mouth to tell him the same but didn't get the chance. His lips pressed down on mine, and his tongue was inside my mouth, tasting, exploring. His hand slipped into my hair, wrapping it around his fist, and he pulled me closer, still.

I locked my arms around him, holding him close. The feeling of his skin against mine was perfect, and my body began to pulse with heat. I exhaled when his lips left mine and fluttered down my neck, below my ear, and dipped down to flutter across my shoulder, feeling some of the day's tension and stress fall from me, only to be replaced with a whole new wonderful kind of tension.

Aidan gave me the heat and the contact that I'd wanted, and I had to say, it was way better than *something good.* And it was exactly what I needed.

CHAPTER 7

AIDAN

My inner-wolf stirred within my chest, and I woke up slowly, chasing a dream that I couldn't quite grasp onto. The fading sounds of wolves howling in the night drifted in and out as the dream dissolved into a groggy, disjointed memory.

I blinked, clearing the sleepy film that layered my eyes. The storm was still going strong, crashing against the house. Rain beat against the windows; thunder rumbled throughout the sky. A flash of lightning lit up my bedroom and then faded, shrouding me once again in darkness. The only light left was coming from the red glow of the digital alarm clock that sat on the nightstand beside me, telling me it was 1:03 in the morning.

Uneasiness unfurled in my gut, and I scrubbed at my face. That dream. The sound of my pack, baying and chasing and tearing into flesh, shifted throughout my conscious mind as if it had been real. It felt real. Sounded real.

Jade was curled up beside me, and as always, she had me right at the edge of the mattress. Her forehead was pressed into my shoulder, and she had an arm thrown over my belly. Her eyes were closed, and her breathing was steady. She was smiling, just a little upward tilt at the corners of her mouth. Peaceful. Content.

A clap of thunder rattled the windows, and I sighed as I listened to it rumble through the sky and fade into the distance. I rubbed at my face again. It was nothing. Just a dream. Probably my subconscious preparing for the inevitable fight my pack was about to embark on. And with that thought, I closed my eyes and drifted back to sleep.

A chorus of howls broke through my sleepy brain, and my eyes snapped open again. That wasn't a dream. I was sure of it. My inner-wolf shifted and stirred again within my chest. He was agitated, urging me up, begging me to move and see what was happening.

I lay still, straining my hearing, waiting, listening ... The wolves' howls sounded again, and I quickly lifted Jade's arm from my stomach and slipped out of bed, careful not to wake her. The muscles in the side of her cheek flexed, and she rolled, flopping onto her back and throwing her arms out wide, before settling back into steady, even breathing.

I felt around the floor, searching for the pajama pants I'd tossed earlier that night. After a moment of searching, I found them at the foot of the bed, tangled with the sheets, and tugged them on before easing out of the room.

My wolves were close. As I crept down the staircase, avoiding the creaking third step from the top, I could smell traces of them. With the rain pounding relentlessly, they had to be within feet of the house for me to pick up their scent. It was watery, weak, and diluted, but it was there. Their baying grew louder. It was excited and frenzied and close. Too close.

In a heartbeat, I leaped down the remaining steps and hurried to the door. Through the small window, I saw a flash of white. The howling stopped abruptly only to be replaced by a low, menacing growl.

I yanked the door open, bolting out into the pouring rain. Air pounded in and out of my lungs in harsh pants. My heart ratcheted up, tripling in beats as I inhaled sharply. Rain. Dead leaves. Blood. Wolves. Green. Bitter. Birchbark. Cougar. The scents assaulted me, and I started to breathe faster and faster as I searched the front yard for any sign of the sources.

The howling started again, coming from the side of the house, getting closer and closer. Paws smacked against the wet ground, the sound almost inaudible over the rain, and suddenly, a mess of beasts, wolves, and cougars, shot past my front deck. My gaze zeroed in on a white wolf — Luken — as he took a leap, tackling one of the cougars. They rolled through the sodden grass, flipping over a few times before springing free from each other again.

Shit! I glanced back at the house as a wave of heat pulsed from within me. All my thoughts centered on Jade. I had to keep her safe. I had to keep them away from her while she slept.

I reached out and pulled the door closed. My skin shuddered, and I started to feel a little shaky from all the adrenaline that pumped through my veins. The shift was coming quickly — quicker than normal — my inner-wolf was jerking against my skin. He wanted out. He needed to protect our mate.

I kicked off my pants. Coarse hair layered my skin. My bones snapped, cracked, lengthened, twisted. I snarled, and my inner-wolf sprang free.

The rain was freezing against my fur-coated skin, soaking me through. I moved to the edge of the deck, tracking the movements of my pack as they tangled with the feline beasts. With a quick scan through the downpour, I counted fifteen wolves and seven ... no ... six cougars.

My wolves were all over the place. There was no center, no organization. They looked as if they were simply reacting to each attack. I didn't understand it. They were struggling, not seeming to gain any ground even with the greater numbers. The cougars were darting around them, quick and efficient, almost as if they were taunting them.

I barked and let my scent thicken in the air, hoping to draw their focus, and I instantly noticed the change in my wolves. Their movements went from sloppy and erratic to alert, and they began to fall into groups, protecting each other's backs and pushing the cougars toward the tree line.

One of the cougars broke off, stalking in my direction. My hackles rose, and the hair along my spine stood on end. The solid, beige-colored cat was large, coming close to my height in wolf form. He was built with sleek muscles, his shoulders packed and powerful. His eyes, a bright green, rimmed with black, were fixed on me.

He stopped a few feet from the deck and hissed. A flash of lightning struck through the black sky, and I caught sight of his long, razor-sharp fangs. He pawed at the muddy ground, growling, and hissing.

My lips curled, and I snarled. I wanted to jump down and tear into the monster, but I couldn't bring myself to move, even for a second, and leave Jade unprotected and sleeping in the house. How did they get this far into town? We'd known that they were coming closer, circling houses on the outskirts, but not this far in. Not with us constantly watching.

Suddenly he leaped at me, a powerful thrust from his hind legs propelling him forward, and before I could move, his fangs struck, burying into my shoulder. I pivoted, tossing him off balance, and just as quickly as he was on me, the cougar was back on the ground a few feet from the deck, hissing again.

My snarl was drowned out by a clap of thunder. My shoulder felt as if it were on fire. A streak of lightning chased through the night, and I saw the big cat push off again, launching toward me.

I shimmied back a couple steps, and as he hit the wooden planks of the deck, I leaped on him. The animal's knees buckled, and he fell to his belly. My heart was pounding in my ears, drowning out the sounds of the fights breaking out around me as I stared down at the cat below me. I bared my teeth, and went to bury them in his neck when I realized that he wasn't fighting, wasn't trying to push me off.

Shit! He was submitting. The beast within me wanted him to struggle, to give me a reason to end his sad little life, but he stayed still. He made a sound that sounded a hell of a lot like a laugh, and he started to shift.

I backed up off him, and he rolled up to his knees. He was older. Probably mid-forties, with a pot-belly and beady black eyes. He had a full head of black hair and a thick salt and pepper beard. He held out his hands, showing surrender, but he never once lowered his eyes from mine.

I noticed my pack was closing in around us from the corner of my eye. With a quick glimpse up, I saw a lump of beige fur about ten feet away lying motionless, and the rest of the cougars were gone.

Disgust rose up around me as I turned my focus back to the man in front of me. His pack abandoned him without even a thought, leaving him at our mercy.

I shifted and rose up to my feet, towering over him. He looked up, a cruel smile on his face, and he laughed. "You should have killed me," the man said, his voice higher than I expected.

Probably, I thought. He deserved death, even if it was only because he came into my territory and attacked me. My aching, bloody shoulder was proof of that. It was enough to end his life, whether he showed signs of submission or not. And if he hadn't shifted, I would have ended him, but it felt sickeningly wrong to do it while he was human. While he had no chance of defending himself.

I gritted my teeth, glowering down at him. "Not sure how you do this in your pack, but here, once someone submits and shifts, we don't kill."

"Pathetic." The man laughed. "Just for the record, I would have killed you." He laughed again, muttering something about me being weak, and then said, "I shifted to give you a message. The girl needs to be with her family, and we will take her back."

Growls erupted, and my wolves stalked closer. Clearly, the bastard had no sense of self-preservation because he started to shift, his face reshaping into that of a large cat. Long fangs descended first, slowly, as if he were taunting me, and then his bones began to break.

Luken was on him as his shift finished, not giving him a chance to run. The others were snarling and snapping around us, ready to take him down. But they didn't need to be. The meaty sound of flesh tearing, ripping, pulling, filled my ears as I watched Luken's white coat stain crimson. The cougar screamed a high-pitched sound that ripped through the air, and then his body went limp.

Jeff sent his cougars in the middle of the night to collect Jade. At that moment, that was the only thought I had. The girl the cougar had been talking about was Jade. I had no doubt about that, and the knowledge rattled me to my core.

I closed my eyes, sucking in breath after breath. The rain felt like pebbles smacking against my bare flesh, stinging my skin. My wolves had quieted, now that the threat was gone, but I could feel them watching me, waiting.

"Aidan, what's going on?" Jade's voice came from behind me, and I spun around. "I heard howling and a scream." She was standing in the doorway wearing only one of my hoodies that hung mid-thigh on her, rubbing sleep from her eyes. Her hands dropped. She paled as she looked past me, most likely at the wolves who were still growling. She turned a little gray as she looked down, spotting the dead cougar on our deck, and then her eyes came up and landed on my shoulder, and her expression changed from sick to concern. "Jesus, what happened?"

"I'm fine," I said, my voice sounding rough and growled. "Just a small flesh wound." I shook my head and stepped toward her. Rainwater dripped from my arms as I lifted a hand to her cheek. The thought of telling her to go inside crossed my mind. She'd been through hell today, and she didn't need anymore, but I couldn't do it. She needed to know, and there was no way I would start hiding things from her again. "It looks like your dad was serious about wanting you home. And I'm thinking he's done with pretending to have an alliance with us."

The sound of bones snapping and reshaping drew Jade's attention from me. I dropped my hand from her face and turned to find Luken, blood caked around his mouth and on his chest, rising to his feet.

He opened his mouth, but I lifted a hand to silence him. "How the hell did they get this close?" I demanded. "And where is the team?"

"Aidan," Jade said softly, her tone, her scent, both urged me to calm down, and I took a deep breath, holding my fury at bay. The other wolves backed up a few steps, dropping their muzzles to the ground. Not one of them shifted, most likely so they wouldn't have to answer me.

Luken cleared his throat, and he looked as if he were regretting not staying in wolf form. "The team ..." he looked down to his toes, let out a breath, and whispered, "We tried to call them when we first spotted the cougars, but we couldn't reach them. The cougars came straight here, Aidan. They knew where they were going."

"I'll call Beck," Jade offered, and she started to shuffle back into the house.

"No," I barked way too harshly, and I instantly felt sick. I turned to her. Her eyes were wide with surprise. "Sorry, sweetheart," I muttered. "Leave them for tonight. We'll talk to them in the morning about it."

Her face fell. She knew exactly what that meant. That I hadn't changed my mind about chatting with them. And I thought she got that not answering a call during an attack seriously didn't help their case. She must have thought it, too, because she didn't argue and nodded in agreement, looking grim but resolved.

She looked back to Luken. "Did anyone else get hurt?" she asked. She was making a conscious effort to keep her eyes on our faces. I could see it in the stiffness of her neck and the stillness of her eyes. There was a slight blush coloring her cheeks, and I thought that it was kind of cute. Even with an animal dead on our deck, she was still acutely aware that she was standing in front of two naked men.

Luken's nostrils flared, and I was sure he was picking up the scent of Jade's unease. It was a tangy smell and hung thick in the air. He shifted from foot to foot, nervously, and looked back at the wolves, gathered around us. "A few scratches," he said after a moment. "Nothing that won't heal. There's another dead cougar on the lawn."

"Can you and the others deal with this?" she asked, waving a hand toward the dead cougar. "And the other one? I want to look at his shoulder."

"Yeah, sure," he said, and he looked at me as if he wanted me to confirm his order.

"Thought we were past this, Luken," I said, my gaze hard and cold, so was my tone. "She gave you an order."

Luken threw up his hands and backed up a step. "I didn't mean any offense. It's just her scent," he said. "It's uncertain. Uneasy."

I chuckled, my anger dissolving. "It's because we're naked," I said and smirked back at Jade. "You really have to get over that, sweetheart."

Jade gave me an adorable dirty look before forcing a smile on Luken. "Sorry, still not used to all of this." She sighed and hugged her arms around her waist, shifting her weight to her right foot. "Bring the dead back to the headquarters." She moved her gaze to my face and blushed a little more. "I want to give them back to my dad, but I don't want my mom there when we do it."

I gave her a little smile. "Sounds like a plan, sweetheart."

CHAPTER 8

JADE

"This is a waste of time, Aidan," I said and swallowed down the rusty taste of guilt that gathered in my mouth. I pulled in a deep breath and shut my eyes for a second. That shivery, breakable feeling filled my chest again. I wasn't one-hundred percent sure exactly where the horrid feeling was stemming from because, well, Aidan wasn't entirely wrong, but I felt it nonetheless.

The feeling first crept in last night, or I guess technically it was this morning, right after we'd left the pack to deal with the dead cougars. While I'd cleaned out the deep gouges that the cougar had left in his shoulder and watched as it healed, Aidan explained why he didn't want me to call Beck, which was basically that they should have been there to start with. He then told me he was exhausted, walked me to bed, pulled me into his arms, and returned to sleep promptly. Surprisingly enough, I fell asleep with him. I didn't know what to make of that, but I thought that it probably had something to do with the fact that I was emotionally tapped out and couldn't bring myself to feel anything about the attack one way or another.

When he woke me up for the second time this morning, he'd been all business, laying out exactly how he felt about the team. He'd explained again why we hadn't called them about the little cougar hiccup that had happened on our front deck last night. I tried to reason with him, telling him that the guys were probably sleeping when Luken had tried them the first time, but Aidan had managed to poke holes in that logic. They were werewolves. They had awesome hearing. The phone ringing would have woken them up. When I tried to say that maybe they'd turned off their phones or at least turned off the ringers, I only managed to make matters worse for the guys. The enforcers always needed to be reachable, so turning off their phones was just as bad as not answering the call.

And not answering the call last night had made Aidan's doubt grow. He needed to be sure about them. Sure that they were loyal. So I'd listened to him and argued my points, but in the end, he stood firm, and I'd relented, agreeing that the meeting was probably a good idea.

Aidan took my hand in his and threaded our fingers together. "We've been over this, Jade," he said, sounding more than a little exasperated. "We're just going to talk to them." He tugged on my hand, pulling me with him as he started across the parking lot.

Dragging my heels, I followed, dreading every single step we took closer to the doors. *Talk to them* was code for deciding whether or not the team still had a future within the pack. Okay, maybe that wasn't entirely right. They would always have a place in Dog Mountain with the pack, just maybe not as enforcers.

I hadn't told Aidan outright, but there was a chance (a teeny, tiny chance) that his concerns were valid. Even though, in the end, the guys had stepped up and done the right thing, they'd also played us. They'd helped Jared. They'd wanted revenge. And if it weren't for the fact that they'd found out that Jared had known where the cougars were, I was pretty sure they would have helped him further or at least continued to turn a blind eye to what he'd been doing. And yeah, it really didn't look good that they'd been called last night and had been unreachable. So I completely got where Aidan was coming from on this issue.

But still, they'd turned over their brother. Their flesh and blood. Even though they knew that he would die for his crimes against the pack.

This morning, the sun was bright, almost too bright, after yesterday's dreary day. The parking lot shimmered, still wet from the storm. In some places, the rain had frozen, leaving a slippery ultra-thin layer of ice on the concrete.

I glanced up at him, squinting against the glare. "Aidan," I said and paused, waiting for a beat, before asking, "Why are you pushing this? They've proven their loyalty to you — to us. What's talking to them going to change?"

Aidan gave me a long, serious look. "I need to be sure. There's too much at stake here. We can't move on your dad without knowing if they'll turn on us again." He paused and let out a slow breath. "I can't trust your judgment when it comes to them, Jade. You care about them too much, and you've been wrong about them before."

His comment stung for a moment. Neither of us would say it out loud, but the whole trust thing was still a raw issue between us. He must have noticed my small wince because right then, I caught a sliver of regret that seeped into his expression. The sliver grew, quickly turning into deep, pained lines that spread like vines from the corners of his eyes, and I knew, just knew that he wasn't trying to hurt me with his words.

Those lines were getting deeper each time they appeared, and seeing them hurt my heart. I knew he was blaming himself for not noticing what Jared had been up to, for not stopping it before it ended in death. He hated himself for taking someone else from the guys, and he figured that if he hated himself, then they must hate him, too. He told me as much in the shower this morning, just before shutting the topic down and refusing to talk about it.

"They don't blame you," I murmured and pulled him to a stop just outside the door of the diner. I stepped in front of him, searching his eyes, but they gave nothing away other than regret.

Aidan watched me with an intense focus. He'd opted for jeans and a blue and gray striped button-down shirt that he'd left untucked. His hair was in its usually carefree mess, and he'd left a day's growth of stubble shadowing his jawline.

"Maybe not," he said with a calm remoteness. "But they hid their blame once, and I'm not going to risk it again."

I nodded, a few fast bobs of my head, not trusting my voice. His detachment, the way he closed me off, hiding everything behind that calm mask, felt like a physical slap, and the intensity of his stare made me wonder if it wasn't just the guys he was worrying about. "I don't ..." I started and then stopped, clearing the prickly lump from my throat. "I don't blame you either." It came out hoarse and whisper-quiet. God, my emotions were going haywire. They had been all over the place since I woke up, and it was driving me batty. His coolness wasn't a personal attack. Logically, I knew that. He was dealing with his demons, but no matter how much my head knew that, my heart didn't want to believe it.

A sad smile played at the corners of his mouth. There was something else in his gaze that I couldn't even begin to understand as he tugged on my hand, pulling me against him. He coiled his arms around me, and I tucked my head in the crook of his neck, breathing in the clean scent of soap and his crisp, sweet aroma of greens, as he pressed a kiss on the top of my head. "I love you, Jade."

"I love you, too," I said. I lifted my head and placed a light kiss on his neck, swallowing down the breakable feeling that was gathering again. His skin felt like velvet against my lips, and although I wanted to stay put, I forced myself out of his arms. If he needed to be sure that the guys were behind him, then I'd give him that. I had to give him that even if it was tearing me up to do it. I leaned in and pecked him lightly on the cheek, avoiding his arms as he tried to capture me again, and pushed the door open with confidence that I really didn't feel.

Inside, the diner was busy, just as I'd hoped. I'd figured the public place would help keep everyone's tempers in check. The place looked warm and inviting with large leather-covered booths and bright lights. The waitress hustled about, and the room was alive with the early breakfast rush chatter.

The waitress greeted us with a bright smile as she rushed forward. She ushered us to a secluded booth in the back corner, chattering away about the day's specials. She was a couple of years older than me, and for the life of me, I couldn't remember her name. Connie ... Corinne ... something like that. She blushed a lot as she spoke and brushed up against Aidan even more as we made our way through the restaurant.

When we reached our table, the team was already there, looking deadly and gorgeous. But despite them looking amazing, there was something dark and lethal in their eyes. I saw it the moment Aidan sat down, and it made my stomach sink a little.

As soon as we were seated, the waitress filled up our water glasses and took our drink orders, oblivious to the silent tension shifting around our table. She smiled, a cheery and more than a little excited smile, and then she rushed off to fill our orders.

"Where's Tommy and Chris?" Aidan asked. His tone was cool, so was his body language, and I nudged him in the ribs, hoping he'd chill out.

"Don't know," Craig said. He smiled a forced smile. He was breathing hard, his nostrils flaring. I thought he was probably trying to pick up the scent of our emotions, and when his eyes fell on me, they frosted over, and his jaw clenched tight.

And it hurt. The team, not a single one of them, looked at me like that. It was as if Craig knew I was about to betray them. I was pretty sure that they all knew. I snagged up a menu, seriously not liking his scrutiny.

Aidan didn't comment on the *don't know* answer, but I felt him stiffen beside me. He dug out his phone and fired off a quick text before placing it on the table.

I kept quiet for a moment, waiting for someone to speak up, but no one did. The tension at our table was building so high that I could barely concentrate on the menu in front of me.

"I'm starving." My voice was overly bright and cheery, and I cringed on the inside hearing it. If my cluttered scent hadn't given away my guilt, I was certain that my voice had. "I think I'm going to get ..."

Landon reached across the table, pushing the menu I was hiding behind down. "You talk to your dad yet?" he asked, eyeing me curiously. His lips curved in a weary smile as he glanced at Aidan and took in my mate's stressed-out vibes.

I shook my head, trying to bring his attention back to me. "No, not yet. We thought ..."

"Jade," Aidan said in warning, stopping me short. His hand went to my thigh, squeezing a little, and I bit my tongue.

The guys sat up a bit straighter, watching us. There was a bit of confusion in their gazes as if they weren't entirely sure why Aidan was cutting me off, but I could also see that they weren't entirely surprised by it either.

"We're not here to discuss how to get those kids out, are we?" Beck asked through his teeth. "What's this about?" His blue eyes clouded with a layer of palpable pain, and his lips were tight as he spoke.

Aidan leaned back in the booth and stretched his arm behind me along the top, letting his hand hang down to graze against my shoulder. His fingertips traced lazy lines, back and forth along the side of my neck as he said, "Nope. I'm giving you a chance to convince me that she's right about you guys."

"Aidan," I hissed, elbowing him again. That was definitely harsher than necessary. That shivery guilt made another appearance, and I pulled in a deep breath, trying to tamp it down.

"Jade, don't," Aidan said softly before I could say anything else. "It's better this way. Blunt and open. We all need to be on the same page here if this is going to work."

There was a breath of silence, and I found myself under the scrutiny of four sets of eyes, and then, after a crazy long minute, Landon finally chuckled. "Haven't you learned anything in the last few days?" he asked with a wide, carefree kind of grin aimed at Aidan. "Jade's always right, even when she's wrong."

I rolled my eyes at him and snorted out a strained laugh. "I'm never wrong."

That earned me a round of chuckles, and I pursed my lips, waiting for their laughter to stop. When it did, I opened my mouth and closed it without saying anything because the waitress scurried over with a tray full of orange juice and coffee. She took her sweet time placing the drinks on the table, casting flirty, mega-watt smiles as she did it. She took our food orders just as slowly, and then, with another round of bright smiles, she finally left.

I poured three big spoons full of sugar into my coffee and stirred, letting my spoon clink against the mug. "Guys, what Aidan was trying to say is that we thought maybe we should disband the team and build a new one. One that doesn't have blood ties to each other or the last alpha."

"Some of us might have wanted to see you crash and burn," Beck said to Aidan as if he were the one who had spoken. He reached for a creamer, opened it, and dumped it into his coffee. "But we're loyal to the pack. You know that. We've proven that to you."

Aidan nodded. "Yeah, you have. But you've also proven that you can be swayed, and I can't risk that happening again."

Landon lifted his shoulders in a lazy shrug. "Do what you need to do, man," he said. "We won't fight it."

"That's it?" Aidan asked. He sounded surprised, and honestly, I didn't know why. They weren't the *talk about your feelings* type. Honestly, I was just happy it was going better than I thought it would. No one was yelling or growling. Eyes weren't flaring, and I didn't see any skin shudders. They might have looked pissed off, but at least they were keeping their inner-wolves in check.

Craig slammed his coffee cup down, the contents sloshing up over the side. "Did you expect us to beg?"

There goes staying calm, I thought more than a little bitterly. I glanced around quickly, hoping no one noticed the rise in Craig's voice and was glad to find no eyes staring in our direction.

Mark swore softly and cut his brother a look that clearly said, *shut up*. Craig saw it. He merely lifted his shoulders in a shrug and gulped water.

"No, I didn't." Aidan sighed. "She sees something good in you guys. I'm just trying to see it, too."

"Aidan," I snapped, and I cut him a dirty look. "You're not making this easy."

"Don't think there's a way to make this easy," said Mark. He reached across the table, took my hand, and gave it a little squeeze. He held his gaze steady on mine. "What do you think about all this?"

That was a good question, and I didn't answer right away, taking a minute to gather my thoughts. When I spoke, I kept my voice at a whisper, making sure no one would overhear. "I think that we have a service for your brother tonight and that your head might not be in the right place."

Mark held my gaze for a moment before nodding and letting go of my hand. "Fair enough."

"Fair enough?" Craig snarled. "You've got to be kidding me!" He turned his glare onto Aidan, tiny flares of gold spread through his eyes. "Haven't you taken enough from us? My dad, my brother, my girl. Now you want to take away the team, too."

"Craig, no one is taking anything away," I murmured. "We just ..."

"Save it, Jade," he growled. "Save your damn sympathy for someone who actually wants it."

Aidan's scent suddenly flared, and his fingers stopped their lazy trail on my neck. His body stiffened. I glanced up at him and opened my mouth, ready to tell him to chill out, but the words died on my tongue.

His eyes were starting to change. Little speckles of gold dotted the soft brown. But he wasn't looking at Craig. He was staring at the entrance of the diner. His face was rock hard, his jaw clenching and unclenching. He moved in his seat slightly, his chest pressing against my shoulder, and I felt the vibration of his soft growl before I heard it.

He nudged me and jerked his chin, signaling me to let him out of the booth. The guys were already standing, their focus fixed on the doors as they swung open.

CHAPTER 9

AIDAN

"What's wrong with you guys?" Jade asked. She was looking at the team and me as if we'd all lost our minds. "Sit down. You're going to make a ..." Her voice trailed off as she sucked in a long, slow breath. Her upper lip started to curl up into a snarl, and her gaze snapped to the door as it banged shut.

"Let me out, sweetheart," I said roughly. I didn't want to push her out of the way, but damn, I would if I had to. I wasn't going to let them anywhere near her. My inner-wolf clawed at my chest, anxious and unnerved. Low growls erupted from the guys as they started to move from our table toward the door.

"You're not going anywhere," she hissed, pushing against my chest. "Sit down, guys." She didn't take the chance that they wouldn't listen to her and used the full force of her new scent to bring their focus back to her. When she had their full attention, she placed her hands on the table, fingers splayed wide, and said, "Sit." Her tone was all command.

The guys didn't waste a second in obeying her. They slid back into the booth quickly, taking their seats, but their gazes never left the doorway.

No one in the restaurant seemed to notice the soft growls that rumbled around our table. Utensils continued to clank against plates. Mugs slapped against tables. People chatted. Just like any other morning at the diner. They didn't have a clue about the threat.

I glanced back at the entrance. The two men had stopped just inside the doorway. Both of them were in their late thirties, cleanly shaven, and dressed in jeans and bright orange hunting jackets. One was tall, gangly looking, and the other, shorter and stubby. Their gazes drifted over the busy restaurant before coming to a rest at our table.

The tall one pulled out a cell phone, thumbed the screen, and brought it to his ear. He kept his eyes on us the entire time. His lips moved, but I couldn't make out anything other than the vague tone of his voice over the clatter from the other patrons.

The call didn't even last a minute, and he shoved his phone back into his pocket. The waitress appeared in front of them, menus in her hand, but they waved her away and took up a post just inside the doors as if they were waiting for friends to show before grabbing a table. And I figured that's exactly what they were doing. Waiting for friends.

"Jade," I said sternly, shifting in the bench seat to face her. "This place is packed. We have to ..."

Jade cut me off. "Aidan, there are only two of them." She waved a hand in their direction. "Not really what I'd call threatening. Even if that phone call he just made was for back-up, the guys could handle it." She huffed out a breath through her nose and folded her arms over her chest. "And we're in public. You can't go all wolfy and attack them here in the diner. People might be used to seeing wolves around town, but they never see the violence. You'll just freak everyone out."

I let out a frustrated growl, and she gave me the eyebrow. It was just one, lifting on the right, and matched with the look in her eyes, it clearly said, *I dare you to argue. You know I'm right.*

Jade, the freakin' voice of reason. When the hell did that happen? She was more of an act first type, and besides that, she'd also been an emotional mess all morning, yelling at me one second and close to tears the next. But now, there wasn't a single trace of nerves in her scent. She was focused. She was thinking. And she was completely in command.

Her gaze swept over the room before returning back to me. "Stop looking at me like I've grown another head," she said with a little laugh, placing a hand on my cheek. "You knew damn well they'd try again after last night. You even told me so this morning."

"Exactly," I said. I was losing patience, so was my inner-wolf. My skin felt as if it were crawling. Coarse hair darkened my forearms, and I was certain my eyes were a nice shade of gold. "Which is exactly why you need to move that cute butt of yours before I move it for you, sweetheart."

I glanced back at the entrance. The men still hadn't moved. They were leaning against the wall to the side of the doorway, with their gazes locked on our table. Waiting.

"What happened last night?" Landon asked. He sounded concerned, but his scent screamed guilt.

I leaned forward, rested my forearms on the table, and glared at him. "If you'd bothered to answer your phone, you wouldn't have to ask."

The others shifted uncomfortably in their seats, making clear efforts not to glance at Jade or me. But Landon ... he was going to argue with me. I could see it. He even muttered something, but his words were lost in a growl that ripped from his throat.

Jade smacked her hands on the table. "Enough," she said, quietly yet fiercely. She waited for a second, making sure we were listening, and then with certainty, she said, "They'll come to us."

"What are they waiting for?" Beck asked.

"I'm guessing they're waiting for more to show." She pulled out her cell phone and started tapping out a message. Seconds after she sent it, her phone chirped with a response. She smiled, looking extremely proud of herself, and she glanced up. "At least half the pack will be outside in five minutes. The rest won't be far behind, so chill out. We will not cause a scene in front of this many people if we don't have to. It wouldn't be good for our image." Her smile faded, and she glared at me then, long and hard, before shifting that glare around the table. "We'll finish our discussion later. Got it?"

The guys nodded and mumbled what sounded like an agreement. It never failed to shock me how quickly the team responded to her orders. It confused me, amazed me, and troubled me all at once. But then, most things to do with Jade left me feeling like that.

"Who'd you message?" I asked, wrapping my arm around her shoulder, attempting to look calm, but I wasn't sure if I succeeded. My inner-wolf was going crazy within me. He wanted to defend our territory. He wanted to protect our mate. He wanted blood. And sitting here doing nothing was putting him (and me) on edge.

Her response was an eye roll as if the answer was obvious, and she said, "Dom."

Jade had been right. The cougars came to us. It took another three minutes for the men to finally push off the wall and make their way over to our table. It seemed to take forever for them to reach us. They moved slowly, with a cocky self-confidence that seemed out of place since it was just the two of them, and there were six of us.

"You've got a good step up out there," the tall one said with a sly smile when he reached us. "Good, but not great. It only took about an hour to slip through your patrols."

"Wait until you try to get back out," Mark drawled with a lazy grin. He lifted his mug and took a sip.

"Don't see that being much of a problem," the short one said. He grabbed a chair, spun it around, and straddled it, resting his arms on the top of the backrest.

I growled. Their scent so close made my skin crawl, and it took everything in me to sit still and keep my arm around Jade. My inner-wolf was jerking against my skin. That guy really needed to stop eyeing Jade's cleavage, or he was going to find himself dead shortly. She was barely showing any skin, dressed in jeans, her plum zip-up hoodie, which was open with a form-fitting black tee underneath. The neckline scooped barely below the crease of her breasts, but the way he was looking at her chest, it was as if she had nothing on.

Jade wiggled against me, and I felt the shudder of her skin as she pressed her back to my chest, facing them. She pushed her palm against my knee as another growl bounced around my chest, and she snapped the fingers on her other hand, drawing the man's attention away from her chest.

"What can we help you with?" she asked sweetly as if she was genuinely interested, but she didn't quite manage to hide the growled roughness of her inner-wolf in her tone.

"You're Jade, right?" the tall one asked from his spot behind the jackass in the chair, arms folded. "Jeff's daughter?"

"That's me," she answered with another sweet as sugar smile.

The one in the chair let his eyes drop to her chest again, and my inner-wolf pressed against my ribs. "Do it again," I snarled. "Check out her chest again, and I swear, you'll be dead before you can suck in one more breath."

"Aidan, baby, chill," Jade said, looking over at me. Her eyes were screaming at me to rein it in, but her tone was still sugar-sweet.

The team watched her curiously, and by their soft chuckles, I thought they were probably getting a kick out of her sweetness, which we all knew was a joke. It wasn't that Jade wasn't sweet. She could be — sometimes — but I thought the fluttery eyelashes were pushing it a little.

I smirked at her, forcing my inner-wolf back. "Jade, sweetheart, I'm completely chilled."

I knew what she was trying to do with her sweet and innocent act. She was buying us time for the pack to show. It was probably smart. No. It was definitely smart. There were too many people here. Too many witnesses to drag them out back and beat the shit out of them like I wanted. Doing something like that would probably ruin the werewolf/human relationship in Dog Mountain.

There was a beat of silence, and then the chubby one in the chair said, "Your dad's pretty worried about you. He sent us to bring you back home."

I laughed at that. So did the guys. But Jade didn't. She gave him a look that was a little sad and a lot concerned. "What did you do to get on my dad's bad side?"

The tall one shook his head in confusion. "Not on his bad side."

"Really?" she said. "It seems to me you have to be." She sighed, and her frown deepened. "I just can't think of any other reason why he'd send you guys in here while I'm with my mate having a meeting with our pack enforcers."

JADE

I almost felt bad for the two men in front of me. Almost. They glanced at the guys, their faces turning a sickly shade of gray. Obviously, my father hadn't bothered to tell them who I'd most likely be with when they tracked me down. It made me hate him even more. I knew he didn't have much concern for human life, but really, did he not even care about his own pack?

I opened my mouth to tell them as much but was stopped short by a high-pitched shout. "Get out of my way, Dominic!" My heart tripped at the panicked voice. Mom. There goes not causing a scene. I swiveled in my seat and winced, catching sight of her pushing and shoving at Dominic's chest, trying and failing to get past him. "I'm serious," she shouted. "Get out of my way!"

I glanced back at the werecougars, taking in their smug grins. Every cell in my body buzzed with awareness. These two weren't here to bring me back to my father. They were only here to track me down. I was sure that my dad knew they'd never stand a chance, just the two of them. And I was also pretty sure that he didn't expect to see them again. They hadn't been calling in reinforcements. They'd been calling for my mother.

I had to admit that it was actually a pretty smart play, sending in someone I loved who couldn't defend themselves against a bunch of shifters. Dad knew I wouldn't ignore her. That I'd protect her. That I'd leave with her to get her out of harm's way.

The tall one chuckled, and I shot him a dirty look. He shrugged. "Like I said, we're not on his bad side. Your mom's pretty worried, too. She wasn't too happy to hear about how your mate manhandled you and tossed you into a car." His expression changed to one of mock concern. "If he does that in public, one can only wonder what kind of a beating he gave you when he got you back home."

I laughed once, feeling sick and cold and a little shaky. "Dom!" I called, drawing his attention. People were starting to look. At us. At Mom and Dominic.

I waved him over. Mom stopped flailing and yelling, and she stepped around him. She rushed toward us with a determined gait. She'd dressed in a hurry. I couldn't remember ever seeing her leave the house in jogging pants before. Her face was splotchy and tear-stained. Her hair was a tangled mess.

I needed to think. If Dominic was here, most of the pack would be with him. I took a quick look out the large front window, spotting the two wolves and a few other pack members in human form pacing the parking lot. People walked by the wolves, barely paying them any attention, as if seeing them in town was a normal occurrence, but then, I guessed it kind of was normal. It should have made me feel better, but at that moment, it really didn't.

When Mom reached our table, Aidan let his arm drop from my shoulder, and he sat a little straighter beside me. "Hi, Pam," he said casually, if not a bit cautiously. He offered her a smile, which actually looked pretty believable, but it didn't fool me. His scent carried a hot spike of anger.

Mom completely ignored him, keeping her tear-filled eyes on me. "Jade, honey. You need to come with me right now." She held out a hand to me, her eyes pleading with me to take it.

I hesitated. I didn't know what to do. She couldn't stay here, and I wasn't going to leave with her and go to my dad. I didn't know what lies she'd been told, but by the way she was glaring at Aidan, I could take a pretty good guess.

"Pam, why don't you sit down for a minute?" Beck said, waving to the empty place beside me.

Mom dropped her outstretched hand. She glanced at Beck and then at the others as if she were only noticing them now. Her face crumbled, and she made a strangled sound from the back of her throat. "I trusted you boys," she whispered. "How could you let this happen to her?"

Resolve settled itself in my belly as I listened to my mom and saw the heartbreak in her eyes. It was time. She needed to know everything. Beck opened his mouth, but I jumped in before he could get anything out. "Aidan, give me your keys."

The werecougar who'd sat down rose from his chair and said, "You're not going anywhere." He folded his arms over his chest. I thought he was probably trying to go for tough, but he failed. He was short, stubby; he might be a shifter, but he clearly wasn't a match for the team or Aidan.

I laughed once, a startling sound, and slid out of the booth. "You really think you can stop me? Look around this table." My voice was rising, coated with anger, and I waved a hand toward the front window. "Look outside."

The men looked to where I pointed, and they cursed under their breath. They started to back away but didn't make it far. Landon and Mark were out of their seats in a blink, blocking their way.

I looked down at Aidan, still sitting in the booth. He hadn't moved to grab his keys. He gave me a look that said he wasn't letting me out of his sight. "I need a pedicure," I said and held out my hand to Aidan.

"Shit," Dominic muttered from his place behind my mom. "Jade, maybe that's not ..."

I cut him a look and didn't let him finish. "It's time, Dom. Call Mac, okay?" I looked back to Aidan and held his eyes, pleading with him not to argue. "Give me your keys," I demanded. "I'm taking Mom back to our place."

He frowned. I knew he was confused. I knew he had no idea what I was doing or thinking. He glanced at Dominic, then at my mom, and then he dug his keys out of his pocket and tossed them to me. "Take Mark and a couple other members with you."

I leaned into him, kissing the corner of his mouth. "Love you, baby."

CHAPTER 10

AIDAN

Jade needed a pedicure.

Not very long ago, I thought that having Jade in my life would never be boring. I wasn't wrong. Since meeting her, I hadn't had a boring day. I hadn't even had a boring hour. I remembered being happy about that, knowing that no two days would ever be the same. I was glad that she didn't back down with me. She challenged me. She surprised me. She kept me on my toes.

Now, though, a part of me wanted the boring. We had two werecougars at our table. We still hadn't come to a decision on what to do with the team. Her mom thought I was abusing her. Her dad was clearly done pretending to be working with us. The werecougars were not only trying to bring in more women but there were three kids, one of them, a young girl within their clutches. And Jade thought now was the time for a freakin' pedicure. I seriously didn't even know what to think about that.

Jade wrapped an arm around her mother's waist and ushered her through the diner, Mark following closely behind her. She didn't look back, not once, and in a few short seconds, she was out the door.

Letting her go went against every protective instinct I had. I wasn't the only one struggling with it either. The team, Dominic, we were all on edge. But that determined glint in her eyes ... I knew if I didn't give her the keys, she would have left anyway. Having the car with locked doors made me feel a bit better, but not much.

I met Dominic's eyes and arched an eyebrow when the door shut behind them. He knew I wanted to know what this *pedicure* crap was about, but he only shook his head. He looked conflicted, as if he weren't entirely sure if he should stop her or let her go. It was obvious that he knew exactly what Jade was up to. He huffed and shook his head again, and then he yanked out his phone, most likely to call Marcy.

"I'm still thinking that these morons pissed off Jeff," Craig said. He rose slowly and stretched his arms over his head lazily.

"Yep," I agreed. "Or he just forgot to give them an exit strategy." I lifted my shoulders in a half-hearted shrug. "Maybe it's just a simple oversight."

I looked at our guests. I didn't have a clue what to do with them. I couldn't just let them go. Except right then, that's exactly what I wanted to do. If only to give me the time to go after Jade and find out what the hell she was up to.

"You all aren't going to do anything," the chubby one sneered. "We're in public."

"We're in a town that loves our pack," Beck said. He was smiling, a manic kind of smile that actually gave me a little chill. He jerked his chin toward the front of the diner, pointing out the wolves still pacing in the parking lot. "No one even blinks at our presence."

The waitress started our way, a couple menus clutched against her chest. Her bright smile was gone, a forced one in its place. She stopped at our table. "Menus?" she asked, looking at our company and then back to me. Her scent told me she was a bit nervous, but she was far from scared. I couldn't really blame her, not after watching Pam's little freak out with Dominic at the door.

"They won't be staying," I said, smiling as warmly as I could. "And we won't be either. Could you put a stop on our order?"

She nodded, and her face fell, disappointed. "Sure."

I pulled out my wallet and tossed a few twenties on the table to cover our bill before standing up. I waved my hand in an *after-you* kind of gesture to our guests and said, "Let's go."

The guys moved in around the werecougars, forcing them to walk through the utterly quiet diner. People watched us move, although it wasn't with fear. It was curious gazes that followed us out, and I found myself thinking that it was actually kind of nice that the town knew about us, trusted us. It sure made some parts of pack life a hell of a lot easier.

The werecougars didn't put up a fight. No. They moved out the doors without a word, heads hanging. I thought they were probably clued into the fact that no one was coming to help them. That Jeff had thrown them to the wolves — literally. At least these two had some sense of self-preservation, unlike the idiot who'd bitten me last night. Or maybe they had just simply given up. The truth? I didn't really care either way.

There were more pack members in wolf form than I'd noticed from inside in the parking lot. Six wolves, all various shades of brown, circled Beck, Craig, and Landon, as they put the cougars into a truck and got in. A couple of the pack members hopped into the truck bed, and then they pulled out of the lot. The wolves loped after them, and I gave out orders for everyone else to head back to the headquarters.

I rode back to the headquarters with Dominic. It was a fairly silent drive, but not entirely. He huffed a lot and clicked his tongue. It was as if he wanted to talk, but he couldn't find the words when he tried. It was weird. Crazy weird. Dominic always had something to say, and he never held back. He looked defeated, I thought, and it made my skin crawl with a bizarre mix of dread and anticipation. "You want to tell me what this pedicure stuff is all about?" I asked.

Dominic chuckled softly and cut me a quick sideways look. "You don't know that girl at all, do you?"

"Sure I do," I said quickly, except it didn't sound believable. "She's mine. Of course, I know her."

From the quick look Dominic gave me, I knew he hadn't expected to hear anything else, and after a few long beats, he muttered, "Pedicure is code for *I'm freaking out and need girl time.*"

"Girl time," I repeated and blinked. "You're kidding me."

"I'm dead serious, Aidan," Dominic said. "Hard conversations take place during *girl time.* They won't answer phones or let anyone in that house until everything that needs to be said is said."

Dominic made a left. Up ahead, I spotted the truck carrying the werecougers as it turned into the headquarters' parking lot. I figured I could lock them up for a bit, but it was only a temporary fix, and I wasn't even sure if keeping them here was a good idea. We had two dead from last night at the building. And now another two alive. I was pretty sure they'd pick up the scent of the dead fairly quickly. Maybe they'd go ballistic when they did, and the pack would solve the *what to do with them* problem quickly?

I scrubbed at my face roughly. Yep, I seriously needed some *boring* when this was over.

"She's going to tell Pam everything." It wasn't a question. I'd seen the determination in her eyes before she left. I'd thought she'd been determined to get her mother away from the enemy. But this ... My lips tugged up at the corners. This was better. "Jade's done protecting her father."

Dominic grunted, "Yep."

More huff-filled silence as he pulled into the parking lot and found a spot. I knew he had something else to say, and for the life of me, I didn't have a clue why he was holding it back. He never had before, and when the next long huff puffed out of him, I snapped, "Just spit it out, Dom."

"Just thinking that this crap with the team needs to end," he said, turning off the car. "You need them. Jade needs them. Hell, the pack might hate them most of the time, but they need those guys, too." I cut him a look, and his hands quickly shot up. He continued with caution. "I'm not saying that we should just forget what they did, but you can't blame them for wanting to help their brother. Not unless you're going to start blaming Jade for stalling with her dad. If you stop and really think about it, they were doing the same thing she's been doing. And don't tell me you haven't let her stall things because we all know you have."

He was not wrong. He knew it. I knew it. I was sure the whole damn pack knew it, too. I knew I didn't look happy when I asked, "What am I supposed to do? I can't just let what they did go. She could have gotten hurt. I could have lost her."

I didn't expect an answer, and I was sure Dominic knew that, but he decided to give me one anyway, and his answer sucked. "Don't really know what you're supposed to do. But you didn't lose her, Aidan. She's fine. And those guys let their brother die to keep her and our pack safe."

I nodded because I really didn't know what to say, and we got out of the car. Groups of pack members huddled around the entrance, watching the team pull our guests out of the truck, and it was at that moment, as I scanned the clusters of people, that I realized Tommy and Chris hadn't shown up yet.

"You see Tommy and Chris today?" I asked as I shut my door.

Dominic glanced over the car with his typical cool mask tightly back in place. "Yeah, sorry. I forgot to tell you. Your dad called them. They're going to be tied up for a few hours."

JADE

It was only 9:17 in the morning, and my day had already turned to crap.

Marcy was standing at the table, noisily sorting through a bag of nail polish that, thankfully, Dominic had told her to bring. She'd been waiting on the front deck with Trevor when Mom and I drove up. I hadn't had to explain what I was about to do. The look she'd given me told me she already knew. I wasn't sure exactly how, but I thought that was probably Dominic's doing as well.

Mom sat in a chair at the kitchen table, her feet submerged in the footbath. She was in a state. She looked dazed and vulnerable and sad. She muttered a lot. Mostly about how sorry she was for pushing me toward the pack — toward Aidan.

"Mom, Aidan would never hit me." It was just a whisper from me, but it was full of sincerity. "And if he tried, he'd be dead. You know the team wouldn't allow it."

I wasn't sure if that was entirely true, but it sounded good. The team loved me. I knew they did, but Aidan was their alpha male, and I was his mate. In the eyes of the pack, Aidan could do pretty much whatever he wanted with me. I was basically his property. But it worked both ways. He was also mine. They probably wouldn't stop me from beating the crap out of him either if I wanted to, which, of course, I didn't.

She didn't believe me. I could see it, feel it, God, I could even smell it. "Ray ..."

"Aidan. Is. Not. Ray." I said it with clear precision, biting each word clean off, with sharp edges and all.

Mom screamed, a short burst of sound that made both Marcy and me jump. It was pure rage and frustration, boiling out of her. Her body shuddered. Her fists clenched. I'd never seen her like this. Never. "Why would your father tell me this if he didn't watch it happen, Jade?"

Mark burst into the kitchen, his breath panting and his eyes focused, searching for a threat. He opened his mouth, most likely to demand what was going on, and I gestured to him, an indication for him not to speak. He frowned, confused, but shut his mouth and propped himself against the doorframe.

My heart was aching, and I pulled in a quick, shaky breath. "I think the better question is why would Dad let me leave with Aidan if he saw that happening to me?"

Mom's eyes widened, and she made a strangled whimpering sound, but she didn't answer my question.

"You know what Mr. Shaw is, Mom," Marcy said. She sounded calm and gentle, and she moved to kneel beside my mom, looking up at her with big, sad eyes. "Don't you?"

Mom nodded. She didn't make a sound. Her gaze was locked on Marcy, waiting breathlessly for some kind of explanation — a link — to make what she thought she knew make sense. And I had that link.

The video.

"Then you know that he could have stepped in easily," Marcy continued delicately. "If Aidan had really punched her in the face like you were told, Mr. Shaw could have stopped it."

I felt myself smile. I had no idea why, because well, this wasn't really a smiling moment, and by no means did I feel happy. But then, maybe the smile was coming from relief. I was going to tell Mom everything. Right now. I wasn't going to have to lie to her anymore.

"Mark," I said. My voice was a little shaky, but I still managed to hold onto that smile. "Can you go upstairs and grab Aidan's laptop? It should be on the dresser in our bedroom."

He nodded to me just a little, and his smile was one of approval and encouragement as he turned and headed for the stairs.

When I looked back at Mom, her face had changed. It went from grief-stricken and enraged to something so twisted with an uncertainty that it made my heartbeat quicken painfully fast. I pulled out a chair and took a seat beside her, clasping her hand in my own. "Mom, there's something I need you to see."

CHAPTER 11

AIDAN

"We should be doing something," Landon said, pacing the floor. We were back in my office with Craig, Beck, and Dominic, trying to figure out the best move, except we weren't getting far. "We should be getting those kids or killing those bastards. We should not be giving them a comfy room and wasting our resources guarding them."

Landon had a point, but unfortunately, the cougars hadn't put up any kind of a fight. The two men were completely and totally compliant as they were led through the headquarters. They kept their mouths shut, and their gazes dropped. I thought they probably knew there was no point in fighting. We outnumbered them too greatly for them to even consider that they might have had a chance at getting away.

Now they were locked up in one of the old bedrooms at the back of the building with four pack members guarding the door. It was a complete waste of man-power, but right then, I really didn't know what else to do with them, and there was just something so ... wrong about killing two men who were showing their submission, even if they did deserve death for the things they'd done with their pack.

"We can't just rush out there," Beck said. He was sitting on the couch, one arm strewn over the back and legs stretched out in front of him. "That's how people get hurt. We need a plan, and yelling about how we should be doing something is not helping."

"We should kill them now!" Craig shouted, from his spot beside Beck, causing Beck to groan and roll his eyes. He wasn't alone with the eye roll.

Craig was twitchy, and his neck had a splash of color slowly creeping up to his face. He was looking at Beck as if he were ready to pummel him for attempting to be reasonable. His fists, clenched and white-knuckled. His jaw flexed so tight the muscles looked as if they were beating under his skin.

"They could be useful," I said from where I leaned against the wall, arms folded across my chest. "We need to consider that before getting rid of them."

Craig moved, jumping up from the couch and crossing the room with speed, and before I could say anything more, he was standing in front of me. The color had reached his cheeks, a bright red. His eyes flared, and he shouted, "They were after your mate, our alpha female. They would have taken her if we hadn't been there."

My eyes narrowed at the thought, and ignoring Craig's outburst, I pushed off the wall, stepped around him, and joined in on Landon's useless pacing. It was true. They had been after her, and if Jade had been alone, they probably would have taken her, although not without one hell of a fight, I was sure.

"But you guys were there, and they didn't take her," Dominic pointed out, drawing all of our gazes. He sat on top of my desk, his hands on his thighs, leaning forward slightly. "No point in fighting over what could have happened."

Dominic fixed me with a look that I tried really hard to ignore as a round of grunted agreement filtered through the guys.

And then there was silence. It was thoughtful and a little tense, and it stretched on longer than any silence really should.

Craig went back to the couch, taking a hard seat. Landon started to pace again, six steps across the room, six steps back. Beck scrubbed at his face, the frown lines deepening.

It struck me then, as I watched them, that these guys were probably more dedicated to the pack than any other member we had. Even now, not knowing whether or not they would still be enforcers tomorrow, they were here, ready to fight. Giving me guidance. And I couldn't ignore that they'd had my back in the diner even after I'd made it clear that I didn't trust them and didn't want them on the team.

Maybe Dominic was on to something. There really wasn't any point in arguing about the *could haves*. When I actually thought about it, most of my anger toward the guys was based on the *could haves*. I could have lost Jade. Jared could have taken the pack from me. The team could have stood by and not said anything about the cougars' location. They could have given Jared more time. They could have taken over his quest for revenge.

But they didn't. None of that happened. I still had Jade and the pack. Jared was gone, and the team was still here, backing me.

The truth? I was starting to think that I'd let my emotions where Jade was concerned run my decisions when it came to these guys, and damn, it made me feel guilty.

"Jade was right," I said, breaking the silence. I went back to my post, leaning against the wall. "I was harsh this morning."

"Don't worry," Beck said, brushing it off with a shrug. "We get it. Emotions are running high all around." He gave me a meaningful look, one that was full of understanding and didn't hold any trace of malice, and for reasons I really didn't want to explore, I found myself looking away. "Aidan, you've got to stop blaming yourself because no one else does."

"He's right," Craig said, still angry. "You made the right call with our dad, and you made it again with Jared." He pulled in a breath and let it out. "But I'm telling you, taking this team apart is not the right call."

"I know." It was all I could say. Tension that I didn't even realize was there eased from my shoulders. Deep down, I thought I'd known that all along.

"Awesome." Landon's voice oozed sarcasm. "Now that we have the obvious out of the way, can someone tell me why Jeff would kick Jade out if he was going to drag her back anyway?" He looked utterly confused. "What was the point?"

What was the point of any of this? If there was one, I couldn't see it. It just didn't make sense. Jeff didn't strike me as a stupid man. Hell, he'd had the pack fooled for years. If it wasn't for that video of him making a deal with Tiffany, we probably still wouldn't have known what this pack was doing. So why now? What was he hoping to gain from having Jade tucked back in his house?

"Aidan?" Dominic called.

I raised a hand. "Hold on." My thoughts started to race. I took a breath and held it as I tried to understand what I was even thinking. Everything was so jumbled. Flashes of the last couple of months. Partial conversation. They all swarmed in and mashed together until everything collided with sharp clarity. I blinked, looked at Dominic, and said, "He needed us mated."

"Why?" Landon asked with barely any patience.

"Because now that we're mated, she carries my scent," I said.

"She doesn't need me to control the entire pack. If he can convince her to work with him, she can force everyone to accept it. Through her, he could run our pack."

"We need to get rid of him, Aidan," Dominic said. There was anger in the statement, but also there was resolution and maybe a little fear. "He needs to be taken out."

"No," I said sharply. "As far as we know, he's the only real authority those bastards have. If we take that, there's no one to keep them in line, no one for them to follow." But as I said it, I had only one clear, crisp thought: *We're going to take him and his pack down.*

JADE

"She took that better than I thought she would," Marcy whispered from beside me as we watched my mom dig through the fridge. The pedicures had been completely forgotten. She'd decided I had to be hungry since she'd interrupted my breakfast and was determined to make a meal.

"I think she's trying not to process it," I whispered back as Mom put a carton of eggs on the counter and kept rummaging through the fridge.

"Jade," Mom called. Her voice was chipper, almost sing-song. "Can you run to the store? We don't have enough eggs for pancakes. Oh, and maybe some more bacon."

"I think we should call Aidan," I said. "Get the guys back here." Not that they would be able to help with this, but honestly, Mom was freaking me out a little. Her scent kept spiking with hot fear, and each time it did, she became a little more frantic, riffling through the fridge.

"Jade?" Mom pulled her head out and looked over her shoulder at me. Her smile was bright and brittle, and her eyes, utterly blank. "Why are you just standing there? Run to the store. Hurry up. We have a lot to do before Jared's service this evening." And with that, she stuck her head back into the fridge and said, "We need orange juice, too."

I heaved a sigh, watching as she pretty much emptied every piece of food that was somewhat breakfast-related onto the counter. Maybe I shouldn't have dumped everything on her all at once, but the thing was, once I'd started talking, I hadn't been able to stop. There was just something so lightening in getting it all out.

After letting her watch the video, I'd launched in, telling her all about the cougars. I explained how they only seemed to change males and locked up women in barbed wire cages. I told her about the kids they had and the *accident*, which left the cougars womanless, and I explained that Dad was their pack leader.

I went on to tell her all about Jared. About how he'd known where the cougars were and hidden it from us. I explained that once his brothers found out, they had turned him in, and then he'd challenged for alpha. Though, I might have left out the little part about my helping Aidan kill him. I couldn't say why exactly, but I thought it might have had something to do with the overwhelming guilt I was feeling over the whole situation. I couldn't help but think that if I hadn't been so consumed with hurting Aidan, I would have seen what Jared had been up to before it was too late.

And then I told her about last night and about the two dead cougars we now had at the headquarters. And finally, I explained that Aidan had only picked me up and tossed me into the car yesterday because I'd basically told Dad that I didn't trust him at all and accused him of protecting those monsters.

Marcy leaned into me and pressed her lips to my ear. "Maybe she's in denial."

"Yeah, maybe," I said, but I wasn't really sure if that was what this was. Actually, going by her scent, I thought she was pretty close to freaking out. This wasn't denial. It was Mom trying to be strong and cope.

A pot clattered to the floor, and Mom bent down to pick it up. She glanced back at us, the pot clutched tightly in her hands. "Go on, honey," she said. She smiled again, another breakable smile. "You're wasting time."

I tried to smile back, but whatever my lips did, it wasn't a smile, and because I really didn't know what else to say, I muttered, "Sure, Mom," as I snagged Marcy's hand and tugged her from the room.

The living room was surprisingly quiet, and it took me a moment to notice Mark sprawled out on the couch, with an arm thrown over his eyes.

Marcy went to the far end and plopped down, not caring that she jostled his feet, but then I thought he probably didn't care either because all he did was readjust, lifting them up and dropping them on her lap.

Marcy made a tragic face, looking at his feet in her lap and then up at him. She looked as if she were going to tell him to get up, but then she shook her head, pursed her lips, and looked at me. "Tell me you're not really going to the store."

"Ummm ..." I took a quick look over my shoulder, seeing Mom rush about the kitchen, and fought back the feeling that I'd just made a really big mistake.

There was a sound, just on the edge of my hearing, and I glanced out the window. It sounded like voices, and at first, I thought it was just the two other pack members that had come with us from the diner. They'd stayed outside under Mark's orders to watch the house. But then it got louder, and there were more voices than just two.

There was a light knock at the door, and then it swung open. "Jade," Erika said with a little nod. She stepped into the house, five other women trailed in behind her. "We need to talk to you."

CHAPTER 12

AIDAN

The phone rang, and for a moment, I felt relieved that something was interrupting me from loading bodies into the bed of Jared's (or I guess it was now Beck's) truck, because really, who wanted to handle dead bodies? But we needed to get rid of them, and bringing them back to Jeff, just as Jade had suggested last night, seemed like a good plan. We were hoping that two more dead bodies to contend with would give us a little extra time to devise and execute a solid plan for extracting the children. According to the team's report, the kids weren't in any immediate danger, but I didn't want to risk waiting. Instead of being manipulative, Jeff was becoming aggressive, and we needed to get those kids out before we retaliated with our own attack. It was safer that way. Fewer distractions. Fewer innocent that could get hurt.

When I dug my phone out of my pocket, my first thought was that it was Jade. Maybe she'd finished up with her mother, and she was calling to see where I was. My second thought was that it could be Tommy or Chris. I'd left them each messages, trying to get a feel on if or when they'd be coming back. You just never knew with my dad. It wouldn't surprise me at all that he'd decide to take them back before I was ready to let them go. He was the master of reneging on a gift.

I cradled my phone in my palm, about to thumb the screen when I read the caller display: *Unknown*. I stared at it for a moment, hesitated, frowned. I usually let unknown calls go to voicemail, and right now, I really didn't have time to politely dismiss a telemarketer. Still, then with everything going on, I didn't want to miss something important, so, curious, I answered, "Hello?"

My greeting was answered by a frustrated sounding groan, and then a familiar and anxious voice said, "Where's Jade?"

I laughed once — stunned. After last night and this morning, I really hadn't expected this call. I thought more along the lines of cougars coming into town trying to fight their way to her. Not an anxious phone call. "If you were looking for Jade, you probably should have called her phone."

"That's who I was calling." Jeff sounded strained, and it was then that I realized that I never removed the call forwarding from Jade's phone last night. All her calls were still being routed to me.

I moved away from the truck and the guys and headed for the back of the building where the picnic table was. I probably shouldn't have. It couldn't have looked good on my part. I was sure they had picked up the unease in my scent when I heard his voice. Still, I guess not trusting the team had become sort of a habit in the last little while, and before I really realized I was doing it, I was sitting on top of the table, listening to Jeff's breathing on the other end of the line.

I waited for a beat for him to tell me what the hell he wanted, but he didn't. Just more heavy breathing. With a huff, I asked, "What do you want, Jeff?"

There was a catch in Jeff's voice. "I-I wanted to talk to my daughter and my wife."

For a moment, I was silent. He sounded … desperate? "Well, we don't always get what we want, do we?" I kept my tone casual, which took a crazy amount of effort. "You're getting sloppy, Jeff, and sloppiness, well, that's a sign of desperation. Honestly, I figured you'd be more worried about what we were doing with the two cougars you sent to get her this morning."

"I didn't …"

"Really?" I blurted, cutting him off. "Are you really going to try to tell me you didn't send them? And I bet you're going to deny filling Pam's head full of lies about me beating up Jade, too."

"I want my daughter home." Jeff's voice shook, and I couldn't tell if it was from anger or nerves. "Give her back, and I'll make sure you never see or hear from the cougars again."

"Is that the deal you were telling Luken about?" I bit out the question sharply and didn't wait for him to answer before I spat, "I'm not scared to fight for what I want, and I will fight for it. For her. For this pack. For this town."

I heard a breath and then utter silence. I pulled the phone away from my ear and glanced at the screen. He hung up. I gazed at it blankly for a moment. Desperate. He was desperate. I was sure of that. But then, if I had four pack members go missing in less than twenty-four hours, I'd probably be desperate, too.

What did that leave them with? The team had come back with a count of twenty, although they hadn't been able to get close enough to be certain of that number. Even so, if we went with that number, it meant that the cougars were down to sixteen, seventeen including Jeff, which, I realized, put his pack back at the exact number that he'd given us to start with.

I wondered if those four had always been expendable. Had he figured he'd lose them all along, or was it just a lucky chance for us?

"Who was that?" Beck asked from behind me.

I pushed my hair back and looked over my shoulder. "Jeff."

Beck rounded the table and hopped up beside me. I could feel his eyes on me, watching, waiting. "In the diner, you said blunt and open," he reminded me after a few beats of silence. He looked very serious, I noticed, as I glanced over at him. "You told Jade it was better that way. Don't you think it's time to use that logic?"

I set my phone down slowly. "Beck ..."

"No," he said, raising up his hands as if they would ward off what I was going to say. "I don't want to hear it. I can't take any more excuses. Ray might have been an asshole, and yeah, I'm glad he's gone, but at least when he ran this pack, everything was out in the open."

"Not everything," I countered. "None of you knew anything about this little deal with Jeff."

"Right." His nostrils flared, and his gaze hardened. "Do you trust me?"

Did I? For the most part, I thought I did, at least to a certain extent. Jade trusted him. Hell, she trusted all of them, and I knew she'd follow them blindly if they asked her to. But even if we'd just sort of cleared the air between us, and even if I thought I could trust him, there was still that small niggling voice chanting in the back of my head. *You killed his father and his brother.*

I sighed. "Beck, I don't think ..."

"I know exactly what you think," he growled. "You think that we're not going to be there when you need us. You think that if you tell us too much, we'll find your weakness and use it against you, just like Jared did. Well, newsflash, Aidan, we all know your weakness, so it's a little too late to try and keep that card close."

And Jade wondered why love should have nothing to do with the alpha pair. It wasn't something I liked to think about, not since I found her and especially not since I claimed her. Besides, it wasn't as if I'd ever want to go back and change what had happened between us. But at times, like this one, it was a struggle to look at everything and see what was best for the pack, not just what was best for her.

I nodded very slowly. "You're right. Everyone knows my weakness. It's not really a secret. But what most don't get is that she's also what keeps me strong. She's what keeps me fighting. I've killed for her, and I'll do it again. In a heartbeat."

"Good." The word was clipped, but his voice was softer when he continued. "Look, you're our alpha. The team and I will follow you, whether you want us to or not. I know you probably won't believe this, but we're glad it's you we're following. No one wanted to follow Ray. The pack, even us, we did it because we didn't have a choice. You and Jade ... you guys, have turned that around. People actually want to follow you." He smiled, chuckled, and shook his head as if the thought was a foreign one. "That's something, Aidan. You didn't know them before. Before, they were just scared. Scared of Ray. Scared of us. You've changed that. You've created a pack based on respect and compassion. Do you have any idea how refreshing it is to see pack members get second chances? I should be dead right now."

I shook my head. "You're alive because of Jade, not me."

Beck shrugged. "Yeah, maybe, but you agreed with her."

"Yes," I said. "Yes, I did." And I was really glad I'd agreed with her.

I looked down at my phone and tapped the screen. 9:42. I considered the phone call with Jeff, mostly because I didn't know what to say about everything Beck had just unloaded. I'd made it clear to Jeff exactly where I stood, and I figured the clock was probably now ticking on the cougars' current location. I wondered if he'd put that piece together yet. Did he realize that we knew where they were hiding? I thought that it could explain why he was taking risks that exposed him outright for what he really was, but still, I hoped that he didn't. We needed to get in and get those kids, fast, before we lost them again.

An idea then struck me, and I glanced up at Beck. "Change of plans. We're not bringing the dead back to Jeff, but I've got an idea on what to do with them."

Beck didn't say anything. He was probably waiting for me to tell him more, and for a moment, I couldn't find the words. My brain was too jumbled, weeding through the new opportunity, trying to find the flaws and the risks, mapping out the details.

When I finally got it out, I'd expected Beck to have an objection because my idea was rocky at best. But he didn't object. He actually seemed excited about the new plan, which was a serious relief, and when I finished, he'd gone back to fill in the rest of the team, leaving me at the picnic table with my cellphone in hand. I needed to know if I'd have Tommy and Chris for this, and there was really only one person that could tell me that.

So I made the call, even though I seriously didn't want to.

"Aidan." His voice was as harsh as a whip slapping against my skin. "Not a good time, son."

"Never is with you, Dad," I said, my phone jammed in between my shoulder and ear as I climbed off the table and started to pace. "But you're going to make time for this call."

He made a noncommittal kind of noise that I knew meant *perhaps*. It was the noise he always made when I demanded his time just before he blew me off.

I sighed. "You'll make time, Dad, or I'll get Mom involved. I'm sure she'd be interested to hear that you called Tommy and Chris away this morning."

"What do you need?" he said, rushed. "Make it quick." He sounded mildly annoyed at me, most likely for pulling the Mom card, but I didn't really care. It worked, and that was all that mattered.

"Tommy and Chris back would be nice," I said, and I maneuvered the phone from its place on my shoulder to my other ear. "If I remember your note correctly, it said they were mine until I was ready to give them back."

"I didn't need them here when I wrote the note," he said. "That changed yesterday."

I stopped pacing and jammed a hand into my pocket. "So you weren't even going to tell me?"

"Obviously, I didn't need to tell you, did I?"

"I thought you actually wanted me to succeed here."

"I do want you to succeed."

"Why'd you pull them out then?" I asked, trying to keep the emotion from my tone. It wasn't working. I could hear the hurt and the anger in my voice, and I was sure he could hear it, too. "You know damn well what I'm facing here, and you know I need them."

"Because," he said, "you're not the only one with problems. I've got a couple rogue wolves here that need dealing with."

"You've got to be shitting me," I blurted. "You called them away to deal with a couple rogues?"

"Pack before blood," he said. "It's always been that way. Always will be. It's not personal."

"Pack before blood," I echoed. I closed my eyes because I felt his words slice through me, and even a deep breath didn't set me right. How many times had he told me that? I couldn't even begin to count. It was pack before blood at my graduation. Pack before blood when my aunt — his sister — died. He hadn't shown at the funeral or my graduation because it was always pack before blood with him. Always. The thing was, the pack hadn't needed him then, but my mom and me, we'd needed him.

It was true. The pack was important, and in the end, I'd always pick what was best for the pack, just like the team had when it came to Jared. Except with my dad, he chose pack even when they didn't need him. And he always would. It was his escape from uncomfortable situations.

"That's never going to change, son," he said. There was a beat of silence, and when he spoke again, his tone was even harsher. "When Tommy shows up there, have him escorted back to me. My enforcers need a word with him."

"What are you talking about?" I asked and started to pace again. "What the hell did he do?"

"He refused to come home," Dad said coolly. "Dropped Chris off at a gas station, said he was done. He turned his back on his pack when he was needed and defied a direct order from me."

"So you're saying he refused to leave me to help you deal with your stupid rogues, and you want to kill him for it."

"That's what I'm saying."

I laughed once. He meant it, and it left me wordless and stunned. Twenty years of service and my father was going to have Tommy killed because he'd decided to help me. There was no way I'd turn my back on him. Not when he was in shit because of me.

There was really only one thing to do, and that was to lay claim before my father could carry out his asinine execution plans, even if the idea of adding Tommy to my pack wasn't one that gave me a warm fuzzy feeling. "Good thing you're not his alpha anymore," I said. "He didn't have to obey you."

"Aidan ..."

"Like you said, pack before blood," I said, cutting him off. "He joined my team. He's part of my pack. If you really want to take him back for your ridiculous prosecution, my mate and I will consider sitting down and discussing it with you and Mom, but I'll tell you now, Jade has a soft spot for Tommy. She won't be handing him over to you." I wasn't entirely sure if that was true, but I knew Jade, and I knew, just knew that she wouldn't hand Tommy over whether she liked him or not.

"If you protect him, son, I'm done with you," Dad said, without a trace of emotion. "You sure you want that?"

"Yeah, Dad, I do," I said. "You were done with me years ago. What I do with Tommy won't change that." I sighed, shaking my head. "You take care of yourself, Dad." And with that, I hung up. It wasn't the first time he told me he was done with me, but right then, I decided it would be the last. And surprisingly enough, I was okay with that.

I fired off a quick text to Tommy: *Talked to my dad. Welcome to the Dog Mountain pack, buddy. We'll talk when you get back. Pack is meeting at my place. Moving out soon.*

And as I tucked my phone into my pocket, I found myself wondering if he would make it back before we made our move on the cougars.

CHAPTER 13

JADE

The backyard was mostly deserted, with only Mark lurking nearby, watching me and the women who'd come with Erika. The air was crisp and clean, and leaves covered the grass in a layer of reds and oranges and greens, with only a few stragglers left clinging to the trees. Erika kicked at them, tossing the ones by her into a small pile, while I waited a little impatiently for her to get to whatever it was that she needed to tell me.

I was feeling a little on edge. After they'd barged into the house, they'd made a point about making sure Aidan wasn't home. Erika claimed that it was a woman's thing they needed me for and that they'd really prefer to talk to me without the male alpha and the team listening in, but my gut (and my inner-wolf) didn't believe her. Hence, the reason for Mark's lurking.

The other females hung around by her — all pack members. There was Whitney, a woman about my mother's age, with silky blond hair that hung past her shoulders and warm, inviting blue eyes. There was Kristen and Stacy, sisters, both in their late twenties, only a year apart. They kept their gazes respectfully dropped, waiting patiently, with their hands clasped behind their backs. There was also Laura, who I didn't know well. She was a newcomer to Dog Mountain, only been here for about nine months, and I thought it was probably the pack that had drawn her to our small town. And then there was Jo — short for ... well, I honestly didn't know what it was short for, but I thought it must be short for something — standing right beside Erika. She was the only one who constantly held my gaze. Her eyes were light green, and they were laughing, kind eyes that made me feel like she held all the secrets of the world and she was dying to tell me them.

I shuffled my weight to my right foot, as I surveyed them. I was a bit surprised that none of the women Erika brought were our age, and I didn't know what or if that meant anything. Erika typically clung to the pack members who were still in school, and it felt ... off that she was here without any of them.

"Erika, she's not going to wait forever," Jo said. Her voice was like bells, and it sounded as kind as her eyes looked. It was sweet and encouraging and full of mystery, and it washed away some of my unease by just hearing the sound. "It would be better if we had her support with this."

Erika said nothing.

"What's wrong?" I asked and stuck my hands in my pockets, not because they were cold, but because I felt an unbelievable need to fidget.

"We didn't say that anything was wrong," Jo murmured in that sweet, bell-like tone, but this time it didn't chase away the sense of foreboding that was starting to settle in my bones.

"You don't need to say it," I muttered. There were times, like this one in particular, that I hated being a werewolf. "I can smell your nerves. You all are on edge. Is it me? Am I that unapproachable? I know the males had issues at first, but I thought you all were okay with me."

Erika groaned and cut me a dirty look. "Sorry if I seem a little nervous, but the last time I stood in front of you like this, you stripped me of my title." She didn't sound sorry, not even a little, and I really hadn't expected it, but suddenly, I felt bad for her.

"I needed you, Erika," I said and shook my head. "I don't know why, but I trusted you. God, I even liked you, and you lied to me." I wanted to say so much more, but I didn't. Now was definitely not the time, so instead, I asked, "Who's looking out for you today?"

"You mean who's babysitting me, right?" Her tone was sarcastic, and I gave her a look that clearly told her to cut it out. "Um, no one," she continued, more cautiously. "With everything going on, I guess you just forgot or whatever."

Crap! I felt my eyes widen. How could I forget something like that?

I opened my mouth, about to apologize, when Erika said, "It's okay. I'm good. The pack has mellowed out a lot since you and Aidan mated, and I made some friends."

"I can see that," I said, not sure of what else to say. The truth?

I was feeling crazy guilty. Erika might not have been someone I actually liked, but she was still part of the pack, and it was me who'd put her in a compromising position by stripping her of her title. There was no excuse for my forgetting to assign someone to watch out for her, even if she was trying to brush it off as if it weren't a big deal.

"Erika came to us yesterday," Jo offered after a second of silence. "She had some ideas on this werecougar mess. Some really good ideas."

"Oh, yeah?" I didn't mean to sound dubious. Honestly, I didn't. It just came out that way. I was sure that Erika could have good ideas. Really, I was. It was just, well, okay, maybe I was holding onto a little bit of a grudge.

Erika glanced vaguely in Mark's direction and then back to me. "Can you get rid of him for a few minutes?" Her voice was barely a whisper, and even with my sensitive ears, I almost missed what she said.

My first thought was to say no, but my gut, well, it was telling me that I needed to hear her out. "Mark," I called over my shoulder, "can you send someone to the store? Mom's going to freak if she doesn't get that stuff for breakfast."

Mark didn't look happy, but he did what I asked. With a jerk of his chin, he took off to the front of the house.

Once he was out of sight, I closed the ten-step distance between the females and me. When I stood in front of her, Erika offered a ghost of a smile and murmured, "Thank you."

I offered up a smile of my own that I hoped looked somewhat sincere and questioned gently, "So what's this idea?" Up close, I could see how tired she looked. Her eyes were ringed with gray shadows, and her complexion was paler than normal.

Erika hesitated for a second, took a deep breath, then blurted, "Well, yesterday when I was with Dom, he made this comment about how he didn't get why your dad hadn't brought more women in for his pack yet, and it got me thinking, maybe he hasn't told them that they won't be getting any of our wolves."

"Okay," I said. The sense of foreboding was coming back full force. "I'm not sure I like where you're going with this."

"Just hear her out, Jade," Jo said, smiling. She looked sideways at Erika, raising her eyebrows. "Go on, doll. Tell her your idea."

Erika closed her eyes, swallowed hard, and then opened them again. She looked a little surer of herself, and firmly she said,

"I thought that if they were still waiting for us, then maybe we should go to them."

"You want to go to them," I stated, not sure I understood. I looked around from one to the other and shook my head. They all seemed excited about this.

"I heard Beck talking last night," Erika said and made a face. "The children ... the little girl. How old do you think she needs to be before they ..." she broke off, swallowing hard and blinking fast. "I wasn't sure if I wanted to do this until then. Now I know I don't have a choice. I have to help. And I will any way I can."

"We'd make one hell of a distraction," Stacy interjected. "Just picture the six of us going in and shifting in front of all those men. I bet it would buy enough time for the team to get the kids out."

Okay, I had to admit that it was actually a pretty good idea. The women could go in. Strut around a little after shifting. It would definitely cause a distraction. But, Jesus, they could get hurt, or worse, they could actually end up in those cages if anything went wrong.

"The team, Aidan, they won't agree to this," I said carefully, not wanting them to think I was blowing them off. "You all know that, right?"

"They will if you're backing it," Laura countered, and I thought that she was entirely wrong on that.

"I think you all believe I hold more power over those boys than I actually do," I said, not unkindly, but with undeniable disbelief. "But," I huffed out a breath, "let's say you're right, and I can convince them, which just to be clear, I'm not saying I will, how do you plan on getting out of there once you're in?"

"The pack," they chorused excitedly.

I looked at them closely. God, they were serious. "Not much of a plan there."

"But it is," said Whitney. "We'll already be in there. When the team is done getting the kids out, the rest of the pack can move in with them. We can attack from both inside and out. It's perfect."

I settled my gaze on Erika. "Why are you doing this?"

"I screwed up," she said simply. "You gave me a second chance, and I want to prove that it wasn't wasted."

"Hey." Mark rounded the corner of the house and stalked over to us. He took one long look at me and asked, "You okay?"

"Yeah," I said, but I wasn't. I felt sick. A little light-headed and nauseated and really, really tense, which I totally blamed on worrying about what was going to happen as the day progressed.

And it didn't help that I was starting to get a hunger headache. Maybe Mom was on to something with the frantic breakfast cooking.

Mark gave me one of those *I know you're lying* looks, but thankfully he didn't call me on it. "Aidan just called," he said. "He's on his way." He looked around our little group and smiled wickedly, if not conspiratorially, and right then, I had a sinking feeling that he'd overheard at least part of our conversation. He then confirmed it. "Just so you know, your idea is the best one I've heard yet." There was a mix of amusement and awe in his voice. "If you're sure about it, I'll back you."

"Mark," I snapped. I really wasn't sure that I wanted to encourage them in this plan. "They could get hurt."

"Yep, but they could get hurt when we attack whether or not they act as a distraction," Mark said and turned back to the house.

No one noticed the sound of the footsteps clomping on the deck until it was too late.

CHAPTER 14

AIDAN

"This doesn't feel like a good idea," Dominic muttered again, looking out over the parking lot.

Looking back on it, I thought I probably should have known that Dominic wouldn't be fully on board with my plan. I'd admit it; there were a few problems with the whole thing. The main one, and the one that I thought Dominic was probably having the biggest problem with, was that I planned on bringing the entire pack with us. That would leave Dog Mountain and the humans within it completely unprotected while we were gone, which might not be the best idea since Jeff had sent cougars into town twice within the last twenty-four hours. But I was taking precautions against another attack — sort of.

The second one was returning the two cougars from the diner still breathing. I knew that was a risk. It would give us two more to fight against, but really, it was the only idea I had to gain access to their location without starting an immediate war. We needed to get the kids safe first, and my hope was that returning the dead with the living would make us look like we were trying to achieve some sort of peace.

"Dom, Jeff sounded really off," I said, looking over at him. "We need to act now." *Off* didn't really describe the desperation I'd heard in Jeff's voice, but I was trying a different approach, one that I seriously hoped Dominic would get, because flat out telling him that Jeff was desperate hadn't worked.

Dominic shook his head in disagreement and said nothing.

It had been about fifteen minutes since we'd made the calls for the pack to gather, and we were still waiting for a handful to arrive. Beck stood a good ten feet away from us, with Craig to his left. Pack members huddled around them, and Beck talked to them; a pep talk of sorts, except, it really wasn't all that peppy. It sounded more like a crash course on how to take someone down quickly. To him, efficiency seemed to be the key to killing, and the pack was eating it up, nodding and asking questions, seeking clarification on tactics. It was impressive and more than a little weird to see an enforcer dishing out the trade secrets, but damn, I was glad for it. Anything that could help prepare them, even if it might be a risk giving out those secrets, was worth it in my mind.

"What exactly is it that you don't like about it?" The question came out more annoyed than I'd meant, but what Dominic didn't seem to be getting was that I was also worried, really worried. Things could go wrong, and I wasn't naive enough to think that we could just charge in there, kill them all, and come out unscathed. Knowing that didn't leave me with a good feeling and having him doubt my plan made it even worse. In fact, I was feeling pretty low.

"I don't like any of it." He made a harsh buzzer kind of sound, and his eyes drifted back to the pack. "Tell me you've at least run this by Jade, and she's all in on it."

I drew in a deep breath and kicked at a random pebble. "Not yet," I said, and yeah, I sounded just as guilty as I felt. "But she'll be on board." Or at least I hoped she would be.

Dominic sighed and gave me a look. "Hope you're right," he said, and then he walked away.

I frowned and ran both hands through my hair, watching Dominic make his way over to Landon. He was off to the right, gathered under a large oak tree with two other pack members. They were huddled closely, listening intently as Landon prepped them on what they needed to accomplish.

As soon as the last few arrived, a scouting team, headed up by Landon, would take off, and the rest of us would head to my place to wait for their confirmation that all the cougars, or at least most of them, were at the hunting camp. I hated wasting time, but I couldn't take the entire pack away without ensuring they were all there. It would be risky and way too reckless with Jeff acting so unstable. I'd figured he'd make a move once Jade and I were mated; I just never thought it would be something like this, something so erratic and unplanned. He'd never struck me as the desperate type. Clearly, I'd read him wrong. But then, with Jade's freak-out yesterday, I guessed that was enough to push him over the edge.

It was surely enough to make him aware that we'd never been playing into his game.

I took my phone out of my pocket and woke the screen. 10:05. It felt like it should have been a hell of a lot later. Only two hours ago, we'd been sitting at the diner about to have breakfast and trying to figure out what to do with the team. Those two hours felt like a lifetime ago.

This is going to work, I thought. *It has to work.*

Fall in Dog Mountain really was beautiful. Even with most of the leaves fallen from the trees and scattered on the ground, the area was full of browns, greens, oranges, and reds. *Nature at its finest moment*, I thought. The air was chilly, but warmer than first thing this morning. There was a good fall breeze pushing through the parking lot, and the sun was out full force, bringing out a shine in the thawing asphalt.

I looked back at my phone and scrolled through my contacts, looking for Mark's number. I thumbed the screen and brought it to my ear when I found it. He answered on the second ring and said, "Tell me you're on your way here."

I laughed once. "That doesn't sound encouraging, Mark," I said. "I was really hoping that it would be safe to show my face there by now."

Mark made an exasperated sound. "Depends on what you mean by safe. Jade told Pam everything, and Pam deals with stress by cooking."

"That doesn't sound so bad." And it didn't, mainly because I was starving. Food would definitely be a good thing right now, and Pam's cooking was amazing. Actually, hearing she was working out her issues by cooking was probably the best news I'd gotten all day.

"Dude, you're going to need to buy another freezer for all the leftovers, and you won't have to cook for months."

That made me laugh. Hard. "It can't be that bad."

"I'm not joking," Mark said. "I just had to send the two guys that came with us to the store for more food. She's cooked everything you had. And that's not all. Erika showed up with five other females demanding to talk to Jade. She's outback with them now."

"Erika's at my house with Jade." It wasn't really a question, more of a stunned statement.

"Yep and those women are all hyped up about something."

That scared me a little bit. Erika and hyped-up wasn't a good combination. Add Jade, Marcy, and Pam, all totally stressed out, and then add another five women to the mix. Well, that sounded like a disaster just waiting to happen. And it was with that thought that I remembered that I never did ask Dominic about the way he'd been watching Erika at the funeral home yesterday.

"Who's supposed to be watching her today?" I asked him, surprised that my voice sounded calm because I sure as hell wasn't feeling it.

"Not sure," Mark said. "Beck dropped her off at the headquarters this morning before going to meet you."

My jaw clenched, and I felt a bud of anger bloom within me. "Let Jade know I'm leaving in a few, and Mark, the rest of the pack's coming with me."

"It's happening now, then," Mark said, in a frighteningly steady tone, not at all unnerved with the possibility of killing or being killed. But then, that was the enforcer mentality, protect the pack at all costs.

"Yep, I've got to go," I said hastily and hung up because Landon was walking toward me, and he didn't look happy.

I studied Landon for a beat, trying and failing to get a read on exactly how unhappy he was, then I pushed off the wall and went to meet him. When we were a few feet apart, I jerked my chin and asked, "What's up?"

In the next second, though, it became clear that he wasn't unhappy — he was focused. "We've got to get moving," he said, with false patience. "Where are the other pack members?"

"Seems Beck didn't bother to make sure someone was here to take over the Erika watch before dropping her off this morning," I said very quietly. *Shit*, I was already restless, so was my inner-wolf, and whatever crap Erika was pulling with running to my mate made it so, so much worse. I felt a growl building inside me, the beast clawing at my chest. Jade had enough on her plate dealing with her mom; she didn't need Erika adding to it. "Erika brought them to see Jade."

Landon considered my words and nodded as if my house seemed like a perfectly reasonable place for them to be, and if Erika hadn't been with them, it probably would have been. "What about Tommy?"

"Nothing yet," I said and sighed. "Can't keep waiting for him."

"No, we can't," Landon agreed, but he sounded less than enthusiastic about it. "Would have been good to have him, though. Another trained enforcer ..." He shrugged. "He would have come in handy."

He was right. He would have. I didn't doubt that for a moment, but we couldn't keep waiting. Jeff had already sent two groups of cougars into Dog Mountain since yesterday, and I doubted he'd stop until we'd killed his entire pack, or they killed us.

I was aware of Dominic coming up behind me, and by the anger, I caught in his scent, I figured he was most likely glaring and shaking his head. Landon's eyes slid past me to focus on him, and his fierce, focused expression faltered.

"You ready for this?" I asked him, drawing his attention away from Dominic.

Landon's grin was tight and predatory when he looked back at me. "Always," he said, and I had no doubt he meant it.

CHAPTER 15

JADE

Mark was halfway across the backyard when the creaky front door opened. He seemed to hesitate in his step for a second as if the sound caught him off guard, and it struck me as odd. We were expecting Aidan, and Mark had just sent someone to the store. People on the deck and the door opening didn't seem odd to me, but his reaction to the sound had my inner-wolf doing backflips in my belly and the hair along my neck prickling my skin.

And that was when I realized that I hadn't heard a vehicle, and it was at that moment that Mark started to run.

Things fell together.

It had only been minutes, five at the most, since whoever was sent to the store left, nowhere near enough time to get there and back. And Aidan, he was coming from the pack headquarters, and he'd only just left. Even speeding, it would take ten minutes to get home.

It took me less than a second to put it together, but by then, Mom was already screaming, and so was Marcy, and I couldn't breathe. A chill took hold of me. All my training, all my skills were suddenly just ... gone. Terror wound around me, washing over me and my legs; they just wouldn't work.

Until ... they did.

And I was moving, running for the back door, and my breath was pushing in and out of my lungs in harsh pants.

"No!" Erika got in my way fast. "No, you can't just run in there." She grabbed me, her hand squeezing tightly around my forearm, and she began yanking me backward, further away from Mom and Marcy and the house.

"I have to," I shrieked, digging my feet into the ground and pulling against her hold. Panic gripped me. Mark was already gone. Vanished inside the house, but the screaming was still screeching through my ears.

Wolves surrounded Erika and me. Closing in, circling. There were five of them, and it took me a second to realize through my panic-induced haze that they were the women I'd just been speaking to.

My wolves.

They were growling. Lips curled, razor-sharp teeth bared. Their heads were turned, watching the house as they positioned themselves around me. *Protecting me*, I thought, but as I listened to the screaming, protection was the last thing I wanted. Marcy and Mom, they were the ones who needed protecting, not me.

"Go help, Mark!" There was no mistaking the command in my tone. The wolves didn't hesitate, not even a little. All five of them lunged forward as a unit, tearing across the grass toward the house.

I started to follow, but Erika's hands clenched tighter on my forearm. Tight enough to bruise. "Jade, don't," she pleaded, sounding desperate and scared.

I looked at her hand, the angle she was gripping me from. I took a breath, tried to calm myself enough to think, and as I let it out, I saw it clearly. All I had to do was twist to the right and yank, and I'd be free of her. And that's exactly what I did.

Erika made a gasping pain-filled sound and pulled her hand back, and before she could shake off the tweak I'd caused in her wrist, I was running again.

An overwhelming smell of blood was the first thing I noticed as I ran into the house, and then I noticed the screaming had changed to whimpering. I could hear growling coming from upstairs and slapping and struggling from the kitchen.

The smell of cougar, sour, lemon, cat, with a hint of birch bark, hit me next. My nostrils flared, and I let out a growl as my gaze landed on a man moving through the living room toward me. He was tall and built like a flippin' tank, moving fast.

I didn't have time to shift before he was on me, although with the way my skin was shuddering, I thought my inner-wolf didn't agree. Adrenaline pounded through my veins, fast and hot, and I braced myself for impact.

But he didn't crash into me. The man stopped just before

hitting me, and his hands shot out, curling around my neck, squeezing, and cutting off my air pipe. “I’ve got her,” he shouted.

I didn’t think, just reacted. I let the adrenaline take hold of me and focused it all on my hands, picturing claws sprouting from my fingertips. I felt the rush as my nails lengthened and thickened, and as my partial shift finished, I took a swipe at his eyes.

He let out a feral scream and dropped his hands from my throat. I doubled over, gasping for air.

“You little bitch.” The growled voice hit my ears a second before I was knocked down, and then the man was on top of me, straddling my stomach.

I bucked up and swiped out again with my claws, dragging them down his neck. He struggled to grab hold of my wrists, but I kept bucking and moving, and he kept missing his target, coming up with only air between his fingers as I continued to attack his throat.

Blood dripped down onto me. Onto my face. Staining my clothes. I could hear the wolves in the house. Scrambling claws on the floors. Growls. Snarls. Busy fighting their own battles. Mom was screaming again from what sounded like the kitchen, and I bucked harder. I needed to get to her. I needed to help her.

The man took hold of my left wrist, slamming it down to the floor and pinning it above my head. He grinned and opened his mouth to speak, but he didn’t get a chance to. I swiped out again with my other hand and dug my claws deep into his throat.

His eyes widened as I tore my hand free, and his hands shot up clutching at the wound. He made a gurgling sound. My stomach heaved as more blood fell onto me, and I shoved him off. He fell to the floor, choking on the blood that must have been pooling in his throat from the gashes and tears I’d given him.

I scrambled back and shot to my feet, expecting him to come at me again, but he didn’t. His throat ... God, I’d torn his throat wide open, and he’d stopped choking and gurgling. And he wasn’t moving.

He’s dead, I thought numbly. *I killed him.*

Mark appeared beside me, causing me to jump. I had no clue where he’d come from, my house seriously wasn’t big enough to sneak up on someone, but somehow he had. He looked at the man and nodded what I thought was approval, and then he held a finger to his lips, telling me to keep quiet, and pointed to the stairs.

A man, medium build, sort of bland, with pasty skin, pale hair, and washed blue jeans, chose that moment to pull my mom from the kitchen. He spotted us, dropped his hold on Mom, and he moved faster than anyone I had ever seen. It was so quick that I didn't even see what had happened. One moment Mark was standing beside me, and the next, he was on the ground. The man went with him, holding him down with his knee pressed into Mark's throat.

I screamed. I couldn't help it, but it turned out that my scream was the right thing to do. Two wolves, one gray and the other light brown came barreling down the stairs, and I suddenly wished I had screamed when the tank had been on top of me.

I didn't even have time to think of shifting before they were on the man, tearing him from Mark, and as soon as he was free, Mark was on his feet. And the man was screaming and kicking at the wolves that were ripping through the flesh and muscles in his calves and thighs.

There was blood. So much blood, staining the carpet and flinging onto the walls. But the man, he was covered in blood, too. His face, his shirt, and it wasn't all fresh, I realized. It wasn't all his.

Mark stood in front of him for a moment, watching the carnage. His face was blank, absolutely void of expression, but then his eyes flared. In a quick motion, Mark reached out, grabbed the man's head, and twisted, and he stopped screaming.

The wolves let go as the man flopped lifelessly to the floor, and they leaped back upstairs. That was when I noticed that I hadn't moved. Not even an inch. I was shaking, and Mom ... I could hear Mom crying.

"Where's Mac?" I asked Mark. My voice sounded calm. Too calm. *I should be freaking out*, I thought, staring down at a man I'd never met, another dead man in my house. But I wasn't freaking out. I felt numb. Completely and totally numb.

"The other one has her upstairs." Mark's voice was growled, and he was already pounding up the stairs.

I spun, about to follow him, when I heard the front door creak, and my gaze snapped to the man who was filling the doorway. My father.

He scanned the room with a quick, thorough glance, and his face twisted up with rage. "Jesus, Jade. You killed them?" His voice was scary calm, not matching his expression. "What's wrong with you?"

I almost told him that I'd only killed the one, but I caught myself and shrugged instead. "They attacked me, Dad. They attacked Mom, too. I was defending myself, my house, and my mother."

His eyes went to Mom, and they darkened with fury. My eyes slid to her, too. She was a sobbing puddle on the floor, halfway between him and me. I didn't think. I ran to her, placing myself directly in between them, and I snapped my gaze back to him.

We stared at each other in tense, angry silence for a few seconds before Dad spoke. "I'd never hurt you or your mother, Jade," he snapped.

"No, you'd just let your monsters do it for you." My inner-wolf was snarling, begging to be let out, but somehow, and I really didn't know how I held her back.

"Jade, I'd never ..." He sighed. "Aidan, he's not thinking clearly. We came here to reason with him. I swear. No one was meant to get hurt."

I said nothing because clearly, that was a lie. Mom and Marcy wouldn't have been screaming if that were true, and there wouldn't be two dead men on my living room floor.

He must have taken my silence as some kind of an invitation because he raised his hands as he stepped into the house, inching the front door shut behind him. "All I've ever wanted was to join our packs, Jade. Wolves and cougars, and more. We could all live together, work together. We could be unstoppable. And Dog Mountain, with the pack living out in the open like they do, it's the perfect place to start. I'm not the monster you think I am."

I laughed, a shocking sound that just blurted out even though I tried really hard to swallow it. "Don't lie to me. The wolves only exposed themselves because of your pack. To keep this town safe from your cougars."

He shrugged. "Times change. We don't care about getting our territory back. That's not what's important now. Uniting shifters is."

"Dog Mountain has never been yours," I spat, not even bothering to acknowledge the rest. There was nothing he could say that would make me consider letting my pack join him and his cougars. I was so sure that it wasn't worth the breath to refute it.

"It was." He dropped his gaze from mine, and I swore he almost looked sad. And if he hadn't glanced back up at me right then, I would have believed he was, but his eyes gave him away. They were cold and flat and unfeeling. "Over one-hundred years ago now, but it was. We were pushed out when the werewolves settled here."

"I don't believe you." It would have been a scream, except that I couldn't get the breath to make that happen. My lungs were just as numb as the rest of me, and I found it hard to pull in any air.

Dad's face flushed an angry red. "Look at what Aidan's doing to us! Look at what he's turned you into. A killer. Tiffany. Jared. They're both dead because of you. And you've just taken two more lives. This is Aidan's fault. All of it. He's turned you against me."

"Get out," Mom said in a small, broken voice. "Just get out." She was still crying, soft, small sobs, and she was still tucked behind me, sitting on the floor right where the man had dropped her.

If Dad heard her, he didn't let on. "Jade, I love you. Please help me. I can't lose my daughter. Please." He stretched out a hand to me, and damn, but I wanted to take it. For half a second, I hesitated. He sounded so sincere, so desperate, that I really wanted to believe him. And I thought he knew that because he smiled a little and took a hesitant step toward me as he continued with his plea. "You're an alpha of this pack. You have his scent now. You can help stop all of this."

I was vaguely aware of the others filing into the living room, and I thought they must have killed the other man that was upstairs because it was really, really quiet in the house suddenly. Only breathing and heartbeats and soft, breathless crying were left.

I swallowed hard. Dad had that look on his face. The one that was always there when I was upset. It was the one that made me want to rush to him and jump into one of his bear hugs. But when I looked into his eyes, really looked, they were still flat, unfeeling, and my heart broke all over again.

"The women ..." My throat clogged up as tears bit at my eyes. I watched him, waiting, desperately wanting him to explain that. It was horrible, but I thought I would have taken anything at that point. Anything to make my heart stitch back together. If it meant that I could keep my dad, mate, and pack. For that sick, twisted second, I thought I would have taken any explanation no matter what it was.

But he didn't have the courtesy to look even a little sorry as he said, "I've been trying to change that."

As it turned out, I wouldn't take just any explanation.

"I've heard," I said. Bile rose up my throat. "Wolves heal faster, right? Less of a chance of us dying on you."

Dad's face went red again, and when he spoke, it looked as if it were a struggle for him not to shout. "Jade, where did you ..."

He didn't get a chance to finish. A savage cry split through the room, and Erika launched herself at him. She shoved him back a step and then cocked her arm back and punched him. Her fist connected with a meaty slap, and he fell back, landing with a thud.

"Don't you dare try to deny it, you bastard!" Erika shrieked. "I was there. I recorded your meeting with Tiffany. We've all seen it! We have proof!"

Erika closed the few steps to where my dad had landed and stood over him. She was vibrating, her hands clenched tight, and her stance, well, she looked as if she were about to kick him.

"Erika!" I shouted. Adrenaline rushed through me — hot and raw. My scent gathered in the air, my imprint heated, and my inner-wolf began to fight me for control. My skin started to shudder, and I knew, just knew, if I didn't pull it together, I'd end up a wolf, and that would not help this situation. I swallowed hard and forced every bit of command I had into my tone as I said, "Enough!"

I wasn't entirely sure if it was Erika I was trying to command or if it was my inner-wolf, but both listened. Erika slid back a step but never took her eyes off my dad, and my inner-wolf backed down, letting me take the lead.

"Why are you doing this, Dad?" My voice came out whisper soft, and I cleared my throat loudly. "The attacks ... the women ... why? I need you to tell me why!"

He held my gaze, and his face contorted with frustration. "I already told you, Jade. I want the shifter community to come together."

"That explains nothing!" I sucked in a breath, trying to rein in my building fury. "Those women weren't shifters. They had nothing to do with your little plan."

"Those women kept my pack happy," he spat, glaring up at me with something that looked a heck of a lot like hatred.

My eyes blurred and prickled. It was at that moment that I realized my father was beyond saving. He was gone. Completely and totally lost within his delusional thoughts. "I don't even know who you are anymore."

"Jade ..." Dad started, but I didn't let him finish because I honestly didn't think I could take any more of his lies.

"You've still got time to run, Dad," I said. "Aidan's on his way home. You better do it while you can. He'll know you were here, and he'll come after you. So run and don't stop because he'll keep hunting you. And you know what? I'm not going to stop him anymore."

"Jade," Erika started to protest, and I held up a hand, stopping her.

I glared at my father and said, "You have three seconds before I let her kill you."

Dad's mouth opened and then closed. He wiped some blood from the corner of his lips and said, "You're making a big mistake, Jade." And then he shocked the hell out of me.

He shifted.

And it wasn't into a big cat.

He shrunk in size, foot by foot. Bones broke, and wings, big feathery wings, sprung from his back.

I blinked, and when my eyes opened again, a hawk hovered in front of me. He beat his wings a few times slowly, holding in place, and then he flew out the back door, which was still wide open.

CHAPTER 16

JADE

It took another three minutes for Aidan to show up after my father flew — *oh my God, he flew* — away.

Mark and I had ushered everyone outside, away from the death and the blood, and that was where we were waiting when Aidan drove up. He wasn't alone. Car after car pulled up into the driveway and onto the grass, and soon our whole front yard was filled with pack members.

Three minutes too late to help.

Aidan got out of a car, so did Beck. He was looking at Beck, laughing at something he'd said. He glanced at the house. His eyes caught mine. He smiled, waved, and then his smile turned scary, somehow. It was all sharp edges and contorted curves. Forced. Wrong. His gaze darted to Mom, sitting on the steps with Marcy huddled in her arms. Then to Mark standing behind them with a hand on Mom's shoulder. Then to Erika and the other women, standing on the grass off to the left of the porch.

His nostrils flared; I thought he was probably catching the scent of the enemy, or maybe he could smell how freaked out we all were. His brown eyes came back to me, and his face went blank, completely and utterly blank, except for his eyes. His eyes were filled with emotion, so much emotion that they were almost scarier than his smile.

"Jade, are you okay?" His voice was hesitant as if he really wasn't sure how to assess the situation. I was sure it looked a bit strange, all of us hanging out in front of the house. I was sure he could see the blood splattered on most of us, and Marcy and Mom were sobbing quietly.

No, I'm not okay. I just saw my dad change into a bird, and there are dead werecougars in my house. That's what I wanted to say, but what I did was shrug, and my voice was all wrong, small and sad and weak, when I said, "I think so."

Aidan took a step, and then he was running, colliding into me, locking me in a breathtakingly tight embrace, so tight that I couldn't even get my arms loose and hug him back. "Tell me you're okay," he said. His voice was tight and growled, and his grip got impossibly tighter.

People were moving around us. Opening the door, going into the house. Growls. Voices. Some shouted. Some whispered. It was suddenly loud, really loud, and it wasn't until Aidan loosened his grip and I snapped my gaze up that I realized I hadn't told him what he wanted to hear.

"I'm okay," I said, and damn, but there were tears in my voice. I swallowed hard and blinked fast, and my voice (thankfully) was stronger when I tried again. "We're all fine, but um ..." I bit my lip and looked to the front door. I opened my mouth, about to tell him what had happened, and probably more importantly, I was going to tell him that I'd let my father get away, but what came out was completely different. "I think we need a new bed, and we definitely need to rip out the nasty carpet in the living room. They're both covered in blood, and, um, there are kind of three dead cougars in human form in the house."

He cupped my face in his big, warm palms and brought my eyes back to his. "Don't care about the bed or the carpet, sweetheart," he said, a small smirk playing at the corner of his lips. He shook his head as if he couldn't believe I was worried about those things. "I don't care if the whole house needs to be torn down and rebuilt. You are the only thing that matters to me." And then he kissed me, and it was full of passion and fear and need, and I was clutching onto him, and him onto me, and for those few seconds, I completely forgot that the pack was all standing by.

But then it ended, and he decided to let me breathe again, although it was a ragged breath at best. He brushed his thumbs across my cheeks, and his expression changed to serious. "Tell me what happened," he said, and with those four words, reality came crashing back.

I told him everything.

Mom put her overcooking to use. With Dominic's help (she refused to go back into the house, not that I blamed her), they fed the pack the food she'd already cooked. They'd found a long, plastic folding table in the garage, along with what I thought had to be a year's supply of throwaway plates and cups and set it up in the backyard. It was loaded with a mix of fruit, eggs, bacon, and pancakes. There were also a lot of steamed vegetables, batches of cookies, and muffins, and I even spotted the ground beef that had been in the freezer and all the fixings for tacos laid out.

While they were setting up the feast, Aidan explained why he'd brought the pack along with the two cougars from the diner, who were currently tied and gagged in the garage, home. He had a plan — a plan that was already in motion. And although the plan was no better or worse than Erika's idea, I really didn't know how to feel about him sending Landon out with only two other wolves without even telling me first.

I tried a few times to tell him about Erika's idea, except I didn't think he listened. He was excited and kind of hyper, and he kept telling me how *huge* it was that my dad was a full shifter (not that I had any clue what that meant), but it seemed to explain a lot to him. I also had to admit that even though he was excited and it was kind of hard to keep his attention, I hadn't tried overly hard to make him listen to me either. Replacing one semi-okay plan with another semi-okay plan didn't make a whole lot of sense, and Aidan was pretty busy trying to organize everyone, so yeah, I didn't really try too hard to get it out.

When Aidan went to help pull the dead from the house and load them in the truck, I snuck away. I needed a moment, or maybe ten, to pull myself together. I felt pretty shaky and really confused, and I was just plain tired. Tired of fighting. Tired of being scared. I was also tired of caring about what happened to my dad.

Numbness would be better, I thought. And right then, I was also feeling pretty numb.

I was standing on the back porch watching my wolves practice their fighting techniques when I felt his hands grip my hips and his chest press against my back. It was a familiar scene in front of me. One I'd participated in countless times, except it had been Jared barking out the instructions, not Beck and Craig, and I'd been the wolf getting my butt kicked.

Aidan's breath was warm against the back of my neck, sending small shivers along my skin. His hands rested lightly on my hips, holding me close against him. He didn't say anything for a long moment, and when he did, it was a whisper in my ear. "How are you holding up?" he asked. He seemed a little calmer, but I was pretty sure he was just trying to mask the excitement he was feeling for my benefit.

"I think I'm pretty much numb," I said, and then, not wanting to explore that topic any further, I continued with, "Thankfully, Mom won't go back into the house, so the cooking has stopped. And the pack's eating everything she already made, so it looks like we won't have to go shopping for a freezer."

Aidan chuckled, a deep, throaty sound that made my knees soft. "I have some good news for you," he murmured as his lips grazed the side of my neck with gentle presses that made my stomach flutter a little.

"Oh, yeah," I said. "What's that?"

He leaned back against the house, pulling me with him. "The team and I are good."

I tilted my head back to look at him and rolled my eyes. "Yeah, I noticed that." And I had, pretty much the moment he'd gotten out of the car and I saw him laughing at something Beck had said. I didn't think I'd ever seen Aidan laugh with one of the enforcers, and I knew I'd never seen one of them try to make him laugh. But them getting along (even if it was awesome) was not really important. Not after finding out my father was not what I thought he was.

Silence fell, and I leaned back, resting my head against his shoulder. I felt sick to my stomach and tired, really, really tired. I tried hard to stay relaxed against him, but cold panic kept jerking at my muscles. I knew, just knew, that he had to hate me for letting my dad go. How couldn't he? If I were him, I'd probably hate me, too. And once his hyperness wore off, he would. I was sure of it.

My hands were shaking, so I folded my arms across my chest in an attempt to hide it. I pulled in a breath, let it out, and broke the silence. "Tell me I didn't screw up."

Aidan actually laughed. "You're kidding me, right? Of course, you didn't screw up."

"Now say it like you mean it," I shot back, shocked, and well, it hurt, like a lot, that he was laughing at me. I tried to wiggle out of his arms, but he held on, his hands moving from my hips to coil around my waist with relentless strength.

"You found out that he can shift into more than just a cougar," he said, an animated pitch coming out in his voice. "That's something, Jade. It's huge, actually. A piece we didn't have before. It explains so much. Like why I couldn't pick up his scent. He's not just one animal. He could be any of them. All of them. It confuses the smells, hides them, and changes them. I should have figured it out. We had a full-blown shifter in my dad's pack when I was seven. If anyone screwed up, it was me. Again."

I wasn't entirely sure what he was talking about, but I knew he was trying to be reasonable, trying to make me feel better. And it was a super nice gesture. It just sucked, though, that it didn't help my trembling hands. "For the record, I'm not sure what you're talking about with the more than one animal smell thing, and I only found out that he could do that because I let him walk away."

Aidan didn't try to explain the animal/smell thing. Instead, he gave me a little squeeze and said, "He's your dad, sweetheart, and your mom was here. I imagine that if it were my dad and my mom was there, I'd do the same thing."

"No, you wouldn't," I said. I swallowed a bubble of panic and tried really hard to make my voice sound reasonable, just like his, and when I spoke again, I even thought I succeeded, sort of. "You hate your father."

"But I love my mother." Again with a reasonable tone. "On the plus side," he continued with a smile in his voice, "we now have a good reason not to put off ripping out that nasty ass carpet."

"Yeah, I guess." I was starting to feel drowsy and almost content leaning against him, but it was hard to completely relax with the sounds of the wolves training in the yard. A constant reminder of what was still to come.

Aidan chuckled and kissed the side of my neck, just below my ear. "What was Erika doing here?" He kept it at a bare whisper as if he wasn't sure he'd really meant to voice the question out loud.

"I tried to tell you earlier," I said. "She had an idea."

"Erika." He sounded surprised, and I tilted my head to the side to see his forehead scrunched up. His eyebrows rose as he looked down at me. "Erika had an idea?"

"Yeah." I dropped my head again and rested it on his shoulder, and then with a long sigh, I told him the idea.

Aidan said nothing when I finished, and I wasn't entirely sure what to make of the change in his scent. It was still heavy with that hyper excitement, but there was something else there now, something I just couldn't place, spicing it up.

His arms dropped from my waist, and I slowly turned around. His face was set, deep in thought, and when he met my eyes, he gave his head a little shake and laughed, a startling kind of sound, and said, "I like it."

"You. Like. It," I repeated slowly, narrowing my eyes. "How can you like this idea?" *But I already knew the answer,*I thought *because it really was a great plan.*

"It could work, Jade." He was staring down at me, but I didn't really think he saw me. His eyes sort of hazed over, and his expression intensified to what I thought of as his *thinking face.* He leaned forward and kissed my cheek absently, and then he walked away. He made it about ten steps before turning back and sending me a quick, unreadable glance. "Come on, Jade. Landon's going to be back anytime now. We need to get ready."

I wasn't sure what *get ready* meant, but I followed him on aching legs down the steps and into the yard, figuring I was probably about to find out.

CHAPTER 17

AIDAN

The yard was as busy as a mall before Christmas. Pack members were gathering in clusters, some looked excited and some right out worried, but all of them were here, and they were all ready to move the second Landon got back.

There was a good-sized group of them in wolf form, training with Beck and Craig. They were like drill sergeants, breaking out training exercises over and over. It was amazing seeing the pack work like this. Together. As a unit. When they did, they looked as if they could take down anything in their path. And I was counting on just that.

"Dom," I called and waved a hand for him to come over when I spotted him in wolf form, running through a drill with Luken. They both stopped at the sound of my voice, and Dominic glanced my way, just a quick turn of his head before he deliberately turned his back to me and squared off with Luken again.

I heard Jade stumble down the steps, following me. I glanced over my shoulder as she did a little hop-skip, catching her balance. She shot me a flustered and slightly confused smile and jogged to catch up. "What's up with him?" she asked warily as she reached me.

I cut her a quick sideways look and grinned. "He's giving me the silent treatment, I think. He's not a fan of my plan." I was too wired to really care. Completely wound up. My entire body was buzzing with energy. My hands, my legs, even the inside of my stomach felt like a live wire, sparking and tingling.

"I'm not entirely sure I like it either." She laughed. It was just a little laugh, and it sounded panicked. "I'm also not even sure I know what it is anymore."

I stayed silent, searching the clusters for Erika. My head was just too full to try and get anything out. Jade's dad was a shifter. A full-blown shifter. That was big. Huge. And Erika's plan, combined with mine ... I had to tell her. Had to talk to her. I needed every little detail.

Jade waited for a moment, and then she let out a long, dramatic sigh. "You want me to talk to him?"

"Nope. He'll get over it." I finally spotted Erika tucked away under a tree while I continued scanning the yard. "Come on, we need to chat with Erika." I reached out and took her hand, and together we skirted the yard.

When I'd first met Jeff, I thought something was wrong with me. I felt like I was losing my senses. I'd been going crazy these last few weeks trying to figure out why I couldn't smell his animal. Had he been taking some kind of drug that masked his scent? Or was there some kind of herb he was using? I knew it had to be something, and I knew it wasn't just me. My pack didn't smell the cougar in him either. But the reason had been simple. The reason was his species.

Jade didn't get it. I knew I probably should have taken the time to try and explain it to her better. But really, I didn't know much more than what I'd already said. Shifters, real, full shifters, carried only the scent of the form they were in while they were in it. It had something to do with the multiple animal thing. That's what the shifter from my dad's pack had told me when I was a kid, and even to him, it had been a mystery of sorts. He'd called it nature, but I remember telling him it was magic.

Damn, I couldn't believe I hadn't put it together. It was all there, staring me right in the face. But in my defense, I hadn't come across a full shifter since I was seven, and that was a long time ago.

What Jeff had said about the wolf pack pushing them out of Dog Mountain could very well be true. From what I'd been told about the Dog Mountain pack history, the cougars had been around tormenting them from before Jeff was even born. And Richard had said the same thing before he died. It would explain the bad blood between my pack and his.

I wondered if the cougars even knew what he was. Shifters weren't a common species to come across. But as Jeff told Jade, times change, so maybe they did know. Maybe he'd promised them world domination or some crap like that, and with the rest of the stuff, he'd spewed at Jade about uniting shifters and being unstoppable ... Well, it kind of made sense that they did know. So even though she told him to run, my gut told me he didn't go far.

And that was exactly why Erika's plan was brilliant. With a few tweaks, we could make it look like Jade had a change of heart after seeing her father. She could deliver the females as a peace offering. The first step in uniting our packs. It was perfect.

But really, uniting shifters was a joke. There was a reason why packs didn't mix, especially wolves. We were too damn territorial. Another pack coming in, all it would lead to is one big pissing contest. Sure, we could work together when necessary, but even then, it wasn't an entirely comfortable union, and it typically ended as soon as the job was done.

The whole unstoppable thing was a joke, too. What did he think? We'd just come out in the open and take over the world? Even if he managed to get enough shifters on board, humans would be an entirely different story. Dog Mountain was unique. They accepted us probably because we didn't let our pack business spill too much into their day-to-day lives. But humans as a whole, in big numbers, they'd panic. And they had a whole lot of guns and testing facilities. Shifters, Weres, we'd never stand a chance against human technology when that panic set in.

So what would that leave him? Maybe he'd be able to rule the shifters. Maybe a few were-packs would join in. But in the end, he'd still be nothing. A blip on the map.

Erika was sitting, tucked under a tree, watching Craig's every movement as if it were the last time she'd ever see him, and she was trying to commit it all to memory. As we reached her, Jade squeezed my hand tightly. I didn't know if it was some kind of warning or her nerves, but I rubbed my thumb in small circles on her palm between our clasped hands, figuring it might soothe her either way and said, "Hey, Erika."

Erika startled and looked up at me with wide eyes. "Oh, hey," she said and faked a smile as she glanced between Jade and me before she let her gaze fall back to Craig.

I watched her faze us out as if she'd already forgotten we were there, and I wondered if she knew how damaged she looked. *Probably not.* It was like her heart wasn't just broken but had been torn clean out and was lying at her feet.

Seeing her damaged managed to tamp down my excitement and made me feel like a piece of crap because it was partly my fault that Craig wouldn't speak to her. I let go of Jade's hand, crouched down beside her, and placed a hand on her bent knee. “If you want to talk to him, I’ll pull him out of there. Mark could take over.”

Erika considered it and then shrugged. “Nah, it’d just piss him off.” She noticed Jade looking at my hand and quickly brushed it from her knee. The fake smile made another appearance. “Besides, it’s just hit 11:00. Landon will be here any time now. No point in Craig wasting his anger on me when he could use it fighting.”

I glanced up at Jade. I was completely lost on what to do here. I didn’t know if this was some secret girl code like the word *fine,* which I knew from experience meant anything but *fine*, or if Erika was serious and she really didn’t want to talk to Craig.

Jade watched us for a long second before she slowly bent down and sat beside Erika. She kept her expression carefully still as Erika shimmied back from me. She didn’t want to scare her, I realized.

When Erika stopped squirming, she said, “I told Aidan about your idea.” Her tone was soothing, sweet even, and just as fake as Erika’s smile. “He said he likes it.”

Erika glanced at me and hesitated. “You like it?” She blinked and smiled for real. “Really?”

I grinned, and the excitement started to bubble up again. I was about to tell her and Jade the new plan that was forming in my mind when Craig, his voice growled, asked from behind me, “What’s going on here?”

Right, I thought. He was always watching her, too, even if she didn’t realize it. My grin widened at the stunned look on Erika’s face as her eyes slid past me to look at him.

I glanced over my shoulder and said, “Grab Beck and Mark and tell Dominic to get over his issues and get over here. There’s been a change in plans.”

JADE

It was nearly 11:15 when Dominic finally shifted and joined us. Fifteen long minutes and my heart was still beating wildly in my throat. I wasn’t sure I liked hyper Aidan. Actually, it was kind of unnerving.

Dominic paused at the edge of our little meeting, and when he noticed that Aidan hadn’t waited for him, I thought he looked disappointed for a quick second, but then his closed-off mask fell back in place.

The pack had formed a semi-circle around Aidan, listening as he explained what we would do. Heads nodded. Grunted agreements sounded. They liked it. Really liked it. And it made me feel sick with worried nerves.

I can do this, I thought, swallowing hard. It was a piece of cake, and I wouldn't be alone. The pack would be close by. The women would be with me. *I can do this.*

I was standing off to the side of the gathering with Marcy and Mom. Marcy clung to my hand. She was shaking, her hand trembling within mine. "He's kind of scary focused," she said in a hushed whisper.

"I know," I whispered back because he was. I thought it was more than just focused, though. He commanded attention. He was determined. He was ready for war. And his vibe summoned the same reaction from the pack. Everyone seemed just as ramped up as he was.

"Jade," Beck said, causing me to blink and look up. He gave me a look as if he were expecting me to answer a question.

"Yes?" I said, and I was sure my face was utterly blank. I felt my heart flutter madly with panic that I'd missed something important. "Sorry, what?"

He grinned that *you're a pain in the ass* grin he had just for me. "Are you good driving Jared's old truck?"

The truck was a monster. It was huge. I hated riding in the passenger seat, and I really wasn't looking forward to attempting to maneuver it down a narrow, hardly used dirt road. I swallowed. "I think so. But I want one of you guys with me so my driving it won't be an issue."

"I don't know about that," Mark said. "I think it might look suspicious."

I quickly shook my head. "No, it wouldn't. I'm just there to deliver the goods. And besides," I shrugged, "I'm also the alpha female. It would look suspicious if I went alone. They'd expect me to bring someone, wouldn't they?"

"His new idea is to send you." Dominic's voice was deathly calm, and his eyes sparked. He tilted his head to look at me. "You've only been a wolf for a couple of weeks, Jade. You can't seriously be considering this."

"I'm not going alone, Dom," I said and waved a hand toward Erika and her group. "They're all coming with me. They're the distraction you all need. And I'm going to give them their dead and the two that are still alive. It'll keep them busy while you guys get those kids, and if it doesn't ..."

"Dammit, Aidan!" he shouted, cutting me off and turning his flaring eyes on my mate. "This is crazy!"

"What am I supposed to do, Dom?" Aidan was shouting, too. His hands curled into fists and his face flushed with color. The muscles along his neck were straining against his skin. His inner-wolf was coming out. I could sense it in my bones, and I could smell it in the air. It was like an electrical current, the power of his scent, the raw authority of his gaze, traveling through the space between him and Dominic.

Dominic threw his hands up in the air. "You're supposed to protect your mate!"

"That's what I'm trying to do," Aidan said. "You really think I want to send her in there? Because I don't. I don't want any of you to have to do this. But the only other option I'm seeing is forcing you guys to move. Except when I think of doing that, it makes me sick. I can't walk away knowing the kind of hell this town would suffer through when we leave."

Dominic growled, and I felt a tremor of pure alpha-energy roll off of Aidan. The pack was getting nervous, fidgeting and twitching. His golden eyes sharpened their focus on Dominic, and he took a step toward him.

"Aidan," I said. I dropped Marcy's hand and walked the few steps to plant myself in front of him, trying to block Dominic from his view. I placed my hand on the swell of his pec, putting pressure on it to draw his attention to me.

"Jade." He was aggravated. I could hear it in his voice and smell the heat of it in his scent. He looked down at me, and there was a warning in his gaze, a warning I knew well.

I chose to ignore it, and I waggled a finger at him, grinning. "Don't even try that *I'm the boss* look with me. It is so not going to work, buddy. Not this time."

Aidan let out a growl, low and frustrated, and his eyes flashed brighter. I thought I was probably pushing it, but I couldn't stop myself. I dropped my hand from his chest, put it on my hip, and pursed my lips. "Did you really just growl at me in front of everyone? Not cool, Aidan."

"Jade." It was Dominic this time, and although his voice was gentler than Aidan's, it held the same aggravation in it.

I spun on him and glowered. "Don't you 'Jade' me." My whole

body was shaking, and I couldn't tell if it was from nerves or if I was just plain angry. "You're being ridiculous. I don't need to be protected. I think I've proven that to all of you a few times now."

Someone chuckled, deep and scratchy, from behind me. "I leave you guys alone for a few hours, and you've already managed to piss her off."

I turned on the voice, feeling something close to fury erupting in my belly. "I'm not pissed off," I growled. My words were followed by a gasped in a breath as I focused on who the voice belonged to. Tommy was back, and with him was Landon.

"Yes, you are," Landon said. He was smiling, and he stuffed his hands casually into the back pockets of his jeans. They sagged a little as he did it. I figured they were Aidan's; I recognized the T-shirt as Aidan's, too, and I realized he must have gone into the house and seen the mess and all the blood before coming out here. "You're all flushed pink and scrunchy-nosed. It's your mad face. I know that face."

My head started to spin, and my blood went cold. I looked from Landon to Tommy to Landon again and finally said, "You're back."

Landon suddenly looked serious and cold and wrong. He exchanged a look with Tommy and then one with Aidan. "Yep, I'm back."

CHAPTER 18

JADE

Aidan stood at the truck window, one arm resting on the door frame, as he spoke to Tommy. When I'd said that I wanted one of them to come with me, I'd meant one of the guys from the team. Someone I knew. Someone that knew me. That someone wasn't Tommy, but Tommy was who I got. I didn't exactly think he was a bad choice. He just wasn't my first.

I stood back a few feet from them. That wasn't my choice either, but they needed to talk, and Aidan had asked for a minute. I couldn't fully make out their conversation over the growing buzz of strategy talk coming from the pack, but from the small piece I did catch, I was pretty sure they were discussing the call Aidan had with his father. I didn't know the whole story on that phone call yet, but I did know that Tommy was now an official member of the Dog Mountain pack because of it.

The front lawn had become an unofficial gathering spot for the pack, which meant that there were groups scattered everywhere. Some in wolf form, others still human, but all of them were doing the same thing: getting ready for action.

"You're thinking you're not ready for this," a cool voice said from behind me.

I sighed and turned to look. Dominic. Aidan's beta, and some days he was also one of my best friends, but lately, he'd taken on the role of the biggest thorn in my side. He was watching Aidan with a critical gaze. He didn't look angry anymore, just worn, as if he'd lost a week of sleep in the last few hours. He wore jeans and a light green T-shirt, and the bare skin on his arms was raised with a layer of goosebumps from the crisp fall breeze that was blowing through the yard.

"You need to be sure, Jade," he said. "Because if you're not sure, those women will feel it. They depend on you."

Those women he was referring to were Erika and her new posse. The six of them were making their way to an SUV that was parked right behind the truck I'd be riding in. They were also the group that I'd be leading. My team.

"I am sure," I said, and I was super glad that my voice conveyed that certainty because my belly was all knotted up, and my palms were starting to sweat. The truth was I was a little scared. Okay, that was a lie. I was more than a little scared. I was terrified.

Dominic shook his head, seeing right through my lie. "Your scent gives you away, honey," he said quietly. He took a step toward me, and his blue eyes were steady on mine. "Run me through it. Every step, okay?"

I hoped I didn't look as crazy relieved as I felt. Pain in the ass or not, Dominic knew exactly what to do to help. He always had. Sometimes I thought he even knew me better than I knew myself.

I pulled in a deep breath. "Yeah, okay," I said and pasted on what was meant to be my *game face* and nodded. "My team is up front. The two cougars who are still alive are riding with the girls to make my offer more believable. We stop at one of the two checkpoints on the way to the hunt camp, where Landon left one of the wolves that went with him. The other five teams will stop at the second checkpoint before fanning out and surrounding the camp. The girls will keep the cougars busy while I jump out at the checkpoint to make sure there's been no movement from the hunting camp."

I hesitated and gritted my teeth. The plan was good. I knew that, but putting my females right in the thick of things ... It wasn't sitting well with me. The truth? My biggest fear about this whole thing was that I wouldn't be able to keep those women safe.

"Good," Dominic said, his eyes still holding steady. "What's next?"

"We drive into the center of their camp," I said and swallowed hard. "The girls are going to park off to the side and back a bit. Tommy and I get out first. I explain that we want the feud to be over. I tell them that my dad was right and that we should be allies, not rivals. I give them their dead, and then I give them the girls and the cougars as a peace offering."

God, what if I fail them? My hands were starting to tremble, and I quickly jammed them into my pockets, trying to hide the shakes, but I didn't think I did it fast enough.

Dominic's gaze flicked down to my hands and then back up to my eyes. "By the time you're done giving them over, the kids will be in the SUV and gone, and the rest of us will move in." His voice sounded normal and steady, and I wondered how he did that, considering what we were about to do. Even his expression was calm. "We've got this, Jade."

I wanted to agree with him because I really did believe that this could work. We doubled the werecougars in numbers. We had a strong group. I really thought that it was possible to win this fight. But instead of agreeing, I asked, "Do you think it's a bad idea to go without assigning a head enforcer to lead the attack?" I knew it was something Dominic had been worried about, and I thought Aidan was, too. The rest of the pack had been divided into five groups, which were to be led by Beck, Craig, Landon, Mark, and Aidan. It was Aidan's idea of a quick fix to choosing a head enforcer. Instead, he made them all leaders to their own teams, hoping it would keep them from undermining each other and pulling the pack in a bunch of different directions while we were out there.

Dominic thought about it for a second. "I think what he's done, splitting them up like this, will work." He folded his arms across his chest. "But, Jade, when this is over, you better make sure he deals with it. A team without a head is like a pack without a mated alpha pair. Things start to fall apart."

"I will," I said, with a bob of my head, and I meant it. The last thing we needed was for things to fall apart with the pack again. We'd just pulled them all back together.

Dominic nodded. He looked away, hesitated for a second, and then reached out for me. He pulled me into a hug and held on tight for a long moment before letting go. "You're going to do great," he said, and then he turned and went back to the group he'd been assigned to.

I waited tensely for Aidan to finish up. It felt like time stopped for about a year while I stood there, watching the muscles in his neck and jaw tense and release only to tense up again.

"Hey, Jade," Marcy called, and I glanced up. She shook her hand in an awkward wave as she edged past a group of wolves, who were pacing around restlessly, then jogged over to me.

"Hey," I said. "Where's Trevor?"

She rolled her eyes and pointed off to her left, where a group of four wolves was gathered. "He's over there with Beck, and Beck thinks I'm a distraction, so he made his group shift."

I snorted out a laugh. "You? A distraction? Never."

Marcy didn't laugh, not even a little. She swiveled on her heels to look at me fully. "You know Mom's inside trying to scrub the blood out of the carpet, right?"

"Yeah," I said and looked back at the house. "She tried to convince us to let her come with us. She says she needs to be a part of this. When Aidan told her no, she started to clean, telling us that she had to do something." I felt an angry heat building in my face, and my stomach started to twist in knots again. "She's blaming herself, Mac. She thinks she should have seen through Dad. She thinks she should have stopped him. I tried to get her to stop, and she whipped a scrub brush at me, yelling at me to get out."

"Oh," she said. She started chewing on her lip so hard it was almost white, and then suddenly, she threw herself at me hard enough that I rocked back a step before I caught my balance. I hugged her back, though, as tightly as I could. She smelled of Trevor, musk and a hint of spice, and a layer of vanilla body spray, with a light undertone of bitter anxiety. "Be safe, Jade," she whispered. "Don't do anything impulsive."

I didn't say anything. I really didn't think there was anything I could say to make her feel better. So I just continued to squeeze her tightly, hoping that it would give her some kind of reassurance.

A throat cleared, and we slowly, reluctantly, pulled apart. Aidan. He looked from me to Marcy as if he weren't quite sure if he should be interrupting us just yet. "I've got Tommy caught up," he said. His voice was gentle, and his gaze, patient. His lips curved very slightly. "He's ready to go ... whenever you are."

"I'm just going to ..." Marcy backed up a couple steps and stopped. She looked utterly lost for a second, but then her eyes brightened a little. "I'm going to go finish the last-minute details for tonight and pick up Jared's remains." Her voice sounded faint and torn, and she started blinking fast, but she looked a little less lost as if she'd found a purpose.

"Thank you, Mac," Aidan said gently. "That would be a really big help."

She just shrugged as if to say it was no big deal. But it was. When we got back, it would be good for the guys, for the whole pack, to put Jared to rest because we would be coming back. And I thought she knew that, too.

"Just bring them all home, okay?" she said.

"We will, Mac," he said. "Promise." And I hoped it wasn't a promise that would end up broken.

Marcy nodded and gave us a weak smile before she turned and headed for Trevor's truck. She waved to us from the driver's seat before starting it up, and then she pulled out of the driveway.

Aidan stepped in behind me, and his arms went around my waist. "Time to go," he said roughly. He gave me a hug that was too quick and not nearly tight enough. "Listen to Tommy. Trust him, okay? He'll watch out for you until I can get back to your side."

"I don't like splitting up," I blurted, turning around to look at him. "I really wish we didn't have to do that."

Aidan's face went still and a little too tight, and I realized that he didn't like it either. "Don't think of it as splitting up," he said. "I'm going to be right there with you. We're going to get through this. I promise you, we will. And when we do, we're going to do something boring. Really, really boring."

"You know," I said, fighting to hide the tension in my voice because the last thing he needed was to worry about me when I needed him to worry about everyone else. I even smiled a little. "Boring actually sounds like fun right about now."

He chuckled, and a flash of what looked like relief passed across his face. He smoothed my hair back and leaned down to kiss me. The kiss was soft and sweet, and it felt so much like a goodbye that it made my chest ache and my throat close up. I clung onto him and dug a hand into his hair, holding his mouth to mine. I didn't want him to stop. I didn't want to lose the connection. I didn't want goodbye.

And it worked for a second, but only a second. He took my wrist gently in his hand and pulled it from his hair, and then he pulled back. "This isn't goodbye, sweetheart," he said as if reading my thought. "I'm going to be right behind you. It's going to work out." He leaned in close then, so close that his lips brushed my ear, and he whispered gruffly, "I'll see you soon, sweetheart. Love you."

And then I stepped back, and I felt all jittery and nervous, but I tried really hard to hide it. I even thought I succeeded — sort of. I shoved back my fear, took a deep breath, and I gave him the best game face I could muster up and said, "Love you, too." And with another quick hug, I turned away from him and walked over to the waiting SUV to get my girls ready.

CHAPTER 19

AIDAN

I was smiling. It was a big smile, and I probably looked goofy, but I couldn't stop it. For a second there, I thought Jade was going to crack. The way she'd kissed me. The way she'd clung onto me. It felt scared and uncertain.

I didn't blame her for that. She hadn't been a werewolf long. She was still growing into it, learning her strengths, figuring out who she was within the pack, but feeling her hesitation made me nervous. Maybe she wasn't ready for this. Maybe she wasn't ready to clean out her father's pack.

But then she walked away. And she seemed okay. Confident. Ready.

It was a tremendous relief.

She was standing at the SUV giving the girls a pep talk, and unlike Beck's pep talk to the pack earlier, this one was actually peppy. The women were relaxing. They were even smiling a little.

Erika and Laura broke off from the group and jogged over to the garage. They lifted the door halfway and ducked underneath, and a moment later, I heard their muffled voices as they set the plan in motion.

They were ready.

I glanced back at the SUV. Jade was looking back at me with an intense, warm focus, and for a second, I felt as if I were the only person there. She had a way of doing that when she looked at me. She made me feel as if I were the only thing she saw. As if I were the only thing worth seeing. It was kind of surreal. Even when we were about to attack — and kill — a pack of werecougars, she could still make me feel as if I were *it* for her just by a look. As if I were her home.

The moment didn't last long. Jade gave me an eye roll and then a little chin jerk. The girls had, I noticed, piled into the SUV. Low growls filled my ears, and a throaty, seductive laugh came from behind me. I knew the laugh. I'd heard it before. Erika.

But those growls ... they needed to stop. I spun on the pack, most of who were already in wolf form. "Enough," I said. I let my scent gather and roll off me quickly in a warning, and the growls died down.

"Come on," Erika said, tugging on the tall one's hand. "I've got some friends waiting to meet you in that SUV over there." She batted her lashes and giggled. "I think you'll like them."

The four of them made their way across the yard, and I was a little surprised to see that the cougars didn't seem at all worried about the wolves scattered around them.

Stupid, I thought and wondered how they'd managed to hide from us for so long. But I figured I knew the answer to that. Jeff. He was obviously the brains behind the whole *uniting shifters* thing, and I bet he was the one who'd kept them on the move, jumping locations and hiding in hunting camps. He was also the one who fed their sick addiction.

My inner-wolf paced restlessly within me, just itching for the moment he could tear into these monsters, and as they got closer, it was a struggle to keep him and my steady gaze in place. "Sorry for the misunderstanding, guys," I said. "Hope there are no hard feelings."

"Not a problem," the short one said, wrapping an arm around Laura. "She'll make up for it." He looked around then, eyeing the wolves curiously. "You guys going somewhere?"

I shrugged. "Nowhere, really. Just a run. Wanted to see the girls off before we left. Make sure they didn't give you any problems."

"Why would we give them problems?" Laura asked, mystified. "We volunteered, and honestly, I can't wait to meet them all." Her scent was screaming excitement, mixed with a little touch of nerves. And the cougars were responding to it, although it wasn't in the way they probably should have been. They were breathing it in, nostrils flaring, their scents matching hers. It was perfect. She mimicked Erika's throaty laugh and smiled demurely.

Yep, definitely stupid.

I chuckled. "Glad to hear it." I glanced at the tall one and smiled a little. "You take care of my girls, now."

"We will," he said, and with that, Erika and Laura tugged them over to the waiting vehicle.

I didn't watch them go. I couldn't. My inner-wolf was pushing to get out, frantic to stop them, and I knew that if I tried to watch, I'd wind up doing something stupid that would ruin everything. So I looked to Jade, and she gave me that warm *you're my home* gaze. She smiled. I smiled. She waved. I waved.

And then she jumped into the truck, and it growled to life, and as it started to inch forward, I turned back to my pack.

"Let's get this done," I said and yanked my shirt off. I pulled the button and zipper open on my jeans, letting them fall. Adrenaline hit me hard and fast, the rush of the shift pulsed through my veins, and I let my inner-wolf spring free.

JADE

The drive would have been so much better if Tommy actually talked.

Tommy wouldn't talk to me. I tried everything. I asked about Chris. His response was two words: *gone home*. I tried to go over the plan, he said three words: *you know it*. I even tried to talk about the weather, and all I got to that was a grunt.

I didn't think it was me exactly. After about five minutes into the drive, I decided that he just really wasn't a talker. The problem with not talking, though, was that the silence was killing me. It was giving me way too much time in my head, imagining all the ways that Aidan or Dominic or Beck or Landon or Erika or Laura or any of the pack members, for that matter, could die.

A week ago, I probably would have laughed off the thought of one of us dying by someone outside of our pack as a bad joke, but then Jared died, and even though it was Aidan who killed him, it made us all a little less invincible to me. Because if an enforcer could die, any of us could.

I had to admit, even though I was crazy nervous, it had been a pretty smooth drive so far. We passed the checkpoint without a hitch, and the girls kept the werecougars occupied during the short stop. Things were going exactly to plan. I wasn't really sure what I'd expected, but since we'd accumulated five dead bodies in the last twelve hours and they were in the back of the truck, smooth and uneventful, wasn't it.

I was fidgeting. Wiggling in my seat. Playing with the window.

Anything to try to distract myself. And when Tommy gave me a five-minute warning, I thought my heart was about ready to give out on me. Then, when the hunting camp came into view, I stopped breathing until my lungs were burning, and I was gasping for breath.

"You've got to relax, Jade," he said as he maneuvered the truck slowly into the small, narrow driveway. He sounded bitter, annoyed, and he cut me a quick look. "I'm not going to let anything happen to you."

"I'm not worried about me," I said. My tone was just short of a shout. "I'm worried about those kids and the girls in the car and the pack. I'm freaked out that I'm going to fail them again. I don't care about my safety. I care about them!"

Tommy put the truck in park and shut it off. He looked at me then, a thorough, invasive look that felt as if he saw right through me. He narrowed his eyes and pulled in a few deep breaths, and then, he nodded as if he'd found whatever he'd been looking for. "I won't let you fail them." And he sounded completely sure of that.

I nodded because, well, I didn't have a clue what to say to that. He must have accepted my nod as some kind of agreement because he looked away. He did a quick, thorough sweep of the area, and for a long moment, there was nothing. No movement, no people. Nothing.

The cabin, a rustic-looking log structure, looked empty — almost deserted. If it weren't for the fire pit blazing and what looked like a pig rotating within the flames, I would have sworn no one was here.

The yard, if you could even call it that, was small. A clothesline was strung up, running from one side of the cabin to the nearest oak, filled with clothing and a few picnic tables that looked set for a meal.

I glanced behind us and spotted the girls parked at the bottom of the driveway, off to the side. Erika was at the wheel, scanning the dense forest beside them, and I wondered, briefly, what the others were doing to keep the cougars distracted and in the SUV. But then I felt like throwing up, and I thought it was probably best not to think about it.

They know what they're doing. They wanted to do this. It was their idea.

"Cabin," Tommy said. "The curtains just moved."

I swiveled back around. He was right. The curtain twitched, parting just a little in the center, and then fluttered closed again.

"What do you think they're waiting for?" I whispered. I wasn't sure why I was whispering, but that's how my voice had chosen to work.

"Probably waiting for us to leave."

"Then we should get out," I said and reached for the door handle.

Tommy's hand clamped down onto my shoulder and held me back. "Not yet," he said. "Aidan's team is to your right. I spotted Beck up ahead and Craig to his left. No sign of Mark and Landon yet. We should wait until they come out. Buy the others some more time to get into place."

I snapped my gaze to the right and peered out the window, searching for Aidan. It took a long second before I spotted a flash of his black coat amongst the trees and foliage, but when I spotted him, my anxiety started to melt, and I felt the game face I'd been faking for the last hour fix into place. My inner-wolf began to stir, urging me to get moving, and I looked back at Tommy. "The girls ..."

"They're fine," he interrupted. "There are six of them in that SUV. Only two cougars in there with them. You're not going to let them down. Trust me, we need to wait."

My inner-wolf didn't like that response. She reared up, clawing and pressing against my chest. She didn't want to wait. She wanted to get outside, get things moving, and get back to her mate, and it took a whole lot of effort to force her back into the pit of my stomach. But I managed and gave him a gasping nod. "Okay. We wait." Because it was probably the smart thing to do, right? We didn't even know if all the werecougars were actually in that cabin.

It took another seven long minutes for more movement from the cabin, but this time it wasn't twitching curtains. The door swung open, and a group of men filed out.

And then there were people all around us, circling the truck and the SUV behind us. It felt like a heck of a lot more than fourteen, but with a quick count, I found out it was fourteen exactly.

Someone stopped next to the truck and peered in the window. It was a lean, medium-height man. He was good-looking, too, maybe twenty-five years old, with dusty-blond hair and startlingly bright green eyes. He had a surprisingly friendly smile, considering we had five of his pack members dead in the bed of the truck. And I had no doubt that he knew they were there even though they were covered up in blankets and tarps. I could smell them, and I had all the windows closed. He was even wearing a faded T-shirt with a big yellow smiley face on it.

Not really what I was expecting.

He waved and tapped on the window. His smile grew, and if it weren't for the overwhelming smell of cougar, I would have thought we were in the wrong place.

I pulled in a deep breath as I reached for the door handle, and again, Tommy grabbed my shoulder and stopped me. I sent him a sharp look, and I swore I saw amusement in his eyes. "Slow down," he said. "Just roll down the window and tell him why we're here."

I shrugged off his hand and pressed the bottom for the window to slide down. As soon as it was open a few inches, the man asked, "You lost?" He had a nice voice. Deep and smooth.

That probably shouldn't have thrown me off, but mixed with his friendly smile and the big smiley face on his shirt, it did for a second. And I found myself genuinely smiling back as I said, "Nope. I'm Jade Shaw, and I'm looking for my dad."

CHAPTER 20

AIDAN

Being stealthy in the fall was seriously not an easy task. Dried-up leaves seemed to be everywhere, and each time one of my wolves stepped on them, the crunching sound was deafening. And with most of the leaves now on the ground, the forest felt open, as if there were no coverage, nothing to keep us hidden.

It sucked.

I circled my group along the west side of the cabin, moving in slowly, creeping as quietly as we could. The place felt almost ... abandoned. Through the trees, the yard looked empty. And it was quiet. Too quiet. The only sounds seemed to be coming from us as we moved into place.

But I could smell them. The cougars were here. That bitter lemon and birch bark scent were thick in the air. Suffocating.

There were two barbed wire cages at the side of the building. They were empty, but seeing them, knowing what they were used for, and knowing that I'd sent some of my females here, tied my stomach into knots.

Don't think about it. They'll never get close enough to see the inside of those cages.

Jade and Tommy were already in place. I could just make out their outlines within the truck from my position. It was parked in the narrow-looking driveway, probably twenty feet from the cabin, and behind it, as close to the tree line as it could get, was the SUV.

Up ahead, I spotted one of the other groups, waiting. Beck's light gray coat stood out, in stark contrast with the forest's browns and reds and oranges. I hadn't spotted any of the other groups yet, but I could hear them. A twig snapping. Dry leaves crumbling. They were here, closing in and surrounding the yard.

Minutes passed, and everything was still. It was as if the entire forest were holding its breath. Waiting. Watching.

It seemed quiet, very, very quiet.

Jade and Tommy still hadn't gotten out of the truck. I figured they were probably seeing something that I couldn't. Something that held them inside. Something that kept them waiting.

They had to be in the cabin, I thought. It was the only place for them to hide. If they were in the woods, we would have come across them. We would have spotted them. With so many of us surrounding the camp, I was sure of that.

A dark, weighted feeling gathered in the pit of my stomach, and I fought the urge to growl. If they were in the cabin, the kids would be, too, and I wasn't entirely sure how to get in, grab them, and get them out without drawing attention. I'd been counting on them being out in the open and using Jade and the girls as a distraction to snatch them away.

Another minute passed. And another. And then, the door on the hunting camp banged open, and a group of men stalked out. They fanned out around the truck as another stream of them spilled out of the building, moving toward the SUV.

I kept my eyes peeled, searching for the children. Waiting for them. But things were happening. People were gathering around both of the vehicles. Talking. Arguing.

Jade, Tommy, the girls, they hadn't gotten out yet, but still, I didn't like what I was seeing, and I could tell that the group with me didn't like it either.

A man, not much older than me, approached the truck, and Jade rolled her window down. She said something to him, something that made him stiffen, and his hands curled into fists.

Everyone else froze. The talking, the arguing, all of it just stopped.

Dominic nudged my side and whimpered quietly. He swung his head toward the truck. I knew exactly what he wanted. Damn, we all wanted to move in, but the kids ...

I thought I heard something, and I froze. So did the others. And a half-second later, I knew I heard something. A light, almost delicate, thump, and then another, and then another, all coming from right behind us.

I exchanged a quick look with the others, and as a unit, we pivoted, teeth bared and deadly growls rolling out.

JADE

Dead silence. My stomach lurched. Everyone outside was frozen, staring at me. And that infectious, friendly smile on the guy standing at my window was changing into something not so friendly — something dark.

He leaned in closer to the window, and the look on his face was hard. The door latch popped, and he yanked it open. "Get out."

I glanced at Tommy. He gave me a small nod, and I turned back to the guy. "Um, yeah, sure. Is my dad here?"

"Depends," he said and gestured for me to get out.

"Depends on what?" I asked as I swung my legs around to hop down. I guessed I wasn't moving fast enough for him because his hands circled my waist, and he lifted me out of the truck.

Tommy growled. It was low and rough and fierce, and by the time my feet hit the ground, he was already out of the truck and beside me. His hand closed around my wrist, yanking me away from the smiley face guy.

"Tommy, I'm good," I said, attempting, and failing, to shake off his too-tight grip. "Seriously, let go. I'm good."

He didn't let go but did loosen up a little. They stared off for an angry moment, and I was uncomfortably aware of the werecougars moving in around us. I also thought I heard a whimper coming from where I'd spotted Aidan, but it was hard to be sure. My blood was pumping fast, my heart, pounding in my ears, and my head was starting to get a little fuzzy from the continuous stream of adrenaline that flooded through me as my inner-wolf fought to come out.

"I want to see my dad," I said and tried to sound demanding. It probably would have been more convincing if I wasn't so frazzled. "He told me to come here if I changed my mind."

The guy raised his eyebrows, and his green eyes sparkled with cold amusement. "I bet he told you to kill some of my pack mates and bring them with you, too."

"No," I said shortly, staring first at him, then at Tommy. We exchanged a look that I didn't understand, and I shrugged helplessly. "Look, it was either them or me." I sighed, looking back to the guy. "I didn't have much of a choice. But I figured you guys might want to bury them or something, so I brought them."

"How considerate of you."

I shook my head in response and found myself looking at Tommy again. He turned his head and looked at me briefly, and I hoped he caught the huge *what the hell?* in my expression. But if he did, he ignored it.

The men were still inching in, and I eased back, shaking off Tommy's hand. No one else was talking. Not even a whispered sound had passed amongst the werecougars since I'd mentioned my name.

The guy, who I assumed was the official werecougars' spokesperson, let out an assumed chuckle. He looked like he was about to say something I wasn't going to like but froze when Tommy grumbled, "She brought a peace offering."

Tommy glanced at the SUV and waved a hand, then leaned back against the truck, folding his arms over his chest, and watched the proceedings with what looked like detached interest.

Erika was the first to come out. She didn't hesitate, strutting toward us, chin high and shoulders back. Laura was next, and attached to her was one of the werecougars. She was giggling and smiling, and if I hadn't known any better, I would have sworn she was actually into the guy.

One by one, my females came forward, smiling, offering little waves. They pushed their way into the circle of men surrounding me and Tommy and the truck. But the two werecougars we'd brought back didn't follow them. They paused and blended into the circle around us.

And still not a sound from the others. They were detached. Quiet. Watching. It was ... confusing. I licked my lips.

I was suddenly hoping that Aidan had found the children. That any second now, the SUV would speed away, and my pack would descend on the werecougars, because this quietness ... I didn't know what to make of it. It was worse than seeing aggression. At least I would have known how to deal with that.

I turned to face the smiley face guy, who was looking at me thoughtfully. "What did you change your mind about?"

I blinked and shook my head, thrown off for a second. "Oh," I said and glanced back at the women. "I'm ready to make the deal. I'm giving you some of our females. In exchange, you all stay the hell out of Dog Mountain."

"Thought they were the peace offering," he said, eyeing me carefully, if not critically.

"Some are," I said and shrugged. "But you don't get them all until I get confirmation from my dad that the deal is still on the table."

He cocked his head slightly, shifting his gaze toward the woods, and then he leaned in close to my ear and said, "Did you hear that?"

I did. It had sounded like a strangled whimper. And a snarl. A vicious snarl that ended in a surprised yip. More whimpering, some growls. Cracks and creaks and crunches. Leaves crumbling. Twigs snapping. The sounds came from every direction. But I looked at him blankly and asked, "Did I hear what?

He was smiling again. The nice one. The infectious one. And it made my blood run cold as ice. "That, Jade Shaw," he said, and his smile grew wider, "is the sound of your pack dying."

CHAPTER 21

AIDAN

My father wasn't a thinker. He had a problem; he fixed it — usually with unnecessary violence — but he didn't think about it. He acted. And as much as that had bothered me in the past, right then, I was seeing the wisdom in his impulsiveness.

I'd taken after my mom, though. I liked to have a plan. I liked to know what I was getting into. But the thing with having a plan was that you think you've got the situation covered. You lose that rush that keeps you on your toes. You miss things. You get cocky. And sometimes planning and strategizing and overthinking gets you to a place that you can't see a way out of.

And right then, I was in that place.

The wolves around me looked a little confused about what they were supposed to do. Dominic was crouched down next to me, a continuous growl rumbling from his chest. Cougars were falling from the trees surrounding us.

With a sharp feeling of alarm, I remembered what Jade had said about the claw marks in the trees. She'd known. She'd told us. We'd even discussed it. And in all the planning and scouting, no one had paid attention to it.

They'd known we were coming. *Dammit*! They'd probably been watching us the whole time while we scouted out the location. I should have known they'd have some kind of security in place. Jeff wasn't stupid. I should have ...

No. I wouldn't think about that. I couldn't think about that. Because if I thought about it, I'd realize that they'd been hiding in the trees all this time and that we were probably staggeringly outnumbered. And if I thought about that, if I let those numbers get into my head, I'd start to worry about Jade and my females who were trapped and surrounded and alone in there.

The wolves in my group were pacing, circling, dodging, growling. Waiting for the signal. Waiting for my command that the fight was on.

I let instinct take over. I channeled my scent and gave the signal to attack — to fight.

And they did.

One of the wolves let out a full-out vicious snarl, and then everything happened quickly. Wolves moved, cougars pounced, and all I could do was hope that the kids were tucked safely in that cabin and they stayed put.

More whisper-soft thumps. Wolves and cougars cried and screamed and snarled. It came from everywhere, all at once.

Something dropped beside me, and I pivoted, crouching down, and bared my teeth. I felt an ugly mix of anger and hatred churn within my belly, and I growled at the beast as it stalked toward me, with all the confident grace of a house cat.

It hissed. I snarled. It circled right. I circled left. I launched forward, and it slipped back. Playing with me.

My blood was pumping hard and fast, and furious energy twisted and curled throughout my body. The sounds of flesh ripping, tearing, pulling, pounded through my ears. Hisses tormented me, a growl filled my chest. I could almost taste the blood that was being spilled all around me.

The cat lunged for me, a blur of beige in the colorful forest, and I twisted and dropped to my belly.

The cougar missed me, landing with a hard thump to my right — not far away, but not on top of me, either. He let out a wail and spun around. His eyes were wild, and his lips were curled back.

I slammed into its body, hard enough to knock it down to the ground. I didn't have long once he was down; the shock of the impact wouldn't keep the beast at bay for more than a second or two. It flinched, trying to shimmy and roll back to its feet, but I didn't let him. I pushed off, landing on top of him, and bit down hard. In a second, the cougar went limp, falling face down into the dirt.

I shot up quickly, scanning the area around us. More wolves were joining our group, and seeing them sent a surge of hope through me. If they were joining, maybe, *maybe,* there hadn't been that many cougars in the trees.

A high-pitched screech came from my left, and I spun toward

the sound. A bird — a large, black bird — dove at me. His talons sunk into my flesh near my neck, and I snarled, tossing my body to the ground and shaking him loose.

The bird let go and then dove at me again, but as it lowered, it started to change. It got bigger. Fur replaced the feathers. Paws replaced the talons, and when the beast hit the ground, its wings seemingly melted away, and I was suddenly standing face to face with a cougar.

Jeff. I knew he wouldn't have run.

I growled, curling my lips back and baring my teeth. He tensed, bracing himself, as I crouched slightly, leveling my eyes with his. He didn't make a sound. No hisses, no snarls. His eyes looked as if they were laughing, full of humor, and I found myself growling again.

It's another game, I told myself. *He's playing with me.* I was sure of it, but his calmness made me uneasy, and for a moment, it kept me rooted in place.

A loud, pain-filled howl erupted from my right, and my eyes darted to the side, just a quick look. I spotted Dominic, falling, tumbling, down. He tried to get up, but he wasn't quick enough. A cougar landed squarely on his back, pinning him.

My heart twisted inside my chest. I glanced back to Jeff, but he was ... gone. Melted into to chaos that surrounded me.

Another agonized howl tore from my best friend, and I launched myself toward Dominic.

A flash of pain rushed through my back leg. I stumbled, fell, and as I started to roll, I felt something sharp dig into my leg. It was crippling. It felt like my leg was being ripped off. I snarled. More pain. Sharp, hot pain.

The cougar tore into Dominic's back, and my hope sputtered and flickered and died.

JADE

I kept my breathing under control, mainly by sternly telling myself that I had to remain completely together. The wolves around the hunting camp weren't my problem. They each had a leader. They each had someone watching their back. My problem, my responsibility, was the women with Tommy and me. I had my breathing more or less managed by the time I spun from the guy, who was still smiling, a far too friendly smile, and I was able to say, "Shift," without making it sound like I was panicking at all.

But the truth was, I was a little panicked.

"I wouldn't do that," a man said and pulled a handgun from the waist of his jeans. He leveled it on me.

That was, for some reason, kind of a shock because, well, he was a werecougar. He could shift and kill me. The gun just seemed really ... unnecessary. "You're kidding me, right?" I blinked. "You're pulling a gun on me?"

"It made them stop, didn't it?" the man with the gun said, his voice sounding antagonistic and a touch condescending.

I could smell Aidan. His alpha scent, that sweet green scent, was rising up around me. Commanding our wolves. The sounds were getting louder. Snarls and painful whimpers. They were in trouble. They hadn't reached the kids. The plan was falling apart.

My entire body was alive with feeling. My pulse was pounding in my ears and temples, and wrists. My skin was buzzing and tingling. Warmth spread from tip to toe, adrenaline chasing through my system.

I took a step and more guns, small handguns, appeared. I laughed once. "Am I really that scary to you all?" I asked and laughed again. "You guys better hope you have perfect aim if you plan on using them."

Smiley face guy chuckled and moved in close to me, so close that I could feel his warm breath puffing against my face. I held his eyes, refusing to flinch. His vibrant eyes were smiling, taunting, cruel, and confident.

He was poison hidden behind pretty eyes and a killer smile.

"I love that sound," he said, and he looked almost ... wistful. His nostrils flared wide as he hauled a full breath into his lungs. "And that smell. I bet some of it's coming from your mate." He licked his lips. "And some from that friend of yours."

He could have been right, but my nose was telling me that the blood wasn't just from wolves, and well, I wasn't even going to consider the possibility that some of that blood could be Aidan's. I just couldn't.

I forced a snide smile. "Nope. Smells like cougar blood to me. I've killed a few of those recently. I know that smell."

He slapped me in the face so quickly that I hadn't even seen him move until he connected with my cheek and sent me staggering back. My whole body quivered, and a growl ripped from my throat. Bones started to break. My ankle went first, then my elbow.

My face was shifting, my teeth lengthening. All around me, I could hear my pack fighting, snarling, and falling. Okay, maybe I couldn't hear them actually falling, but my brain was conjuring up a pretty vivid image of wolves lying motionless on the ground, blood pooling, cougars watching ...

I hardly noticed the guns anymore. Somewhere in the back of my mind, I knew they were still trained on me, but I didn't care. I let my scent gather, and I was about to force my wolves to shift when Tommy said, "Jade, don't."

He was still leaning back against the truck, and I had to admit, it shocked me. At some point, he'd raised his hands, carefully holding his palms out in surrender. But those hands had claws now, and coarse, dark hair layered the tops. His face was like stone, set in a murderous expression, and his eyes blazed gold.

The man — Mr. Smiley Spokesperson — barked out a laugh. "Yeah," he agreed. "Don't." He didn't seem to notice how close Tommy and I were to shifting, or maybe he just didn't think that any of us were a threat at all. He actually turned his back on us and looked at my girls, who I noticed, were just barely holding onto their skin.

Underestimating us was a stupid, stupid mistake.

My breath caught. A string of pops and snaps rang through the air. Fabric tore. Flares of heat shot through my limbs.

The guns opened fire. Shots rattled against the truck, and the windshield exploded into cracks. But by the time the first searing bullet grazed my skin, the guy who turned his back on me was already falling.

CHAPTER 22

AIDAN

I could only stare. The body lying not even ten feet from me — Dominic's — didn't look to be alive. He wasn't moving. He didn't look as if he were breathing. The rusty-brown wolf had fallen to his side. His muzzle was open slightly, his eyes were shut, and his legs and paws looked loose and relaxed. He almost looked as if he were sleeping, and if it weren't for the chunk of flesh and fur missing from in between his shoulders and the blood soaking into the ground around him, I might have thought he was.

Except he wasn't moving at all. Not even a quiver of his chest from a shallow breath.

I squeezed my eyes shut. This couldn't be happening. He couldn't be dead. He just couldn't be. But when I opened my eyes, Dominic was still on the ground, and he still wasn't moving.

I hadn't felt scared during the attack. Not really. Not until now. I'd been focused, determined. But now ... now I was terrified. My mouth was dry, shriveled up, and so was my throat. Dominic was my friend, the best friend I had in Dog Mountain, and he was ... I let out a painful whimper.

Somewhere in the back of my mind, I was aware that gunshots were still ringing out, but I couldn't pull my eyes away from him.

Seeing him so still, hurt worse than anything I'd ever felt before. I should have saved him. I was his alpha, his friend. I should have gotten to him. I should have ...

Jade.

My heart started to pound, and my chest constricted with dread. She was still in there with her team. I needed to get to them. Get them away from the bullets. I needed to get them out of there.

I tore my eyes from my best friend, my beta, and surveyed my surroundings with a quick, swiping scan. I was surrounded by death. Cougars and wolves. Bodies and blood. My wolves were everywhere. Some lying on the ground, injured, some still fighting.

I tried to stand up, but the pain in my back legs seized me up tight. They were broken. I could feel the bones grinding as I tried to get to my feet again, and when I glanced down and saw how not straight they were, I winced. They were a mess, bones snapped, and flesh was torn up.

I growled. I was useless to Jade, to my pack, like this. I needed to shift and let my broken bones reset and mend.

I wasn't sure what had happened. One second I had one of those bastards trying to gnaw off my legs, and the next, there'd been a series of cracks that sounded a heck of a lot like gunfire, and the cougar had let me go.

It felt like it took hours for my body to change forms, but I was sure it was just a few seconds. My inner-wolf fought against the shift, struggling to stay in control. All he wanted was to fight, kill, and claim back what was ours.

Each broken bone in my legs burned as it snapped again and reset itself, and by the time I finished, I was covered in a thin sheen of sweat, and my breath was strained and labored.

Another round of sharp, loud cracks came from the direction of the hunting camp. Panic welled up inside me. I pushed up to my feet, and a twinge of pain shot through me as I put my weight on my legs, but it wasn't unbearable. My legs were moving before my brain could catch up, and I was running toward the edge of the forest.

I saw her — my mate — through the trees. She was in wolf form, just lying there on the ground. A man — it was the man who'd been at her window — was standing over her. The shoulder of his T-shirt was drenched in blood, I noticed, as he bent down beside her. He reached out to touch her midnight black coat, and I felt the wildest, strongest impulse to rip him apart from limb to limb. I could visualize it, and it was alarming and so very satisfying.

And then Jade moved. Her skin started to crawl, and she began to shake. She was shifting, I realized, and I felt myself run faster.

I reached the edge of the tree line just as a set of arms wrapped around my chest, hauling me back. "Aidan, stop!" Mark said.

"Let go of me," I commanded, my tone firm, direct, and full of fury. My imprint was blazing, and my scent, thick in the air. "Let go!"

"They won't hurt her," he growled. His eyes were red and blurred with exhaustion. "They need her. Stop and think, Aidan!"

Mark started to pant, and his arms were weakening. I twisted and yanked my body free of his grasp, and as I did, Craig darted in front of me and shoved me back a step. "You can't help her, or any of us, if you're dead." He was straining, too. Fighting to stay strong and on his feet under the force of my alpha scent. "Look around!" he shouted, panicked and flailing his arm to point behind me. "They need you more than she does right now!"

When I only growled, Craig shoved me again. He puffed out his chest, squaring off with me, and pointed behind me again. I wasn't sure what he wanted me to see. I wasn't sure if I even cared. In the back of my mind, I knew that if the enforcers thought Jade was in real danger, they wouldn't be stopping me. They'd be killing anything that stood in their way to get to my girl. She was one of theirs just as much as she was mine.

My nostrils flared, and every muscle in my body was strung tight as I did a slow circle, looking to where he'd pointed.

There was movement all around me. Whimpering. Heavy breathing. Disturbed leaves crunched and crumbled. *My wolves.* They were stirring, limping to their feet, healing.

And the cougars that had been hiding in the trees were dead. All of them.

Someone coughed, a hacking, painful cough, and the sound made my breath hitch. My gaze snapped to Dominic. Beck was standing by him now, his bloodstained muzzle nudging at Dominic's shoulder.

A strangled sound worked up through my chest, and my eyes started to burn. Dominic wasn't dead. I blinked and then blinked again. He'd managed to shift and pull himself into a sitting position, resting his head in his hands. He was breathing hard, sweating, shaking, coughing. But he wasn't dead.

Silence fell. Complete silence. The gunshots stopped. The screams silenced. I swallowed hard and looked back to where Jade was lying to see the man drape a blanket over her. And the other females were being lifted and carried to the cabin. They weren't being hurt. The men looked as though they were being careful, gentle even, now that my females were unconscious.

And everything snapped into hot, sharp clarity.

Uniting the shifters. Jeff didn't want us dead. He wanted us to join him. But he wouldn't be that stupid, right? Keeping the girls, even if they were wounded, was dangerous. They'd heal, and he had to know that we'd come for them.

Craig's hand fell on my shoulder and tightened. "We've got to move."

"What?" I asked and turned my head to look at him. I felt rage, so hot, so pure, it felt like I was burning from the inside out, and it felt terrifyingly good. "We're not going anywhere without our females."

He saw my rage. His hand skittered away from my shoulder, and his eyes dropped to the ground. "They can't fight," he said. "Most of them are struggling to walk. We need to fall back."

"I'm not leaving her." My voice was growled, and my eyes flared. "We're not leaving any of them, the girls or the kids."

Craig didn't say anything, but he hadn't moved out of my way, either. I felt my face go red, and the muscles in my clenched jaw fluttered. My scent ramped up, my imprint blazed.

"Aidan," Mark said in a soft, tentative voice from behind me. "Look at them. They've got to heal. We can't help the kids if we're dead, and you need to trust Jade to do her job. She'll keep those girls safe."

I didn't turn. I couldn't. I knew what I'd see. I knew he was right. But leaving Jade ... My inner-wolf was going crazy, clawing at my chest and pressing against my skin at the thought.

Another hand gripped my shoulder and tugged me around. "Look," Mark said. "Dammit, Aidan, look!"

And I did. I looked at my pack, bleeding and cut up. Some were limping; some could barely stand. Dominic was hunched over, his back torn up and bleeding. My pack was a mess, and I knew damn well if I forced them to attack now, we'd lose. We'd lose the war, and we'd put the girls in even more danger.

My pack needed me, but I couldn't just walk away. Not from her. Not from any of them.

I swallowed hard and jogged over to Dominic, dropping to my knees beside him. "You good?" I asked, which was probably a stupid question seeing as I'd been pretty certain that he was dead only a few minutes ago.

"Yeah," he said. "I'm good." He was still breathing roughly, but he looked better — steadier. More color in his cheeks. More of the typical coolness in his gaze. He looked more like Dominic and, well, less dead.

"Good." I reached out and clasped his shoulder. "I need you to do something for me."

Dominic nodded. It didn't look like an agreement, but more that he knew that now wasn't the time to disagree.

"Take them back to that hunting camp we passed about five miles out. Get them shifting. Get them healed as fast as you can."

Dominic looked sick, and he wouldn't look at me. "Don't," he said faintly and pulled back from me. "Don't ask me to leave her."

"I'm not asking, Dom," I said. "Go."

♥

There was a dull thump of flesh hitting the ground, and then another.

Beck and Mark were breathing hard beside me, and low growls rumbled in their chest. I wasn't one hundred percent sure if those growls were a warning for me to stay hidden or if they were caused by what was happening just past the tree line from where we were crouched, watching in disbelief.

The cougars hadn't been taking the girls to the cabin. They'd been taking them to the cages.

My lips were curled back in a silent snarl, and I pawed at the ground restlessly, watching as, one by one, my females landed into the cages with a fleshy thump.

And still, the enforcers wouldn't let me attack.

Craig's teeth were pressing against my leg, holding onto the spot where the break had only just healed. The three of them had held back to help me, they said, but I knew the truth. They were here to make sure I didn't do anything stupid, and Craig's sharp teeth were a constant reminder of that.

Seventeen men were surrounding the cages, watching and laughing when the man who'd been talking to Jade at her window carried her over. She was relaxed into unconsciousness, her head resting lightly at his neck. He didn't drop her like the others. Instead, he set her down gently and brushed the hair from her face tenderly. It looked as if he actually cared about her. His hand lingered at her cheek for a moment that was way too long, and then he pulled a blanket around her.

My silent snarl turned into a loud growl. *I'm going to kill them all.*

I started forward, and Craig's teeth tightened onto my leg, pinching into my skin. I spun, snapping out at him. My heart was racing. *No one touched her like that. No one but me.* My inner-wolf wanted blood, and right then, all I could see was red.

Footsteps pounded in our direction and then slowed as if the men couldn't figure out where the sound of my growl had come from. And Craig, damn him, he wasn't backing down. His teeth dug in deeper, and he started dragging me backward.

Beck launched at me then, growling and snarling, and Mark was right there with him. I let my scent roll off of me, growling at them to back down, but they didn't. My damn enforcers just kept coming, pushing and pulling me back, shuddering through the effort to ignore my commands. And it was then that I realized they were doing exactly what they were meant to do. Protecting my pack from me. Stopping me from making a move that could hurt them all.

And as they dragged me away before the cougars could find us, I didn't know whether I hated them or loved them for doing their damn job.

CHAPTER 23

JADE

I came awake feeling sick, achy, and cold. Someone was poking thick, blunt needles into my skin, or at least that's what it felt like, and when I tried to move, the world tilted and spun around me.

I blinked my eyes and groaned. It wasn't needles poking at me. It was wire. I was in one of those damned barbed wire cages.

I tilted my head slowly to the side and swallowed down the well of panic that bubbled up inside me when I realized that I wasn't alone. Curled up in the fetal position, Erika was pressing into the corner of the cage I was in. She was head to head with Laura, who was lying crookedly, bending with the other corner, and both were still out of it. And beside us in a second cage was Kristen, Stacy, Jo, and Whitney, all curled together in the center, unconscious.

I swallowed thickly and closed my eyes. How had it come down to this? My team, all six of them, were with me, split up and crammed into cages.

"You promised," I whispered, blinking away the sting of tears that bit at my eyelids. "You told me you wouldn't let me fail them." But Tommy wasn't here to hear me, and all I could do at that moment was hope that he'd gotten away. Maybe he'd found Aidan. Maybe he was safe. *Please let him be okay.*

Someone had draped a blanket over me, covering me up, and as I scanned over the girls, I noticed they had them, too. It was still daylight. The sun was high in the sky. I couldn't have been out long. No more than thirty minutes, I guessed. Everything felt foggy. I remembered the smiley face guy, and I remembered attacking him. The girls had started to shift. Tommy had been beside me, snarling. And then there was pain. Burning, hot pain.

"You shouldn't have brought them here," a deep, smooth voice said, and I blinked my eyes open again. It was smiley face guy, but he wasn't smiling, and for just a second, I thought that I saw something in him. Something other than the poison. He was looking at me with something that looked a lot like ... remorse?

"I shouldn't have brought who here?" I asked and sat up, swallowing down nausea that washed over me from the movement.

"Your mate, his males." He shook his head. "You shouldn't have brought them." His voice was very quiet, thoughtful, and almost sad. "We're going to have to kill them now."

My heart started racing. "I don't know what you're talking about." I almost shouted it, and I gritted my teeth, attempting to control my tone. "The only male I brought was in the truck with me. Where is he? Where's Tommy?"

He ignored my question and moved closer to the cage. He gave me an amused look and chuckled softly. "Yes, you do. You know exactly what I'm talking about." His right shoulder was covered in dried blood, and for a beat, I felt a bubble of delight, knowing that I'd caused at least a little damage before I'd been taken down. "We're going to find him," he said. He smiled then, a friendly, welcoming kind of smile that was more than a little confusing given the fact that he'd locked me up in a cage. "And we'll kill him when we do."

"Find who?" I asked, but I thought I already knew the answer to that. Even though it was terrifying to do that with him so close, I closed my eyes. I didn't want him to see what I felt, even if he could smell it. I didn't want to give him the satisfaction of seeing the way his words were ripping me in half.

Aidan left us here. He. Left. Us.

"Your mate," he said after a long moment. "It's too bad, though. We really could have used you both." He seemed so rational. Even his scent. It was calm. And it was ... my nostrils flared. I could smell cougars all around, but his scent, it was different. It was human.

My dad wasn't the only real shifter here.

I suddenly felt as though I'd been punched in the gut, and all my insides had been torn out. I felt hollow, empty.

And stupid. Really, really stupid.

Of course, Dad wouldn't leave his pack for days, or even weeks at a time without someone else here to keep them loyal. Things started to make sense. The fast changes in the cougars' location, even when Dad was home. He never seemed frazzled, always confident that he'd win his sickening games, and I guessed that was because he wasn't the only one playing them. He had someone else, someone like him who was after the same goal.

I opened my eyes. "You're like my dad, aren't you?" It came out as a half-whisper, half-shout. "You're not a werecougar. You smell like them, but it's not as strong. You're probably wearing clothes they'd worn, or maybe it's a transfer scent from being closed up with them in that small cabin. But you smell ..." I shook my head and pulled in another breath. "You smell more human right now than anything else. You've been calling the shots here while my dad was in Dog Mountain playing his games with my pack."

He didn't say anything, but his widening smile and soft chuckle were enough of a response for me to know that I was right.

"What's your name?" I asked, and my voice sounded all wrong. It was higher than normal, scratchy, too. My throat was dry, rough, and I swallowed — hard.

"It's Jason," he said and moved closer until he was right next to the cage. He rested his hands on top, bending his fingers loosely into the squared mesh, carefully avoiding the barbs, and looked straight down at me.

I fought back the urge to whimper and scuttled back. If Aidan and the team left me here, it was because they knew I could keep the girls safe, and I wasn't going to let this jerk think anything different, even if I was the one in a cage. "What happened to Tommy?" I demanded, and he raised his brows. "Where's the guy that came with me, Jason?"

Jason locked his gaze on mine and held it, losing his amused expression. "He's fine for now, and he'll stay fine if you cooperate."

I sucked in a breath. I bet it wasn't hard to miss the wave of misery that came from my scent because that was exactly how I felt — miserable. "I brought you what you asked for," I said and waved a hand toward the girls, but my voice totally lacked the conviction it needed to make the statement even semi-believable.

"It's not about the girls," he said. His voice started out soft but quickly hardened. "And we both know they were never meant to stay here. Your pack wouldn't have been hiding in the woods if they were." He paused and stared down at me for an uncomfortable minute. "Jeff told you what he wants. What we want." He crouched down beside me, and his eyes flared with heat. Then he shrugged. "You should have thought of that before you tried to fool us with that stupid deal of yours."

Right, I thought, and then dread hit me. *He wants our packs to join together.*

"Where's my dad?" I asked. "I want to talk to him. Now."

"He's out hunting your mate." Jason sounded calm enough, but the tips of his ears were turning red, and the look in his eyes had gone completely insane.

I couldn't find any words. I just sat there shivering, staring into those crazy eyes. They were cold and calculating, searching my face like an invasive probe, and after a second, I found myself looking down.

"You can stop this," he said softly. "Order your males to join us. Make your females behave. If you work with me, I'll see what I can do about these cages."

I raised my head very slowly. "What?"

"Help me, and I'll let them out. This doesn't have to be ..." he paused and licked his lips, his hard eyes heating further. "Uncomfortable."

"Those bastards aren't going to find him, Jade," Erika said, and I jumped, twisting around to see her still curled in the fetal position. "Don't make a deal with this asshole." She glared at me. Her eyes were rimmed with red, but they were dry and really angry. "Don't you dare give up on Aidan or on us."

She stopped talking, and her eyes refocused on Jason, who stood up and was striding toward her. He watched her for a second, and she seemed to be holding her breath until he glanced back at me, and it whooshed out of her.

"Think about it, Jade," he said. "I'd be a good ally to have." And then he walked away.

By the time he vanished around the corner, my brain was working in overdrive. We had to get out of here before they found Aidan and the rest of the pack. There were no two ways about that. I looked at the cage, the chains, the barbs, the locks ...

An idea, not much of one, but it was something nonetheless, started to form. I looked back to Erika. "Wake up the girls," I said. "We've got to get out of here and help the others." I might have sounded calm and neutral, but right then, I was anything but. And I was pretty sure Erika knew that because she didn't waste a second in doing what I asked.

CHAPTER 24

AIDAN

Dominic stepped back from the door and closed it. He'd been hovering since I'd arrived. "They're close," he said. "A few more shifts, and we should be ready to move."

"How about you?" I asked, scanning his back. "Your back's still raw. You should be out there shifting with them."

"I should be with Jade." It wasn't the first time he'd said that since I'd gotten here and I hated hearing it. His tone held so much loathing, and his hatred was just boiling over. It wasn't making the call I'd made to send the pack away any easier to deal with.

I took a deliberate breath and then let it out, trying to keep my inner-wolf locked up tight. "You think it was easy leaving her there?" I asked. "You think I wanted to walk away? What was I supposed to do, Dom? Force you all to go in there when most of you could barely walk? How well do you think that would have played out?"

I felt sick leaving the girls. Utterly sick. Leaving them with those monsters was almost worse than seeing Dominic motionless on the ground. Almost. The only thing that made it not as bad was that I knew, *I knew*, that Jeff wouldn't let them get hurt until he had what he wanted — my pack. And I wasn't going to give him that.

Beck, Mark, and Craig had dragged me, biting and clawing, pretty much the whole five miles to where my pack was holed up, trying to heal. They'd fought me hard every step of the way. Pushing through my scent, struggling against my commands. If I wasn't so pissed about it, I'd probably be amazed at how strong they were as a team. When one started to cave under my command, the others had picked up the slack, sensing each other's shortfalls and filling in the weaknesses. Yeah, okay, even if I was pissed off about it, it was still pretty amazing. They really were great together as a team.

But even if they were right, and we'd needed to regroup to be of any use to the girls, it felt ... sick leaving them and the kids there. Sick and wrong and cruel.

Right now, I had the pack outside shifting over and over. Deep cuts and bad breaks could take hours to heal, but shifting, well, it sped up the healing process, forcing the ripped-up skin and broken bones to reshape and mold and mend with each shift until they snapped back to how they were supposed to be.

My leg and all the new bites the enforcers had given me as they forced me back were as good as new after three shifts, but Dominic wouldn't do it. He was too damn focused on hating me to look after himself.

Dominic's hands curled into fists, and his face flushed an ugly red. "She's in a cage! They're all in a cage! You saw them put her in there, and you walked away."

A sudden surge of illness swept over me as the vision of Jade being carried and placed in that cage filled my head. She'd been out cold, and I'd watched as that guy that had stood at her truck window brush her hair back from her face with a tender sweep of his hand, and then he'd laid a blanket over her body.

It had taken everything in Beck, Mark, and Craig to stop me from charging in and trying to kill them all to get to her. There'd been seventeen cougars by the cages, watching my females being locked up. *Seventeen.* I hadn't spotted Tommy, but I had to assume that they'd have others watching him. There were thirty of us, including Jade, Tommy, and me. I didn't know where Tommy was exactly, and seven of my wolves were now in cages. If I was playing the numbers game, which I definitely was not doing anymore, I'd have to say our packs were close in numbers now. We'd killed another thirteen of them during their tree jumping stunt, but there were still at least those seventeen left.

And then I saw Dominic lying on the forest floor, not moving, and I remembered thinking he was dead, and I felt as if I were going to throw up.

"Yeah, Dom," I said, swallowing hard. "They're in cages, and that means that the cougars want to keep them alive. They're probably safer there right now than they would be with us." I scrubbed at my face, and when I looked back at him, Dominic started to speak, but I held up my hand to stop him. "I already thought I'd lost you once today. Couldn't go through that again, man. I just couldn't. They would have killed you if I'd let you go in after her. But they won't kill her. They need her to command our pack."

That threw him off for a second. His eyes went vague and unfocused. His hands started to uncurl, and his lips parted. "Is that ..."

"Dominic," I said, my voice deadly soft. "What I need right now is you backing me, not fighting me. That girl trapped in that damn cage means everything to me." I swallowed, and I pushed off the wall, turning away from him, mainly because my eyes had started to burn, and I seriously didn't want him to see it. "She's my home. I'm going to get her out of there."

There was silence for a long second before Dominic cleared his throat. "Um, is it safe to speak yet, or are you going to bite my head off?"

"What?" I asked, and all the breath left me in an audible huff with the word.

"Is that what you thought?" he asked hesitantly. "That I was dead?"

"Yeah," I said, and damn, I had to squeeze my eyes shut for a moment. I was fighting with all kinds of emotions — anger at Jade's dad, frustration with the entire situation, fury that my dad had pulled Chris home before I was ready, outright fear that I was going to lose someone close to me. So far, not one of my pack members had died today, and it scared the hell out of me that that could still happen.

"Shit, that must have sucked," he said and laughed a little, but there was no humor in the sound.

"Yep." I turned to him, and somehow I managed a small smile. "It did."

His blue eyes searched mine, and I knew he could see the emotion, but he didn't call me on it. "So," he said. "I'm going to go shift a few times, see if I can fix the gaping hole in my back. Five minutes and we should be good to go."

He started for the door, stopped, and grabbed me in a hug. I rocked back a little from the impact, but I hung on for a few beats, and with a couple of back slaps, we stepped apart.

"I thought you were dead," I said, and damn, my voice was all choked, but I found myself repeating it. "I thought you were dead."

"Yeah, we established that." Dominic gave me a half-smile that looked kind of grim. "Come on," he said. "Let's go see if they're ready."

♥

I wasn't sure if the pack that stood before me was ready exactly, but they were determined, and I figured that had to count for something.

The sun was starting to fall on the horizon, and with only a couple hours of daylight left, we really needed to move. There was no way that I'd leave the girls there overnight, and by the looks set on my werewolves' faces, they weren't about to do that either.

There were twenty-two of us, all semi-dressed in a mix of camouflage and worn denim, that we'd found in the cabin. The air was cool with a breeze, and the forest around us was silent and still.

I thought I should say something epic and probably something motivating, but as I stared at them watching me, waiting, the only thing that came out of my mouth was, "I love her."

As it turned out, the pack thought those words were, in fact, epic. Cheers rose in the air, clapping and shouting, followed. I heard rumbles about alpha pairs and love and true partnership, and something about a new dawn for our pack. And for a brief moment, I was stunned silent.

"I can't promise you that we'll all walk away from this," I said, shouting over the cheers. I waited for a second for them to tamper down and continued. "And if you want to walk away, I won't blame you. You've all fought hard, and I'm grateful. But I can't ... I won't leave without our females and those kids. I won't go home without my mate." I paused for a moment and scanned the crowd, and then asked, "Are you with me?"

"Hell yeah," Beck shouted. "Wouldn't miss a good fight for anything."

But the rest of the pack was quiet, thoughtful. I was starting to get a little nervous that they would give up and go home, and then Phil walked up to me, and I had to admit that my nervousness tripled. He wasn't all for Jade being alpha, and he'd made that pretty clear in front of everyone when she'd walked into the headquarters with me after she'd moved out of her dad's house.

He stood in front of me for a moment, his eyes giving nothing away, and then he smiled. It wasn't really a happy smile, but it was an easy one. He extended his hand, and I took it in a shake. "I'm with you, kid, till the end."

More cheers, louder this time, and I smiled a real, full smile. They were with me. Even after all the bullshit Jade and I had made them suffer through, they were with me.

CHAPTER 25

JADE

The blankets were old and fraying, and they were really easy to tear.

The edges of the cages were wired together with more of the same sharp barbs that lined the walls. They weren't huge, at least not for three or four people, but they weren't small, either. The cage doors were chained closed with heavy locks securing them. Breaking those locks was a no-go. I'd tried. We'd all tried. We'd also tried to bend the barbed wire walls, pulling and tugging, but we couldn't break it. The damn thing just bent, and with the way the wire crisscrossed in small squares, even with bending the wire, we couldn't get an opening big enough to squeeze more than an arm through.

So now we were tearing up the blankets, wrapping our hands, and slowly untwisting the barbs that held the cages together along the edges. It was tedious and painful and frustrating as all hell, and I really didn't think a human would have the strength in their fingers to do it, but we did. And it was working. So far, we'd managed to loosen the top four inches on each cage door.

Erika hissed and jerked her hand back. "They couldn't have left us thicker blankets," she muttered under her breath, glaring at the corner of our cage and sucking on a finger. She huffed loudly. "We're never getting out of here." She sounded like she was fighting hard to sound normal, but she missed her mark. I could hear the panic building in her voice. I could smell it, too. And that bittersweet scent was choking me.

"Yes, we will," I said. I didn't sound normal, either. I sounded angry and hurt, and betrayed. I swallowed hard and attempted to ignore the sting that Aidan's leaving me here caused. He had his reasons. I knew that. If he thought he'd be able to get in and get us out safely, he would have. And I had no doubt he'd come back. He wouldn't just leave us here. But it still stung.

Keep it together! Be strong for them. I swallowed down the pain and whispered fiercely, "I'm going to get you all out of this." And I would, definitely, hopefully.

Erika shook her head. "Jade ..."

"I want cookies," Laura blurted suddenly and made a loud, frustrated sound from the back of her throat. "You'd think they'd at least give us comfort food after locking us up in these stupid cages."

I heard the shuffling footsteps coming behind me, and alarm shot through me. I scrambled, just like the others were, to pull my blanket up around me and hide the torn strips under it. Laura had taken up the job as our lookout, and since she loved to bake, she'd chosen *cookies* as the code for *someone was coming*, claiming that she'd be able to ramble on about them easily if anyone came by. She hadn't been lying. So far, she'd given out five recipes, talked about oven temperatures for baking them, and she'd even listed off her favorites and why.

"Really, Laura," Kristen said and rolled her eyes. "Cookies again? Can't you find something else to go on about?"

Laura laughed as the man stalked by us, but it was a little strained. She shrugged. "What can I say? I love cookies."

He didn't come close to the cages. None of them had yet. Not since Jason had been here. This one looked a bit older than Jason but of a similar build and height. He didn't smile. He didn't frown. His expression was as flat as his muted brown eyes. Those eyes, though, stayed fixed on the girls right up until he rounded the corner and disappeared from sight.

At least they were leaving us alone. It was the best we could hope for, really, but it was also the one thing that knotted me up the most.

Because if they were leaving us alone, it meant that they were busy doing something else — like hunting my mate.

Once he'd turned the corner, Erika reached out for me, clutching onto me as if she thought that if she let go, she'd fall. Her head bent, and she rested it on my shoulder. She was shivering, and the shudders went right through me.

For a second, I was shocked because, well, it was Erika, and we weren't really on hugging terms, but the shock faded. I pulled her closer and held on just as tight. "It's going to be okay," I said. "I'm going to get you guys home."

She leaned back and looked at me. Her eyes were rimmed red, and she looked hollow and exhausted. "Jade, I-I'm so sorry."

I blinked in surprise. "You? Sorry?" I studied her for a second. "Sweetie, you've got nothing to be sorry for."

"Yes, I do," she said. "I'm sorry for ignoring your calls and for messing around with Aidan and for being a crappy beta." She wiggled away from me and grabbed the edge of a blanket, tearing off another strip. "I shouldn't have let him in that day. I should have answered the phone. I shouldn't have told you I was studying. I was just ..."

"Erika, stop," I said, taking her trembling hand and squeezing it. "Just stop. It's over. We're good, okay? None of that matters anymore." I meant it, and by the look she gave me, I knew she was aware that I was serious. Whatever happened before was over, done, buried. The whole thing seemed kind of ridiculous now, given our situation.

I squeezed her hand one more time, and then I snagged up one of the strips of fabric and quickly wrapped up my fingers before shifting back over to the corner I'd been working on and starting in on the next barb.

She was silent for a moment, and then almost awkwardly, she said, "When Aidan showed up at my door, he looked so wrecked, and you ... you were being so stupid. God, Jade, you walked away from him. He's the best thing that's ever happened to you. We all saw it. The way you looked at him like he was *it* for you, and he saw you, too. It was like no one else existed for him except you, and you just walked away. I was so mad at you for that. I would have killed to have what you two have." She laughed then, a strangled kind of laugh. "Turns out I did. I just didn't realize it until it was too late."

I looked at Erika, really looked at her, and I saw something. Something in her teary eyes made me feel a little helpless. And guilty. Crazy guilty. The truth was that I kind of hated me, too, for walking away. If I had have stuck it out, forgiven Aidan sooner, and worked with him to stop my dad, instead of unknowingly helping Jared inflict his revenge, we probably wouldn't have been stuck in a cage.

I didn't even know what to say.

But I did know who she was referring to. Craig. I knew she was really hung up on him, and I thought the other women knew that, too. They were all looking at her with that *you poor thing* look, and all I wanted to do was fix it for her. It was … weird and really unexpected, but she was mine. My female, my wolf, part of my pack, and it tore me up seeing her so … sad.

"It's kind of scary, isn't it?" I said. "Loving someone that much." I shook my head. "I wasted so much time with Jared, you know? Time that I could have had with Aidan. At first, I told myself it was because I wanted to stop my dad, and Jared was the way to do that, but really it was because I was scared. Terrified, actually. Aidan lied to me, manipulated me into fighting for him, for the pack, and for you guys." I laughed once. "Turns out it was probably the best thing he'd ever done."

"Yeah," she breathed. "It's freakin' terrifying."

I looked back at the corner and started twisting the wire again. "If you want my advice, don't stop fighting, Erika. Never stop fighting. Life is too short not to spend it with the person who makes you whole."

"She's right," Jo said. "If he's important, you need to fight for him. But if you ask me, Craig's the one screwing this up. Not you. The way I heard it, he hadn't even told you that he wanted you as his mate until after the Aidan thing."

"We were sort of seeing each other," Erika said. "It was casual, but it was still something."

Kristen snorted. "Casual. All that means is that he's too chicken to make a commitment. When you get that boy back, you make sure he knows you aren't playing around this time."

"Did you bring me cookies this time?" Laura shouted, and we all jumped and shuffled, hiding our escape efforts as fast as we could.

It was a long, long afternoon. Eventually, the men stopped walking by. I wasn't really sure if that was a good thing or not, but without their constant observation, we made headway on our exit strategy. Another ten minutes or so, and we'd be able to shove the doors open. We didn't talk much, just worked. There didn't seem to be a lot to talk about after the girls had determined that it was Craig that was being an idiot. I wasn't entirely sure if I completely agreed with that. She'd hurt him. Crushed him, actually. But it made Erika a little less teary-eyed to hear it, so it was good.

The sun was starting to fall when I heard the bell-like laughter. It was sweet, almost like wind chimes, and it was followed by a full-bellied, rumbling laugh that I'd have known anywhere.

I froze mid-twist and whispered, "Shush. My dad's here." I

didn't know what else to say, but the round of fast, suction-like breaths made me very aware that the girls knew that him being here probably wasn't a good thing.

Because if he was here, then the chances were good that he'd found my pack, and Aidan wasn't coming back for us.

Dad had his arm around a tiny young girl with a head of blond, ringlet curls. She couldn't have been more than twelve. He was smiling down at her as he strode toward us. It was the smile he'd always given me. The one that said I was the absolute center of his world. The one that made me feel warm and loved, and safe. And seeing it directed at someone else stung — bad. So bad that my chest ached and my eyes burned.

Behind him were a bunch of his cougars, eight, no, there were nine of them. They looked happy and really excited. And it made my inner-wolf, and me, hurt, a deep, sharp ache that filled every part of my body.

I tried (and failed) to bury the feeling as I lifted my chin and gave Whitney a narrowed smile. She quickly slid back, covering the corner of the cage they'd been working on, and at the same time, Laura took up the position in our cage.

Dad stopped and crouched down in front of the girl. "Go see what your brothers are getting into, pumpkin," he said. "I'll be in soon, okay?"

She smiled, a radiant, sunshine kind of smile, and giggled. "Will you play that card game with me?" Her voice was just like her laugh, sweet and bell-like.

"Sure," he said. "Now, go on." And with a quick kiss on his cheek, she turned and ran back around the corner, and a second later, I heard the door to the cabin open and then slam shut.

"Did I miss a chapter?" Erika whispered. "Because that looked like a man who loves that little girl."

"Yeah, it did," I said quietly, not wanting him to overhear. I felt sick. Cold and sick and hurt. "That was exactly how he was with me until I met Aidan." And I couldn't help but wonder if that girl was meant to be more than a girl who wound up in a cage because I was sure there had to be something more to that kindness, just like there had been when he used it with me. For me, he'd used it to steer me closer to Dominic and the pack, and I was sure he was using it on her to point her in whatever direction he needed her to go in. His pushes for me had always been subtle and always hidden behind that *I love you* smile, but when I thought about it, really thought about it, they'd been there. Always. For years now.

Dad asked where Jason was, and I didn't think he liked the answer because his eyes hit mine then, and they were bright with anger. He closed the distance to the cage with a long, determined stride and pointed at me. "Stand up, move to the door, and don't you give me any lip, Jade. I'm not going to tolerate it."

I didn't stand up. Instead, I only blinked, stunned by the harshness in his voice. Was he completely done pretending to care about me? Had he ever actually cared? There wasn't a trace, not even a tiny speck of warmth in his eyes as he glared at me. Nothing. It was as if I meant nothing to him anymore, and I found myself crouching, getting ready to shift if I had to. The girls were silent, stiff, and ready, too.

"You should have listened to me, Dad," I said. "You should have run."

He gave me a long, frowning look. "Stand up, Jade. It's time we come to some kind of agreement here."

"I'm not leaving my girls in here," I shot back with a touch of a growl, deepening my tone. "You want to talk to me, talk because I'm not going anywhere without them."

His eyes narrowed. "I'm not giving you a choice. I've played your little game long enough."

"My game!" I shouted. There was something in his tone that made my spine snap straight, and my entire body tensed up tight. "I was never playing a damn game."

"Watch that tone with me, Jade," Dad growled. "I'm still your father even if you choose to pretend I'm not."

I crossed my arms, holding the blanket snuggly in place. "It's a little late for fatherly lectures, Dad. You lost that right the moment you threw me out of the house and pushed me into becoming Aidan's mate."

Dad lowered his voice, and his eyes were suddenly intense. "I did that for you." He sounded like he actually meant that. "None of this would be possible if you weren't mated to him. I've given you power. I've given you the backbone you needed to run your pack and mine."

"Why the hell would I want to run a pack of sick male cougars who think it's okay to lock women in cages and use them as toys?" I glanced past him to the men who'd gathered behind him and snarled. "What's wrong with you people?"

At one time, I'd wondered if maybe they weren't all evil. I'd hoped for it, actually. But as I looked at them, they didn't even have the decency to look ashamed. A few of them even chuckled.

These weren't good but misguided people. They were monsters. All of them.

"Everyone has their vices, pumpkin." Dad had the courtesy to look away, but I really wondered if it was only because his left eye had started to twitch, and he didn't want me to see it.

I shook my head. "This isn't a vice. In the real world, it's called kidnapping, rape, and murder."

"We're shifters, pumpkin." His voice softened, and he moved, rounding the cage to the doorway. He still wasn't looking directly at me, only watching me from the corner of his eye. "The rules are different for us."

He sounded as if he actually believed the garbage he was spewing at me. Like this was normal behavior, accepted even. How scary was that? The man who raised me, loved me, cared for me, actually thought that what he was doing, what he allowed his pack to do, was okay.

"Do you actually hear yourself?" I asked. I aimed for disgust, except my voice came out as a whisper. "Shifter or not, this isn't okay, Dad."

"I'm done discussing this with you," he snapped. His face grew red and furious as he reached into his pants pocket and fished out a key. "If you want to see Aidan again, you'll stand up and come over to the door."

Panic, blind, hot panic set in as he leaned forward to unlock my door. We'd left the wires on, but loose, to keep the doors looking solid as the men walked by, but if he grabbed it, the top half would flutter and give.

"He's not here," I said, scrambling forward and blocking the girls in my cage behind me and out of his reach. "I'd scent him if he was." I was glad I sounded confident in that because I didn't feel it. My heart was hammering so hard that it hurt to breathe.

"Well," Dad said, taking hold of the lock, "you can believe that if you want to, pumpkin, but he's here. My boys found him, and they're here for their reward. You can come with me and see him, or you can stay here and watch."

The door started to bend as he fiddled with the key, and his eyes, blazing with fury, snapped to mine. He opened his mouth, probably to yell at me, but didn't get a chance. "No!" Whitney shouted. "No, don't touch me!" And the wire door on the second cage clambered to the ground.

"Look at this," one of the men said. The disbelief was obvious in his voice. "These girls were fixing to escape."

And then everything seemed to blur together. There was laughter, cold, cruel laughter, bones breaking, and growls sounding. The men crowded the cage; the girls shifted.

Dad tore off the door to my cage, and he dropped to his knees. He glared at me long and hard, and then he pressed forward. His arm leaped out, and he wrapped his hand around my ankle, pulling hard.

"Back up," I growled, kicking out of his hold. "Don't make me hurt you."

But he didn't back up. He only laughed. And it was then that I decided that he was dead to me. Completely and officially dead to me.

CHAPTER 26

AIDAN

It was a calm, easy trek back to the werecougars' location, though I had to admit, I was waiting for something to go wrong. As we reached the edge of the forest where the cougars had hidden in the trees, I thought that we'd face another attack.

But nothing happened.

The only thing we found waiting for us were the dead we'd left behind. The cougars hadn't even bothered to collect their pack members. I almost felt bad for the dead — almost.

Most of the space around the cages was taken up by the werecougars. Some were shaking the structures, taunting the girls trapped inside. They'd shifted to wolves, and were growling, a low, deadly threat that didn't seem to faze the werecougars. A few of the men stood by and watched, but all of them looked ... hungry, greedy, eager.

Jeff himself was on his knees, half in and half out of the cage Jade was in. He had a hand on her ankle, and he was pulling as if he thought he could physically drag her from the confines of the barbed wire enclosure.

He wasn't getting far.

Jade looked stubborn, but there was something else there, too. Despair. I could smell it. She was putting up a good fight, but she struggled to keep it together. She kicked wildly at her father as he pulled at her legs, but she wasn't making any of the kicks count. And she was yelling, except I had no idea what she was saying. It was garbled and frantic, a string of sounds that didn't quite sound like words. She had Erika, and I was pretty sure Laura, trapped behind her. They were snapping out at Jeff, though, they couldn't quite reach around Jade to hit their intended mark.

I growled. I could almost feel her fear, and I wanted, no, I needed her to calm down and focus. I channeled my alpha scent, letting it pour out of me. There was a good breeze flowing through the forest, and I figured it would only take a few seconds for her to pick up my scent, and I seriously hoped smelling me close by would be enough to make her chill out.

It worked.

Suddenly, Jade just stopped. She stopped yelling. She stopped struggling. She looked toward me, her eyes squinting as she scanned the trees, and she laughed a little hysterically.

The other females were snarling, snapping, growling, within the other cage, but as Jade laughed, they stopped, too, sitting back on their hind legs, panting.

They knew we were here.

As evidence to that, Jade laughed again, looked straight at her father, and said loudly, "You better let go of me now." She sounded a little sad but also really furious. "Aidan's not really a fan of people trying to hurt what's his, and neither is my pack. When they find out what you were planning to do, they'll kill you all."

For a beat, there was nothing but silence. The men paused in their taunting. They turned, following the females' gazes, but they didn't move.

And then I noticed that it wasn't just Jade's cage that was open. The doors, both of them, were completely off and lying on the ground. Maybe that was the reason they hadn't moved; nothing would be blocking the exit for my females if they did.

"Ignore her," Jeff growled. "Man up and get those wolves under control." He started pulling at Jade again, but when she kicked, she hit him square in the face. He sat back, and his hand shot up to his nose, and he shouted, "You little brat!"

I felt a dark, bloodthirsty thrill spread through my belly, and I let the rush of adrenaline wash over me. I started to shift. It was probably crazy taking my human form now, but I wanted Jeff to know it was me. I didn't want there to be any doubt in his mind that the wolf who ended his sick, miserable life was me. And my inner-wolf, well, it seemed he wanted that, too. He didn't put up a fight; instead, he pushed the shift along, giving up all his control.

A soft tingle spread along my skin as the coarse black fur that covered my body began to recede. The snapping of my bones sounded extra loud, bouncing through the silent forest, but all I felt was the rush of the shift.

When my human body solidified, I got up to my feet and rolled my shoulders. I let out a slow breath, surveying the group. There were only nine of them, plus Jeff, by the cages, but I figured the others would come running the moment we attacked. Actually, I was counting on it.

Dominic growled and made a chomping sound with his teeth. He looked up at me and gave me a lopsided dog smile. He was ready to go. I just smiled back, although it probably looked a little feral. "Find the kids," I said. "Keep them away from the cages." And then, keeping my human form, I strode forward.

The werecougars seemed confused. Maybe they thought I was crazy, walking out into their midst; I wasn't sure. But then they looked past me, and alarm replaced the confusion. One of them made a startled sound, and they started to move, drawing back and flinching as my pack followed me, moving in from every direction. We moved in calmly. None of my wolves threatened. No one attacked. They were just there, a quiet, deadly presence at my back.

"You won't be keeping them, Jeff," I said with a lazy smirk, stopping a few feet from his back. "Step away from them before something ... unfortunate happens."

He didn't seem to care one way or another that I was standing there, which was odd, I thought, and definitely stupid. He barely even looked at me, keeping most of his focus on Jade.

But Jade was looking at me. Her eyes raked down my body, and a flush shaded her cheeks. "Hey, baby," she said and laughed a little. She sounded pretty close to insane, breakable, and stressed. Really, really stressed. She gave me a look that was half warm and half cold and crossed her arms, ignoring her father completely. "Took you long enough."

I grinned and shook my head. "Sorry, sweetheart. Won't happen again."

"You're darn right it won't." Her nose scrunched up, and she waved a hand widely around her. "Can you believe these guys actually think keeping me in a cage will convince me to force our wolves to join them?" She huffed. "And guess what else? Our females are supposed to be their reward for hunting you guys down. Dad here even said you were here, and he was going to let me see you if I let his beasts have our girls."

I chuckled. "Is that so?" *She was good at this*, I thought. Good at acting as if everything was normal, and she had the situation under control when she was really coming close to full-out panic. I could smell it. I could hear it in her laugh and see it in her eyes.

"Yep," she said and grinned. "But you don't look like you've been hunted down and caught, so I'm thinking he's full of crap."

A couple of my wolves pressed in closer to the cage beside Jade's, forcing the werecougars back with a few low growls, and as they moved further away from the cage, the females sprang free and quickly melted in with the rest of the pack.

"Sweetheart," I said gently. "You can go on and shift now. I've got this."

"Aidan," Jeff said, and finally leaned fully out of the cage and looked at me. He sounded annoyed, as if the last threads of his patience were thin and about to snap. "Don't encourage her. She's not leaving this camp. None of you are."

"Step away from my mate, Jeff," I said and took another step toward him. I gave him a second, only a second, to obey, and then I lunged forward, grabbed his ankles, and yanked him away from Jade.

He shouted, just a small, quick burst of sound. He kicked out at me, but it was too late. I already had him flipped onto his back and pinned to the ground.

The realization that I wasn't just here for my females must have dawned on him as my bones began to break and change. He looked up at me wide-eyed and pretty obviously scared. His fear smelled bittersweet. He tried to slide out from underneath me, but his panic made him slow, sloppy, and completely uncoordinated.

"What are you idiots waiting for?" he shouted. "Get this beast off me!"

CHAPTER 27

JADE

I couldn't shift.

It wasn't that I didn't want to, because I did. I really did. And my inner-wolf, well, she wanted out, and she wasn't being quiet about it either. My skin was crawling, and raw adrenaline was pumping through my body, but I just couldn't do it.

There was chaos all around me. Wolves and cougars. Snarling and hissing. My pack was taking them down faster than my brain could process. None of the cougars were running to help my dad. Okay, that wasn't entirely true. They were trying to get to him, but my wolves were taking them down before reaching their target.

Beck, a large dusty-gray wolf, stood at the cage door. He was whimpering and nudging at the bottom side of my foot, urging me to come out.

But I couldn't make myself move.

Those monsters were going to take my girls, and I hadn't been able to do anything to stop them.

Suddenly Aidan let out a war cry and threw a hard elbow right into my dad's jaw, and then he shifted. It all happened so quickly I almost missed the change. His body hazed, bones broke, bent, changed, midnight black fur replaced tanned skin. He was snarling, growling, and pinning my dad down.

I watched it all, and I felt nothing.

This was it. My mate was going to kill my father, and I felt nothing.

Absolutely nothing.

I expected to feel something. Sadness or relief or anger. Something. Anything. But all I felt was numb.

Was it wrong that most of me wanted him to die? He was a monster. He'd kidnapped, raped, and killed, or he at least organized those horrible things, and his victims were innocent people — humans that had no chance of defending themselves against his pack. He deserved death. They all did.

Erika and Laura were nudging at me, trying to push me out of their way without hurting me. They wanted out. They wanted to help our pack, but I was frozen, caught up within my numbness, and blocking their exit.

Aidan's jaw was opened wide, and he was lowering, ready to rip out my dad's throat, but suddenly he made a painful sound, somewhere in the middle of a snarl and a whimper, and stumbled backward, rolling off my father.

Dad scrambled to his feet. He was holding a sharp-looking pocketknife in his hand that was stained and dripping scarlet liquid from its blade. He was bloody, too, and he looked weakened, but he was moving, and the sight sent my inner-wolf into a rage-endured frenzy within my chest. That man — my father — had been about to offer my wolves to his pack of beasts as a reward. He didn't deserve to be moving.

And that's when I felt something. Something dark and a little crazed, and it compounded into something that was totally insane.

I scrambled from the cage, the barbs tearing at my knees and catching at the blanket that was tucked snugly around me, almost ripping from my body.

My eyes were locked on the knife clasped in my dad's hand. "Who the hell brings a knife to a shifter fight?"

Dad didn't answer, but then I guess I didn't expect him to. He wasn't paying any attention to me, and he didn't seem to notice Erika and Laura, either. The girls were pressed to my side, snarling at him, as I advanced.

"Stand up to them!" he cried. He looked around, frantically waving the knife. "Make them submit."

The cougars were shifting, and more were coming. Running across the small yard, tearing off their clothes. The sound of bones snapping, so many at once, was a sickening sound, echoing back from the cabin and the forest walls.

"You're destroying everything, Aidan," Dad shouted, turning as Aidan got back to his feet and stalked toward him. He held his hands out, still clasping the small knife in one, as though his hands could stop my mate from coming closer. "Your emotions are clouding your judgment and stopping you from doing your job. You're supposed to be leading them, not fighting for a girl. Alpha pairs aren't about love. Strength and dominance are all that matters." His voice was rising, tinted with fear. "You said that yourself not so long ago in my living room. Be the dominant male you're meant to be and control your mate! Stop fighting me for a girl!"

Aidan's lips curled, and he let out a vicious snarl. I couldn't see his wound through his thick black fur, but I knew it was there. I could smell it, his pain and his blood, but he didn't let it show. He stalked toward my dad, and that was when my dad stumbled back, crashing into the cage that had held me captive. He dropped his knife, and it clattered through the wire, just as the cage bent, and then collapsed under his weight. He let out an agonized cry as the barbed wire tore through his clothing and ripped into his skin.

"No, Dad," I said. "You're wrong." I quickly rushed to Aidan's side, pressing my leg against his fur. He glanced at me, just a quick look, before letting out another growl at my father. "His emotions aren't clouding his judgment. They're making him see what's important. Leading a pack isn't all about power and control."

Dad tried to stand up, but he couldn't. Erika and Laura snarled and snapped each time he moved, pushing him back down. Dots of blood began to well up from where the barbs had dug into his skin. The more he struggled, the worse it got.

"You asked me about the women," he said. "This is why they aren't changed. This is why they don't live with us. He's going to lose everything because of you. Because he thinks he loves you."

I almost corrected him. Almost. But I didn't. It wasn't worth the breath to tell him that Aidan didn't *think* he loved me. He knew he did, just like I knew with him. I almost asked him about Mom, too, but again, I thought I probably didn't want to know. I didn't want to know if he actually cared about her or why he'd married her. I was sure the answer would only make me sick.

Instead, I looked over my shoulder and said softly, "Look around, Dad. We aren't exactly losing anything."

And we weren't. In minutes, my pack had taken down over half of Dad's forces, and they were still attacking with vehemence fervor.

That was when a cougar broke through my wolves and charged at us. He hit Laura first with a hard knock into her side that threw her to the ground. Erika spun away from my dad, baring her teeth, but she hesitated.

We all hesitated.

Because it wasn't a werecougar. It was a shifter. It was Jason. In mid-leap, he shifted into a bird, a big ugly looking bird. He flew upward and disappeared into the forest.

His little stunt gave Dad an opening. Dad launched from the cage and rushed at Aidan. He started to shift, and it cost him his life. Aidan might think twice about killing someone in human form, all of us would, but once the shift started, it was over.

I thought Dad knew that, too. He glanced at me, just a quick look that was cold and emotionless, and it told me he didn't regret anything he'd done, and then he was taken down.

Beck and Erika, who'd been circling around us, lunged forward to attack, and they latched onto his calves, causing him to fall. And then more wolves descended, biting into him and tearing at his flesh.

He started to scream, but it sounded all wrong. His voice wasn't human. It was rough and pitched and screechy. His face wasn't his anymore; it was something else, something not quite human and not fully animal, as though it had frozen in mid-shift, and I wasn't entirely sure what he'd intended to turn into.

I clamped my hand to my mouth, holding in my own scream. I wanted to look away, but I couldn't. It was as if I needed to see this, even if I didn't want to. I needed to know the terror he'd caused was over. I heard his last breath, and I saw his struggle stop. It was fast, and it was deadly, and it was a horrible way to die, being torn apart.

CHAPTER 28

AIDAN

It would have been better if Jade hadn't watched.

Jade wouldn't look away, even after her father took his last breath. Her eyes were wide and filled with horror. It was as if she were frozen, not wanting to watch and not able to move. I could hear her heart pounding within her chest, and her scent was thick and bitter.

A sickening crack filled the air, and she flinched, but still, she didn't look away.

I trotted over to her side and rubbed up against her leg, nudging her and nipping at the torn wool blanket that was wrapped snugly under her arms.

Her hand fell to my head, and that's when she finally tore her eyes away from her dad. They hit mine, and the horror faded into something that looked like worry. But she smiled a little. "I'm fine, Aidan," she said, and her body trembled through a shudder. She gave my head an absent little pat. "Go help the others." And then she turned and started to walk away.

I opened my mouth and let out a loud growl, protesting. She didn't look fine. She looked lost and kind of defeated, and if she looked around, she'd see that the pack didn't really need my help. The cougars were falling quickly, and the last few still fighting were battling against the team. Some of our pack had even started shifting back to human. The fight was pretty much over.

She stopped short at the sound of my growl and spun back to face me. "Don't growl at me," she said, placing a hand on her hip. She smiled tightly, the strain showing clearly in her features. "Go on. Find Tommy. I need to go and meet the kids."

I growled again, but it was useless. Her face was set in that stubborn determination. I knew that face, and I knew it well. No matter what I did or said, she would do what she thought she needed to do.

But still, I shifted anyway.

My inner-wolf didn't even try to stop me. I thought he was probably just as worried about her as I was.

With her hand still on her hip, Jade noticed and waited for me to get to my feet. I figured she knew I'd only chase after her if she started to walk away again. And as she waited, those big brown eyes of hers never left mine.

I stepped in close and pulled her into my arms. She didn't protest, not even a little. As soon as I touched her, her hand fell from her hip, and she wrapped her arms around my waist, holding onto me tightly.

"I wish you didn't watch that," I said, pressing my nose to her hair and breathing in a deep drag of her scent. "I'm sorry you did."

"I needed to see it." Her voice was freakishly composed, and she pressed her hand to my chest, pushing gently until I let her go. "Please find Tommy," she said. "I really want to go make sure those kids are okay."

I studied her for a moment and then nodded. "Sure, sweetheart." And even though the last thing I wanted was to let her go, I stayed put and watched her walk away, although the entire time, I thought I should probably follow her. Actually, it was a serious effort not to follow her.

But I didn't, because well, I believed her. She really was okay.

My girl is okay.

When she rounded the corner of the cabin, I turned back to the yard, surveying the scene. Mark and Craig were finishing off the last werecougar standing. They were doing it quickly, efficiently, and with two well-placed bites, the beast laid limp on the ground.

And it was over.

All those weeks of games with Jeff, and it was finally over. It felt ... good. I felt ... lighter, knowing we'd stopped those monsters before they could hurt anyone else.

Beck had shifted, and he was jogging the tree line, with Landon on his heels. They were counting the dead, I realized, watching their lips move with the silent numbers. Beck noticed me and veered my way. "We got the thirteen from the tree jumping ambush and another sixteen down here," he said when he reached me. "But it looks like that other full shifter got away."

"What about our pack?" I asked. "Is everyone okay?"

"A few cuts, but nothing that won't heal," Landon said. "We found Tommy. He got snagged up in one of those tree snares. Everyone's accounted for."

I nodded and swallowed a few quick swallows. "Let's get the dead buried then," I said. Tension that I hadn't even realized was there melted from my shoulders and the knots in my gut loosened. "And then we go home. We've got some ashes to spread tonight."

Beck smiled. "Sure thing, boss," he said, and as they took off, I turned back to the cabin and went to meet the kids.

JADE

Dominic and Luken were playing Go Fish, and they were losing.

I found the kids inside the cabin with Dominic and Luken. It wasn't much. One large room with bunk beds lining the back wall and what looked like a sleeping loft with a log-style ladder leading up. A propane stove, a small sink, and a large wooden fold-up table surrounded by chairs.

Dominic grumbled something under his breath as the girl with the blond ringlet curls snatched a card from his hand. He'd dressed — kind of — in an orange jacket that was open and far too small and a pair of camouflage pants, which were identical to Luken's get-up. The girl giggled, a delighted little giggle, and her cheeks were stained with an excited blush.

Not really what I'd expected to find, that was for sure.

A little boy, maybe three, tiptoed up beside Dominic and rose up on his toes. He had curly red hair, and his chubby little cheeks were dotted with freckles. He held a hand over his mouth, trying to hold in his giggles as he peeked at Dominic's cards.

He took a good look, and then, he ran over to the girl and whispered loudly, in a way only a child could. "He's got a two of hearts."

I laughed. I couldn't help it. As the one boy whispered, not so quietly, another boy about the same age was doing the tiptoe thing to Luken. He was adorable, with white-blond hair and crisp blue eyes, and he had a heart-stopping smile, with two little dimples.

Luken shifted in his chair, ever so slightly, and passed his cards from one hand to another, so the boy could get a better look without being too obvious about it.

I laughed again, harder this time, and Dominic looked up at me, grinning widely. "Tara's kicking my butt at cards," he said. "And Joel and Cody are helping her do it. They're all little cheats!"

"Is that Jade?" Tara asked. She looked up at me, and her pretty little smile vanished.

"That's her," Dominic said. He put his cards down and leaned back in the rickety-looking wooden chair.

She fixed me with a cool stare and folded her arms over her chest. "He said that you're going to make us go to school. He said we're going to live with your pack now. Is that true?"

"Do you want it to be true?" I asked hesitantly because I really couldn't tell if she liked the idea or not. Her scent said she was excited, but the body language ... well, it was cold and a little angry.

"Will my dads be coming with us?" she asked, her sweet-sounding voice turning harsh.

"Um ..." I started and then just stopped. I didn't know how to answer that. I wasn't sure if I should tell her the truth or sugarcoat it. I thought she probably heard the commotion outside, and I figured she was old enough to know what had happened. But still ... she was just a kid.

I looked to Dominic for some help, but he only shrugged as if to say he had no idea how to proceed.

As it turned out, I didn't have to say anything.

Suddenly, Aidan's warm weight settled in at my back, and his solid arm looped around my waist. "No, sweetheart," he said, "they won't be coming with us." His tone was gentle, soft even. "Your dads had to go away."

She snorted and rolled her eyes. "You mean they're dead."

Somehow I hadn't quite expected the snark in her response or her blunt statement. I thought she'd be upset, maybe even shed some tears. I'd seen the way she'd been with my dad. I'd noticed the smile and the eager expression. And yes, I'd really thought it had been real.

But I was beginning to think that maybe she'd been playing the *sweet and innocent* card because the bottomless look in her eyes right then told me that she'd seen more horror in her short life than anyone should have seen.

I wasn't the only one that was left speechless by her statement. Dominic's eyes widened, and he sucked in a quick, sharp breath. Luken's jaw dropped, stunned.

I saw Erika, Laura, and Jo inch forward from the corner of my eye. They'd come in, probably behind Aidan, and I hadn't even noticed. I glanced over my shoulder quickly to find all of the females from my pack squashed in behind Aidan and me, and outside there were quite a few of the males hovering.

I felt equally shocked and proud at that moment, seeing my pack crowding into and around the cabin, making sure the kids were okay, that we were all okay, and it sent tingles all over my body.

If Tara had noticed them, she wasn't letting on. She kept her eyes fixed on Aidan, waiting for an answer.

He hesitated for a second, and then he sighed. "Yes, they're dead. They hurt a lot of people, sweetheart, and they weren't going to stop."

"I know." She looked down at her cards and frowned. "I saw Jade and her friends in the cages. I know what happens to the girls that go in there. My mom died in one of them a few months ago." She lifted her tiny shoulders in a shrug. "Too bad you didn't come sooner."

And right then, my heart broke. Just shattered.

There was a round of gasps from the pack, and the scent of their heartbreak spiked in the air. *I'm sorry* was murmured over and over, and I heard a few sobs, too.

"Sweetheart ..." Aidan said. His voice cracked, and his arm loosened from my waist. He started to step around me to go to her, and I noticed he'd fastened one of the blankets from the cages around his waist, covering him up.

But Tara didn't seem to want his sympathy. She held up a hand, asking him silently to stop, and said, "I like the idea of going to school. Dominic said there would be other girls my age there. Can I have my own bedroom when we move from here?"

"You can have anything you want, baby," I said, and there were tears in my voice. "Anything."

She nodded and watched me wearily for a moment before turning to her brothers. "Come on, boys," she said, standing up. "The faster you pack your things, the faster you'll get to play with that fire truck Dominic told you about."

They didn't waste any time jumping into action. As I watched them rush around packing up their belongings, I realized that not only had we killed my father and defeated the werecougars, but thanks to my incredible pack, we were going to give these three children a chance at real life.

After all the pain and misery, things were finally starting to look up, and I thought that today just might have been one of the worst, and probably the best, day of my life.

EPILOGUE

JADE

Aidan had promised that we'd do something boring when the battle with my dad was over. I couldn't say that boring was what I got, but I did get normal, and normal, well, that was just as good as boring.

The hallways in the pack headquarters were abnormally quiet for a Saturday. Everyone was tiptoeing around and whispering, and that could only mean one thing: the boys were having a nap.

I glanced back over my shoulder, taking one last peek at Tara as she strutted out of my temporary bedroom in her new knit dress. Dominic let out a whistle of approval, and I smiled, and then, I snuck away down the hall to track down Aidan and the two sleeping monsters.

It had been just over a week since we'd brought the kids home, and it had been nothing short of chaotic. We'd held Jared's service right after we got back from the hunting camp, spreading his ashes in the clearing. I'd been right; it had been a good thing for the team and for the pack. A little closure after a lot of death. And thanks to Marcy, it all went smoothly.

Mom had taken the kids during the service, and well, I was pretty sure she fell in love with them during those two short hours. The kids, all three of them, were now living with her. She'd been adamant about it, and although both Aidan and I were planning on taking them in, we were also glad she'd said no to that idea, because well, we might be the alpha pair, but we were just barely adults ourselves, and definitely not ready to look after three children on a full-time basis. But being a big sister and brother was a heck of a lot of fun.

After the kids' living arrangements were settled, there were shopping trips and school registrations to handle. At first, those two things hadn't seemed like a lot, but it was. The kids had never been to a store. They'd literally lived their lives in the bush.

On the first trip to a mall, I thought I would have to rush Tara to the hospital. She'd hyperventilated herself into unconsciousness, passing out in the first store we went to that sold girls' clothing. Who would have thought buying a dress could be that epic? Well, for Tara, it was. She even told me so, over and over and over, and well, over again.

And the boys ... Aidan had taken them to a toy store, and let's just say that nothing — absolutely nothing — could have prepared him for that one.

During that experience, I decided that my mom wasn't just awesome; she was a superstar. Aidan had called her, explained the nightmare he'd found himself in, and she'd come to the rescue and quickly wrangled the boys.

On top of getting the kids settled in, Aidan and I had been living at the pack headquarters because our house was currently undertaking a massive overhaul. The carpets were being torn out, the walls repainted. Even the kitchen and bedrooms were being renovated. And today was the day we'd finally get to move back in. I had to admit, I was crazy excited about that.

But even if it was hectic, it was normal, it was fun, and having the kids around, even if they weren't living with us, made everything a little ... better, easier. The kids were going to be okay, which made what we did, what the pack did, to stop my father, worth it.

As for the pack, well, life just went on. Some went back to work, others went back to school. Things just went back to normal. Okay, maybe not entirely normal; we were werewolves after all, but it was all pretty ordinary other than the whole changing into a wolf thing.

The team was back to training, and each day they spent time hunting Jason, the full shifter who got away. So far, they hadn't found him, but they weren't giving up, and if Jason was ever stupid enough to come back into our territory, they'd catch him.

They'd also added Tommy and Luken to their ranks, and as for the head enforcer, we'd let the guys vote. Surprisingly, they'd voted Landon into the position. I'd expected it to be Beck, but I had to admit, Landon was doing a fan-freakin-tastic job at it so far. Since he'd taken over, the rest of the pack were warming up to them, talking to them. They no longer walked in the other direction when they saw an enforcer coming.

It was nice. A nice and much-needed change.

Somehow I hadn't expected things to just go on. But I guessed that was how life worked. You went on. You moved forward. And ultimately, you became stronger for it.

I reached Aidan's office, and I inched open the door, trying to keep quiet. The last thing I wanted to do was wake the boys again before Mom got here to pick them up. They were both sprawled out on the couch, breathing evenly, and Cody had a thumb stuck in his mouth. It was probably evil of us to let them sleep now. They'd be crazy hyper when they woke up, but secretly, I thought Mom liked it that way.

Mom hadn't asked about Dad yet. She didn't question us on what happened or ask where the werecougars were. But I thought she probably already knew. Actually, I was sure she'd figured it out the moment we brought the kids home with us.

Aidan glanced up from his computer and smiled. It was a relaxed, contented smile, and seeing it made my entire body warm. I'd never seen him so content, so happy, and I loved it. Simply loved it.

I went straight to his desk, pulled out the chair he was sitting on, and plopped down on his lap, exhausted.

"Where's Tara?" he whispered, wrapping his arms around my waist, and pressing a light kiss onto my neck, just below my ear.

"Modeling her new clothes for Dom," I whispered back. "He's helping her pick what to wear for her first day at school on Monday."

Aidan chuckled and shook his head. "You're a very mean girl, Jade Shaw."

"No, I'm not." I cut him a look. "He likes it, I swear. He used to do it with Mac and me all the time." I snuggled into him, resting my head on his shoulder. "Anything interesting happen while we were gone?"

"Maybe," he said with a mischievous edge to his voice. I wiggled on his lap and looked up at him, arching a brow, and he chuckled. "I thought Mac was the gossiper."

"Spill it, buddy," I said in the sternest voice I could manage, which really wasn't that stern since I was still whispering. "I mean it. Tell me, or you'll be sleeping here tonight."

He made a face that clearly told me he knew that was an empty threat, and he leaned into me and kissed me in that place just behind my ear, that place that always made me shiver.

"I might have walked in on Erika and Craig in the gym changing room this afternoon," he said.

"And what were they doing in the gym changing room, Aidan?" I asked, trying not to let his kisses distract me.

It wasn't working.

He continued to feather those light lip touches down my neck, and as he did, I felt as if I were falling, falling into that wonderful, warm place that I only ever found within his arms.

"I think you can figure that out," he whispered.

No kidding, I thought. I had a pretty good idea. Erika had been pretty relentless in her pursuit for his attention over the last week, and I knew it was only a matter of time before Craig stopped pretending he didn't care.

The door opened, and Mom breezed through. I jumped, and heat rushed to my cheeks. Aidan dislodged his lips from my neck but chuckled as I tried to wiggle off his lap, and he tightened his arms around my waist. I gave him a *look*, he smirked and gave me a *look*, and I rolled my eyes, and then I settled back against him.

Mom glanced at the boys, smiled, and then turned a scowl on us. "You let them sleep?" she asked. I thought she was trying for annoyance but didn't quite hit the mark. "Really, Aidan, it's too late for a nap. They'll be up all night now."

"You love it," he said, laughing. The boys began to stir, yawning loudly, and he laughed again.

"You're right," she muttered. "I do." She crossed over to the couch and smiled down at them. "Who's ready for some pizza?"

And there it was. The magic word.

The boys sprang to life, jumping off the couch, shouting, "Me," and ran for the door.

Mom laughed and waved a quick goodbye before chasing after them and telling them to go find their sister, which immediately led to both boys screaming out for Tara because that was, of course, easier than actually looking for her.

I sighed and shook my head, but I was smiling, a big, wide smile. I hadn't really expected it, at least not so soon, but we were okay. Mom, the kids, the pack ... We were really okay.

Aidan gave me a quick kiss as he leaned around me and started saving his work and shutting down the computer. "You ready to go home?" he asked. "The house should be ready for us by now."

I pulled his arms back around me when the computer shut

down. His arms were always solid and safe and warm, and having them around me was like being wrapped up in comfort. "Yeah," I said. "I can't wait to see it."

I leaned back into him with a sigh, and his chest vibrated against my back as he chuckled. He rested his chin on my shoulder and whispered, "You know you're going to have to stand up if we're going home, right?"

I nodded. "I know." But I turned in his arms and kissed him, a sweet blend of heat and softness. I loved this. Bubbles of joy spread through me as his lips played with mine. I loved him. It had been a rough couple of months since he'd moved to town, and we'd both stumbled and fell and even crashed a few times, but it was worth it. The fight, the heartache, all of it was worth it to be here at this moment, feeling those bubbles tingle throughout my body.

When the kiss finally ended, we both dragged in a strained breath, and he seemed to have trouble letting me go. His eyes, flecked with gold, searched my rosy cheeks. "You know," he said, cupping my face in his big warm hands, "I'm very lucky you love me."

"Yes. Yes, you are," I said, fixing my face in my most serious expression, which totally failed because my body was shaking with silent laughter as my happy bubbles began to burst and fill me with a giggly kind of bliss. "And I guess I'm pretty lucky you love me, too."

And then, as my laughter quieted and we got to our feet, I wondered what the future might hold for Aidan and me and our pack. I was pretty sure it wouldn't always be easy, but with his arm around my shoulder, holding me close to his side as we walked to the car, I felt completely at home, and that was more than enough for me.

Acknowledgments

An enormous thank you goes to my family and friends. Thank you for your unwavering support and encouragement. I'm truly grateful to have you all in my life, and I love you all.

To my husband, Jordan, thank you for having so much patience and understanding, especially when I ignored you for days while working on *Deadly Pack*. You are the best!

And to my editor, Kathryn, I couldn't have finished this book without you. Thank you for being an invaluable member of my team.

Last, but not least, a huge thank you to all of my fabulous readers. You guys rock!

Note from the Author

Thank you for reading *Deadly Trilogy*. If you enjoyed this book (or even if you didn't) please consider leaving a review on the site where you purchased it. Word-of-mouth is crucial for any author to succeed and your review, even if it's only a sentence or two, makes a huge difference in helping new readers make the decision to read my books. Many thanks for your support.

XOXO,

Ashley Stoyanoff

About the Author

Romance author Ashley Stoyanoff is the recipient of two Royal Dragonfly Book Awards for young adult and newbie fiction. Her first book, *The Soul's Mark: FOUND*, came out in 2012. Her other passions include reading and shopping for the latest fashions. Learn more about Ashley and her work at ashleystoyanoff.com.

Further Reading: Going Rogue

Did you love *Deadly Trilogy*? Then you should read *Going Rogue* by Ashley Stoyanoff!

We all die. Some of us sooner than later.

Alexa Cross never thought her existence would revolve around death. In life, as a nurse, she helped save people. But life has a funny way of throwing the unexpected because, in the afterlife, she spends her time watching people die and collecting their souls. As much as she wants to stop the deaths, she knows death is inevitable, and it cannot be stopped.

However, when a serial killer decides to take up shop in her district, Alexa can't sit back and do nothing. No one should die like that, and she's determined to alter Death's timeline. But, to do that, she needs to embrace who she is now and break some rules. It's the only chance she has of stopping the person responsible for the vicious murders.

www.ingramcontent.com/pod-product-compliance
Lightning Source LLC
Chambersburg PA
CBHW060209030726
47499CB00004B/969

* 9 7 8 1 9 2 7 8 0 6 1 6 6 *